TREASURE OF GOR

TREASURE OF GOR

GOREAN SAGA * BOOK 38

John Norman

ISBN: 978-1-5040-8949-4

This edition published in 2024 by Open Road Integrated Media, Inc.
180 Maiden Lane
New York, NY 10038
www.openroadmedia.com

TREASURE OF GOR

CHAPTER ONE

"You will need a collar for her," he said.

"Of course," he said.

He meant a new collar, of course.

I was already collared.

I had been put in my first collar shortly after my arrival on the planet Gor.

I had never expected, on my former world, to be collared. Who would expect that? And certainly I had never expected to be brought to this world, as, in effect, a form of livestock.

As the Goreans say, "The orchards of Earth are ill-guarded."

I had not even suspected that the planet Gor existed, until shortly before my abduction, or, as the Goreans would have it, my 'acquisition.' After all, a hunter does not abduct his prey, nor does a trapper abduct his catch.

I had now begun to dream in Gorean.

I knelt at his thigh, my head down.

Would he take me to a city?

I hoped so.

I wanted clothing. In public, in a city or town, as I understood it, we were almost always given clothing, though, to be sure, clothing appropriate to our station, our situation, our condition. We were not to be confused with free women, the lofty, abundantly robed, switch-bearing Ubaras in the streets. But even a brief tunic, a short, open-sided camisk, belted with binding fiber, the rag of a ta-teera, any mockery of a garment, is precious to us.

Why were we dressed so?

Clearly for the pleasure of men.

It pleases them to have us so.

Too, in such a garb it is clear that we are different from them, that we are quite different from them, that we are marvelously, excitingly different from them, that we are females, and, for such as I, only females.

Soon, despite our intended degradation and abasement, we do not object to being clothed, if clothed, as we are. We accept our bodies and revel in the preciousness of our sex.

So, we are dressed for the pleasure of men.

Let it be so.

We love it.

But what woman truly objects to being dressed for the pleasure of men? What woman does not wish to be attractive to men, even if, in her public *persona,* she would wish to appear to hate them? Surely the colors and textures, the careful foldings and artful drapings, the splendors of the Robes of Concealment, are intended, in their way, to interest and attract men, as much as the simpler garb deemed suitable for us, the occupants of collars. We are given no choice in what we wear, and no choice, even, as to whether or not we will be clothed.

We are animals.

Animals need not be clothed.

Why should free women hate us so?

Is it because we belong to men and men treat us as they wish? Do they wish to belong to men and be treated as men wish?

I do not know.

Men treat us, in this civilization, in the way of nature. Men treat them, in this civilization, in the way of civilization. Sometimes I suspect that free women envy us. Perhaps that is why they hate us so.

Nature can be denied, but I do not think she can be escaped.

"*Kajira,*" said a voice.

I lifted my head, but did not meet his eyes. It was the voice of he before whom I knelt. There were three men in the tent, he before whom I knelt, he at whose side I knelt, and a third man, who stood to the side.

"*La Kajira,*" were the first words I had learned on this world.

When I had first been ordered to utter them, I did not understand them.

I understand them now.

The words had been said.

That was enough.

"You are a barbarian," said the voice.

"She is," said he beside whom I knelt.

"What were you called on the far world?" asked the first man, he before whom I knelt.

"My name," I said, "was Agnes Morrison Atherton."

"Ag-nes-mor-iss-on-ath-er-ton," said the first man, carefully.

"Many barbarian names are similar," said the third man. "They are clumsy and lengthy. It is a wonder they can remember them."

"I call her 'Janet,'" said he at whose side I knelt. "It is a barbarian name, and thus, I think, suitable. Too, it is simple, and easily said."

"What is your name?" asked the first man, he before whom I knelt.

"'Janet,'" I said.

"If it pleases us?" he asked.

"Yes," I said, "if it pleases you." I was uneasy. Had I erred? I did not wish to be whipped.

I put my head down, again. I was reluctant to meet his eyes. What if he should be displeased?

I had been disappointed with the men of my world. I found them, on the whole, and, in particular, the more educated, refined ones, uncertain, conflicted, tamed, diffident, self-alienated, and weak. I do not think that this was their fault. As I now realized, they had been trained so, conditioned so, socially engineered so, in such a way as to be circumscribed and limited, in a sense, stunted and crippled. It seemed the point of this was to turn lions into lambs, but I did not think this was much in the interest of lions. In a neutered world, there was no use for men and women, entities so dynamically, radically, and sexually dimorphic, but only non-men and non-women. Most humans seek to live their own lives. Some humans seek to determine the nature of the lives that others may live.

The men of this world I found quite different, on the whole, from the men I had known on my former world. I had no doubt, however, that these men and those of my former world were of the same race or species. The differences between them, I was sure, were cultural, not genetic. Too, it seems clear that Goreans were originally of Earth origin, their ancestors somehow having been brought to this world. Many customs and practices suggested this. Too, the linguistic evidence was overwhelmingly persuasive, as I had encountered many expressions in Gorean which were the same or very similar to those found in one or another of the languages of Earth. How then, could I explain to myself that the men of Gor seemed to me in many ways superior to most of the men I had known on Earth, in strength, virility, power, passion, and intelligence. I suspect three reasons might be involved. First, those brought to Gor may not have been a representative sample of the human race, but represented a selection with certain criteria in mind; for example, if one were to select plants or animals to stock a given garden or preserve, would one not, insofar as it was possible, select such specimens with care, having in mind such criteria as vitality and health? Secondly, Gor is a fresh, clean world, innocent of pollution and contamination, one in which air and water are not fouled, and food is free of poisons and adulterations. Such a world does not slow and depress organisms; such a world does not do war on health and energy. And, thirdly, in the Gorean world, as in certain cultures of Earth's past, sensuality and the body are not overlooked, disparaged, or frowned upon, but celebrated. There is nothing wrong with strength, vitality, and health. Accordingly, those who share such an *ethos*, who prize health, energy, and passion, and live accordingly, are commonly, without pausing to give it thought, healthy, energetic, and passionate.

On my left thigh, high, under the hip, I was marked. It was the common *kef*, small and lovely, the staff and fronds, beauty subject to discipline, the most common mark on Gor for one such as I. As soon as the searing iron, cleanly and precisely, had been drawn from my thigh, I knew I could never again be what I had been. I was now marked, unmistakably, as what I was. I could never be the same again. I pulled against the straps, helplessly. I had been marked *kajira*. I knew there was no escape for one such as I on this world. I had been marked *kajira*. It hurt so! It had been done to me. I wept. The tears ran profusely down my cheeks. I had had no say in this. I had been given no choice. I cried, and cried, but, as stunning, and as shocking, as it might seem, as incomprehensible as it might seem, mingled in the storm of my tears, choking, and sobbing, was gladness. I had now come home to what I was, and wanted to be, what in my deepest heart I knew I was, despite years of denying it, despite years of trying to force it from my conscious mind. I had known since puberty, even before I knew the word, that I was *kajira*. Now I was on a world where *kajirae* were familiar, where they were a significant, ingredient component in a rich, vivid, complex culture, where they had their place, a place from which, for them, there was no escape. I sobbed, but I was overjoyed. I was *kajira*. Now I was marked *kajira*.

"Is she the slave of interest?" asked the man before whom I knelt, presumably this of the man at whose thigh I knelt.

"Yes," said he at whose side I knelt.

I did not know what this meant. Of what interest could I be on this world, other than, I supposed, slave interest.

"Beyond that?" asked the man before whom I knelt, presumably this of the man at whose thigh I knelt.

"She is a barbarian," said the second man, at whose side I knelt. "She knows little of Gor. She is intelligent. She is comely. The hair is nice. The slight pocking on her face will not lower her price. It will make her more interesting. She juices at the snapping of fingers."

My bared body suddenly burned red. How revealed I was! What right had he to speak so of me, and in my presence? Then I recalled I was a beast, an animal. Such things were to be as open to appraisers, bystanders, sellers, buyers, to anyone, as much so as the color of my eyes or hair. I recalled, shuddering, my sale, the wide, gently concave, sawdust-filled surface of the block, worn by the bared feet of many women, illuminated by torches, the crowd, little of which I could see, the voice of the auctioneer, his hands on my body, handling me as the goods I was. Then, I had screamed and shuddered. Suddenly, without warning, he had forced me to reveal my latent vitality. I had then collapsed to the block, shattered, trembling, sobbing, holding my hands about me. I could hear, in my misery, in my dismay, the sudden upsurge, the new urgency, in bidding. I could not help myself. What had been done to me? Who, now, could respect me? How could I respect myself? Pretense was gone. I had been revealed as a hot, needful animal, one of several, for whom men were bidding.

On my former world a myth exists that the more educated, learned, or intellectual a woman is, the less sexual. On Gor, buyers are well aware of the falsity of that myth, or, perhaps one should say, they quickly force the woman herself to demonstrate its falsity.

I was uneasy.

My belly was restless.

A *kajira* is not permitted to pretend to inertness, or frigidity. Gorean men are not patient. They take her swiftly in hand. She soon finds herself to be as helpless, as hot and sexual, as the collared animal she is.

I knew I would respond, helplessly, to any of the men in the tent. Had I met such men on Earth I might have put myself to their feet. Had they deigned to recognize me and pointed to the ground before them, I would have knelt, gratefully, head down before them, and pressed my lips to their feet, acknowledging what we were, what they were, and what I was.

"How does she train?" asked he before whom I knelt, whom I shall refer to as the first man.

"Excellently," said he at whose thigh I knelt, whom I shall refer to as the second man.

Momentarily anger fused up within me. How dare they speak of 'training.' Did they think I was an animal?

But, of course, I was an animal.

I hoped that the momentary stiffening of my body had not been noticed.

"Beware, *kajira*," said the second man. Again I hoped I would not be whipped. They knew I was new to this world. I think they were thus lenient with me. I did not think that would long continue.

"She has received the attentions of the Green Caste?" said the first man.

"Yes," said the second man.

Most Goreans, at least in the cities and towns, and in the environs of such, have a caste. The 'Green Caste' was that of the Physicians, supposedly one of the 'high castes' of Gor. I knew very little of the caste structure of Gor, nor of the clan structure within the caste structure. The Physicians had examined me and administered a set of injections referred to as the Stabilization Serums. I did not know their purpose. I was also forced to imbibe a hideous brew. Its purpose, I was told, was to prevent conception. The breeding of women such as I, I learned, is supervised and controlled. I suppose that is not unusual in the case of certain animals. When conception is permitted or desired, another drink is administered, called a 'Releaser.' I am told it is delicious. Then a woman such as I is commonly blindfolded, gagged, and sent to the straw of the breeding shed. She is also hooded during labor and birth. In this way she will know neither the sire of the child, who was also blindfolded and gagged, nor the child.

"That she knows little of Gor," said the first man, "is imminently suitable to our purposes, but, paradoxically, if she knows too little, she may frustrate the same purposes, say, by unwittingly courting danger, by eating poisoned fruit or roots, exposing herself to theft, naively crossing the path of wild animals, stepping into a stand of leech plants, touching an ost, even attempting to escape. Such errors would provide our project with little profit. We would require a new *kajira* and time is short."

"She is ignorant, suitably so, but not stupid," said the second man. "Too, she has been informed of some things, such as the capacities of *sleen*."

I shuddered. My hands bound behind me, I had been thrust into a *sleen* pen. I feared to be eaten alive. The large, serpentine, six-legged, fanged thing rushed to me, thrusting its snout against my body. "Do not be afraid," had called the second man. I was half dead with fright. I was drawn from the pen, because I could not move. I lay outside the gate, in the grass. The second man had then pointed to me, and cried out the name 'Janet' several times. He then turned to me. "You will run into the woods," he said. "I will not give the *sleen* the 'hunt and kill' command, but the 'hunt and herd' command. The *sleen* will then return you to my feet. Do not dally, or the *sleen* will feed."

"Please untie my hands," I had begged.

"Run!" he had said.

How helpless one is when one's hands are tied behind one! And how casually, snugly and effectively they impose this simple tie on us! Some inches of cord and we are at their mercy!

I had run, awkwardly, into the woods and had run no more than a few minutes, when, to my terror, I saw the *sleen* in front of me, snarling. In my running I had lost my way. I had no idea where the small encampment with its pen was. But the *sleen* knew. Then, driven, sobbing, frightened, the animal nipping at my ankles and calves, bloodying them, I was herded back to the encampment, and fell to my knees, gasping, before the second man. "*Kajira*," said he, "the *sleen* is Gor's finest tracker. It can follow a scent months old. It is single-minded and tenacious. It will follow the scent of a single *verr* through a flock of *tabuk* without a thought, for it is the *verr*'s scent to which it had first addressed itself. Beware the *sleen*." He then cast a slab of meat to the *sleen* which pounced on it, held it down with its forepaws, and tore it apart.

I had then, overcome, fainted at his feet.

I still did not know what a *verr* or *tabuk* was.

"What of tarns?" asked the first man. "For you may have to move by tarn."

"Do not fear," said the second man. "I will hood her, and move with care."

"She is unlikely to encounter animals in the wild," said the third man, he standing to the side.

"I take it, she is illiterate," said the first man.

"Yes," said the second man.

"Good," said the first man.

I had never thought of myself as illiterate, but it was true, I could not read Gorean. In that sense I was indeed illiterate.

Many Goreans are illiterate, incidentally, particularly in the lower castes. There is, however, a caste called the 'Scribes,' the members of which, for a remuneration, can write letters, make wills, draft documents, and such. The Scribes, the 'Blue Caste,' as I understand it, is also, like the Physicians, a 'high caste.'

"*Kajira*," said the first man, "much is afoot. Danger will abound. Trails are twisted and will lead afar. Wealth and life are at stake. Surely you are curious. Surely you wish to ask questions. You may now ask questions."

A thousand questions burned within me.

I lifted my head, but did not meet his eyes.

"Curiosity," I said, "is not becoming in a *kajira*."

The three men then began to discuss a number of details having to do with things I did not understand.

My thoughts strayed back to the observatory on Earth. It was there that these things had begun.

After a time, their conversation seemingly concluded, the man who had been before me turned to the side, to confer with the third man, he who had contributed little to the discourse. He was shortly bearded, and wore a fine, but simple, reddish-brown tunic. He also wore a short red cloak. His limited accouterments were a dagger, short sword, and wallet. I would learn later that he was the most important of the three. Kneeling away from him I had not paid much attention to him, and, for a time, I would not much recall him.

I pressed the side of my cheek against the thigh of he beside whom I knelt.

"Perhaps later," he said.

"Yes, Master," I said.

CHAPTER TWO

I waited at the office door for a moment.

I put my glasses on.

I did not need them. They were of plain glass. They made me look more sophisticated, more learned, more professional.

Then I knocked, four times, sharply, clearly. That seemed appropriate. I had a folder, with images and papers with me.

I am not sure how long ago this was.

How does one assess days when one is unconscious? On Earth one might note a given time and compare it with the new time, the time of regaining consciousness. One need only consult the calendar. But what if there is no calendar, or, more frighteningly, the calendar is different, and is not intelligible to you?

I had petitioned for this meeting.

In one sense I supposed that that was not wise. In another sense, I did not think that I had much choice, however dubious from their point of view might seem my credentials, however in doubt they might hold, or profess to hold, my competence.

Data are data.

Their interpretation may be problematic.

I waited outside the door, listening.

It would be a fourth meeting. I feared there might not be a fifth. I sensed that the patience of Dr. Jameson, the director of the small, private observatory in the southwestern portion of the United States, was less than inexhaustible. At the second and third of our meetings, he had invited the two other senior members of the staff to attend, Drs. Townsend and Archer. I suspected that they would be in attendance this afternoon, as well. I feared that my position, my internship, was in jeopardy. Its terms permitted them to terminate it at their discretion. On the other hand, were they not scientists? As scientists, surely they were not free to dismiss unfamiliar explanations or alternative theories. Data are data, no matter how unusual or surprising. Must not seeming anomalies be somehow drawn within the compass of science? My findings, if findings they were, surely did not threaten the fabric of knowledge. They necessitated no wholesale abandonment of a worldview. They begged for no novel and unprecedented, transforming paradigm to suddenly illuminate a mysterious universe anew. Quite the contrary. They merely requested, so to speak, in all diffidence and with all courtesy, an explanation, and one ideally posing not the least threat to received modalities of scientific discourse. Surely science accepts that the world has its wonders, and merely trusts, if not insists, that these wonders can eventually be rationally ordered and find their place on one of science's familiar, sturdy shelves. It is obvious that the improbable is, in its way, probable. Consider one hundred numbers in a jar. The chance of drawing any one of these numbers is a hundred to one. But, the probably of drawing one of those numbers is '1,' namely, absolute certainty. But what if one of those unlikely numbers shows up more than once, even frequently?

My work involved radar imaging.

Let me digress briefly.

The existence of asteroids has been known since at least the early years of the Nineteenth Century. The first asteroid recognized in modern times is Ceres, discovered in 1801. It remains, to date, the largest known asteroid, measuring some six hundred miles in diameter. Others, Vesta and Pallas, were discovered in 1802, Juno in 1804, and so on. Today there are well over a million asteroids known. They are commonly sorted into three major types, C, M and S, the carbon-rich, metallic, and stony. Whereas there are asteroids, or asteroidlike bodies, throughout the solar system, most inhabit what is called the Asteroid Belt, which is located between Mars and Jupiter. NEAs are 'Near Earth Asteroids.' It is commonly thought that the closest of these 'NEAs' lie in an orbit closer to the orbit of Mars than to that of Jupiter. My research suggests that certain NEAs may actually orbit not between Mars and Jupiter but between Mars and Earth, and that some such NEAs, not all, are anomalous in certain major aspects. Of that, more anon.

I knocked, again, this time more timidly.

"Come in," said a voice. I recognized it as the voice of Dr. Jameson, the director.

The voice sounded pleasant, and this, to some extent, allayed my fears.

I was young, and a woman, but I was prepared, as I could, to stand my ground, cognitively. Truth, in all its casual indecency, does not wear either pants or a skirt. I had never understood, except politically, the value of genderizing knowledge and suggesting that epistemologies, or theories of learning, were gender or class based. It seemed to me unlikely that the boiling point of water, so to speak, would change depending on the sex of the cook. Similarly I found it difficult to understand the premises underlying the so-called 'sociology of knowledge' unless semanticism was involved, essentially changing the meaning of words. I suppose that one could, if one wished, change the meaning of 'truth' from what is the case to what is thought to be the case. Thus, the world gets flat if people think it is flat, and round or cubical if people take it to be round or cubical. But I did not see how that could change the shape of the earth.

The director had agreed to schedule this fourth meeting so, I think, he and his colleagues might now be prepared to take my data seriously. After all, something which does not fit now might fit later, somewhere else.

Or was I to be dismissed?

So I entered the room.

I trust that I appeared severe, and businesslike.

Surely one must present a suitable *persona*, or attempt to do so, if one is to be taken seriously, even if one is uncomfortable with the selected *persona*.

In any event, I had no intention of allowing myself to be regarded as I had been in previous meetings, as though I might be uninformed, simplistic, confused, or naive. It is infuriating to be blatantly tolerated, indulged, or patronized. My work, my data, must be taken seriously. If I were somehow in error, which was surely possible, I was, at least, owed an explanation. Let them correct me; as colleagues to colleague, let them explain my error. Surely I was owed at least that much. Might not science proceed by climbing a staircase of mistakes? One hears of 'pessimistic induction,' a concept extracted from the history of science, and that 'today's science is tomorrow's fallacy,' and so on, but does not that, in itself, suggest that each step may lead to a higher, better step?

To my surprise, atop the desk of the director, about which he and his two colleagues sat, seemed to be a light collation, sandwiches, dried fruit, some pastry, coffee, tea, and such. I knew he and his fellows often took lunch together in his office, but it was now after two in the afternoon.

I had no idea how to interpret this seeming anomaly in the usually meticulously observed schedule of the observatory. Apparently some delay had occurred, a late delivery perhaps, or some unexpected matters which, however trivial, required prompt attention. I looked at the pastry. Then I realized what must be the case. Something like a half an hour ago, a small, white bakery van had drawn into the small parking lot of the observatory. Presumably it had left by now. Dr. Jameson and his colleagues, I suspected, must have been holding off, waiting for that van. Scientists, it seemed, might, as much as others, have a sweet tooth. I envied them in a way. Calories, it seemed, were my enemy. Why should I care about such things? I did not care for men, of course, and proved it by the severity of my garb and the professionalism of my attitudes and demeanor, but, oddly, I wanted to be attractive to them. Biology is hard to root out. But why, I wondered, should it be rooted out? Once biology is rooted out, what is left behind? Many women barter their sex for privileges and favors. I suppose it is their right. Many use their sex, implicitly or explicitly, to obtain political, social, and economic advancement. What is wrong with that? Why should they not avail themselves of their assets? Is it wrong for the bird to use its wings, the gazelle its speed, the cat her claws? Yet, for some reason, I did not feel justified in doing so. I hoped I had not, perhaps inadvertently, or unconsciously, done so. It is hard to know about such things. Some things cannot be helped, and, perhaps, should not be helped. One is what one is, who one is.

But if the men were eating, why did they not so inform me, ask me to wait for a time, or reschedule our meeting?

That would have been simple enough.

But they had not done so.

Why would they not have done so?

"Has this some meaning," I wondered, "and, if so, what? Are they marginalizing me, trivializing me, implicitly insulting me by relegating my presence and importance to that of something which can be attended to between more important matters, such as light banter, and a lunch's sips and bites, was that their message to me, or is this a token of implicit welcome, one of informal collegiality, admitting me at last to, say, a coveted sanctum, a place where I could be one scientist amongst others?"

"Forgive me," I said. "I did not mean to intrude. I can come back later, or tomorrow."

"Nonsense, Atherton," said the director, Dr. Jameson, affably enough. "Come in and sit down. Help yourself to something, if you wish." He gestured expansively to the makeshift luncheon table into which he had transformed his desk. "It is we who apologize," he said. "We are late. We are sorry."

I sat down.

I placed my folder with its images and papers, on Dr. Jameson's desk, before me.

"While in the midst of apologizing," said Dr. Jameson, "permit me to tender another, one more deserved and more profound."

"Sir?" I said.

"We have, in the last few days, more carefully reviewed your work."

"Thank you," I said.

I was nervous. I took off my glasses, polished them with my handkerchief, put them back on.

"You can understand, of course," he said, "my, and then our, initial reactions."

"Yes, sir," I said.

"Many," he said, "would regard your hypotheses, your proposals, absurd, and, if taken seriously, troubling."

"I fear so," I said.

"Why are you so patient with her?" snapped Dr. Townsend, sharply. "She is a spy and thief!"

"No!" I said.

"I am sure she meant no harm," said Dr. Jameson, leaning back, and removing a pipe from a tray to the side.

"Let her explain herself," suggested Dr. Archer.

"What am I to explain?" I asked.

Dr. Jameson filled the pipe from a pouch and tamped the tobacco down.

"You have accessed computers and equipment several times, often privately, late at night," said Dr. Townsend.

"Yes," I said, "but on my own time."

"You lacked authorization!" said Dr. Townsend.

"Be fair to Atherton," said Dr. Archer. "We have never required authorizations of the sort you suggest. We have never discouraged independent research, as long as it did not interfere with the work of the observatory. We are not some sort of diminutive police state. This is not some secret government enclave, embarked on sensitive projects involving national or global security."

I did not understand the remark about global security.

"The opportunity to engage in private research, time-and-equipment access permitting," I said, "was one of the reasons I applied for my internship."

"There you have it," said Dr. Archer.

"It is not so simple," said Dr. Jameson, lighting his pipe. He then regarded me. "The sky, my dear Atherton," he said, "is a large place. We are all familiar with the problem of locating the needle in the haystack. Now, consider the problem of finding a needle somewhere in ten thousand haystacks. You see the difficulty."

"Certainly," I said.

"Two possibilities suggest themselves," said Dr. Jameson, blowing some smoke thoughtfully about.

Dr. Archer took the opportunity to take a sip of tea.

"You might," said Dr. Jameson, "find the one needle in the ten thousand haystacks by luck, an event which might occur once in several billion times, or you might know where to look."

"I did not know what I was looking for," I said. "I did know where I might look, for something, perhaps something interesting, whatever it might be. I was curious."

"You are extremely curious, it seems," said Dr. Townsend.

"Perhaps," I said.

Was not curiosity the first step on a road which might lead to knowledge?

Dr. Archer smiled.

His smile made me uneasy.

Radar imaging, a procedure in which I, as many others, was adept, is an invaluable instrument in the toolbox of the astronomer and astrophysicist. By means of it, applied, for example, to the study of asteroids, conjoined with measurement and other techniques, one can determine the size, shape, path, motion, speed, and such, of an asteroid. One can, in effect, produce an image of such a body, analogous to that of a rock in flight.

"I do not think I did anything wrong," I said.

"But perhaps something a bit untoward or irregular?" asked Dr. Archer.

"Perhaps," I said. "But I have been open about everything. I have shown you the images. I have given you the calculations to review."

"We have examined them," said Dr. Townsend.

"I concealed nothing," I said.

"One thing perhaps, my dear," said Dr. Jameson, from behind a wreath of smoke. "You did not specify your source for the original coordinates."

"I see no secret, let alone any anomaly or indiscretion, in this," I said. "I came on the coordinates in a folder, in a file drawer, in the observatory library."

"A drawer with a lock," said Dr. Townsend.

"It had a lock," I said. "It was not locked. It was ajar. I needed only draw the drawer open."

"And you did so!" said Dr. Townsend.

"The cabinet was not locked," I said.

"You removed a particular folder," said Dr. Townsend.

"I replaced it," I said.

"But not, it seems," said Dr. Townsend, "until after you had examined it."

"Cursorily," I said.

"You noted certain figures," said Dr. Townsend.

"I wondered about their significance, if any," I said.

Also, in the margin of a page, in pencil, I had noted the word 'Tunguska.' I made nothing of this at the time. I did not mention this to my colleagues.

"Why that envelope?" asked Dr. Archer. "What was important about that envelope?"

"I had seen it, more than once, on Dr. Jameson's desk," I said. "I was intrigued. Nothing was marked 'confidential.'"

"That is true," said Dr. Archer.

"Distinguishing something as 'confidential,'" said Dr. Townsend, "would call attention to it. Better, let there be nothing remarkable about it. Let it be filed inconspicuously amongst others, but let the door to the cabinet be locked."

"I did not realize confidentiality might be involved," I said. "I gather that I should have asked permission. I am sorry."

"She had no way of knowing," said Dr. Archer.

"The drawer should have been locked," said Dr. Townsend.

"I gave the envelope to Miss Bennett, for filing," said Dr. Jameson. "She apparently filed it but neglected to lock the cabinet afterwards. Perhaps she was distracted."

Miss Bennett was the observatory librarian. She was a trained reference librarian, but had no particular expertise in the technical work of the observatory. She was, I suppose, an attractive young woman, but, too, one clearly not unaware of her attractiveness. I had tried not to look down upon her. She was efficient, but, I thought, might have been more aloof and soberly dressed. She was blond and blue-eyed. I was sure she was not a natural blonde. And I was sure, very sure, she was not oblivious to her possible effect on men. I had sensed that she had carried on flirtations with more than one of the men on the junior staff at the institution. I knew of only one who had proved immune to her charms, a young astrophysicist named Maxwell Holt. Perhaps that was how she might have been distracted, if she had been distracted. She would not have had the background or understanding to meaningfully peruse the folder in question.

"Miss Bennett is no longer with us," said Dr. Townsend.

"Dismissed, discharged?" I said, startled, upset.

"That sort of thing," said Dr. Jameson.

It occurred to me that I had not seen her for several days. I assumed she was on vacation, leave, or such. A young male was attending to the library, I assumed temporarily.

"For so small a thing?" I asked. "For so brief a lapse? Surely not."

"Do not concern yourself," said Dr. Jameson.

"It is a matter of principal," said Dr. Archer. "Carelessness is unacceptable. Suppose something of importance had been involved."

"I feel responsible," I said. "If only as a favor to me, please hire her back, with my apology."

"That would be difficult," smiled Dr. Townsend.

"Do not blame yourself," said Dr. Archer. "It has nothing to do with you. Miss Bennett was remiss in her duties. That is all."

"I should have locked the cabinet myself," I said. I had, of course, left things as I had found them.

"It would have made no difference," said Dr. Jameson. "Miss Bennett's mistake or lapse became evident days ago, indeed, as soon as you began to share your questions and seeming findings with us, which would not have been possible if the antecedent breach had not occurred."

"Forgive me," I said, "but I do not approve of scientific secrets, of research espionage, of one scientific team competing with others, each spying, and stealing marches, if possible, on the others, as if some sort of game, or war, was involved. Is priority so precious? What does it matter who is first, or second, or third? Science salutes objectivity and truth; she hails cooperation, collaboration, and fellowship, not competition, strife, and jealousy."

"Do not be naive, Atherton," said Dr. Jameson. "Prestige, reputation, appointments, salaries, positions, donations, promotions, contributions, grants, prizes, awards, and such, are at stake."

I was not naive. I was angry.

I was well aware that science, particularly the social sciences, might be politicized, that ideologies often influenced what was studied, how it was studied, and by whom it was studied, and not unoften implicitly prescribed results which scientists were well advised to reach, certainly if they wished to procure advancement, obtain further grants, and such. It was no secret that experimental designs could be arranged with certain ends in view, and that unwelcome results could be dismissed, ignored, or explained away. Had not Dr. Jameson, and the others, later, days ago, dealt with my findings in such a way, so negatively. Sometimes, too, data were actually manipulated, tailored to an end, falsified, or simply invented. It is said that truth crushed to earth will rise again. But what if it did not? How would one know? What if it were not permitted to rise?

"Perhaps, Atherton," said Dr. Townsend, "you are angling for your name to be listed amongst the authors of remarkable, even seminal, papers. That is understandable. Why should you not crave reputation? Why should a clever young woman like yourself not become recognized, easily and cheaply, merely by inserting herself meretriciously into the work of others? What does it matter if you do not pay for the feather you are eager to put in your cap?"

"I seek nothing," I said. "I am misunderstood. And certainly I would look for no recognition to which I am not entitled."

"Perhaps you are poised to rush into print prematurely," said Dr. Townsend. "You would seem to wish to place us in an embarrassing, difficult, if not untenable, situation. First, we are not ready to publish. Second, it seems you wish to be given credit for achievements not really your own. Thirdly, implicitly, you threaten to proceed independently. Perhaps you could explain to us how this differs from blackmail."

"You do not understand," I said, half choking.

"Do not cry," said Dr. Archer.

I fought back tears.

I removed my glasses.

I was humiliated. I was misunderstood. I respected these men. They were my superiors. They were colleagues. I would have done nothing to hurt them.

"I had no intention, then or now," I said, "of stealing research. That was not, and is not now, my intention. I did nothing wrong. Perhaps I should have asked permission to examine the file. It did not really occur to me to do that. I did not think that that was necessary. It would have been embarrassing. I thought that that might seem presumptuous. I was just curious. I meant no harm. Is not science to be free, public, and open?"

Then, to my humiliation and shame, I burst into tears.

How much then of a scientist was I?

But scientists are human. They have their likes and dislikes, their loves and hates, their ambitions, their hopes and fears, their resentments and jealousies, their pettinesses and spites, their petulances and annoyances, their prides, as much as any others. Certainly a degree in some science or other did not automatically remove its recipient from the human race, with its flaws and frailties. As it is said, science does not lie, but scientists can.

I angrily, as I could, wiped away my tears.

I put my glasses back on.

My tears had obviously embarrassed the men. I was enraged with myself, for this unexpected and unrestrainable display of weakness. How could they now respect me as a colleague? Had I not now reinforced some masculine stereotype of women? I knew that many enclaves of men in academia and the sciences honestly did not welcome women as colleagues, being uneasy as to the effects of their inclusion. What should now be said and what now should not be said? What new restrictions were to be imposed on speech and behavior? Were now the meadows of open, hale, and frank fellowship to be transformed into political minefields? How now could one examine and review work objectively when any criticism might be viewed as evidence of bias? And how now could a male compete fairly and honestly with a colleague not only backed by law and scrutinizing agents poised to spring into action, but armed with, and willing to utilize, the weaponries of sexual desirability? And now I had wept before them. What must they think of me now? Were a woman's tears, classically and traditionally, not touted to be one of the most common and least resistible of her weapons? I hated myself.

Predictable responses were not long delayed.

"Don't cry," said Dr. Jameson, concerned.

"We apologize," said Dr. Archer. "We are not truly cads, boors, or insensitive brutes. We meant no harm. Please forgive us. I assure you, Dr. Townsend did not mean to be rude."

Dr. Townsend, happily, had the decency to respect me. He sat back, silent, and angry. He, at least, did not bring into play the hypocritical platitudes and cliches deemed appropriate on such occasions.

I felt like striking Dr. Archer.

"It is I who apologize," I said. "I apologize. I am sorry. I behaved in an unseemly way. But I am guilty of no wrongdoing, certainly not knowingly so."

"Of course, you are not," said Dr. Archer. "We all recognize that. Put it from your mind. If there is any fault here, it is surely ours. All you owed to us was, so to speak, an address in the sky, a set of coordinates. Everything else is yours. If, in any respect, your work infringed upon or duplicated ours, it was no more than would be expected. The path to a house may be discovered by more than one traveler. Independent seekers may find the same treasure."

"I want no credit," I said. "I thought my work interesting, and exciting, even fresh and original. That is why I wanted so much to call it to your attention. I did not realize that so much might have been anticipated."

"And how much do you think might have been anticipated?" asked Dr. Jameson, kindly, relighting his pipe.

"I am not sure," I said. "I do not know."

"Does your folder," asked Dr. Jameson, indicating the folder I had brought with me to the office, with its images and notes, now on his desk, between some pastry and empty coffee cups, "contain some new material?"

"Some," I said.

I began to tremble. I hoped for some review of certain calculations. Too, I now had available some sharper, more recently obtained images. The two objects were now not only surprisingly placed, as before, but more clearly defined, having arrived at an orbital position favoring imaging.

"I think that I am more familiar with certain details of your work than my colleagues," said Dr. Jameson. "Perhaps then, in the name of wholeness, you might summarize some aspects of your work for us, remind us of the sort of things going on, and bring us up to date on any new developments."

"My pleasure," I said, gratefully, eagerly.

I had scarcely dared to hope for such encouragement.

I then felt, for the first time, that these men were prepared to take my work seriously.

"But why now," I wondered.

"First," I said.

"Wait," said Dr. Jameson. He depressed one of a row of switches on the small, flat com-box to his right, and I heard a woman's voice respond, "Sir?"

"Coffee, tea, again, Mildred," he said. She, Mildred Brown, a middle-aged woman, managed the small canteen or cafeteria in the basement of the observatory. He then turned the switch off.

"Have some pastry," he suggested.

I remembered the bakery truck, the small, white van, in the lot. I supposed it had left by now.

"Thank you," I said.

"Now, let's talk," said Dr. Jameson.

"By all means," I said.

Let it be understood that there are more than a million asteroids, and many would place their count in the millions. Some of these are cataloged but most are not. Would you give names and numbers to the grains of sand on a beach or the leaves in a forest? For several days, or rather week-ends and nights, when I was not engaged in my normal work, I had pursued the matter of the mysterious coordinates extracted from the folder in the unlocked file cabinet. Days passed and I found nothing unusual at the specified 'address,' so to speak. There were asteroids aplenty, but where in the asteroid belt were there not? I grew despondent. I decided to abandon my project. What then was the point of the coordinates, or of the folder itself, which I had seen occasionally on Dr. Jameson's desk? Perhaps some error or mistake had occurred. But that seemed unlikely. Who in their right mind would provide specific instructions to nowhere? Perhaps something had been at those coordinates but was no longer there? Perhaps they were outdated? But the folder seemed current. Then, late on the very night after which I had decided to abandon my project, I began to toy with the coordinates. Perhaps something analogous to a substitution cypher, hopefully a simple one, might be involved. The figures, rather like letters, might be displaced somewhat, either forward or backward. The next morning I sorted through the preceding evening's images. Most were nondescript and uninteresting, but then, suddenly, my hands shook, and I felt giddy, and was afraid I might faint. Imaged as clearly as might be an illuminated rock at night were two unusual asteroids. The next night, and the following nights, excited and exhilarated, I bent to my inquiries with unrestrained zest. The two unusual asteroids were of similar size, some miles in diameter, and were in proximity to one another, and had emerged, seemingly, from somewhere within the asteroid belt. As they were on the Earthside of Mars, they were unusually located. Moreover their paths seemed anomalous. Their motion seemed coordinated, but surprising. I did not think they were the prisoners of an orbit, or certainly not of a familiar or expected one. These were no normal asteroids. Common asteroids are not planetoids. They are irregular in shape, like rocky trash; they are like debris, like the possible remains of a shattered world. They range from pebbles in space to orbiting mountains, even to, as in the case of Ceres, miniature orbiting continents. These asteroids, interestingly, though clearly rock-like asteroids, were *spherical*.

After a time, I leaned back in the chair before Dr. Jameson's desk.

"Interesting," said Dr. Jameson.

During my exposition, coffee and tea, following Dr. Jameson's request, had been brought to the office. We abated our discussion until the waiter left.

"Those images have been faked," said Dr. Townsend.

"I beg," I said, "to differ."

"Certainly not faked," said Dr. Archer, "but perhaps explicable in terms of some malfunction of equipment, some distortion or confusion of images, or such."

"I think that is unlikely," said Dr. Jameson.

I was grateful for this opinion.

"Granting that these images are authentic, that they are what they seem to be," said Dr. Archer, "I think that we should invite Miss Atherton to favor us with an interpretation."

"Magic," said Dr. Townsend.

"Scarcely," said Dr. Archer.

"Atherton?" said Dr. Jameson.

"These are clearly asteroids," I said, "natural, astronomical bodies, physical bodies with size, shape, mass, and motion. That is clear from the imaging. They are, however, unusual in five ways. First, their shape is unusual; second, their similarity to one another is unusual, as they have much the same diameter; third, their location, is unusual, lying between Mars and Earth; and, fourth, their proximity to one another is unusual. One such body is remarkable. That two should be found together, in association, so to speak, is even more remarkable."

"Have some coffee," suggested Dr. Archer.

"Thank you," I said.

"Nature," said Dr. Jameson, "is vast and mysterious; it is replete with surprises and improbabilities. Consider the shapes of asteroids. Bodies are shattered, shaped, and carved over thousands of years in thousands of ways. There are millions of asteroids. Is it so strange then that one or more might be spherical or near spherical in shape?"

"But," I said, "there are two, rather together."

"They might have been similarly formed by similar forces," said Dr. Archer, "in the same part of space, at nearly the same time, astronomically speaking."

"Yes," I said, "I think so."

"I do not think that their location, on the earth side of Mars is a cause for particular concern," said Dr. Jameson. "Many denizens of the Asteroid Belt, given the passing of large bodies might be gravitationally drawn from their original orbits. Too, solid bodies in space are not unusual. Consider comets and meteors."

"Too, their proximity to one another, that is, proximity astronomically speaking," said Dr. Archer, "is easily explained, as suggested, in virtue of a presumed similar origin, and their likely subjection to similar forces."

"I think so," I said.

I took another swallow of coffee.

"Excuse me," said Dr. Townsend, "but I thought you said these bodies were unusual in five respects."

"Yes!" I said, eagerly.

"Four such respects, as I recall," said Dr. Jameson, "were shape, similarity, location, and proximity, their aggregation, astronomically speaking, of course."

"The fifth," I said, "is doubtless the most important point, the greatest anomaly. But I am less sure of it. The measurements, the calculations, are subtle. I fear I am in error. I must be. Yet the math seems clear. Certainly it is here that I am most in need of your help." I was reasonably sure that their own calculations would not have entered into the dimension of inquiry which I had in mind. Why would it have? I felt I might be a fool. Had I made some egregious error, overlooked something obvious, made a mistake which would henceforth diminish me irremediably in their estimation? Had it not been for subtle deviancies from the expected flight paths of the asteroids, I would not even have considered the matter. Who would even think of openly putting such matters into the hands, so to speak, of the observatory computer? But I had done so. And, as I had said, the math seemed clear. There must be some alternative explanation. My calculations had been based on the size of the bodies and, consequently, on their supposed mass. Gravity, so to speak, takes mass seriously.

"What is this mysterious fifth respect?" asked Dr. Jameson.

"It is nothing," I said. "I must look into the matter further."

"You have raised the point, Miss Atherton," said Dr. Townsend, shortly. "Proceed, by all means. Expatiate."

"You are among friends and colleagues," said Dr. Jameson. "Please continue."

"I do so with hesitation," I said. I fear I blushed.

I took another sip of coffee, anything to delay matters. The coffee seemed to have a subtly odd taste. I had not noticed that before.

"Please, Atherton," said Dr. Jameson.

"It seems," I said, "if I am not mistaken, that we are confronted with two very unusual asteroids, perhaps asteroids of a hitherto unknown type."

"How so?" asked Dr. Jameson.

"There is a discrepancy between size and assumed mass," I said, "reflected in the movements of the bodies."

"And how would you explain this discrepancy?" asked Dr. Townsend.

"I do not know," I said.

"The action of relevant, undetected bodies," said Dr. Archer.

"I do not think so," I said, "not within the solar system."

"What then?" asked Dr. Archer.

"I will tell you what it is like," I said.

"What is it like?" asked Dr. Townsend.

"It is like," I said, "—the asteroids were hollow."

Dr. Archer burst into laughter.

I felt shamed and miserable.

"I am sorry," I said.

I took another sip of coffee. What else was there to do?

I was not sure I could rise from my chair.

I did not understand this.

"I am sorry," said Dr. Archer. "I could not help myself."

I removed my glasses and put them back on.

"Actually, it is not geologically impossible," said Dr. Jameson. "Volcanic action might be involved. In a low-gravity environment, particularly, lava might be spewed forth in such a way as to find itself beyond the grasp of the parent body, after which gravity would nurse the debris into a sphere."

"Not a hollow sphere," said Dr. Townsend.

"True," said Dr. Jameson.

"Perhaps there might have been an unexpected gravitational anomaly," said Dr. Archer.

"Unlikely," said Dr. Townsend.

"There must be some natural explanation," I said.

"I am sure there is," said Dr. Townsend, "in a way."

"Are you all right?" asked Dr. Jameson.

"Yes," I said, shaking my head a little.

"We knew you were utilizing equipment privately, at unusual hours," said Dr. Townsend.

"I made no secret of it," I said. "I thought it permissible, being a member of the staff."

"As it was," said Dr. Archer.

"We did not realize the purport of your research until later," said Dr. Townsend.

"When I first brought it to the attention of Dr. Jameson," I said.

"Which demonstrated your frankness, and openness," said Dr. Archer.

"Yes," I said.

"There is one point here," said Dr. Townsend, "on which we have failed to touch."

"What is that?" asked Dr. Archer.

"The coordinates extracted from the folder would not have brought Miss Atherton directly to the asteroids."

"True," said Dr. Jameson.

"We congratulate you, Miss Atherton," said Dr. Townsend, "on your perspicacity. You realized that the coordinates in the folder were not those of interest, but, rather, were the key to those of interest."

"I suspected that," I said. "I did not know."

"Why do you think the true coordinates might have been concealed?" he asked.

"Presumably," I said, "in the interests of privacy, or confidentiality."

"Or secrecy?" he asked.

"I did not really think about that," I said. "If I did, I ignored it, in my excitement. I was curious I wanted to know."

"Perhaps," said Dr. Archer, "you assumed, naturally enough and with good reason, that nothing should be, or would be, concealed from qualified members of the staff."

"I could not resist," I said. "My desire to know carried me away. If there is something wrong here, or some indiscretion, I am sorry, truly sorry."

My speech slurred a little. I shook my head a bit.

"Are you well?" asked Dr. Archer.

"Yes," I said. "I think so."

"Have some more coffee," suggested Dr. Archer.

"No, thank you," I said.

"You have learned a great deal, Miss Atherton," said Dr. Townsend, "perhaps more than it is in your best interest to know."

I did not understand that remark. I would, later.

"Do you think so little of me?" I asked. "I am not a thief. I would not steal your research. I would not rush into print. I could not do so if I wished. Serious journals, respected journals, refereed journals, would not credit my credentials, or my work, without investigation, without first checking with my superiors, my sponsoring institution. I want no credit for your work. I do, however, urge you to publish. The world has a right to know these things."

"You are really sure you are well?" asked Dr. Archer, solicitously.

"Yes," I said, insistently. Briefly, there was a dark rim or edge about the periphery of my vision, but I shook my head again, and it disappeared.

I removed my glasses again, wiped them, and replaced them.

I then realized that Dr. Jameson had put aside his pipe, opened the top drawer of his desk, and pulled forth a set of large, numbered photographs.

"Let us suppose," said he, "for our convenience, that we name your two asteroids, Alpha and Beta. What I have here, then, enhanced, enlarged, glossied, in color, are several photographs of Beta."

"Photographs?" I asked.

"Yes," he said.

"That cannot be," I said. "To get images like that you would need a vehicle, a space craft, manned or unmanned. You would need a flyby of some sort. There are no flybys of our two asteroids. If there were, I would know, the world would know. It would be public knowledge."

"Not at all, Atherton," said Dr. Jameson. "You are right, to get such images, you would need a flyby. You are wrong if you think that such a flyby must be public knowledge."

"You are the victim of a hoax," I said. "Those photographs are fakes."

"I fear not," said Dr. Jameson.

"Perhaps," said Dr. Townsend, "you think that all flybys are of terrestrial origin."

"I do not understand," I said.

"Let us look at some of the photographs," said Dr. Jameson. He spread out four such photographs before me, facing me.

I felt sick, faint, shaking.

"These photographs date back six months," said Dr. Jameson, "even from the time that our asteroids were nicely concealed in the asteroid belt. Beta had recently received the glancing blow of a sizable meteorite. Her rocky shielding is blasted away, torn away, on one side. You can see the exposed, curved steel."

"It is hollow," I whispered.

"It is an artificial asteroid," said Dr. Archer.

"That accident set back certain plans for several months," said

Dr. Townsend. "Now, as you know, from your own radar imaging, the damage has been repaired. It seems again an unusual, but natural body."

"But closer now to Earth," said Dr. Archer.

"Who could build such things?" I asked. "Who would build such things?"

"A race which wished to survive, which sensed that its own world was in jeopardy," said Dr. Archer.

"Aliens," I whispered.

"If you like," said Dr. Jameson. "But from their point of view it is we who are the aliens, just as a Frenchman is foreign to an Englishman, and an Englishman is foreign to a Frenchman."

"What do they look like?" I asked.

"Presumably much like us," said Dr. Archer.

"Convergent evolution," said Dr. Jameson.

"We have never seen one," said Dr. Townsend.

"They still exist?" I asked.

"Very much so," said Dr. Jameson.

"We have only dealt with intermediaries, who are clearly human," said Dr. Archer.

"I believe none of this," I said.

"What does that matter?" asked Dr. Townsend.

"Alpha and Beta, if we wish to use those denominations, exist," said Dr. Archer.

"Your own work has proven that," said Dr. Jameson.

"I understand nothing of this," I said.

"You know a great deal," said Dr. Townsend, "far more than it is in your own best interest to know."

I tried to rise, but my body did not allow it.

"By now," said Dr. Townsend, "you doubtless realize you have been drugged."

"The coffee," I said.

"You will lapse into unconsciousness shortly," said Dr. Jameson. "Perhaps, before that occurs, I might entertain you with a story."

"Let me go," I said. I twisted in the chair. "What is going on? What are you going to do with me?"

"Long ago," said Dr. Jameson, "much where the Asteroid Belt is now, there was once a fine, fresh, beautiful world, one not too unlike Earth, one neither too close nor too far from its star, neither frozen nor scalding, a world where water might exist in its liquid form, and a world small enough to allow the escape of hydrogen, and large enough to retain oxygen. On this world, several forms of life evolved, competing in their diverse ways, consciously or blindly, for survival and resources. That is a process in which some are successful and others are reduced, marginalized, replaced, exterminated, put aside, and, not unoften, eaten. As would be expected, one of these forms of life, eventually, by means of its intelligence, energy, and ruthlessness, came to the top of the food chain. Ironically, the same properties, cruelty, envy, self-seeking, competitiveness, jealousy, aggression, covetousness, and such, unchecked, which bring, or accompany, a species to the top of the food chain eventually, as intraspecies rivalries persist, and technology and weaponry advance, threaten the survival of the species, at least its survival in an advanced state of civilization. Perhaps you have wondered why, in a universe with similar elements and laws, and billions of habitable planets, we have not found ourselves deluged with messages and signals, if not visitors, from other worlds."

A darkness hinted itself in my peripheral vision. I moved my head a little. I closed my eyes, hard, and then opened them. The darkness was gone. Dr. Jameson was still speaking.

"Due to wars, the ravaging of resources, the fouling of air and water, the inability or unwillingness of factions to cooperate and address a thousand problems, over the centuries, it became clear that the world was becoming uninhabitable. Further, destructive forces were coming into existence by means of which the world itself might be literally torn asunder. The warring factions, each with an eye to its own survival, over centuries, began, in space, to build refuges, habitable fortresses, satellites, colonies, artificial worlds, steel worlds. Then, as one might suppose, eventually, factions, hoping to blow others from the face of the world, thus triumphing in an ultimate war, unleashed forces dooming the plant. Blow followed counterblow, and the world began to tremble and burn. Remnants of decimated populations, with only hours left, as they could, fled to the steel worlds, to join their fellows. And then night became flaming day, and a hundred steel worlds rocked in the blast, and a world was gone, and the asteroid belt was formed, silently orbiting the sun, between Mars and mighty Jupiter."

"I will not believe this," I said.

"You need not," said Dr. Townsend.

"There is a bit more to this story," said Dr. Jameson. "Another world entered our solar system, perhaps near the same time, a world from somewhere in outerspace, a world ship, so to speak, guided and governed by aliens of prodigious intelligence, knowledge, and power, spoken of as Priest-Kings, bringing with it its own atmosphere, life forms, ecosystem, and such."

"It is called 'Gor,'" said Dr. Archer.

"We have never seen Priest-Kings," said Dr. Archer. "But, presumably, being intelligent, they are much like us."

"Convergent evolution," said Dr. Jameson.

"The artificial worlds," said Dr. Townsend, "alarmed, recognizing the power and sophistication required to move planets, withdrew more deeply into the concealing debris of their shattered planet, and, soon, as they could, disguised their worlds that they might reside more imperceptibly amongst the orbiting ruins of their former world."

"Interestingly," said Dr. Jameson, "the steel worlds had been preparing an invasion fleet by means of which they intended to seize and claim the then-pristine Earth, an Earth on which, at that time, humans were no more than a few scattered, warring tribes, with flint knives and stone axes."

"But the armada from the steel worlds failed of its purpose," said Dr. Archer.

"It was encountered, blasted in space and melted in flight, by Priest-Kings," said Dr. Townsend.

"Millennia passed," said Dr. Jameson. "Earth stood within the aegis of Priest-Kings. Unknown to herself, she was protected by mighty forces. But, too, as time passed, Earth became less and less desirable from the point of view of the steel worlds. They began to covet, however, the fresh, green, lovely world of Gor, so much like their original world. They still covet it."

"There is no mysterious, unrecognized world, Gor," I said. "You cannot hide a planet in the solar system. A thousand effects would give away its existence and location."

"Not at all," said Dr. Jameson. "The presence of Gor, visually and gravitationally, is masked."

"Impossible," I said.

"Not given the science of the Priest-Kings," said Dr. Jameson. "Visually the presence of Gor is masked by its location, being opposite the Earth, always keeping the sun between it and the Earth. Gravitationally its existence is masked by the overwhelmingly powerful gravitational field of the sun. To use a visual metaphor, who will note the light of match behind the towering rage of a forest fire."

"Orbits are elliptical," I said. "That sort of thing would necessitate periodic adjustments in a planet's orbit."

"Of course," said Dr. Jameson.

"Impossible," I said.

"Not to a form of life," said Dr. Townsend, "which can move planets from star to star."

"No one knows of Gor," I said.

"We do," said Dr. Archer.

"Thousands do," said Dr. Jameson.

"Contacts have been made," said Dr. Archer. "Too, its existence has been theorized since ancient times. It is usually referred to as the 'Counterearth.' The Greek expression is '*Antichthon*.'"

"Let me go," I said, weakly. "I meant no harm. Don't hurt me. Let me go."

Dr. Archer reached out and removed my glasses. He looked at them. "They are plain glass," he said.

"I thought so," said Dr. Townsend.

"Why, Atherton," asked Dr. Jameson, "did you meddle in these matters?"

"I was a fool," I said. "I wanted to do something. I wanted you to be proud of me. I wanted you to support me, to further my career. I wanted to impress you."

"We are proud of you," said Dr. Jameson. "You have done quite well."

"Let me go," I said, finding it difficult to form the words.

"You know too much," said Dr. Townsend.

"Why did you wear glasses you did not need?" asked Dr. Archer.

"I wanted men to take me seriously," I said. "I wanted to look severe, prim, professional."

"She is a female," said Dr. Townsend. "She is vain, worthless. I know what such are for."

What was I for? What did he mean?

Dr. Jameson tapped out a number on his cellphone. "Bring the van around," he said, "to the back entrance."

"Don't hurt me," I said.

"She has good ankles, and lovely eyes," said Dr. Archer.

How dare they speak so? Did they not know the law? I could sue them.

"She would look well in a collar," said Dr. Townsend.

What could they mean by that?

Oddly I was terrified, and thrilled, imagining myself collared. What would a collar mean? What would I be, if I were collared?

I must desperately turn the conversation away, to other things.

"The asteroids," I said, "Alpha and Beta, are they artificial worlds?"

"You seem to take such things more seriously now," said Dr. Townsend.

"Are they?" I begged.

"Not really," said Dr. Jameson. "They could be, but are not. They are hollow, of course."

"They are empty, not inhabited," said Dr. Archer.

"What then is their purpose?" I asked.

"At the moment, they are inert, poised, waiting," said Dr. Jameson.

"I do not understand," I said.

"You must not tell her more," said Dr. Townsend.

"It will not matter, will it?" asked Dr. Archer.

"No, I suppose not," said Dr. Townsend.

"You are very sleepy, are you not?" asked Dr. Jameson. He glanced at his watch.

"Release me," I said. "Let me go."

"Why do you wear your hair so pulled back, so tightly bunned?" asked Dr. Archer. "Why do you dress so severely?"

I did not try to answer.

"She has a very nice figure," said Dr. Jameson.

Did he not know that men were not supposed to notice such things?

"I think she will make a nice item of livestock," said Dr. Townsend.

I did not understand this. I was afraid to understand this. I feared I understood this. I did understand this. I felt reduced to my utter essentials. I was dismayed. I was thrilled. I was excited.

"Do you remember the extensive tests, intellectual, emotional, psychological, and such, to which you were subjected while applying for a position here?" asked Dr. Jameson.

I nodded. What more could I manage?

"You have needs and desires, depths," said Dr. Jameson, "of which you have scarcely dared to dream."

"She is no Miss Bennett," said Dr. Townsend, "but, for a man who is looking for a fine mind in the shapely, collared beast who is begging permission to lick his feet, she will do very nicely."

Dr. Archer threw my glasses into the wastebasket at the side of Dr. Jameson's desk."You will not need these any longer," he said.

"The van should now be in place," said Dr. Townsend.

Dr. Archer was regarding me. "It is a shame," he said. "She is quite intelligent."

"It will raise her price," said Dr. Townsend.

"When she accepted the internship," said Dr. Archer, "presumably she did not anticipate that she might one day find herself exhibited, collared and stripped, on a slave block."

"The fault is hers," said Dr. Jameson. "She left us no choice."

"True," said Dr. Townsend.

"She learned too much," said Dr. Archer.

"By far," said Dr. Townsend.

"Perhaps she will not be overly distressed," said Dr. Jameson.

"What do you mean?" asked Dr. Townsend.

"Consider her psychological profile," said Dr. Jameson.

"In what respect?" asked Dr. Archer.

"Profound needs and desires," said Dr. Jameson, "feared, and desperately fought."

"I do not understand," said Dr. Archer.

"It does not matter," said Dr. Jameson.

"I think she is still conscious," said Dr. Archer. "Her eyes are open."

"I wonder what, in her deepest heart, she most desperately wants," said Dr. Jameson, "what would most satisfy her?"

"What she wants no longer matters," said Dr. Townsend.

"True," said Dr. Jameson.

I could neither speak nor move.

I closed my eyes.

I lost consciousness.

CHAPTER THREE

"Oh!" I wept, suddenly.

The sting of the switch had been swift, and painful.

I was on all fours, in the grass.

"Let me strike her, Master," said Rika, who was 'First Girl' in the camp.

Many native Gorean *kajirae* do not much care for their barbarian sisters.

"Get to your work," snapped Bakron.

"Yes, Master," said Rika, and hurried away.

"Please do not strike me again, Master," I begged.

"Barbarians are so stupid," he said.

"Yes, Master," I said.

"They know nothing," he said. "They are confused, petty, and worthless. They have a thousand babbling tongues and cannot even speak to one another, let alone understand one another. They despoil and ruin their world. The men dress dully, awkwardly. The women shamelessly bare their faces and do not conceal their ankles. They do not acknowledge what is obvious and important, and waste their time on the inane and miniscule."

"Yet their females are of interest," I said.

"Only as groveling, worthless slaves," he said. "Only in collars are they worth something, and, even then, very little."

"Yes, Master," I said.

"Let them be slaves, serving their Masters," he said.

"Yes, Master," I said.

"Of what use elsewise might be a female of Earth?" he said. "At least in collars they are good for something, if not much, for the first time in their lives."

I did not want to be struck again. It is not simply the pain, but it is also the humiliation. Well does it remind us that we are mere slaves. We are struck as animals. But, of course, we are animals.

"Forgive me, Master," I begged.

I had asked for clothing, a tunic, a camisk, a ta-teera, anything. I was the only slave in the camp kept stripped.

On my former world, I had been of some importance. I was intelligent and educated. I was sophisticated. I held degrees. I was a scientist, in a demanding discipline. I held a position, however tenuously, in a recognized institution. I was valued for my work and respected by colleagues.

Why had I not been given clothing?

I am sure that it had had something to do with my attitude, carriage, or demeanor. I had dared to look directly into the eyes of a male. I had stood before a male as a free woman, not a slave. I had not fallen to my knees immediately in the presence of a male. I had then been whipped and taught that I was a slave, in every legality. Clothing was withheld from me. Such things now, like my food and drink, what I might need, what I might require, depended not on me, but on others. My first days in the camp had been miserable. I learned well how to fear the will and might of the free. My pride and self-esteem were being stripped from me, as had been my clothing. I had been close-shackled, my ankles separated by no more than six inches of chain. I had then been hurried about, awkwardly, often falling, to attend to numerous petty tasks about the camp. I learned to fear the other slaves and, in particular, Rika, the first girl. I was chained to a post at night, in the open. In the morning, before dawn, I was awakened by a kick or a blow of the switch. Four times I had been put under the five-stranded Gorean slave whip, for, as nearly as I could tell, no reason. What had I done? How had I failed? Perhaps this was to inform me that Masters needed no reason to whip a slave. I was made more and more afraid. I did not want to be beaten. Nor did I want to be scorned and abused, scolded, ridiculed, and spat upon. Was this suitable for one such as I? It seemed so. I tried harder and harder to please them. Could I never do enough? Would they never be pleased? I found that I desperately wanted to please them. What had become of the proud, sophisticated Agnes Morrison Atherton? Where had she gone? Had I once been her? I was aware, of course, that I was being subjected to a regimen of psychological techniques. But, too, I knew that such techniques were efficient and effective, just as much as snapping a wrist or breaking a leg. I would be changed, helplessly, willing or not. I could not help myself. I was afraid. The Goreans know well how to take a proud free woman and turn her into a groveling, frightened slave. At night, after the campfires were extinguished, I would be chained again to the post between the tents. I would lie there, miserable, weeping myself to sleep. Yes, I was a slave. Could I not have known that, from the collar on my neck, the mark on my thigh? But, as the days and nights passed, I became aware, given what was being done to me, what I was helpless to resist, that there was a thousand times more to being a slave than having a collar on one's neck, a mark on one's thigh. I, once Agnes Morrison Atherton, now one who had no name in her own right, no more than a pig or dog, was beginning to think slave. I was beginning to be slave. Then one night, late, I awakened at the post. I lay there, on my chain, looking up at the three moons, the White Moon, the Yellow Moon, and the tiny Prison Moon. I shook with comprehension. I realized then, for the first time, suddenly, profoundly, and incontrovertibly, I was no longer a free woman, merely collared and marked. I had become a slave. It had been done to me. I was a slave. If I had been presented to Drs. Jameson, Archer, and Townsend, even on Earth, I would have immediately fallen to my knees before them, naturally and appropriately, and waited to be commanded. Had they made a certain gesture I would have pressed my lips to their shoes. Had they asked anything of me, including any sexual service whatsoever, I would immediately, unquestioningly, humbly, obediently, fervently, joyfully, have done all I could to please them. I was no longer free. I was now a belonging, a property, owned by others. I no longer had pride and self-esteem. I no longer needed pride and self-esteem. I no longer wanted them. I had become a slave. I was a slave. And, oddly enough, I felt a profound relief, and peace. The techniques imposed on me had not been so much enforced causalities but, in their way, a key which had allowed me to unlock depths within myself, depths I had hitherto only sensed. The fighting, the war was over. I was now what I should be, what I had longed to be. It was as though artificialities and conventions, imposed, external prescriptions, trainings and conditionings, had crumbled away from me. In the loss of a self, I had discovered a self. In my categorical, complete, inconvertible defeat lay my victory.

I had become what, in my heart, I had always wanted to be and what, in my heart, I had always been.

A slave!

Bakron turned away from me, and I lay on the grass. I was no longer shackled. I looked about the camp.

It was a small camp. There were five tents. They were round, and striped. Small pennons flew from the projecting center poles of the tents. I did not know the significance of the pennons, if any. I had learned, some days ago, not to be too forward in my questions. Curiosity, supposedly, was not becoming in a *kajira*. That is interesting, as what can be more curious, more insistent, more desirous of knowing, than a *kajira*? Perhaps depriving *kajirae* of information helps them to keep in mind that they are slaves. But who, anyway, would wish to explain things in detail to slaves? Who, for example, would wish to explain things in detail to domestic animals?

I counted twenty men in the camp.

They were diversely armed.

I did not think they were of the Scarlet Caste, that of the Warriors. The only Warrior I had seen in the camp had been the short-bearded fellow some days ago, who had stood back, rather out of view, in the tent while Bakron, at whose side I had knelt, had presented me to the camp leader, Philip. Many Gorean names are identifiable as Earth names. Names can have long histories. Doubtless many go back hundreds of years, even before being brought to Gor.

I did not know why I had been purchased and brought to this camp. It clearly was not for simple girl purposes, at least not entirely. There had been several slaves in my lot who were clearly superior to me, certainly in beauty, or at least in the sense of being higher-priced collar meat. Two, for example, had had auburn hair, which tends to bring higher prices in the market, and three were trained pleasure slaves, one who had once been sold from a minor block in the Cerulean, a famous market in Ar, the most populous city in Gor's northern hemisphere. And certainly I had not been purchased because I was the cheapest, as there were some who had sold more cheaply than I. I think I had sold in the bottom third of the prices. I think the facts that I was a barbarian, spoke, already, at that time, a passable Gorean, and had not been long on Gor, influenced my purchase. I had gathered that sort of thing from my interview, or presentation, in the tent some days ago.

There were six slaves in the camp, including myself. If I were Gorean, or passing for Gorean, or if my Gorean were better, I might have pressed the other slaves for information. But I suspected that they knew no more than I why I had been purchased. They presumably assumed that I, as I supposed they, had been purchased for the usual purposes men buy girls, for work and pleasure, inordinate pleasure.

No one was watching me.

My ankles were no longer hobbled by close-shackles.

I could have risen to my feet, walked to the edge of the camp, and slipped away into the woods. I would not do so, of course. I was well aware that there was no escape for a Gorean slave girl. We were marked and collared, and clad, if clad, as slaves. Where would we go? What could we do? Into what family, clan, or caste could we fit? Society saw us as slaves and would see that we were kept as slaves. There is, of course, another reason why many *kajirae* do not attempt to escape. They do not wish to escape. There is something many men do not understand, how precious bondage and a collar can be to a woman.

We are not males; we are females. We are quite different from males. Evolution has its consequences, if not its purposes.

I saw a shadow.

I sensed that Bakron had returned. I went to my knees. He was behind me. I knelt with my knees closely together. I did not dare go to *nadu*, the position of the Gorean pleasure slave, kneeling, knees spread, back on heels, back straight, palms of hands down on thighs.

"First obeisance position," he said.

I put my head to the grass, kneeling, the palms of my hands down on the grass, on each side of my head. Second obeisance position requires the slave to lie on her belly, prostrate.

I was uneasy.

I did not dare turn about.

First obeisance position can also serve as a punishment position.

I did not want to be whipped.

I should not have begged clothing before. What right had I to clothing?

"What is your name?" he asked.

"'Janet,'" I said, "if it pleases, Master."

"I think," said he, "you can well please a Master."

"A slave," I said, "hopes to please a Master."

No lash fell.

I was becoming excited.

I felt myself oiling.

My body was preparing to receive him. It anticipated him. It wanted him.

"Do you beg use?" he asked.

"Yes," I said, "I beg use."

"'Yes?'" he said.

"Yes, I beg use," I said, "—*Master.*"

I was then put to use.

He was quick. I wanted more. I so much wanted more. I dared not speak. I was a slave. I dared not turn around.

"May I speak?" I asked.

"Yes," he said.

"Do I belong to you?" I asked.

After my interview, or presentation, in the tent I had been put in a new collar. I was not told what it said. The new collar had been snapped about my neck before the old collar was removed. Thus, there was no moment in which I was not collared.

"No," he said. "You are the property of Bazi Imports."

I knew nothing of 'Bazi Imports.' I did wish, as any slave, I suppose, to be the one slave of a single, private Master, to love and serve such a Master with my whole heart, and have him all to myself.

"May I ask what my collar says?" I asked.

"It says," he said, "'I am the slave of Bazi Imports.'"

Something struck me as a bit odd in this arrangement. The typical collar, as I understood it, tended to be a bit more specific, or personal, and would be likely to contain one or more proper names. For example, if there was a slave, Linda, and a Master, Flavion, say, of Corcyrus, one would expect a collar to read something like, 'I am Linda. I belong to Flavion of Corcyrus,' or, simply, 'I am the slave of Flavion of Corcyrus.' Consider something like 'I am a slave of the city of Corcyrus.' That seems very general. Presumably there might be several slaves of a city such as Corcyrus, or Ar, or Argentum, and so on. Specificity makes it easier, for example, to return a particular slave, perhaps stolen or lost, to a particular Master. In the case of a company, say, Bazi Imports, it seemed to me the collar might better read something like 'I am Janet. I belong to Bazi Imports,' or such.

"May I turn about?" I asked.

"Stay as you are," he said.

I, kneeling, but now with head up and palms of hands on my thighs, looked ahead.

My knees were still closed.

I hoped, one day, to be ordered to *nadu*. How vulnerable and exposed, how primed, how ready, is a woman kneeling so before a man, a Master.

"Does Bazi Imports have many slaves?" I asked.

"Hundreds," he said.

I had overheard no talk of 'Bazi Imports' in the camp. Too, I had seen nothing in the camp which suggested a branch of, or a mission of, a company. Should there not be desks and ledgers about, which suggested records and bookkeeping? Should there not be goods, imported or not, in evidence? Should there not be agents or clients coming and going in the camp? What of wagons, or such, to move goods about, and so on? I would have been even more intrigued, or alarmed, had I known more of Gor. We were in the northern hemisphere of Gor, and Bazi, noted for its plantations, and, in particular, for its teas, was south of the equator. Thus, a collar such as mine in Bazi or its vicinity would presumably be quite common; on the other hand, in the northern hemisphere, it would, without specifically identifying either a slave or a Master by name, be almost unique. Thus, a slave in such a collar, lost, strayed, fled, stolen, or such, might be easily recognized and apprehended, even without revealing her or her Master by name. Thus, such a collar, in the north, would provide an interesting combination of both specificity and anonymity.

I wondered if I were truly the slave of 'Bazi Imports.'

"Why was I purchased?" I asked.

"Straighten your hair," he said.

I did so, carefully, perhaps a little ostentatiously. Then I returned my hands to my thighs. A girl can be very proud of her hair. She can intrigue with her hair. She can flirt with her hair. I wanted to impress Bakron. He was one of the better-looking men in the camp. On Earth I had worn my hair publicly in a tight bun at the back of my head. That was an aspect of the *persona* I had been concerned to cultivate, that of an individual efficient and formal, cool and severely professional. For some reason I had not wanted to cut it short like many professional women, possibly to project a more mannish image. Sometimes, I had privately loosened it and played with it in the mirror. I had wondered if a man might like it. I had heard that much may be done with hair in the furs. One of the punishments most feared by a female slave is that her hair will be cropped or her head will be shaved. Her hair, like the girl herself, can be sold. Sometimes free women of the lower castes will sell their own hair. Its absence can be concealed with scarves and hoods.

"May I speak again?" I asked.

"Yes," he said.

"Why was I purchased?"

"Your flanks are not without interest," he said.

That was a common way in Gorean of conveying the notion that a girl, a slave, of course, or a captured, stripped free woman was attractive.

"Beyond that," I said. "Days ago, in the tent, when you first presented me before Master Philip, I gathered more might be involved."

"What is not becoming in a *kajira*?" he asked.

"Curiosity," I said. "Forgive me, Master."

"You will soon be leaving the camp," he said. "Do not turn around."

There was a tiny shadow, such as might be cast by a passing bird. Something had fluttered over my head and fallen to the grass before me.

My heart leaped. I was frightened. I rejoiced. I hoped.

I looked at the bit of cloth.

"You may break position," said Bakron.

I raced to the bit of cloth, sobbing with relief and laughter, seized it up, held it, pressed it to my lips, and kissed it, and slipped it on, over my head.

"Thank you, thank you, Master!" I cried.

I turned about, but he had gone elsewhere.

I smoothed down and adjusted the garment. It was of *rep*-cloth. It was brief and sleeveless. It was clinging and form-revealing. Perhaps a free woman, awakening in some public place, finding herself clad in so little, might have fled away, terrified, seeking shelter, or might have collapsed in place, sobbing and shrieking in shame, but I, or one such as I, found it welcome and precious. To be sure, in such a garment, it was clear that its occupant was a slave, but, of course, it was designed to leave no doubt as to that.

It is interesting that a garment which was, at least in theory, I supposed, designed to degrade, debase, and humiliate a slave, a garment certainly intended to emphasize the distinction between the worthless slave and the exalted free woman, is so marvelously exciting and sexual. Is not a woman in a slave garment a thousand times more attractive than one clad in the multitudinous bundlings of the colorful Robes of Concealment? And what if, too, she is in a collar, is ownable, a belonging? What can compare with the sexual excitement of such a thing? But perhaps men have something to do with this. They will have females, if they are slaves, as they want them, half naked and blatantly revealed in all their desirability, exhibited for their delectation, exposed for their perusal and appraisal. Why not? After all, they are men, and the Masters.

Now I had a tunic, as tiny as it was, which raised me, in its way, to the level of the other slaves, barbarian or no.

I had never known, on Earth, if I was sexually attractive or not. But I had learned on Gor that I was, and, apparently, keenly so. There was no mistaking it. I had seen the eyes of men on me. Too, I was now collared.

I wondered what Drs. Jameson, Archer, and Townsend might think, if they saw me as I now was, as a slave. Perhaps at the observatory, as I had moved about, attending to my duties, they had mentally removed my clothing, had, idly, bemusedly, mentally stripped and collared me. I suspected they would have been pleased with what they saw. Had they imagined me at their feet, stripped and collared, pressing my lips to their shoes?

I had no doubt that, at the end, they knew well what they were doing to me, and what would become of me. I wondered if they found that amusing. I did not think that I was the first Earth female whom they might have seen fit to convey to a market on Gor, as no more than meaningless, shapely female livestock.

I had been too inquisitive. Supposedly I knew too much, but, in reality, I knew almost nothing. I had not the least understanding then, or now, of what I had stumbled on. I was grateful that they had not killed me. But why should they do that? Might I not have value, some value of a sort, however minimal, however negligible?

I could be sold, and I had been sold.

Now I, an Earth female, found myself for the first time amongst men who were as nature permitted men to be, proud, free, strong, unassuming, mighty, self-assured, unselfconsciously, naturally commanding, thoughtlessly, powerfully, severely, uncompromisingly, naturally dominant. They were natural Masters and I now knew myself to be a natural slave. This thrilled me to the core. Too, to such men what could a woman such as I, a mere Earth female, a barbarian, so different from a Gorean free woman, be but a slave?

I now had clothing, though a tiny, shameful tunic, brazenly exhibiting me for the frank, perusal of men.

I did not object.

There was a collar on my neck.

I could not remove it.

I did not object.

There was a mark on my thigh.

I could not remove it.

I did not object.

I looked about the camp, the tents, the grass, the encompassing woods.

I had learned here, on this world, on Gor, what I had always suspected on Earth, that I should be a slave, that I wanted to be a slave, and that I was a slave, a natural slave.

That is what I was.

I wanted to be a good slave.

Masters, of course, would give me no choice.

They had whips and chains.

That pleased me.

I wanted no choice.

"It is time to help with supper, Janet," said Rika.

"Yes, Mistress," I said. The 'First Girl' is often addressed as 'Mistress' by the slaves in her charge. She is not free, but she is in a position of authority. The practice is presumably good for discipline.

Masters seldom desire to involve themselves directly in the matters of slaves, in their work, their squabbles, disagreements, and such. Such matters ae commonly left to the 'First Girl.'

Rika was actually civil.

The 'First Girl' usually wears a *talmit*, a folded band of cloth tied about her head, across her forehead and knotted behind the back of the head.

I followed Rika.

My standing in the camp, I gathered, had risen. I had even been given clothing, such as it was.

I hoped that I was as attractive in my tunic as the others were in theirs. I saw no reason to doubt it.

Master Bakron had said I was soon to leave the camp.

He had not said that the camp was to be broken, or moved. He had just said that I was soon to leave the camp.

I did not understand that.

CHAPTER FOUR

I was kneeling on the grass between two of the round, colorful, pennon-bearing tents in the encampment, polishing the boots of one of the lesser men in the camp. I was not allowed to polish the boots of Philip, leader in the camp, or those of Bakron, who apparently stood close to him in rank. That privilege was not mine. Girls will fight for the prestige of serving a more handsome, richer or higher-order Master. In this camp, duties were dispensed by Rika, our First Girl. I do not think that Rika was now ill-disposed toward me, but why should I, a barbarian, have the honor of polishing the boots of a Philip or Bakron? In Gorean society, rank, distance, and hierarchy are taken seriously. Society tends to be stratified. This is not simply a matter of caste, of low and high castes, for example, but even within castes, organizations, bands, prides, groups, and such. The notion of a nondescript, undifferentiated 'horizontal' democracy in which it is pretended that everyone is equal to everyone else, despite obvious differences in ability, talent, intelligence, resources, influence, energy, placement, family, and such, and in which each is encouraged to compete with and out do the others, would be likely to strike the average Gorean as a recipe for instability and unrest. Why encourage thousands to strive for a prize which, it is clear, few can win? Are those who lose, the great many, then reduced, diminished, shown to be less than the others? How better could one produce envy, frustration, distress, hatred, disappointment, and widespread thwarted ambition? Gorean society, for better or for worse, is a stabler, more traditional, less frustrated, more content, less volatile society than the one with which I was hitherto familiar. In any event, most Goreans inhabit a tiered 'vertical' aristocracy in which each tier is regarded as important and worthy of occupancy. Whereas there are provisions for altering or raising caste, most Goreans would not wish to take advantage of them. It would not be in accord with tradition. It would not be in accord with the 'way.' What would others think? They are generally content with, and proud of, their role in society, a role without which society would be less fruitful and more impoverished, perhaps even impossible. So the Cloth Worker weaves and the Metal

Worker works metals; each fits and each contributes; and who else could weave so well or work his metals so cunningly?

He apparently waited until I had finished the pair of boots on which I had been working. He had come up behind me. I had just set aside the last boot beside its fellow. I had not noticed his approach. Then as I half cried out, startled, in alarm, the dark hood was thrust down, completely, over my head, adjusted, and buckled shut behind the back of my neck.

"Be silent, slave," said a male voice.

I was then thrust to my belly on the grass and my hands were pulled behind me and tied together. Next, my ankles were crossed and bound.

"She is ready," said a voice.

I then heard a long, sharp sound, presumably issuing from a whistle.

I did not know its meaning.

"May I speak?" I begged.

"No," said a voice.

I sensed that there were at least three men about.

I lay amongst them, prone, at their feet.

Even had I not been bound, hand and foot, I would have been helpless, disoriented, dismayed, in the hood.

I could see nothing.

How casually they do such things to a slave!

I suddenly feared I was being stolen. A slave can be stolen. She is a property, like a horse or dog. But a moment's reflection disabused me of that thought. I was in the camp. The men about seemed at ease. I had not been gagged. Then there had been the long, shrieking whistle, whatever it meant.

I remembered Master Bakron's remark, that I was soon to leave the camp.

"I see it now," said a voice.

"There, to the east," said another.

"What do they want of her?" asked a man.

"I do not know," said another.

"Even Philip might not know," said another. Philip was first in the camp. It was before him that I had first been presented.

"He would know," said another.

"It circles," said one of the three.

"It observes; it reconnoiters," said another.

"The note on the whistle, its length, its pitch, should have been sufficient," said another.

"Let care be exercised," said another.

"It is satisfied; it is coming down," said one of the men.

"Summon Philip," said another. I sensed that one of the men left the group.

Almost at the same time three things occurred. I heard a snapping, as of a flag tormented in the wind, of a stout cloth jerked tight, once, then twice, then again. I felt a blast of wind engulfing myself and the others, a tearing at grass, and I sensed a leaping up of dust and debris. I sensed the men had struggled to keep their footing. My bared, bound limbs felt a cold air.

"It is bulky," said one of the men.

"It will be slow," said another.

"Too," said a third man, "it is encumbered by the basket."

"Did you expect a war tarn," said a another, "bred for battle and speed?"

"Such a beast would be noted," said another.

"*Tal*, Philip," said one of the men.

"*Tal*, Bakron," said another.

There was then, unexpectedly, a sudden, shrill, piercing, deafening, startling cry, a screech that might have held lions in their place.

I cried out in terror and thrashed, hooded, bound, in the grass.

"Steady, slave," said a voice, that of Bakron.

I lay still.

"Who is the tarnsman, the basketeer?" asked Bakron.

"We are not to know," said Philip, "neither his name nor his Home Stone, nor he ours. We will identify one another differently."

Shortly thereafter, Philip said, "The *larl* is not blue."

"Nor," said a harsh voice, "is the *jard* green."

"Can you read?" asked Philip.

"Yes," said the voice. I did not care for its tone. Had the question been regarded as insulting?

"Here," said Philip, "are the instructions, written, as specified. Peruse them. Make certain that all is clear."

I supposed that the instructions had been written, that they might be more conveniently referred to, or reread. Also, of course, they might have been written that they might not be spoken aloud, where others might hear them.

"All is clear?" asked Philip.

"Yes," said the harsh voice.

I heard some papers thrust into a tunic, or perhaps a wallet.

"Can you make the delivery in fifteen days?" asked Philip.

"Easily," said the harsh voice.

I heard some coins moved about, perhaps being withdrawn from a small sack or perhaps from a waist-hung wallet, of the sort carried by many men.

"Forty copper tarsks, as agreed," said Philip.

"Two silver tarsks," said the harsh voice.

"Thief!" cried Bakron. "The slave herself would not sell for that much."

"Kill him," said a man.

"Cut his throat," said another.

"To leech plants with him," said another.

"Release the *sleen*. Set the *sleen* on him," urged another.

Law on Gor, I would later learn, often reached no further than the compass of one's sword.

"That is dishonorable," said Philip, quietly, soberly. The way he said that, I gathered that, on Gor, there were few, if any, arguments so persuasive, so weighty, so compelling.

"I think it unlikely," said the harsh voice, "that we share a Home Stone."

I had heard of Home Stones, but I knew little about them. I gathered that they were important to Goreans, or many Goreans.

"Run him naked for the *sleen*," said a man.

"Explain to me what this business is all about," said the harsh voice.

"I know little more than you," said Philip.

"Do you wish to pay three silver tarsks?" asked the harsh voice, or perhaps a gold tarn, of the mintage of Ar?"

"Do you wish to leave this camp alive?" asked Bakron.

"What is the importance of this slave, and to whom?" asked the harsh voice.

"Do not concern yourself," said Philip.

"Two silver tarsks," said the harsh voice.

"Do not!" cried Bakron.

"Two silver tarsks," said Philip.

"Good," said the harsh voice. "Give me the key to her collar."

I gathered that this was done. Would I then be put in another collar? Would I be renamed? Who could be interested in me, and why? It was clear to me now that I must have been somewhere, somehow, recognized and pointed out, and then deliberately purchased and brought to the camp, to be held for a future delivery somewhere. I understood nothing. I feared much. Who could want me, now no more than a humble, rightless, obedient Gorean slave girl, and for what? I had only sold for sixty copper tarsks, plus twenty tarsk-bits, Brundisium. I did not know where I had been delivered on Gor nor where I had been sold. I did not even know the location of the camp I now occupied. I knew so little of Gor. I was so helpless. I was a slave. Masters would do with me what they wished.

"Put her in the basket," said the harsh voice. "Secure her within, tightly. I would not want her to struggle about and fall. It is a long way from the clouds to the ground." He laughed. "That would be a waste of collar meat."

Bound, prone, hooded, and helpless, I knew little of what was transpiring. I did not understand the remark about clouds or falling. That surely suggested an aerial transportation or aerial journey of some sort. But I had heard the sound of no plane which might have landed nearby, no roar of a helicopter, or such. I was apprehensive. I did not know what a tarn was. And what was this talk of a basket? But I had heard, unmistakably, the arrival of some large, possibly dangerous form of life, which had apparently responded to the piercing blast of a whistle heard earlier.

I felt myself lifted, lightly, in a man's arms.

"Masters?" I whimpered.

"Silence," said a voice.

I pulled a little, squirming, at my bonds.

"Steady, *kajira,*" said he in whose arms I was held. I ceased struggling. It was pointless to do so. I was helpless. I had been tied by a Gorean male.

I was carried a few yards and then laid supine, gently, on a folded blanket, apparently, as far as I could tell, within some sort of heavy wickerlike cage. My ankles were then tied with a length of rope, one end of which, as I later discovered, was fastened within the cage, toward the upper rail. I did not know at the time how large the cage was. Had I stood in it, it would have come approximately to my collar.

"I wish you well, *kajira,*" said he who had placed me in the wickerlike enclosure. I would later come to understand that the basket, as it was woven, combined the features of strength and lightness.

He who had placed me in the basket then folded the blanket about me. "It will be cold," he said.

Something then, like a side or gate, was fastened shut. Thus, I gathered, the cage, was closed.

I heard what sounded like the squeak of a ladder.

"Stand away!" commanded the harsh voice, from some feet before and above me. This made little sense to me.

There was silence. If a departure were imminent, I heard no farewells. Friends seldom take their leave of one another in silence. On Gor, as on Earth, there are social rituals which are almost invariably observed when encountering one another or taking one's leave from one another.

Suddenly I heard a repetition of that hideous, sudden, half-deafening screech or cry which I had heard a few minutes before. In the wild, by means of such cries, a tarn, which is an enormous, crested, fierce bird, often announces its presence and, before taking flight, often notifies the sky of its pending arrival. There are varieties of tarns, even in the wild, some, where food is abundant, as in the mountains of Thentis, tending to flock, and others, in leaner environments, tending to be aggressively territorial. Domesticated tarns, in so far as such monsters can be domesticated, are bred for different features. There are draft tarns, racing tarns, hunting tarns, light, long-flighted 'spy' or reconnaissance tarns, war tarns, and such. The 'spy' or reconnaissance tarns, and war tarns, incidentally, are trained to alight and take flight in silence.

I screamed with misery, and, suddenly, the basket began to jar and jerk, and rush on its runners through the grass, and then, suddenly, swinging, was airborne.

I then, perhaps overcome with fear and stress, lost consciousness.

CHAPTER FIVE

I do not know how long I slept but, when I awakened, I was cold and it was night.

I was still in the basket, swinging, aloft.

Bound and hooded as I was, it was not easy to rearrange the blankets, which had become dislodged, but I squirmed about, and, turning and rolling, and thrusting, managed to wad or pile them to one side and then, as I could, slip between them. I was well satisfied with my efforts. I did not dare call myself to the attention of the controlling rider, or driver. I was not a free woman. I was a slave, with much to fear. I was sure he would land if and when he wished, not when I might wish. One wants a Master to be strong with one, firm with one, even severe with one, but one does not want him to be cruel or heartless. That would not be a Gorean Master. The slave, after all, is an owned animal, and few Masters will treat such an owned animal badly. Indeed, many are quite fond of their animals, their pets, so to speak. One would not treat a dog or horse badly, so why should one treat another sort of animal, the slave, badly, assuming of course, that the slave is trying to do her best to be a good slave, is trying to please her Master fully, and in every way? I longed for a good Master. But we cannot choose our Masters. We are helpless. We are slaves. We must hope to be purchased by a good Master. It is they who choose, not we. A free woman has the power of refusing. We do not. A free woman may, of course, in virtue of slave raids, internecine warfare, and such, be enslaved. She might even then be purchased by a formerly rebuffed suitor. In such a case, she will learn to lick and kiss his feet well.

I was now fairly warm.

I knew the Gorean night through which we flew was beautiful, having seen it many times in the camp, with its stars and one or more of its lovely moons visible.

I wished I could see it now.

I had no idea what direction we flew or where we were. I suspected that it might not be without intention that I had been hooded. But even had I not been hooded I would have had little understanding of from where we had flown, or toward what we might be flying.

Twice, as I lay awake, it seemed to me that he who controlled our flight had abruptly and inexplicably changed our altitude and direction, and each time, I sensed, from the dampness of the air as I could feel it, we might have ascended into a roiling forest of clouds. Once, too, I heard two distant horns, seemingly responding to one another.

We fled away from them.

I wondered why I had been taken from the camp. Where were we bound? What was to be my fate? It would be one over which I had no control. The driver had apparently, independently, altered the terms of some antecedent agreement and charged what was apparently an extortionate fee for my passage, for my shipment somewhere. How had he dared to do so? What did he know, or sense, that others did not? Why had Master Philip agreed so readily? He had not refused. He had not had the driver beaten or slain. I was relatively cheap goods. Surely I was of no importance. What importance could a slave have? What was going on?

Such reveries were suddenly disrupted for the driver cried out in anger and swerved in flight, a maneuver which caused the basket to swing sickeningly to the side. "Away!" he cried. "Away!"

I half sat up, the blankets flung about, the air suddenly cold. I struggled in the ropes. I felt helpless in the hood.

Again the driver abruptly altered the trajectory of the flight, and the basket tipped, as we ascended.

I think I screamed.

Again I sensed we were climbing into a cool fog of clouds. But this time I sensed we were not alone.

"Away!" cried the driver. "May you fly out to sea and fail to find your way back! May your eggs be crushed!"

Again the basket swung wildly.

"May the *tabuk* elude you!" cried the driver. "May you fail to detect *verr*!"

Then I again heard the snapping sound, like the air being beaten, like the smiting of clouds, and there was a screech answered by another.

Something buffeted the basket.

This time I know I screamed.

The driver was agitated, not so much frightened as wary and angry. There was another abrupt shift in flight, and the basket was jerked another way. I rolled to the side of the basket, over the blankets.

"May your feathers be infested with vermin!" shouted the driver. "May the west wind blow your nest apart!"

His cries made little sense to me.

"Begone!" he cried. "May your eggs be twice crushed! We have nothing here you want. Be patient! We do not claim your air. We want no more of it than the span of our wings and for no longer than it takes to leave it behind!"

At that point some large body, screeching, struck the basket and, a moment later, I felt the basket seized in two places, as if by monstrous hands, and, to my horror, one side and the bottom of the basket was torn away, and I, screaming, felt myself slipping, and then plunging away from the basket into the damp, cold air. I fell some twenty feet screaming, and then the length of rope which had been bound about my ankles when I had been placed in the basket, to keep me in the basket, jerked tight, and I swung, upside down, bound and hooded, in the night.

CHAPTER SIX

Moments later I felt myself being hauled upward, foot by foot.

"Master!" I wept. "Master!"

"Be silent," I was told.

I felt myself, by several coils of rope, being tied upright to what seemed a thick, wickerlike railing in the remains of the basket. The driver had, somehow, descended to the damaged basket, retrieved me, and fastened me in what was left of the basket. He then departed from my side, climbing above the basket. The blankets were gone, fallen away somewhere to the earth. The wickerlike webbing on which I stood was soon painful to my feet, and I alternated between suspending my weight between the ropes and the ribbing.

"Master!" I called upward. "I am hungry. I am cold. I am miserable! Be kind! Have pity on a poor slave!"

There was no answer.

Whatever had attacked the basket seemed to have departed. Our progress through the night seemed much as before. Perhaps it had been driven away. Perhaps it had been satisfied, thinking it might have disemboweled a foe in the night. Perhaps it was satisfied that it had driven away a territorial intruder. I was grateful that it was gone, for whatever reason.

"Please, Master!" I wept, calling upward.

I was bound, I could see nothing.

"Obey well," he said, "or I shall feed you to the tarn."

The tarn, I gathered, was the large, winged thing that drew the basket though the air. I had never seen it. I did not know if it were some sort of flying mammal or gigantic bird. Whatever it was, it was swift, powerful, and enormous, and, I suspected, dangerous. Given his interactions with the basket's attacker, speaking of eggs, a nest, and such, I supposed the attacker had been some sort of bird. Probably, too, then, the attacked beast, that which drew the basket, was a bird. Territoriality is commonly intraspecific. One does not expect stags to defend territory against bears, nor bears against stags.

I did not take his threat seriously.

I must be important to him.

What good would I be dead?

I suspected he had risked his life to climb down to the basket, return me to a safer custody, and then make his way back to the sconce from which he controlled the gigantic, winged beast.

I thought I had little to fear from him unless it be a beating or two.

Master Philip had paid two silver tarsks for my delivery somewhere, and the driver, I supposed, would also expect to receive, or extort, some remuneration at the point of delivery. Too, did not many business transactions involve a fee, part of which was paid in advance and another after the business' completion? I had little fear then of being fed to a tarn, whatever that was, or a *sleen*, or such, the latter beast being one I was already only too fearfully familiar with. I was, however, uneasy with the realization that the tarn, whatever that was, was carnivorous. I felt safe, at least until my delivery. And, I supposed, I would be safe beyond that as well, at least as safe as any other domestic animal on this strange and wonderful world. Indeed, I would later learn that slaves, in many situations, such as war and the sacking of cities, were safer than free women. Sometimes, in the fall of a city, when slaughter reigns and the blood lust of the victors is still unslaked, free women will disguise themselves as slaves that they may not be slain as free citizens but spared as acquired livestock, a disguise which is not infrequently replaced with the reality of the mark and collar. And woe to the false slave, the free woman, if her deception is penetrated by actual slaves, for she will be beaten and dragged to the burning iron. Then, collared, she will find herself little more than a slave of slaves, slaves eager to avenge themselves on a formerly hated and feared free woman.

After a time, the mood of the driver became expansive and civil.

"It is morning, *kajira*," he called down to me. "We will descend and make camp. It will be amongst trees, away from paths and roads. Thus, reclusive, remote and shaded, unseen from the air, it will be well concealed. I will tether the tarn. I will have breakfast, and give you some gruel. We will rest, and then, come nightfall, we will once again climb the sky."

I hoped we would land soon.

If I were to eat, I would be freed, at least partly, of the hood.

I coveted such relief.

I gathered that, in this area, wherever it was, he preferred to fly at night. I recalled the horns I had heard a few hours ago. I sensed that, on Gor, at least in sparsely inhabited areas, there might be danger on the ground, and possibly, too, downward from the air. Why else would one wish a camp to be well concealed? Too, it seemed danger might lurk abroad in the sky. Why else would one wish to fly at night?

"Do your thighs burn?" he called down.

"I do not understand, Master," I said. I hoped I did not understand him. I feared I understood him only too well.

"You are a barbarian," he said, "fresh to Gor."

"Yes, Master," I said.

"I thought it would be so," he said.

Why would that be, I wondered.

I did not know how much he knew.

"My collar," I said, "says that I belong to Bazi Imports."

"Do you?" he asked.

"I do not think so," I said.

"To whom do you think that you belong?" he asked.

"I do not know," I said. "I think to Master Philip, he who paid you two silver tarsks."

"He will have relinquished your ownership, as instructed," said the driver. "You are a slave between Masters."

"How can that be?" I asked.

"One who can be literally, legally, seized, claimed, captured, and sold, such things," he said.

"How is it that I am placed in such a status?" I asked.

"Presumably," said he, "to obscure antecedents, to cover a trail, to make it harder to trace you. It will be as though you, a slave, had appeared from nowhere, susceptible to being claimed by anyone."

"But you are to deliver me to a specific individual?" I said.

"Yes," he said.

"Who?" I asked.

"Curiosity is not becoming in a *kajira*," he said.

"Forgive me," I said.

"Do you like being in a collar?" he asked.

"What does that matter?" I asked.

"It matters naught," he said.

"We have no choice as to our collaring, nor as to what collar is put on our neck," I said.

"That is as it should be," he said.

"Yes, Master," I said.

"Do you like being in a collar?" he asked, again.

"I am a natural slave," I said. "I belong in a collar."

"But do you like it?" he asked.

It was almost as though I stood at the edge of a cliff. It was almost as though I was poised to dive into deep water. Free women may lie with impunity. Slave girls may not.

"Yes, Master," I said.

"Do you love it?" he asked.

"Yes, Master," I said.

"You are meaningless, and worthless," he said.

"Yes, Master," I said. How could I explain to him my desire for a Master, my need for a Master, my wanting to surrender and belong, to serve and love, to give all to another, to a Master?

"Are you white silk?" he asked.

"No, Master," I said.

"Good," he said.

I had pretended on Earth to be prim and cool, even when I longed for ropes and chains, for the touch of a Master. But I had been white silk on Earth. I had been casually and routinely, brutally, if you like, red-silked shortly after arriving on Gor.

"Tell me of your slave fires," he said.

"Men have lit them," I said. "I am helpless."

"Good," he said.

He then began to reduce altitude.

I gathered that we would land shortly.

CHAPTER SEVEN

How marvelous it was to be relieved of the hood!

It was morning and the air was fresh. Dew still adhered to branches and leaves. Rocks were damp, and, in the intermittent shafts of light, glistened.

My ankles were unbound. My wrists were still tied behind me.

The tarn was tethered some yards away, amongst the trees.

It had already been cared for.

It was a gigantic, taloned, hook-billed, crested bird. It was the first one I had seen. I had no doubt that it was dangerous. I would have feared to approach it.

I was kneeling.

My captor, or custodian, was muscular, coarsely featured, dark-haired and dark-eyed, short-bearded, and long armed. I took him to be of some low caste. I did not think he was of the Warriors. He did not, at least, have the carriage or demeanor which had characterized the red-cloaked man I had seen days ago in the tent of Master Philip. There was an easy menace about him. A metal-studded wristlet encircled his left wrist. I conjectured he would be no stranger to a variety of primitive weapons.

"How do they speak you?" he asked.

"I am Janet," I said, "—if it pleases Master."

"It will do," he said.

"May I inquire the name of Master?" I asked.

I lowered my head before his frown.

"Forgive me, Master," I said. Had I been longer on Gor, I would have known that if a man wishes you to know his name, say, he has just bought you, he will give it to you. Otherwise, it is presumptuous for a slave to inquire. Indeed, it is often viewed as presumptuous for a slave to address any free person, particularly a stranger. I wanted, of course, to learn all I could. Much seemed mysterious. In what intrigues or plans might I be enmeshed? One name might lead to another name and that name to a place, or an occupation, and so on. At this time, I did not know that many Goreans, particularly of the lower castes, have two names, a public name or 'use name,' and a real name. Spells, enchantments, curses, and such, were usually regarded as inefficacious when used against a public name or 'use name.' The case is often regarded as quite otherwise if the real name is known; hence, the common precaution of concealing the 'real name.'

As my captor, or custodian, had made no attempt to conceal his features from me, either by masking himself or blindfolding me, I had supposed my request to have been both innocent and natural, which supposition, I had now gathered, had been in error.

"Thank you for unbinding my ankles," I said.

I supposed that I was soon to be put to use.

"Do not think to rise up and hurry away," he said. "In these woods there are *sleen* and *larls*."

I had no intention, my hands tied behind me, of wandering about in a strange woods.

I was apprehensive, however, that he had even suggested the possibility. Did he know something which, if I knew it, would have tempted me to so forlorn and foolish an act?

I did not know what a *larl* might be but I well understood what a *sleen* was. I would not have cared to meet one in the woods, in the wild, one not handled by a keeper, one not responsive to, a keeper's voice, a keeper's will.

On Gor I had seen no rifles, pistols, or such. Beasts then, I supposed, must be hunted, or dealt with, by means little superior to those employed by earlier humans on Earth, hunting, or defending themselves against, the cave bear, the lion, the aurochs, the mammoth, even the saber-toothed tiger. On this world then, women, lovely and soft, statistically smaller and weaker than men, whether slave or free, had need of the protection of men. Men were important. On my former world, they were subtly encouraged to regard themselves as unimportant, as unnecessary, even obsolete. How was an unemployed hunter to occupy himself?

My captor, or custodian, then turned his back, and busied himself about the camp, looking through two leather satchels which, I supposed, had been removed from amongst the accouterments of the tarn.

Was he inviting me to leap up and run?

I remained kneeling.

He removed various objects from one of the matched satchels, dishes, a rounded sack, possibly of meal, a bota, presumably of water.

Then I saw him extract, and unfold, a five-stranded Gorean slave whip.

"Do you know what this is?" he asked.

"Very much so," I said.

To my relief he refolded it and replaced it in the satchel.

"You are new to Gor," he said, "an ignorant, foolish, barbarian slave."

"Yes, Master," I said. Surely I was ignorant and, from the Gorean point of view, a barbarian. I did not, however, regard myself as foolish. If there had been any foolishness in me it had been removed at Master Philip's camp.

"At least," he said, "you are not as foolish as you might be."

"No, Master," I said.

"Sometimes," he said, "a new acquisition from the Slave World does not yet understand, at least fully, the depth and perfection of her bondage."

"Yes, Master," I said.

"They must be taught," he said. "Thus I offered you the opportunity to flee, the opportunity to try to escape. I would recapture you, of course, in moments, and then I would have stripped you, tied you to a tree, and given you a lashing the memory of which would be such that you would not thereafter even dare to think of escape."

"Master tests a slave," I said.

I was relieved that it had been a test, as I had suspected it might be.

Thus, as far as I knew, I had nothing to fear, at least no more than the common *kajira*. In any event, I was sure that I faced no mortal peril at least until the journey was completed. It was then that I supposed that he would receive some remuneration for my delivery.

"We are *kajirae*," I said. "There is no escape for us. The world will keep us *kajirae*."

He then strode to me and stood before me.

He was strong, and a man of Gor.

I looked up, frightened, helpless.

I was kneeling, my hands were tied behind me.

"Please me, Earth Woman," he said.

"Yes, Master," I said.

I thrust my head up, under his tunic.

Afterwards he thrust me to my right side, to the grass in that small clearing that was the site of our camp.

"May I speak?" I asked.

"If you wish," he said.

"It is well known," I said, "that *kajirae* are curious."

"Like she-*sleen*," he said.

"I know I may not ask your name, or city, or town," I said.

"Nor my Home Stone," he said.

"But may I ask where you are taking me, and to whom you are taking me, and for what reason?"

"No," he said.

"I see," I said.

"I do not know the reason," he said.

"I am afraid," I said.

"Were you stolen from some foolishly enamored Master who might want you found and returned?"

"No," I said.

"Have you offended someone, far away, or long ago?" he asked.

"I do not think so," I said.

"Do you know of some free woman's unwise or forbidden tryst, of some treasurer guilty of peculation, of some seller of poisons, of a secretly hired Assassin, of a suborned general?"

"No, Master," I said.

He then put me to my stomach and untied my hands.

"Thank you, Master," I said. "May I not now tidy the camp, gather grass and leaves for bedding, prepare food?"

"We will eat and rest," he said.

"Master may now shackle me," I said, "and I will gather firewood."

"There will be no fire," he said.

"Yes, Master," I said. I recalled that the camp was to be discreet and inconspicuous, and was to be abandoned with the fall of night.

I remained on my belly. I had not been given permission to change my position. One learns such things. One is 'bound by the Master's Will.' Too, of course, from such a position, it is difficult to leap up and run. I gathered he was not sure of me. I was now free of physical tethers, chains, and such. He would take no chances with me.

He looked about, at the woods.

He then withdrew some meat and bread from a satchel and fed. He drank from the bota. I did not think that it contained aught but water. *Paga, ka-la-na,* and such can soften the edges of reality.

Why should one, in an alien or unfamiliar environment, put oneself into a condition where one might not notice a movement in the brush, not hear the snapping of a twig?

I was very hungry.

I lay quietly.

When he was finished, he wiped his hands, rose up, and set forth two bowls. He filled the first bowl with liquid from the bota. Into the second bowl he poured some meal. This meal he then moistened from the bota.

"Feed," he said, "pretty animal."

How well he insulted and diminished me!

How the word 'pretty' seemed to trivialize me! Was I 'pretty?' Did I want to be 'pretty?' How demeaning it was to be 'pretty!' I did want, I knew, to be beautiful, to be interesting to men, to be desirable to men, to be exciting to men. But 'pretty?'

I was no child.

It was a way of reducing me, of course, another way to let me know that I was no more than a slave.

I was more than pretty.

Of that I was sure.

I was not a toy or bauble.

And I well knew that I was a slave.

I was determined not to internalize my trivialization.

"Yes, Master," I said, rising.

"No," he said, "down, on all fours, crawl to the bowls."

I did so.

"Now, pretty animal," he said, "on all fours, feed."

"Yes, Master," I said.

In this fashion I could not use my hands and they were, so to speak, held in place.

The average slave eats much what the Master eats. That is to be expected. Indeed, she will almost always have prepared the meal. Too, they will commonly eat together, though he will take the first bite or drink.

I was familiar with slave meal, or slave gruel, from the camp of Master Philip. It tends to be bland, but it is filling and nourishing. It is designed for the feeding of domestic stock. Occasionally they mixed in a bit of meat or fruit. In the camp, like the other girls, I was allowed to use my hands and fingers. That I was now to feed as an animal, pretty or not, was not lost on me.

Well then was I in yet another way reminded that I was no more than a beast, a slave.

It amuses Masters to see a former free woman, perhaps one once selfish and arrogant, one once perhaps proud and lofty, so feed.

My captor, or custodian, well knew how to treat a slave.

My eyes began to fill with tears, but I was ravenously hungry and much desired to feed. I lapped at the water and thrust my face, biting, into the mush. Then I stopped feeding, startled. He was behind me. I felt the bit of skirt of the tunic flung up, over my back. His hands gripped me.

"No, please, Master," I wept. "Not so!"

"Continue to feed, slave," he said.

How could I do so? I thrust my head down, trying to obey. I was rocked. Water spilled. What was left of the meal bowl tipped, some of the meal sliding from the bowl into the grass.

"Clumsy," he commented.

Then I could not even try to eat. I clung to the grass. I endured. I tried not to feel. Then, so fiercely dominated as the slave I was, I could not help but feel. I cried out my shame, my yielding, my gratitude. I wanted it to go on, endlessly. But then it was over.

I wondered, what if Drs. Jameson, Archer, and Townsend had witnessed this? Would they have been dismayed, scandalized, or amused? Had they ever, in their imaginations, I wondered, put the young, attractive, cool, aloof, professional, Ms. Agnes Morrison Atherton, so to their pleasure?

How clear it was to me then that there was a collar on my neck, that I was marked.

I whimpered for more, plaintively, but he was done with me.

I lay on my stomach.

"You juice nicely," he said. "A Master would be well pleased with you. You are worth every copper tarsk they would pay for you. You are a hot, pretty little animal."

I lay there, on the grass, in tears of degradation, and recollected my ecstasy. Perhaps, I thought to myself, I am a pretty little animal. Perhaps that is all, really, I am.

"Pick up the bowls," he said. "Rinse them out, dry them with grass, and return them to the satchel. When you are finished, crawl to that small tree at the edge of the clearing and wait there, on all fours."

A bit later he approached me where I awaited him, near the small tree he had indicated. He carried some loops of chain in his hand. He wound one end of the chain twice about my neck and secured it in place with a heavy padlock. He then wrapped the other end of the chain twice about the narrow trunk of the tree and secured in place, too, with another padlock. Some four feet of chain then, in a gentle loop, stretched between my neck and the tree. I was then as might be a she-quadruped, tethered in place.

"You may break position," he said.

I sat on the grass by the tree.

"Have I still permission to speak?" I asked.

"Until revoked," he said.

I was anxious to learn all I could which might be pertinent to my future or fate.

"May I inquire Master's caste?" I asked.

"No," he said.

"I thought it might be the Merchants," I said.

I detected no flash of response on his features which might suggest that I had struck sparks from some flint of truth.

"How so?" he asked.

"Master seems a shrewd businessman," I said, "as well as handsome and strong."

He smiled.

Any woman knows it is easy to flatter a man. Will they not believe almost anything which redounds to their credit or benefit?

Most Masters, of course, are neither, really, handsome nor ugly. He, however, did shade somewhat toward ugly.

He smiled, again. I hoped I would not be beaten. I recalled, uneasily, that I must be careful. I was not dealing with a typical man of Earth, subdued and undermined, eager to receive any commendation or compliment, no matter how far-fetched or absurd it might be.

"I gather," I said, "Master was expected to accept a prearranged fee for my transportation, one of forty copper tarsks, but Master solicited, successfully, a fee of two silver tarsks." I recalled that I had had only sold for sixty copper tarsks, plus twenty tarsk-bits, Brundisium. The 'Brundisium' business, I understood, had to do with the number of tarsk-bits to a copper tarsk, which, apparently, can vary from city to city.

"So?" he said.

"Thus," I said, "Master was both shrewd and, I think, brave."

"I should have demanded more," he said. "And I was not really brave. I had gathered that there was much secrecy in this affair, and, accordingly, that I would be the only operative in this portion of the affair, for they would be reluctant to double or triple the risks of disclosure. Secrets seldom keep themselves. They are like the ost. They like to warm themselves in the sun."

The ost, I gathered, was some sort of snake or lizard.

Why, I wondered, was secrecy involved in this matter?

"So you surmised," I said, "that they had little or no choice but to succumb, to pay whatever you might demand, because of the privacy involved, or even, too, perhaps, because of some sensed urgency in the matter under consideration."

"Precisely," he said.

"Forgive me," I said, "but it seems you broke a word, that you failed to keep a commitment or agreement, that you were dishonest, that you cheated them, that you betrayed them, that you swindled them."

"We did not share a Home Stone," he said.

"But did you not then place yourself in jeopardy?" I asked.

"You are in little danger of a sword which cannot reach you," he said.

"You were to accept forty copper tarsks for my transportation," I said. "How much are you due for my delivery?"

"The balance of my fee," he said, "the second forty tarsks."

"It would be difficult for you to heighten that fee and survive," I said, "as you would then be pretty much within the grasp of your principal."

"True," he said. "I have given the matter some thought."

"I gather," I said, "that the journey to the point of my delivery will last several days."

"It would," he said.

I did not quite understand that.

"Master Philip, the camp master," I said, "asked if you could make the journey in fifteen days, and you said, 'easily.'"

"I recall," he said.

"Do you think it will take ten days, or twelve days, or such?" I asked.

"We have already put several Ahn in flight," he said. "From here, given decent weather and typical winds, I would conjecture the journey could be made in, say, eleven days."

"The basket is ruined," I said. I really did not wish to be tied to the remains of the basket as I had been last night. Perhaps it could be repaired or somehow replaced.

"Rest now," he said. "We leave in a few Ahn."

"Yes, Master," I said, reclining on the grass.

I did not immediately go to sleep.

Something was troubling me.

I knew not what it was.

I dropped off to sleep.

I dreamed I was half-naked and was chained to a tree on a far, fresh, beautiful world, and then I awakened, suddenly, and half stifled a scream. I yanked at the chain. I was half-naked and chained to a tree on a far, fresh, beautiful world. It was already dark. My captor, or custodian, was up, attending to the tarn.

I think I suddenly realized, frightened, what had been troubling me, what seemed, an idea, an understanding, a fear, like a threatening beast creeping about, just outside the light of a fire. It seemed as if I saw its eyes blazing in the darkness. Then it approached, and it seemed I saw the lowered head, the lowered body with arched shoulders, the massive hindlegs gathered beneath that long, sinuous, excited, trembling body, poised as though to spring. It suddenly became clear to me what I feared. Knowing little or nothing, I must yet know too much. Two large, mysterious artificial asteroids, whatever their purpose or intent, were out of position, were between Mars and Earth. What were they doing there? Intelligence, calculation, and intent seemed involved. And was there not, supposedly, a distant, silent war being waged, one in which the fate of worlds might hang in the balance? In such a war what might be the role, if any, of those large, mysterious, artificial bodies? On Earth I had stumbled on things I did not understand. Even so, as ignorant as I was, my scrap of knowledge, not even understood, had been enough to send me to the markets of Gor. Now, on Gor, that same scrap of knowledge, which I did not understand, might be a piece in a puzzle of which I knew nothing, yet a piece which might be terribly meaningful to others. My bit of knowledge, unbeknownst to me, might threaten powerful forces or beings. I was now sure that I had been hunted, and was now caught! Perhaps Drs. Jameson, Archer, and Townsend had been castigated. They had not killed me. Had they then, inadvertently, put at risk large, dark plans, due to the indulgence with which they had treated a foolish intruder who did not even know what she was doing? Doubtless they had erred. Were they still alive? What was one life in the scales, easy enough to snuff out, against the weight of worlds? So that was the solution of the mystery! So that explained all! That was why I was wanted! I was a possible threat. What now was my life worth? I felt cold. I was sick. I trembled. I wept. I yanked at the chain, futilely.

"What is wrong, *kajira*?" inquired my captor, or custodian, who had now approached, unnoted, his doings with the tarn doubtless concluded.

I continued to pull at the chain, wildly, weeping.

"Stop," he said.

"Let me go!" I wept. "Let me go!"

I could not help myself. Had I been able to look upon myself, I would have seen what any dispassionate observer would have seen, a piteous, beside-herself, hysterical slave. I who had so often prided myself on the walls of my self-control had now witnessed those walls collapse. Horror and fear shook me as a dog might have a cat.

His hand was then in my hair and he turned my face to him and, with the palm and back of his right hand, he struck me, sharply, four times, back and forth, left cheek, right cheek, left cheek, right cheek, and then, released, I sank to the grass before him, a quieted, cuffed slave.

He then went to the tarn and returned, shortly, with a small flask.

He lifted me up to my knees and put his hand behind the back of my head. "Here," he said, bringing the flask to my lips. "Drink this. It will calm you."

I swallowed the contents of the flask. As far as I could tell it was only water.

"It will take at least ten days to convey me to the agreed-upon delivery point, will it not?" I asked.

"It would take something like that," he said. "Why?"

"I was curious," I said.

"What frightened you?" he asked. "You were upset."

"Forgive me, Master," I said.

"If you carry on like that," he said, "it will lower your price. You might be beaten. You might be fed to *sleen*."

"Forgive me, Master," I said.

"Things are better now," he said.

"Yes, Master," I said.

Somehow I was no longer upset, no longer afraid.

"The drink!" I whispered.

"Steady," he said. "It is harmless."

"You drugged me," I said.

"I have helped you to relax," he said.

"What is it?" I asked.

"*Tassa* powder," he said, "a little, in solution. In wine, it is often used by slavers in the acquisition of free women."

"Is Master of the Slavers?" I asked.

"No," he said. "But I have done various things at various times. One picks up one's coins where one finds them."

I did not doubt that of such a man.

"Are you still afraid?" he asked.

"No, Master," I said, and lapsed into unconsciousness.

CHAPTER EIGHT

I awakened in flight.

I was not in a tarn basket, nor tied in the shambles of one as I had been last night.

The remains of the tarn basket had been discarded.

I lay on my back, stretched over a broad convex sheet of leather which was part of the saddle. My hands were chained back, over my head, to a ring, and my ankles were chained, as well, to another ring.

I was naked.

Happily I was not hooded.

I could see little of the tarn, but there was no mistaking the large, broad wings which, stroke by stroke, sped us through the air.

The reins of the tarn, a set of straps ran over my belly.

"It is time you awakened, *kajira*," he said. "I trust you slept well. I trust you have recovered from your indisposition of yesterday evening."

"Yes, Master," I said.

"What was wrong?" he asked.

Suddenly my fear again swept over me. I began to cry.

"Are you mad?" he asked.

"I do not want to die," I wept.

"You are not unique," he said. "Few regard that prospect with zest. What is wrong?"

"They want to kill me," I said.

"Who?" he asked.

"Those to whom you are to deliver me," I said.

"How do you know?" he asked.

"It must be," I said.

What could he know of secret wars, of intrigues which might be both subtle and vast? How could I speak to him of depths which I myself could not fathom?

"Please, please do not give me over to those who await me," I begged.

"Do you bargain?" he asked.

"No, Master," I said. Could a dog bargain with her Master? I was not a free woman. I had nothing with which to bargain. I did not even own my own collar. I could not dangle my favors tantalizingly before him. Already I lay before him, naked and chained, his to do with as he might please.

"But you might plead?" he said.

"Yes, yes, yes, Master!" I said.

"What a slave wishes does not matter," he said.

"Yes, Master," I wept.

Who did not know that?

"You are very stupid," he said.

"How so?" I asked.

"Or, more likely, you think me unbelievably stupid," he said.

"No, Master," I said.

"Think," he said. "It need not cause pain."

"I do not understand," I said.

"I am not stupid," he said. "I am shrewd, I am clever."

"Yes, Master," I said.

"I was to pick you up for forty copper tarsks, a fee that attracts little attention," he said. "But I suspected a *sleen* in the vicinity. When you see the snout of a *sleen*, the rest is not far behind. I gambled. I won. I extorted two silver tarsks. I was clever, I was shrewd. Do you think then I will deliver you somewhere for the paltry sum of another forty copper tarsks? I would be a fool to do so. I could sell you for more."

"Master!" I sobbed suddenly, joyfully.

He made some adjustment to the reins of the bird.

"Then you have no intention of delivering me to the contracted party?" I said, the morning suddenly become bright.

"No," he said.

"And Master's trick," I said, uneasily, "might not work twice."

"No," he said. "Definitely not. It would not be favored by the odds. You would be in the vicinity, available for discovery, and seizure, and I would be within range of retaliation."

"And word of your brilliance, your economic coup, might even now be speeding from the camp of Master Philip to the point of delivery."

"I think not," he said. "Much here is secret. I do not think that Philip would know fully the point of delivery, the parties involved, or such things."

"Even so," I said, "the delivery unmade, you have placed yourself at risk."

"It will be many days before it is even realized at the delivery point that the delivery is late, let alone that it will not be made. By then I could be anywhere, in the mountains of Thentis, in the Tahari, in the Barrens, in far Turia, even at the World's End."

"I am unutterably grateful," I said.

"It will not be easy for you to be traced," he said.

"My collar," I said, "identifies me as the property of Bazi Imports, a collar supposedly rare this far north."

"I have the key," he said. "I will remove it and scrape away the legend. Such collars, defaced, re-lettered, and so on, are not rare, particularly amongst the Peasants."

"I am marked with the *kef*," I said.

"Do not concern yourself," he said. "It is the most common slave brand on Gor."

"Master will sell me?" I said.

"As soon as possible," he said.

"I am content," I said, happily.

"I will cause the bird to veer," he said. "Look then, as you can, below."

I was pleased to look forward to this, as I had seen little so far but clouds, and an occasional bird.

Suddenly the bird shifted flight, and I gasped, but, swung in the chains and rings, I looked down, eagerly, to my left.

"Those are ripening *sa-tarna* fields," he said, "there, in the Vosk basin, south of the river. Some of the richest farmland on Gor lies in the Vosk basin. Look further and you can see the river, like a silver ribbon, in the distance. It seems narrow from here but it is a mighty river, often four or five *pasangs* in breadth. It drains most of a continent. It goes past dozens of towns and villages. It empties into the vast marshland of the delta, and, beyond, into the Tamber Gulf and then into Thassa, the sea."

"It is beautiful," I said.

At the moment I suspected that anything would look beautiful, even were it not as beautiful as the broad, lush golden fields below.

Then the bird, guided by the reins, righted its flight, and I sank back over the heavy, convex sheet of leather over which I was chained. It struck me as I did so how my body, arched over the leather, was lifted before the controller of the bird, as though for his perusal or casual touch.

"This is a beautiful world," I said.

"We intend to keep it that way," he said, angrily.

I was startled. I wondered if he had ever been to my former world. Perhaps he had heard stories of its economic pillaging and the vile failures of the stewardship to which it had been subjected. What was one to make of creatures which fouled their own dens or nests? There was a saying on Gor that the females of Earth were fit only to be the slaves of men of Gor. But is it not always the case that the females of the enemy become the vulnerable, helpless slaves of the victors? And is not that as it should be? Women are properly slaves and loot. Let them understand themselves so. What woman does not know in her heart that she is the proper slave of a Master?

"Oh!" I said, for I had been touched.

"I am going to prime you," he said, "and bring you to the point of yielding, to the point where you beg to yield, and then I shall desist."

"No, Master!" I begged. "Do not do so! Please do not do so! Do not be cruel! Have mercy on a poor slave!"

"Do not concern yourself," he said. "It will not last long. I would not even have begun had I not noted below that for which I have been searching."

How could I not concern myself?

For what had he been searching?

"Do not begin what you will not finish," I begged.

"Be silent," he said.

I gasped.

I twisted in the chains and rings.

I whimpered.

I lay at his mercy.

CHAPTER NINE

"Will a leash be necessary?" he asked.

"No," I said. "I will heel you."

"Make certain that you do not brush against my body," he said. "I know that trick."

I was kneeling in the grass, naked, my hands bound behind me.

I whimpered.

"No," he said.

I struggled a foot or two toward him, and put down my head, pressing my lips to his bootlike sandals. "Please, Master," I begged.

"No," he said. "On your feet."

I had to follow him only a short way. I was pleased for that. It was not easy to walk. It was painful in my heightened state of induced arousal. I feared I might shatter and burst. If I did so, I was sure that I would feel his belt, savagely. Perhaps, I thought, the relief would be worth the ensuing pain. But I would struggle to contain myself. I was a woman of Earth. I had now met men of Gor. I feared to displease one. How right and necessary it seemed to me to obey them. Then, mercifully, he stopped.

It was no accident he had brought the tarn down where he had.

Standing in the grass, waiting, I viewed a sight which I had never anticipated viewing, a sight which on Earth had not been seen for perhaps a thousand years.

The line was quite long.

I began to tremble and was afraid, but the demeanor of my captor, or custodian, made it clear that, from his point of view, nothing unusual or amiss was occurring.

The long line was flanked by some dozen or so helmeted and lance-bearing riders mounted on what seemed to be agile, bipedalian lizards of some sort. The heavy, clawed feet of the mounts, I was sure, could crush a human being. There were no trees in the vast grassy plain now stretching about us, seemingly endlessly, nothing to climb, to avoid the peril of an interaction with such large, scaled, plated beasts. My captor, or custodian, seemed calm. One of the riders noted us, for he turned his mount slowly in our direction. My captor, or custodian, lifted his hand. The rider acknowledged this overture by dipping and lifting the point of his lance. I could scarcely conjecture what might be the shock of a massed charge of such beasts, fierce and mighty, with lancers astride. Yet here the beasts were amply separated, a few on each side of the long line. This first rider was then joined by a second rider, one with a helmet crested with the hair of some animal. Both approached us. The impact of one of their lances, couched, with the weight of the mount, say, running, would be formidable. Both riders had stirrups, which would keep the lancer in the saddle.

"*Tal*," said my captor, or custodian.

"*Tal*," said the newcomers.

In the presence of free males, I knelt.

I noted that both riders, had, slung at the side of the saddle, amongst other accouterments, a coil of rope and what appeared to be a net of some sort. I supposed that that might be used in hunting, for example, to net a running animal.

"Split your knees a little," said my captor, or custodian.

I did so, a little.

A tear came to my eye.

He did not want my thighs to touch. He knew well what might be the consequence of that. More than once I had been on the brink of shattering. Several times, when I had lain before him, helpless in the chains and rings, he had brought me almost to the point of explosion and had then denied me the release I craved. My begging had been ignored. He had been amused. What power he held over me, a poor slave!

Now, once again, my tensions were coiling and knotting and weeping in my belly, and, it seemed, engulfing my entire body.

He put his hand lightly, casually, as though inadvertently, on my shoulder, and I wanted to scream.

The men of Gor had done their work with me. They had ignited slave fires, which could be conveniently rekindled.

The long line was now making its way past us, some twenty yards away. In that line there may have been better than four hundred female slaves, naked, and chained together by the neck, their wrists thonged together, as were mine, behind their back.

Some looked idly upon us.

There was nothing unusual in what they saw, three men, one afoot and two recently dismounted, a pair of large, agile saddle lizards, and a kneeling, stripped, tied, slave.

But there was much unusual from my point of view in what I saw. What on my dismal, gray, crowded, polluted world, so sanctimonious and smug, so short-sighted, selfish, and self-satisfied, had prepared me for this, a lengthy, single-file coffle of lovely, naked, chained, tied, slaves? Had these been culled from a hundred slave camps? Was this this the harvest of a season's raids? Was this the loot extracted from a hundred smoldering villages and towns? Had a city fallen, its walls breached, its gates smote asunder, its edifices looted, its temples burned, its daughters gathered and marked as slaves? Perhaps I was most struck by the remarkable beauty of the coffle, but I would learn later that the only thing really unusual about this coffle was its length. Just as many wagons may join in caravans for the sake of safety, so, too, several slave houses may move their goods together to certain markets, to minimize the risk of theft. Each of those slaves, I later learned, had inscribed on her left breast, in bold, grease pencil, the emblem of the house which owned her. Thus, perhaps as many as ten to fifteen houses might be moving their goods in this one coffle. In Gorean, there is an expression 'slave beautiful.' The meaning obviously is that the woman to whom it is applied is assessed as being beautiful enough to be a slave. Goreans are seldom interested in ugly slaves, or, for that matter, in stupid slaves. Neither sells well. Sometimes, to her chagrin, a captured free woman is released as being 'unworthy of the collar.' The collar is, accordingly, taken as a badge of female desirability. As the slave is valuable, slave theft is not unknown on Gor. The slave, of course, is seldom easily stolen. She may be chained to the foot of her Master's couch, chained to slave posts in public places, while the Master goes about his business, and so on. The slaves in the coffle now passing, for example, were chained together by the neck. This not only prevents escape but reduces the risk of theft. Also, as I would learn, the coffle chaining was secured not by locks and keys but by hammering. This also minimizes the risk of theft. Woman theft, incidentally, like the theft of other valuables, vessels of gold, plates of silver, rolls of silk, and so on, is not without its risks. One of the putative justifications for the differences between the attire of slaves and free women is to protect free women. A raider, for example, scouting a slave, can see what he would be getting, what he would be risking his life for. In the case of the free woman, on the other hand, he may not know. Few men are willing, at least in private raids, to risk castration and impalement for a woman who might turn out to be as ugly as a she-tarsk. Accordingly, espionage of a sort may take place, cultivating dressing slaves, spying at women's public baths, and such.

"What do you want for her?" asked the dismounted rider with the helmet crested with hair. The cresting was apparently a sign of rank. I would later learn that the most common cresting is fashioned from *sleen* hair.

"Three silver tarsks," said my captor, or custodian. For ease of identification, if not of accuracy, I will now refer to him briefly, as 'my captor.' He made no pretense of being my owner. I was, as I recalled, at least in some sense, 'between Masters.'

"Three silver tarsks," said my captor, once more.

"Too much," said the fellow with the crested helmet, whom I shall now refer to as the first man, and his fellow as the 'second man.'

"That is much what I paid for her," said my captor.

"What did he pay for you, girl?" asked the first man.

"I do not know," I said. That seemed to me the safest thing to say. Actually, of course, he had paid nothing for me. In my sale, I had only sold for sixty copper tarsks, plus twenty tarsk-bits, Brundisium, whatever that meant. I did not even know where I had been sold.

"Her face is pocked," said the second man.

That was the result of an illness I had had as a girl, connected with food poisoning.

"No one claims she is a gold-tarn girl," said my captor.

He began to move his fingers on my shoulder.

I would have much preferred that he had not done so.

I had been well primed.

"What do you think you are worth, girl?" asked the first man. "Three silver tarsks?"

"Whatever Masters will pay for me," I said.

"And what if they pay nothing?" he asked.

"Then nothing," I said.

"Her blemishing," said my captor, "is scarcely noticeable. If anything, it makes her more attractive, in a particular way. On a dark night are not the stars more beautiful? Is not the striped jungle *sleen* more beautiful than the tawny prairie *sleen* or the snow *sleen* of Ax Glacier?"

From what I had seen of a *sleen* in Master Philip's camp, I was not at all sure that I could find any *sleen* to be beautiful. Terrible perhaps, but beautiful? How could beauty be conjoined with that serpentine, six-legged body, those claws, that fanged maw?

At my first sale, and in Philip's camp, no one had objected to my face, not even the other slaves. As far as I could tell, no one had even noticed.

Is it not the business of the seller to raise the price, as he can, and that of the buyer to reduce it, as he can?

I thought I was beautiful.

Certainly, several men had seemed to think so.

"Three silver tarsks," said my captor.

"She is a copper-tarsk girl," said the first man.

"Two silver tarsks," said my captor.

"Twenty copper tarsks," said the first man.

"Absurd," said my captor. "One might as well sell her for *sleen* feed."

The second man pointed to the passing coffle. "There are four hundred and twenty slaves in the coffle. We do not need another."

"One silver tarsk," said my captor.

"Twenty copper tarsks," said the first man.

"She is as hot as a Tahari dancer," said my captor, "as hot as a *paga* slave from Brundisium or Port Kar. She juices promptly, splendidly. Two days in a slave box and she will scream with need. She begs for chains. Imagine her crawling to you, needfully, whimpering, the whip in her teeth."

"Twenty copper tarsks," repeated the first man.

My captor then took me by the hair and forced me down to the grass and, at the same time, placed his hand on me.

"Yes!" I shrieked, and pressed gratefully, forcefully, against him. He removed his hand and I writhed in the grass.

"Sixty copper tarsks," said the first man.

"Ninety," said my captor.

"You primed her," said the second man.

"Eighty," said the first man.

"Done!" said my captor.

That was more than I had originally sold for.

"What is her collar?" asked the first man.

"That is not important," said my captor.

"May I see it?" asked the first man.

"That is not necessary," said my captor. "I will remove it."

"And scrape it?" asked the first man, amused.

"I have a file," said my captor.

"You never bought her," said the first man. "You stole her. I thought it would be so."

I supposed that, in a sense, I had been stolen.

"Does that matter?" asked my captor.

"Not to the house of Kleon," said the first man.

"We do not inquire into such matters," said the second man.

"I found her wandering about," said my captor.

"Of course," said the first man.

"Who, seeing a pretty bauble," said my captor, "will not stoop to pick it up?"

"Remain here," said the first man. "We will send a rider back to pick her up."

"With eighty copper tarsks," said my captor.

"With eighty copper tarsks," said the first man. He and his companion then remounted their strange steeds and rode away, toward the head of the passing coffle.

I, now subsided, lay quietly in the grass.

Well had I demonstrated that I was a slave.

I had not been able to help myself.

I did not care.

I did not want to help myself.

"I have been sold," I thought. My life was now to take a new turn.

Then I became afraid.

"I am afraid," I said.

"What are you afraid of now?" asked he to whom I have referred as my captor.

"I am afraid I will be found, and apprehended," I said.

"Dismiss that fear," he said. "That is extremely unlikely. I flew in the direction of the point to which I was to deliver you only until I could no longer be seen from the camp. Then I changed my direction."

"To meet this chain?" I asked.

"Only to the vicinity," he said.

"You did not tell them I was a barbarian," I said.

"They did not ask," he said. "They need not know."

"Thank you, Master," I said. "That will make me less conspicuous, make me harder to trace."

"I thought it might lower your price," he said.

"I see," I said.

"A rider approaches," he said. "Kneel up."

The approaching rider was astride another of those unusual mounts.

My captor removed a small key from his waist wallet and, a moment later, freed my neck of the collar. It was the first time since my original collaring on Gor that I, as far as I knew, had not been collared. He then slipped the collar into his tunic.

I was, of course, naked, tied, and well marked.

"I do not wish to be traced either," he said.

The new rider hauled back on the reins of his beast, and it reared, and then its heavy, clawed forelimbs struck back, down, hard, into the turf.

He wore no helmet and carried no lance. A wide blue scarf ran from his right shoulder to his left hip. On the left side of his saddle was a purse and, on the right side, a rope and slave whip.

He dismounted easily and freed the purse, from which he counted, doubtless, eighty copper tarsks.

My captor then housed these in his waist wallet.

The newcomer regarded me.

"Is she free?" he asked. "She has no collar."

"No," said my captor.

I knelt quietly while a new collar was snapped about my neck.

"It says," said the newcomer, "I am owned by the House of Kleon."

"Yes, Master," I said.

He then took a grease pencil from a rectangular case hooked at his belt, and traced, deeply, some design on my left breast.

"That is the mark of the House of Kleon," he said, placing the pencil back in its rectangular case.

"Yes, Master," I said.

That mark could be recognized several feet away.

"The coffle is large and the guards few," said my captor. "Do you not fear slave theft?"

"No," said the newcomer. "Theft is impractical. First, the coffle is too large to steal. What common band of brigands could essay such a task? How could they hope to make away with, and conceal, better than four hundred slaves? You would need the resources of a city. Size is safety. Second, the slaves are chained together, and the linkages of their chaining are closed by hammering. Tools and time would be needed. It is not practical for brigands to address themselves to the task. It is not as though they could cut a few *kaiila* out of the herd and make away with them."

The newcomer then drew shut the purse, or coin sack, and replaced it at the left side of the saddle, and, coming about the right side of the mount, removed the slave whip and rope from the saddle. Scarcely regarding me, he held the whip to my lips and I kissed it, routinely acknowledging my slavery and submission. He then replaced the whip at the saddle and tied one end of the rope about my neck. He then had me rise and led me to the left side of the saddle, where he tied the free end of the rope to the left stirrup.

I was uneasy, being so close to the large reptilian mount.

"What is wrong, slave girl?" asked the newcomer. "Have you never seen a *tharlarion* before?"

"Forgive me, Master," I said.

The newcomer climbed to the saddle, and was then high above me, to my right.

"So that is a *tharlarion*," I thought. I would later learn that there were many *tharlarion*, of diverse types on Gor, bred and trained for a variety of purposes.

"I wish you well," said my captor.

"I wish you well, Master," I said.

The newcomer then kicked back in the stirrups and the beast began to move forward.

I hurried in order not to lose my footing.

Soon my captor was well behind us.

I looked back once and saw him standing in the grass, watching us leave.

I did not expect to see him again.

I did not even know his name.

CHAPTER TEN

"What is your collar?" she asked.

"House of Kleon," I said.

The mud in the large, palisaded slave pen was ankle-deep. It had rained heavily the last two days.

"A minor House, an inferior House," she said. "Mine is the House of Ho-Turik."

"That is a better House?" I asked.

"Everyone knows that," she said.

"A guard arranged for my purchase, in the fields, three days before we reached the river," I said.

"The guards work for the various houses," she said. "He was probably a House-of-Kleon guard."

I supposed that was likely.

"He was authorized to purchase," I said.

"Many are," she said. "Did he have a helmet crested with *sleen*-hair?"

"It was crested," I said.

"*Sleen* hair," she said.

"I do not know," I said.

"*Sleen* hair," she said, "if he bought for a house."

I was muchly pleased to be out of the coffle.

Many of the slaves had been in it for weeks, trekking overland. In this respect I was very fortunate.

"It is going to rain again," she said.

I shuddered. In the pen we were nude. The small blanket I had been issued was still damp. In the coffle we had not been given blankets. Slaves are often nude in slave pens and in coffles, particularly when the coffles are in the open country, away from towns and cities. There is thus less soilage from sweat and dust. We had been brought into the small river port of Victoria Minor after darkness, presumably to avoid offending the sensibilities of free women. Victoria Minor is on the south shore of the Vosk. It is not to be confused with Victoria on the north shore, across from it, which is one of the major ports on the Vosk, noted in particular for its slave markets, serving much of the Vosk Basin. Most slaves reach Victoria from east on the river, brought downstream on oared river boats. Some are floated downstream on flatboats which, at the end of the journey, be it at Victoria or further downriver, are sold for scrap or burned. Victoria Minor, on the other hand, given its location, provides a practical transit point to Victoria, across the river, for overland traffic from the east.

"What is Victoria like?" I asked her.

"I do not know," she said. "I have never been sold there."

"Many are sold in lots there," said another slave.

I did not know whether that would be to my advantage or not.

One thing was for certain. I would have nothing to say about it.

"When are we to cross the river?" asked Luta, she to whom I had been speaking, of the other slave.

"I think, soon," said the other.

"It is raining," said Luta, angrily.

The weather took no note of her displeasure.

Indeed, it began to rain more heavily.

It was now dusk.

We had been in the pen for two days. We put our small blankets over our heads and about our shoulders. Our ankles and calves were spattered with mud. Other than our blankets there was no shelter from the direct fall of rain, but, when the wind whipped the rain about, we could go to one or another of the interior walls of the palisade and take advantage of what shielding was provided by its twelve-foot-high palings. To be sure, as there was something like nine hundred slaves in the pen now, there was often a good deal of pushing and shoving. The larger, stronger girls would work their way in, closest to the palings. We hoped they would be purchased by Peasants.

Just then a bell rang, and Luta sped away toward the sound.

Happily, in this pen there were no feeding troughs. Such invite disputes for positions at the trough and the stronger, more aggressive girls commonly fight for, and obtain, a disproportionate share of the food. They may even warn others away from the food. Thus, by controlling the supply of food, dispensing or withholding it, they can obtain sycophants and dependents for themselves. In such a way, groups, or gangs, are easily formed. Here, however, a line would be formed and each girl, in passing the serving slaves, holds out her cupped hands and is given what she can hold. Some girls even hold their forearms and wrists together, hoping to obtain larger portions and prevent spillage. Still, it is not advisable to be the last in line as the food is limited and may run short.

Drinking water is plentiful in the pen, being available in slave pans. One is not allowed to scoop out the water, but must go to all fours and drink in the manner of the she-quadruped. One supposes that such things are intended to help the slaves keep in mind that they are slaves. But of that, I assure you, we were in no danger.

I lost little time in following Luta and I, the former Agnes Morrison Atherton, was soon holding out my cupped hands to a serving slave and was receiving a precious double handful of gruel. The rain which was falling mixed in with the gruel. I went to a place near the palisade wall and, crouching down in the blanket, now soaked with rain, fed.

I then lay down in the mud, the blanket clutched about me.

I must try to sleep.

I did not think I could do so.

CHAPTER ELEVEN

It must have been some hours later, when I awoke, suddenly.

"Guards," had whispered a slave near me, to another.

It was dark.

It was still raining, but not heavily.

A yellowish moon was in the overcast sky. The planet has three moons. One, oddly called the Prison Moon for some reason, was comparatively tiny and was not always easily visible.

It was unusual for guards to enter the pen, particularly at night.

I sat up in the mud and pulled the blanket more about me.

Several yards to my left I saw three men, in hoods and rain cloaks. One of them bore a lantern.

They stopped by one slave or another and were apparently entering into some form of discourse with her.

I became apprehensive.

They turned in my direction.

I regretted that I had not changed my position when they were elsewhere engaged. But what good might that have done, particularly if they had noticed me moving, or that I had moved? Might that not have attracted their attention; might that not have aroused their interest or suspicion?

The lantern was coming closer. Its light was reflected, sparkling, in the light rain falling in the darkness.

I went to my knees so that I would be suitably positioned. They were free. I wrapped the blanket about me. Once I was illuminated by the lantern I expected that they would tell me to discard it, to thrust it down over my knees.

Then the light shone on me.

I put down my head. I pulled the blanket more closely about me. I was silent.

"Look up," I was told.

I did so, closing my eyes a little against the light of the lantern.

"Collar," said one of the men, one of those not holding the lantern. I could see in the light that a swirl of hair crested the helmet.

"House of Kleon, Master," I said.

"We are searching for a barbarian," he said. "Do you know any barbarians in the pen?"

I was frightened.

I feared to respond.

"Do you?" he asked.

"No, Master," I said.

"What is your name?" he asked, I thought, suspiciously.

"'Mira,'" I said, "if it pleases Master."

This was the name of a slave I had met in the camp of Master Philip.

There are doubtless various languages spoken on Gor, but there is one major language on the planet, which, naturally enough, is denominated 'Gorean.' In what I take to be the myths of this world, this dominance of a single language is ascribed to the 'Will of Priest-Kings,' supposedly mysterious denizens of the palisaded Sardar Mountains, forbidden to mortals. 'Priest-Kings,' doubtless, were invented by the caste of Initiates, a high caste, the 'White Caste,' as a brilliant hoax by means of which they might, with little trouble to themselves, prosper and profit by the risks and labors of others. The Initiates, who eschew sex and beans, and purify themselves by the study of mathematics, claim to be intermediaries between 'Priest-Kings,' the supposed gods of Gor, and mortals. Given this important role, it is only natural that their temples should be generously supported. They also solicit and accept offerings. When the raiders of one city return home laden with plunder from another city, it is natural for the Initiates to appear, and await their share. They also sell their prayers and spells to mortals. For a fee, proportionate to the resources of the petitioner, Initiates will invoke Priest-Kings to thaw the heart of Tullia to the suit of desperate Quintus, to assure a plentiful olive crop to Zeuxis, to assure victory in the tarn races to the Blues, to inflict scurvy on a zealous creditor, to give victory in the courts to Nexus, the embezzler, to blight the *sa-tarna* fields of Bram the Diligent, to cause the song-drama of Ho-Sito to fare ill with the critics, to cause Tassack, the runner, to break a leg before the city games, and so on. Too, if the devotion of the faithful seems to be growing lukewarm or gifts seem lacking or insufficient, Initiates will warn of the dangers likely to ensue should the Priest-Kings be displeased, and so on. In any event, Gorean tends to be standardized by convocations of Scribes at the four great fairs of the Gorean year, the major fair being that of En'Kara, associated with the vernal equinox. Thus, superstition, not understood as superstition, namely, conformance to an alleged Will of Priest-Kings, can have profound social utility, in this case, bringing about a language which is almost universal on Gor. Despite the universality, or near universality, of

Gorean on the planet, a number of dialects exist. For example, those of Kassau and Shendi are quite different, that of Jad on Cos easily distinguished from that of mighty Ar, and so on. In this way, I hoped that my own accent, which I had modeled on a sort of amalgam of those of various slaves I had encountered, would not attract undue attention. Too, as far as I could tell, my Gorean, so to speak, was honestly better than passable. At any rate, most of the slaves I had met in the coffle or here, in the pen, took me as Gorean. There was a certain satisfaction in that, vainly, and particularly as it might enable me to fade from the sight of possible pursuers.

"Where are you from?" he asked.

"Here and there, from wherever I am chained," I said, "and far off."

"Where originally?" he asked.

I thought wildly for a moment. Then I said, "Market of Semris."

One of the girls in the coffle was from Market of Semris. I had even tried to imitate her accent.

"That is not far off," he said.

"Forgive me, Master," I said. "It seems far off for one afoot, on a chain."

"Doubtless," said the fellow with the lantern.

One of the men laughed.

I was pleased.

On Earth I had known several individuals whose English was so good that I had naturally, but mistakenly, taken them for native speakers. I hoped something along those lines might be the case on Gor, as well. If one is interested in the matter, of course, it is seldom difficult to tell a 'barbarian' from a native Gorean, that on the basis of background information. The native Gorean will know many things of which the 'barbarian,' a newcomer to the culture, would be ignorant.

"May I speak?" I asked.

"You are bold," said the fellow in the helmet crested with a swirl of hair.

I hoped I would not be struck.

At the least, I expected that they would now tell me to pull down the blanket.

Such things help a girl to keep in mind that she is a slave.

It was still raining, lightly.

"Forgive me, Master," I said.

"You may speak," he said.

"May I ask why Masters search for a barbarian," I asked, "and what might be the name of the barbarian?"

"No," said the man with the crested helmet.

"Forgive me, Master," I said.

"If you should learn of a barbarian in the pen," said the man in the crested helmet, "you are to inform the guards, immediately. Do you understand?"

"Yes, Master," I said.

"Let us continue our search," said the fellow who stood next to the lantern bearer. "Time grows short. I fear the silver tarsk will not be ours."

Many girls do not sell for a silver tarsk. Thus, the apprehension of the sought barbarian must be a matter of some importance to someone.

And I feared it might be of great importance to someone.

"One who can recognize the barbarian by sight will be here in the morning," said the man with the lantern, not pleased.

So, I thought, that explains the appearance of the guards at night.

It was as though I had been struck.

Someone could recognize me by sight!

"That," I thought, shaken, "must be either the man with the wristlet, hired anew, whose name I did not know, or someone from the camp of Master Philip. Who else could recognize me by sight?"

"How early in the morning?" asked the fellow who stood next to the lantern bearer.

"Well before the arrival and departure of the river boats," said the man with the crested helmet.

"He will have time then, as they file past him, to examine every slave in the pen," said the man with the lantern.

"We will look further," said the man with the crested helmet, and the three of them turned away and, a moment later, they were discoursing with another slave.

I remained kneeling in the mud, the light gone, the blanket clutched about me and pulled half over my head, as well. It was soaked. Too, my hair was sopped, and water ran down my face, and some of it consisted of tears, tears of fright, of terror, of despair.

I had learned, however inadvertently, it seemed, something that would have been of great interest in the pen, that tomorrow river boats were to arrive and depart. It seemed then that the coffle, and the others in the pen, brought overland to the south shore of the Vosk, were to be ferried across the river to Victoria, site of one of the largest and most active slave markets on Gor, serving, it seems, much of the Vosk Basin.

"So," I thought, "tomorrow the matter is done. I am penned. I cannot escape. Tomorrow I am to be recognized, identified, and apprehended. Tomorrow, the former Agnes Morrison Atherton, stupid fool that she was, to dabble in dark and terrible things,

things she does not even understand, is due to pay the price of her curiosity."

I pulled the blanket more about me. It seemed cold. They had not asked me to remove the blanket. They had had more important things on their mind.

I had not even sold for as much as a silver tarsk!

CHAPTER TWELVE

It was still dark when it began.

In Gorean chronometry, it was shortly after the second Ahn.

I had not been able to sleep after being interrogated by the three guards. I sat alone, my knees drawn up, huddled in the blanket, a few feet within the twelve-foot-high palings of the pen, frightened and miserable.

In a few hours he would arrive, the man who could identify the sought slave by sight.

Would it be the man with the studded wristlet or someone from the camp of Master Philip, perhaps even Master Philip himself, or his deputy, Bakron? It made little difference to me.

I thought I heard a man shout somewhere.

I lifted my head.

Then it was quiet.

I listened, intently.

I heard nothing.

I had scarcely lain down, the blanket wrapped about me, when every sense became acutely alert.

Then I heard it again, a sound like groaning wood.

I sprang to my feet, slipping briefly in the mud, then regaining my balance. I turned about. Against the disk of the White Moon, now in the sky, I caught sight of the palings of the pen. They had moved! I heard a straining of wood. I screamed, and sped away from the wall. The wood was inclining inward. Other slaves awakened, and leapt to their feet, looking about, and then, perhaps better apprising themselves of the danger than I had, screamed, too, and fled from the palings, which suddenly then, over a width of some seven or eight feet underwent an abrupt, radical transformation, some splintering, and breaking, and others pressed forward until, showering dirt about, they sprang from the surface of the soil in which they had been anchored. Some girls, screaming, were trapped under ruptured or uprooted posts. In at least two other points in the pen the palings, too, were being afflicted from the outside by some prodigious, pressing, unknown force. Then I saw a large, ponderous body with a comparatively small head mounted on a long, sinuous neck. Its forelimbs were massive and half buried in wreckage. I darted to the side, to be out of the path of the monster should it proceed. This enabled me to see another such beast, risen on its hind legs with its forelegs pressing against wood. And shortly thereafter another portion of the pen burst inward, splintering palings. Some of these palings were trampled into the soil. Others tilted inward, their pointed ends suggesting a defensive bulwark, inclined forward, as if prepared to slow or fend the charge even of the bipedalian lizards ridden by the coffle guards.

Then I head the cries of the men. "Out of the pen, *kajirae*! Empty the pen! Run between the lanterns! Stay between the lanterns! Now! Hurry! Hurry! Run!"

Some men entered the pen with whips. Shouting, and not sparing the lash, they began driving the slaves out of the pen through the breaches in the wall. "Run little *vulos*!" they cried.

"Hurry, *tastas*! Amaze the bounding *hurt*! Let the fleet *tabuk* envy your speed! Faster! Faster! Stay between the lanterns! No blankets! No blankets!"

Why the admonition about lanterns?

Why no blankets?

Perhaps they did not want the slaves to be encumbered in their flight?

"Raiders!" cried a slave, rushing past me.

In that moment much became clear to me. The long coffle had not been heavily guarded. Apparently, it had not needed to be. It was large and unwieldly and its occupants were chained together by hammered-shut linkages. Thus, it would require a considerable investment of time and effort even to attack the coffle, let alone attempt to seize it and profit by it. How much easier then to break into a pen and run off some untethered stock! And who would expect an attack inside the presumably safe precincts of a town? Might not surprise be an element of theft as well as of war? And I did not doubt that the attack took place this night, or early morning, as the raiders may have learned of the soon-impending transfer of the slaves across the river to Victoria.

"Run, you fool!" said Luta, hurrying past me, her blanket discarded.

Two more slaves rushed past me.

I could see the funnel of lanterns outside the palisade.

I heard the snapping of a whip, sharp, loud, like the report of a rifle, only feet away. I started. I saw him draw back his hand. The next act of the whip, I was sure, would not be a warning. Half stumbling, I threw down the blanket, slipped in the mud, recaptured my balance, and ran toward the funnel of lanterns. I half cried out as my shoulder brushed the forelimb of one of the ponderous beasts whose weight had shattered parts of the palisade, and ran toward the funnel of lanterns.

Many animals, and some human beings, will impose limits on their behavior which are largely of their own making. They see walls, so to speak, which do not exist. They will assume things cannot be done which reality, in fact, does not at all preclude. An example is the tendency of many animals, and some human beings, to respect the nonexistent boundaries of the 'hunting funnel.' Some primitive hunters construct such a funnel, wide at one end, the entering end, and narrow at the other end, the closing end. Piles of rock, topped by turf, may constitute the pylons of such a funnel. Perhaps a running, driven animal, say, a caribou, confuses these constructions with hunters. It is not known. In any event, many caribou, driven into the wide mouth of the funnel, usually by noise-making women and children, will stay within the pylons, the space between which becomes progressively narrower, until the end is reached, where the hunters wait. At any point, a caribou could simply leave the funnel, but many do not.

I did not even consider departing from the funnel of lanterns. It was not that I was a driven, heedless animal, or that I feared that, beyond the lanterns, in the darkness, guards might wait, with whips and edged steel. It was rather that I saw that my best chance of life would be to be taken by the raiders and carried into a new slavery. Within hours, someone who could recognize the sought slave would be in Victoria Minor and I would have to file past him. Better then to be carried away or driven away to some foreign pen where I would be safe, as safe as any other stolen beast.

So I, with others, muchly in darkness, hurried down the narrowing funnel of lanterns.

In moments, I would be at the closed end of the funnel.

At the end of the funnel, the caribou, crowded together, cease running, turn one way or the other, are confused, and begin to mill. The hunters then, with bullets or arrows, begin to harvest the meat, often at point-blank range.

As far as I could tell, the slaves, driven from the pen into the funnel of lanterns, remained in the funnel, and presumably much more so than might a driven herd of caribou. I think this is because the slave girl knows it is much safer to obey than not to obey. She knows, in her intelligence, she is not being driven to her death, but merely to a different slavery, which might be better or worse than, or not really much different from, the one in which she would find herself in the normal train of events. It is thus her intelligence and not her ignorance which keeps her in the funnel. In my own case, I had the additional, forceful motivation of wanting to avoid being in Victoria Minor in the morning. I might mention, in passing, that Goreans tend to prize intelligence in a slave. It makes her far more valuable. It is a familiar criterion in slave selection and hunting. Some men rank it higher than beauty, perhaps because it is usually associated with helpless sexual responsiveness. There is nothing surprising in this because high intelligence is often linked with high vitality and high vitality with acute sexuality.

As I ran down the funnel, sometimes slipping, sometimes jostled by other slaves, I wondered that the pen guards had not been more active, if they had been active at all, in guarding their stock. Too, where were the guardsmen of Victoria Minor? By now it seemed there must be some awareness in the town that a raid was in progress.

Surely there was no army to deal with.

Might not guardsmen be approaching, even now?

All too suddenly, unexpectedly, we were stopped, crowded together, at the bottom of the funnel.

"Down, down!" cried a voice.

We knelt down, crowded together, in the mud.

Several men, some with lanterns, others with coils of rope, began to force their way amongst us. "That one! That one!" said a fellow with a crested helmet. As he designated one slave or another, other men, with ropes, began to coffle the designated slaves together by the neck.

We had not been permitted to bring our blankets, small as they were, with us. I supposed that was not only that we be less encumbered in our flight, but that we could be more easily assessed at its culmination. Also, in this way, there would be less to identify us as slaves from the large pen at Victoria Minor. Also, in this fashion, we would have, once our collars were removed, nothing from others. We would be completely dependent, for anything, for everything, on our new owners, or claimers.

"That one! That one!" said the fellow in the crested helmet. "Get them with the *tharlarion* to the barges! Be quick! Hurry!"

Outside the light, away from the lanterns, I sensed the movement of large bodies.

Suddenly, kneeling there in the mud, I became afraid.

Clearly the raiders were hurrying.

They were pressed for time.

Clearly then they had not taken the town.

They hurried.

They were afraid.

What if I were not chosen?

Even now marshalled forces, guardsmen and others, might be afoot. Possibly aid might even be on its way from Victoria, across the river.

The fellow in the crested helmet continued selecting slaves.

I conjectured, as I could, that the raiders, while not few, might be no more than fifty or sixty in number. That many might be dealt with, I supposed, by local guardsmen, and certainly so if they were reinforced from Victoria.

Too, it seemed unlikely that the limited number of raiders could manage the entire stock from the large pen, something in the neighborhood of nine hundred slaves. Presumably then it was a lightning strike, hoping to breach the pen, seize prize stock, and make away before encountering any practical resistance.

What then, if I were not chosen?

How could I, unclad, well collared, hope to escape?

In neither of my prior sales had I brought my seller even as much as a silver tarsk.

Why should I be chosen?

At that point, those raiders within my purview suddenly stopped, and stood still, heads lifted, listening.

"Be quiet!" said one of them to a whimpering slave.

I strained my hearing, and then, far off, the sound, faint, carrying over the river, I heard a ringing, as though hammers might be striking large, hanging bars.

"There is time," said a man. "It will take an Ahn to cross the river."

"Less," said another man. "And they may be under way."

The lantern was lifted higher.

"That one! That one!" was heard again. Slaves were pulled by the hair up, out of the crowd, and into line. Loops were swiftly knotted about their necks. They were then conducted through the darkness, toward the river.

"That one!" I heard. "That one! Her!"

There was now a clear urgency in the doings of the men.

There was then, apparently from some quarter in the town, the sound of a distant trumpet, which was answered by another.

"Guardsmen assemble!" cried a man.

"To the barges!" cried a man.

"That one! That one!" I heard.

"We have over a hundred!" cried a man.

"We will be cut off from the barges!" cried another.

"We have enough! To the barges!" cried another.

"*Harta!*" cried a man. "*Harta!* Haste, away!"

"*Harta! Harta!*" called another.

Those raiders whom I could see began, hurriedly, to withdraw.

"No!" I cried, rising up, trying to thrust my way through the kneeling, crowded slaves. "Wait! Wait!"

"Fool!" cried a slave.

"Do not break position!" warned another.

"Better to be sold in Victoria!" said a slave.

"That is a known market," said another.

I was seized by more than one slave. "Stay where you are!" said one. "Remain on your knees!" said another. "You will have us all whipped!" said another. "Hold her," said another. "Force her down, on her knees!" cried another. "She is mad," said another. "You do not understand!" I screamed. "Let me go! Let me go!" But I was pulled down and held down, prostrate, in the mud. "Be still!" I was told. "Be quiet!"

I could not rise.

Some minutes passed.

"They will be gone," I said.

"Lie still," I was told. "Do not attract attention to yourself or to us."

"Let me kneel," I said.

"Let her kneel," said one of the slaves. "She is quiet now."

I rose to my knees.

"Where were our guards?" asked one of the slaves.

"I do not know," said another.

Attention was not now on me.

I could still hear, faintly, the ringing of the bar from across the river.

"Our guards were suborned," said one of the slaves.

"Never," said another.

I heard the two trumpets, much closer now.

"Guardsmen," whispered a slave.

"Keep quiet," said another.

I pushed aside one of the slaves, springing to my feet, and forced my way through kneeling bodies, and, in a moment, had broken through to the ground which had lain at the closed end of the 'hunting funnel.' The lanterns were now gone. Lamps had been lit in some nearby houses. I could see a street before me, bending to my left. I hurried after the raiders. I could smell the river.

I sped amongst buildings.

Then, suddenly, clouds breaking, I saw the mighty Vosk, like a narrow ocean on one shore of which I stood. In the distance, down-river, in the light of the White Moon, I saw four barges.

"Wait!" I called after them. "Take me with you! Take me with you!"

The planking of a wharf was under my feet.

I then heard the trumpets again, even closer.

Weeping, I spun about. I fled away from the trumpets. I feared Victoria Minor. And I feared the shore, for its buildings and its now-awakened populace, who, doubtless, would soon be about. It was near dawn. I must avoid capture at all costs. I fled south, to put Victoria Minor and the shore behind me. I must reach the open country.

CHAPTER THIRTEEN

He wound the several coils of rope about my upper body. My upper body was then swathed with rope. It was coarse and tight. He jerked tight the last knot.

"Stop crying," he said.

Before he bound me he had put me to slave use in the high grass. He had not been pleased. He had cuffed me twice, slapping my face back and forth. "You are cold and tight," he said. "What is wrong with you?"

I had been miserable, distraught. All was lost. I had been caught. But what else, a little sooner or a little later, could I have expected, marked, collared, naked, a slave?

He had then slapped me twice more, sharply.

I, a slave, had been displeasing!

"Forgive me, Master," I wept.

I was a slave. I was desperate to be pleasing to the free. Let those who cannot understand that find themselves in a collar on Gor.

He then knotted a rope on my neck and tied the free end to the stirrup of his bipedalian *tharlarion*.

"We must hurry, *kajira*," he said. "The tenth Ahn is near, the boats prepare to embark."

He then climbed to the saddle.

I doubted that I was more than half a mile from Victoria Minor.

I had tried to hide in the tall grass, but he, from the vantage point on the high saddle, looking down, had seen me easily. I suspected, too, that he had had little difficulty in following me, given the presumed disturbances my passage had wrought in the rain-soaked grass.

"You were a fool to run," he said.

"Yes, Master," I said. But what choice, really, had I had?

His voice was high above me, and to my right, he in the high saddle. I did not know him or recognize him. On the other hand, his carriage, appearance, livery, demeanor, lance, and accouterments, such as the rope which had been at his saddle, and the netting which was still in its place, presumably useful in snaring running prey, had marked him well enough as a guard from one of the houses whose goods had been threatened, or lost, in the night. I did not think him a guard associated with the House of Kleon. I did not know how many houses had been represented in the great pen.

"I do not mark you stupid," he said. "Why did you run?"

"I was afraid," I said.

He kicked his heels back, and the *tharlarion* began to stalk forward, back toward Victoria Minor.

I hastened, as I could, to keep up. It would be unpleasant to fall, and be dragged through the grass, even for a few feet.

"You are not a free woman," he said. "Of what were you afraid?"

"I do not know," I said.

Kajirae are livestock, two-legged cattle, of a sort, domestic animals. They have value. They have little to fear from men. A free woman, on the other hand, might be slain as an enemy. To be sure, most men will spare a surrendered, pleading free woman, a submitting free woman, for the collar.

"Sometimes *kajirae* stampede," he said. "Fear sweeps through them inexplicably. Perhaps something small starts it, an unidentified sound, a rumbling in the earth, the nearby strike of lightning, a rumor, that a *larl* is nearby, that wild *tharlarion*, bellowing and trampling, are rushing toward a compound, something. I have seen it happen twice."

He seemed in an expansive mood.

I was miserable.

I tried to watch my footing.

The ropes were tight and coarse. He had probably tied me as he had, having been disappointed with my usage. It was, I supposed, a way of punishing me, of expressing his disappointment, even his displeasure.

"Four fled," he said. "You are the last to be captured."

"Yes, Master," I said, trying not to stumble. The high grass did not make the footing easy.

"The raiders struck and escaped," he said. "They made off with better than a hundred *kajirae*. The loss was grievous. The house of Ho-Turik was hardest hit."

The way he said that led me to believe that he was not of the House of Ho-Turik.

I recalled that Luta was owned by that house. I wondered if she had been carried off.

"Most of the pen guards were trapped in the guards' quarters," he said. "The entrances and exits, narrow portals, were held by raiders. Town guardsmen, relatively few, some seventy or so, unsure of the strength of the raiders, sent to Victoria for help before engaging, by means of passenger *vulos*."

"Yes, Master," I said.

I thought it wise to assure him that I was attending his words. I had, of course, other things on my mind.

"I wonder," he said, "why the raiders did not take you."

"Oh?" I said.

"It was dark," he said, "and they may not have had time to get to you."

"Perhaps," I said.

"Perhaps they tested you and found you disappointing and inert," he said.

"They did not test me," I said.

"Are you annoyed?" he asked.

"No, Master," I lied.

"You are appealing to the eye," he said. "If you were not inert, you might go for as much as a silver tarsk fifty in Victoria."

I was not sure what a silver tarsk fifty might be, but it was surely more than a silver tarsk.

"I will not be sold in Victoria, Master," I said.

"There is still time to catch the boats to Victoria," he said.

"Nonetheless," I said.

"I do not understand," he said.

"It has to do with an agent come to Victoria to apprehend a missing slave," I said.

"The one for the return of whom a whole silver tarsk was offered?" he asked.

"Yes," I said.

"What is that to you?" he asked.

"Nothing," I said.

"She is a barbarian," he said.

"Yes, Master," I said.

"She has been taken," he said.

"What!" I said.

"She was apprehended before I left Victoria Minor," he said. "She is Courtney, a blond-haired, blue-eyed barbarian slave of Achaeus, a silver merchant of Argentum. She fled two passage hands ago. The whip, if not the hamstringing knives, will soon welcome her home, where she will be cast, chained, to the feet of her Master."

"Master!" I cried.

He looked down, puzzled.

I looked up, wildly.

"What is wrong with you?" he asked.

"I am not an inert slave, Master," I cried, pressing my lips to his stirrup. "I am an obedient, needful slave! I am helpless. My slave fires rage! Have pity on me! Take me! I beg it! Use me as the worthless slave I am!"

He pulled the *tharlarion* up short.

I flung myself to my knees in the grass.

"How am I to understand this?" he asked.

"Surely," I said, "Master has seen a needful, begging slave before. I oil! I gush! I beg!"

He slipped from the saddle.

He stood before me.

"Please, Master," I begged.

Then he took me by the hair and flung me to my back on the grass. He took my left ankle in his right hand and my right ankle in his left hand.

He held my ankles closely together. I strained but could not split my legs for him. I writhed in the ropes on the grass.

"Please be merciful to a poor slave," I begged.

"Hold your ankles together," he said, "tightly."

I tried but he widened them easily.

"That is enough," he said.

I then lay before him, supine, his, my ankles in his grip, my legs spread.

"Please, Master," I said.

"I think we have time," he said.

"Oh, yes, Master!" I said. "Yes, Master!"

CHAPTER FOURTEEN

We were close to the river, waiting to be embarked for Victoria, on the northern shore of the Vosk.

Now that I was safe, and had nothing to fear, my thoughts were eagerly roving about. I hoped to be purchased by a fine, strong Master, one who would well fulfil my slave needs, so neglected, so starved, so concealed, on my former world. Too, I would like to be his single slave. Who cares to compete for the attention, and the caresses, of a Master? It would not hurt, either, however, if he were well fixed and had a fine house. On the other hand, if he were well fixed and had a fine house, he would be likely to have more than one slave. If so, presumably, on the favoring side, there would be less work for each. There were many options to consider, pluses and minuses, so to speak. If I were a free woman, I would have much to say concerning such matters. I could bargain as I pleased, sell myself as I wanted, hold out for as long as I wished, wait for the best offer, and so on. As a slave, on the other hand, others would choose me or not, buy me or not. I would have no say in such matters. We must wait to see by whom we will be taken off the block. I, of course, still hoped to wear my collar in a city. Victoria Minor was a town, not a city. Victoria was larger, considerably, but, as I understood it, it was no Ar, no Brundisium, no Turia. I had heard of the lofty towers of the high cities, and the bridges interlaced amongst them. I wondered if I would have the courage to walk the high bridges. There were worlds to know about Gor and its culture. My curiosity was boundless. But I dared not inquire too widely or deeply for fear I would be recognized as a barbarian. Barbarian *kajirae* do not always fare well at the hands of Gorean *kajirae*. Is there not often suspicion of, or fear of, the stranger, the different? I suspect that that has been selected for in the course of evolution. How else explain how widespread it is? In Gorean, interestingly, as in many languages of Earth, there is a single word for 'stranger' and 'enemy.' Accordingly, I tried to piece together as many facts, as much information, as I could, subtly, from what I heard, often casually, in the talk of Masters, in the gossip of slaves.

"Into the water," said a male voice, "clean off the dried mud, the dirt, the filth, from your bodies. Stay within the barred enclosure! Stay away from the bars!"

Each of us had been given a cloth.

There were some forty slaves in my group, the last group. It was well past noon. Apparently several boats had left earlier.

We made our way down the slippery bank, cloth in hand, and waded into the barred enclosure, it being open on the shore side. I saw no point to the enclosure. It was daylight. No slave was likely to attempt to escape. There were some guards about, and a variety of free men, docksmen, warehouse workers, and such. It would be a great relief to clean off the mud and grime of the large pen. I wondered if it were still occupied. I supposed not. Certainly, eventually, it would have to undergo serious repair.

"Wash your hair," we heard. "Stay away from the bars."

I am sure none of us needed any encouragement to clean our bodies and wash our hair. This opportunity was much appreciated, but it was no substitute for a clear stream, a quiet pool, or tub of clean water. The Vosk is a mighty river, draining much of a continent, and, like any such river, it washes its share of sediment, silt, and salt to the sea, in its case, first passing through the delta and the Tamber Gulf, and thence to Thassa, the sea.

I applied the cloth I had been given, wiping away grime and dirt.

"Look," said a slave, pointing. "A round ship!"

I looked. It was a ship with two masts, but no sails set. Its oars were inboard. Apparently, it was utilizing the current. To move upstream, it would use its sails, which depend from long sloping yards, and its oars. I did not see why they called it a round ship, as it was not round.

"I know little of ships," I said. "Why do they call it a round ship?"

"See its size, the height of its bulwarks, the width of its beam," said one slave.

"Are you from the mountains or the Tahari?" asked a slave.

I gathered that this was an insult. At the least, it was a comment on my stupidity or ignorance.

"No," I said.

I continued to wipe away the grime and dirt.

"It is a cargo ship," said another slave, as though that would clarify matters.

"Where is its guard ship?" asked another slave, shading her eyes. It is sometimes hard to see, given the reflection of the sun on the water.

"Following, fool," said the slave. "Thus it can move easily to either side, to whichever side it might be, from which danger might threaten."

I could now see a second ship, but I had not seen it at first. It was low in the water; it was comparatively long and narrow. Its prow was concave. No masts were visible. It reminded me of something alive, half unseen, gliding through the water. There seemed a menace about it.

"See it?" asked a slave of me.

"Yes," I said.

"That is a ram ship, a knife ship, a fighting ship," said the slave.

"It is quite different from the round ship," said another.

"Yes," I said.

"It is lovely," said a slave.

"Frightening," said another.

"Both ships have an eye on one side," I said.

"On both sides," said a blond slave, laughing.

"You are from faraway," said a slave.

"Why do the ships have eyes on them?" I asked.

"How else could they see their way?" asked another slave.

I did not respond but I thought that I then understood something I did not understand before, something about the relationship between a mariner and his vessel. The wood had come alive.

I rinsed out the cloth I was using, and wrapped it about my left wrist.

I immersed my head twice, parting and rinsing my hair under water. Then I straightened up, leaned backwards, and shook my hair behind me.

"She-sleen!" laughed a guard.

Quickly I waded farther out into the water, toward the bars closing the water end of the enclosure. I stopped when I was shoulder deep and well concealed.

He did not own me, and would not be likely to do so.

I did suppose he could afford me.

I gathered that I was not expensive.

But surely there was something to be said for me.

The pen guard who had recaptured me, he who had been mounted on the *tharlarion*, had not regarded me as unappealing, at least to the eye.

One of the slaves, laughing, splashed water on another and her victim, shrieking and laughing, responded immediately, clearly outdoing her attacker. Several of the slaves then joined in, and the rectangular area within the bars erupted in a drenching tumult.

One of the noncombatants called out, "Stop splashing! Stop splashing!"

I did not care for the furor or uproar either, but I saw no point in discouraging it.

Let them find their amusement as they would.

"Stay away from the bars," called the guard, laughing.

The rag I had wrapped about my left wrist came loose in the water, and I reached out and snatched it.

Most of the slaves, including myself, moved away from the combatants, the havoc of them now dominating the center of the enclosure. In doing so, many of us backed to the end or sides of the enclosure.

I took the rag I held and began to fold it in squares, to use it again as a wash cloth before we were ordered from the enclosure. A ship, oared and single-masted, was moored at a nearby pier, and I supposed it was waiting for us, to provide us with our projected passage across the river. Other ships were at other piers, further upriver.

In the meantime, the game of splashing one another, to the accompaniment of shrieks, laughter, and insults, had become wilder, less stable, less defined, and more intrusive.

"Stop it, stop it, stop splashing," cried she whom I took to be our local spoilsport, reiterating her earlier disapproval, but, oddly, her face was not now reddened by indignation or anger, but had a cast of apprehension, even of fear. She was the slave who had explained the reason for the location of the guardship, the ram snip, in the wake of the round ship. She knew, it seemed, something of such things, something perhaps of the river.

There must have been at least fifteen or twenty of the slaves in the enclosure who were churning the water, engaged in the small water war within the bars. As in such cases, even actual skirmishes and battles, melees, and such, with charges and retreats, the center of gravity, so to speak, will move back and forth, and forward and backwards. As a result, the chaos in the enclosure began, with no explicit intention, to shift toward the river end of the enclosure, which, in turn, pressed several of the other slaves, who were nonparticipants in the fray, including myself, closer to the bars on the river side of the enclosure.

"Stay away from the bars!" screamed the slave who had seemed so prudishly, or intolerantly, opposed to the light-hearted banter and play of her collar sisters. At the same time one of the players stumbled backward in the water, buffeting me, and, as I flung out my hands and tried to recover, my footing gone, swept by the water, I lost my grip on the washrag, and tried to snatch it back from between the bars before it might begin to drift downstream. I did not want to risk its loss. I feared I might be punished. A slave will do much to avoid the fearsome kiss of the five-stranded slave lash. No sooner than my hand had clutched the rag a great toothed body had rolled on its side and snapped at my hand and the rag. For an instant, my hand and the rag were clearly within a gigantic, toothed maw which could not close its bite because of two vertical, parallel bars, about which were its jaws, and between which were my hand and the rag. The bars were bitten at and wrestled about, jerking the enclosure. At the same time I screamed and jerked my hand back. I felt instantly sick, threw up in the water, and, as I did so, frenzied, I half swam and half ran back toward the shore. The other slaves, too, fled back to the shore. There was much screaming. The damp sand of the shore beneath our feet, we turned back, to see the barred enclosure rocking under blows and, in two places, visibly, bent inward. We could see several dorsal fins cutting the surface of the water, then disappearing as bodies rolled to the side and threw themselves against the bars. Other dorsal fins could be seen approaching from upstream and downstream, and from across the current. The Gorean shark is nine-gilled and not five-gilled. I feel justified in referring to these creatures as sharks because of their resemblance to Earth sharks. One supposes that such an optimum design for marine predation might be produced independently on numerous worlds due to the parameters of convergent evolution.

I found myself standing on the sloping sand next to she who had discouraged the splashing in the enclosure, she who had seemed informed about the rationale of the guardship's location.

"You tried to warn them," I said.

"Much good it did," she laughed, bitterly.

After a time, some five or ten slaves returned to the enclosure, in water to their waist or thighs. They kept well to the center of the enclosure, away from the bars.

Our sisters are brave," I said.

"They are stupid," she said.

The enclosure now seemed placid enough. But we could see an occasional dorsal fin outside the bars.

How did you know there would be a guardship following the round ship?" I asked.

"I did not know," she said. "Normally there is not. But, of late, river pirates have become more active."

"Why now?" I asked.

"It is spring," she said. "Much loot is found on the river, silver, gold, silks, jewels, and other loot."

"Other loot?" I said.

"You and I," she said, "slaves."

I had not much thought of myself as loot before, but, of course, as I was a property, I could surely become such. Indeed, even a free woman, I supposed, could count as loot. Were not the women of a conquered city, stripped and chained, the loot of the victors?

"This is the major slaving season," she said. "Sometimes wars are fought with the slaving season in mind."

"You knew the position of the guardship," I said, "following, to be able to quickly reach the side from which danger might threaten."

"If the location of danger is not known," she said, "otherwise, naturally, the guardship places itself between the danger or the likely quarter from which danger might be expected."

"The guardship follows, and does not lead," I said.

"One does not wish the round ship to be attacked from the rear," she said.

"Come back in the water!" called one of the slaves from within the enclosure, the water to her waist.

"It is safe now," called another, the water to her thighs.

"The sharks are gone," said another.

"They are fools," said my interlocutor.

"How so?" I asked.

Surely the sharks were mostly gone, and the enclosure, though bent in places, was mostly intact.

"River eels are mostly on the north shore of the Vosk," she said, "where they can scavenge from the settlements. On the other hand, while they will not dispute a hunting ground with the shark, they will often follow the shark to a putative food source."

"Should you not warn the girls to come ashore?" I asked.

"Many eels," she said, "will not pass between bars, and some are too large to do so."

"Still," I said.

"Object lessons," she said, "are often the best learned. They are seldom forgotten."

"Come back in the water," called a slave.

"Do not be afraid," called another. "Our transport is still moored!"

"Frightened *vulos*!" called another.

"Do not be afraid," called another. "Do not be a timid *verr*."

Some more of the slaves returned to the water.

I still clutched the rag I had been given. I did not move.

"Why do you not join them?" asked my interlocutor. "Why do you not enter the water?"

"I am disinclined to do so," I said. "I have listened to a woman wiser than I."

"It seems safe," she said.

"I gather that it may not be so," I said.

At that moment there was a shriek of pain from the enclosure and one of the slaves in the water began to splash frenziedly toward the shore dragging something thrashing, glistening, wet, rubbery, snake-like, half emerged, its fangs sunk in her calf. A moment later another slave screamed and fled toward the shore trying to jerk loose the serpentine thing clinging to the side of her waist. Another slave was striking down in the water and yet another was kicking at something I could not see. Shortly the enclosure was emptied of slaves, and the guard, with his knife, was forcing loose the grip of the two living tenacious things whose mouths were filled with flesh and blood.

"Sometimes," said my interlocutor, "there is much to learn from the frightened *vulo* and the timid *verr*. Why is the *vulo* frightened? Why is the *verr* timid?"

"My name is Mira," I said.

"That is odd," she said.

"Why?" I asked, a little tensely. I feared her. She seemed to know more than I cared to suppose.

"It is a Gorean name," she said.

"So?" I said.

"A Master must have been pleased with you, to give it to you."

"I do not understand," I said.

"You are a barbarian," she said.

I feared to deny it.

"Few notice that," I said.

"Some will," she said. "I advise you not to pretend otherwise. Some Masters will not be pleased. You are not a free woman."

Free women, as I understood it, might lie and mislead with impunity. This was not the case, as I understood it, with *kajirae*.

"How did you know?" I asked.

"Subtleties of accent," she said.

"Do not give me away," I said.

"I do not need to," she said. "You have already done so."

"Many think me Gorean," I said.

"Naturally," she said. "Your Gorean is quite good."

I hoped that few could detect my imposture. It was a barbarian who had been extracted from the camp of Master Philip; it was a barbarian who had been fastened in a Bazi-Imports collar; it was a barbarian, one who knew little but seemingly too much, who was to be delivered to some mysterious destination. Therefore, let me be Gorean. Therefore, let me keep my Earth origin secret. I did not care to participate in games and intrigues I did not understand; I did not care to be sought and possibly silenced for something the importance of which I did not even grasp.

"Thank you," I said.

"'Calla,'" she said.

"Thank you, Calla," I said.

I did not think that Calla would give me away. I feared that I might give myself away. I resolved to continue as had been my wont, to allow myself to be understood as Gorean, but not to risk denying that I was such.

How many people could detect me as barbarian?

Few, or many?

I did not know.

This made me uneasy.

"My collar," I said, "is a House-of-Kleon collar."

"Mine," she said, "is that of the House of Temione."

"'Temione' is a woman's name," I said.

"She is a slaver," said Calla. "She specializes in female field slaves."

"You do not look like a field slave," I said. "You are quite beautiful."

"She is a woman who hates beautiful female slaves," said Calla. "She also hates men who care for such slaves."

"She is very ugly herself?" I asked.

"I have only seen her veiled, with her whip," she said.

"Perhaps she hates men but wishes to be one," I said. I knew little of these things but I had heard that there were such women, unusual women, unless social engineers, for political purposes, would have society understand them as not unusual, women who loathed their sex, and sex itself, who despised and envied men, and despised and hated women, women who feared to be women.

"I do not know," said Calla, "but she wishes to deny beautiful women to men and wishes to deny Masters to beautiful women. Thus, she buys the most beautiful, most desirable women, the most needful women, as she can, and consigns them to heavy labors in remote fields. Thus, in denying nature and warring with reality, she attempts to frustrate both men and women."

"What is the point of this?" I asked.

"I do not know," she said.

On Gor, as I understood it, such women had little political power.

Presumably, gratifications of one sort or another were involved.

At that point, we heard a bell from several yards away, to our right, as we faced the river.

"That will be the signal to board the slaves," said Calla. "Ours is the last shipment from the great pen, until it is filled again."

"Rags in the basket!" called a guard.

We put the rags we had been issued in the basket.

"Single file," called the guard. "Hand coffle!"

"What is 'hand coffle?'" I asked.

"Not only are you a barbarian," said Calla, "but you have not been long on Gor. Get in line. After that, remember left hand to left hand, right hand to right hand. One of your hands will grasp that of the girl in front of you or be grasped by the girl behind;

your other hand will be grasped by the girl behind you or will grasp that of the girl before you. Thus, unless you are either at the beginning of the line or at the end of end of the line, both your hands will be occupied, one grasping, one being grasped. This suffices for short distances."

"In line, in line!" called a guard.

I fell into line and, as the girl before me extended her left hand back I grasped it with my left hand and put my own right hand back, and felt it grasped by Calla. In this way each hand either grasped or was grasped, in an alternating fashion.

In a few minutes we were on the pier where the ship was moored, waiting for us. A guard's word released us from the hand coffle, and we milled on the planks. I had not spoken in coffle. I might not have been on Gor long, but I knew enough not to speak in coffle. Such can bring a lashing. Now, however, while a fellow in a blue tunic with a clip-board was conferring with a mariner near the rail of the ship, the slaves chatted. Two of them had had the ravages wrought by the eels treated, these lacerations having been painted with some dark substance. I did not think that these blemishes would lower their value. Normally only collectors and connoisseurs concern themselves with such trivialities. For example, I doubted that many buyers would be concerned that my complexion was less than pellucid. Indeed, some might find that of interest. Most, I was sure, would not even notice. Most, I supposed, would be more interested in the thought of what the girl would be like in their arms than how she might appear under a strong glass. In any event, I was what I was, and I saw little point in worrying about it. I doubted that Doctors Jameson, Archer, and Townsend had given the matter much thought. I did suppose, now, that, being men, they might have undressed me for their pleasure, in their imagination, as I moved about in the observatory, attending to my duties. I certainly had little doubt that they might have done so with Miss Bennett, our librarian, who was not only lovely but, in my opinion, all too ready to turn her not inconsiderable charms to her advantage. Could I have been envious of her, jealous of her? Certainly not. But are not all women, in a sense, rivals? Has evolution not made us so?

"I wonder how many trips across the river this ship made today," I said to Calla.

"Probably none," she said.

"How wide is the river?" I asked, puzzled.

"Here," she said, "some two *pasangs*."

I did not know how long a *pasang* was but I supposed that two *pasangs* would be something over a mile in length.

"It is narrow for the Vosk," she said. "That is doubtless why a settlement, in this case, Victoria, arose at this point, on the northern shore, and, obviously, Victoria Minor, the lesser Victoria, on the southern shore."

"It is hard to see the opposite shore," I said.

"It is better seen from the top of a watch station or tower," she said.

"'Watch station?'" I asked.

"Such keep the Vosk under surveillance," she said, "and can transmit fire signals as need be."

"I saw a high wooden structure, of several levels," I said, "on the way here. "Was that a watch station?"

"Yes," said Calla. "Oddly, it did not seem to be manned."

The ship we were waiting to board had a single, apparently fixed mast, with a long, inclined yard. Interestingly, sails are hauled from the deck by ropes to the yard. In this way, mariners need not ascend rigging. I did not know it at the time, but this arrangement apparently allows smaller crews and, in the case of naval warfare, the crew can be better shielded. As the ship, too, seemed to be lightly oared, it seemed it would rely more on its canvas than its oars. This, too, of course, allows a smaller crew. Larger galleys, multiply oared galleys, may have as many as four or five men to an oar. This redounds not only to the speed and power of such a galley, but to the number of men on hand to either effect a boarding or resist one.

"Be ready," said Calla. "We board."

"House of Ho-Turic," said a mariner, he near the rail, glancing at the collar of the first slave in the boarding line. The fellow in the blue tunic then made a mark on the paper fastened to his clipboard. The slave was then conducted to a place at the foot of a boarding plank."

"Can you swim?" asked Calla.

"Yes," I said. "Why?"

"It is nothing," she said.

"Why has this ship not made more crossings, ferrying slaves to Victoria?" I asked.

"The river is wide," she said.

"House of Quintus," said the mariner, looking at a collar. "House of Rutilius. House of Sorak."

"The slaves seem unusually fair," I said.

"They are," said Calla. "That is no mistake. The best are often saved for last, to make sure the crossing is tried and safe."

"I do not belong amongst them," I said.

"You fled, as did four others," she said. "All were recaptured. You were recaptured last, but, happily, in time to be included in the last ship."

"My captor used me for his pleasure, twice," I said.

"Doubtless that delayed matters," said Calla.

"Doubtless," I said.

"House of Siba," said the mariner. "House of Kleon. House of Ho-Turic."

"Do not be annoyed," said Calla. "It is not at all inconceivable that you might have been assigned to the last ship."

"Thank you," I said.

I was then before the mariner. "House of Kleon," he said, and the fellow in the blue tunic jotted down a mark on his clipboard.

Briefly I thought how strange it was that I gave so little thought to the fact that I was standing before clothed men, naked, a collar on my neck, a locked collar, one I could not remove, being boarded on a galley as a domestic beast, with other domestic beasts, a slave. I had internalized my bondage. I was a slave, wholly a slave, and nothing more. I gave no thought to freedom. Gone was my former life. I was a slave, as a dog is a dog and a horse a horse. It was what I was. And I knew, deep in my heart, it was what I was, and wanted to be. I longed for a Master before whom I might kneel, whose boots I might kiss, whom I might love and serve, selflessly, devotedly, with the whole slave of me, with all that I was and wanted to be.

Calla was behind me.

"House of Temione," said the mariner. "How is that?"

"There was only one in the pen," said the man in the blue tunic, making a note on his papers. "This is obviously she."

"She is extraordinarily beautiful," said the mariner.

Calla lowered her head.

"Such slaves are rare in the markets," said the fellow in blue. "Lady Temione buys but she seldom sells."

"She is selling this one," said the mariner. "This one is destined, like the others, for Market of Demetrius in Victoria." Market of Demetrius was a major market in Victoria, handling mostly slaves brought overland from south of the Vosk.

I thought I saw Calla smile.

I did not understand this.

"I might bid on her myself," said the mariner.

"Would that it might be so, Master," she said.

"You could not afford her," said the fellow in blue.

"Where slaves are many, prices are low," said the mariner. "She might be sold off a minor block by accident. Such things can happen."

"May you bask in the light of fortune," said the man in blue.

"Next," said the mariner.

I was a little before Calla.

We went to the line before the boarding plank.

"You may have a bidder," I said to Calla, "the fellow who checked our collars."

"He will never bid on me," she said.

"He seemed serious," I said.

"He will never have the opportunity," she said.

"Why not?" I asked.

"Do not concern yourself," she said.

"I wonder what it will be, to be sold in Victoria," I said. "I have been sold twice, but never in a major market."

"Do not concern yourself," she said.

Shortly thereafter, the last of the collars were checked, and we filed over the boarding plank. On deck, we were put to our knees, our rows encircling the fixed mast.

"The great pen," I said, "is now empty, or little occupied."

"It will be repaired before the arrival of fresh coffles," said Calla. "It is the season."

One of the two slaves who had been attacked by eels, she who had been bitten at the waist, was kneeling some feet from us.

"They must change the bathing enclosure," I said.

"Why?" asked Calla.

"Eels," I said.

"No need," said Calla. "Eels will depart when there is nothing to eat there. Eels are more common on the northern shore of the Vosk, anyway, where there are more settlements. They are not likely to return unless following sharks attracted to activity in the water."

"Be silent," said a mariner. "We do not care to hear the clattering of female tongues."

I looked about. The cargo was indeed fair, unusually fair. Calla had suggested that there was no mystery to this, that it had to do with an earlier essaying of the safety of the river. In any event I did not think that I belonged in so specialized a lading. I recalled that I was the last recaptured of four fled slaves. Our flight, or at least mine, had presumably delayed matters somewhat. I had doubtless missed my scheduled shipping. I had been returned to Victoria Minor after the first several boats had already embarked for Victoria.

At this point, two of the mariners, one of whom had aided in the checking of collars, lifted up a heavy hatch. This led downward into a lightless interior.

"Masters, may I speak?" begged Calla, suddenly, clearly disturbed.

"Yes," said he who had aided in the checking of collars. The man in blue was nowhere in sight. He had left, possibly returning to an office or a place where he might submit or file his records. Two docksmen were loosening ropes from the mooring cleats. Oarsmen were taking their place on the benches.

"Not the hold, Master," she said. "Do not put us there. It will be cold, damp, and dark, and it is too small for our number. Rather, be kind, be merciful, and let us remain on deck, in the sunlight and fresh air."

"Yes, Master," pleaded several of the slaves.

"Perhaps," said the mariner.

I am sure that it had not escaped his attention that the original request had been uttered by Calla. I supposed that beautiful women, even slaves, were more likely to have their requests acceded to than those of their plainer sisters. The man was clearly ready to allow us to remain on deck. I hoped we would be permitted to do so.

"What is going on here?" asked a fellow, seemingly in authority. His garb and gear were no different from that of the others, but his attitude was one of command, and he clearly expected to be deferred to. I supposed him to be the captain or, at least, the second officer. The ship was not large. It had only eight oars, four to a side. Two mariners stood by, ready to haul the sail onto the sloping yard. I suspected that the sail, nursing its packing of wind, would be the prime mover of the vessel. Given the size and weight of the boat, even though it was not large, certainly no massive 'round ship,' it seemed likely that the primary function of the oars would be to manage the vessel in leaving and entering a port. The two fellows who had freed the mooring ropes now had two long poles, with which they would press the boat from the wharf, opening space for the oars, in this case on the starboard side. In larger ships, four such poles are commonly used from within the ship, to thrust the ship away from the wharfage.

"The slaves wish to remain on deck," said the fellow who had helped with the collars.

"Since when," asked the newcomer, "does cargo direct its own stowage; since when do she-tarsks choose their own pen?"

"Never, Captain," said he who had helped with the collars. Then he addressed himself to the slaves. "Get below," he said. "Down the ladder, be careful."

Some moans escaped the slaves.

"Learn," said the captain, "though you may be prime merchandise, you are still only merchandise, as much as the lowest kettle-and-mat girl. Learn what you are, domestic animals, vendible beasts, slaves!"

"Get below, now," said the fellow who had helped with the collars. "Be careful, but be quick. Hurry! *Har-ta! Har-ta!*"

In my turn I descended the ladder. Happily, the steps, the cross-pieces, were flat. I felt damp sand as I stepped off the ladder. Presumably it was serving as ballast. Shortly thereafter, the heavy hatch cover was dropped into place. The hold was then plunged into total darkness. Some whimpering escaped the slaves. We then heard a rattle of chain, so I supposed the hatch cover had been chained in place. I did not think that that precaution was necessary. It was unlikely that any of us, from the ladder, could have pushed the cover up and away from its lodging. We heard orders being uttered; we sensed, in the darkness, the movement of the vessel. There was a sudden scream in the darkness. "*Urt!*" I heard. "*Urts!*"

"Be silent," warned Calla. "You will panic the others. The *urts* are more afraid of you than you of them. They are not aggressive. They are not starving; you are not bound helplessly. This is a hold, not a prison, not a punishment place. Be silent!"

"You are not first girl!" said a voice in the darkness, angrily.

"First girl or not," said Calla, "listen to me! We will soon be abroad in the river, not easily marked from the shore. Come to the steps, near my voice, as you can. The hatch is nearly amidships. Stay away from the sides of the hold." We heard a shaking of chains.

"Chains!" said a voice.

"Thank the Priest-Kings," said Calla, "that you are not in them, that you are not chained in place. Stay toward the steps, near my voice, towards the center of the hold."

"Why?" asked a voice.

"We are crowded as it is," said another voice.

"Do as I say," said Calla. I suddenly uttered an inadvertent cry. A tiny thing had scampered over my left foot. "Who is that?" asked Calla, angrily.

"I, Mira," I said. "Forgive me." I had almost said 'Janet.' I feared seemingly so slight a slip might prove disastrous. Someone in the darkness, a few feet away, began to sob.

"Stop it," said Calla. "Be quiet."

"You be quiet!" said an angry voice.

"She is not first girl," said a voice. "Let us tear out her hair and scratch her to pieces. It is dark. The Masters will not know who is to blame."

"Let her alone," said another voice. "We would all be punished."

I shuddered. In punishing all, the guilty person was certain to be punished. Too, the guilty person would later be at the mercy of those who had been punished in her place. Such a custom, I realized, uneasily, helps to keep order amongst slaves. Harsh as it may seem, its existence redounds statistically to their safety and welfare.

Minutes crept by.

Some of the slaves began to talk amongst themselves.

"Gather toward the center of the hold," said Calla.

"Do not listen to her," said a voice in the darkness.

I moved more to the center of the hold.

I think fifteen minutes passed.

I could sense the movement of the ship. One could feel its adjusting in the crossing, compensating for the soft pressing of the current to starboard. There are rapids in the Vosk, as, for example, west of White Water, but for most of its lengthy journey from the Voltai to the delta it is comfortably navigable. It rises in its banks in the late spring, but seldom to any extent which would threaten its many riverside settlements.

"Calla," I whispered, "how long does it take to reach the other side?"

"It would take something like an Ahn," she said.

This was something longer than an hour, assuming the rotation of Gor and Earth were comparable, as there are twenty Ahn in the Gorean day.

"Thank you," I said.

"We are not going to reach the other side," said Calla.

"What?" I said.

"Listen," said Calla.

There was stirring above, on the deck. I heard shouting. The ship began to turn about. The slaves stopped chatting.

The ship was single ruddered, like the ships of Torvaldsland, with their steering boards. Most Gorean ships, on the other hand, particularly those that dare stormy, turbulent Thassa, the sea, are double ruddered. This provides for closer turns, important in naval duels and, should one rudder be disabled, the ship may make do with the other.

"What do you mean?" I asked Calla.

"Come to the ladder," cried Calla. "Make your way to the sound of my voice! Come to the sound to my voice!"

"What is going on?" cried a voice from the darkness.

There was more shouting from above, on the deck. We heard cursing.

The ship veered west, downriver.

"What is going on!" demanded the voice from the darkness.

"Come to the sound of my voice!" cried Calla.

A slave screamed.

"This way! Here! Here!" cried Calla.

At that moment there was a deafening, horrendous crash, a sound louder and more terrible than any I had ever heard before, accompanied by a rupturing, a bursting in, a splintering, of plankage, and light and water flooded into the hold. I blinked my eyes against the sudden painful light and saw, through half-closed eyes, and felt, as I reached out, a wet, heavy, hideous snout of iron intruding into the hold. I saw oars outside, a long tier of them, thundering into the water. The snout of iron, rocking, drew back, through wreckage and water, and I found myself staring into a large, backward-moving, quiet, placid, painted eye.

CHAPTER FIFTEEN

I recoiled, screaming and sobbing, the violent running pain, following from the stroke of the lash, coursing through my body, turning it into a shaken receptacle of misery. "Please, Master, no more, I beg of you! Please, no more, Master!" The pain enveloped me, from the back of my neck to my ankles. I was a broken, beaten slave. I was naked, my wrists crossed and bound together over my head, fastened to an oar set between two tripods of timber. "Oh, no, no more, Master, please!" I begged.

"What is your name, wretched she-tarsk?" he asked.

"Mira, if it pleases Master," I wept.

"What are you?" he asked.

"A slave, Master!" I said.

"And what else?" he asked.

"Nothing else," I said. "I am a slave and only a slave, Master!"

"To whom do you belong?" he asked.

"I belong to Lady Temione of Hammerfest," I said.

"What does your collar say?" he asked.

I could not read Gorean, but I had been told what it said. "I am the property of Temione of Hammerfest. Return me to my Mistress."

"It is a special privilege to belong to Lady Temione of Hammerfest," he said.

"Yes, Master," I said.

"Do you rejoice in your good fortune?" he asked.

"Yes, Master," I said.

"Do you know why you were beaten?" he asked.

"No, Master," I said.

"What?" he asked.

"Forgive me, Master," I said. "A slave may be beaten for any reason or for no reason."

"You were beaten," he said, "because you are sexually desirable, because you are the sort of worthless animal on which men bid ardently."

Another fellow then freed my wrists from the oar and I, my body burning with pain, slipped to my knees.

He who had lashed me then held the whip to my lips and I kissed it, frightened, again and again. He then pointed to his feet with the coiled disciplining device, and I covered them with kisses.

"I think," he then said, to his fellow, he who had freed my wrists from the oar, "she will do nicely."

"They all belong in collars," said his fellow.

When the ram had broken through the hull and the hold was suddenly filled with intense, painful light, rushing water, and splintered, floating planking, chaos, hysteria, terror, and screaming had reigned in that opened, ruptured wooden cave that had been the hold. Slaves rushed toward the ladder. Calla and I were thrust to the side. I lost my footing in the forceful water and then regained it. "Be calm! Be still!" cried Calla. Of all in the hold, she alone kept her head. Slaves, crowding, tried to climb the ladder; some six, scrambling, fighting, scratching and pulling hair, managed to win a place on its ascent. Others clung to its sides. Two, sharing a higher step, were trying unsuccessfully to push up the hatch cover. Its weight alone held it in place.

"Fools!" shouted Calla. "It is too heavy for you."

"Let me try!" cried slaves, clustered about the ladder.

"Even were you ten times stronger," said Calla. "It is chained shut!"

"We are lost!" cried a slave.

"We will drown!" cried another.

"We are all going to die!" cried another.

"Do not be stupid!" cried Calla. "No one needs to die! They want you alive! You are worthless to them if you are dead!"

"The ship is sinking!" cried a slave.

"Call to them to unchain the hatch cover!" cried Calla.

"Free us! Let us out!" cried slaves.

"There is no answer," moaned a slave.

"The ship is wounded," said Calla. "It dies! Seize wreckage or swim. Escape through the wound!"

"Not into the river!" cried a slave.

"Raiders wait to pick you up!" said Calla. "Hurry!"

"There are sharks, eels, river *tharlarion*!" cried a slave.

"Soon," said Calla. "Not now! Be quick! Move!"

The water was rising in the remains of the hold and the ship began to incline.

"Toward the light!" cried Calla. "Make your way toward the light!"

I and several others, half-swimming, some clinging to wreckage, clambered toward the massive rupture in the hull, and, a moment later, I was in the river, swimming toward the long, lean, placid-eyed predator, rocking in the river, who had struck so terrible a blow in the hull of the ship on which we had been boarded less than an hour ago in Victoria Minor, the lesser Victoria. Over the prow and over bulwarks of the knife ship, between oars, were dangling several knotted ropes. "Hold to the ropes!" called a man's voice. I seized an oar whose blade was under water. "The ropes!" called a man. "The ropes!" I thrashed my way to one of the dangling ropes and seized it just above one of the knots. Hardly had I done so than I, dripping water, half-blinded by the river water, chilled, felt myself being drawn upward. Strong male hands then pulled me forcibly from the rope to which I desperately, half hysterically, clung. I was then, a hand on my upper left arm, sped amidships and flung to my knees. This was in the vicinity of a mast socket, with its chocks, near which, horizontal on the deck, were a removable mast and yard. On such vessels it is common for the mast, or masts, to be lowered before engaging in combat. Also, the mast, or masts, lowered, the ship, low in the water to begin with, is more difficult to see. Accordingly, the mast, or masts, are commonly lowered when one wishes to surreptitiously approach an enemy vessel or prey vessel. Similarly, such an action can be useful in eluding pursuit.

"Lower the longboat," said a man. "Get the *kajirae* out of the water. Then get the others off the planks and beams if you have to burn or scrape them off. Get them aboard, all of them."

"Sharks," said a mariner, pointing.

"Keep them away from the *kajirae* as you can. Use the lances."

"Hold to the rope!" I heard a man cry, from somewhere forward.

"We took her beautifully, amidships," said a mariner.

"Better the slaves had been kept on deck," said another.

"They did not even have time to unchain the hatch cover," said another.

"Nor needed they," said another man. "It was clear. We made their cargo an exit through which a *tharlarion* might tread, through which a regiment might march."

"Our benefactors make away on their longboat, abeam," said a man.

"Wish them well," said a man. "Perhaps they will have another shipment for us anon."

A fellow laughed.

"Watch for ships of the Vosk League," said a man.

"They are upriver, east," said a mariner. "She has seen to it with the spreading of rumors."

"She employs agents well," said a mariner. "Who can match her in the *kaissa* of the river?"

"I hope no *kajirae* are lost," said a man who, I think, had some priority amongst the others.

"She will not be pleased if that is the case," said a mariner.

"Calla will save as many as possible," said a man.

"The last slave is being boarded," called a man from somewhere to starboard.

"It is Calla," said another.

"The ship goes under," observed a fellow.

I could not see this from where I knelt.

Three or four of the mariners removed their caps.

"She will be reborn," said a mariner, "awakening to a new life when somewhere, sometime, eyes are painted anew."

"Look, to the stern castle," said a man. "She is there."

"She surveys her domain," said another.

We turned aft. On the high deck of the stern castle there stood a female figure, erect, proud, and commanding, a figure which could not be but that of a free woman. She was well robed, but lightly. At her left, at her waist, there hung a light scimitar. In her right hand was a whip. She was hooded and veiled. At the distance I had no idea what might be the color and aspect of her eyes.

The figure was imposing. It was viewed in silence and with deference.

This was, as it turned out, my first glimpse of one of the Vosk's wealthiest oligarchs, the owner of hundreds of slaves, the proprietor of a well-known slaving house, the owner of a great farm, one of the largest in the Vosk basin, and the Mistress of Calla, the Lady Temione of Hammerfest.

Regally, carefully, she descended the steps of the stern castle, between the two helmsmen on the helm deck, and, attaining the main deck, approached us.

We lowered our heads.

"Look up, misbegotten, silken urts," she said.

We raised our heads.

"An excellent catch," she said. "They will look well in sacks with digging sticks in their hands."

One or another slave whimpered.

"Say good-bye to perfume, beads, and ankle bells, she-urts," she said. "You are not to be purchased by rich, handsome fellows, to patter about on marble floors, to reside in opulent cities, to look on vistas from high bridges, to nibble on dainties stolen from great kitchens, to be ravished by Masters who will make you scream in ecstasy. No. Beautiful as you are, and you are beautiful, every one of you, you will be refused to men and men will be denied to you."

She then turned to one of the men, and snapped, "Bring Calla, the she-tarsk, to me."

In a moment Calla stood before her.

"Get on your knees," she said.

Immediately Calla knelt.

"How dared you stand before me, slave?" she said.

"Forgive me, Mistress," said Calla.

"But I think you performed your task well," said the Lady Temione.

"It is my hope that I did so," said Calla.

"So, account," said Lady Temione.

"I was entered into one of the long coffles bound for the great pen at Victoria Minor," said Calla. "I learned and communicated to your agents the day of arrival in Victoria Minor, the day of shipping to Victoria, the ships that would be employed, and the name of, and scheduling of, the ship intended to carry the most valuable cargo. I tried to get the slaves permission to remain on deck in the intended crossing, but could not do so. I did my best to calm, protect, direct, and save them."

"Forty-two slaves, including yourself," said Lady Temione.

"Forty-three, Mistress," said Calla. "One, a recovered fugitive, was added shortly before embarkation."

"And how many have we on board," asked Lady Temione of one of the men.

"Forty-three," he said, "counting the slave, Calla."

"Excellent," said the Lady Temione. "We have lost not one lovely digger of *suls*." She then turned to a tall man in a yellow scarf. "We shall tarry here no longer, Captain," she said. "Raise the mast and yard. Let the wind kiss our sail. Fly the pennon of Jort's Ferry. That will do as well as any. Let our progress be unhurried and stately, as befits our pose of innocent merchantry."

"Meanwhile," laughed a man, "let the Vosk League risk her hulls at White Water."

"No ball of flaming tar will cross our bow," said a mariner.

"No scout ship can object to our transporting cheap field slaves west," said a man.

"They are cheap, indeed," laughed a fellow, "as they cost nothing."

"Nonetheless," said the Lady Temione, "we will cover them."

"Shall we gag them?" asked a man.

"No," said Lady Temione. "If we should be boarded, and scrutinized, that would arouse suspicion."

"What if one cries out?" asked a man.

"Then cut the throat of the lot," said Lady Temione.

"They do not appear to be common field slaves," said a man.

"It is well known," said Lady Temione, "that Temione of Hammerfest buys field slaves for their beauty, to enhance the appearance of her fields. Such is her wont."

"You could sell these with high profit in a dozen markets on the Vosk," said a man, "far from Victoria."

"I do not choose to do so," said Lady Temione.

"Why?" asked a man.

"It is my wont," she said. She then said, "Fit the she-tarsks with chains."

"What of the slave, Calla?" asked a man.

"Chain her with the rest," said the Lady Temione. Following this, she turned about and retraced her steps aft and disappeared through the portal of the stern-castle cabin.

Men then set about fitting us with chains.

I was close to Calla.

Metal clasped my wrists and ankles. Eventually a chain would be threaded through the shackled legs of the slaves, this putting us on a single chain.

The men did not warn us to silence.

"You knew these things," I said to Calla, reproachfully. "You betrayed us, bringing us into the possession of the free woman, the Lady Temione. We are now in her chains."

"I, too, am their prisoner, and feel their weight on my limbs," she said.

Interestingly, I spoke of 'the free woman, the Lady Temione.' How naturally I spoke of her awesome status, that of freedom, and how naturally I spoke of her using the lofty expression 'Lady.' I scarcely dared speak of her. Her name and station frightened me. She was free, and Gorean. Many of my former world would not even have understood the chasm that separated the free from the bond on this world. They would have been unable to understand that gap. But let them be here and collared and they would learn it quickly. The Lady Temione was of a different order of existence from me. Legally, the difference was that between the free person, the lofty citizen, with rights, and the rightless, vendible domestic animal. I now, on Gor, lived and understood a distinction which would have been inconceivable to me when I had been free on Earth. I now knew myself to be no more than a Gorean slave, a beast in her collar. The Lady Temione, and others like her, were not simply higher than me, immeasurably higher than me, but other than me. The difference was not one of quality or degree, but one of kind. The free person is not higher than the pig, but other than the pig. The Lady Temione was a free person. I was not. I was a slave.

"I did not think you capable of such things," I said to Calla.

"I betrayed no one," she said. "I obeyed my Mistress. What else is a slave to do?"

"Still," I said.

"I did not wish to die by inches for days," she said.

"Oh, Calla," I said, then understanding, "I am sorry."

"Mistress Temione," she said, "finds pleasure in depriving needful, longing slaves of Masters. She wants them kept from men and men kept from them. The more beautiful and needful the slave, the more she is driven to deliver her to the miseries of heavy labor in remote fields."

"I do not understand that," I said.

"Nor I," she said.

But I wondered if there were not cultures which, subject to complex, specific, unnatural unfoldings, socially and historically, did much the same, striving to keep slaves from their Masters and Masters from their slaves.

"How many slaves does Lady Temione have?" I asked.

"I do not know," said Calla, moving a little in her chains. "I think she must have some eleven hundred field slaves and perhaps forty or fifty house slaves."

"And she chooses her slaves with care, for beauty, needfulness, and such?"

"As she can," said Calla.

"Her stock then, her slaves, must be of great value," I said.

"The expense must have been enormous," said Calla.

"We cost her nothing," I said.

"It is only in the past year that Mistress Temione has ventured into piracy," said Calla, "allying herself with Einar, Sleen of the Vosk."

"I have not heard of him," I said.

"That is because you know nothing of the Vosk," she said. "Few know his true identity or whereabouts. The Vosk League searches for him in vain."

"Are there many such captains?" I asked.

"Piracy on the Vosk has been much diminished since the foundation of the Vosk League," said Calla, "but it still exists. At one time piracy was much more open, even rampant, even the setting forth of fleets of ships, but now it is mostly carefully calculated and judiciously ventured. The wharfage of Master Einar is secret, but it is thought to be in the vicinity of the fields of Mistress Temione."

"How is it," I asked, "that Lady Temione dares deal with a pirate?"

"Greed," she said. "Has she not added forty-three slaves to her livestock even today, and prize stock for which men might kill? A plausible cost for such stock would be well over a hundred silver tarsks."

"I take it," I said, "the captain of this ship is not he who calls himself the Sleen of the Vosk."

"No," said Calla, "but the wealth of Master Einar is doubtless behind the ship and crew."

"Is it wise for the Lady Temione to ally herself with one such as Master Einar?"

"One blinded by the blaze of gold," said Calla, "often fails to note the ost at his feet."

"The action was done," I said, "before Lady Temione made her presence known."

"Of course," said Calla. "Her implication in dark matters is to be concealed. What if she were recognized? The Vosk knows her only as a dealer in field slaves, the maintenance of a house for such, and the wealthy mistress of a Great Farm."

"Lady Temione must be grossly ugly," I said.

"Why do you say that?" asked Calla.

"Have you seen her unveiled?" I asked.

"No," said Calla.

"Because of her hatred of beautiful slaves," I said. "She must envy them for possessing the beauty she so markedly lacks. She punishes them for possessing a desirability not her own. She hates them so, and men so, that she will deny them to Masters and will deny Masters to them."

"It seems strange and unnatural," said Calla. "Why should slaves not have Masters, and why should Masters not have slaves?"

"She frustrates the longings of both Masters and slaves," I said.

"It is interesting," said Calla. "In one way, she disguises, as she can, the beauty of slaves and, in another, proclaims it."

"I do not understand," I said.

"Surely," said Calla, "you are aware of the common nature of slave garments, designed by men to set off and display the beauty of their properties, tunics, camisks, ta-teeras, and such?"

"I know of tunics," I said. "I have heard of camisks and ta-teeras." I was well aware of the excitements of tunics, both as to their nature and their meaning, that their occupants were belongings, that they were owned.

"Well," said Calla, "in the fields, the slaves are put in rough, coarse garments, unattractive garments, like sacks, to conceal, as much as possible, their enticing charms, but, paradoxically, their hair is not cut short nor are their heads shaved as one might expect. Their hair is to be as clean, and as bushed and combed, as if they were to be put on the block within the Ahn."

"I think I know why that might be," I said.

"Why?" asked Calla.

"To further frustrate the slaves," I said. "Let them realize that not only do they remain as beautiful as ever under the insult and disgrace of an unflattering garment, but that they can look about and see one another as attractive, as possessing an attractiveness which pleases them, which delights and thrills them, which they know would be of great interest to men, but an attractiveness which will not be permitted to reap its common consequences, those of ardent bids and the eventual subjection of the objects of those bids in the arms of strong Masters."

Calla smiled, ruefully.

"She wants them to be attractive," I said, "and know that they are attractive, but also to know that, to their frustration, their attractiveness, in their present situation, in their current rounds of imposed toils, will be without consequence, that it will be meaningless."

"Your explanation is rational," said Calla. "It would satisfy many minds. It may even be true, as far as it reaches. Indeed, I suspect that that is the case. Surely it answers an obvious question, 'Why should she not want them to be in every way attractive or in every way unattractive?' But I think that there may be a deeper truth, an independent, more concealed explanation."

"How so?" I asked.

"An explanation which underlies an explanation," she said.

"I do not understand," I said.

"An uncertainty, a double ambivalence, within Lady Temione herself," said Calla. "It seems she fears, hates, and despises men, and yet finds them, perhaps to her consternation, attractive, and that she fears, hates, and despises women, as well, and, in so doing, fears, hates, and despises herself. She, a woman, rejects womanhood, and yet longs for her fulfillment as a woman. She is torn in two, trying not to be what she knows she is, and what, in her heart, she wants to be."

"A simpler explanation might be," I suggested, "that she is dreadfully homely, and is thus an enemy to all that is whole, healthy, and beautiful."

"I have never seen her unveiled," said Calla.

"It is clear enough from her behavior," I said.

"Every woman is beautiful in one way or another," said Calla. "Public criteria are like nets through which many lovely things may slip."

"In any event," I said, "I am pleased that our hair will not be cut short or our heads shaved."

"On the great farm of Lady Temione," said Calla, "there is only one slave whose hair is shamelessly short."

"She was punished?" I asked.

"No," said Calla. "When she was purchased, she was bald. Her head had been shaved. Her hair is grown out a little now."

"I thought Lady Temione only purchased lovely slaves," I said.

"That is true," said Calla. "But the hair of this slave will grow out."

I moved my ankles a little in their shackles; I lifted my wrists a bit, hearing the sound, feeling the weight, of the closely linked wrist rings.

"Kneel up, she-tarsks," said a male voice. "Spread those pretty thighs."

Calla and I knelt up, and the long coffle chain was looped about our ankle chain and passed on to the next girl.

In a few minutes the long chain, looped about our ankle chain, had been similarly looped and threaded between the legs of the forty-three slaves.

I knelt on the deck, now back on my heels, near the mast, chained hand and foot, a common chain now running between my legs, by means of which I was attached to the others.

Earth was faraway, somewhere on the other side of blazing Tor-tu-Gor, or, if one wishes, Sol, a small, yellow G2 star, the common star of Earth and Gor. I recalled Earth, and the observatory, and allusions to an altercation or war I did not even understand. I recalled those two large, seemingly out-of-place, spherical satellites whose nature I had perhaps unwisely investigated. I did not understand their nature or purpose. They seemed harmless enough, quiet enough, in their orbits, orbits they had assumed, orbits from which I was sure they could depart. It was almost as though they were waiting, poised and patient, but I had no idea for what they might be waiting.

And so I knelt on the deck, near the mast, chained hand and foot, a common chain now running between my legs, by means of which I was attached to the others, a slave.

"Men approach with canvas," said Calla. "They will cover us. We will not be noted from the shore or by passing ships."

"I am afraid," I said.

"Do not be so," had said Calla. "You are a lovely slave. You look well, naked, marked, chained, and collared. What have you to fear then, other than perhaps having failed to be fully pleasing, in all ways?"

"You will be quiet," had said a male voice.

Calla and I were then silent.

The canvas had then been drawn over us.

Another fellow then freed my wrists from the oar and I, my body burning with pain, slipped to my knees.

He who had lashed me then held the whip to my lips and I kissed at it, frightened, again and again. He then pointed to his feet with the coiled disciplining device, and I covered them with kisses.

"I think," he then said, to his fellow, he who had freed my wrists from the oar, "she will do nicely."

"They all belong in collars," said his fellow.

He who had lashed me then put his hand in my hair and pulled my head up, so that it was lifted to him. I turned my head to the side, not daring to look into his eyes. He was a free man. I was a slave. Then, a moment later, as though for some reason annoyed, he released my hair and I put my head down, gratefully.

I whimpered.

I trembled at his feet, my back afire.

"It is a shame to use such slaves in the field," said he who had released me from the oar.

"It is the wont of Lady Temione," said he who had lashed me. Then, angrily, seemingly frustrated, infuriated by something I did not understand, he, with a blow of his heavy, bootlike sandal, struck me rudely to my side on the ground.

I looked up at him, frightened.

I did not understand why he had done what he had done.

Why was he angry?

What had I done?

"You will be issued a body sack and a blanket," he said.

"Yes, Master, thank you, Master," I whispered.

"Take her to the kennels," he said.

I was pulled to my feet by the hair and then I was bent over, my head being held at the left hip of the fellow who had released me from the oar.

It was the standard Gorean slave-leading position.

I was then, in the custody of my keeper, led away.

There seemed tensions about, severe, painful tensions, which I did not understand.

In any event, it was thus that I was introduced to the fields of the Lady Temione of Hammerfest.

CHAPTER SIXTEEN

I saw her from a distance, another slave, from behind.

I paused in my digging, my back aching, my *sul* bag, heavy, looped over my shoulder.

Some slaves were about, digging in nearby furrows. From where I worked, I could see our group's *sul* cart, into which our *suls* would be later deposited, with its four harnessed field slaves. What struck me about her was that, in contrast to most, if not all, of the slaves on the farm, she had only a short brush of hair. It was brown, and was perhaps only a quarter of an inch in height. I recalled that Calla, on the ship moving downstream, had told me that there was only one slave amongst the slaves of the Lady Temione who had so little hair. I looked about. None of our male overseers were close. Curious, digging stick in hand, I approached the figure. When I was a few feet from her, perhaps five or six feet, I stopped. "*Tal*," I said.

She turned about.

"Bennett?" I said. "Bennett!" I half cried out.

She squinted against the sun.

"Xanthe!" she said, alarmed, her *sul* sack swinging at her waist. "Men might hear."

"Do you not recognize me?" I said. "Agnes Morrison Atherton! Intern. The library, Earth, the observatory!"

"I know you," she said.

"And I you," I said.

"There is a collar on your neck," she said. "Agnes Morrison Atherton no longer exists. Who are you?"

"Mira," I said.

"You are a slave are you not?" she said.

"Yes," I said.

"A domestic animal," she said.

"Yes," I said.

"As am I, thanks to you," she said.

"Surely you cannot blame me for that," I said.

"A drawer was left ajar," she said. "It was trivial, unimportant, an accident. You stole something from it! That was the difference!"

"I wanted to see something," I said. "I was curious."

"I was blamed," she said.

"I knew nothing of that," I said. "When I did not see you about, I thought you were on vacation or leave. I did not know you had been discharged, certainly not for so small an inadvertence. I was distraught. When I learned that you had been let go, which was much to my dismay, I tried to intervene on your behalf. I was terribly upset."

"Let go?" she said. "Discharged? A small inadvertence? I found myself in a van, stripped and in chains!"

"It is not my fault that you were shamelessly careless in attending to your responsibilities," I said, "that you neglected your work, that you were derelict in your duties, that you were off somewhere, maybe in the kitchen, flirting with male junior staff members."

"I am pleased to see you here in a sack and collar," she said. "But I cannot see what they would want with one such as you."

"Masters have been pleased with me," I said. "Muchly so!"

"I find that hard to believe," she said. "Where is your bound-back hair, your severe garb, your superior demeanor, your glasses? A sack becomes you."

"And who could wear a plain, shapeless, coarse sack as stunningly as you?" I asked. "And where is your long, luxurious, abundant hair?"

"My head was shaved," she said.

"Why?" I asked. "What had you done?"

"Nothing," she said. "My hair had been dyed. I was not truly a blonde. This angered men. If I was sold so, the merchant feared that he would be exiled and his business burned to the ground. And the colored nail polish was scraped from my nails."

"Goreans like honesty, authenticity, truth," I said.

"They are dolts, prudes," she said.

"They like to know what they are buying" I said. "They do not like being fooled or defrauded."

"It will grow out," she said.

"And soon, I am sure," I said. "It is a lovely brown."

"I am far more beautiful than you," she said.

"Leave that to the men to decide," I said.

"Surely you do not doubt it," she said.

"I see no reason to accept it," I said.

"You thought yourself so clever, so proper, so unattainable, so superior," she said.

"We knew different things," I said. "What I knew was more germane to the work and purposes of the observatory."

"You were more important than I," she said.

"Only in the context of the observatory," I said.

"You are not more important now," she said.

"No," I said, "I am not more important now."

"I hated you," she said.

"I am sorry" I said.

"You despised me for my attractiveness, for the interest of the men in me, for my beauty," she said.

"Annoyed with you, perhaps," I said. "Envied you a little, perhaps."

"You looked down on me," she said.

"What if I did?" I asked. "I was entitled to do so. My work was of greater importance to the observatory. I was of greater importance. You could not even understand the papers you kept so poorly. You were not much more than a clerk. Of course, you were less than I. Why should I not have looked down on you?"

"You were jealous!" she said.

"I could at least lock the drawer of a filing cabinet," I said.

"You were so superior, so unattainable," she said. "You are not so superior now, so unattainable now."

"No," I said, "I am not so superior now, not so unattainable now."

"Masters, on a whim, can tear off your sack, throw you to the ground and make you squeak and beg," she said.

"Now," I said, "at an amorous glance you would kneel, juice, and beg, very different from teasing the junior men at the observatory, testing your powers, arousing them and then, for your amusement, leaving them unsatisfied."

"Masters have done it to me," she said.

"They have kindled your slave fires," I said.

"And what of yours?" she asked.

"They burned even on Earth," I said.

"Worthless slave!" she hissed.

"I have found myself in a collar," I said. "I would not be otherwise."

"I did not know a worthless, needful slave lurked beneath your cool, lofty mien, your refined sober garb," she said.

"How terrible and brutal," I thought, "can be the trammels of convention and civilization, both on Earth and on Gor. Why should one who is a slave, knows she is a slave, and wants to be a slave, fear to kneel before a man and beg a collar?"

"What did you sell for?" I asked.

"Twenty silver tarsks," she said.

"You are a liar," I said. "I doubt that any of the slaves of the Lady Temione of Hammerfest would bring twenty silver tarsks. And surely not one with her head shaved."

We lifted our digging sticks, but neither struck the other. There were Masters about, guards, overseers, and we feared to be punished.

"I have not been put to a Master's pleasure since I was brought to the great farm," she said.

"Nor I," I said.

"I have seen men look at me," she said, "even as I am, in a sack, and seemingly shorn."

"It must be hard on the men, as it is on the slaves," I said.

"They can patronize the taverns and brothels of Hammerfest," she said. "We can do little other than weep in the darkness of our kennels."

"The Lady Temione is without mercy," I said.

"She hates women, especially lovely slaves," she said.

"She must be terribly ugly," I said.

"Yes," she said.

"I have received the inoculations of the Stabilizations Serums," I said. "Have you?"

"Of course," she said.

"Do you believe what they say of them?"

"Yes," she said. "There is unquestioned, universal consensus on the matter, even amongst the castes, and there is no reason to lie. More importantly, we have seen thousands of Goreans, slave and free. How many have you seen, slowed and ravaged by the depredations of age?"

"Perhaps one, or two," I said. "I do not know."

"They administer such serums even to slaves," she said.

"Is that not strange?" I asked.

"Not at all," she said. "They own us. We are their properties. What owner does not wish his properties to retain their value?"

"How is it possible that such things exist?" I asked.

I was not really sure that they did exist.

"Some say that the caste of Physicians, the Green Caste, perhaps over centuries, viewed aging not as a fate to be lamented but as a condition to be rectified. Eventually they came on a cure for what they called the drying and withering disease. Others say the serums were a gift from the Priest-Kings."

"Who are the Priest-Kings?" I asked.

"The gods of Gor," she said. "I do not know if they exist or not. Supposedly they live in the Sardar Mountains, a palisaded, mysterious, dark, forbidden terrain."

"On Earth," I said, "such serums, if they exist, would be of incalculable value. Fortunes would be spent to obtain them. Many, without a second thought, would lie, cheat, steal, and kill for them. Kings and politicians, magnates and generals, would vie for them. Mass movements and revolutions would spring up to demand them. Borders would be crossed, cities would be burned, ships seized, to get them."

"Undoubtedly," she said.

"Some on Earth might possess them already," I said.

"How so?" she said.

"We are here," I said. "And what road can go in but one direction?"

"We knew of no such person or persons," she said.

"The secret would be well kept," I said. "Were you the recipient of such serums on Earth would you advertise that fact? Would you dangle that golden apple before populations? Media would go mad. Social upheavals would occur. Calamity would ensue. Civilizations would collapse and perish. You would be apprehended, to become the object of extensive experimentation, and doubtless, eventually, of a fruitless dissection."

She stood in the furrow, clutching her digging stick.

"What are you thinking?" I asked.

"What I had not thought of much before," she said, "that if I had not left open the drawer of a filing cabinet, I would not be standing here, barefoot in the dirt, a slave, but yet one in possession of a gift which I had not earned and for which I had done nothing, a gift which would be priceless on my former world, a youth and beauty not subject to the ravages of time."

I wondered if such a thing could be true.

Certainly I had heard of it.

Could it be the case?

"For that boon," I said, "many a woman would beg the collar."

"But it is bestowed on us for the benefit of Masters," she said, "not for anything which we have done or deserved."

"True," I said.

She pulled at her collar. "But I am owned! I am a slave!" she said.

"You cannot remove it," I said. "It is on you. It is locked."

"I know," she said, angrily.

I seldom resented my collar. I knew that I belonged in it. It gave me a sense of rightfulness. It was important to me that I could not remove it. I wanted to have no choice but to be a slave. Thus, as I was choiceless, my slavery was more real.

"I trust that you do not blame me for your bondage," I said.

"Why not?" she asked.

"You are very beautiful, you know," I said.

"Even as I am?" she asked.

"Of course," I said. "It is obvious."

"Why should I not charge you with bringing about my shameful bondage?" she asked.

"Others could have been hired for the position you held," I said, "older women, more conscientious women, more diligent women, more experienced women, better credentialed women."

"Beauty casts flowers on many a path," she said. "Should I complain if men can see better than they can think?"

"I think they can think quite well," I said. "It is merely that they may not be thinking what you think they should be thinking. Who are we to tell a man how he should think?"

"Men are monsters," she said, "and we are their prey."

"You are not yet grateful prey," I said.

"I do not need a Master," she said.

"Yet," I said, "you long for one."

She regarded me, angrily, but did not dispute my assertion.

I stepped back, regarding her.

"No," I said. "I do not think you should blame me for your bondage."

"Why not?" she snapped. "I do not understand."

"Even as you are," I said, "clad in a gross sack, your hair so short, much betrays your beauty, your collared throat, your features, your trim ankles. What male, regarding you, could but, in his imagination, set you stripped on a sales block, being turned about, being exhibited for his perusal?"

"What are you trying to say?" she asked. "I do not understand."

"Much was going on in the observatory of which we know little," I said. "I do not think it so anomalous that you were hired before others. You may blame me for your bondage but, if anything, I think my action did no more than precipitate an already impending outcome. From the moment you were hired, I am sure that that fate was in store for you, sooner or later. While you flirted on Earth and amused yourself, toying with the emotions of men, chains and a marking iron were waiting for you on Gor."

"And what of you, Miss High, Proud, and Mighty?" she asked. "Had your employers, your mentors, and sponsors, no interest in your flanks, no thought of how you might look, naked, chained, at their feet?"

"Certainly not!" I said, aghast, outraged. "My position, my appointment, had absolutely nothing to do with such matters! Everything was purely professional. There was no thought of such things. Such considerations were immaterial. They were absolutely irrelevant to my appointment!"

"How do you know?" she asked.

"It must be so!" I said.

"I would not be sure of that, if I were you," she said.

"I took care to dress and act in such a way as to discourage even the slightest of hints of such things! I did my best!"

"Perhaps it was not good enough," she said.

"You are hateful!" I said.

"I saw you moving about, differently before men than when alone, standing, turning out a hip, glancing over your shoulder, the little smile. I was not fooled by your pretended primness, your playing with your glasses."

"No!" I said. "No!"

"We are not so different," she said. "I doubt that you managed to fool even yourself."

"I hate you!" I said.

"And I you," she said, "fraud."

I cast down my digging stick and hurled myself, weeping, on her, screaming, flailing, trying to seize her, to strike her, to bite and scratch her, anything. We rolled in the furrows, *suls* scattering about. I could not seize her hair but she had no difficulty in getting her hands into mine, and, in a moment, I was on my knees in the dirt, shrieking in pain, she on her feet, her hands, knotted and twisted, in my hair. "Please stop!" I wept. "Stop!"

"Fraud, fraud!" she screamed. "Admit you are a liar and a fraud!"

"Yes, yes, stop it!" I cried.

"I am a liar and a fraud. Stop, stop!"

"Beg me to stop," she screamed. "Beg it as a slave, the slave you are!"

"I beg it!" I screamed.

"As the slave you are!" she said.

"Yes," I cried, "I beg it! As a slave! As the slave I am! Stop, please stop!"

"Who is more beautiful?" she asked.

"You, you!" I wept. "Please do not hurt me more!"

"Mistress!" she said.

"Mistress, Mistress!" I conceded.

Then a male voice said, "Stop squabbling, foolish *kajirae*!" The former Bennett, once Eileen Bennett, now Xanthe, instantly releasing her grip, was pulled bodily away from me and thrown back into the furrows. She rose immediately to her knees and put her head down. I, too, who was already on my knees, lowered my head. We were in the presence of a free man.

Some other slaves, nearby, who had not interfered in our altercation, went to their knees, heads down, as well.

Aside from the lingering pain I felt, my scalp afire, I felt miserably foolish. How could I, once Agnes Morrison Atherton, have behaved so? What nerve had been touched? What veil had been torn away. I felt ashamed, but, too, relieved. It was as though I had looked in a mirror but denied that the image could be my own. Was it not a mirror in which I dared not look? Why had I howled at a reflection which could only be my own? I admitted to myself then what I had, on some rejected level, long understood. My appearance had not been immaterial to my appointment. Nor had I really wanted it to be so. I expected it to be relevant, and I had hoped it would be. On the other hand, I knew that I was intelligent, diligent, motivated, well prepared, and fully qualified to do the work. Even had I been plainer or a male, I would have been a suitable, even excellent, candidate for the position. But I did not, really, object to the fact that my appearance might have served me well. Why should I do so? What woman in her right mind would object to being sexually desirable, if she might be such, in view of the many social and economic benefits and privileges associated with so fortunate a status? But what a difference between the free and the slave! When a woman is free, she may profit from, and exploit, such a status as she wishes. She may use her beauty to bargain for benefits and advance her fortunes, to put herself on the market and sell herself, so to speak, for her own profit. But the slave is put on the market by others, and sold not for her profit, but for that of another. She is owned. She is merchandise. I revisited my altercation with Xanthe. I pondered. It seemed to me likely that, as I had earlier suggested, the former Eileen Bennett, so tantalizingly attractive, might have been added, even from the beginning, to the staff of the observatory with a Gorean market in mind. But what then of me? Could the senior staff at the observatory, Doctors Jameson, Archer, and Townsend, have had such an outcome in mind for me? Surely not! But I did not know. I thought it was possible. Could I be that attractive, worthy of a collar on Gor? I did not know. In any event, one thing was clear. The former Eileen Bennett and the former Agnes Morrison Atherton were now on Gor, both of them, marked and collared slaves.

The free man, a guard, did not ask us what the difficulty or problem might be. It was of no interest to him.

"I was annoyed," he said.

"Forgive us, Master," we said.

"You should both be lashed," he said.

We trembled, heads down.

"It grows late," he said. "Tor-tu-Gor will soon rest. Gather up your *suls* and take them to the cart."

"Yes, Master," we said.

He looked about, at the others. "The light goes," he said. "Take your *suls* to the cart. Do not let your gruel grow cold."

He then left.

"He did not lash us," said Xanthe.

"He did not have a whip," I said.

"He could have used his belt," she said.

"I think he would have liked to put one or the other of us to his pleasure," I said.

"Or both," she said.

"It must be hard for the men, that we are denied to them," I said.

"It is hard for us, too," she said, "that we are denied to them."

"Thanks to Mistress Temione," I said.

"What difference could it make to her?" asked Xanthe.

"It seems she takes pleasure in denying pleasure to others," I said, "perhaps pleasures for which she herself longs, but fears, and will not permit herself."

"How long can men tolerate such deprivation?" asked Xanthe.

"I do not know," I said.

We rose to our feet, and began to gather the scattered *suls*, returning them to our bags.

We were then a few feet from one another.

"Eileen," I said.

"Xanthe," she said.

"I am sorry I lost my temper," I said. "It seemed important to me to hide myself from myself. I was a fraud, and a liar, mostly to myself. Many times I pretended to be oblivious of the needs which seethed within me. Often in my fantasies I was marked and collared, and knelt naked before Masters."

"I, too," she said, "but I despised the men of Earth for the socially engineered weaklings they permitted themselves to be. Thus I enjoyed exploiting them, humiliating them, and tormenting them."

"Here men are different," I said.

"Very different," she said.

I then went to her.

"I am sorry," I said. "I behaved badly."

"I, too, am sorry," she said. "I, too, behaved badly."

"Do not hate me," I said.

"Nor you me," she said.

We kissed one another, I think both with tears in our eyes.

"Earth is behind us," I said.

"Far behind us," she said.

"I did not even know this world existed," I said.

"Nor I," she said.

"We now know it is real," I said.

"And here," she said, "on this world, we are slaves."

"Goreans," I said, "think that the women of Earth are vain, petty, and spoiled, that they are worthless except as collared slaves."

"To Gorean men," she said, "what could women such as we be but slaves?"

"They do with us as they wish," I said, "they use us as they please."

"Of course," she said. "We are slaves."

"Marketable barbarians," I said.

"We had better hurry," she said. "The *sul* cart will be leaving shortly."

"Look to the sky," I said, pointing.

"I see," she said, "a lone tarnsman."

"What is he doing?" I asked.

"I do not know," she said, "but I have seen them before, always alone."

"I am sorry your hair was shaved away," I said.

"It will grow out," she said.

We then hurried to the *sul* cart.

We did not wish our gruel to grow cold.

CHAPTER SEVENTEEN

"Who is Gordon?" I asked.

Calla moved a little in her harness, with a sound of bells. "Administrator of Hammerfest," she said, "one of the twenty-two oligarchs of the Vosk, one of the richest men on the river."

"What is the occasion," I asked.

"It is much like a visit of state," said Calla. "Mistress Temione wishes to be accepted as the twenty-third oligarch of the river. The favor of Gordon of Hammerfest would be invaluable in securing that recognition."

"Surely Mistress Temione is rich enough," I said. "What does it matter whether or not she is acknowledged as an Oligarch of the river?"

"It matters to her," said Calla.

"Vanity," I said.

"Of course," she said.

"She is probably richer now than some of the already accepted Oligarchs of the Vosk," I said.

"I would not be surprised," said Calla.

"I would not think it wise for Mistress Temione to advertise the extent of her wealth."

"I am sure that Gordon of Hammerfest is discreet and trustworthy. This survey, brief, small, and partial, as it will be, is confidential."

"The survey may be confidential," I said, "but if she is designated an Oligarch of the Vosk, her wealth will not be in dispute. It will be, in effect, a matter of public surmise, if not of public record."

"The confidentiality of the survey," said Calla, "is in case her wealth does not qualify. It would be embarrassing to make known the results of the survey if they were insufficient to win the coveted recognition."

"Look," I said, with a stirring of bells, "there is Mistress Temione."

"Stay in place, and look forward," said Calla.

"Who is with her," I asked, "so large a man, so seemingly severe, and in such splendent robing?"

"He with her," said Calla, "is Gordon of Hammerfest."

"I would fear to belong to such a man," I said.

"Keep your eyes forward," she said.

"If Mistress Temione is so rich," I said, "why does she not have beasts, draft *tharlarion*, draw her carriage?"

"She does have beasts to draw her carriage," said Calla, "our variety of beasts."

"Stand up," said our driver, seated beside his fellow, from the wide driver's bench of the carriage.

The twenty of us, ten to a line, stood, with a jangle of harness bells. The carriage was flanked by ten guards, five to a side.

"Mistress Temione and Master Gordon seemed in earnest converse," I said.

"No longer," said Calla. "Only when they could not be overheard by guards or slaves."

"I sensed tension in their conversation," I said.

"Be quiet," said Calla. "You will have us all beaten."

Lady Temione and Gordon of Hammerfest were then at the side of the carriage. I did not turn to look at them. I did not think that that would have been wise. Too it was difficult to move without the betraying tinkling of the harness bells. My hands, as were those of the others, were tied behind me.

"I see, noble Lady," said Gordon, now lightly, offhandedly, with little sign of tension in his discourse, "you utilize *kajirae* as draft beasts."

"It is one of the few things they are good for," she said. "They can understand simple commands, and are responsive to the blows of the whip."

"One draft *tharlarion* could outdraw fifty such beasts," he said.

"Draft *tharlarion* are expensive," she said.

"I trust that you could afford such with ease," he said.

"Many times over," she said.

"I trust then that your practice of utilizing *kajirae* as draft beasts is not a matter of economy."

"Certainly not," she said.

"A matter of preference then," he said.

"Quite," she said.

"May I inquire into the grounds of your preference?" he asked.

"Ascribe it to the whims of a woman," she said.

"There is a rumor," he said, "that you commonly pay far more than is usual for field slaves, that you stock your kennels with merchandise which might bring fine coin in most markets."

"Dismiss such rumors," she said.

"They would suggest that your motivations were other than economic."

"Let us ascend to the carriage," she said.

"Commonly," he said, "when *kajirae* are utilized as draft beasts, certainly a strenuous, sweaty labor, they are naked. Yet you conceal the possible charms of these *kajirae* by cloaking them in gross sacks."

"To hide the imperfections of their bodies," she said.

"Yet," he said, "their ankles, and their features, and hair, would seem to suggest that what is seen might auger well for what is now unseen."

"Though I am a woman," she said, "I believe I can convince you that my resources are such as to place me high amongst the oligarchs of the river."

"To ascertain this is the point of my visit, noble lady," he said.

"I do not think you will be disappointed," she said.

"I trust not," he said.

"You will be fair, of course," she said.

"My office as Administrator of Hammerfest guarantees that," he said.

"I sense an edge in your voice," she said. "I wonder if you like me."

"I assure you," said he, "I hold you in the fullest extent of the esteem you deserve."

"Should my holdings prove superior to yours," she said, "as you are an accepted oligarch, you will salute me as a fellow oligarch, will you not?"

"Even were your holdings somewhat less than mine," he said.

"I do not expect them to be less than yours," she said.

"Then there could be no question of the matter," he said.

"I have better than twenty-five hundred *vielts* under cultivation," she said. "I have over eleven hundred and fifty slaves, field slaves and house slaves. Indeed, as a part of our tour, along our route, we shall pass between two lines of kneeling slaves, a corridor of slaves, so to speak, who will cry out joyfully, wishing us well, as we pass. Too, I have over two hundred men in my employ, overseers, guards, accountants, clerks, drovers, wagoners, and such. I am the major supplier of produce for a hundred *pasangs* east and west on the Vosk."

"Surely the major supplier," said he, "are the thousands of peasants for a hundred *pasangs* east and west on the river, in their palisaded villages, those with individually tended fields, or those with shared fields."

"Single major supplier," she said. "Even the largest of peasant villages could not begin to equal the extent of my *vielts*."

"I am sure that is true," he said.

"It is," she said. "And I have four blockhouses situated to defend the farm, and my house, my palace, is a fortress in itself, capable of withstanding the siege of a thousand men."

"I have heard of your house," he said.

"You shall see it this evening, after our tour," she said, "while we sup."

"I shall look forward to it," he said. "Are your house slaves also adorned with the lovely sacking wasted on the field slaves?"

"Their bodies are similarly covered though with less coarse, but similarly concealing, material," she said. "I would not care to look upon, or be inadvertently brushed by, field sacking."

"I will look forward to supper," he said.

"For entertainment," she said, "I will have a house slave play the *kalika*."

"Splendid," said Gordon, Administrator of Hammerfest, dryly.

"I think you will find my house impressive," she said.

"I have familiarized myself with its gates, its walls, its battlements, its defenses," he said.

"So like a man," she said. "Better to attend to its gardens, its décor, its tapestries."

"Doubtless," he said.

"You may assist me into the carriage," she said.

"Before we begin our tour, with its attendant survey, partial as it must be," he said, "I think it imperative to return to a matter on which we earlier, and, unfortunately, somewhat heatedly, touched."

"Not that," she said, impatiently.

"I am sorry," he said. "But it is not I alone who am concerned in the matter. The High Council of Hammerfest has imposed an obligation on me to clarify the matter."

"Proceed," she snapped.

"Perhaps we should withdraw a little," he said. "Others might overhear. The matter is delicate."

"I have nothing to hide," she said, curtly.

"You are, of course," he said, "familiar with certain troubling rumors."

"Rumors baseless and false," she said.

"Nonetheless," he said, "gossip persists. You must understand that to be acknowledged an accepted oligarch by the municipalities enrolled in the Vosk league, as merely social as the denomination may be, there can be no taint of wrongdoing, no hint of ill-gotten gains. The point of the title is to celebrate riches honestly earned, this being a credit to the holder of the title and an incentive to others to emulate his success. Thus it encourages others to enterprise, imagination, vision, and hard work."

"It is easier to envy and hate the successful," said Lady Temione.

"With many it is so," said Gordon. "But if it is acceptable to hail the triumphant soldier, cheer the victor in city games, celebrate the *kaissa* master, glorify singers and poets, why is it not appropriate to rejoice at the existence of the great merchant, the founder of a business, the creator of wealth, which, by its very existence, profits so many?"

"Seeking the title of oligarch," she said, "I could not agree with you more."

"You are willing to be envied and hated?" he asked.

"What is large is always hated by the small," she said. "Let the *urt* disparage the *larl*. It does not diminish the strength and glory of the *larl*."

"Some, I fear," said Gordon, "resent the influence of wealth on the state."

"The state is founded on wealth," she said. "To deny the influence of wealth, whether of gold or steel, is to deny the fact of the state, even its legitimacy."

"Perhaps," said Gordon.

"Wealth can buy many things," she said, "amongst them the state."

"The danger," said Gordon, "is when the purchases of wealth are made secretly, when they are concealed or denied. That is the most evil of treacheries. Explicit oligarchy, regardless of how it is viewed, disdains subterfuge."

"I trust," she said, "that you will tender me your support, that I may attain to the public distinction of being denominated an Oligarch of the Vosk. I deem my wealth altogether sufficient to justify that title, and I expect you to recognize that fact."

"But," said Gordon, "the wealth, if that of a true oligarch of the river, must be legitimately acquired. It must be won honestly."

"Or at least appear to have been won honestly," she said.

"In that remark," said Gordon, "I trust that you do not refer to a possibly dubious origin of some of your own resources."

"Certainly not," she said angrily.

"That brings us to our difficulty," said Gordon, the Administrator of Hammerfest, "and to certain rumors."

"Baseless and false rumors," said Lady Temione.

"Undoubtedly," said the Administrator of Hammerfest, "but rumors nonetheless."

"Speak clearly," said Lady Temione.

"Here?" he said.

"Yes," she said. "I hide nothing. I fear nothing."

"In particular," said Gordon, "it is hinted, in shadows of speech, in tavern gossip, in hollow whispers heard in alleys and about the docks, amongst low, furtive men, that you are in league with the infamous Einar, who calls himself the Sleen of the Vosk."

"Rubbish," said Lady Temione. "That is river talk."

"The talk is real," he said.

"But false," she said. "There is not one particle of evidence to link me with Einar."

"The lack of evidence does not imply innocence," said Gordon. "It is claimed that you have dealt with the dreaded Einar, the so-called 'Sleen of the Vosk,' by means of agents."

"That is categorically and absolutely false," she said.

"I am relieved to hear that," said Gordon.

"I know nothing of Einar," she said.

"Few do," said Gordon, Administrator of Hammerfest. "He is a mysterious figure, seemingly lurking in the shadows. Yet his influence seems everywhere."

"I have heard so," said the freewoman, Mistress Lady Temione of Hammerfest.

"You have never had dealings with Einar or his agents?" asked Gordon.

"Certainly not," she said.

"You swear so?" he asked.

"Of course," she said.

"By the veracity of the free woman?" he asked.

"Yes," she said.

"And by the Home Stone of Hammerfest?"

"Certainly," she said.

"I am pleased to hear it," he said.

"I would not know Einar, the Sleen of the Vosk," she said, "if I were speaking face to face with him."

"I am sorry for having raised the issue," he said, "but I trust that you understand that I had no choice but to do so."

"Of course," she said, "you were charged to do so by the High Council of Hammerfest."

"Unpleasantries happily out of the way," he said, "let us enjoy the afternoon, conducting our small, sampling survey whose favorable outcome is, I presume, already assured, and look forward to a pleasant supper and evening."

"I will have a slave play the *kalika*," she said.

"Splendid," he said. "Incidentally, may I congratulate you on the richness and tastefulness of your robing and veils?"

"Thank you," she said. "You may now assist me into the carriage."

"It will be my pleasure to do so," he said.

"I think you will find my resources and holdings more than sufficient to be those of an Oligarch of the Vosk."

"I am sure I will," he said.

"I hope you will permit me to recompense you for your time, inconvenience, and effort, say, by the token of a hundred gold tarns of distant Ar, tarns of double weight."

"*Ela*, lady," he said, "I must decline your kind offer, lest it be misinterpreted by the small minded and cynical as an attempt to tarnish the objectivity of my assessment."

"Such coins are rare along the river," she said.

"Even so," he said.

"As you will," she said.

"My lady," he said, politely.

"Thank you," she said.

There was then, a moment later, the sudden unexpected crack of a whip, and the harness bells jangled wildly, as the slaves reacted.

We heard a woman's laugh, doubtless that of the Lady Temione.

The whip had not struck anyone, but it did convey its message. The stroke of some whips can literally cut open the sacking on a girl's back.

"Forward, *kajirae*," said the driver. "Move."

We put our weight into the straps and, after a frightening first moment when we feared we could not move the carriage, the wheels began to turn, and then we, bent over, hands tied behind our backs, began to propel the carriage forward.

CHAPTER EIGHTEEN

"Fire! Fire!" screamed a slave.

I awakened, wildly, abruptly, painfully, casting my blanket aside, struggling to my feet, my body sore and aching from the exertions of the day, having been one of the *kajirae* who had drawn the carriage of the Lady Temione of Hammerfest.

I saw nothing of fire.

It was dark in the kennel.

"Fire!" came the cry, again.

I smelled smoke. Somewhere in the darkness I heard something which was like a crackling of twigs or stirring of wind.

Slaves pushed past me in the darkness, making their way toward the door of the kennel.

It was shortly after that that I saw the first sign of flame, a horizontal, enlarging streak of red, back, at the far end of the kennel where the tarlike caulking between the heavy, tiered logs was melting away.

Slaves were screaming and pounding on the door, which consisted of a door within a door. The 'high door,' when opened, would admit two slaves to pass through at a time, coming or going. The 'low door,' on the other hand, which was close to the ground and built into the high door, would allow the passage of only one slave, or one person, say, one guard, at a time, crawling, on their hands and knees. This arrangement was most likely suggested by a feature utilized in some 'communal halls' or 'keeps' in peasant villages where there is, however, only one door, much like the 'low door' of the kennel. The point in the peasant villages is one of security and defense. Only one enemy or interloper can crawl through the opening at a time, which would limit the speed of entry and place the entrant, on his hands and knees, much at the mercy of the knives and axes of the peasants within. The 'low door' in the kennel, when utilized, seemed to have two purposes, one to remind slaves that they are slaves and, secondly, to make it easier to control their movements, to tether them, and so on. Some slave cages are similarly constructed.

"Let us out! Let us out!" cried slaves pounding on the door.

I moved a little closer to the center of the kennel, where a ventilation shaft opened to the night sky. The flames were not close. I saw no point in entering into the frenzy at the door. Looking up I could see the stars of the night sky. A shift of the wind carried some smoke across the opening between the kennel and the stars. I also saw some brief sparks in flight. A slave screamed, apparently burned by a droplet of hot tar fallen from the roof.

"Move back from the door. Calm yourselves! Be patient! Be apart! You will injure one another! The door will be opened before the flames can reach you!" cried a woman's voice, that of Calla.

Few heeded her.

I had no idea how the fire had started. I ruled out the possibility of an accident. There had been no storm with lightning. Cooking was not done in or near the kennel. But who might set such a fire, and why? Just as on Earth few in their right mind would set fire to a stable of valuable horses, so, too, few in their right mind on this world would set fire to a kennel of *kajirae*, many of whom, like Calla, were valuable. I then heard, some yards away, to my left, on the other side of the door, the pounding of a heavy hammer on metal, and the rattle of chains.

"Stay calm!" shouted Calla. "The door will be opened!"

There was pounding, over and over, the brutal strike of a heavy hammer on stout metal.

Men of Lady Temione would have had the key to the great padlock securing the door on the outside.

Thus, those who strove to free the door were not of her employ.

My mind darted back to Victoria Minor and the raid on the great pen. "Raiders!" I thought. I coughed. My eyes were starting to sting. I wondered if the raiders were those who had attacked the great pen in Victoria Minor. Yet here, on the *vielts* of Lady Temione, there would be no succor from an aroused city militia or from mighty Victoria across the river. I feared the fire but it did not, certainly as of yet, constitute a mortal threat. Rather I saw this eventuation as providing a surcease of the miserable labors of the farm. I was hoping I might be sold in an opulent market and then, clothed, though doubtless in the brief, proclamatory tunic of a slave, wear my collar in some city, preferably in one of the tower cities of which I had heard so much and knew so little.

I began to cough and my eyes stung more. "Let them free the door," I thought. "Get it open! Get it open!" I wanted the night air, the stars, the cold grass!

Then there was a collapse of logs at the far end of the kennel, and I saw, clearly, for the first time, flames.

More screaming ensued. I do not even know if I added to the screaming or not. I might have. I do remember being suddenly terrified.

Then the pounding stopped and there was a rattle of chain as it was drawn through heavy staples.

The low door in the high door was then swung open.

There was fighting, clawing, and scratching as slaves, soon to be on their hands and knees, fought to make their way through the small, cleared portal.

"There is time!" shouted Calla. "Be patient. Step back. One after the other!"

"One at a time, she-sleen," barked a man's voice. "One at a time!"

The sound of this man's voice, deep, abrupt, definitive, and authoritative, clearly that of a free man, a possible Master, addressing slaves, a voice redolent of command, one not to be questioned, one brooking no demur, struck silence into the slaves. It instantly was met with abject, frightened compliance. Order was restored.

Calla stood within the kennel and, in the wild, reddish light, indicated a slave. "You," she said. "Now you. Next. You. Now you!"

I took my place in line, on all fours.

Before I made my way through the tiny portal the far end of the kennel was enveloped in flames.

It had been no accident that the fire had been set as far as possible from the exit of the kennel.

This protected the portal as long as possible and would drive the occupants toward it.

As I gratefully emerged from the kennel, sucking in the night air, clenching my eyelids together, trying to soothe my smarting eyes, crawling on my hands and knees, a rope was knotted about my neck, and I was added to what would prove to be a coffle of five. Earlier coffles of five were already added to others. The last girl in one coffle of five was then tied by the neck to the first girl in the next coffle of five, and so on. In this way there was one long coffle, in this case, given the occupants of my kennel, one of fifty slaves. Similar arrangements, I would learn, were managed at the other kennels.

Calla, the last to emerge from the kennel, was the last of her coffle of five, which would be the last of the coffles, which would eventually put her at the end of the longer coffle.

"Are there any more inside?" she was asked.

"No, Master," she said.

"You have determined this?" she was asked.

"Yes, Master," she said.

I had much respect for Calla.

She had waited to be the last to leave.

She was intelligent, brave, and kindly. I had no doubt that in the ramming of the ship on the river, she had saved lives, and she may have done so as well in the firing of the kennel. The kennel had been fired, I assumed, in order to expedite the acquisition of the kennel's occupants. She had also kept the secret that I was of barbarous origin. I thought she would make a fine first girl, one firm but fair, one solicitous of her charges and yet one who, avoiding favoritism, would impose an impartial discipline. Some Masters, incidentally, who have several slaves, will, from time to time, change the 'first girl.' This puts something of a curb on the governance of a given 'first girl,' for she may eventually find herself subject to a former subordinate with an aggrieved recollection, a subordinate eager to express herself in retaliation.

I, now kneeling in my place, looked about. There were perhaps twenty raiders I could make out. Certainly I did not, in the light of the now muchly flaming kennel, see any guards or overseers I recognized.

I knew that Lady Temione had some two hundred men or so in fee, but these were not all men at arms. I did not know the numbers of the raiders. I conjectured, based on what I was later able to estimate, that there might be three or four hundred. I saw no sign of the retainers of Lady Temione. It seems they had withdrawn, been driven away, or were engaged elsewhere. Indeed, perhaps they had been closed in or neutralized as had been the case at Victoria Minor. It was possible, too, that they had been suborned or even dissuaded from offering what would clearly have been, at least outside the palace, a futile, token resistance.

"Coffle!" snapped a voice.

We rose to our feet.

"We will house these *kajirae* temporarily in the palace," said a tall, bearded fellow who was apparently in authority.

"Has the palace then, that fortress touted to be capable of standing a siege of a thousand men, been taken?" I wondered. "Has it fallen? Could that be?"

This was the night of the day on which I had served in the belled harness of the Lady Temione's carriage. This, too, was the night of her supper with Gordon, the Administrator of Hammerfest. Was the supper in progress? Did Lady Temione even know what was occurring, or had occurred, elsewhere in her broad, spreading *vielts*?

A man pointed toward the palace, or fortress, several hundred yards away.

The coffle adjusted itself.

"Move," he said.

We moved.

The first step is taken with the left foot.

CHAPTER NINETEEN

I, a field slave, had never been in the walled palace of the Lady Temione.

I had, of course, seen it at a distance.

I think it was something after midnight when our coffle was halted before the central gate of the palace. The two leaves of the large gate were swung back, one to either side. It was dark within the gate. Whereas the palace might be referred to as a fortress of sorts, it was more of a fortified palace. There was, for example, no moat, no drawbridge, no portcullis.

A frantic female figure, clad in a soft, white, sacklike garment, suddenly darted out of the darkness, clutching a stringed musical instrument of some sort. Then, seeing us, she stopped, abruptly, startled, confused. In her haste to depart from the palace, she had not realized our presence. One of the men seized her upper right arm and dragged her stumbling to the coffle, to which she was promptly added. She started to whimper, but was instantly warned to silence. She was then amongst us, neck roped. She continued to clutch her instrument. "Spoiled house slave," said a slave near me. "Take that silken sack away from her and beat her until she begs to sweat in the fields," said another slave. "Filthy *sul* diggers," responded the girl in white. "Be silent," said a man, interposing his arm between the slaves who seemed prepared to attack one another. I knew there was a hierarchy amongst slaves, but I had not hitherto realized that that hierarchy might be so fiercely redolent of a mutual acrimony. The house slaves commonly look down on the field slaves with contempt, feeling themselves far superior to their benighted sisters toiling in the fields and the field slaves, for their part, tend to despise their loftier sisters as smug, pampered she-urts undeserving of their soft lot.

A man strode forth from within the gate.

"How many have you?" he asked.

"Fifty, no, fifty-one," said our coffle master.

"You are the sixth kennel to arrive," said the fellow who had just joined us. He had a helmet crested with flowing hair. "Take your coffle inside and put them in the garden, near the pool."

"A splendid haul," said a man.

"Better than Victoria Minor," said another.

"That is enough," said the fellow in the crested helmet, sharply.

"By now," said a man, uneasily, "word may have reached Hammerfest."

"No," said the man in the crested helmet. "Have no fear. It will not have done so."

I wondered why this might be, why he had spoken with such assurance. I certainly hoped word had not yet reached Hammerfest. I did not care to be 'rescued,' to be returned to the fields of Lady Temione.

Soon our coffle was conducted within the palace grounds and put with other coffles, those of our predecessors.

"If thirsty, drink from the fountain," said a man. "Do not seek to satisfy your thirst from the pool. You might find your hands or face bitten away."

"Carnivorous eels," whispered a slave near me.

I suddenly did not envy the house slaves as much as before. It is unpleasant to 'swim with the eels,' as it is said.

We were scarcely settled in the garden, sitting, kneeling, or reclining, when another coffle was ushered through the gate.

"We must feed this stock in the morning," said a man.

"Easily done," said another. "The great kitchen is nigh and the pantry is at hand."

A man turned to us. "How many of you miserable field slaves were once house slaves?" he asked.

With the exception of myself, I think all the slaves within earshot were identifying themselves as having been house slaves. I thought that this was highly probable, for Lady Temione, in her strange desire to humiliate unusually beautiful women and deny them the satisfaction of their needs, wished to populate her fields with women who, off the block, might have gone for well over a silver tarsk, namely, women whose background would almost certainly not have been the labors of the fields.

"How many here know grates, stoves, and ovens?" he asked. "How many can create a feast?"

"I, I, Master! I, Master!" cried dozens of voices.

The point of slave training is to enable the girl to please her Master, and thus her training is seldom limited to bathing him, serving him at the foot of his couch on the furs, and such. She is also likely to be versed in domestic chores such as laundering, ironing, cooking, cleaning, shopping, and so on. Beyond such things, some Masters like to have her trained in song, literature, music, and dance. Needless to say, intelligent, talented, educated slaves often sell well. An interesting feature of some slave trainings is, so to speak, sensitivity training, encouraging the girl to become more aware of her world, more radiantly alive, more aware of scents, colors, flavors, feels, ambiances, atmospheres, and so on. Consider, for example, the smoothness and shine of leather, the touch of silk, the sound of a chain's linkage, the clasp of a slave bracelet on one's wrist, and so on.

Ten of the slaves were released from the coffle and sped away to the kitchen and pantry.

One of the men who had ushered us from the kennel had been standing about. It was he who had questioned Calla as to whether or not the last of the slaves had been accounted for.

"May I speak, Master?" asked the slave in white-silk sacking, she with the musical instrument.

"Do not let her speak, Master!" said a field slave.

He cuffed the field slave, and his blow left blood at her lip. She then, kneeling, head down, shrank back.

"Certainly," he said.

"I was in the banqueting hall," she said. "I fled. The Mistress, together with the Administrator of Hammerfest, and others, is there. The Mistress knows something is amiss, from the absence of retainers, from the silence of the corridors, but not what. She grows suspicious. She becomes alarmed. She fears to investigate. There are many viands, dainty, sumptuous, and rare, on the plates of the guests. Masters might consider adding them to their anticipated repast."

"Excellent," said the man. "You are a fine, lovely slave."

"Thank you, Master," she said. "I also play the *kalika*."

"She sells herself well," I thought. "She is interested in him. She wants him for her Master. But wait until she is alone with the other slaves. I suspect her silk sacking will soon be torn and soiled, if not removed." I did not blame her, of course, for trying to call herself to his attention. It is hard to make clear to the free how deeply, fully, profoundly, and desperately a slave can desire a Master. Yet she is so helpless, she whose desire is love and service, she whose desire is to submit and belong to another. She cannot buy; she cannot choose; it is she who is bought, she who is chosen. And what of a free woman who kneels before a man, holding his ankles, kissing his boots? She must first confess herself a slave, by which confession she becomes a slave, and then beg to be his slave. But what if he is not interested? He can then strip her, take her to a market and sell her. Why not? She is a slave. How I had wept in the kennel for arms in which I was not enfolded.

The fellow to whom the white-clad slave had addressed herself made his way, in the light of the White Moon, to the end of our coffle where he released Calla. "Girl," said he to her, "pick four sisters, fellow chain-daughters, and follow me into the palace. We are going upstairs to do some shopping." I think that he had been impressed with Calla earlier, she who had been the last to depart from the kennel, she who had not left until all others had been accounted for. Her beauty, too, I suspect, even so much concealed in her coarse sacking, did little to dissuade him from his choice. I was amongst the four slaves she selected. This did not surprise me because, despite our disparate origins, we had become friends. Although she had never entered into the matter, requesting an explanation, or such, I think she sensed that I felt myself in some possible danger, and wished to do what she could to keep me safe. Certainly she had never revealed her knowledge of my barbarous origin. Aside from the pleasures of our friendship, I was much indebted to her generous mentoring. She frequently instructed me. From her, as she intended, I learned much about Gor and Gorean ways.

The five of us, heeling him to the left, followed the raider, treading carefully about the edge of the pool.

The garden was more crowded now, as further coffles had been brought in from other kennels.

We were soon ascending broad stairs within the palace. The stairs were lit by *tharlarion*-oil lamps. We met no one on the stairs. Shadows were flung about, eerily. The raider seemed to have little doubt as to his way. I suspected he was familiar with the palace, or, at least, a map of the palace. As his weapon remained sheathed, I took it that this portion of the palace had been secured.

At the top of the stairs were the two leaves of a decorated portal, these now closed. On the door were pictures of, to me, unusual animals and flowers. The holding of Temione of Hammerfest, as hinted earlier, was more of a palace than a fortress. Its exquisite taste, as well as its nature, suggested not the sternness of a man, perhaps a commandant or warlord, but a woman, and one of taste, sensitivity, and intelligence. At this threshold, the raider stopped, and lifted his hand, warning us to silence. In a bit he lowered his hand and then, his head inclined a bit to the left and toward the portal, remained standing, in an attitude of attention.

I soon realized that one could hear, sometimes clearly, sometimes less distinctly, voices from the other side of the panel.

A voice which I recognized as that of Gordon, the Administrator of Hammerfest, seemed to be trying to pacify someone, to allay unwarranted apprehensions.

"Dear Lady Temione," he said, "do not fear. I am sure that all is in order. Return to your dining couch. I am sure all will soon become clear."

"The bell is not being answered!" I heard. "Why is the bell not answered?"

"I do not know," said Gordon.

"Where are the serving slaves?"

"Perhaps they have temporarily withdrawn, and are soon to return," said Gordon.

"I hear nothing from outside," she said. "I fear that the palace is deserted, that the corridors are empty."

"Surely not," said Gordon. "Let us return to dessert. Liqueurs are at hand."

"It is so, Lady," said one of the men in the room. "Let us complete our repast. Continue to eat and drink behind the modesty of your veils, which you do so daintily."

"I am afraid," she said. "Who knows what lies outside the door, if anything?"

"Do not fear," said Gordon. "I am sure that all is as it should be."

"Return to your couch, dear lady," said another male voice. "Be at ease, recline without fear."

I did not know how many might be at this collation, presumably in honor of the Administrator of Hammerfest, whose opinion with respect to one's worthiness to be recognized as an Oligarch of the Vosk seemed to be of such value, but I thought the number would be small.

"I am going to ring the gong!" said Lady Temione. "Its alarm will shake the palace, carry for a *pasang* across the fields!"

"That is unnecessary," said Gordon.

"Finish your wine," suggested another male voice.

There was then the sound of a hammer striking, again and again, against an apparently large piece of metal, I think, suspended, and I cried out in misery and covered my ears with my hands. It is unpleasant, even acutely painful, to be so close to the origin of such a sound. The leaves of the closed portal did little to mitigate the shock of such an offense to the stillness of the night.

"Help! Help! Men! Men! Where are you! Where are you!" cried a gasping Lady Temione of Hammerfest, apparently frightened and doubtless shaken and sore from so unaccustomed an exertion.

"Desist, Lady," said Gordon. "Be easy, I beg of you. All is under control. All is as it should be. I have men at hand!"

At this point, he who had led us upstairs to the threshold of the hall, opened the leaves of the portal and stepped inside. We followed him, bunched together.

Lady Temione, distraught in her colorful veils and swirling robes, pointed to our guide.

"He is not one of my men!" she screamed. "He is a thief, an interloper, a raider!"

"Surely not," said Gordon. "*Tal*," he said to our guide.

"Tal," responded our guide.

There were four reclining on the couches, all male, besides Gordon, Administrator of Hammerfest. Lady Temione was afoot, in consternation, in her colorful veils and swirling robes, still clutching the metal mallet with which she had smitten the gong so many times.

"Forgive the intrusion," said our guide.

I and the other slaves, being in the presence of free persons, knelt.

"Who are you? What are you doing here?" screamed Lady Temione.

"Forgive me," said our guide. You need not be privy to my identity. My presence here is easily explained. Many are hungry in the garden. We hoped we might gather in some of the leavings of your table. I trust that there is no objection to that."

"There is little left," said Gordon, "but you are welcome to what there is. And there is, hopefully, a bit more in the side room which was supplied from the kitchen. To be sure, I would not expect too much, given the fabled parsimony of our hostess."

Lady Temione looked to us, the slaves.

"What are you doing here?" she said. "You know that you are not permitted in the house. You are dirty field slaves. Do you beg to be cast into the eel pool for this effrontery!"

"Thank you, noble Master," said our guide.

"It is nothing," said Gordon, Administrator of Hammerfest.

It was interesting, I thought, that Master Gordon had so generously dispensed leftover provender to our guide, as one would have supposed that any discretion in such a matter would have lain with the mistress of the house.

"Get out!" cried Lady Temione.

"Forgive me, Lady," said our guide. "I am not yet ready to do so."

Lady Temione screamed with rage and hurled the gong mallet at our guide. It went wide of its mark and struck the wall behind him, to the right of the portal as one would face it from within.

She then backed away, toward the dining couches.

"Do you know who that is?" she said, threateningly, to our guide, pointing to the Administrator of Hammerfest.

"Yes, noble lady," said our guide. "He is well known on the river. He is the honorable Gordon, noble administrator of the port of Hammerfest."

Lady Temione glanced to the men in the room. Might she depend on them to leap up, to spring into action, to protect her, to deal with this intruder? "Are you alone?" she asked our guide.

"No, noble lady," said our guide.

"How many of you are there?" asked Lady Temione.

"Several," he said.

A dark look crossed her features.

"Do not fear," said Gordon to our guide. "We have no intention of attacking you with Turian eating prongs."

"I would gather what I came for, if it pleases Masters," said our guide.

"By all means," said Gordon.

"You are not after food, he-tarsk," said Lady Temione. "I am not stupid! There, at the table, reclines Gordon, the Administrator of Hammerfest. With him are four members of the High Council of Hammerfest. All are rich. Satiate there, if you must, your hunger for gold. I am poor! My produce rots, my fields are barren. I have little or nothing. My coffers are empty. I am bankrupt. Take what you can from me, a few coins, a jewel or two, and leave. Let you and your fellows, if you must, despoil these others, not me. They, not I, are the true masters of wealth."

"I expected you, or others, somewhat earlier," said Gordon.

"I feared we might be already too early," said our guide.

"What?" said Lady Temione.

At this point we heard several footsteps on the stairs approaching the hall. There was, too, a jangle of weapons and accouterments.

"Someone comes!" exclaimed Lady Temione.

"Those will be my men," said Gordon.

"Thanks be to the Priest-Kings," cried Lady Temione. "The palace has been retaken! It is ours once more. Surround the raiders. Cut their throats! Let not one live! Slay them to a man!"

Several men poured into the room, armed, weapons unsheathed.

"*Tal*," said the leader of the newcomers.

"*Tal*," said Gordon, amiably, finishing a sip of wine, and rising from the dinner couch.

Our guide showed no sign of uneasiness.

Could these be the men of Gordon, Administrator of Hammerfest? They were not. I noted, in the livery of guardsmen. Indeed, I recognized two of them from the galley on which I and other slaves had been boarded, following the ramming and sinking of the transport ship bound across the river for Victoria.

"Sheathe your weapons," said Gordon to the newcomers.

"No!" cried Lady Temione. "Set yourselves on interlopers! Find them! Kill them!"

Weapons were sheathed.

"What is going on?" demanded the Lady Temione of Hammerfest.

"We must conduct something in the nature of a trial," said Gordon.

"I do not understand," she said. "Turn your men against the interlopers. Clear the palace! Clear my lands! Slay them all!"

"What are we to make of you?" asked Gordon of the Lady Temione.

"Where are my retainers?" she cried.

"Apparently," said one of the four fellows still reclining on their dining couches, "the retainers of the noble Lady Temione did not care to die for her."

"And it seems," said another, "that her house was not as defensively strong as rumored."

"Let us not disparage her house," said Gordon. "A small sack of silver is often enough to open a postern gate, through which men might silently file."

"One earns loyalty by character and deeds," said another, "not through scorn and pay."

"My dear Lady Temione," said Gordon, "if I may call you that for a time, I found your plea of penury to a presumed interloper surprising, for my tour of your resources, as short and minimal as it was, convinced me that you are the proprietor of one of the major fortunes on the Vosk."

"I am," said Lady Temione.

"You are not then nigh destitute, nor bankrupt, nor on the verge of bankruptcy?"

"Certainly not," she said.

"You would have turned the predatory avarice of marauding interlopers away from yourself, onto dinner guests?" he said.

"Only as a trick," she said, "provisional and clearly temporary in duration."

"I am relieved to hear that," he said.

"One must be clever," said Lady Temione.

"A property which, in your view, you are far from lacking," he said.

"Certainly," she said.

"I see," he said.

"Order your men to hunt down and slay the interlopers," she said.

"Rather," said Gordon, "let us address ourselves to the business of the evening."

"What business?" she asked.

"That," said Gordon, "of your worthiness to be entitled 'Oligarch of the Vosk.'"

"What of my palace? What of the interlopers?" cried Lady Temione.

"My examination of your resources, cursory as was," said Gordon, "has fully convinced me that you are more than worthy of the distinction you covet so earnestly, that of being denominated an Oligarch of the Vosk."

"Excellent," she said. "The matter is then done."

"Not quite," said Gordon. "You may remember that whereas wealth is a requirement for being an Oligarch of the Vosk, it is not the only requirement for that distinction. We would not want just any vulgar holder of wealth to bear so honorable a title. For example, the wealth must have been won honorably and, if it is to be applied in such a way as to attempt to influence the course of the state, it must be done openly, not by means of private devices and secret briberies. For example, any bargain made with a legislator or official, moneys paid and services therewith purchased, must be a matter of public record, that the governed, through their caste councils and such, must weigh its approval or disapproval. To be a mere oligarch might be compatible with dishonesty, crime, and secrecy, but any such thing or practice would instantly disqualify anyone aspiring to the honorable title of 'Oligarch of the Vosk.'"

"Granted, to be sure," said Lady Temione.

"That would be subscribed to by any major polity on the Vosk," said Gordon.

"Certainly," said the Lady Temione.

"The title is intended to salute both a considerable economic achievement; legitimately obtained, of course, and social concern, a willingness to apply wealth productively in such a way as to redound, sooner or later, in one way or another, to the public welfare. Wealth is not to be confiscated, leading to eventual stagnation and poverty, but increased, that it may multiply and flourish, that there will be more to share, that more will profit from its existence."

"I assure you," said Lady Temione, "that every tarsk-bit of my fortune, which you acknowledge is considerable, has been acquired frankly, fairly, openly, and honestly."

"There are rumors," said Gordon, "that you have been enleagued with the notorious pirate of the Vosk, he who calls himself Einar, the Sleen of the Vosk."

"False," she said. "I am wholly innocent of any such arrangement, relationship, or connection. I know nothing of such a loathed, dreaded, and hateful fellow."

"You deny that you have had dealings with the agents of Einar, Sleen of the Vosk?"

"Certainly," she said.

"I find that of great interest," he said.

"Why so?" she asked.

"Because," said he, "you have had dealings with my agents."

"I do not understand," she said.

"I am Einar, Sleen of the Vosk," he said.

CHAPTER TWENTY

"Revive her," said Gordon, Administrator of Hammerfest.

The leader of the men who had recently come to the dining hall, those who had been gratefully welcomed by Lady Temione, those who had treated Gordon, the Administrator of Hammerfest, with deference, poured the remainder of a decanter of wine over her unconscious figure. I and the others who had accompanied our guide from the garden outside into the palace and upstairs to the dining hall, winced in dismay seeing the abundant and resplendent robes of the Lady Temione so soiled. What a terrible thing to befall a raiment so rich and beautiful! And what might have been, I wondered, the punishment of a slave who had, however inadvertently, spilled even a bit of wine on so marvelous a garmenture. The horror of this desecration, I am sure, afflicted my fellow slaves even more than I, as they were Gorean and doubtless more attuned than I to the status and loveliness of such a raiment and the gravity of so dreadful an offense.

Two men lifted a sputtering, frightened Lady Temione to her feet. She regarded Gordon, the Administrator of Hammerfest, wildly. Then, recovering herself, she adjusted her veils and smoothed down her robes.

I admired her boldness.

"What," I wondered, "was going on inside her?"

She drew herself up, angrily, proudly. Despite her wealth and power, she was of average height for a woman, perhaps, like myself, a bit less.

She would, I gathered, put a brave front on matters.

"What is the meaning of this?" she asked. "I demand an explanation! This is a poor jest, indeed! I will have you removed from office!"

"Remove your veils," said Gordon.

"Never!" she said.

"Shall I have a slave do so?" he asked.

"Permit me to do so, Master," said Calla.

"No!" cried the Lady Temione.

Slowly, one after another, she unpinned and unwound her veils. Then she dropped them to the side and threw back her head.

I gasped, as did the other slaves and the men in the room. Even Calla reacted. How wrong my conjectures of the Lady Temione had been!

Several of the men struck their left shoulders three and four times with the flat of their right hand.

Lady Temione of Hammerfest was not ugly. She was outstandingly, awesomely, beautiful!

She then thrust back her hood, and long, yellow hair tumbled back over the dangling hood, and the collar of her robes.

This was met with further gentle applause by the men in the room.

She looked about, to the men in the room.

Resentment flashed in her blue eyes.

Then she again faced Gordon, Administrator of Hammerfest.

She stood before him, as the Goreans say, face-stripped.

Veiling in public is common, though not universal, amongst Gorean free women, particularly if they are of high caste.

I was somewhat surprised that she had retained veiling during the supper, as she apparently had, eating and supping behind it, as the supper was small, informal, and private, and the guests few and presumably familiar. I assumed she had done this in order to conceal her features, which, as I understood it, was her wont.

"Was it so terrible," I wondered, "to be a beautiful woman?" Perhaps she did not wish to be defined by her unusual beauty.

I might mention, in passing, that facial veiling is denied to slaves. Would one veil animals, say, dogs, cats, horses, and such? Too, veiling or not, as differences in garmenture, tends to reinforce the distinction between free and slave. Too, some say that veiling is denied to slaves in order that raiders and slavers will see them as a more natural and reliable prey, as a captured free woman might turn out to be too plain to sell well in the markets. Why should one put one's life at risk for so little gain? The fact that most women of Earth do not veil themselves not only makes slaving on Earth easier but suggests to many Goreans that the women of Earth are natural slaves. Who but an amorous slave would dare to brandish her features so brazenly? To be sure, there are many Goreans, predominantly males, who believe all women are natural slaves, that it is in their nature to be slaves, that nature designed them for Masters, and that they would be incomplete and forlorn until they find themselves at the feet of Masters.

How well stood the Lady Temione of Hammerfest!

"How proud and insolent," I thought, "is a free woman."

How I felt myself slave, so slave, so worthless, so meaningless, before such!

"You may now," said Gordon, Administrator of Hammerfest, to the Lady Temione of Hammerfest, "remove your clothing."

"No!" she cried. "No!"

"Completely," he said. "Every particle, every thread, every last stitch."

"Never," she said. "Never!"

"Now," he said, "unless you wish to be lashed as a slave."

"I am free," she said. "You would not dare!"

"Fetch a whip," said Gordon to one of the men.

"If you wish my garments removed, noble Gordon, exalted administrator," she said, "feel free to do so yourself."

"Beware!" cried more than one man in the room.

"My dear Lady Temione," said Gordon, "I decline to accept your invitation. I have it on the authority of your most trusted serving slave, Sira, whom men of mine saw fit to question, that your garments contain eleven poisoned needles, the scratch of any one of which will produce excruciating pain followed shortly by a bursting of arteries and death."

"Surely you do not believe that," she said.

"Word of the penchants of certain high-caste women in the tower cities reaches even to the remote courses of the mighty Vosk," he said.

"Master," said Calla, "I was once the high serving slave of Mistress Temione. I believe I can remove the secret needles without danger either to myself or to Mistress Temione."

"Do not!" said he who was our guide, he who had supervised the emptying of our kennel, he who had added Calla to the coffle.

"Master," whispered Calla.

Something, I suddenly sensed, had occurred between our guide and Calla. Bondage has mysterious chemistries. Seeing her he would long to own her. Seeing him she would long to be his slave.

"Lady Temione will be familiar with the task," said Gordon. "Proceed, Lady Temione."

"No!" she wept. "I am afraid!"

"Very well," said Gordon. He then addressed his men. "Use knives and swords," he said. "Cut the garments from her. Be careful. Then burn the whole, and bury the ashes."

Four men rushed forward, blades drawn.

Lady Temione spun about, one way and the other, screaming and twisting, recoiling and turning, blades flashing about her, robes being shredded from her, horrified at her stripping, and terrified that she might be cut and scared, even slain, in what must have seemed a frenzied onslaught of wicked, swift steel.

Then she stood, shaken and bared, her knees slightly bent, the remnants of veils and robes about her. Even her hose and slippers had been removed.

"Easily two silver tarsks," whispered Calla to me.

Then the Lady Temione sank to her knees, bent over, head down, trembling, thighs clenched together, trying to cover her body with her hands, on the broad, smooth, colorful tiles before the dining couches.

"She dallied," said Gordon. "Lash her as a slave, and then bind her, hand and foot."

At the first stroke Lady Temione howled in disbelief, and then, for the next three or four strokes, begged for a surcease of the pain, and then, for the last two strokes she was silent, scratching at the tear-stained tiles.

She did not resist as her ankles were crossed and bound, and her wrists, behind her, were served similarly. She then lay prone, naked and bound, hand and foot, whipped, before Gordon, the Administrator of Hammerfest.

"Lady Temione," said Gordon, "you have perjured yourself before an officer of the port of Hammerfest, profoundly and repeatedly. You have proposed yourself as a candidate for the honor of being denominated an Oligarch of the Vosk, in spite of being manifestly unqualified for so priceless an honor. Further, you have been found to have been in league with pirates, and to have profited from their dark work. Perhaps you believed, if one is in league with pirates, one has nothing to fear from pirates. Such an opinion is mistaken. Your lands and properties will be confiscated by the state."

A murmur of approval coursed through the men in the room.

"Have you anything to say?" asked Gordon.

"I have," she said, "tarsk."

"I encourage you to show respect before the law," said Gordon.

"I am a free woman," she said. "Unbind me, and bring me clothing."

"Help her to her knees," said Gordon.

Lady Temione was lifted to her knees.

I did not think she was accustomed to kneeling, naked and bound, before a man.

"Unbind me, bring me clothing befitting my station," she said.

"You may speak," he said.

"I am a free woman," she said. "I do not need permission to speak."

"You may speak," he said.

"Am I to speak to Gordon, the Administrator of Hammerfest, or to Einar, the Sleen of the Vosk?" she asked.

"To either or both," said Gordon.

"Let me first then," said she, "address myself to Einar, the Sleen of the Vosk. Your career of terror and plunder is soon to end. You, and your ships and men, and your base, depend much on the support of the Administrator of Hammerfest, but that is nearly over for I shall inform on him and see that he is brought to justice. Thus, as your patron is undone so, too, will be you. Secondly, let me address myself to Gordon, the Administrator of Hammerfest. I shall report him to the Vosk League, revealing that he is the mysterious and elusive Einar, the Sleen of the Vosk. Thus do I reveal secrets and bring peace once more to the Vosk."

"Peace is unlikely on the Vosk," said Gordon. "There are riches to be reaped on the river. Where there are riches to be reaped there will always be reapers to reap them."

"But I trust," said Lady Temione, "though I am stripped, whipped, and bound, I am not without power. I trust that both Gordon of Hammerfest and Einar, the Sleen of the Vosk, fear me."

"I assure you," said Gordon, "we will take the matter under consideration."

"You are now to free and clothe me, and restore my lands and properties," she said. "Also, as I have been insulted and discomfited, you are to deliver to me half of the public treasury of Hammerfest."

"Your silence would seem to be costly," he said. "Is there anything more?"

"Half of the riches you reap on the river," she said.

"Take her down to the garden," he said, "and cast her into the eel pool."

CHAPTER TWENTY-ONE

The Lady Temione, squirming and screaming, was carried from the hall and down the stairs.

"Hc cannot do that!" I wept to Calla.

"He holds the sword," said Calla.

Gordon, Administrator of Hammerfest, stood toward the center of the hall, conversing with the four members of the High Council of Hammerfest, now risen from the dining couches, and certain of his men, high men apparently, from amongst those who had recently ascended to the hall.

"Gather up what food you can," said our guide, "from the tables, and the serving room, to the side."

"She will be eaten alive!" I said to Calla.

"Obey the Master," said Calla, availing herself of the rectangular gap between the three narrow tables, on which the three dining couches abutted. It is from this gap between the tables that the tables may be served. Two individuals may recline on each of the three couches. Two men of the High Council had shared each of the side couches, and the Administrator of Hammerfest and the Lady Temione of Hammerfest had shared the end, or high, couch.

Miserable and distraught, I followed Calla.

She began to shift food from various plates to a larger plate.

"Did you notice," she asked me, "how she was carried from the room in a man's arms, as a free woman? She was not thrust over his left shoulder, her head to the rear, as would be a slave."

"The Administrator must spare her!" I wept.

"If he pleases," said she, "otherwise not."

"I must throw myself to his feet and beg her life!" I said.

"It would do you no good," she said. "Who would listen to you? Who would pay you attention? These things are not for you. It is a matter amongst the free. You are a beast, a slave. At the least you would receive a lashing for your presumption. And, more likely, you would be bound and join her in the pool."

"The Administrator dallies," I said. "He exchanges pleasantries with his fellows. He will not be in time to intervene or rescind his order!"

"Help me with the plates," said Calla.

"Time is short!" I said.

"Do not fear," she said. "The well-deserved execution of Mistress Temione will not take place before the noble Gordon of Hammerfest is present. He and his fellows would wish to see her thrash in the water, screaming, as a hundred eels flock to her, each to compete for its mouthfuls of flesh."

"I do not feel well," I said.

"You are hungry," said Calla. "Take a bite of the food. I do not think anyone will notice."

By the time that Calla, and her four cohorts, including me, had brought food, heaped on plates and wrapped in dining cloths, and wines and liqueurs, poured into decanters and figured *craters*, to the garden, the raiders, additional men of the Administrator, and even slaves were in the midst of a revelry, devouring streams of food emerged from, and emerging from, the palace kitchen.

"This is not slave gruel," said Calla. "Feast, feast while you can, before Masters recall you are in a collar."

But I had little appetite.

Some of the raiders were singing.

Not a yard from me a slave was seized by the arm. "Let us see what is in this sack!" cried a raider, and a moment later I heard a slave scream with ecstasy.

I turned away.

"Calla!" I wept.

"What is wrong?" asked Calla.

"Lady Temione is to be cast to eels!" I said.

"It is not our concern," she said.

Another slave was seized nearby.

It was dark.

Some torches, with the feasting, had been lit in the garden. Here and there, a fellow had a lantern.

It must have been an hour or two before dawn.

Most of the slaves were still in their rope coffles.

"I am a stranger to this world," I said. "I am afraid. A woman is to be fed to eels. I am miserable. I cannot stand it!"

"That is understandable," said Calla. "You are a barbarian. You know little of this world. Run. Try to escape, if you wish."

"There is no escape for a slave girl," I said.

"I wonder if you believe it," said Calla.

I made my way, desolate, to the edge of the eel pool.

I could see the reflection of torchlight in the water. The pool seemed calm. It gave no clue as to what might lie beneath its surface.

"It looks calm, does it not?" asked a man.

"Yes, Master," I said.

"Watch your step," he said.

"Yes, Master," I said.

I hurried further about its edge.

The men about showed little apprehension or concern. They were not anxious to withdraw. Clearly this was quite different from the raid at Victoria Minor, the Lesser Victoria. What had the raiders, and the others, here, to fear from Hammerfest?

I expected, shortly, that the slaves generally, even coffled, would be thrown to the garden turf and put to slavc use.

Vigilance would be put aside.

It would be easy for me, uncoffled, to slip away.

I wondered if I might escape.

Where was there to escape to?

"Gordon arrives!" said a male voice. "The Administrator is nigh," said another voice. "Bring the trussed *vulo*," said another. "Let us watch," said another.

I could see, in the torchlight, Gordon, Administrator of Hammerfest, the four members of the High Council of Hammerfest, and others, approaching.

Not feet from where I stood I saw a man emerge from the half-darkness, the bound, naked body of the Lady Temione cradled in his arms. The honor of being so carried was accorded to her, I gathered, from what Calla had said earlier, in deference to her status as a free woman.

He laid her gently on her back beside the pool.

It seemed he did not wish to bruise her. She was free.

I felt I should flee away, but I found myself unable to move. I did, happily, remember to kneel, for free men were close at hand.

Briefly my eyes and those of the Lady Temione met. Her eyes were frantic with fear.

A moment later Gordon, with others, arrived at the edge of the pool. He looked down on the Lady Temione. "What have we here?" he asked.

"A little *vulo*," said a fellow, "well-trussed."

"Mercy!" shrieked Lady Temione.

"She is a pretty *vulo*," said Gordon.

"Mercy! Mercy! I beg for mercy!" cried the Lady Temione.

"Has this *vulo* a name?" asked Gordon.

"It is the Lady Temione of Hammerfest," said a man, as though helpfully.

"Surely not," said Gordon. "The Lady Temione of Hammerfest would not so appear in public."

"Nonetheless, it is she," said a man.

"Where are your robes, where are your veils, Lady Temione?" asked Gordon, chidingly. "Do you not know that men might look freely upon you? You are as naked as a slave."

"Do not kill me!" she shrieked. "Do not put me in the pool! Do not feed me to eels!"

"Pity the poor eels," said a man.

"How so?" asked a man.

"They must be hungry," he said. "And there will be so little on which to feed."

"Mercy!" shrieked the Lady Temione. "Let me go! You have my lands, my goods! Welcome to them! I ask only my life. I plead for my life! Mercy! I will never betray your identity, noble Gordon, noble Einar!"

"You do not want to disappoint the eels, do you, Lady Temione?" asked a man.

"They are your eels," said another.

There was laughter.

A crowd had now gathered at the pool. Interestingly, I saw no slaves. I knew that many, and surely most, of the slaves hated the Lady Temione. But, too, it seemed, they did not care to see her immersed in the pool. I did not dare rise in the presence of free men without permission, even had I the capacity to do so, and, somehow, I could not utter a sound. Words hid in some inaccessible place. My throat was like wood. I wanted to flee, and could not move.

"Shall we have some food and wine for the Lady Temione?" asked Gordon. "I fear we have been inhospitable." He then turned to the supine captive. "Dear Lady Temione," he said, "would you not like a sip of wine, a tasty viand before you take your leave, to sport with the eels?"

"Spare me!" she cried.

"But, of course, you have little appetite," he said. "Forgive me. I had forgotten that you had recently supped."

"Mercy! Please, mercy! Mercy!" she cried.

"You two," said Gordon to two of his men, "lift her up. On the count of three, hurl her forth, far and deep, out, into the pool."

"No, no!" cried Lady Temione.

"One!" said Gordon. "Two!"

"How have I failed to please you?" shrieked the Lady Temione.

"Hold!" said Gordon. "What strange words are these, uttered by the Lady Temione?"

"The words sound," said a man, "much like the words of a slave."

"They are!" wept the Lady Temione. "I am a slave, a slave! I pronounce myself so. It is done. It cannot be undone. I am now a slave! Have mercy on a poor slave!"

"How can this be?" asked Gordon.

"I have always been a slave!" she wept. "I am a natural slave. I have known it for years. I fought it. I rejected it! But it whispered itself to me, over and over. You are a slave. You are a slave. I know it is true."

"You cannot be a slave," said Gordon. "You have no brand, no collar." He then pointed to me. "Look there," he said, "that is a slave. See the collar on her neck?" Then he snapped, "Brand!"

Instantly, wildly, suddenly able to move, I shifted my weight to my right knee and extended my left leg, fully, toward Gordon, pulling up the gross sacklike garment imposed on me as a field slave, revealing my brand.

"The common *kef*," said Gordon. Then he faced she who had been shortly before the Lady Temione. "Where is your brand?" he asked. "Where is your collar? I see no collar, no brand. Thus, you cannot be a slave."

"I am a slave, Master," she cried. "What have brands and collars to do with bondage? Bondage is of the heart. Mark me! Collar me! Put the certifications of law on me so that all may see me, despise me, and know me slave. Let legal niceties make public and visible what has hitherto been secret and concealed."

"If such is done," said Gordon, "you would no longer be able to deny your bondage, even if you wished. You could not then conceal your status, no matter how much you might desire to do so. You would be absolutely helpless. Your condition would then be not only inalterable, as it is now, but publicly, visibly, inalterable."

"Yes, Master," she wept, held upright by the two men. Her knees were bent, as though she would kneel.

"Release her," said Gordon.

The slave fell to her knees and then flung herself to her belly and, bound as she was, hand and foot, squirmed to the feet of Gordon, Administrator of Hammerfest, and, putting her head down over his feet, began, weeping, to cover them with kisses, fervent and desperate.

Men laughed, and slaves, suddenly, began to appear near the pool, relieved, much pleased, and eager to look on.

"We were to execute a free and worthless female criminal," said Gordon, "the rich, selfish, proud, cruel, haughty Lady Temione of Hammerfest, but she vanished, and in her place we found a mere slave. What shall we do with this mere slave?"

"Throw her to the eels," laughed a man.

"No, Master!" said the slave, lifting her head. "Please, no! I will strive to be pleasing, in all ways! In all ways!"

"Perhaps she is frigid," said a man.

"It will be easy enough to kindle her slave fires," said a man.

"Please be kind, Masters," she begged. "I am only a helpless slave."

"You do not yet know what it is to be a helpless slave," said a man.

"Master?" she said.

"Once your slave fires are kindled," said a man, "you will be more of a helpless slave than you could now understand or dream."

My body suddenly ached with need. How deprived I had been! I had always been keenly cognizant of my sexual needs, even on Earth, so seething, global, and complex, so insistent and demanding. But I had struggled against them, had striven to distract myself from their imperatives, had endeavored to drive them, and their searing demands, from my mind, heart, and body! But on Gor I could be lashed for not being the vital, sexual animal I knew myself to be. Collared, on Gor, I was a thousand times freer than I had been on Earth. On this strange, fresh, wonderful, beautiful, natural, perilous world I was marked and collared. I now existed for the pleasure of men. It was what I was for. I knew how on this world a slave could crawl to the feet even of a cruel, hated Master, moaning and begging for his least caress. Let those on Earth scoff at such things but they had never knelt at the feet of a Gorean male. How radiant and alive I was on Gor! Had I not been bred for such things through thousands of natural selections? What was the point of being a slave if one were not treated as a slave, dominated as a slave, used as a slave? How I longed to give all of myself, and serve. How I longed for a Master!

"I am no stranger to slave fires," said the slave. "I have known men before whom I had desired to kneel and kiss their feet, but I was free and dared not do so."

"That impediment has now been removed," said a man.

"I am the gift of my hereditary coils," she said. "I know I was made to be owned by men."

She again put her head down to continue her ministrations to the bootlike sandals of Gordon, Administrator of Hammerfest.

"Enough," said Gordon. "Desist!"

Clearly he did not wish to be aroused. The slave, in her way, has powers. What slave at the feet of her Master does not know that? Sometimes, given the anger of the Master, sensing what power the slave might exert over him, she is taken to the market and sold.

A man pulled the slave up to her knees, and she lifted her head, confused and bewildered.

"Bring a length of rope," said Gordon.

A length of rope was brought.

"Behold, slave," said Gordon, "I wrap this rope six times about your neck and knot it, one loop for each letter in the word *'kajira.'* It will serve until we can have a suitable metal circlet locked on your neck. Later, an iron will be heated and it will be pressed into your thigh, firmly and deeply, smoking and hissing, marking you as the beast you are."

"Yes, Master," said the slave. "Let me be marked. I beg to be marked!"

"Now," said Gordon, "let her be greeted by her sister slaves."

Several slaves rushed forward, crowding about she who had recently been the Lady Temione of Hammerfest, eager to vent a long pent-up hatred on her.

"Hold, hold!" said Gordon.

I think he had not anticipated the venom with which the slave might be attacked. Could the Lady Temione have been so hated?

I think he feared they would maim or scar her, perhaps even kill her.

Someone snapped a whip and the slaves, frightened, melted swiftly away, back into the shadows.

The former Lady Temione, illuminated in the torchlight, now supine, bound, gasping, bruised and sore, spat upon, maligned and berated, was shuddering with pain and misery.

Certainly she had learned how one slave can be at the mercy of other slaves. She must look to men then to protect her not only from the abuse of free women, but, in certain cases, from that of other slaves, as well.

"Untie her," said Gordon.

She was put to her belly and relieved of her bonds.

"Kneel, she-tarsk," said a man. "Get on your knees!"

She struggled to her knees.

"Now," said Gordon, "let her be thrown to the lowest of men, after which she will serve our feast, close-shackled, lest she, not yet metal-collared and marked, be tempted to try to run."

In 'close shackling,' the girl's ankles are fastened closely together, usually six inches to a foot apart.

"May I not be clothed, Master?" pleaded the slave.

She was cuffed.

Blood was at her lip.

Did she not know enough to ask permission to speak?

"You will be the only naked slave in the garden," he said.

She knelt before him, head down.

"Surely you know," he said, "that the women of the enemy serve the victory banquet of the conquerors naked, either before or after they are collared and marked."

I am given to understand that this is normally done before they are collared and marked. This is to impose an excruciating humiliation on them that they, though free, must serve as naked slaves. This also suggests that the women of the enemy may be freely stripped and are worthy only of being slaves to the conquerors.

"Yes, Master," she said. "Forgive me, Master."

"Now," said he, "who amongst the lowest men wishes to show this she-tarsk what it is to be a slave?"

A large number of fellows responded, enthusiastically.

"I see that there are few high men in the camp," said Gordon. There was much laughter in response to this supposed observation. "Very well," he said. "It is impractical to throw her to your feet. Draw lots then for her usage. In the meantime, let not other *kajirae* doubt their charms. Feast! Seize those you like. Warm the grass. Let the wine flow! In an Ahn it will be light and we had best make away."

By far the greatest number of the slaves were still in their rope coffles. I and a few others who had been freed to fetch and serve were not. Both those who had been field slaves and those who had been house slaves then slipped their sacklike gowns, whether of loosely woven, coarse material or silk, up to their necks and back, behind them, as they could, welcoming the men who rushed upon them. The long, painful sexual draught which had been imposed upon them by the depriving cruelties of the Lady Temione were at an end. Rain, so to speak, fell plentifully upon welcoming, thirsting fields.

"As part of your pay, good fellows," announced Gordon, magnanimously, "each of you may select a slave for your own, yours to do with as you please, to keep, sell, trade, or whatever you wish. The only exception is the former Lady Temione of Hammerfest, whom I wish to see put naked on a public block and auctioned therefrom, a pleasure to which I have long looked forward."

This offer was warmly greeted.

Almost immediately, under the light of torches and lanterns, an uproar ensued, tempers flared, and haggling began.

Some Ubars, Administrators, High Merchants, and such have considerable resources. This makes it possible for them to maintain regular troops, professional guardsmen, and even Warriors, members of the Scarlet Caste. This is commonly the case in larger cities and towns, and certainly in the 'tower cities.' On the other hand, the pay of mercenaries, free swords, so to speak, is commonly small, and may be unreliable. Accordingly, in taking fee, they expect to supplement their income by means of loot. This tends to produce situations which are rarely encountered in more civil arrangements, situations such as mercenary captains leaving one venue in which they are engaged to seek another more promising, even to changing sides in the same conflict, not to mention having to face mutinies and desertions when success seems improbable or likely to be too long postponed. And, needless to say, mercenaries tend to follow pennons leading to suitable sites, those where resistance is likely to be weak and loot plentiful. Given such considerations it was easier to understand how a Gordon of Hammerfest or an Einar of the Vosk might wish to be generous, or seemingly generous, with their followers and, as in the case of the raiders, their colleagues. Too, the allegiance bought by Gordon's seeming generosity, over and above the pay of his men, was cheaply obtained, considering the lands of the former Lady Temione, her palace, and her coin and material wealth. The balance of the unclaimed slaves would presumably accrue to the raiders for their assistance. A remark I had earlier heard made it clear to me that the raiders were the same as had raided the great pen at Victoria Minor.

Slaves were being selected and ravished.

I did hear, from time to time, not only angry shouts, and, even, four times, the clash of steel. I knew that men could kill for slaves. This thought dismayed me. On the other hand, I recalled, from the camp of Master Philip, one slave who had claimed, proudly, that six men had died for her. Others had proclaimed her a liar. I certainly hoped that she was lying. On the other hand, I knew that men could kill for gold and silver, even copper. Therefore, it was not inconceivable that they might kill for other goods, as well, *sleen*, tarns, slaves, and such.

I moved about the edge of the pool.

Many slaves, of course, were not claimed.

"Me, Master! Select me, Master!" I heard.

Here and there, men cast marked stones. One fellow, it seemed, had won five slaves.

I saw one man lying on the grass, a slave binding up his wounds.

Few men looked at me. I remained, as I could, out of the light.

Wine was abundant. It was even being thrust down the throats of slaves. Here and there, there were the remains of coarse sackings which had been torn from, or cut from, slaves. A slave, feet away, to my left, was moaning, lost in pleasure. Another slave, farther away, was begging, "More, more, Master!"

No man pursued me. No man ordered me to his feet. One man looked at me, drunk, staggering, but I am not sure he even saw me. A moment later he collapsed to the grass.

I looked about.

One might almost have thought that gates had been breached and a city fallen. But there were no burning buildings, no looters with bulging sacks of utensils, plates, and vessels, no screaming, weeping, unveiled, half-clad women being whip-herded to collection points. No. In this garden, unruly and wild as it might seem, there were no free women, screaming and weeping, being taught that they were women. There were instead free men and, in their arms, women in collars, women who had no doubt that they were women, women who would never be given any doubt about it, the most raw, reduced, and basic of women, the woman who is owned, the woman who is goods, the most radically female of all women, the most marvelously desirable of all women, the female slave.

And I, too, was a slave!

In every fiber of my being.

But I was a miserable, inferior slave! I knew that I did not belong with the choice slaves about me. I knew I had not belonged with those slaves who had been saved for the last, safest transportation to Victoria. I had merely fled, and had been recaptured. I had not belonged with them. I did not even belong with the expensive, carefully selected field slaves who had been owned by the Lady Temione of Hammerfest, she wishing to deny them to men, perhaps hating their beauty, as possibly approaching hers. I did not deserve to be here. It was an accident. What man could want me, except as a kettle-and-mat girl? I was even a barbarian.

Suddenly, out of the darkness, I saw Calla approaching me, her sacking half torn away.

"I have been looking for you," she said.

"Why?" I said. "I do not understand."

"Why are you still in that ugly sacking?" she said. "Are you hiding? Do you not wish to feel the grip of men on your slave body?"

"I am ugly," I said.

"You are stupid," she said. "Many men would kill to get their collar on your neck."

"Surely not," I said.

"I have little time to speak," she said. "I must hurry back to my Master. I do not wish to be whipped."

"Your Master?" I said.

"Flavius, of Venna," she said. "He is high amongst the raiders."

"He could then lead you away in chains," I said.

That seemed so final to me.

She was my friend. Now she could be simply led away, like a horse or dog. Tears sprang into my eyes. I was on Gor, a slave.

"We met at the kennel," she said. "He found me a slave of interest. Soon he wanted to own me, every bit of me. One can tell. You know him. He led us into the palace, to obtain food from the dining hall. I think he will be my Love Master."

"'Love Master?'" I said.

"But if I am not pleasing," she said, "I fear he will sell me or give me away. I must hurry back to him. I am eager to feel the weight of his chains."

When a woman wears a man's chains there is little doubt of his interest. Few women misunderstand their own chaining.

"You were selected then," I said.

"Instantly," she said, and added, proudly, "and none dared to do contest over the matter."

"I am pleased for you," I said.

"I have sought you out," she said, "not merely to wish you well, for I do not think we shall ever see one another again, but to tell you something I overheard."

"What is that?" I asked.

"It may be unimportant," she said. "It must be unimportant. But I was afraid for you."

"What is it?" I asked.

"Have you ever heard of a Kur?" she asked.

"No," I said.

"I have never seen one," she said, "but I have heard of them. They are large, dangerous beasts, rare and of unknown origin, fanged and clawed, speeched and minded, calculating and purposeful, said to have fallen from the stars."

"I do not think there are such things," I said.

"One raider claims not only to have seen one, four days ago in the darkness, but to have spoken with it."

"If it a beast," I said, "how could he speak with it?"

"By means of an enchanted box," she said, "which turned the sounds of a beast into Gorean and Gorean into the sounds of a beast."

I began to be afraid. I had no difficulty in dismissing the notion of 'enchanted boxes,' whatever they might be, but I could easily conceive of a sophisticated technology which might move from the phonemes of one language into those of another.

"Why do you speak to me of these things?" I asked.

"I do not want to know your name when you were free," she said.

"I do not understand," I said.

"It is best for me to know little of these things," she said. "What I do not know cannot be extracted from me, even should I be torn by torture."

"You are making me afraid," I said.

"The beast was looking for a barbarian," she said.

I shuddered.

I knew that my Gorean, if imperfect, was quite good. Few, I knew, would take me for a barbarian. Most Goreans seemed to attribute anything unusual in my speech to a difference amongst dialects. My greatest danger was a lack of historical and cultural background. I was unfamiliar with Gorean games and songs; I knew nothing of the exploits of legendary heroes; I did not even know small poems and stories familiar to most Gorean children.

"Why would a beast be interested in a barbarian?" I asked.

"I do not know," she said.

"What," I wondered, "would a beast, an animal of some sort, have to do with worlds, their intrigues and fates? Does a *sleen*, or such, have such concerns?"

"There are many barbarians on Gor," I said, "perhaps thousands."

"The beast, it was said," she said, "was interested in one barbarian in particular."

"Why?" I asked.

"I do not know," she said. "The beast knew little of his quarry other than a fragment of her name when free."

"That," I said, "is surely little to go on."

"Agreed," said Calla.

"It had no pictures, no sketches, no descriptions of the barbarian?" I asked.

"Only," she said, "that the barbarian was of medium height, or slightly less, a brunette, and had a figure that begged for the collar."

"That is nothing," I said, "many women are of medium height or a little less, and most women are brunettes, and, if they are brought to Gor from Earth, they would have, at least in the view of slavers, a figure that begged for the collar."

"The fragment of the free name," said Calla, "was something like 'Ag-nas.'"

"'Agnes!'" I said.

"I did not hear your cry," said Calla. "I heard it not!" Then she regarded me, puzzled. "Why should you, or some barbarian, be of interest to a beast?"

"Or others," I said, in misery. "I am wanted, too, by others."

"Why?" asked Calla.

"I fear I know things I should not know," I said.

"It is said," said Calla, "that the beast is of a species which can feed on humans, as we might feed on *vulos* or *verr*."

"How can I run?" I asked. "How can I escape? I am collared. I am marked. I am a slave! Must I wait to be discovered? Must I content myself with hoping to be overlooked? If found, I could be stolen or slain, even routinely purchased!"

"I wish you well, dear Mira," she said. She embraced me, gave me a quick kiss, and then turned about, and fled away into the darkness.

"I wish you well," I whispered.

I hoped she would not be whipped.

I looked about myself. The camp was quieter now. Many slaves lay at the feet of new Masters. Were I to guess, I speculated that there had been some three hundred raiders and two hundred, or so, men of Gordon, the Administrator of Hammerfest. That would be some five hundred men altogether, each of whom had selected one particular personal slave. On the supposition that the Lady Temione of Hammerfest had had eleven hundred and fifty or so slaves, that meant that the raiders and their captains retained some six hundred and fifty slaves for marketing, that constituting a plunder equivalent to what might be accrued from the taking of a town or small city. Too, given the wealth and the cruel proclivities of the Lady Temione of Hammerfest, those slaves would almost uniformly be prize merchandise. The loot, so to speak, would doubtless be divided amongst several markets, to best conceal its origins. Almost all of the slaves, I was sure, would be much pleased to put the labors of the fields behind them, preferring to be sold into a lighter, more congenial bondage. I myself, I was sure, had recently, eagerly, entertained similar hopes. But now it seemed clear that pursuit was in the vicinity and markets might be under observation.

I knew something, though not much, of the planetary intrigues, perhaps even martial interactions, in which I found myself unwillingly embroiled, but I had naturally supposed them limited to humans, or something much like humans. Now, it seemed possible that something quite different from what was supposed in my possibly naive assumptions might be involved. What if, reaching out in the night, one touched not a hand, but a paw?

It was shortly before dawn.

If I were to run, I should do so before light.

What was I to do?

I hurried stealthily to the scene of the revelry, picked up a cup, and folded some viands into a piece of ripped silk, apparently torn from the sacking of a house slave. I then returned to the eel pool and, carefully, softly, dipped the cup into the water. I was preparing to dip it in again when I sensed a subtle movement in the water. I leapt back. I saw nothing, but I knew something was there, waiting. I put the cup down on the edge of the pool and backed away. I clutched the improvised sack with its provisions. I was afraid to run, but, if I were to run, there was no time to waste.

I heard a sound, I think a whimper, away from the pool, to my right. Had I been seen? There was another whimper. I approached the sound. I did not wish to be seen leaving the camp. Happily, the men of Gordon and the raiders did not have *sleen*. Guard *sleen* can be trained to prowl the perimeters of a camp. In this way, they can attack intruders and any, too, who might attempt to leave the camp without authorization, deserters, fleeing slaves, spies, and such.

I heard a sound of chain.

I stepped carefully. I did not want to cut my feet. The ground was strewn with shards, pieces of broken pottery, each an ostracon.

Though I could not read the scribbling on the ostraca I assumed it had to do with numbers.

A kneeling figure was swathed with chains.

They could have secured a *tharlarion*.

As one could not well put a slave to use who was so chained, they must have been put on her after the men had finished with her, either using her or, afterwards, being served by her.

Too, there was a heavy chain about her neck, and another about her left ankle. These two chains were fastened into posts driven deep into the ground.

The chained slave was the former Lady Temione of Hammerfest.

She whimpered again, a small noise, a slave noise.

She would fear to cry out. She might be beaten.

How rudely she had been introduced into her new life, that of a slave!

I pitied her.

Then, upon a brief reflection, I did not pity her, but was muchly pleased. She had been the cruel Lady Temione of Hammerfest. She had pronounced herself slave. Now let her learn what it was to be a slave, a Gorean slave.

I turned about.

I would make my way west, past the structure, now abandoned, the citadel of, the palace and fortress of, the Lady Temione of Hammerfest. Its bulk would shield me from the sight of the camp.

It was now beginning to be light.

I sped away.

CHAPTER TWENTY-TWO

I kept moving west, keeping the mighty Vosk on my right.

Occasionally it rained, but not heavily.

Every so often I waded across a small creek, it adding its diminutive contribution to the flow of the enormous Vosk. Hundreds of such rivulets, and rivers, larger and smaller, over thousands of square miles, fed the waters of the Vosk, waters sometimes wide and sluggish, sometimes plunging, narrow, and fierce, eventually reaching the marshes of the vast delta, and, beyond that, the Tamber Gulf and Thassa, the sea herself. I hoped to encounter no rivers, or larger bodies of water. I could swim but I was not a strong swimmer. Currents could be strong and dangerous, and dash one against rocks, or hurl one over falls, and, in slower waters, one did not know what might lurk beneath the surface. I did not think I could, in most places, swim the Vosk itself. I was sure I could not have done so from Victoria Minor, even if one discounted the dangers of river sharks, eels, and *tharlarion*. Twice I avoided peasant villages. Life for a slave there I supposed would not be much different from that in the *vielts* of the Lady Temione of Hammerfest, and might well be worse, due to the hostility of the free women of the peasantry, often large, strong women unfavorably inclined toward slighter, more attractive women, and thus more than ready to wield the punishment stick or whip. I knew I was far from the delta, but had no idea how far.

I looked up.

It must be about noon.

It had now ceased raining.

After not having been put to slave use yesterday, I had become uneasy concerning my desirability. I knew I was not a prize slave like Calla, the former Lady Temione, Bennett, or Xanthe, as I gathered she had been named, or Luta, or many others whom I remembered from the great pen at Victoria Minor, and the *vielts* of the Lady Temione, but I thought myself comely, and not without attractions. All women, I suppose, wish to be found desirable. I do not think that this is a mere matter of happenstance vanity. I suspect it has also been selected for amongst the many courses of evolution. In any event, desirability is often in a woman's best interest, biologically and otherwise. Certainly the free woman cultivates and enhances her attractions, as she can, to open doors and smooth her path, to improve her prospects, so to speak, and the slave, a property, hopes to become a more delicious property, that she can interest and obtain, or keep, the Master of her dreams.

I continued on.

The sun was warm.

I did not think I could long be loose.

I still wore the collar of the Lady Temione of Hammerfest, and my only garment was the coarse sacking of a field slave.

I was not sure why I had run.

It was doubtless foolish to have done so, but a concatenation of circumstances had encouraged me to do so. I was uncoffled and unsupervised; it was dark; the opportunity to slip away was obvious; I was angry and distressed that I had not been selected for, or even seized for, slave sport during the revelry; my slave needs wept for satisfaction; I felt forlorn, neglected, miserable, and scorned; I wanted to flee, to get away, to somewhere, anywhere; and, perhaps most important, I had been terribly disturbed by the communication which had been imparted to me by Calla, about a beast inquiring after a barbarian slave, a fragment of whose name when free had been 'Agnes.' All of my original terrors of being discovered and done away with had returned forcibly and dismayingly, worsened by the intelligence that my pursuer was not even human but a beast of some sort, of a kind which might feed on human flesh. Was I to remain inert, perhaps to find myself on a chain where I could easily be recognized and from which it would be impossible for me to escape? It seemed important to me to run if only to find myself in a different venue, differently caged or chained. Perhaps I should have remained with the raiders. Perhaps amongst such numbers I would be less conspicuous, and more easily overlooked. And if I were taken to be Gorean, what had I to fear from anyone who might seek a barbarian? Had I been foolish? I did not know. But I had run. That had been done. I trusted that when my inevitable recapture occurred, I marked, slave clad, and collared, as it must, I would not be hamstrung or have my nose and ears cut off. I did not think that that would happen. That would substantially lower my price. Who would wish to maim, mutilate, or scar an animal of at least some value? I wondered then if some others might have also fled, perhaps some who had not been selected, or selected by Masters to whom they feared to belong. Surely amongst so many slaves on so wild a night one or more might have fled, however foolishly, hoping to improve their lot with a different Master, or such?

I had not walked much farther when I came on another small creek. Happily, in my flight I had had no difficulty in obtaining water. Indeed, somewhere to my right lay the Vosk itself, perhaps no more than a few miles away. I sat down on the grass, to feed on some of the viands I had stolen from the garden of the palace of the Lady Temione of Hammerfest. Carefully rationed, they might last me three or four days. I wanted to have my meal before wading to the other side of the small waterway. This seemed best to me, in case I might lose my footing, or fall, in which case I might lose or soak my small store of provender or part of it. What I had stolen from the garden was a far cry from the bland, if nourishing, porridges of slave gruel. Indeed, as many Goreans in rural areas make do for the most part with simple, plain foods, cheeses, soups, vegetables, fruits, nuts, grains, breads, and such, much of which is not all that different from what is fed to slaves, I was banqueting, contrarywise, on provender such as might grace the tables of the wealthy, as was easily understood as it had, in effect, been removed from just such tables. Shortly thereafter I folded the remainder of the food in the piece of torn silk sacking from the garden, and rose up a bit. I carefully checked the surrounding terrain. It was clear. I then went to the creek and satisfied my thirst. Following that, I pulled my garment up about my neck to keep it out of the water, and, holding the silk-wrapped package of food at shoulder level, began to wade slowly, carefully, across the creek. I knew that I had not left prints where I had entered the water because the soil there had pretty much dried from the recent rains. The water, for the most part, came no higher than my waist. I slipped once where the bottom unexpectedly slipped to the side, but regained my balance, and soon arrived at the other side, my food and garment dry. I was well satisfied with myself, and prepared to continue on my way, west.

I looked back, across the creek, and east. I saw nothing. This pleased me. I had, of course, left prints where I had emerged, soaked and dripping, from the water. I wiped these away with a handful of fresh grass. On my hands and knees I did so. Then I noticed that certain reeds to my right were broken and trampled. I presumed some animal must have done this, either in pausing to drink or in crossing the creek, certainly something which was not, whether wisely or not, concerned about concealing its presence or passage. Curious, I looked about. Moments later, I cried out, softly, frightened. There were indeed prints here, and they were not mine. They had been left at the edge of the creek before the soil had dried. The prints were clearly those of an animal. One could tell that from the impression of claws. Claws, too, I knew, indicated a carnivorous animal. Too, from the depth and breadth of the prints, it seemed to be a large animal. I was not happy at the thought that I might be sharing the local *vielts* with a large, dangerous animal. Would that a fellow were nearby, armed with that heavy spear which seemed to be a Gorean's frequent weapon of choice. I thought of a *sleen*, or perhaps a *larl*, an animal I had never seen. But I was sure the prints could not belong to either beast. It seemed that this animal moved, at least for the most part, on two limbs. Thus, it appeared to be essentially bipedalian. I recalled the 'enchanted box' of which Calla had spoken. To manipulate controls on such a device would presumably require hands, or something much like hands, and that suggested that the possessor of the 'enchanted box,' the 'Kur,' would be, at least for the most part, bipedalian. The prints had been clearly impressed on soil which at that time had been soft and wet, but, apparently, as the prints had not been reduced or washed away, shortly before the rain stopped or shortly after the rain had stopped, before the ground could dry, which suggested that they had been left some two or three hours ago. I noted to my relief that the prints were oriented eastward. I wondered if the beast might have seen me. Certainly I had not seen it. Its interrogations, if any, I was sure, would be addressed not to *kajirae*, but to Masters. Too, it might have seen other slaves about. I was reasonably sure that I would not be the only slave who had availed herself, for one reason or another, of the chance to slip away from the garden near the palace of the Lady Temione of Hammerfest.

The beast had been moving east. I was moving west. Each step we took separated us more and more from the other.

I was thus much pleased.

I was in little danger.

Too, my Gorean was excellent. I could pass for a Gorean, even with most Goreans. It should not be hard then to do so with an alien lifeform, should I encounter one, to whom humans, free or slave, might seem much the same. Too, the beast seemed to have little to go on, little other than a fragment of a name. And were there not thousands of *kajirae* on Gor, native and barbarian? And, too, I doubted that the beast could easily pursue its inquiries. At night it had paused and accosted a single raider. If such an animal, large and monstrous in aspect, should approach a peasant village or the gates of a town or city, might it not be slain out of hand? The tiger's jungle is doubtless dangerous for a human, but I suspect that the streets of the human are far more dangerous for the tiger. It is easier to kill and cage than question and confer. The human being is good at killing; it has had thousands of years to practice.

I was safe.

I continued on my way, west.

CHAPTER TWENTY-THREE

I saw them from far off, in the late afternoon of my third day of freedom, insofar as a slave girl can be free, the rider of a saddle *tharlarion*, and, following behind him, on foot, five naked female slaves, their wrists fastened behind their backs, each on her own neck rope, some fifteen feet in length, three of these ropes attached to a heavy ring at the left side of the saddle and two attached to a similar ring on the right side of the saddle.

I had exhausted my small store of food.

I stood up, hungry and miserable.

The rider must have seen me for he had turned his *tharlarion* toward me, and begun to approach in a leisurely manner.

When he was a few feet away, I knelt and lowered my head.

"Get up," he said.

I rose to my feet, careful not to meet his eyes directly. Some Masters regard direct eye contact as suggesting insolence on the part of a slave. Is she a free woman who dares look so boldly into the eyes of a free man? Others do not seem to mind it, at all. I supposed it might depend on the sort of eye contact. One does not know at first, of course.

The slaves tied by the neck to his saddle stood, watching, but, apparently, not much interested. If he had turned to face them, I assumed they would, under his gaze, have knelt. Most slaves will do much to avoid a whipping. A slave seldom braves the whip but once.

He remained in the saddle.

At the side of his saddle were the rope and netting that I recalled from the guards accompanying the coffle bound earlier to Victoria Minor.

Such things are common to slave hunters.

There was, too, a long, muchly coiled whip there the function of which I did not understand. It did not seem a practical implement.

"What does your collar read?" he asked.

"I am told," I said, "it says 'I am the property of Temione of Hammerfest. Return me to my Mistress.'"

"You are illiterate," he said.

"Yes Master," I said.

"Recently," he said, "the lands and palace of the Lady Temione of Hammerfest were overrun, apparently by marauding pirates venturing ashore. She has disappeared. Her chattels were scattered. I have five behind me, tied to my saddle rings now. Her lands, as needs to be the case, have been confiscated by Gordon, Administrator of Hammerfest, in the name of the High Council of Hammerfest."

"I did not know that," I said. To be sure, I was not surprised.

"What are you doing here?" he asked.

"In terror, in the fighting, fleeing for my life, I fled," I said.

"Just as the others behind me," he said.

"I would not know," I said.

"You are all liars," he said. "You are fugitives."

"Surely not, Master," I said.

"Why did you not travel at night?" he asked.

"I was afraid," I said. "I was afraid of the dark. I was afraid of animals."

"You saw me," he said. "Why did you not attempt to escape?"

"I knew I could not elude you," I said.

"We shall see," he said.

"Master?" I said.

"Those behind my mount tried," he said. "Now they are my catches."

"I could not expect to succeed where so many failed," I said.

"Are you alone?" he asked, looking around.

"Yes, Master," I said.

I was uneasy, being on my feet before a free man. Those in collars will understand this.

"You seem frail, weak, frightened, forlorn," he said.

I made no response to this. Certainly I was tired, starving, and miserable. I must have made a pathetic figure standing before him, he looking down on me from that high proud saddle.

"You have run far enough," he said.

"Yes, Master," I said. I knew I was tired of 'running.' And I knew the outcome, sooner or later, would be the same. I would be caught. There was no escape for the Gorean slave girl.

"You are hungry," he said.

"Very much so, Master," I said.

"You have surrendered to me," he said. "Thus, you have denied me the sport of the chase."

"Forgive me, Master," I said.

"Why did you deny me that pleasure?" he asked.

"I am safer on a chain than loose in the fields," I said.

"That is true," he said, "but you are such that you belong on a chain."

"Yes, Master," I said. I wondered if he knew how true that was. On Gor, I could be the slave I truly was. On Gor I need not deny my slave.

He then swung his legs over the side of the mount and descended the four-rung saddle ladder.

He then stood before me.

"No," he said, "do not kneel."

"I am not a free woman," I said.

"That is obvious," he said.

"I beg to kneel," I said.

"Stay on your feet," he said.

"Yes, Master," I said.

"Let us see your hands," he said.

I held them out to him, palms up.

"The hands of a field slave."

"Yes, Master," I said.

"Soothing oils and creams will remedy that," he said. "By the next passage hand, they could be as soft as those of a *paga* slave in Ar."

I did not fully understand that. I did know that Ar, a tower city, was the greatest metropolis in Gor's northern hemisphere, as Turia was in her southern hemisphere.

"I do not think they will put you on the block until then," he said.

"I hope to be pleasing to Masters," I said.

"You have not been pleasing to me," he said, "as you have not run."

"Forgive me, Master," I said.

"Your features are not unpleasant," he said, "and your ankles are of interest, but that long, brown, gross, coarse, loosely woven *sul* sack in which you are hiding leaves much undisclosed and problematic."

"Thus Lady Temione of Hammerfest clothed her field slaves," I said, "and such sacking was similarly flung over her house slaves, though their sacking was of silk."

"Two of my catches," he said, gesturing back toward the tethered slaves tied to his saddle rings, "were house slaves."

"Yes, Master," I said.

"You cannot tell which two, can you?" he asked.

"No, Master," I said.

I expected that two of the slaves bound to the saddle rings would not have been pleased to hear that.

"You can tell from the hands," he said.

"Yes, Master," I said.

"It is said," he said, "that the Lady Temione of Hammerfest purchased only beauties, that she even, for some reason, put beauties in the fields."

"I was not purchased by her," I said. "It was an accident of sorts, an untoward circumstance, that brought me to her fields."

"Do you like your garment?" he asked.

"It is precious," I said. "It covers me."

"But a slave," he said, "has no right to covering."

I knew that to be true. A slave was, legally, an animal, a domestic animal.

"We shall see," he said, "if there is anything of interest between those ankles and your hair and features."

"Master?" I said.

He seized the garment. I tried to draw back. He whipped out a knife. I cried out in dismay and fear. In a moment, he holding to the garment, pulling it out from my body, had cut it away and thrown it to the side. I had been 'knife stripped.'

"Turn before me, slave girl," he said.

I did so, terrified. Several times the knife, stabbing, poking, and slashing, had come terribly close to my body. But neither the blade nor point in all their frightening speeds had touched me. I realized then I could not have been the first woman he had 'knife stripped.'

I felt the grass beneath my bare feet, the warmth of the sun on my shoulders, the grassland's soft wind flowing over my body.

"Again, and better," he said.

I turned again, this time as a slave.

I hoped he liked what he saw.

He was a man, a Master.

"How different this was from Earth," I thought.

She who had been Agnes Morrison Atherton of Earth, now a slave, unclothed, on the planet Gor, had turned slowly before a man, exhibiting herself as the sentient, living object she now was.

I stood before him.

There was nothing before him but a girl, a light, close-fitting collar on her neck.

"Now," he said, "you may kneel."

Gratefully I fell to my knees, my head down.

I knelt before him, a naked slave before a Master.

He then turned away and went to the saddle *tharlarion* and led it forward by the reins, muchly to where I knelt. I shuddered. I could almost have reached out and touched one of those heavy, clawed feet. The rider's action, naturally, brought the other slaves, on their neck-ropes, near me, as well. They too, put in place, knelt.

"What a sorry lot of she-tarsks," he said.

Two of the slaves laughed. They were not unaware of their charms or of the prices they might bring in an open auction.

"You are all stupid little *vulos*," he said, "mindless *tastas*."

I knew that *vulos* were domestic fowls. There were apparently several varieties of such. I had no idea what a *tasta* might be.

"You were so stupid," he said, "that you ran. But why should I object? I get ten copper tarsks for each of you pretty little things I bring back to Sulport."

I think that Sulport was downriver from Hammerfest. Why should we not be returned to Hammerfest? The nearest large town upriver from Hammerfest, I had heard, was Fina. Victoria was much further upriver.

"Does not Master ride for the House of Ho-Turik?" asked a slave.

I had heard of this house in the great pen at Victoria Minor. Luta had been owned by this house. She had thought it superior to that of Kleon, whose collar I had worn at the time.

As the slave had spoken without requesting permission, I gathered that this Master was either indulgent, or, more likely, that the slaves had a standing permission to speak, one revokable, of course, at his whim. I did not know if I were included within that permission or not. If one is unclear as to such matters, it is wise to request permission to speak. There are few things that more impress our slavery on us, incidentally, than this possible curb on our speech, that we must have our Master's permission to speak.

"Occasionally," he said. "The house sometimes hires, and sometimes, as now, has enough riders. One picks up copper tarsks as one can, when one can."

I wondered if he had helped guard the long coffle approaching Victoria Minor. Some of the riders, I knew, had been of the House of Ho-Turik.

"We have trekked far, Master," said a slave. "May we not be rested now, and fed and watered?"

"You ran well," he said, admiringly.

"But I am now on your rope," she said.

She did not seem upset about this.

"Do you beg it, prettily?"

"Very prettily, Master," she said.

I decided I hated her. I doubted that she had run so well. Free women, not slaves, I suspected, would be the most earnest and desperate of runners, even if clumsy and not skilled, women frantic to retain their freedom. To be sure, I supposed that a slave might try to flee from a hated or cruel Master, seriously enough, hoping to fall into a better bondage. Unfortunately, the captured fugitive slave, if not returned to her former Master, which is almost overwhelmingly the case, would be likely, as a caught runaway, to fall into a heavier and more stringent slavery, one more onerous than that from which she had originally fled.

"Very well," said the rider, and he began to busy himself about the packs fastened behind the saddle.

"Thank you, Master!" called a slave.

"Be as you will," he called over his shoulder.

The slaves then assumed what attitudes they would, as far as their restraints permitted.

As I took myself to be included in this welcome, issued permission, I sat in the grass.

Occasionally, as one or another of the slaves moved, I saw that her wrists were not pinioned behind her body by thongs as I had expected, but by slave bracelets. Such bracelets tend to be more comfortable than thongings, and they are, of course, more effective as constraints, not because the prisoner is not unutterably helpless in thongs, but because they cannot be untied or cut loose by another party. Slave bracelets are much lighter than the manacles which are commonly used in the case of male prisoners, but, like those manacles, they render their commonly smaller, lighter occupants similarly helpless. Whereas the slave bracelets confining the catches of the rider were plain, slave bracelets often supplement their custodial aspects with aspects one might more normally associate with jewelry. Imagine, if you will, two lovely matching bracelets, one on each wrist, but joined by a metal linkage. Some slave bracelets are enameled, engraved, plated, set with jewels, and so on. It is not unusual for a Master to desire to enhance the beauty of his properties by various means, jeweled collars, and such. In promenades, Masters are commonly accompanied by leashed slaves, often strikingly adorned.

The rider then put down bowls into which he poured water from a large bota and into which he shook some brown pellets. The slaves then, kneeling, head down, both fed and drank.

I was the only slave who was not trammeled.

I was also the only slave who was not fed and watered.

"Master, may I speak?" I asked.

"No," he said. "And kneel."

I knelt.

There was laughter.

After a time, he pointed to me and addressed the others. "What do you think of my latest catch?" he asked.

"She was not a catch, Master," said one woman.

"She was a surrender," said another.

"Who would want her?" inquired another.

"I could have caught her myself," said another.

I doubted that.

"It is true," he said, "that she denied me sport."

"Whip her," said one of the slaves.

I remained as I was, positioned.

I did not much care for the slave's recommendation.

"Masters will treat us kindly, will they not," asked a slave, "as we did not really run away, but merely fled in terror to escape pirates?"

"And kept on fleeing," he said, "for one or more days?"

The slaves, I noted, did not seem too distraught. I wondered if they had truly tried to elude the rider. Why were they not, on their ropes, if not outraged and in tears, shaken and in consternation, or at least sullenly bitter at having been apprehended? Surely a free woman being led into bondage might be expected to grievously lament her lot, perhaps even to howling her terror and misery to the sky. The rider was a stalwart, handsome fellow, but I thought that that would have had little to do with the slaves' apparent complacency. His features might even have been concealed in a wind scarf. Most likely, I conjectured, they, like myself, had had no serious hope of escaping, but, like myself, had availed themselves of a beckoningly easy exit from the garden of the Lady Temione of Hammerfest, and its presumably distressing memories, and hoped, after an interlude of freedom, to obtain a new, lighter, more pleasant bondage. Supposedly fleeing from pirates would provide them with at least the semblance of a suitable motivation for flight. Thus, when caught and claimed, they might even escape a serious whipping. In my case, of course, I had a very serious motivation for wanting to put a great distance between me and the fields of the Lady Temione of Hammerfest. I wanted to remove myself as far as possible from the compass of a beast's inquiries.

The rider went to the side of his saddle and removed a whip from a small ring there. It was the long, several-times-coiled whip I had earlier noted. Certainly it was not the usual slave whip with its five broad blades which slaves learn quickly to fear. Indeed, it seemed to me an unwieldy device. At the time, I did not realize it was a capture whip, and that it was not intended for disciplining a slave.

He held it out, toward me, and I bent swiftly toward it, grasped the coils in my two hands, lifted them to my lips, and, putting down my head, licked and kissed it, humbly, fervently, hoping to be found pleasing. Too, even as hungry as I was, this act of obeisance enflamed me.

"A worthless slave!" laughed one of the girls on her neck rope.

He jerked the whip from me, which startled me. "Master?" I said.

"Get up, and run!" he said. "Run! Escape!"

"Run!" cried several of the slaves.

I stood up, confused.

The slaves had apparently seen this sort of thing before.

"Run!" cried more than one.

"You are slow to obey," said the rider. "Hurry to the feet of my mount, kneel down, and clean its claws with your lips, tongue, mouth, and teeth."

Wildly I spun about and fled.

I do not know why I did this. Perhaps, I had hoped that it was not too late to run. Perhaps I had been seized by the mad notion that I might somehow escape. But I do not really think I was thinking at all. My reaction was not rational; it was immediate; it was visceral. The *tharlarion* filled me with awe and terror. I had no idea how it might respond to my attempting to comply with the Master's command. I could be trampled. It might crush me with one movement of one of those mighty appendages. It might reach down and seize me in its jaws. I was a horrified, terrified animal. Was it the rider's intent to feed me to the beast?

I had scarcely taken five steps when that long, snakelike lash snapped about my ankles and I fell rudely, abruptly, helplessly to the ground and was drawn back a yard or so toward the rider. I thrust away the encircling leather, sprang to my feet, and, weeping, darted away. A moment later the leather whirled about my body and I was hauled up short, two coils tight about my stomach, wrenching into my flesh. I thrust the coils down over my legs, to the grass, and tried again to flee, when I suddenly stopped short, fearing that I might strangle myself, and I tried to pull the coils from my throat, but I felt myself drawn gently backward, until the rider was within an arm's reach of me. I then, well captured, knowing myself his, turned about and flung myself to my knees, and, putting my head down, a yielded quarry, humbly kissed the rider's feet.

"Must a command be repeated?" he asked.

"No, Master," I said.

I had no desire to feel the lash.

I crawled to the two massive feet of the saddle *tharlarion* and, head down, with lips, tongue, teeth, and mouth, began to clean its thick, heavy claws.

"The whip," said the rider, "is a capture whip. It may be used even from the first rung of the mounting ladder, the mount in motion. Many slaves are not familiar with the implement. Had you been so, you would not have dared to run, unless, of course, you were ordered to do so."

I threw up in the grass, which wrenched my stomach, because of my lack of food, and then continued with my work.

When I had finished, and had had my work inspected for quality, the rider, by the hair, drew me up, back, and away from the *tharlarion*, and flung me to my side in the grass.

He looked down on me and I, from my side, looked up at him.

"Would you like permission to speak?" he asked.

"Yes, Master," I said.

"I grant you a standing permission to do so," he said, "but do not abuse the privilege."

"I am tired, weak, and hungry," I said. "I beg to be fed and watered."

"On your belly," he said. Spread those pretty legs. More widely."

My body was shocked, again and again, blows like thunder, and then, as he rose and left, I lay as I was, prone, shattered, on the grass.

He was done with me, for the time.

He returned after a time and drew my wrists behind my back, where he snapped them into slave bracelets. After that he ran a rope from a ring on the right side of the saddle to my neck, and knotted it in place. In this way, there were three slaves neck-roped on each side of the saddle. He then put a bowl near me and poured some water and pellets into it, and left. I struggled to my knees, went to the bowl, and, putting down my head, gratefully, fed and drank. It was now evening, and the other slaves were resting or asleep. The Master, it seemed, given the hour, was content to stay in place. Presumably it is difficult to hunt at night. Too, given the footing, it is difficult to move captures in the darkness. I noted that he had lit no fire. Might there be other hunters abroad?

She who runs by night must sleep by day. She also requires water. The hunter, as I would learn, over the next few days, usually traverses parallel lines to flush his prey, and sharpens and narrows his pattern when in the vicinity of water. From the high saddle of the *tharlarion* he can also survey a compass of ground much superior to that of a hunter afoot, this making it easier to detect a sleeping body or the signs of a quarry's passage.

CHAPTER TWENTY-FOUR

I was awakened, startled, by the heavy hand held closely over my mouth.

"Make no sound," said a voice, "or I will cut your throat." I felt the thin, fine, uncovered edge of steel gently but unmistakably pressed to my throat.

I remained absolutely quiet, rigid, terrified.

"I am cutting your neck rope," whispered the voice. "You will then rise up and face south. There, in the night, you will see a small, intermittent point of light. Go to that light; be quick; be silent."

It had now been four days since my capture or surrender. This afternoon, the rider of the *tharlarion* had informed us that he was returning to Sulport, to turn us in and claim his capture fees. He did not explain to us the motivation for this decision, nor would he be likely to do so, as we were slaves. Similarly, it would not occur to drovers to explain such matters to cattle or horses. As he still had only the same six captures tied to his saddle, his decision might have been based on the seeming lack of quarries. Perhaps the runners from the garden near Hammerfest had all been caught by now. That was possible. That might become clear at Sulport. On the other hand, after a dry hunting spell, he might simply wish to collect some coin and avail himself of the taverns of Sulport. Or, I suspect, particularly now, that he had had some grounds for surmising that he was not alone in the grassland, perhaps from something sighted, some spoor discovered, the marks of a camp now abandoned, or such, and that the mostly hard-won fruits of his work might be in jeopardy. A coin, after all, can be grasped by more than one hand, and the coin is indifferent as to the hand that grasps it.

Obedient to the command I had received, fearing for my life, I made my way, stumbling, back-braceleted, trying not to fall, through the grass in the darkness to the spot of light which seemed to come and go. Its source, as it turned out, was much farther away than I had supposed. It is difficult to judge such things in the darkness. Eventually, after several hundred yards, I reached the source of the light. "Kneel down," said a figure in the darkness. "There, and be quiet." I knelt down. As I did so, I was aware I was near another kneeling figure, doubtless one earlier ordered to this place, as I had been. As the minutes passed, another, and another, joined us and was knelt in our group.

"That is six," said one of two men in the darkness.

"All of them," said the other.

"With our eleven," said the first man, "it has been well managed."

"Let fools do our work for us, scratching the countryside for prizes," said the second man.

"The wise man," said the other, "reaps crops others have sown."

"Plenius and Hanran should be back by now," said the second man."

"They are greedy tarsks who linger to loot the camp and secure the *tharlarion*," said the first man.

"That could wait until morning," said the other.

"Not if you want first pick of the saddle bags," snarled the first man.

"So let them empty their purses when light," said the second man, "revealing their contents to our knives."

My blood chilled as I gathered from their conversation that they lay in wait for hunters returning to Sulport, and perhaps other settlements. They had already slain two hunters in the past few days, from one of whom they had obtained four trophies, and from the other seven. The men were four in number. In this way they were well prepared to deal with any single hunter. Pairs of hunters or larger numbers of hunters, they let pass without incident. Their approach to their work was simple. They would move at night, in the darkness. One was dispatched to deal with the hunter, hoping to slay him in his sleep; another, particularly in case the hunter was not discovered or not easily slain, was to silence and direct slaves, for who knew what parties other than their own might be about in the darkness; and, surely, one would not wish to accept the inconvenience of scattering, frightened, screaming slaves; the third man, the leader, coordinated matters and maintained the signal lantern; and the last man would herd and supervise the slaves, those being acquired and the others previously acquired.

"Someone is coming," said the second man, the fellow in charge of the slaves.

"Who is there?" called the man with the lantern, it now shuttered, he who was the leader.

"Plenius," called a voice from the darkness.

"Advance," said the leader, sliding the lantern panel open.

The newcomer was he who had cut away my neck-rope and, presumably, those of the other slaves.

The newcomer looked about. "Where is Hanran?" he asked.

"I do not know," said the leader.

"He should have preceded me," said the newcomer, Plenius. "It takes only an Ihn to cut a throat, but Ehn to loosen and herd slaves."

"I do not like it," said the leader.

"Perhaps the hunter was not in the camp or, restless, had exited the folds of his blanket," said he in charge of the slaves.

"Go back, look," said the leader to Plenius.

"Not I, not alone, not in the darkness," said Plenius.

I sensed a knife was whipped from a sheath.

And then a second knife.

"Sheath your blades," pleaded he who was in charge of the slaves. "We do not know what is in the darkness."

"Wait," said Plenius. "Hanran may dally at the camp. He is doubtless shortly behind me."

Knives were sheathed.

After a minute or two a voice called from the darkness, haltingly. "Aesil," it said.

"Here!" said the leader.

"Hanran!" said Plenius, gratefully.

A man came slowly forth, emerging from the darkness. Then, at the edge of the light, he sank down slowly, and then sat down, cross-legged, as Gorean males often do.

I did not think him well.

"You dallied," said Aesil. "We will examine your purse in the morning."

"And that of Plenius, too," said the fellow in charge of the slaves.

"My knife is prepared to deny you that privilege, Livius," said Plenius.

"We will do with such matters in the morning," said Aesil. "As for now, we are again four and are again well joined. Our affairs prosper. We have obtained, with the new six, seventeen slaves, quality slaves, whom we can sell downriver in Port Cos or Turmus, at the delta."

"No modest finding fees for us," laughed Plenius.

"Shall I add the new slaves to the others?" asked Livius.

"Later," said Aesil. "I am eager to see if one slave in particular is amongst them."

"Who would pay ten silver tarsks for a single slave?" asked Plenius.

"A beast," said Aesil.

Suddenly the night felt cold.

I began to shudder.

"What is wrong?" asked Livius.

"I am cold," I said.

The leader then began to interrogate us, one at a time. I was the fourth slave questioned. He crouched before me, I kneeling, like the others. "Are you a barbarian?" he asked, fiercely, his face not six inches from mine.

"No," I said, in such a way as to suggest that I found the question demeaning, if not offensive.

"Say a few sentences," he said to me.

"Any sentences?" I asked.

"Any sentences," he said. I knew he would be looking for some trace of an accent with which he might be unfamiliar. I spoke a little of the *vielts* of the Lady Temione of Hammerfest.

"Enough," he snapped. "Are you aware of any barbarian slaves encountered recently?"

"No, Master," I said. I would certainly not tell him of Xanthe, who had been Eileen Bennett on Earth. She knew me only too well as the former Agnes Morrison Atherton.

"Does the word 'ag-nas' mean anything to you?" he asked.

"No, Master," I said. He then went on to the next slave.

He later stood up, his interrogations having proved thus far fruitless. "I think that there are no barbarians here," he said. "But we will pursue the matter further in the morning. There are many barbarians who do not even know the sign of the Priest-Kings, the name of the Ubar of Cos, that of the former adopted daughter of Marlenus of Ar, who are unfamiliar with the love poems of Dina of Ar and the songs of Andreas of Tor, who are unable even to name the twenty pieces of *kaissa*."

I knew none of these things and, even if I had known them, I was sure there would be thousands of others with which I would be unfamiliar.

I felt sick with fear.

"Livius," said Aesil, "fetch the other eleven slaves. We will bind all together and in the morning we will march to a ferry point from which to cross the Vosk. With good weather, we can reach it in two days."

Livius turned about and disappeared into the darkness.

Aesil then turned to the figure of Hanran, he who had come last to the point of light.

"You dallied," said Aesil. "You were late to return. Did the *tharlarion* stray? Was it hard to recover it in the darkness, or, more likely, you rifled the saddle packs of a tethered beast or the clothing and purse of the slain hunter, or both, to enrich yourself at our expense. You know we are to divide loot into five parts, two for me, as leader, and one each for you, Plenius, and Livius."

"I took nothing," said Plenius. "I would wait until morning, as always, when all is open and clear, when all is gathered, when all may be distributed as agreed."

"Good," said Aesil. "Then you will not object to emptying your purse as soon as it is light." He then turned to the cross-legged, now half-slumped figure of Hanran. "Hanran," he said, "you loitered. I am not pleased. Do you question the agreed-upon rules of division? You are quiet. Do you sleep? Speak. Do you fear to speak?"

Aesil reached out, impatiently, to shake Hanran awake.

Then he drew his hand back.

The figure of Hanran fell to the side.

Plenius rushed forward, turning the body to its back. I and two others cried out in fear. The chest of the body, as could be seen in the lantern light, was covered with blood.

"He is dead," said Plenius.

Instantly Aesil slid the panels of the lantern shut, and all was darkness.

"The hunter must have awakened," said Plenius.

"Or been waiting," said Aesil.

"The hunter," said Plenius, "is not likely to believe that Hanran would be alone. He will suspect confederates. Thus he will have saved himself. He will have fled."

"I think that likely," said Aesil.

"We are three, he is one," said Plenius. "We are more than enough to deal with a single foe. Too, for all he knows we might be ten or twelve in number."

"Unless," said Aesil, "while we scouted him, he scouted us."

"We are, in any event, three to one," said Plenius.

"Call Livius," said Aesil.

"Livius! Livius!" called Plenius into the darkness.

There was only darkness and silence.

"I fear," said Aesil, "he did not flee."

"Then we are two to one," said Plenius.

"Draw your weapon," said Aesil. "Be silent. Keep close."

CHAPTER TWENTY-FIVE

"There!" cried Plenius, rising in the stirrups, pointing.

"I see him," said Aesil.

Four times the mounted hunter had appeared, a lonely figure astride his *tharlarion*, in the distance, but had not approached.

And four times Aesil and Plenius had veered to the right, to avoid closing with the stranger.

This was the afternoon of the day after the raid on the hunter's camp. I had little doubt but what Aesil and Plenius feared the night, the coming of darkness.

"He is herding us toward Sulport," said Plenius.

"No more," said Aesil. "We have had enough."

"He is too far for a fair shot," said Plenius.

"We shall parley," said Aesil. "That will bring him within range."

Both Aesil and Plenius had bows concealed beneath blankets. These blankets were cast before them, over their saddle aprons. The saddle apron may be used for additional packing space. Its expanse may also be used for tethering a female captive, usually belly up, her ankles and wrists fastened to rings on either side of the saddle. These bows were short, stubby weapons, which would be fired from the shoulder, much like a rifle. Each had a projectile in its guide, short, metal, and thrice-finned.

Aesil's small entourage consisted of himself and Plenius, both mounted, two *tharlarion* with empty saddles, which beasts were tied behind Plenius' *tharlarion*, and seventeen slaves, eleven of whom were back-thonged and six of whom were back-braceleted. The slaves all wore the collar of the Lady Temione of Hammerfest; of the seventeen slaves fifteen had been field slaves and two house slaves. The seventeen slaves were tied together by means of a single loop of rope threaded between their arms, the wrists of which were either back-thonged or back-braceleted. In this way, the loop of slaves was such that it might, in theory, move independently of the entourage, even flee from it. On the other hand, it was unlikely to avail itself of such an opportunity. To do so would be a cause for discipline, and, strung together, it might be conveniently recovered. Where would it go, what could it do? The point of the arrangement was primarily to guarantee that it could not compromise the maneuverability of the *tharlarion* of Aesil and Plenius. A last oddity connected with the slaves was that each was gagged. In this way they could not, even if they dared to do so, interfere by cries or shouts with the doings of the men. As slaves are almost never gagged in coffle, I trusted that the hunter would not be unaware of this anomaly and would give some thought as to its possible motivation.

Aesil lifted a green cloth and shook it, over his head. He then thrust the cloth in his belt and led his small entourage slowly toward the hunter. I saw Plenius' hand slip beneath the blanket on the saddle apron. When the hunter and Aesil were separated by some fifty yards the hunter held up his hand, palm toward Aesil, and pointed to the ground. Aesil dismounted. The hunter then, facing Plenius, who was behind and to the side of Aesil, repeated the gesture. "Get down," said Aesil, over his shoulder. Reluctantly Plenius dismounted. The hunter, too, then dismounted. "Bring the catches," said Aesil to Plenius. "We shall negotiate." Following the gesture of Plenius we took our place before Aesil. "Forward," said Aesil to us. We then made our way through the grass toward the hunter. Later Aesil said, "Stop, kneel." He and the hunter were then some ten yards apart, and we seventeen slaves on the loop of rope, kneeling, were between them. Plenius was close to Aesil, on his right. All three men loosened their swords in their sheaths.

"*Tal*," said Aesil, pleasantly.

"*Tal*," said the rider, affably.

"We are both reasonable men," said Aesil.

"I trust so," said the hunter.

"Behold the slaves," said Aesil.

"They are beheld," said the hunter.

"Each," said Aesil, "was a property of the Lady Temione of Hammerfest."

"I will take your word for that," said the hunter.

"—a Mistress noted east and west on the Vosk for the choiceness of her slaves."

"I have heard that," said the hunter.

"To begin," said Aesil, "as we are two and you are one, we may kill you at our leisure, promptly and easily."

"You are welcome to try," said the hunter.

"Yet," said Aesil, "as we are brothers, fellow merchants in a way, we are willing to grant you your life, if you withdraw now and have no further dealings with us."

"You are generous," said the hunter. "But why, then, have you set slaves between us, presumably for my perusal."

"Because," said Aesil, "we wish to avoid unpleasantness. You may choose one and then withdraw, with your life and a slave, never to bother us again."

"But you made off with six of my catches," said the hunter.

"Surely you do not expect six slaves for nothing," said Aesil.

"In a few Ahn," said the hunter, "it will be dark."

"You killed two of my men," said Aesil.

"Who were doubtless involved in the slayings of others," said the hunter. "Few hunters are fortunate enough to have eleven catches."

"Surely you do not wish our conversation to become a matter of blood," said Aesil.

"It is hard to judge these things," said the hunter, "for your skills are unknown to me, as are mine to you. Are you eager to wager?"

"The wager of steel?" asked Aesil.

"Of course," said the hunter.

"We are two and you are one," said Aesil.

"I am willing to wait until darkness," said the hunter.

"You may take your six," said Aesil, angrily. "Take them and be away, troubling us no further."

"I have been troubled," said the hunter. "Thus I will take seventeen."

"You jest," said Aesil.

"Yes," said the hunter, "until darkness."

"Wait," said Aesil. "We have not only slaves, but gold, much gold in our saddle packs."

Then he turned to Plenius, and said, "Bring our *tharlarion* here, that we may buy our way free of this madman."

"Immediately," said Plenius.

"Hold," said the hunter.

Plenius whirled back.

"It is a rare hunter who carries gold into the grasslands or expects to find it there," said the hunter.

"You will see. We will fetch it," said Aesil.

"I see your saddle aprons are cold," said the hunter, "for each is covered with a blanket."

"Tarsk!" cried Aesil.

Plenius, sword drawn, turned and ran back to his *tharlarion*.

"Slaves," said Aesil, "go with Plenius." He then, sword drawn, eyeing the hunter, walked slowly backward, step by step, through the grass.

The hunter then turned about, mounted his *tharlarion*, and, a few minutes later, disappeared toward the west.

* * *

It was night.

The slaves lay to the side. They were still on their rope loop, but they could not rise as the ankles of each were tied together.

"He is somewhere about," said Plenius. "I know it."

"Let him be about," said Aesil. 'We are together, not separate. We are safe."

"He could spring out of the darkness, and kill us both before we could respond," said Plenius.

"He cannot even find us in the darkness," said Aesil. "We have not lit the lamp."

"He will hear the grunting of the *tharlarion*," said Plenius.

"They are not at hand," said Aesil.

"The slaves are near," said Plenius.

"And well that is," said Aesil. "They are now ungagged and uneasy. Their cries, inadvertent or not, will inform us of the presence of any intruder."

"There is one way in which he cannot kill us both," said Plenius.

"And what is that?" said Aesil.

"We separate," said Plenius. "In that way one of us is bound to escape."

"Brave Plenius," said Aesil. "Our foe knows that I am first, that it is I who am leader here. Thus it is I whom he would track and kill. You would condemn me to meeting him alone, while you make your escape."

"No," said Plenius. "He will not know who he is following, until it is too late. And he might not be able to track either of us."

"Thus at least one survives," said Aesil.

"One hopes both will survive," said Plenius. "And your skills with the sword are far superior to mine."

"What of the slaves?" asked Aesil.

"We divide them," said Plenius. 'You may have nine and I only eight."

"If I have the most slaves," said Aesil, "our foe would be more likely to follow me."

"Then I will take nine and you take eight," said Plenius.

"I, the leader, have less?" said Aesil.

"Take the most then," said Plenius.

"What if I want all?" asked Aesil.

"Take all then," said Plenius. "I want only to be on my way."

"You wager," said Aesil.

"Much in life is a wager," said Plenius.

"You are embarked on this course?" asked Aesil.

"Yes," said Plenius.

"So be it, friend," said Aesil.

"You are not angry?" asked Plenius.

"No," said Aesil. "I cannot see you in the darkness. Hold forth your hand that I may once more grasp it in hearty fellowship."

Shortly thereafter I heard a soft cry, and then silence.

"I do not wager," said Aesil.

I sensed a body being gently lowered to the grass.

"I wish you well, dear friend," said Aesil. He then began to awaken slaves, warning them to silence. He then removed the ropes on their ankles. Shortly thereafter he gathered together the four *tharlarion*.

We were then ready to leave.

"We trek," he said. "By dawn we will be far from here."

CHAPTER TWENTY-SIX

In the midmorning, Aesil disengaged the rope on his saddle which led back to three *tharlarion*, these, roped together, following us in tandem. He had released the rope for he had seen the hunter. The slaves were still held in proximity to one another by the rope which, in its knotted loop, had been threaded between their arms. They were not, however, as on the day before, gagged. They needed not be. A crossbow, loaded, was slung openly on each side of Aesil's saddle. Many Gorean warriors do not regard the bow, either the rifle bow or the straight bow, as a fit weapon, presumably because it kills from afar, which seems to them a form of cheating in the game of war. Their weapons of choice are the spear and sword. The Gorean peasantry, on the other hand, has no compunction about relying on so fierce and devasting a weapon used in defending their villages and Home Stones. The crossbow or rifle bow is looked down upon by many Goreans because it is supposedly easier to master than the straight bow, and also, one suspects, because it is commonly associated with the Black Caste, the caste of Assassins. A major advantage of the crossbow is that it may remain quiescent, loaded, so to speak, the quarrel or bolt patient in its guide. Its major disadvantage is that it cannot match the long bow's rapidity of fire.

It soon became evident that the hunter, who had at first seemed small in the distance, was now approaching, and swiftly.

Aesil lifted up one of the two crossbows with its set quarrel.

I was sure he would prefer to deal with the hunter before he might come within the compass of the latter's steel.

The gait of the running bipedalian *tharlarion* is not a smooth one, but more in the nature of a bounding, lurching one. It would be extremely difficult, I supposed, to strike the rider of such a mount at any considerable distance, particularly if the rider, bent down, was approaching head on, and was much obscured by the massive fanged head of the beast. Presumably Aesil would wait until he could fire at point-blank range.

But he did not.

He had no intention of striking the rider.

At some forty yards he pulled the trigger on the bow and the quarrel, that metal-finned missile, lodged itself in the wide chest of the charging beast. I thought this a lapse of judgment on the part of Aesil for how could so small an object much affect that ponderous avalanche of muscle and bone which was bounding toward him?

The *tharlarion* spun about, with a wild, grunting bellow, and then, responding to the rider, realigned itself with its target. The plunging weight and bulk of such a beast could snap a small tree or shatter a palisade. But, oddly, it burst forward only a bound or two, when it slowed, and then stopped. It swung its head back and forth, as though puzzled, and its breathing became less breathing than a labored medley of stentorian noises. The hunter tried to urge the beast forward toward Aesil, but his efforts were unavailing. The beast shuddered, and went into its position of somnolence, or sleep, in which it stands upright on two legs, its position stabilized, tripod-like, by the heavy tail. I did not realize it at the time but the beast was dying. Aesil cried out in triumph, seized his second crossbow, the quarrel of which was already in place, and slipped from the saddle of his *tharlarion*. At the same time, the hunter, disdaining the mounting ladder, leapt from the saddle, but struck the ground heavily, unevenly, his face contorted with pain. I feared he had broken his leg. In that moment, or almost at that moment, the body of the beast tensed, stiffened, and then fell to the side. It lies so only when dead or dying. The hunter cried out in pain and dismay. One of his legs was trapped between the *tharlarion* and the ground. Aesil, afoot, the crossbow ready, hurried to the dying beast by whose weight the hunter's leg was pinned to the ground. The *tharlarion*, clearly, was still alive. I could see the rising and falling of its torso. The noise of its breathing was intermittent, and hideous.

"Do not reach for your sword or knife," said Aesil, standing almost over the hunter, his crossbow pointed down, toward the hunter's heart.

"Savor your triumph," said the hunter.

"I shall," said Aesil.

"The crossbow is unknown in the grasslands," said the hunter.

"Not to me," said Aesil.

"How could a single bolt slow, let alone stop, a *tharlarion*?" asked the hunter, wincing.

"You wish to talk?" asked Aesil.

"Surely, given the circumstances, you cannot begrudge me that desire," said the hunter.

"A swift poison, deadly in its effect," said Aesil. "It cost me a tarn of gold, of double weight, of the mintage of Ar. It is amongst the most potent serums brewed by the Caste of Poisoners."

"One of Gor's secret castes," said the hunter.

"Shall I now loose the quarrel?" asked Aesil.

"I think you are in no hurry to so do," said the hunter.

"Perhaps not," said Aesil.

I did not believe that the hunter's conversation with Aesil was merely to win a postponement of the inevitable, but I knew not what else it could be.

"I gather that your business," said the hunter, "is to gather in slaves not to return them to authorities for return fees, but to sell them in some independent venue."

"It is the difference between silver tarsks and copper tarsks," said Aesil.

"Then," said the hunter, "you are, simply put, a thief."

"You are perceptive," said Aesil.

"And you are a murderer," said the hunter.

"Few willingly relinquish valuables," said Aesil.

"And, in killing," said the hunter, "you eliminate witnesses and preclude retaliation or pursuit."

"Exactly," said Aesil.

As this unusual conversation took place, the breathing of the dying *tharlarion* became louder, more rapid, more labored, and more hideous. It was though it was building up to some point beyond which I knew not what might occur. I thought of the hand on a boiler's gauge jerking higher and higher, darting increment by darting increment.

"But now," said the hunter, "it seems you are out of business."

"How so?" asked Aesil.

"Three of your men are dead," said the hunter, "two by my hand and, I gather, from visiting your camp this morning, one by yours."

"There was a disagreement," said Aesil.

"A disagreement cut short by steel," said the hunter.

"As it happened," said Aesil.

"How will you fare now?" asked the hunter.

"I do not understand," said Aesil.

"You are now bereft of colleagues," said the hunter.

"Temporarily," said Aesil. "But after I slay you, I will go to Port Cos, where I can enrich myself by the sale of four *tharlarion*, each worth a dozen slaves, and seventeen slaves. After that it will be easy to recruit allies. I know taverns in Port Cos infested by eager, hungry urts, each ready to kill for a tarsk-bit."

The breathing of the stricken *tharlarion* became more and more disjointed and tumultuous.

"What is wrong with the *tharlarion*?" asked Aesil, stepping back.

"You know little of *tharlarion*," said the hunter.

"It is dying," said Aesil.

"Have you never seen a *tharlarion* die, not quickly, but as of illness?" asked the hunter.

"No," said Aesil, "only of a blow to the heart or throat, as by an ax or a planted, sharpened stake, or its having its throat torn out by another *tharlarion*."

"Wait," said the hunter. "The moment is near."

"Let us be done with this," said Aesil. "You have been outsmarted. You have lost. I have won. What you possess in persistence and courage you lack in cunning. The world belongs not only to the brave and tenacious but to the clever, as well." He then aimed the bow, with its set quarrel, at the heart of the hunter. He smiled. His finger tightened on the trigger of the weapon.

At that point the last throbbing of the beast's mighty heart denied death for the last time and the *tharlarion*, with a wild bellow struggled upright and then, an instant later, collapsed. dead.

In that wild moment the hunter, his leg freed, his face contorted with pain, scrambled limping to his feet, and lunged awkwardly toward Aesil, who, startled, frightened by the sudden unexpected, spasmodic movement of that enormous, scaled body, had stumbled back a pace, his weapon losing its alignment. Aesil quickly, desperately, regained his balance. But then, as he endeavored to swing the weapon back into play, the hunter, now before him, struck the bow up and away just as, with a sharp, humming snap, the quarrel sprang from the guide and disappeared somewhere in the grass. The hunter flung Aesil back into the grass and drew his sword. He waited for Aesil to regain his feet and draw his own sword, and then the two men faced each other, swords drawn, across three or four yards of grass.

"Why did you not attack while you had the chance?" asked Aesil.

"You were not ready," said the hunter.

"Again," said Aesil, "you are a fool."

"It is a foolishness I chose," said the hunter.

"You will discover I am not unskilled," said Aesil.

"There are tiers of skill," said the hunter. "Many are skilled at *kaissa*, and marvelously so, but few so much as Centius of Cos or Scormus of Ar."

"You limp, you are injured," said Aesil.

"Do not concern yourself," said the hunter.

"I shall not," said Aesil. "But it will lessen my sport."

I feared much for the hunter, for though I knew little of swordsmanship, I knew that one fights not only with the eye and arm, but with the entire body.

There was a sudden, sharp flash of steel.

Aesil drew back, turning white.

"You could have struck," he said.

"I did not choose to do so," said the hunter.

I could not see that there was any difference between their skills.

There was another brief exchange.

"You could have struck," said Aesil.

"I did not choose to do so," said the hunter.

Aesil backed away. He threw his sword into the grass. "Let me live," he said.

"You were a party to the slaying of sleeping men," said the hunter.

Aesil suddenly turned about and hurried toward the *tharlarion* from which he had dismounted some minutes earlier.

"Master," I cried. "Beware! Beware! There is another bow, another bolt or arrow!"

The slaves regarded me, startled.

I suddenly realized, to my horror, that, in the fear and agitation of the moment, I had cried out in English. I had shown myself a barbarian, though doubtless of a sort not clear to the others.

The hunter was hobbling after the running Aesil. My warning to him, as I now realize, would not only have been unintelligible to him, of course, but would have been unnecessary. Surely he would recollect better than anyone save perhaps Aesil himself that the bow which had fired the first quarrel, that which had resulted in the death of the hunter's *tharlarion*, would still be at Aesil's saddle where, doubtless, too, ammunition for it would be at hand.

The hunter, with his labored gait, was yards behind Aesil, who, reaching the *tharlarion* first, tore the bow from the saddle and seized a bolt. He then thrust his left foot into the bow stirrup, holding it to the ground. He was in the process of drawing the heavy, curved metal into place when the hunter was but feet away. Aesil looked up, wildly. He hurled the short, stubby bow at the hunter, who bent to evade the improvised missile. Aesil then ran into the encompassing field. I assumed that he was concerned only to effect an escape, but, a moment later, I realized his action had a deeper import. He was hurrying to that part of the field into which the quarrel loosed during his struggle with the hunter had disappeared. It was quite possible that that quarrel, like its fellow, was unusual, that it was coated, too, with a poison so deadly that its cost was measured not in copper but gold. If that were the case it might, handled or thrown, constitute a fearful weapon. If it could bring about the death of so large and powerful a beast as the hunter's *tharlarion* in a few minutes, its least scratch might kill a human in a much shorter time.

Aesil now began to search in the field, frantically, bending down, scratching, tearing up clots of grass.

The hunter mounted Aesil's *tharlarion* and guided it slowly toward where Aesil was rummaging through the grass. Aesil looked up from his knees at the towering weight of the ponderous beast in whose shadow he found himself.

"No!" he cried. "No! The blade! Let it be by steel!"

I, and the others, strung on our rope loop, our hands confined behind us, had followed the *tharlarion* now ridden by the hunter.

"No!" screamed Aesil. "No!"

The hunter urged the *tharlarion* forward.

I, and many others, looked away.

The hunter dismounted and examined the body. Then he turned to face us. "I would not dishonor my blade by staining it with the blood of an urt," he said.

He then looked about a bit, and then bent down. He lifted the quarrel from the grass. "He almost found it," he said. He then wiped the head of the bolt on the grass, ridding it of the pastelike substance with which it was coated. He then tossed the object away. "We can reach Sulport in less than five days," he said.

CHAPTER TWENTY-SEVEN

"*Ela*, fine ladies," he said, "we have no oils and cloths. But grass will do. And waste no time."

The hunter, or rider, as I shall revert to speaking of him, was in a pleasant mood. Instead of returning to the pens of Sulport with six captures, which would be remarkable in itself, he would, following the crossing of the Vosk, pass the gate with four *tharlarion*, three to the good, and seventeen slaves. He had also, I gathered, increased of late the weight of his purse. One does not leave silver and gold lying about in the deep grass. The trampled carcass of Aesil himself had contributed better than a gold stater of Brundisium and four silver tarsks to this cause.

"Wash away the sweat and grime," he said. "This is the clearest water this side of the Vosk. Sparkle, *kajirae*, sparkle. You will not see better until the slave pools of Sulport."

Supposedly we would reach the ferry station by noon tomorrow.

I, in my turn, at the edge of the cool, swift-flowing rivulet, was released from the common tether rope and my wrists were freed of the plain but sturdy slave bracelets which had confined them behind my back. Occasionally in the trek, to relieve aching muscles, the rider would march two or three of us at a time front-braceleted or even unbraceleted, then held only by a neck rope. Today, however, as we were only a day's trek to the Vosk, he was more attentive to our custody. Once the pen gates closed on us, we knew that opportunities for escape, if any of us were so foolish as to think of escape, were all but closed for us. We would be caged or chained; men would be about; walls would be high; gates would be watched or closed; we would be sold; we would have new collars, new Masters. I hoped for a good Master, one firm but kind, one who would treat the slave of me as it should be treated, as it wanted to be treated.

I seized up a handful of grass.

I stepped into the water, ankle deep.

I was miserable.

I had betrayed myself.

Days ago, crying out, I had revealed myself as a barbarian.

"At the ferry station," the rider said, raising his voice that all might hear, "you will receive tunics, light and brief though they may be."

"Thank you, Master!" cried several slaves.

"We do not want your appearance to scandalize the noble free women of Sulport," he said.

"No, Master!" responded several slaves.

I had not been clothed since I had been 'knife stripped' by the rider days ago, shortly after he had acquired me.

"And," said the rider, "let us pique the curiosity of the good fellows of Sulport. Let them visit the pens and exhibition cages if they wish to confirm their speculations."

There was laughter.

But I was in no mood for mirth, if mirth it was.

Since yesterday I had been sick with fear. My outburst, so natural and fluent, uttered in a language unintelligible to its auditors, had identified me as a barbarian. Fortunately, I had never, at least since Victoria Minor, weeks ago, pretended to be a native Gorean, then claiming I was from Market of Semris, so I did not fear being punished for an explicit falsehood. I had merely allowed others to assume that I was Gorean which, given my facility with the language, was a natural assumption. Surely I was under no obligation to disabuse others of mistaken assumptions, particularly if by so doing I would be likely to fare less well at the hands of sister slaves, who tend to be contemptuous of barbarians, or, worse, given what I knew and wished I did not know, place my life in jeopardy.

I was the only slave free at the moment. Those who had already bathed or were waiting to bathe were still back-braceleted, or back-thonged, with the rope loop threaded through their confined arms.

I waded further into the rivulet, bent down, splashed water about my body, and began using the grass to loosen the grime on my body, which I then began to rinse away.

I had detested the gross sack, or sacklike garment, the Lady Temione of Hammerfest had imposed on her field slaves. It was difficult to imagine a more unflattering garment. On the other hand, it was a garment. I would much have preferred, however, a more typical Gorean slave garment, one of the several sorts of brief tunics in which the charms of slaves were more than hinted at. I had heard of ta-teeras and camisks but had never seen one, let alone been placed in one. Gamenture is interesting in its meanings and suggestions. Obviously there is a world of difference between the free woman's colorful and abundant 'robes of concealment' and the slave's tunic. So, too, there is a world of difference between the gray smock of the toiling Metal Worker, the white and yellow robe of the negotiating Merchant, and the flowing scarlet parade cape of the Warrior. Also, the same garmenture can have quite different effects on different occupants. A free woman might find herself wholly at ease in given robes whereas a slave, forced against her will to don such robes, might tremble in terror, knowing not only that they are not for her, that she does not belong in them, for they are for the free, but that she could be punished terribly if found in them. Similarly, a free woman forced to don a slave garment might collapse, swooning or weeping in shame, whereas a slave, happy in her health and beauty, and reveling in her desirability, might wear the same garment brazenly and delightedly.

I turned about in the water, now to my knees, and looked back, toward the others. The *tharlarion* were quiescent, in their sleep position, tethered; the slaves were sitting on the grass, chatting, some bathed and others waiting; and the rider was busied, his back to me, reordering the items in a pack. I backed through the water, approaching the farther side of the rivulet. I was happy to know that at the ferry point the slaves would be clothed, even if slave clad. I envied them. I, too, would much want a garment, even so slight and degrading a garment. But at the ferry point there would be too many men; we would be too carefully watched; we would be herded together, and boarded so, and, across the river, would be the slave pens of Sulport. I must escape this group, where I had foolishly, inadvertently, revealed my barbarous origin. I had no hope of remaining indefinitely free, naked, branded, and collared, but that was not necessary. I needed only be free long enough to fall in with different Masters, where, I was sure, I could easily, uncritically, be taken for a fugitive Gorean girl. I would then be safe. I did not think that the rider, this close to Sulport, would wish to abandon his trove to the risks of the open grassland while pursuing a single slave and perhaps the least of his herd.

I continued to back through the water until I felt the silt of the farther shore beneath my feet.

No one was watching me.

No one noticed me.

I was rested and well fed.

I turned about, and fled away.

CHAPTER TWENTY-EIGHT

By now I was at least an hour's distance from the rider's camp.

I was pleased.

The first hour would have been the most hazardous, when I, still close to the rider's camp, might have been most promptly and conveniently recovered.

I was sure I had adjudged a certain matter correctly. He would not wish to risk the *tharlarion* and the other slaves falling into other hands.

Accordingly he would refrain from following me, presumably the most negligible of his charges.

It was only necessary now to see to it that I, seemingly inadvertently, cross the path of some other group. This close to Sulport, a day's trek or so, I was sure that would be possible. If necessary, I need only approach the river, near which there would be numerous settlements. It had been my good fortune that the rider had been so intently occupied that he had not noticed my departure.

I continued on, wading through the grass.

I recalled Earth, with its hatreds and divisions, its lies and competitions, its poisons and pollutions. I wondered if it were not, in some deep sense, far more of a barbarity than fresh, green, honest Gor. Perhaps I had come from a more barbarous world than I had realized, one far more barbarous than I had understood and far more barbarous than many Goreans suspected.

But were there not always worlds and worlds within worlds?

Consider a towering world of glass and steel, harboring citadels of finance and bastions of industry. Is it the same world as that of the fishing village, the mountain retreat, the crowded slum? My world, an academic, scholarly world, as I had now come to realize, was an incredibly naive world, a world in which ideas were substituted for realities, a world in which lovely abstractions replaced facts, a world of theories anchored not in truth but in unquestioned fantasies. Did not these children of the universities, who inhabited one school after another, who had been sheltered in, and protected by, one school after another, who had never been out of a school, and knew nothing of the real world and the true nature of living men, ambitious, possessive, hungry, determined, competitive, and grasping, blithely impose their fictions and simplicities on one generation of students after another, sending them forth like dazzled lambs into a world of wolves and lions, a world in which, to ascend and thrive, they, too, their fantasies quickly disabused, must become a wolf or lion?

I saw a rider far off, before me.

Should I approach him, calling myself to his attention, lest he overlook me, or follow him so that I might, when I chose, eventually surrender to his rope or chain, or should I allow myself to be seen, and then, as though startled or dismayed, feign flight, which would doubtless encourage him to my pursuit?

From far off, behind me, I heard, faintly, a tinkling of bells. I looked back and saw a small caravan, of some three wagons, drawn by quadrupedalian *tharlarion*, and two outriders mounted on bipedalian *tharlarion*.

As the caravan, as far as I knew, might harbor one or more free women, I decided I would cast my lot with the male. As a slave, even before I had had much contact with them, I very much feared free women. Certainly I had heard dreadful stories about them and their hatred for female slaves. The only free woman with whom I had had personal contact, at least of a sort, had been the Lady Temione of Hammerfest.

I stood up, straight, and lifted my arm, waving, smiling, to the rider before me, some one hundred and fifty yards away. As I walked toward him, he guided his *tharlarion* toward me. I had walked only a few more yards when I stopped, apprehensive. The *tharlarion* continued to move toward me with a slow, stately gait. As it approached, I became more and more frightened. I was then, suddenly, sure. I looked wildly back, behind me, at the caravan. Then I looked forward, again. The rider who was approaching did not call out to me, or give any sign that he recognized me. But I recognized him, and I had no doubt that he recognized me. It was the rider from whose camp I had recently fled. He had circled about, so that, if I ran, I would be running back, toward his camp.

With my outburst, earlier, days ago, I had given my barbarous origin away.

Even the slaves in his camp knew that.

Strangers, on the other hand, would doubtless take me for Gorean.

My origin then could remain concealed.

I would then be safe once more.

I spun about, and, wildly, frenziedly, raced toward the small caravan. The rider did not own me. If anyone owned me, it would be the port of Hammerfest, which had, I surmised, confiscated the lands and chattels of the Lady Temione of Hammerfest. I must try to reach the caravan or one of its outriders before the rider could take me into custody. If I could manage to do so, he would be deprived of his capture right. That right would accrue to any free person into whose keeping I might first come.

The rider, behind me, uttered a cry, but it was not a cry of anger or surprise, or warning; rather it seemed more like a cry of satisfaction, even elation.

I sped through the grass, toward the wagons, and the outriders, now before me.

I heard the grunt of the *tharlarion* behind me, doubtless urged to speed.

I knew I could not outrun the *tharlarion*. In a single bounding stride it could cover twenty to thirty feet.

I heard its bellow behind me, and then a succession of staccato hissing gasps, coming closer and closer.

I could also hear the impact of those two gigantic, clawed feet slashing, trampling, through the grass, pounding the earth.

The two outriders had arrested their mounts, and even the small caravan had paused.

Why had the two outriders not rushed toward me?

They sat still on their mounts.

The *tharlarion* was coming up behind me on my left. Of course, for the rider, as most humans, was right-handed!

The turf was torn, the ground pounded.

The breathing of the *tharlarion* was loud and ghastly.

Then, suddenly, I threw myself to the grass, and I was aware of the roped and weighted net flashing past me and striking the grass.

"Excellent!" cried the rider. "You are not as stupid as I feared."

The net was attached to a long cord, and the rider immediately began to haul the net back to his grasp.

I sprang to my feet, cast a wild look at my goal, the wagons and outriders, and then sped again toward them.

But a moment later the rider, his net again in hand, placed his mount between me and my goal. I then stood, quietly, gasping, tensely, in the grass. I then, giving no warning, fled suddenly to the left side of the *tharlarion*. It is quite possible to cast the net overhand across the saddle, but this gives the quarry an extra fraction of a second to see it and avoid its clutches. Also, it is difficult to net a quarry when it understands the net, is several feet away, and is watching. The net spun toward me. I evaded it. "Good," he said. "Well done." He drew in the net again. I threw another glance toward the wagons and the two outriders. They were passive, but attentive. I dashed toward them but was again cut off by the bulk of the *tharlarion*. "You are quick," said the rider, "but the *tharlarion* is quicker." I backed away. The rider spread the net and swung it loosely. To my dismay he urged the *tharlarion* closer. This would give me less time to evade the net. I must thus, at so close a distance, to avoid the net, anticipate the cast. The net flashed toward me, like a small cloud of hemp and iron, but I evaded it, leaping to my right. "Marvelous!" said the rider, drawing in the net. "You are a clever little beast. Look, the audience applauds." I looked quickly, wildly, toward the outriders, both of whom were gently, respectfully, striking their left shoulders with the palm of their right hand. "However, you should not have taken your eye off me, however briefly," said the rider. "You will note that I chose to refrain from taking advantage of your error. Too, I might have been lying. You should not overlook such a possibility." I cried out in exasperation, turned about, and began to flee about the side of the *tharlarion* toward the wagons and outriders, but, to my misery, I slipped and sprawled to the grass. The *tharlarion* and its rider loomed over me. I would not have time to rise to my feet. I was caught! I sobbed. "Get up," said the rider. I rose unsteadily to my feet, tottering in the grass. "Which way will you dart this time?" asked the rider. I had darted to my right a moment ago. I became confused. What should I do? Did that not depend on what he expected me to do? But what would he expect me to do?

Situations of this sort can lead to labyrinths of reasoning. Two can match wits, back and forth, between this and that, from A to B, from B to A, and from A back to B, and so on, leading, so to speak, from decimal point to decimal point, from complexity to ever greater complexity, each trying to outguess the other. Some individuals are much better than others at this sort of thing, winning drinks or coins from others, or, in some instances, living or dying.

I sprang to my right, and the weighted net spun about me, encumbering my arms and legs, and I fell, tangled, distraught, netted, into the grass. I struggled, unavailingly. The rider clambered down the mounting ladder, a bit awkwardly, from his injury of some days ago, and wound the net cunningly, tightly, about my upper body and, with the weights, fastened it shut, holding my arms to my sides.

He then looked down on me, netted, helpless at his feet.

"You did quite well," he said. "I had thought you might. You seem intelligent though it is stupid to run, as there is no escape for such as you. But you must have had some good reason, or you thought so, to do anything so absurd."

I squirmed a little in the net at his feet, miserable.

"Be careful," he said, "lest you excite me, or others."

I lay still.

I then became aware, looking up, that the two outriders had now brought their mounts close.

"Are you going to cut the tendons behind her knees?" asked one.

"It is difficult for a slave to dance when so crippled," said the rider.

I knew little or nothing of slave dance, save that it could drive a man wild with desire. No wonder it was eschewed, even denounced, by free women.

"She runs cleverly," said the other. "You should enter her in the contests."

"I thought she might," said the rider. "But when I first apprehended her, days ago, she did not run. It was a great disappointment to me. She cost me the sport of the catch. This morning I removed her constraints, the bracelets and tether rope, supposedly that she could wash her body, and then pretended to busy myself about the camp, to tempt her to flee, of which temptation she, however foolishly, availed herself."

I was not pleased to hear this.

Things had transpired as he had wished.

I felt foolish.

"As you arranged matters," said the first outrider, "perhaps she need not be lashed severely."

"But she did run," said the rider.

"That is true," said the first outrider.

The two outriders then turned their *tharlarion* about and withdrew.

"May I speak?" I asked.

"Certainly," said the rider. "You were given that standing permission days ago."

"The men did not challenge you for me," I said. "Am I so unattractive?"

"Why should they have done so?" he asked. "To do so, in this situation, after my free catch, would not have been honorable."

"I did not think you would follow me," I said.

"Why is that?" I asked.

"You placed three *tharlarion* and sixteen slaves at risk of appropriation," I said. "They were left undefended in the grasslands. Am I so attractive to you that you would risk such treasures merely to return me to your rope?"

"They were in little danger," he said. "The *tharlarion* were tethered, the slaves were in constraints and linked together. What would they do? Where would they go? It is unpleasant to starve. And few hunters would be incapable of following a trail of sixteen coffled slaves."

"They could be stolen," I said.

"We are near Sulport, in civil lands," he said. "And do not judge all Goreans by killers and thieves. No society can exist if its population is not overwhelmingly attentive to the protocols of decency and respect."

"Still," I said.

"There was little risk," he said, "particularly as I knew I could bring you in in an Ahn or so."

"You wanted to hunt me," I said.

"Yes," he said. "You once denied me that pleasure."

"One which you have now obtained," I said.

"Gratifyingly so," he said.

"Do you find me attractive?" I asked.

"Of course," he said. "You are slave beautiful. That makes the catch even more pleasant. Lie still."

"You outthought me," I said.

"How so?" he asked.

"How did you know I would spring to the right again?" I asked.

"I did not know," he said.

"You guessed?" I said.

"No," he said.

"I do not understand," I said.

"The human tends to be a creature of pattern," he said. "Thus, if one can detect his pattern, it is possible to anticipate his actions, and act accordingly."

"I did not know I had a pattern," I said.

"Such things are subtle," he said, "and often obscure or even undiscernible to the person himself."

"And you detected my pattern?" I said.

"Not at all," he said.

"Master?" I said.

"It is impossible to detect a pattern, yours or mine," he said, "if there is no pattern."

"I do not understand," I said.

"Let chance rule," he said. "Cast the marked stones. Let them have their say."

I looked up at him, puzzled. I was on my back. The net was fastened tight about my upper body.

"Look for something external, over which you have no control," he said. "I looked upward, north or south, or east or west. If I saw a bird, I would cast the net to the right; if I saw no bird, I would cast the net to the left. In this way, chance directed my action."

"You saw a bird," I said.

"And so cast the net to the right," he said.

"Then it was a matter of chance that you won," I said.

"Yes," he said. "But the point is that you could not detect a pattern and use it to outguess me, for I had no pattern. Recourse to such things is useful in scheduling patrols and reconnaissances, in minimizing the dangers of overhunting or underhunting herd animals, and so on."

He then lifted me to my feet and, with a generous length of the long cord attached to the net, that by means of which he could retrieve it, fastened me to his stirrup. My tether was then some eight or ten feet in length.

He mounted to the saddle of the *tharlarion*.

"We will now return to camp," he said.

The *tharlarion* turned about and began to move west. It moved with a slow, ponderous, stately gait. I, on my tether, could match its pace. I knew he could make the return to the camp a misery for me, but he did not do so, or, at least, not yet. I felt foolish, chagrined, on the tether. I had not only failed to escape, but had been unable to elude capture for even a full day. How amused, how scornful, would be the other slaves to see me, a barbarian, returned so promptly, so easily, to the common rope.

Is that not what one would expect in the case of a foolish, hapless barbarian?

"You seem despondent," said the rider.

"I am caught," I said. "I am helpless. I am on a rope."

"Surely you did not expect to escape," he said.

"I hoped to escape you," I said, "and then, after a time, to fall to some eventual other."

"I gave you a good start," he said.

"You wanted me loose to hunt me," I said, "for your sport. It was a game!"

We continued on.

"I am not a toy!" I said bitterly.

"You are mistaken," he said. "You are a toy, a beast, an object, a property. As you are a slave girl, you are all of these things, or whatever a Master wishes. Get it through your lovely head that you are owned, owned like a goblet or boot. I do not know who or what you were in the past but now you are goods, well-curved, delicious goods, exciting, attractive goods, to be bought and sold, to be bartered, to be exchanged or given away, and as what you are, goods and only goods, goods to be done with as Masters might please."

I cried out in anguish.

"You are a lying little hypocrite," he said.

"Master?" I said.

"Do you not know yourself?" he asked.

I looked at him, wildly, tears in my eyes, in his net, on his rope.

"You are a natural slave," he said. "One need only look upon you to see that. You are a slave in every drop of your blood, in every fiber of your being."

"Surely not, Master!" I said.

"You are a slave and you want to be a slave," he said.

I put down my head.

Were these ruminations not reminiscent of the wars I had fought with myself for years, fighting to remain bound by prescribed conventions, trying to remain held within invisible chains forged by an unnatural culture, struggling to remain true to views of me which were alien to my deepest, most real self? Then, on Gor, I had been freed to accept myself as what I was and had always wanted to be. But that is one thing. It is quite another to admit publicly what I had discovered to be true privately. Gor had released my slave and would see to it that it was treated as it should be treated. Behaving as a slave I had become the slave I wanted to be. Now when I knelt before a man I was not acting as a slave, but was a slave. But it was another thing to acknowledge my inner reality explicitly, openly.

"Would you care to acknowledge yourself a natural slave, freely and openly?" asked the rider.

"Certainly not," I said.

We continued on.

"Master," I said.

"Yes," he said.

"I acknowledge myself a natural slave, freely and openly," I said.

"Do you not feel better now?" he asked.

"Yes, Master," I said.

I suddenly felt as though I had discarded a weight, cast away an onerous burden, as though I was suddenly, marvelously, free.

I found myself excited and thrilled to be a slave. I welcomed being goods.

Too, how simple and real everything then became! I now knew how to speak and act. I now knew what to do, and how to behave. At last I had an identity, one well defined, socially and culturally.

But, in a sense, what did my feelings matter, one way or the other? I was marked and collared. I was at the mercy of the free. Even so simple a thing as to whether or not I would be clothed was up to the free.

I wanted no choice.

But, even had I wanted a choice, I knew I had no choice. I was a slave.

"Slave," said the rider, "should I increase the pace of the *tharlarion*?"

"Please do not, Master!" I begged. I knew the rider had hitherto been kind. On the other hand, if he should urge the *tharlarion* to speed, I could run only so far or so fast, and would then lose my footing and be dragged through the grass.

After something like an hour, the rider halted the *tharlarion*. "Beyond the next rise," he said, "is the camp."

"I dread being returned to it," I said.

"The views of the other slaves?" he said.

"Yes," I said.

"You will not be long exposed to their contempt and ridicule," he said. "By noon tomorrow, we will reach the ferry station and cross the river to Sulport. Things will then be much easier for you."

"Am I so unattractive?" I asked.

"I do not understand," he said.

"You caught me, fairly," I said. "Is there no prize for you in your game? Am I not to be put to use? Am I not the defeated, who must now be summarily taught her foolishness, her futility and negligibility?"

"I will collect my winnings later," he said.

"I long for the arms of a Master," I said.

"In a few days," he said, "you will doubtless be marketed, presumably after your hands are softened, after they prove other than those of a field slave."

I moaned, softly.

"You flame?" he asked.

I was surprised that he had heard me. He must have keen hearing.

"Each day more," I said.

"So," he said, "our small catch is slave-girl hot?"

"Yes, Master," I said. As the slave is not a free woman, she may speak openly of such matters. It is, I suppose, a privilege of the collar.

"If you scream your need like the kenneled girls awaiting their sale," he said, "I will beat you."

"Yes, Master," I said. "Forgive me, Master."

Once our slave fires have been kindled, once we are so fiercely tormented by our raging needs, as Masters will have it, how much then we are helplessly owned by men!

We need their touch. We will crawl, and whine, and beg for it. We have been given no choice. We are needful slaves.

"We shall now return to camp," he said. "Prepare."

"Master?" I asked.

How was I to prepare?

From his high saddle on the *tharlarion* I do not doubt but what he could see over the rise and peruse the camp.

He suddenly urged the *tharlarion* ahead and I was jerked off my feet, and was being dragged helplessly through the grass. In a moment he had surmounted the rise and was plunging down the incline toward the camp. A moment later the *tharlarion* was splashing through the small rivulet in which I and others had bathed, I dragged behind him, choking and sputtering, on the net rope through the water, reeds, and mud. Then I was drawn to the center of the camp and the rider dismounted, freed the net rope from the stirrup, pulled me to my feet by the hair, and exhibited me, bedraggled, muddy, soaked, fatigued, frightened, unsteady, my hair tangled and sopped, turning me about, to the other slaves. There was much laughter and jeering. "What a stupid slave! What a silly slave!" called slaves. "Were you a *pasang* out of your rope," called one, "or just a half of a *pasang*?" "Beat her, Master," called another. "Lash her to the bone!"

"Are you hungry?" called the rider to the slaves.

"Yes, Master!" called several of the slaves, and I was no longer an object of interest to them.

"When I have tended to the *tharlarion*," he said.

The rider drew me to the edge of the camp, put me to my back on the grass, and, with the net rope, crossed my ankles and tied them together. He then returned to the main part of the camp to see to his mount and the slaves.

I lay alone, abandoned, my ankles tied together. I could not rise to my feet. I mused on how easily, and so simply, a girl can be subdued and bound, the binding of her ankles rendering her so helpless.

I listened to the laughter and chatting of the slaves as they were fed.

I, too, was hungry.

I was weary, muchly worn by my attempt to escape, my capture, and the return to the camp.

It grew late.

The Yellow Moon was in the sky.

I fell asleep and dreamed that my ankles were unbound and that I found myself somehow in a crowded, lamplit tavern, and that a whip was pressed to my lips, which whip I fearfully kissed and licked, a whip to which I knew I must soon dance. And then I rose to my feet before the men. I was terrified. I knew nothing of the whip dances of Gor. The whip snapped, and I danced. Then the men, aroused and eager, swarmed about me, and made of me a vessel on which they slaked their lust, and I moaned, ravished and grateful.

I awakened, suddenly, in the darkness in the grass, to my ankles being unbound.

I threw them apart.

"Slave," said the rider, scornfully.

"Yes," Master," I said. "I am not a free woman. I may be as I want to be, the slave I am."

"Close your legs," he said. "And get to your knees."

"Yes, Master," I said.

I looked at him, in the light of the Yellow Moon.

"Use me," I begged.

He put a bowl of gruel on the grass.

"Please," I said.

"Feed," he said.

I struggled, as I could, in the reticulated cords which swathed my upper body. "The net," I protested.

He put his hand in my hair and forced my face down to the bowl, and then thrust my face into the gruel.

I had dallied.

He then released my hair and I lifted my head from the bowl.

"Forgive me, Master," I said.

I then put my head down again and, biting and lapping at the gruel, fed.

When I had finished, he wiped the gruel from my face, and thrust me, kneeling, a yard or so from him.

I did not think he bore me rancor.

"Master?" I said.

"Perhaps later," he said, sitting cross-legged.

A soft moan escaped me.

"You are a hot little pudding are you not?" he asked.

"I am needful," I said. "Men have made me so. I cannot help it."

"Nor do you wish to do so," he said.

"No, Master," I said.

"I find you of interest," he said. "I wish to speak to you."

"As I am," I asked, "naked, kneeling, and helpless?"

"Yes," he said, "such things make the conversation more pleasant."

"I ran away," I said. "Am I to be lashed?"

"No," he said, "nor starved, close-chained, nor crippled. You did precisely what I wanted you to do, attempt to elude me."

"I failed to do so," I said.

"I think you are highly intelligent," he said.

"I, a mere slave, intelligent?" I asked.

"Certainly," he said. "Do you think the intelligence of a woman changes when she is collared and thrown to a man's feet where she belongs?"

"No, Master," I said.

"It is pleasant to take a highly intelligent woman," he said, "and teach her the slave she is."

"We cannot help that we are women," I said.

"But I do not understand you," he said. "If you are so intelligent, why were you so stupid as to run? Do you think you can outrun your brand and collar?"

"I had a reason," I said, "one sufficient, in my mind, to justify the risks."

"It must be a weighty reason indeed," he said, "for you to risk the lash, even crippling."

"It has to do with my origin," I said.

"That you are a barbarian?" he asked.

"Yes," I said. "I endeavored to conceal that fact, but I gave myself away when I cried out, in a language alien to you, to warn you that your enemy had a second bow."

"In conditions of emergency or stress," he said, "it is not unusual for one to revert to a first language. I could not understand your words, but your intent was clearly to call something to my attention, to alert me or warn me, or such. But I would be mad to find anything reprehensible in that. I gather you wished to conceal your barbarous origin in order not to be scorned or abused by your fellow slaves."

"Partly," I said.

"I knew you were a barbarian before," he said.

"Master?" I said.

"From subtleties in your speech," he said.

"Many cannot tell," I said.

"Apparently not," he said. I was unsettled by his asseveration. I knew that Calla had recognized that I was not natively Gorean. I trusted that few could tell. "Do not be so concerned about the matter," he said. "One encounters barbarians on Gor. Some rich men collect them. They add variety to a pleasure garden. And do not worry so much about your sister slaves. They will have their sport, spoil your gruel, hide your blanket, tell their jokes, ventilate their jealousies and annoyances, for a time, but, a bit later, they will see you as no more than another collar sister, one who will sell for a little more or a little less than themselves."

"There is more," I said. "There are those who search for a particular barbarian, to do away with her, and, as barbarians are rare, I fear they will take me as that barbarian."

"Thus, you fled," he said.

"Yes, Master," I said.

"Your secret, if it is a secret," he said, "is safe with me."

"Thank you, Master," I whispered, relievedly, deeply grateful.

"Several slaves will be penned in Sulport," he said. "You will be unimportant amongst them."

"A girl is pleased," I said.

"As you know," he said, "the lands and properties of the Lady

Temione of Hammerfest were confiscated by Gordon, Administrator of Hammerfest, in the name of the High Council of Hammerfest."

"Yes, Master," I said.

"What you are unlikely to know," he said, "is that Hammerfest has contracted with the house of Ho-Turik, a major slave house, to handle the sales of the slaves of the former Lady Temione of Hammerfest."

"I did not know that," I said. I had heard of the house of Ho-Turik. I supposed that it made sense to market the Lady Temione's slaves through an agent or dealer. A river port such as Hammerfest would be unlikely to do that directly.

"The sales will probably take place east on the river, upriver, in Victoria," he said. "Prices tend to be higher in Victoria. It is the major market on the river. Buyers come from all over Gor to buy there. In the press, the crowdings, and transactions, there will be few, if any, who would know you are a barbarian or care whether or not you are. There, I suspect, you can easily pass as Gorean, and will be safe from whatever dangers might concern you."

"A slave is grateful, Master," I said.

"Let us speak no further of this," he said. "I suspect that the less I know of the matter the better it will be for the both of us."

"We should be at the ferry station by noon tomorrow?" I asked.

"Easily," he said.

I was pleased.

I would be safe.

"Gor is beautiful," I said.

"Are not all worlds beautiful?" he asked.

"Some more so than others," I said.

"You ran well," he said.

"But I was well netted," I said.

"Sooner or later," he said, "they all are. It is just a matter of time. There is no escape from the net."

"Master did not use the 'capture whip,'" I said.

"Not from the saddle," he said.

"I understand that the slaves will receive tunics at the ferry station."

"Yes," he said.

"I hope that I, too, may be so fortunate, so privileged," I said.

"Is that important to you?" he asked.

"Very much so," I said.

"That is interesting," he said, "slaves, and clothing. Did you know that many slaves do not care to be naked in public?"

"I am not surprised," I said.

"But they are slaves, beasts," he said.

"Even so," I said.

"What difference could it make?" he asked.

"I assure, Master," I said, "it can make a difference."

"I acknowledge," he said, "that tunics can be attractive on a slave."

"Very much so," I said.

Men found them exciting on a woman, and not simply, I suspected, because they left little of an occupant's charms to the imagination, but, also, because of their meaning. The woman so exhibited was, legally, a domestic animal, a property, something vendible, something purchasable. Are not such garments made to be removed?

It might be noted, in passing, that, aside from the obvious contrast between the garmenture of the free woman and that of the slave, there are also contrasts within the garmenture of free women and within the garmenture of slaves. The robes of a rich man's daughter and those of a poor man's daughter are not likely to be identical, nor is the tunic of a rich man's slave likely to be confused with that of a poor man's property.

There is clearly a sociology of garmenture, as there is of wearing the hair, the mode of speech, and so on.

I suspect that the vanity of women is greater, if possible, than that of men.

The normal, healthy woman desires to be attractive to men. Biology has seen to that. And there are diverse ways of being attractive. The free woman is not unaware of the enhancing effects of her veils and robes, in their arrangements, colors, and textures, and the slave is more than aware of the material, length, and cut of her tunic.

I longed for a tunic, or such, as slight as such a garment might be, not only for its token of covering my body, but because I was well aware of its effect on men, and how exciting it made me look and feel.

I struggled a bit in the net wound about my upper body.

"She-*sleen*," he said.

"I am needful," I said.

"You beg to be put to use?" he asked.

"Yes, Master," I said. "Very much so, Master."

I squirmed in the net, I fear, piteously. My needs were much on me.

"I shall think about satisfying your needs," he said. "If I decide not to do so, you will remain needful."

"You would so torture me?" I said.

"If it pleases me," he said, "slave."

"Master," I said.

"Yes?" he said.

"If you touch me, and bring me bit by bit, relentlessly, to the helpless brink of my earthquake and explosion, please, please, do not stop. Be kind. Let me explode. I beg it so!"

"I will do what I please," he said. "And you will accept it, and endure it, slave."

"Yes, Master," I said. "Please, please, Master!"

"Remember, you are in a collar," he said.

"Yes, Master," I said.

"I think I will have you," he said.

"But I am netted," I said. "I am helpless."

"That makes no difference," he said.

CHAPTER TWENTY-NINE

"You cannot do this to me!" she cried. "I am the Lady Temione of Hammerfest!"

"You are a nameless slut of a slave," said the attendant. "You do not even have a name. But perhaps a Master will one day give you one."

"I am the Mistress of estates, the owner of over a thousand slaves!"

"You do not even own the collar locked on your neck," said the attendant.

"Clothe me!" she demanded.

"Perhaps someday someone may do so," he said, "if you behave suitably, if you are sufficiently pleasing."

"Give me back even that tiny, shameful tunic," she cried.

"So now," said another attendant, "you want it?"

"Yes!"

"Do you beg it?" asked the other attendant.

"Yes," she wept. "Yes!"

Her plea was met with derision.

"Where are you taking me?" she wept.

"To your sale," said an attendant.

"I cannot be sold," she said. "I am a free woman!"

"Tell it to the brand on your thigh, the collar on your neck."

"You cannot show me to men like this!" she cried.

"Few men buy slaves clothed," said an attendant.

"None in his right mind," said another.

"What do you think she will bring?" asked an attendant.

"The blond hair, the blue eyes, are interesting, the figure is superb," said one of the men, "perhaps three silver tarsks."

"I am free! I cannot be sold," she cried.

"I wonder if so much," said another.

"Come along," said an attendant.

"Take your hands off me!" she cried.

"Put her in leading position," said one of the men.

"Do not dare!" she cried. "I am free! I am not a slave! I do not even like men!"

"That is of no interest," said a man. "They will use you for their pleasure as often as they wish and however they wish."

"You will learn to crawl to them on your belly and lick their feet," said another.

"Never, never!" she cried.

"Be silent, collar slut," said the attendant.

"What is going on here," asked a male voice, which bore a natural tone of authority.

"An unruly slave," said an attendant. "I fear she may disturb the others."

I and others were standing in the corridor leading to the auditorium, our right shoulders to the wall. In the same line stood Luta, whom I knew from the great pen in Victoria Minor, the lesser Victoria, and the former Eileen Bennett, who must now answer to her only name, 'Xanthe,' whom I had known from the observatory on Earth, where she had served as the observatory librarian. The farther exit of this corridor, as I understood it, led to an area at the foot of the sales block. I could hear, at intervals, the ringing of the bell which announced that one sale was concluded and that another might begin.

I was supposed to be pleased, for having the honor of being sold in Victoria. I was pleased, of course, but not for the esteemed honor of being sold in Victoria, but, rather, because, as I understood it, buyers often came from far away to purchase in Victoria, and I hoped I might be purchased by someone who would take me far from the river, far the former estates of the Lady Temione, far from a prowling beast, and so on. Too, I had never lost my hope that I might one day see and serve in one of Gor's tower cities.

How lovely that would be!

What more could a slave desire?

He who had recently arrived and whose voice held that ring of authority regarded the former Lady Temione of Hammerfest, openly and appraisingly, as one might look on a slave.

How outraged, and furious, she was!

"Have you something to say?" he asked.

"Yes!" she cried.

"It is appropriate for one such as you," he said, "to address a free man from her knees."

"I am free!" she said.

"Get on your knees," he said, sharply.

The former Lady Temione, suddenly frightened, went to her knees.

"I am free!" he said.

"Then why are you on your knees?" he asked.

She went to rise.

"Stay on our knees, slave," he snapped.

Quickly she returned to her knees, looking up at his stern visage.

"You may now ask for forgiveness," he said.

"I ask for forgiveness," she said.

When a woman is naked and on her knees before a fully clothed man it is difficult for her to be anything but a naked woman on her knees before a fully clothed man.

It is certainly hard to conduct a conversation on an equal level.

"Yes?" he said.

She dared not meet his eyes, those of a Master. His gaze might have melted steel.

"I beg for forgiveness," she said, "—Master."

"You will be quickly taught that you are a slave," he said.

"Yes, Master," she whispered.

"At the least indication of recalcitrance or resistance," he said, to the attendants, "she is to be lashed."

"But before her sale?" asked an attendant.

"Yes," said the newcomer, and then continued on his way.

"Get up, slave," said one of the attendants.

The former Lady Temione of Hammerfest rose to her feet. She was thrust into line before me.

I heard a bell ring; another sale had been concluded.

We all shuffled ahead a pace or so.

She tried to cover the collar before her by her hair, as though that would make it go away, but that, of course, only made it more obvious behind her.

She wore a Victoria sales collar, as did the rest of us. Our former collars, many of those being the collar of the Lady Temione of Hammerfest, had been removed from our necks after the Victoria sales collar had been fastened on us. In this way there was no moment in which at least one collar was not on us.

My hands were now much less roughened than hitherto. This was due to time and the soothing lotions with which they had been treated by certain members of the Green Caste, that of the Physicians, those who specialized in the care of animals.

I heard the bell ring again, and again we moved a bit forward, toward the door at the end of the hall.

I had been sold, at least knowingly, twice before, once from an open-air, crossroads market, and once later by the alighting tarnsman in a field near the Vosk. I did not know my original point of arrival on Gor nor the exact location, a few days later, of my first sale at the crossroads market. At the time of my first sale, at least of those known to me, I had been taught only a few words of Gorean, mainly, I suspect, to help me understand what was wanted of me and to avoid the whip. I had been sold, I later learned, for sixty copper tarsks, plus twenty tarsk-bits, Brundisium. I did not, at the time, understand the monetary values involved. I later learned that the sum was a modest one. At that time, of course, I knew little Gorean. My vanity, at any rate, welcomes such an assuagement. My second sale, at least of those that I knew of, was that of the alighting tarnsman, for eighty copper tarsks.

Monetary values, markets, and such, differ considerably with location and time. I learned that in most localities there were four to eight tarsk-bits to a copper tarsk, and the copper tarsk might be literally divided in accordance with this ratio. In Brundisium, on the other hand, there were one hundred tarsk-bits to a copper tarsk, probably to facilitate commerce in a large, commercial port. As nearly as I can tell, Goreans use a base-ten mathematics, this presumably reflecting an Earth origin, if not one of an original anatomical convenience. It is not unusual in markets to see scales being used to weigh coins. Some coins have been shaved and occasionally there is a suspicion that a currency may have been debased. Much commerce on Gor, particularly outside the cities and towns, is done with barter. I have heard that some peasants in remote areas keep a coin or two on hand to show children how foolish are the populations of cities and towns. What peasant would be so stupid as to trade a *verr*, or *bosk*, or even a *vulo* for a tiny, inedible disk of metal?

I have wondered, sometimes, if Drs. Jameson, Archer, and Townsend sold me to Gorean slavers, or just delivered me to them. I suspect the latter. If they sold me to them, which they might have done as an amusement, would they have, say, done so for a tarsk-bit? Would that not have pleased them, to sell the prim, arch, lithe, svelte, intellectual Miss Agnes Morrison Atherton to Gorean slavers for a tarsk-bit, which they might then keep in a drawer, to look at occasionally? And might they not have parted similarly with the luscious, attractive Miss Eileen Bennett? Perhaps there was more than one tarsk-bit in that drawer.

Did we mean so little to them? Were we worth so little to them?

But, of course, for we were to be slaves.

On Gor I had learned much more about men than I had dreamed of on Earth. I now understood how men, strong, ambitious, aggressive, healthy, virile men looked at women.

They saw us as objects of desire, as things to seize with joy, as things to possess and put through our paces, as things to own and master.

I now had no doubt that Drs. Jameson, Archer, and Townsend had studied me and Miss Bennett, how we carried ourselves, and moved, and spoke, and considered our possible dispositions. Were we not, as they saw us, walking and moving before them, slaves? Did they not see us, beneath our clothes, barefoot, and in tunics and collars? Did they not think of us as kneeling before them, owned?

Again the bell rang and we moved forward.

"Up the stairs, slave," said an attendant to the former Lady Temione of Hammerfest, at the foot of the huge sales block, its surface some ten feet above us.

"No, no, no," she wept, sinking to her knees.

How small and piteous now seemed the former Lady Temione of Hammerfest, once so haughty and arrogant, once so regal and commanding, once so severe and formidable a free woman of Gor, now on her knees, weeping and shuddering, at the foot of the stairs.

"No, no!" she sobbed.

Then she cried out in pain as the attendant put his hand in her hair and dragged her behind him up the stairs.

Then she was thrust to the surface of the torchlit block. The attendant then returned downstairs to where I and two others awaited our turn to be exhibited to the crowd. "Tenalian of Ar," he said to his fellow near us, "is in the house."

"He buys once a year in Victoria," said the other. At the time I did not know who this was. Had I known, how my heart would have leaped, how I would have hoped! On the block were two men, prominently the auctioneer and, in the background, a burly whipmaster.

I supposed that the transition between veils and a collar, between robes and chains, between freedom and slavery must be harrowingly miserable for a Gorean free woman, doubtless much more so than for a typical free woman of Earth, the Gorean woman having been so accustomed to status, prestige, power, and station.

On Gor, too, you see, the chasm between slave and free is profound and unbridgeable.

Imagine then the feelings of a Gorean woman used to despising and commanding slaves, to beating and humiliating them, to regarding them as meaningless, negligible animals, and to treating them as such, finding herself suddenly one of them.

I supposed I should feel sorry for the former Lady Temione of Hammerfest but I did not do so. "Let her," I thought, "learn what it is to fear as a slave, to work as a slave, to obey as a slave, to serve as a slave, to beg as a slave, to be vulnerable as a slave, to be treated as a slave, the slave she is."

From my position at the foot of the block, I could see the semicircular, ascending tiers. Seated centrally in the fourth tier up was Gordon, the Administrator of Hammerfest. Apparently he had come upriver all the way from Hammerfest to observe the sales. Had he not, not really so long ago, expressed his wish to see the former

Lady Temione of Hammerfest put naked on a public block and auctioned? Was that not a pleasure to which he had long looked forward? With him were several men I remembered from the palace and garden of the Lady Temione of Hammerfest.

From my position I could not well see the former Lady Temione on the block, but it was easy to hear the auctioneer and observe the crowd.

"I am free! I cannot be sold!" screamed the former Lady Temione.

The crowd roared with laughter.

When the mirth subsided, the auctioneer cried out, "*Ela*, I fear some monstrous injustice may have been perpetrated, that some terrible mistake may have taken place. Have we here a free woman?"

"No!" cried several in the crowd, including women.

There was more laughter.

"Do not let her cover her slave body with her hands!" cried a woman from somewhere in the tiers. "Do *sleen* and tarsks cover themselves so?" asked another.

There was more laughter.

"She claims to be a free woman," said the auctioneer, "but we find her naked on a slave block; we find there is a brand on her thigh; and we find there is a collar locked about her pretty neck! What can we do? What shall we do? Let me appeal to one of our noblest and most esteemed guests, the honorable Gordon, Administrator of Hammerfest."

"Yes," cried many in the crowd.

I had no doubt that Gordon had been forewarned of this appeal.

"I myself heard her, of her own free will, pronounce herself slave in the environs of Hammerfest," said Gordon.

"I, too," said several of the men with him.

"Noble Gordon, dearest friend," wept the former Lady Temione of Hammerfest, holding out her hands, "be kind, be merciful! Let Hammerfest keep my lands, my palace, my wealth, my slaves, all my properties, but let me be free, if only as a despised pauper, a destitute vagabond, a despised vagrant, begging for scraps in the alleys and streets of the lowest ports on the river."

"Do not dare to compare yourself to the free!" cried a woman. "Such are a thousand times above you!"

"What shall we do, noble Masters?" said the auctioneer.

"Sell her," said Gordon.

"Sell her!" cried the crowd.

"No, no!" cried the former Lady Temione of Hammerfest."

"Behold," called the auctioneer, "the blond hair, common in the north but rare on the river, gold like ripe *sa-tarna*; eyes as blue as the sky; note the slim ankles, the width of the hips, the narrowness of the waist; the sweetness of the bosom! I turn this lovely, meaningless beast before you. Would you not like to have your own collar on her neck? Would you not like to have her greet you on your return home, kneeling and hoping to be noticed? Would you not like to have her chained to the foot of your bed, whimpering for your caress?"

I was surprised that bids did not storm forth from the crowd. Surely the former Lady Temione of Hammerfest was a most attractive piece of merchandise, an excellent buy.

After a time, the auctioneer stopped.

The audience waited.

Then he spoke again. "Now, noble patrons, gentle friends, and astute buyers," he said, "we shall open the bidding. Thank you for your patience. The first bid is accorded to our honored guest from far downriver, Gordon, the noble Administrator of Hammerfest."

Gordon rose to his feet.

"One tarsk-bit," he said, clearly, decisively.

"I have a bid of one tarsk-bit," said the auctioneer.

The crowd was silent.

"Now," said Gordon, "I have expressed my view of the worth of the slave. Now my vengeance on she who was a criminal, one who conspired with the notorious Einar, *Sleen* of the Vosk, is almost complete. Remember, whoever buys her, she is a self-confessed natural slave who dared for years to masquerade as a free woman. Consider then how she is to be treated. The bids may now begin. When she is sold, my vengeance will be complete."

"Sleen, tarsk, urt!" screamed the former Lady Temione of Hammerfest.

At this point the burly whipmaster with whom the auctioneer and slave shared the surface the large block rushed forward and the five broad blades of the typical Gorean slave whip struck the former Lady Temione of Hammerfest again and again, each stroke like a bursting bolt of fire.

The slave shrieked with pain. "Stop! Stop!" she begged. "Please, stop!" From what I gathered, and the little I could see, I gathered that she lay under the whip, squirming, rolling and writhing, on the block.

"Enough!" called Gordon, and the whipmaster desisted.

"Thank the noble, kindly Administrator of Hammerfest, slave," said the auctioneer.

"Thank you, Master, thank you, kind and noble Master!" wept the former Lady Temione.

"Do you like being lashed?" asked the auctioneer.

"No!" wept the former Lady Temione. "No! Please do not lash me more!"

"Surely you had your own slaves lashed," said the auctioneer.

"But they were slaves," she said.

"And what now are you?" he asked.

"A slave, Master," she wept.

"And what else?" he asked.

"Nothing else, Master," she said, "only a slave, Master."

The former Lady Temione of Hammerfest now knew she was a slave. She had discovered that she, as other slaves, was subject to the whip.

"You are now going to be sold," said the auctioneer. "You will obey me with perfection. You will do exactly as you are told. You are going to smile. You are going to pose. You are going to exhibit yourself. You are going to impress buyers. You are going to convince them that you are worth owning, that you are a succulent slab of collar meat. Do you understand?"

"Yes, Master," she said.

"Let the bids begin," said Gordon.

And thus began a storm of bidding.

CHAPTER THIRTY

"Do not lie so long on the deck," said a keeper. "You will cook like a *sul*."

I rose to my feet. I then stood on the small sheet on which I had been lying.

This was the fourth day in the delta.

The days were long and hot. The humidity was oppressive.

"Let me see your hands," he said.

I held them out to him, palms up.

"Good," he said. "A few more days and they will be as soft as the underbelly of a she-sleen."

I supposed that was good.

"May I cover myself?" I asked.

"Yes," he said.

I then bent down, picked up the sheet, and put it about me. I did this slowly and gracefully, as I had been taught.

"May I speak?" I asked.

"Yes," he said.

"Why am I, and other stock on the barges not tethered?" I asked.

"You are," he said.

"I do not understand," I said.

"Come here, to the rail, and look," he said.

I joined him at the low rail, about ankle high. That was not high, but it would suffice to keep a sleeping person from rolling off the deck, into the water.

He shook out the blades of his whip, and dangled them in the water. He then shook them slightly, and then, quickly, jerked them back.

Jaws snapped, like the flinging shut of a wooden box.

I leaped back, startled, crying out.

Briefly I had seen the long, narrow snout of the *tharlarion*, and the eyes, emerged, and then the creature sank back, deeper, under the water, no longer visible from the surface.

"That is your tether," he said. "The delta, and its denizens."

"It was there," I said.

"Probably more than one," he said. "They tend to follow the larger rafts and barges, particularly if they are linked, as in our flotilla. Mostly they are looking for garbage. Almost always they take their prey in the water. When one throws itself unto the deck they are terribly dangerous. It is important to kill any who have learned to exploit that possibility. *Rencers* will follow such a one relentlessly."

"Who are *Rencers*?" I asked.

"They inhabit the delta," he said. "They live in villages on islands formed from plaited, woven stalks of the *rence* plant. As the *rence* rots at the bottom, new *rence* is added to the top."

"I have not seen any," I said.

"They are there," he said. "Have no doubt that they have seen us. The *rence* islands can be moved about, for fishing and hunting, for concealment, for gatherings, for festivals, for mutual defense, and such."

"Whither are we bound?" I asked.

"Through the delta to the Tamber Gulf," he said.

"And thence?" I asked.

"What is not becoming to a *kajira*?" he asked.

"I have been told," I said, "curiosity."

"I have heard that, as well," he said.

"Yet," I said, "it is well known that we are uncommonly curious."

"Through the Tamber Gulf, past Port Kar, to Thassa, the Sea, and thence south along the coast to Brundisium," he said.

"As in 'Brundisium of the hundred tarsk-bits?'" I asked.

"Yes," he said.

"And thence overland?" I asked.

"Perhaps," he said. "But perhaps, too, to Tyros or Cos, or the Farther Islands, or even to the World's End."

"East?" I said. "Overland east?"

"Perhaps," he said.

"Then why," I asked, "do we go downriver, through the delta, west?"

"Clearly," said he, "girl, that the shipment be secret."

"Raiders, thieves?" I said.

"Assuredly," he said. "To take a large number of prize slaves upriver past dozens of towns and ports is to risk much for little gain."

"Pirates," I said, "such as Einar, the Sleen of the Vosk?"

"And others," he said. "Even now four vessels, rumored to have prize slaves chained in their holds, are proceeding upriver."

"Decoys," I said.

"Yes," he said.

"Surely such a secret would be hard to keep," I said.

"Few are privy to so sensitive a plan," he said.

"Perhaps only Administrators, Admirals, and such," I said.

"Yes," he said.

"Such as Gordon of Hammerfest?" I said.

"Undoubtedly," he said. "But even were it not so, few pirates would dare follow barges into the delta. Aside from *Rencers* and beasts, it is a labyrinth of high *rence* and uncertain, confusing channels, and there are thousands of square *pasangs* where the water is too shallow to float even a river ship."

"But you show no lights after dark," I said.

"A precaution," he said. "Too, one does not wish to attract beasts."

"I heard slaves speak, who had overheard Masters," I said. "They claim that we, those on these linked barges, were all purchased by Tenalian of Ar, or his agents."

"The tongues of men are often loosened by *paga*," he said, "and some fellows pay too little attention to those who serve the *paga*."

"Happily," I said.

"Tenalian of Ar," he said, "often uses agents to purchase for him, in order to conceal the number of his own purchases, which are often considerable."

"I think," I said, "that after landing at Brundisium, we will proceed overland, east."

"By slave wagon," he said.

"For Ar is east," I said.

"East and to the south," he said.

"We are bound for Ar," I said.

"That is possible," he said.

"Because," I said, "Tenalian is of Ar."

"A few drops of *paga*, and an attentive slave," he said, "and the greatest of secrets blazes forth like the delta sun at noon."

"A girl is pleased," I said.

"What difference does it make," he asked, "where you wear your collar? What difference does it make to a *tarsk* where lies its pen, or to a *bosk* or *kaiila* where it grazes?"

"We may be domestic animals," I said, "but we are not *tarsks*, nor *bosk*, nor *kaiila*. I assure Master it makes a great deal of difference, at least to us, where we wear our collars."

"Yes," he said, "I suppose that in Ar there are fewer *tarsks* to feed, fewer burdens to bear, fewer *suls* to dig and harvest."

"Yes, Master," I said.

How could I tell him of what I had heard of the tower cities, the soaring buildings, the graceful, arching bridges, the boulevards, the parks and markets, the song dramas, the theaters, the concerts, the tarn races, festivals, and dances; the contests of plays, poetry, and lyric song, with prizes of golden tripods, even oddities, unintelligible to me, like public *kaissa* matches in stadiums, attended by thousands of citizens?

"Do not count on reaching Ar," he said.

"Why not?" I asked, apprehensively.

"The tolls charged by *Rencers* for allowing us to traverse the delta," he said, "tolls which may be paid with female slaves. The *Rencers* may exact a toll of some two hundred *kajirae* at this time of year. They use *kajirae* on ropes in the water, as bait when hunting *tharlarion*, much as those of Port Kar use slaves when hunting giant canal *urts*."

I felt faint.

"I jest, of course," he said.

"I did not know that," I said.

"I thought you might not," he said. "Is my humor not delicious?"

"Perhaps more so to the humorist," I said, "than to its victim."

At that point a large shadow soared across the deck of the barge. It was there, for a moment, and then gone.

My interlocutor, shading his eyes, looked after the object, like a winged kite. I had never seen such things until the delta, save in artists' fantasies or reconstructions. I recalled stories I had heard of the presumably mythical Priest-Kings and their doubtless mythical voyages of acquisition, in which they, perhaps with scholarly or aesthetic interests in mind, had, over countless millennia, stocked their world with diverse forms of life, from various worlds. The stories must be false, even absurd, but it did not seem likely to me that humans were originally native to Gor. So how had they, or their ancestors, reached this world? And had the swift, serpentine, six-legged *sleen* its origin on Gor or on some other world? Certainly few animals on Gor had six legs. And what of the mighty tarns? Surely their strength, so astounding on Gor, suggested a large-world origin. "A winged *tharlarion*," I said, looking after the flying monster, "an ul."

"They can be dangerous," he said.

"Master sports again with a slave," I said. "Not to humans, surely."

"To whatever it can clasp in its claws," he said. "Do you think it is only for purposes of reconnaissance, to have eyes in the delta, that we have two tarnsmen on the last of the linked barges?"

"I did not know we had two tarnsmen with the barges," I said.

"Now you know," he said, "and I wager that now every slave on this barge and on any barge within earshot will know it, too, within an Ehn."

"Should the slaves not be warned?" I asked.

"Perhaps now," he said. "Normally one waits some days, until one is deeper in the delta, in order not to alarm them prematurely."

"That was an ul," I said.

"I do not understand it," he said. "Normally uls are not found in the eastern delta."

"There must be a reason," I said.

"I shall inform the Shipment Master," he said.

"It is permissible for me to speak of this?" I asked.

"Yes," he said. "And there are two things to keep in mind. One, if an ul is about, if possible, take shelter. Two, if you are in the open, crouch down, or lie down, and do not move. Do not contrast with, or emerge from, the background."

"You mentioned tarnsmen," I said. "What is their role in all this?"

"If a slave or keeper should be so careless as to be seized," he said, "a trumpet blast alerts the tarnsmen to take flight and further blasts specify the azimuth of the *tharlarion*'s flight. As the ul takes its prey to its nest for feeding, this provides the pursuing tarnsman some Ihn to attempt a rescue."

"I trust that these rescues are frequently successful," I said.

"Seldom," he said. "On the other hand, whereas the slave, or such, is usually eaten or half eaten by the time the tarnsmen arrive, the *tharlarion* is still feeding, or is inert and sluggish, having fed, and is thus easily killed. Thus it makes only one such strike."

"I see," I said. "But sometimes the rescue is successful?"

"Certainly," he said.

"One can always hope that things will work out well," I said.

"Certainly," he said.

He turned away, but then, after a moment, turned back.

"Watches will be set," he said. "When an ul is sighted, a whistle will be blown, this alerting the barges."

"That is wise," I said.

"I do not know what the ul is doing in the eastern delta," he said. "That seems to me mysterious. Now, I shall report what we have seen to the Shipment Master, in case he is unaware of it, and you may now, much to the chagrin of your collar sisters, have the exquisite pleasure of imparting to them the anomaly of the misplaced ul."

"I will mention the matter to the blond slave," I said, "that she will have that exquisite pleasure."

"I know that one," he said, "the former Lady Temione of Hammerfest, a she-tarsk. I do not know what Tenalian wanted with her."

"She is very beautiful," I said.

"So is a mountain of ice," he said.

"Properly handled," I said, "she will soon be tortured with need."

"As you are?" he said.

"I am a slave," I said.

"She will not credit you as the source of the gossip," he said.

"That is why I chose her," I said, "because she will not do so."

"I do not understand you," he said. "Why do you hide in the shadows, so to speak, why do you conceal yourself amongst others; why do you seek to be unseen, to be unnoted?"

"Perhaps that I will not be noticed by a passing ul," I said.

What could I tell him?

I must not stand out.

I must be taken as Gorean. Too, even in my freedom, on Earth, I was shy, and retiring.

Let others seek plaudits and compete for attention.

I shunned such things.

Let each be himself.

"The blond slave is not popular," he said.

"Perhaps in imparting a new, singular intelligence to eagerly listening others, she will become more popular," I said.

"No," he said. "It will make her more arrogant. She despises slaves and holds herself above them."

"She was once quite powerful," I said.

"She is now in a collar," he said, "only one slave amongst others."

"I do not think she sees herself so," I said.

"Whether she does so or not," said he, "a collar is now on her neck."

I was then alone.

Shortly thereafter, gathering my sheet more closely about me, I sought out the former Lady Temione of Hammerfest.

"How dare you address me?" she asked.

"Doubtless to curry favor," I said.

"What do you want?" she asked.

"A flying *tharlarion*, an ul, has been sighted," I said.

"What is that to me?" she asked.

"I am told they are dangerous," I said. "It behooves us to be watchful. If one is about, hide, or, if that is not practical, make yourself inconspicuous, and do not move."

"I have not seen one," she said.

"Yet one was seen," I said.

"I am not afraid of an ul," she said.

"Then you are courageous," I said. Then I added, "I am told they are rare in this part of the delta."

"What is it doing here then?" she asked.

"It is not known," I said. "Watches will be set. A whistle will signify a sighting."

"You may address me as 'Mistress,'" she said.

"I do not care to do so," I said.

"Get out of my sight," she said.

"That is not easily done on a barge," I said.

"Did you hear me?" she asked.

"Clearly," I said.

"Remove yourself from my sight!" she said.

"You may do so yourself, and simply," I said. "Look in another direction."

"Insolent slave," she said.

"To me," I said, "you are neither Mistress nor Master."

"She-tarsk!" she hissed. She angrily raised her hands, the fingers like claws.

"If you attack me," I said, "be warned. I will defend myself."

"You would not dare!" she said.

"You are not a free person, to whose abuse I must unquestionably and docilely submit," I said. "And, I assure you, your price would be considerably reduced should half your hair be torn out, or should you lose an eye, or have an ear bitten away."

"My price!" she said, outraged.

"Precisely," I said. "Then a *tharlarion* groom could afford you."

"I am larger and stronger than you are," she said.

"Not all that much so," I said. "Too, keep in mind that slave girls who fight are often whipped by Masters. Thus, peace is kept in a house."

She clenched her small fists.

"You have few friends on the barge," I said. "If I were you, I would not wander too close to the edge of the barge, particularly after dark."

She turned white.

"It is something to keep in mind," I said.

"Collar meat," she said.

"Collar meat," I said. "Blond, blue-eyed collar meat."

"I am more valuable than you," she said.

"The farther you go north the less so," I said. "And you do not even have a name yet!"

"I am the Lady Temione of Hammerfest," she said.

"Only if some owner put that name on you," I said.

She turned away, angrily.

After a time, she approached other slaves, some of whom were larger and stronger than she, who would be likely candidates for an appointment to the post of 'first girl,' should such an appointment be made.

Comparisons of size and strength do not figure only amongst men.

I was sure that the former Lady Temione of Hammerfest was now concerned to inform the other slaves about uls, dangers, anomalies, and such. To possess knowledge not known to other slaves, and to impart such knowledge, perhaps furtively and secretly, bit by bit, and especially prematurely, commonly, exponentially, enhances the status, prestige, and importance of a slave amongst her collar sisters, especially if it is knowledge, gossip, or such, which Masters would presumably wish have withheld from them. On the other hand, I was confident that the former Lady Temione of Hammerfest, being she, would perform this normally delightful action in such a way that she would appear to her auditors less a confiding fellow slave sharing an exquisite secret with them than an intolerably condescending informant, one clearly interested in impressing her superiority on inferior auditors.

I did not actually fear, incidentally, that the former Lady Temione of Hammerfest was in danger, or much danger, of being thrust overboard by her fellow slaves, but I had thought that the remark might be chasteningly useful in reminding her of a slave's vulnerability.

A slave is likely to fare much better as a slave if she understands that she is a slave.

My sale in Victoria had gone well. I had sold for a silver tarsk, six, namely, a silver tarsk and six copper tarsks.

Mostly I was pleased that I had not been sold as a barbarian. The *tharlarion* rider had kept his word. He had not revealed my Earth origin.

Far off, in the sky, I saw an object in flight.

I shaded my eyes.

It was another ul.

CHAPTER THIRTY-ONE

There was a shrill blast of whistles!

"Another!" exclaimed a keeper.

I scanned the sky.

Yesterday two uls had been seen. Today six had been noted.

"Is there no end of them?" he grumbled.

"They are migrating," proposed another keeper.

"Uls do not migrate," he was told.

"Keep watch," said an officer.

The most recent of these flighted, gray, wide-winged, featherless monsters continued east. They had long necks and large, backward-crested heads with long, tapering, narrow beaks, which were toothless. I was told that these monsters were hollow-boned and light for their size. Converting quantities from Gorean to English, some of the larger uls had a wing span of some forty feet and a weight of as much as a thousand pounds. They were warm-blooded like birds, and laid eggs, but, unlike birds, did not feed or raise their young. In this way they were typical *tharlarion* and differed from birds, from fleer, *jards*, tarns, and such.

It was nearly but not yet noon.

Interestingly, the linked barges of Tenalian's shipment were still in their night position, joined together in what was much like a large, squarish fortress formed from flat, floating blocks. In this way the area exposed to possible boarders was minimized and Tenalian's forces could be deployed promptly and efficiently, from point to point, as might seem appropriate. Light was not shown after dark. I think I suggested that earlier. In this way the position of the island of barges might be concealed from possibly unwelcome visitors, human or otherwise. What provoked my curiosity was why, now, well after daylight, our journey through the delta toward the Tamber Gulf had not been resumed.

Also of interest was the fact that the slaves, to their pleasure, had been issued tunics. It was wonderful, once again, to be clothed, however clothed, be it only as a slave. Slaves, as animals, are not entitled to modesty, but few of us, I assure you, are without that characteristic. It is one thing to be naked before our Master, and quite another to be naked in public. I did not understand, at the time, why this had been done, as we were still in transport. For example, slaves marched overland in coffle would commonly be nude. Thus, tunics would not be soiled, would not be exposed to dust, sweat, rain, mud, and such. Why were we then, in transit, given clothing? We were not in civilization, so to speak, not in a village, town, or city, not on a well-traveled road, not in the vicinity of a free woman, not in a caravanserai, or such, but yet we had been issued tunics.

I supposed that it was not for us, as slaves, to look into such matters, but, surely, we were entitled to wonder about them.

And in the meantime, let us rejoice.

Clothing, and its lack, are interesting.

Whereas a free woman might be dismayed or scandalized to look upon the garment of a slave and might swoon with shame to consider herself placed in such a garment, the case is quite otherwise with the slave once she learns her collar, once she understands, in the fullest sense, it is locked on her neck. She then loves her garment because she knows how it enhances her charms. She can now be as proud, free, bold, and brazen as she wishes. She has been freed from convention. She is no longer permitted reservations and inhibitions. She knows that in it she is exciting and desirable, and available, even for purchasing; she knows she enflames men; and she, in her garment, is enflamed herself; she discovers she is a profoundly sexual creature, and knows, as a slave, how helpless and vulnerable she is. She kneels, kisses the whip, and begs to serve. She is content. She is happy at her Master's feet, where she belongs. She is a slave.

In our 'shipment' there were some four hundred slaves distributed over six linked barges.

We were all in the collar of Tenalian of Ar.

He personally, and through certain agents, had purchased heavily at Victoria. Apparently many bargains had been taken off the block. It was, it seemed, at least temporarily, a buyers' market. This was, I gather, primarily due to the acquisition of the many slaves formerly belonging to the Lady Temione of Hammerfest by the Council of Hammerfest. An overabundance of goods, at a given time and place, tends to depress prices. Market forces assert themselves, whether dealing with *suls, tarsks,* or slaves. Accordingly, given the generally high quality of the slaves of the Lady Temione of Hammerfest, bargains were seemingly plentiful. It was rumored that Tenalian, and his agents, availing themselves of these market conditions might have overpurchased. Buying cheaply and expecting to sell dear presupposes it is possible to bring the goods, potentially valuable goods which were purchased cheaply, to the dear market. That might not always be easy to do.

Even now Tenalian's purchases, supposedly proceeding upriver from Victoria were actually deep in the delta of the Vosk.

One of the advantages of the 'Night Position,' from the slaves' point of view, were two intervals of about an hour each, first, when it was early in the morning and it had not yet been broken, and, second, when it was early in the evening and it had just been formed, was the chance to cross from barge to barge, move about, and visit with other slaves. This was not permitted in actual darkness. As you have gathered, I and the former Lady Temione of Hammerfest were on the same barge, which, incidentally, was the lead barge when the flotilla of barges moved toward the Tamber Gulf. Luta, whom I knew from the great pen at Victoria Minor was on the fourth barge, and Xanthe, the former Eileen Bennett, was on the fifth barge. I avoided the former Miss Bennett for fear she might speak to me in English or, in some other way destroy or jeopardize my attempt to be taken as natively Gorean.

I was sure that I was still sought, and not for the reason that a slave might be most often sought.

It was, as I mentioned, shortly before noon.

I was still puzzled as to why the barges were, at this late hour, in the 'Night Position.'

Perhaps it had to do with the large number of uls observed, which, I gathered, was anomalous at any time, but particularly so in this part of the delta.

For those interested in such matters, I might mention that the barges, when underway, commonly drift with the current toward the Tamber Gulf. When necessary, to free them or propel them under certain conditions, one uses poles, pressing into the mud or sand. One does not paddle or row barges. At the end of the trip, the barges are commonly dismantled for their wood. Where the depth permits, ships may move about under oars. *Rencers* commonly use small craft formed from the cut-and-bound stalks of the *rence* plant, the same material which is used for creating the *rence* islands on which they have their small villages of *rence* huts. These small craft, commonly carrying one but occasionally two individuals, are paddled.

I approached Bortak, a keeper, and sometimes poleman, with whom I had spoken before. He was standing, shading his eyes, looking west. I knelt beside him. I was sure he knew I was there. "May I speak?" I asked.

"If you wish," he said.

"It seems," I said, "that we are still in the 'night position.'"

"It does not merely seem so," he said. "It is actually the case."

I thought it most judicious to remain silent.

"Have you just discovered that?" he asked.

"No," I said.

"Most *kajirae*," he said, "noticed that long ago."

"I am sure they did," I said.

"You are fetching in that tunic," he said.

"It is a girl's hope that Master is pleased," I said.

"It is, however, too generous, too long, is it not?" he said.

"A girl has no say in such things," I said.

"Perhaps," he said, "I will explain that to you."

I waited, but no explanation was forthcoming.

"What do you want?" he asked.

"I am wondering why we are still in the 'night position,'" I said.

"Do you wish to feel the lash?" he asked.

"Not at all," I said. "Many uls have been sighted," I said. "Does that have anything to do with our pause, with our anchoring?"

"The many uls seen, and particularly in this part of the delta, is unusual. I do not understand it. But that is not why we remain at anchor."

There was then a shrill blast of a whistle, and we looked up quickly, scanning the sky. A large ul, its broad, leatherish wings spread, soared some seventy feet in the air over the two barges farthest to the north. Then the wings snapped and it smote its way past.

"They grow bold," he said.

"I wonder if they are hungry," I said.

"Uls are always hungry," he said.

He then returned his attention to the delta, looking westward.

"I do not wish to risk a lashing," I said, "but I am curious to know why our progress has been arrested. Why have the barges not been separated, and then, linked together, continued on their way toward the Tamber Gulf?"

"There," he said, "look," pointing.

I saw, coming through the *rence*, a single boat, a reed boat, small and formed of the bound-and-bundled stalks of the *rence* plant.

A single man paddled it to within some five yards of our barge.

"*Tal*," he called, lifting his hand.

"*Tal*," responded the keeper, near whom I knelt. Then he said to the newcomer, "Hold, officers approach."

Tenalian himself was not on the barges. He, as I understood it, was with the four decoy ships moving east on the Vosk, doubtless to assure observers that that fleet contained his purchases, and perhaps to organize and mount a defense against possible predation. He was not the sort of man, I had gathered, who would expose his followers to risks he himself was unwilling to sustain.

In a moment, several men, and some slaves, were at the ankle-high rail of the barge.

"I come in the name of Ho-Hak, he of the large ears," said the man in the reed boat, "he, Ubar of the Marshes."

"The delta is wide," said a man with a helmet crested with *sleen* hair.

"But not so wide as the sky," said the figure in the boat.

"The delta is long," said the officer.

"But not so long as the Vosk," said the man in the boat.

"The waters of the delta are slow," said the officer.

"But not so slow as the growth of the Tur tree," said the fellow in the boat, his paddle across his knees.

"Excellent," said the officer. "Eighty copper tarsks, forty now, and forty once across the flats." He then tossed a purse to the fellow in the reed boat. The fellow in the reed boat thrust it in his purse, not bothering to count it.

"There are many uls about," said the officer.

"Too many," said the man in the boat. "They are fleeing something."

"What could terrify an ul?" asked the officer.

"We do not know," said the fellow in the reed boat.

The officer then turned about and addressed the men with him. "Prepare to get underway," he said.

Shortly thereafter the keeper and I were alone.

"We were waiting for the pilot," he said, looking out over the marshes. "He will find us channels to get through the 'flats.' Without a pilot, trying to find our own way, we might be slowed by days, even weeks."

"He did not understand the uls," I said.

"No," said the keeper.

"The man in the boat was a *Rencer*?" I asked.

"Yes," said the keeper. "They know the delta, or parts of it, the way a free woman of Ar knows the shops along the Avenue of the Central Cylinder."

"He did not count the copper tarsks," I said.

"Nor should he," said the keeper. "It would be insulting to the payer to count the tarsks, as it would be insulting to a shopsman for a customer to count his change."

"Of course," I said. I was apprehensive. I hoped I had not given myself away. Surely a Gorean would know that.

"If there are not forty copper tarsks in that purse," he said, "unfortunate consequences would be sure to ensue. One does not care to be cheated. It is not merely that future arrangements would be jeopardized, but that we might be led astray in the delta and be irretrievably abandoned in its most dangerous labyrinths. Too, it would be easy for *Rencers*, skilled with the great bow, hiding in the *rence*, to exact whatever toll of lives they might wish. Too, further east, it is not unknown for *Rencers* to fasten a recreant or undesirable to a pole, leaving him for uls, or aquatic *tharlarion*."

"I see," I said.

"And now, too," he said, "you see why the slaves were given generous tunics this morning."

"Master?" I said.

"*Rencers*, after all," he said, "are men."

"I see," I said.

The tunics were generous indeed, falling to the calves. They even had sleeves, unusual in a slave garment.

At that point there was another blast on the warning whistle.

The keeper crouched down.

"Stay low," he said.

"Yes, Master," I said.

"Look!" said he. "That ul is flying west. It is going back. It is returning!"

I watched it disappear over the *rence*.

"Others will follow," he said. "I am sure of it."

"It no longer flees," I said.

"It seems not," he said.

"From what were such fearsome beasts fleeing?" I asked.

"I do not know," he said, "nor, it seems, do the *Rencers*."

"The uls will now return?" I said.

"I think so," he said. "One, then two, then others. The ul is territorial. It will return to its part of the delta, to its hunting ground, its cliff, its nest."

"Then the danger which threatened them is now past," I said.

"It seems so," he said.

"I wonder what could have frightened them," I said.

"That is known to hundreds," he said, "perhaps thousands."

"To so many?" I asked.

"Yes," he said.

"Who?" I asked.

"Are you so stupid as not to know?" he asked.

"Apparently," I said.

"It is known to the uls themselves," he said.

I was annoyed. "Master smiles," I said.

"You look well on your knees," he said.

"I am before a free man," I said.

"I think I will tie your hands behind your back."

"I am a slave," I said. "Master may do as he wishes."

"There," he said. "It is done."

"I am now bound, helpless, kneeling before Master," I said.

"I now give you permission to please me," he said.

"Yes, Master," I said. "Thank you, Master."

CHAPTER THIRTY-TWO

"You have heard the whistle," I said. "Crouch down, lie on the deck, seek shelter."

Several uls had already flown past, each heading in the direction the barges themselves were bound, to the west.

"Did you request permission to address me?" she asked.

"It slipped my mind," I said.

"Insolent slave," said the former Lady Temione of Hammerfest.

"I need no more permission to address you than to address an *urt* or *tarsk*," I said.

"Uls feed on fish, birds, and small *tharlarion*," she said. "To humans they are harmless."

"The Masters believe otherwise," I said.

"Wharf rats, vagabonds, polemen, slave keepers, and louts," she said.

The barges, now aligned, were making their way slowly through the *rence*, following the pilot in his small, light craft.

"I spoke in your own best interest," I said.

"I am grateful and flattered," she said. "Your solicitude is as touching as absurd. Next, warn me of the threats of flowers or the enmity of moons."

"I speak only as the men would speak," I said.

"Men are brutes and fools," she said. "I hate them."

"Surely you know what they can do to you," I said, "how they can turn you into a begging slave."

"Never," she said.

"You set a poor example to other slaves," I said. "You do not obey. You scorn warnings. You never make yourself small. You never lie on the deck. You never seek shelter. You do not remain still. You walk about, upright, arrogant, and unconcerned."

"Uls pose no danger to humans," she said.

"I am sure the *Rencers*, the people of the delta, fear them," I said.

"*Rencers* are ignorant," she said. "They cannot even read."

There was then another shrill sound but there seemed something anomalous in it, which I only understood a moment or so later.

"See," said the former Lady Temione, pointing at a huge form soaring past, some hundred feet or so to our left.

I, bent low, followed her gesture.

It was then, not looking back, that it came to me, suddenly, to my terror, the explanation of the unusual sound I had heard a moment ago.

I spun about.

The sound had been that of a second whistle, its blast almost coterminous with the first whistle.

I screamed as the large, ridged, narrow jaws of the ul closed on the body of the former Lady Temione.

Heavy clawed feet scratched the deck. Wide, featherless wings blocked out the sky.

The former Lady Temione screamed, her eyes wild with terror, her body clenched in those long narrow jaws, she drawn from her feet, lifted from the deck.

I heard men shouting, racing towards us.

Surely their poles could poke and strike the beast, forcing it to relinquish its prey; surely their knives, swords, and spears could stab and cut it before it could snap those mighty wings and, dashing the air behind it, rise from the barge.

Again the Lady Temione screamed.

The eyes of the beast seemed tiny, wild, and bright, in that large, elongated skull with its bone-like projection stretching behind it for better than a yard.

I was sure that the beast, confused and angry, would take to the air any moment, its jaws clutching its prey, putting behind itself an unwelcome din, seeking the familiar, reassuring safety of flight.

Tarnsmen sometimes speak of their mounts as 'saddling the wind.'

Tarns are not native to the delta.

In the delta, the ul, monstrous and horrifying, is the king of the sky.

In the delta, it is they, not the majestic tarn, who saddle the wind.

Is the wind affrighted, one wonders, to have so terrible a companion?

In an instant those wide wings, vast, gray and leathery, would beat and the monster would ascend.

In that wild, confusing moment I acted without thinking. In certain moments there is no time nor place for thought. I suspect that in such moments, one does not think but responds, does not reflect but act.

If there is a time for thought, a time for reasoned decision, it seems one might give some sense to distinguishing between cowards and heroes, if it pleases one to do so arrogant a thing. But what if there is no thought? What if the body explodes blindly into movement? In such a case, are there cowards and heroes? In such a case, does it make sense either to scorn the one or praise the other? In such moments I do not think that a person who flees from danger is to be criticized nor one who confronts danger is to be praised.

As those great featherless wings spread to lash the air, I flung myself forward and, as they struck back and down, the rush of wind scattering men back, I had seized one of those claw-footed legs. Perhaps I had hoped to impede the monster, to stop its flight, to anchor it to the deck, if only for an instant that the men might reach it with their weaponry, their poles or spears, or swords, anything to disable or kill it. I do not know.

I knew I was in flight, giddy and terrified, the barge below, slipping back and away from me.

I was over the water.

Higher smote the monster.

Perhaps I should have let go instantly.

But I had not.

Now I was afraid to let go.

Given the shallowness of the delta, I feared the fall would be one to the death, and, even were one to survive the fall, broken and helpless, I did not think I would long be alone, not in the waters of the delta. The denizens of the delta quickly remark anomalies in their environment.

As we left the vicinity of the barges, I heard, far behind, not warning whistles but diverse blasts on more than one horn, signal blasts.

My heart leaped.

I remembered the keeper's telling me of the tarnsmen, two of them, with the barges, tarnsmen kept largely for reconnoitering, but who could, too, respond to signals. Already they must be informed of the ul attack. Already must they have been apprised of the direction of the ul's flight. They must be on the wing even now. The ul, as I understood it, conveys its prey to its nest for feeding, perhaps to be alone with it, away from other uls. The interval of time between the ul's seizing a victim and feeding on it, would, in theory, provide tarnsmen an opportunity, however slight, to effect a rescue. If not, they might arrive in time to kill the ul, thus preventing another such attack. The theory seems to be that an ul who has once fed on human flesh would be likely to do so again.

"There is hope!" I cried to the former Lady Temione of Hammerfest. "Be brave! Live! Tarnsmen will be aflight!"

But there was no response from the Lady Temione. I feared she was dead.

The monster sped on its way, the delta far below.

The ul drew its legs up beneath it, as is done in flight. This put me pressed against its body. I could smell it. I was aware of its breathing, drawing back, then pressing against me. I was aware of the beating of its heart, now, in flight, smooth and slow. I do not think that it was aware of my weight, at least in any direct or serious sense, as it would have been negligible to him, given his strength and bulk. I did suppose, however, that it was probably aware of something about its leg, but I do not think it was really aware of what it was, that it was a conscious, living person lofted with him, clinging there. That was doubtless fortunate for me. Too, if he had utilized his jaws to tear away some sensed encumbrance tangled with, or caught about, his leg, might he not have lost his prey, it falling to the marsh far below?

It did not scratch at me with its other claw-footed leg. Perhaps it was not aware of me nor my weight.

It sped on.

I looked back, as I could. We were now far beyond the barges. The sky seemed clear behind me. Where were the tarnsmen? Were there tarnsmen?

I knew not how long it might take the ul to reach its nest. There had been several flights of uls moving east, for some days. Then, recently, uls were seen flying west, presumably returning to the hunting grounds, or territories, from which, earlier, for some reason, they had fled.

We had been aflight an hour or so and I had heard no sound from the former Lady Temione. I assumed she was dead. If so, she would be spared the horror of being eaten alive.

I was not, at the time, afraid of falling, as I was pressed between the body of the monster and the drawn-up leg to which I clung. Even had I somehow fallen asleep in this dreadful ensconcement, I did not think it likely I would have slipped and plunged to the delta. At the first sense of hazard, I am sure I would have been jarred awake. I did consider risking the fall and the delta, if only to escape being eaten, but this option seemed to promise little more than a quicker death. While I was alive, I would try to stay alive. Too, as I now suspected, the monster might not even know it bore a passenger. Perhaps while it occupied itself with feeding on the body of the former Lady Temione, I might be able to slip away, if only to succumb to another of its sort.

I would try to maintain my current position.

It is common, I suppose, for a human being to prefer an indisputable security, one even temporary, for just a little longer, than rush into a threatening darkness of unseen perils.

I saw nothing of tarnsmen.

"No, no, no!" I heard, a scream whose source was no more than feet from me.

The former Lady Temione was alive!

She must have lost consciousness and only now recovered it, perhaps awakening from some nightmare into a reality far more fearful.

Suddenly, overwhelmingly, irresistibly, overpoweringly, I hated her for being alive.

How natural this was, how terrible it was!

No longer now could I hope to slip away unnoticed. Whatever she might be, or however she might or might not act in the same circumstances, I knew I could not simply abandon her. She was as human as I, and I must try to help her. Surely I could intervene in some way. At the least I could try to distract the beast or lead it away from her. Might not the tiny brain of the beast be confused, undecided between quarries, permitting at least one prey animal to escape?

But little did I know then of the height and precipitate steepness of the cliff in which its lodging was placed.

Had I known that, perhaps, yielding to weakness and despair, I would have relinquished my position and slipped from its nestled limb to the delta far below.

Despite the heat of the day it was chilly in flight.

I did not know how far we had come from the barges, but they were now far behind. I also suspected that we had flown over the mysterious 'flats' through which some *Rencer* was even now guiding the barges. I did not know it at the time, but there were several areas in the vast delta in which the services of a pilot were desirable, if not necessary. A pilot, aware of suitable courses, can shorten a journey by days or even weeks. Whereas most waters of the delta will eventually debouch in the Tamber Gulf, there are numerous eddies, pools, lakes, and lagoons. One may also encounter occasional cross currents, commonly angling south. Traversing the delta can be not only time-consuming and tedious, but confusing and dangerous. In places, the height, thickness and tangles of marsh growth, reducing visibility to a matter of feet or yards, can be almost impenetrable. One supposes that even an army could be lost in the mazes of the delta.

As we sped on, I soon became aware of an unmistakable odor, that of smoke, the sort that can linger for days in a burned building or ruined forest.

I saw no active fires but clearly there must have been a sizable, active conflagration in the vicinity within the last few days. I could almost taste smoke on my tongue. An unpleasant residue of smoke lingered. It hung like an oppression in the atmosphere. Looking down I could see in places a grayness like ash, and, here and there, the remains of a delta lace tree, roots in water, whose intricate, colored, fibrous filaments had been burned away. Occasionally we flew over a hillock, watched over now by the stark, black remains of trunks and branches of *ka-la-na* trees, once yellow with flowers and fruit. The land was rent, disfigured, and scarred. I could not understand what I saw for fires in the delta are rare. They pose a considerable threat to *rence* villages where the *rence* is dry, but seldom to the delta itself. But here it seemed that wild *rence* itself might have been burned down to the level of the water. Many stalks of blackened *rence* floated in the waters below. I supposed that, days ago, this area might have been insufferably unlivable. Then I realized that I knew what those of the barges and, apparently, many *Rencers* did not, what explained the mysterious flights of uls and their sudden appearance so far east in the delta. They, the mighty uls, had met an unexpected foe, one incomprehensible to them, a foe that they could neither claw nor bite, a foe invulnerable to their weaponry, a foe fierce, spreading, and unstoppable, the red beast, mindless, unassailable, and pitiless, fire. What I could not understand was how this fire could have occurred or, if occurring, spread so widely. The currents in the delta separate thousands of stands of combustibles. How then could the fire have been so wide-spread? How could it, in seeking its tinder, have crossed thousands of barriers of water? I then saw another ul in flight. That alarmed me. I then became aware that we were stroking our way amongst cliffs, several of which had shelflike ledges. And, here and there, there seemed recesses, crevices, or caves, in those cliffs. I saw an ul emerge from such an opening and, spreading its wings, it soared below us, and was then lost to sight.

I was terrified.

At that point the ul began to descend.

CHAPTER THIRTY-THREE

Wings snapping, the ul literally paused in flight, hovering, a sheer clifflike wall before it, some thirty feet away, and then it approached the wall, and, lowering its legs, I clinging to one of them, alit on a wide shelflike projection, behind which yawned a large cavelike opening.

The shelf was wide and deep, and the opening behind it, for most of its extent, at least a hundred feet, was large, yards high, wide, and deep. It was so large that the ul might have stood erect and extended its wings within it, until, far from the opening, in the darkness, it began to narrow and the ceiling sloped downward. There was also, I would discover, several feet within, a narrow break in the rock to the right. I had little doubt that this lodging was amongst the most choice in the cliff, which, to my dismay, was some three or four hundred feet high, steep, smooth, precipitous, and unscalable. To be the master of such a domicile amongst a population of such winged monsters, spoke much for its standing amongst its peers, a standing doubtless earned by bulk and ferocity.

A moment after the beast landed on the shelf, I released the leg and slipped behind it, catching my balance on the shelf. I was unsteady from the flight. I do not think the monster was even aware of me. It then, folding its wings, the former Lady Temione dangling from its jaws, stalked within the opening. I followed it, looking wildly about. I saw a rock or two, a man's fist size. There were bones, too. Some of the bones appeared to be human. So much, I thought, for the notion that uls did not prey on humans. Some yards within the cavernous opening, to the extent light penetrated, it opened his jaws and dropped its burden to the stone floor. It lifted its head and moved it about, stretching its neck, and opening and closing its jaws several times. Its neck and jaws possibly ached from the flight, reacting to the prolonged near rigidity of neck musculature, and the strain of a tensed, unloosening grip for so long. Doubtless it commonly captured prey and bore it aloft for far shorter periods of time. The tunic of the former Lady Temione was bloody, but the blood was now dry. After the barge, in the grip of the ul's jaws, given the ul's toothless grip, I think she had lost little blood. The eyes of the former

Lady Temione were glazed with terror. She emitted a tiny, whimpering sound, and tried to move, but, instantly, one clawed foot of the ul pressed down on her, pinning her in place.

Why, I wondered, could she not have died in flight? Why must she be alive now? Might I not hide, for a time, while the ul fed on a lifeless body? But she was alive! Thus I knew my body would try to interfere, however ill-fated, however brief and unavailing, might be so absurd an intervention. But what difference did it all make? We could not kill the ul and, if we could, there would be another, and another. This lofty domicile would be a most desirable lodging, and it, if free or abandoned, would attract others. And I had seen the cliff. There was no escape there, unless it be the escape of death, flinging oneself to the stones below, to escape being eaten. Too, there was no place in this domicile where one might hide indefinitely. One would die of thirst or hunger.

As the ul bent down to pull at the living flesh of the former Lady Temione, I seized up a rock and hurled it, from inches away, point blank, at the monster's head. It struck him alongside the long, poised beak. The ul drew back, more startled than injured. I then realized it had been unaware of my presence, until I had betokened it by an act which might well be regarded quite as meaningless as it was futile.

The ul straightened up and swung his long beak toward me. Doubtless to him it seemed that I had appeared from nowhere. The close-set beady eyes in that narrow head regarded me. I did not expect it to reflect on my surprising presence, or, puzzled, to try to interpret it or explain it to himself. It would simply accept it, and then act.

I backed away.

The ul followed me one pace. This took the heavy, clawed foot off the body of the former Lady Temione of Hammerfest.

"Get up, she-urt," I said. "Run, crawl, go to the low part of the cave where the ul cannot reach you!"

"I cannot move!" she wept.

"Very well," I said. "Stay where you are and get eaten."

I backed farther away.

She rolled to her side, struggled to all fours and began to make her way to the back of the cave.

I had my eye on the narrow, vertical crevice near the opening of the cave, to the side, to my right as I was backing away.

The ul took another step toward me.

I shouted and waved my arms, which demonstration I trusted the ul would find aversive. Was not withdrawal from strong stimuli, a movement, a noise, an unexpected shadow, or motion, a response pervasive in the kingdom of life, such stimuli often being linked to the possible strike of a predator? Had not hundreds of uls withdrawn, for example, from the stimuli of raging flames, most presumably without having been burned? Whereas my theory seemed plausible to me, the ul, rather obviously, did not take it as seriously as I did. It did not take long for the error in my reasoning to become apparent. The ul, as was evident, while perhaps annoyed, was not really surprised or startled. No longer could the response be immediate or reflexive. The source of the noise and motion was before him, easily comprehended. While the ul might be puzzled by, or might disapprove of, my actions, they were nothing likely to elicit a survival response.

The beast once more moved toward me.

I reached down and picked up a second rock and hurled it as hard as I could at that large, narrow head. This, even if it did not engage the withdrawal response, arrested the monster's advance. Then, no sooner had the stone struck the ul's head, just below the right eye, than I spun about and darted into the narrow crevice near the cave's entrance. It was about eight or nine feet deep and, whereas it would admit the ul's beak, head, and neck, it would not admit its shoulders, wings, or body. I turned and backed into the crevice until I felt the stone at my back. I could go no further. The angry beak jabbed into the crevice, snapping. It could not reach me, but I could have reached out and touched it. I collapsed, laughing, and crying. It took the small brain of the ul better than an hour before it realized that it could not reach me, and drew back from the opening. Soon thereafter it spread its wings and left the cave, presumably to hunt. When it did so, I came forward, out of the crevice. The former Lady Temione of Hammerfest was well back, under the low roof at the back of the cave. I think that the monster had forgotten about her.

"It has gone," I called to her.

She crawled forth from her ensconcement.

I went to the opening of the cave. "I will watch," I said. "Then you will watch."

"Are we safe?" she said.

"For now," I said.

"Can we climb down?" she asked.

"No," I said.

"Then it is a matter of time," she said.

"Tarnsmen were aflight," I said. "I heard the signal horns."

"They should have been here," she said, "long ago."

I could not gainsay that.

"What is the smell," she asked.

"Ul leavings, the stink of death, bones, cave odors," I said.

"No," she said.

"Ash, soot, burned vegetation," I said.

"Much?" she said.

"The ravages were extensive," I said.

"That is strange in the delta," she said.

"I would not know," I said.

"How is it that you are here?" she said.

"You were seized by the ul," I said. "I tried to hold it in place. I failed."

"You were a fool," she said, "to attempt that."

"I did not stop to deliberate," I said.

"Where are the tarnsmen?" she asked.

"They must have lost the sky trail," I said.

"I do not think so," she said.

"I do not understand," I said.

"I think they chose not to find us," she said.

"Why would that be?" I asked.

"I am not sure," she said.

"We must hope for their arrival," I said.

"They will not appear," she said.

"Surely you are mistaken," I said.

"I do not think so," she said.

"Why would they not appear?" I asked.

"I am not sure," she said.

"We may hope," I said.

"The ul is large, easy to see, its flight direct," she said, "the tarnsmen would have been swiftly in the saddle."

"Let us hope," I said.

"That costs little," she said.

"That is one of the perquisites of hope," I said.

"You called me a she-urt," she said.

"I managed to get your attention," I said.

"I am not a she-urt," she said.

"I apologize," I said. "But not much, and not enthusiastically."

"You saved my life," she said.

"Not for long, I fear," I said.

"Still," she said.

"I did not think much what I was doing at the time," I said.

"You may address me without permission," she said.

"Thank you," I said.

"I am not generous with that permission," she said.

"Do you know there is a collar on your neck?" I asked.

"You are a natural slave," she said. "It is obvious. You are born for the collar. Anyone could see that. You will never be fulfilled until it is on your neck. But I am different. I am not a natural slave."

"Yet you are a woman," I said.

"I am too beautiful to be a slave," she said.

"Men believe that the most beautiful women are slaves," I said. "That is why they enslave them. The collar is a badge of quality. It says that men have found that woman acceptable to be collared. She is worth owning. She is desirable. They want to possess her, every bit of her. Therefore, get on your knees, kiss the whip, and be done with it."

"Never," she said.

"In your heart," I said, "do you not long for a Master?"

"I am the most beautiful of all the women on the barges," she said.

"There is one," I said, "who is your superior." I was thinking of the former Eileen Bennett.

"Who is that?" she asked.

"Xanthe," I said.

"I know her, from the pens," said the former Lady Temione of Hammerfest. "She is a she-tarsk."

"Hardly," I said.

"Definitely," she said.

"I think that she, when free, had great sport with men, teasing them, tantalizing them, taunting them, raising and dashing hopes, promising much and delivering little, or nothing, and so on."

"I suspect that things have changed for her now," said the former Lady Temione of Hammerfest.

"I expect so," I said. It was easy to imagine the former Miss Eileen Bennett now, naked at the feet of a Gorean Master, looking up, seeing the whip in his hand, hoping not to be beaten.

"I am Temione," said the former Lady Temione of Hammerfest. "Masters will have it so."

"I am Mira," I said. "Masters will have it so."

"Then it is so," she said.

"You are doubtless sore and miserable from your journey," I said.

"Yes," she said, "but I can move about now. I can help watch. If I see the ul returning, I will call out and we can hurry to our refuges. The tunic is soiled, and bloodied, but it is sleeved, and the grip of the ul in flight, while firm, is not lacerating."

"Many aerial predators," I said, "bring their prey alive to their nest, den, or lodging. Perhaps the meat is fresher, or somehow flavored by the victim's struggles and terror."

"I see little hope for us," said Temione.

"What of rescuing tarnsmen?" I said.

"Were there such," she said, "we would be tied to saddle rings and on our way back to the barges by now."

"Do not despair," I said.

"I gather that the cliff cannot be scaled," she said. "Thus we are prisoners here, helpless prisoners. There is nothing to eat or drink. If the ul does not devour us, we can do little but hide and wait to die. Better to fling ourselves over the cliff and avoid a far more terrible death, one either lingering or one quicker, one within the wrenching jaws of the ul."

"Cling to hope," I said.

"And why?" she asked.

"An ul brought us here, to these heights," I said. "Perhaps an ul can effect our descent."

"That is absurd," said Temione. "Fear has addled your wits. You are mad."

"To be sure," I said, "we will need a dead ul."

"What can kill an ul?" she asked.

"Another ul," I said.

CHAPTER THIRTY-FOUR

"Our winged friend has left," I said. "I do not think it to be soon returned. It has had a long, tiresome journey followed by frustration. Its mood will be unpleasant and it is doubtless hungry. Accordingly, I think it will be foraging for a time."

"It seems much has been burned," she said, from her coign of security at the back of the cave.

The atmosphere was still oppressive.

"It will do the best it can," I said.

I was now near the arched opening of the cave and the broad, flat, ledge beyond the opening, having left the narrow crevice in which I had hitherto taken refuge.

The sky was very blue.

"Is it safe?" she asked.

"For now," I said.

"You have a plan?" she said, crawling forth onto the floor of the cave, from her coign of security.

"I am counting on the patience of an ul," I said, "its determination to feed, its unwillingness to be cheated, its willingness to wait."

"As did the ul which brought us here," she said.

"Precisely," I said. "Very much so."

"I think few uls would care to enter here," she said.

"They must be lured to do so," I said.

"How can that be done?" she asked, approaching me.

"With bait," I said.

"But we have no bait," she said.

"You are mistaken," I said.

"What bait?" she said.

"I will do very nicely," I said.

"I am afraid," she said.

"I trust less so than I," I said. "When I call to you, return to your hiding place."

"And what of you?" she asked.

"I shall return to mine," I said.

"But an ul can see us, smell us, sense us," she said.

"That is essential to my plan," I said. "We must seem near, available, at hand, on the verge of accessibility, vulnerable, inviting, only a snap or bite away, so fresh and tantalizing that its senses will reel, so that it cannot bear to tear itself away."

"What if more than one ul comes?" she said.

"What if no ul comes?" I said.

"Your plan is precarious, fragile, and unlikely of success," she said.

"I am sure our estimations on that matter are in agreement," I said.

"I am far more beautiful than you," she said. "Should I not be the bait?"

"I am not sure that you are so much more beautiful," I said.

"Do not be absurd," she said.

"What of lovely Xanthe?" I said.

"A she-tarsk," she said.

"Appraisals, and such things," I said, "we will leave to the Masters. In any event we are dealing here with uls and not lustful fellows eager to get their collar on a catch. For all I know, the male ul may be driven to distraction by odors or hisses, by the look of wings or claws, or the shape of a beak."

"Which of us looks more edible?" she asked.

"I am sure I do not know," I said. "I suspect that there is little to choose between us on that score. In any event, we may leave that to the uls."

"It was I who was seized on the barge," she said.

"That is because you were stupid," I said, "standing upright, moving about, not paying attention."

"I am not stupid," she said.

"Very well," I said. "But you feigned the matter brilliantly. I was completely fooled."

"If you insist on being the bait," she said, "I shall not object."

"It has nothing to do with beauty, or such," I said.

"Clearly not," she said.

"My niche of refuge is closer to the opening than yours," I said. "I can reach it much more quickly."

"What if the ul is small, or half-grown?" she asked.

"Then I shall hope to be inconspicuous," I said.

"Do your best to be of interest only to a large ul," she said.

"Do not fear," I said. "I have no wish to share my shelter with an ul of any size."

"Nor I mine," she said.

"When I call out," I said, "hasten to your refuge."

"I feel your plan is deeply flawed," she said.

"I have several better," I said, "but each requires the services of several large fellows with spears."

* * *

I screamed, casting myself bodily into the narrow opening. In my haste, my left shoulder was abraded on the stone. The sleeve of my tunic was torn open. There was smeared blood on the rock. The hissing was monstrous, but a yard away, like steam rushing from a valve, and the beak poked toward me, biting and snapping, and claws scratched at the stone of my small shelter. I had not expected the suddenness of the charge. Several uls, each of which I had deemed to be suitable to my purposes, had exited from or entered into openings in the cliffs. Given the half mile or so of cliffage to my left and right, below me and above me, I conjectured a population of hundreds of uls might house in these rude habitats. Some had flown past, most ignoring me. Two or three had hovered nearby. I began to suspect that not all uls would feed on human flesh. Many, at least, did not seem to regard creatures such as I as within their prey range. Several times I had stood outside the cave, emerged from its shadows, on the broad, bright ledge, crying out, gesticulating, trying to call myself to the attention of denizens of these high, remote cliffs. Then, a few moments ago, one such monster had swung about, altering its soaring flight, and, in flight, approached the cave opening, where it paused, hovering, regarding me. I redoubled my efforts to call myself to its attention. As I watched it, at a given point, I suddenly became terrified. Its head and neck began to extend toward me, the huge wings beating, holding it in place. "It is going to dart toward me!" I thought. I spun about, fleeing back into the cave. "Run!" I screamed to Temione. I heard the vast wings snap and a fierce shadow darkened the shelf. To this day, I feel I had somehow anticipated its charge, but it is possible, of course, that I had simply, in the stress, lost my nerve, and broke away, and that it was my flight which had automatically triggered its pursuit response. In any event I managed to reach my place between the rocks, with almost nothing to spare. The breath of the monster was sickening. After a moment or two it stopped snapping and scratching at the rocks. It then tried wedging itself into the crevice, but it soon realized it could not do so, not to any extent which would permit its beak to close about my body. It then drew back. It was unaware of Temione who had managed to crawl back into the narrow opening at the back of the cave, where the ceiling of the cave sloped gradually down to the floor. The new arrival was somewhat smaller than the monster who had transported Temione and me to the cave, but it was, in any case, large and formidable. From its smaller size I sensed that it might be younger than the other. The monster turned about. What if it found feeding impractical? Would it leave? Was it hungry? Would it give up on feeding here, and go elsewhere to hunt and eat? I had counted on its remaining in the cave until the larger ul returned. But perhaps, if it were younger, it might be less patient than the older ul and more ready to divert its energies to a newer hunt, perhaps one sooner consummated and more profitable. I thrust myself closer to the opening of the crevice. The closest he could come to me before was within a yard, I drawn back as far as I could manage. Now, if I remained where I was, it could actually bring its beak into play. "Hold, winged *tarsk*!" I cried. "Your beak is ugly. Your eyes are too small. Why does your skull go back so far? Did it not know when to stop? Some uls, I have heard, have teeth, shiny and sharp as knives. Why then does your sort make do with bony ridges?" Naturally the ul had no idea of what I was saying but I hoped to keep its attention and, to the extent I could, keep it in the cave. Then Temione, doubtless with the same intent, began, purringly, to call out to the ul. "Beautiful monster," she called out. "Do not deprive us of your company! Stay! Let us admire you! How handsome are your beak and wings! Your eyes sparkle. How keen they must be. Are you not the finest of all uls in all the cliffs?"

Then she shrieked in terror, squeezing back into her low-ceilinged niche, as the ul, perhaps then only aware of her presence, snapped its wings, flew at her a foot above the cave floor, and, landing with an arresting scratch of claws, snapped at her with the long narrow beak.

"I was almost killed!" cried Temione.

"Watch out," I said. "The ul is quick." Certainly I had had personal experience of that.

"I spoke soothingly," she said. "Why should it attack me?"

"It suspected you were insincere," I said. "It is well-known that uls despise idle flattery."

"She-urt!" she cried.

"She-tarsk!" I responded.

"I am larger and stronger than you," she said.

"Not that much so," I said.

"I can scratch the flesh off your bones," she said.

"I do not think so," I said. Surely I could get my hands in her hair first.

"I can," she said.

"Not if you are eaten first," I said.

"We are lost," she said.

"A small chance is gigantic," I said, "when compared to no chance. You were very brave. Try to keep the monster in the cave. But be careful. Dangle a hand or foot, if necessary, but be careful. You much assisted my plan when you dared to make your presence known. The ul, with two possible feedings in view, is far more likely to remain in the cave."

"Your plan, whatever it is," she said, "is absurd."

"If you do not know what it is," I said, "how do you know it is absurd?"

"Because it is your plan," she said.

"Better an absurd plan than no plan," I said.

"Stay back!" cried Temione.

"It has been an Ahn," I said. "The ul has lost patience. It prepares to leave."

"We have done all we can," said Temione. "We have spoken to the monster, we have teased it, we have taunted it, we have risked emerging from our shelters again and again, only to rush back in time. The ul is tired. It has been patient. Now it will leave."

"We must not let it do so," I said.

"Get back in the rocks," said Temione. "We can do nothing further. Tempt it no longer. Get back in the rocks."

"Do not fear," I said. "I am quick. I can do so."

"You are too far from the rocks," said Temione. "Get back!"

"I can do so," I said, tensely. I hoped I could do so.

"Ho, monster," I said, "turn about. See how far I am from the rocks. Can you catch me? Are you afraid to look? You are stupid. In that great skull of yours, your brain is the size of a *tospit*. That is why you are no match for a human."

But the monster did not turn about. Rather it spun about, without looking, like a hurricane, and smote its way across the floor of the cave.

I heard Temione, standing at the rear of the cave, scream.

I felt myself lifted from the floor of the cave, seized in the jaws of the ul.

CHAPTER THIRTY-FIVE

Scarcely had I felt the long, narrow, ridged jaws of the ul close about me, lifting me, than a vast shadow blotted out the light at the cave entrance and our huge, original captor, it which had snatched Temione from the deck of the barge, with a snap of wings, from the shelf outside the cave entrance, burst into the cave, crashing into the ul in whose grasp I was. The force of this blow turned my captor half about and it, its wings snapping and spreading, turned back to face the returned proprietor of this dreadful, bone-strewn lodging. Each beast spread its wings, widely, perhaps to enlarge its aspect and intimidate the other. The ul in whose keeping I was, with a sudden twist of its neck, flung me behind it, over its left wing, and I struck the floor, skidding, abraded, and rolled toward the back of the cave, half stunned. In this way, its jaws were readied for war, and its body was placed in such a way as to deny its adversary an uncontested access to its prey. "Here, be quick, here," whispered Temione, "hide, hide," rousing me to crawl back near her into the low-ceilinged part of the cave. I did so, half without thought, only half aware of what was occurring. I saw her frightened eyes. "Awake," I thought to myself, "awake!" Then, sharply, recovering, suddenly feeling pain and thrusting it to the side, I shook myself free of shock. The ul, like the newcomer, was now opening its jaws, hissing, and exposing the ridges of those jaws, presenting a mien awesomely threatening. I had little doubt that in nature the largest and fiercest of such displays might often win the day without bloodshed, causing the seeming lesser of the opponents to withdraw, however reluctantly or grudgingly, a result statistically likely to be in the best interest of the species, but I did not think that that could take place in this encounter. This was no neutral ground. A border had been crossed. Too, the younger ul, assuming it was younger, as it was smaller, was cornered. In this place, no gradual giving of ground was practical. If a lodging had been violated, might it not be again violated? Too, prey was involved.

"They will kill each other," said Temione.

"Then we are the safer," I said.

"But we will be no better off," said Temione.

"We might be much better off," I said.

There was a storm of twisting, striking bodies, of hissings and gruntings, of bolts of expelled air, a snapping of beaks, a flailing of clawed feet. Sometimes these monsters spun about, seemingly in one another's grasp. Sometimes they were inverted, or rolling together as might have contesting aquatic *tharlarion*. At other times they rose yards from the floor of the cave, continuing their altercation with wings and skulls scraping against the roof of the cave. Occasionally, for some reason, they separated, facing one another, and then, for no apparent reason, would again fly wildly, hissing and biting, at one another.

I doubt that this dispute continued for more than half an hour but, given the harrows of our vicarious participation, our lives being at stake, the flurries and interstices in the combat, and its inevitable ebb and flow, it seemed interminable to us.

"It is a battle of Ubars," said Temione.

"Were it in the sky," I said, "the clouds would bleed."

"The ul of the barge is the larger," she said. "Size favors it."

"The smaller is quicker, and, I think, less fatigued," I said.

"They are well matched," said Temione.

"It must soon end," I said.

"There!" said Temione.

"Oh!" I gasped.

The beak of the larger ul had slipped like a thrusting, parried blade off that of the smaller ul and its jaws had now, somehow, closed on the throat of the younger. I did not think this was a sought, instinctual closure, as it might be with dogs or wolves, but, given the vulnerability of that region and the ul's fashion of biting and laceration, it might supply the key to victory.

"The smaller is dead," said Temione. "It will bleed to death."

"No," I said. "Not yet. See its fear and desperation."

"Why does the large ul not release the throat, and bite it?" asked Temione.

"I do not know," I said. "I think, in its tiny brain, it senses something else."

"What?" asked Temione.

"The grip of death," I said.

"Behold the smaller," said Temione.

"I see," I whispered.

The body of the slighter ul, as it was held, was pressed against that of the larger ul. It brought up its clawed feet as though to push the larger body away. Then, in its stress, it, perhaps in virtue of an unexpected reflex, began, frenziedly, to claw and tear at the belly of the larger.

"Do not look," I warned Temione.

I myself looked away, but then looked back.

The larger ul had released its grip on the throat of the smaller ul, and backed away, dragging a cargo of intestines behind it, like coils of glistening hosing. It backed away, slowly, and then, across the sunlit shelf, outside the cave entrance, tried to spread its wings, failed to do so, and then stiffened, and toppled sidewise from the shelf.

The smaller ul, a flow of pulsing blood emerging on its neck with each breath, moved toward the shelf.

Temione and I crawled forth from our low, cramped shelter.

The smaller ul, patches of blood behind him, tottered at the edge of the shelf.

"No!" I cried. "Come back!"

"Let it go!" said Temione.

"No!" I cried.

"Do not interfere," she said. "Let it alone. Be away with it!"

"Never!" I cried, rising and running to the center of the cave. "Can you not see that it will fly, or fall!"

"Beg the Priest-Kings that it do so!" cried Temione. "We are then free!"

"Free to die," I said.

I rushed out on the shelf.

"Come back, noble monster!" I cried. "The cave and all within it are yours! You have defeated a mighty champion! Victory is yours! The foe has succumbed! Return and claim your world, your Ubarate, your city!"

"Are you mad?" cried Temione. "He cannot understand you!"

"How do I know what it understands?" I asked. "If it cannot understand words, let it understand triumph, reality, a situation, tones of voice, celebration, a conclusion!"

"You are mad," she said.

"If nothing else," I said. "I remind it that we live."

"Better it not be so reminded," said Temione, now near me, toward the center of the cave.

Slowly the smaller ul, bleeding with each breath, turned toward us.

"This lodging is yours," I called to it. "Claim it. Is it not one of the finest palaces in all the cliffs? Now it is yours! How mighty you are, how renowned!"

"Back away!" said Temione. "It is still alive. It is dangerous!"

"It is dying," I said.

"It is not dead," she said.

Both of us backed away.

"Approach, Ubar of the Delta, companion of clouds, brother of the wind," I said, "come deeper into your domain."

"It is alive. It will charge," said Temione.

"Withdraw slowly," I said. "Threaten it with no possible loss. Above all, do not turn and run."

"Come with me. Follow me," whispered Temione.

I reached out and placed my hand on the large, narrow, lowered beak. The blood now ceased to flow from the torn throat of the ul.

It raised its head and spread its wings, and looked about, as though surveying the cave, its now-conquered, palatial world, and then, slowly, it lowered its head and sank to the floor.

"It is dead," I said.

"Thus we cannot, as in your foolish, wild words, fly it from the cave," she said. "What madness that was. I was a fool, as mad as you, to even dream a speck of such a thing. My fear, my terror, my hope, subverted reason and scorned judgment. How beneath me! How unworthy of me! Hurry now. Help me drag this monster to the edge of the shelf, where we can plunge it to the delta below."

"Not at all," I said. "Our work now begins. Once stones were saws and knives. Let them be so again. There is much to be done. Weight must be lost, cut away. Tissues must serve as cords. Wings must be stiffened with tied bones. We must have a frame. Let it be that built by nature for the mighty ul. We shall make use of it. As he soared, so, too, if all goes well, shall we!"

CHAPTER THIRTY-SIX

The water was to our knees.

"Ai!" cried Temione.

"Do not let that thing fasten itself in your calf," I said. "We have no metal to heat, no salt to discomfit it."

"We are lost," said Temione. "The sun is cruel."

We were making our way east, small island by island, hoping to intercept the barges moving west, toward the Tamber Gulf. We could see the ul cliffs behind us.

The foliage here was still muchly burned away. The fire in the delta, seemingly anomalous, had wrought destruction over an extensive area, certainly over several square miles. Its origins remined mysterious.

"If we rendezvous with the barges, we will soon be returned to cages and chains," said Temione. "Our collars will be more on us than before."

"Keep your staff ready," I said. "Watch out for *tharlarion*."

"Bits of wood will do little to protect us," she said.

"Not all *tharlarion* are large," I said.

We continued to trek east.

"Stop. Be still," I whispered. "Good," I said. "It has passed."

"I saw it," she said.

"It is hard to miss a dorsal fin," I said.

"I did not miss it," she said.

"Try to move like water. Do not splash, or muchly so." I remembered the bathing pool at the southern shore of the Vosk, near Victoria Minor.

"They are most dangerous in the early morning and early evening," she said, "in the early morning because hungry after the night, and in the early evening to carry themselves through the night."

"I hope they are aware of that," I said. "It is my impression that they are ready to eat in any light, at any time."

"This water is too shallow for them," she said.

"Our recent visitor was apparently unaware of that," I said.

"It seems they do not need much water," she said.

"It is well to keep that in mind," I said.

"The delta steams," she said, wiping her forehead.

"If I may resume our conversation," I said, "much depends on who cages or chains you, whose collar you wear."

"That is the difference between us," she said. "I am a natural free woman and you are a natural slave."

"Yet," I said, "you are a woman."

"A free woman," she said.

"In clear water," I said, "regard yourself. You will discover a mark on your thigh and a collar on your neck."

"No man can master me," she said.

"Perhaps no man you have yet met," I said.

"You are fortunate the larger ul arrived when it did," said Temione.

"Perhaps," I said. "But I rather think, given the time involved, and the eyesight of aerial predators, the larger ul may have realized an intruder was in the cave, and was waiting to deal with it in flight, in the open, rather than in the confines of the cave. I suspect its action was precipitated when it saw me seized. Was it to surrender its prey to an intruder, prey it had so extensively and unsuccessfully sought in its own lodging?"

"Perhaps," she said.

We continued on.

"Stop!" she said.

We paused, immediately.

"Did you hear it?" she asked.

"The cry of the Vosk gull?" I said.

"No" she said. "Listen."

"Yes!" I said. "Voices!"

"I am not an ul," had said Temione.

"Nor am I," I had said.

"Perhaps tarnsmen will arrive," she said.

"And perhaps you will thirst to death or be fed upon by the next ul choosing to visit this lair," I said. "When I give the signal, cling to our device, its ropes of sinew about you, carry it rapidly across the shelf, and launch it over the cliff."

"We will then fall to our death," she said.

"If all goes well," I said, "we will soar to our life."

"I do not think this thing will work," she said.

"It may not," I said. "It may come to pieces, it may not take the air, it may plummet, but the principles involved are tried, familiar, and sound. I assure you, this is no simple fantasy of mine, but a makeshift version of a form of artifact both practical and well-tested."

"Where?" she asked. "I know such things not."

I thought quickly.

"You are familiar, of course," I said, "with the Voltai Mountains." I had heard them referred to. Beyond that I knew nothing of them.

"No," she said, "I am of the Vosk Basin."

"Excellent," I thought. I then spoke. "Knew you more of the Voltai Mountains," I said, "you would be familiar with a sport enjoyed there by local lads, called the sport of sky sailing."

"I have never heard of it," she said.

"Of course not," I said. "You are not of the Voltai Mountains."

"What is sky sailing?" she asked.

"Large, light devices are built," I said, "frames, resembling wings, built of wooden strips, stout cordage, and thick canvas. One climbs up, fastens oneself within the frame, and leaps out, into the air, and floats about, like a leaf or feather."

"I do not believe you," she said.

I was muchly concerned to conceal my barbarian origin. Some, I knew, sought me. They sought a 'barbarian.' Thus I wished to be taken as Gorean. Accordingly, in order not to give myself away, I wished to invent a Gorean background, or provenance, so to speak, for what I had in mind.

"It can be done," I said. As far as I knew, of course, those of the Voltai knew as little about such things as Temione.

"It sounds dangerous," she said.

"Accidents can happen," I said. "Are you ready to help?"

"It is a wagon of the air?" she said.

"In a way," I said.

"The lads of the Voltai do this?" she asked.

"Frequently," I said. "Surely you do not doubt me."

"Can you guide this thing?" she asked.

"We will let the device take us where it wishes," I said. "That will be acceptable, doubtless even best." Despite a couple of handles and attached lengths of sinew, I had no confidence in my ability to manage the thing.

"And where will it take us?" she asked.

"Eventually down, I trust," I said. I saw no point in alarming Temione with speculations having to do with side currents, updrafts, and such. Let the trip be as uneventful as possible.

"Stay within the sinew, and hold tightly," I said.

"Will the uls not see us?" she asked.

"We will leave in darkness," I said. "I do not think that uls hunt at night. If an ul should see us, say, in the light of a moon, it will merely think us another ul, one in soaring flight."

"I hope that is true," she said.

I, too, hoped that it was true.

"I am hungry," she said.

"Eat a bit if the ul meat," I suggested.

"I am not that hungry," she said.

"As you wish," I said.

"I am thirsty," she said.

"At this point, the water in the delta below will be fresh," I said. "It is not yet mixed with that of the Tamber Gulf."

"That does me little good now," she said.

"Perhaps later," I said.

"Why are you not eating?" she asked.

"I am not that hungry," I said.

Some two hours later it was night. Two moons were in the sky, the White Moon and the Yellow Moon. Occasionally, clouds dimmed the light of one moon or the other.

"Ready?" I asked.

It seemed to me about as dark as it was likely to get.

"We will carry the device over the shelf quickly, and, holding to it, and fastened therein, leap from the cliff."

"I think I shall stay behind," she said.

"Remember," I said. "The lads of the Voltai do this all the time."

"You are sure of this?" she said.

"Certainly," I said.

"I am ready," she said.

Little of the carved, butchered ul was left but the wings, which I had done my best to stabilize, with bone and sinew.

"Now!" I said.

We managed to carry our device swiftly over the flat shelf outside the cave, but, instead of continuing, utilizing the momentum of this rushing charge, as I had planned, we stopped short at the edge of the shelf.

"Why did you stop?" she asked.

"Why did you?" I asked.

"I was afraid," she said.

"I, too," I said.

"Remember the lads of the Voltai," she said. "Let us take courage from them."

"Yes," I said. "Let us do so."

"If they can do it, so, too, can we," she said.

"When I give the word," I said, "thrust the device out from the cliff." It would not do for it to strike the cliff and be broken, collapsed, or torn to pieces."

"I am ready," she said.

"Now!" I said.

It was a terrifying, sickening moment, realizing that the flat, firm, solid shelf outside the cave entrance was no longer beneath us. It was like a frightening step into nothingness. I hoped we would clear the cliff. And then, suddenly, we felt as if we were yanked upward a foot of so in the air, and we sensed the wings of the ul, air beneath them, swelling upward, and we began to glide through the night, leaving the cave and cliff behind us. Our flight was not long, but much longer than I had expected. I had thought we would land relatively close to the foot of the cliff, perhaps a hundred or yards or so from its base but, given the breadth of the ul's wings, our relatively slight weight, and the nature of the air which sustained us, we must have extended our flight by three or fourfold. We began our long, sloping descent, the wind in our hair, our tunics swept back. The terrain below us grew closer and closer, seeming to fly back behind us, and then our sky steed crashed into a stand of darkened *rence*, and we found our feet in the water and the large wing on the right buckled and broken. Pathetic and amateurish as was our performance, and crude and awkward as was our landing, we were now several hundred yards from the cliffs. Temione was no longer at my side. I was alarmed. I feared she might have fallen. "Temione," I called, "where are you, are you all right?"

"I am here, I am drinking water," she said, from the darkness.

I disengaged myself from the sinew harnessing, and, kneeling down, cupping my hands, brought water to my parched lips.

"Are you all right?" asked Temione.

"Yes," I said.

"Was our alighting not uneasy?" she asked.

"Somewhat," I said.

"Is this sort of thing not dangerous?" she asked.

"Sometimes," I said.

"Do the lads in the Voltai who go sky sailing alight similarly?" she asked.

"I have never heard of one of them getting a scratch," I said.

"They must be skilled," she said.

"I have never heard of one of them who was not," I said.

"Doubtless they practice diligently," she said.

"I have never heard of one of them who did not," I said.

"At least, we are safe," she said.

"We do not know what might be in the darkness," I said.

We had paused.

"Did you hear it?" she had asked.

"The cry of the Vosk gull?" I said.

"No" she said. "Listen."

"Yes!" I said. "Voices!"

"*Rencers*?" she asked.

"I do not think so," I said. "I doubt that *Rencers* inhabit this area. Presumably *Rencers* communicate with one another, from village to village. But the *Rencer* who dealt with the barge-master knew no reason for the anomalous flights of uls, and thus knew nothing of the fire."

"The delta is vast," she said.

"*Rencers* might avoid areas where uls are plentiful," I said.

"It would not do to fall into the hands of *Rencers*," she said. "I understand them to be savages, suspicious, skilled in stealth, dangerous with the bow. I have heard they shun strangers and cast displeasing slaves to *tharlarion*. Who would care to live so simply, so primitively, on tiny straw islands, in so fearful an area, so remote from the amenities of life?"

"What is peril to one," I said, "may be security to another. For those who reject or abhor civilization, its absence is neither a hardship nor a tribulation. Loneliness is not a burden to those who prize and seek it. To those who trust no one, distance is a measure not of suffering and misfortune but of comfort and safety."

"Many are the monsters of the delta," she said, "and prominent amongst them are *Rencers*."

"Every culture has its ways," I said. "Children have nothing to say about the garments into which they are born."

"I fear and loathe *Rencers*," she said.

"As you are marked and collared," I said, "I am sure they would know what to do with you."

She blanched.

"I doubt that the voices are those of *Rencers*," I said.

"Surely the barges are not yet at hand," she said.

"Not so soon," I said, "given the length and speed of the ul's flight."

"Then whose voices drift to us from behind the *rence* and over the waters?" she asked.

"We shall see," I said. "Let us proceed carefully."

CHAPTER THIRTY-SEVEN

"Ships," whispered Temione.

"Five," I said.

"Knife ships," she said. "See the rams, the shearing blades."

"The water is too shallow for ships," I said.

"Here," she said, "not there."

"It is a lagoon," I guessed.

"There are lagoons," she said. "But that is a channel, probably its end, backing into the Tamber itself."

"There are such channels," I said.

"Some," she said. "The delta is wide."

"I did not think ships could ply the delta," I said.

"Those cannot," she said. "They are ships for the sea, for Thassa herself, not delta ships, almost barges."

"They are at anchor," I said.

"They are stopped," she said. "They will go no further."

"Perhaps they could be hauled by ropes, drawn by male slaves," I said, "or avail themselves of portages, being dissembled at one point and reassembled at another."

"They are not delta ships," she said. "They are ships of war."

"From Port Kar?" I asked.

"Port Kar is now at peace with the delta," she said.

"It was not always so?" I asked.

"The delta did not always have the great bow," she said. "And Port Kar did not always have a Home Stone."

"What ships are they then?" I asked.

"I do not know," she said. "But they must have come into the delta from the Tamber Gulf, and thus from Thassa herself."

"From Cos or Tyros?" I said. I had heard of these Ubarates.

"Bold would be ships of Cos or Tyros to venture into the waters of Port Kar," she said.

"Not from Cos or Tyros then?" I said.

"I do not think so," she said.

"What are they doing here?" I asked.

"I think," she said, "they are waiting."

"For the barges," I said, "the barges of Tenalian!"

"I think so," she said.

"The barges," I said, "could avoid the ships. They need not access the channel."

"See the camp to the side," she said. "It is large. It is fortified. See the setting of sharpened stakes, to fend against *tharlarion*."

"There are several men, many men," I said.

"Counting crews and men at arms," she said, "perhaps three to four hundred."

"More than enough to subdue the guards and keepers on the barges," I said.

"When the barges are close enough," she said, "they will wade the waters to intercept them. Then, with loot and spoil they will return to the ships."

"Defense will be stout on the barges," I said.

"It will be overwhelmed," she said. "The raiders will attack at night, in numbers. They will have the advantage of surprise and will create fearful diversions, spreading terror and shattering resistance."

"I understand the business of numbers and attacking at night," I said, "but how could they, with so many men, so large a camp, and several ships, enlist surprise amongst their options?"

"What if their scouts, their points, and outriders, their tarnsmen and tarns on reconnaissance, were blind? What would they see?"

"Nothing," I said.

"And would it not be much the same if they refused to report what they saw?"

"Yes," I said.

"No tarnsmen," she said, "came to our rescue."

"We had seen too much," I said. "—the burning of *rence*, possibly even a camp, and ships, or might see them, from tarnback, on a return to the barges."

"Behold the camp," said Temione, parting the *rence* a tiny bit, "a tarn. To the right. I wager it is that of one of the two tarnsmen with the barges."

"I see," I said.

"I am sure they were suborned," said Temione. "Why should they not be paid twice, not carry two purses, one from Tenalian, the other from the lurking raiders?"

"Honor," I said.

"Some men know not its name," said Temione.

"You spoke of diversions," I said, "fearful diversions."

"See some of the stakes," she said, "those upright, buried deeply in the ground, with heavy ropes trailing into the water?"

I looked more closely. "Yes," I said.

"When I was free," she said, "I heard stories of such things from men who heard them in the taverns."

"What things?" I asked.

"From when *Rencer* village might be pitted against *Rencer* village, before the unifying of *Rencers* under a delta lord named Ho-Hak."

"I do not understand," I said.

"*Rencers* live in apprehension," she said, "should an unusually aggressive *tharlarion*, or one abnormal, climb the *rence* to enter a village. They will relentlessly hunt down and kill such a beast, lest its example be followed by others, lest even such a tendency be somehow transmitted to offspring."

"I have heard something like that," I said.

"The ropes in the water," said Temione, "lead to captive *tharlarion*, hungry, with their jaws strapped shut. These will be conveyed to the barges where, their jaws freed, they will be thrust onto one or more barges. When the men of the barges discover the danger and spend themselves resisting what they take to be a surprising, unfortunate, natural attack of beasts, the raiders will attack from another point. It is a tactic known to *Rencers* but unlikely to be understood by, or expected by, those not of the delta."

"That is a fearful diversion, indeed," I said.

"The barges are doomed," said Temione.

"On the decks of the ships," I said, "there seem to be stores of some sort, covered over with tarpaulins."

"Housings for such as we, I wager," said Temione.

"Slave cages?" I said.

"I think so," said Temione.

"I do not think I would care to be so housed," I said.

"Get used to it," she said. "You are a slave. You would look pretty housed naked in a tiny slave cage. Men like to see us helplessly so. It helps you to better understand your rightful subjugation to men."

"And yours?" I said.

"I am a free woman in a collar," she said.

"You are a slave in a collar," I said.

"You are a slave whether in a collar or not," she said.

"I welcome the collar," I said. "I want no choice."

"That is fortunate," she said, "For you have none, slave."

"Nor do you," I said, "slave."

"Slave!" she hissed.

"To be dominated by a male thrills me," I said, "as nothing else. I never feel so meaningful, so real, so female than when at the feet of a male, a master, one to whom I belong, one who will do with me as he pleases."

"That is the difference between us, slave," she said.

"I think there is little difference between us, slave," I said. "Wait until a handsome, mighty male seizes your hair and forces your lips to his feet."

"I was the Lady Temione of Hammerfest," she said.

"And you are now naught but a collared slave," I said. "You are nothing. You can be bought and sold like a boot or goblet."

"We had best dally no longer," she said. "Let us now approach those of the camp and ships."

"How so?" I said.

"It is better than dying in the delta," she said.

"We know much now," I said, "that is unknown to those of the barges."

"Doubtless," she said.

"We know the reason for the flight of the uls," I said, "the red enemy, fire. And we may surmise from its nature, its extent, and the inability of natural barriers, abundant courses of water, to constrain it, that this fire was deliberately set."

"Why would it have been set?" she asked.

"Probably for various reasons," I said, "perhaps to clear the area of possible *Rencers*, possibly to drive away dangerous, predatory uls, perhaps to devastate and render useless, burned and barren, a swath of land through which a large expedition might venture, placidly and safely, undetected. Who would care to enter into, or traverse, so terrible a terrain? Within such a land might not a large beast, or beasts, dwell and wait, their station prepared, their resources gathered, readying themselves to pounce when the opportunity presents itself?"

"The uls returned," she said.

"Not for days," I said.

"But they came back," she said.

"Perhaps the raiders underestimated the strength of the call of territoriality," I said.

"Let us now call ourselves to the attention of the raiders," she said. "We are slaves. We have value. They will not harm us, lest perhaps to give us an instructive lashing, to remind us we are slaves. We will merely be the first in their cages."

"I think not," I said.

"I do not understand," she said.

"The barges must be warned," I said.

"Why?" she said.

"The barges will be surprised," I said. "Without the honest services of their scouts, their hired tarnsmen, they are blind. Blood will flow. Men will die."

"The delta is no stranger to such things," she said.

"I would preclude slaughter," I said.

"The delta is dangerous," she said. "You do not even know the location of the barges. If you are noted in the marshes, say, seen from above by scouting tarnsmen, they would kill you instantly, lest you reveal their plans. Come with me to the camp of the raiders. This war is not ours. Let us seek our cages."

"You would have us leave the barges to their fate?" I said.

"The delta is vast and unkind," she said. "We do not know her. In her marshes we are no more than wandering, imperiled beasts. Unguided, we might miss the barges entirely. We have no choice."

"Sometimes," I said, "it is when one has no choice that one must choose."

"Attend my words," she said. "They are not feathers in the wind, they are weighty, like rocks and sand."

"Perhaps your counsel is wise," I said, "but I cannot accept it."

"Why?" she asked. "Are you so eager to wander lost in the delta, perhaps for weeks, until eaten or snared in the coarse ropes of *Rencers*?"

"I would do my best to save lives," I said.

"Why?" she asked. "They are not your own. Men kill one another frequently. It is the way of men. They are beasts. Do not concern yourself."

"Some know honor," I said.

"The fools amongst them," she said.

"Even were I free," I said, "I would wear no mantle stained with innocent blood. It leaves deep stains."

"Ah!" she said. "You think if the barges were warned, they would free you!"

"I think only of saving lives," I said, "or, at least, of warning others of danger."

"You would not be freed," she said. "Only a fool frees a slave girl. Not for nothing is that a common saying. They want us in collars. Once a man has tasted slave, he becomes a *larl*. He is henceforth satisfied with nothing less."

"Were I freed," I said, "I would remove my clothing, kneel, and name myself slave."

"Slave!" she sneered.

"Yes," I said. "What is wrong?" I asked.

"When I hear such things," she said, "something within me quivers."

"It is the sensing of your deepest self," I said.

"I cannot admit that," she said.

She touched her collar.

"The time will come," I said, "when you can no longer deny it, when you will no longer wish to deny it."

"I do not know what to do," she said.

"Let us close the *rence* and withdraw," I said. "The barges cannot be far away."

CHAPTER THIRTY-EIGHT

"Where are the two slaves, Mira and Temione?" called the keeper.

"Here," said a second keeper, beside us.

We were prepared to be summoned.

Instantly, from our knees, as we were in the presence of free men, we both went to first obeisance position, our heads to the deck, palms of our hands flat on the deck beside our heads.

"Tie their hands behind their backs," said the keeper. "Then tie them together by the neck. Then attach a rope to the neck rope and bring them before the barge-master."

"We are to be rewarded," whispered Temione to me, her head besides mine, both of our heads to the deck. "I shall demand freedom and riches."

Our hands were then being tied behind our backs.

How simply and effectively this is done!

We were then tied together by the neck.

"Get up, heads down," we were ordered.

The heads-down position is one of humility, thus appropriate for slaves. Also, heads down, one is unlikely to meet the eye of a free person.

Another length of rope was tied to the center of the rope that tied us together.

A moment later we were being led to the table of the barge-master, where we knelt.

Both of us, and the other slaves on the barges, were now no longer in the ample, sleeved tunics in which we had been placed to make us less exciting to *Rencers*, less tempting, but in typically scanty slave tunics, the sort which leaves no doubt in the observer's mind that we are properties, domestic animals.

From where we were I could see one of the hundreds of tiny *rence*-strewn islands amongst which the mighty Vosk, in its many streams and floods debouches into the Tamber Gulf. Many of these small islands have names, and all have locations and coordinates. In this way, wary businessmen may choose amongst several points for loading or unloading cargo, which measure, as I understand it, much facilitates security, stealth, and secrecy. I could see three ships at anchor west of the island. These were not delta ships. Delta ships, rafts, and barges seldom, if ever, access the open waters of the gulf. I understood that if one were to trace the shoreline of the Tamber Gulf further to the north and west one would eventually reach many-canaled Port Kar.

"You did well, slaves," said the barge-master. "You may look up."

I looked up, but took care not to meet his eyes. Temione, too, looked up, but, I suspected, somewhat more boldly.

"The foe, whatever be his nature or identity, attacked six nights ago," he said, "but encountered only darkness and air. We have that on the authority of *Rencers* to whom the foe appealed for intelligence."

The barges had not held their normal 'night position,' but had moved in the darkness south and away from the channel in which the five ships of the raiders lay at anchor. They had then adjusted their course to continue on to the Tamber Gulf. In this way, an altercation was avoided in which, doubtless, a considerable expenditure of human life would have taken place. Too, given the numbers involved, it seemed more than likely that the guards and keepers on the barges, if not wiped out to a man, would have been driven from the barges and scattered into the nocturnal marshes.

"Had we not been warned in time," said the barge-master, "as we would not have been, given the treachery of the tarn scouts on which we depended for vigilance, calamity might have befallen. But, warned, and by mere slaves, disaster was averted. We expedited movement and changed our course, putting us well beyond the wading, trekking range of the foe. Now we have successfully negotiated the delta and made our way to the noble Tenalian's secret, prearranged rendezvous point where his ships await. Without your aid, without the intelligence you supplied, our enterprise might well have failed."

"May I speak, Master?" asked Temione.

I suspected that the boldness of this initiative might have surprised the barge-master.

"—Yes," he said.

"I, with my follower, my colleague and associate, Mira," she said.

"Your worthless collar sister," he said.

"Yes, Master," she said, "I, followed by my worthless collar sister, Mira—escaping many dangers and fierce uls, discovering a formidable enemy lying in wait for your fleet of barges, transporting the goods of the noble Master, Tenalian, put aside all thoughts of personal safety and, at great personal risk, in the lonely, vast, trackless, watery wilderness of the delta, imperiled by *tharlarion*, quicksand, serpents, sharks, and *Rencers*, fought my way to your side, to bring you intelligence without which you would surely have been destroyed."

"Might have been sorely discomfited," suggested the barge-master.

"Forgive the detail, Master," she said, "but I wish it to be clear, for my sake and that of simple truth, the extent of the risk, sacrifice, hardship, and heroism involved in my saving the barges, and, doubtless, many lives, including that of my collar sister, Mira."

"We have some understanding, however imperfect," said the barge-master, "of what was involved."

"Thus Master," she said, "I am confident that I may depend upon your sense of honor, so prized by you as an officer, and your recognition of fittingness, so precious to you as a man of probity and judgment, to express your appreciation of my deed, and recompense me accordingly."

"What of your collar sister?" he asked.

"She, too, surely," said Temione.

"It was for such a reason," said he, "that I had you brought before me this morning."

"But kneeling, scarcely clad, bound, neck-roped?" she said.

"You are slaves," he said.

"Mira is a slave," said Temione. "You can see it in every curve of her body, in every expression on her face. But I am a free woman, though in a collar."

"If you are in a collar," he said, "you are a slave."

"Master?" said Temione.

"How can I recompense you for your service?" he asked.

"Free me!" she said.

"But," he said, "if you are already a free woman as you aver, how could I free you? One cannot free the free."

"Very well," she said. "I am a slave."

"Are you a slave, wholly, and nothing else?" he asked.

"Yes, Master," she said, "I am a slave, wholly, and nothing else."

"You acknowledge that?"

"Yes, Master."

"Fully, and completely?"

"Yes, Master," said Temione.

"And might you, beside your freedom, desire aught else?" he asked.

"Only what I deserve, gold, silver, jewels, riches," she said.

"And what of the slave, Mira?" he asked.

"You can give her to me and I could sell her somewhere," she said.

"And what have you, Mira, to say of all this?" he asked.

"I am a slave," I said, "it will be done with me as Masters or Mistresses please."

"Mira," he asked, "should I free you?"

"I do not think Master is a fool," I said.

"Free me!" exclaimed Temione.

"What does your collar say?" he asked.

"That I am the property of Tenalian of Ar," she said.

"How then could I free you?" he asked.

"In the name of Tenalian!" she said.

The barge-master then turned to one of the nearby keepers. "Take this slave," he said, indicating Temione, "strip her, and tie her on her belly at a low railing, and then give her ten lashes."

Temione regarded the barge-master and shook her head wildly, negatively.

"Do you protest the decision of a free man?" he asked.

"No, Master!" she wept.

"Should we shave her head?" asked a keeper. "As an extra punishment?"

The barge-master thought for moment, and then said, "No, it would lower her price. Let her keep her hair, but, for allowing her to keep her hair, add five more lashes to her punishment."

"Please, no, Master!" begged Temione. "Did I not serve you well? Is this how I am paid for what I did?"

"A slave is to serve her Master or Mistress," said the barge-master. "You did no more than you should have done."

Temione was then cut loose from me, and pulled to her feet by the hair.

"After your lashing," said the barge-master, "you will be kept naked and will serve as a slave to slaves. You will learn well, my dear, what it is to be a slave. In two days, you will beg to kiss the feet of a man, any man. In three days, you will beg to serve the pleasure of a man, any man." He then addressed himself to the keeper at hand. "Take the seductive she-tarsk away," he said.

Temione then, in leading position, bent over, the keeper's hand in her hair, was conducted from his presence.

"You are Mira?" he said.

"If it pleases, Master," I said.

"I fear your collar sister was displeasing," he said.

I shuddered.

"I know from those to whom you first reported," he said, "how prominent was your role in reaching and warning us."

I said nothing.

"More so," he said, "than that of the other."

Again I remained silent.

"Open your mouth," he said.

I did so, prepared to serve his pleasure.

I was a slave.

"No," he smiled, and placed a round, hard candy in my mouth. Slaves will not kill for such a candy, but they will steal and fight for one.

"You did well," he said.

I looked up, from his feet, gratefully, tears in my eyes.

How much relativity there is in such things, with respect to what is precious and what is not! Not negligible to one in a tunic and collar is a candy, a kind word, a smile, a hand in her hair, affectionately shaking her head, such things. The former Agnes Morrison Atherton, of Earth, young, adept, urbane, refined, sophisticated, well-educated, cool and professional, now on a foreign world, now a Gorean slave girl, now helplessly subject to heats and needs, knelt before a free man, a female before a true man, knelt rightfully, thankfully, and honestly. How shallow and empty then seemed Earth, with its thousands of prescribed lies and hypocrisies. How unreal then seemed Earth, and how true, vivid, and real was Gor.

I, a woman, was at the feet of a Master.

I knew I was where I belonged.

"Unrope, untether, the slave," said the barge-master to a keeper. "Ankle chain her on Barge Two."

I was startled and grateful.

When I was freed, I went to the feet of the barge-master and kissed them, again and again.

"Enough," he said. "Follow the keeper to your new chaining."

"Yes, Master," I said.

How I loved using the word 'Master' to a man. Why should one not use such a word? They are the Masters.

Barge Two was reserved for slaves regarded as more valuable. This accounted for the chaining. How could one run, or be easily stolen, if one is chained to several others? On Barge Six chaining was also known, but the chaining of slaves there was heavier, and their treatment was harsher. It was, in its way, at least in certain sections, a punishment barge, where might be found slaves who, in one way or another, often, in my view, in seemingly trivial ways, perhaps guilty of an indiscreet expression or tone of voice, a hesitation or dalliance in complying with a command, or such, had not been found fully pleasing by a Master. It was a dreaded barge, one from which errant slaves, eager to mend their ways, hoped to be soon freed, and one to which other slaves feared they might be consigned. I hoped that Temione would not be put on Barge Six. She must hone her slave skills, and, more importantly, come to see herself as a slave, and become a slave, through and through, unquestioningly, until she not only accepted her bondage, but wanted and cherished it, until she treasured her servitude, until she yearned for her subjugation.

A slave finds her wholeness and redemption in submission. To be a slave is her meaning, her identity, her nature, and joy. But then I shuddered in terror, realizing I was an object, that I could be bought and sold like a pig, fitting for me, as I was an animal. I was a slave! How paradoxical and wondrous is being a slave! I wanted to be a slave. I feared to be a slave. I was a slave. It had been decided for me. I did not object.

I hoped that Temione would be consigned to Barge Two. She was certainly beautiful enough to justify such a consignment. And I could probably get soothing lotions from a keeper to tend her back. I wished that a Master would take her in hand and conquer her, until she, well knowing herself conquered, could understand and welcome herself slave.

As I followed the keeper to Barge Two, I winced, hearing the falling of the lash on Temione.

A few moments later, as I sat on the deck of Barge Two, a manacle was snapped about my ankle.

"Please, Master," I asked, chained, "may I speak?"

"Yes," he said.

"May not," I asked, "the slave, Temione, be put here, on Barge Two?"

"No," he said. "She has been found displeasing. She will be chained, heavily, and nude, on Barge Six. There she, with others, will be fed little, and on garbage, and will frequently feel the switch or whip. Do you wish to join her?"

"No, Master!" I said.

"Then see that you are pleasing," he said.

"Yes, Master," I said.

"Do not concern yourself," he said.

"Yes, Master," I said.

"After that," he said, "for a time, kept naked, she will serve as a slave to slaves."

I was silent.

How far now was the vulnerable collar-girl, blond-haired, blue-eyed Temione, from the wealthy, imperious Lady Temione of Hammerfest, possibly to be considered for the honor of being denominated an Oligarch of the Vosk!

"Belly and lick," he said.

I went to my belly and licked and kissed his feet.

Then he strode away.

I lay there on the warm deck.

CHAPTER THIRTY-NINE

"Gruel?" asked Temione.

"Yes," I said.

She steadied herself, because of the rocking of the ship.

She put a ladleful of slave porridge in my cupped hands.

"Thank you," I said.

Temione looked at me, gratefully.

"You do not thank a slave," said a girl next to me in the hold of the round ship.

"Are you a barbarian?" asked another.

"The naked she-tarsk will scorn you," said another.

"Keep her small and frightened," said another.

"She is one of us," I said. "We are all slaves."

"Slave!" called one of the slaves to Temione.

"Yes, Mistress?" said Temione.

"More gruel," said the slave.

"I may not, Mistress," said Temione. "You have had your serving."

"I want another," said the slave.

"I may not, Mistress," said Temione.

"Few eat," said the slave. "Much is left."

This was true. Several of the slaves, sick with the pitching and rolling of the ship, had little or no appetite. Even now, four moaned in the half-darkness, their huddled shapes dimly discernable in the light of the small, swinging lantern. Nearby was the broad-stepped ladder leading up to the hatch by means of which, when opened, the deck might be accessed.

"Even so, Mistress," said Temione.

"Come here, slave," said the girl.

Temione made her way to her side.

"You once owned me," said the girl.

Instantly Temione, with her small pail of gruel and ladle, knelt before her. "Forgive me, Mistress," she begged.

"Now you are little better than a slaves' slave," said the girl.

"Be merciful," said Temione. She was naked, but so, too, were we all, in the filth and squalor of the crowded hold.

"Have you eaten?" asked the girl.

"I may not, until all have been served," said Temione.

"I wonder if the Masters will believe you?" said the girl.

"Mistress?" said Temione.

The girl then reached into the small pail, scooped up a moist wad of the porridge, and rubbed it about Temione's face.

"Stop!" I said.

But I could not hasten to Temione's aid because some hands behind me seized my hair and pulled be back, and, twisting, I was held to the floor of the hold, my head afire.

"Do not interfere," said a girl.

"She was a house slave," said another girl.

"I was not!" I said. "I was a field slave! Let me go! Please, let me go!" The former house slaves, or palace slaves, of the Lady Temione of Hammerfest did not fare well when exposed to her former field slaves. Indeed, most house, or palace, slaves, when mixed with former field slaves, pretended to have labored in the fields.

I watched, as I could, held down, as the remains of the pail were poured over Temione's head, hair, and shoulders.

"Beware," I said, "the Masters will not be pleased!"

"She is right," said a slave.

Those in the hold, within the circle of the tiny lamp's light, were instantly subdued.

"Go to the water keg," said she who had discomfited Temione, "and clean yourself well, and say nothing to the Masters, or, when we are allowed on deck for fresh air and sunlight, in our lots, you might fall overboard."

"Yes, Mistress," wept Temione, trembling, struggling to her feet.

At the same time, my hair was released.

We were not chained in the hold. First, there would have been little point in doing so. Second, should the ship find itself in jeopardy, perhaps having run on rocks or having been rammed, we, the hatch opened, would be in less danger of going down with the ship. Third, our freedom from chains made it easier for small lots of us to be brought back and forth between the hold and the deck.

There were three ships, round ships, in our small convoy. We had been moving south along the coast for six days now, toward, as I understood it, a major port, one named Brundisium. For the first three days of our journey, in the Tamber Gulf, and thence breasting Thassa, the sea, we had been escorted by two knife ships from Port Kar. On the fourth day two knife ships from Brundisium had met us, and the ships from Port Kar had put about and withdrawn, presumably to return to their home base. One mariner had expressed his relief at their departure, saying that such an escort was like 'setting *sleen* to guard *verr*,' but another had reminded him 'that Port Kar now had a

Home Stone.' One of the ships from Port Kar was well known in these waters, the *Dorna,* said to be frequently captained by someone called Bosk, of Port Kar, apparently a ranking member of the Council of Captains, the body sovereign in Port Kar. It was not known, however, whether or not this Bosk of Port Kar was on board at the time.

There was still speculation about the nature of the five ships which had been at anchor in the delta, at a channel's end, those apparently waiting to intercept the six barges of Tenalian's fleet. In any event, it was now clear that Tenalian's ruse of shipping east on the Vosk had been a signal failure. Clearly a serious breach of security had been involved. In our journey south toward Brundisium, there had been no sign of those five ships. Their quarry had eluded them.

In a few minutes, Temione, rinsed clean, her body freed of gruel, with her pail and ladle, was approaching the broad steps leading up to the overhead hatch.

"Hold!" cried the girl who had been her tormenter.

"Mistress?" said Temione, stopped at the foot of the stairs.

"Come here," said the girl.

Temione put down the pail and ladle and went to the girl, before whom, as slave to Mistress, she knelt.

"You look well, Lady Temione of Hammerfest," said the girl, "naked, and collared, on your knees before me."

"I am not the Lady Temione of Hammerfest," said Temione. "I am only Temione, a slave."

"True," said the girl, "and you were a displeasing slave."

"How so, Mistress?" asked Temione.

"I was displeased," said the girl.

"Forgive me, Mistress," said Temione, frightened.

The girl then put her hands in Temione's hair and twisted and shook her head, cruelly, and then, with the front and back of her hand, struck her, again and again, until, I gather, her hand burned, and she stopped.

To all this, Temione, trembling, shuddering, and weeping, submitted. She kept her hands down, not even raising them to fend a blow. She, a slave, before one who was to her as free, dared not offer, or even suggest, the least resistance, not by word or deed, or by even the tiniest expression. She did not even turn her head away. As a slave she knew she might not protest, or even demur, not to one who was to her as free.

"Now, get out of my sight, slave," said Temione's tormenter.

"Yes, Mistress," said Temione.

She had barely reached the foot of the stairs where she had left the pail and ladle when her tormenter cried out to her, "Hold!"

Miserable, Temione turned about and knelt, humbly, head down.

A ripple of mirth coursed through the hold.

"Have you not forgotten something?" inquired Temione's tormenter.

"Mistress?" said Temione, raising her head.

"You have not yet thanked me for disciplining you," said the girl.

"Forgive me, Mistress," said Temione. "Thank you for disciplining me."

"You will now, I trust," said the girl, "strive to be more pleasing."

"Yes, Mistress," said Temione.

"Say so then," said the girl, "and as what you are."

"I will strive to be more pleasing, Mistress," said Temione, "and as what I am, a slave."

"She is being taught she is a slave," whispered the slave behind me.

"Be kind," I said.

"Are you her friend?" asked the girl behind me.

"I know her," I said.

"One thing more," called Temione's tormenter.

"Mistress?" said Temione, in misery.

"On the deck," said the girl, "you will fling yourself to the feet of the crew. You will have five Ehn, and five Ehn only, to interest a man, any man, in your use, in your full use. If you are not in a man's arms being put to full use in five Ehn, you will be deemed displeasing."

"No, Mistress, please, no!" cried Temione.

"It is unfair," I said. "Men may not wish to be bothered. They may feign disinterest. A slave is helpless. She is nothing. It sometimes pleases men to let a slave crawl and roll, whine and moan, in need. It primes her for a yet more devastating subjugation. It is cruel."

"Five Ehn!" laughed Temione's tormenter. "And remember, she-tarsk, you will be returned to the hold. You must sleep amongst us, within range of our nails and fists, and more easily might rest a tethered *verr* amongst ravenous *sleen*."

Sobbing, Temione snatched up her pail and ladle, rushed up the broad steps to the overhead hatch, and began to beat on it, pleading that it be opened.

"Not even five Ehn now!" called out her tormenter.

It was wonderful, in my lot's turn, to be admitted to the deck, to be in the sun, to inhale the fresh air.

Our ship, one of the three we had boarded near the outlet of the delta, was between the other two, one to the port side, a bit behind our ship, the other somewhat ahead of our ship, to starboard. It had eased past us in the last few minutes. This was not unusual. With the currents, the winds, the amount of canvas exposed on the long lateen-rigged yard, and with differences in rowing, changing shifts of oarsmen, and such, the ships often changed position with respect to one another. They did, however, always remain in sight of one another, indeed, within hailing distance of one another. Knife ships, warships, often beached at night. Round ships, broader beamed, deeper keeled, seldom did. As nearly as I could gather, our three ships were 'medium-class' round ships. In any event, we did not beach at night. At night, we either lay to, or continued our voyage, keeping track of one another with lanterns or calls. Smaller round ships occasionally did beach at night. In any event, we did not. Far to starboard, low in the water, hard to detect, were two knife ships from Brundisium, our current escort. They were posted between us and the dangers which might unexpectedly sweep toward us from mighty Thassa. On our left, we could see occasional villages. This far south there was little to fear from them, unless we ran aground or had to deal for water or supplies. Our high gunwales, common on round ships, protected us from boarding parties on small boats, and a rocket or two fired into the air, could bring our escorting warships to investigate. Our trip was uneventful, perhaps because of the sheltering fighting ships from Brundisium. They had sighted, we were told, one knife ship from Tyros, but it had remained far off.

I saw Xanthe, the former Eileen Bennett, crouching near the single fixed mast of the round ship. She looked about, almost as if she might spring to her feet. But where, on the ship, was there to run? Then she slumped down in place, sitting at the foot of the mast, her head forward, in her hands. I did not understand this. As Eileen was clearly, given her Gorean, a barbarian, I avoided her company. She was highly intelligent, but even the most intelligent can occasionally be guilty of a dangerous, revealing lapse. What if she inadvertently spoke English to me, or mentioned something to me that a native Gorean might find foreign or incomprehensible? Accordingly, we seldom interacted. We did have much in common, of course. We were both in Gorean collars.

I regarded her.

I did not understand why she had acted as she had.

What could explain that?

What had disturbed her?

Surely it could have had nothing to do with the ship to starboard which had recently slipped a bit ahead of us. Many times it, like its fellow to our left, had eased ahead of us or slipped behind us, to one degree or another.

She was still sitting at the foot of the mast, her head in her hands. I saw her shoulders move. Was she trembling?

What, if anything, was wrong with her?

I turned my attention away from her.

I looked about.

Temione was nearby, sitting near the rail.

The three of us, Xanthe, Temione, and I, were in the same deck lot.

I approached her.

She looked at me, and, frightened, quickly knelt, her head bowed.

"No," I said. "Do not kneel to me."

"Slaves aboard are to be as Mistress to me," she said.

"Not I," I said.

"If I break position," she said, "you will not beat me?"

"Certainly not," I said. "We are both nothing, only worthless properties, only slaves. Sit here, beside me, by the rail. Do not be afraid."

"Yes, Mistress," she said.

"Mira," I said. "Do not cry."

She sat down, beside me, on the deck.

"You were kind yesterday, in the hold," she said.

"You were poorly treated," I said. The barge-master had not been pleased with Temione, her assertiveness, and her preposterous charge to him that she should be freed, and even enriched. After her lashing, he had had her consigned to Barge Six. As a continuance of her punishment, she was to be kept naked and serve 'as a slave to slaves.' This condition, to Temione's misery, had been prolonged after our boarding the ships which were to convey us to Brundisium. I trusted that after our landing, she would be returned to her earlier condition of being simply one slave amongst others. How grateful the former Lady Temione of Hammerfest, once so arrogant, would be of that! Her nudity amongst tunicked slaves would no longer sting and shame her, of course, for we were all kept naked on board, as is common with livestock being marched or transported. "I think," I said, "things will be easier for you once we reach Brundisium. I think that different keepers will be involved, and that they will see no reason to treat you differently from other slaves."

"Let it be so," she whispered.

"I heard a mariner say that we should reach Brundisium by noon tomorrow," I said.

"It is a great port," she said.

"Have you been there?" I asked.

"No," she said. "But I had hoped sometime to visit."

"You will," I said.

"On a chain," she said.

"Our Master, Tenalian," I said, "is of Ar. I am eager to see Ar. I have heard it is large, populous, rich, splendid, opulent, marvelous, wondrous."

"Perhaps we shall first see it," she said, "our hoods removed, from the surface of a sales block, while men bid upon us, while we are being sold."

"If you still think of yourself as a free woman in a collar, it will be hard for you," I said.

"I no longer think of myself as a free woman in a collar," she said. "I now think of myself as a slave in her collar."

I turned to regard her.

"I have changed," she said.

"If it is hard for you to say these things," I said," you need not speak."

"Yesterday," she said, "I was given but five Ehn to interest a man, only five Ehn to have myself violently seized and put to abject slave use."

"I know," I said. "It was terribly cruel of the other slaves."

"I fled frenziedly to the deck," she said. "I put myself to my knees and belly, I wept and begged for use, I flung myself to the feet of one man after another, whining, licking and kissing, placing a foot upon my head, weeping, begging! Ehn fled, one by one, and no Master would deign to use me. Was I so gross, so shapeless, and ugly? There was but an Ehn left, and I collapsed, weeping, to the deck. Was I, once the Lady Temione of Hammerfest, of no interest, of not the least interest, to a man? Then I felt a hand in my hair and I was turned to my back."

"'What are you?' I was asked," she said. "'I am a slave!' I shrieked, reaching for him. 'I am a needful, begging slave! I beg use! I beg use! Please, Master, be merciful, be kind, to a pleading, worthless slave!'"

"And then?" I said.

"And then," she said, "he, with a scornful laugh, worthless as I was, put me to use!"

"Good," I said. "I feared what might have been done with you had you returned to the hold as a failed slave. You were successful. You garnered a usage. You won. You were clever."

"No," she said. "You do not understand. I found myself a slave. I wanted a man. I wanted a Master. I wanted to be claimed and ravished! I wanted to be owned. I wanted it! I was a slave and wanted it!"

"In nature," I said, "we belong to men. We hope to find the man to whom we would belong."

She began to sob, uncontrollably.

I let her weep for a time.

Then I said, "Be pleased. Supposedly we will reach Brundisium by noon tomorrow."

She wiped her eyes.

"Think now of other things," I said.

She smiled. "I have much wondered about one thing," she said.

"What is that?" I asked.

"Who were those who lay in wait for the barges of Tenalian in the delta?" she said.

"We do not know," I said. "But they were foiled. Do not concern yourself about them."

"Substantial resources were invested in its nocturnal foray," she said.

"It failed," I said. "The barges had slipped away."

"Would they be so easily discouraged?" she asked.

"They have no choice," I said. "The stones were cast. The game was done."

"Perhaps they could not catch us," she said. "Perhaps they did not care to risk an encounter with the knife ships of Port Kar or Brundisium."

"We are safe now," I said.

"Ar is far away," she said.

"Where are you going?" I asked.

"Down, in the hold," she said. "I have been informed that goods such as air and sunlight should not be unduly expended on one such as I. In the hold, there is hair to be combed, water to be distributed, straw to be arranged for the bedding of my betters, many things. Should I loiter I risk a beating."

Temione then rose to her feet, and hurried to the opened hatch.

I rose to my feet and looked about. Our deck lot, I was sure, would soon be replaced by another.

To my surprise, Xanthe, the former Eileen Bennett, once the research librarian at the observatory, was much as before, sitting with her back to the mast, her head in her hands. From time to time her body shook. I could not tell if she were weeping or trembling. As there was no one about, certainly in the immediate vicinity, I went to her. "Eileen, Xanthe," I whispered. "Is something wrong?"

She looked up, frightened.

"Tell me," I said, "in English, if you wish. If one should approach, turn to Gorean."

"Your secret," she said.

"Of course," I said.

"I open my mouth," she said, "and I mark myself a barbarian, something suitable to be mocked, scorned, and beaten."

"Your Gorean is intelligent and good," I said. "It is a matter of your accent. In time, with attention and care, it will improve, if you should wish it to do so."

"If I should wish it?" she said.

"Some men are fond of Earth women," I said. "They enjoy having them as abject slaves. Sometimes we sell better than Gorean girls."

"Which does not endear us to Gorean girls," she said.

"I have a special reason for attempting to keep my origin secret," I said. "Please do not question me on the matter. Just accept it and respect it."

"You were so much superior to me at the observatory," she said. "You had status. You had respect. You stood higher. I resented you. You angered me."

"Dismiss such memories from your mind," I said. "Here we are the same. Here we are equal. Our status, legally and socially, is identical. Here, we are both slaves. Here, if anything, you, with your beauty, stand higher than I."

"Yes," she said. "And do not forget it, once high and lofty Agnes Morrison Atherton. Here our roles are reversed. Here you are clearly less than I."

"That is for men to decide," I said. "I am comely."

"I can reveal your secret," she said. "I could tell others that you are only a barbarian, to be despised on this world."

"Some know it already," I said.

"I can tell it to a thousand," she said.

"Please do not do so," I said. "It could mean my life."

"That is ridiculous, preposterous," she said.

"You do not understand," I said.

"It does not matter to me," she said, "if you care to lie about your Earth origin."

"I am not lying," I said. "I just let others think what they will."

"A way of lying," she said, "as you know they will take you as Gorean."

"Not all do," I said, "and I do not see it as a lie."

"Perhaps I shall make the matter broadcast," she said.

"Be kind, be merciful," I said.

"Have no fear," she said. "I will keep your secret. That may save you a beating or two."

"Thank you," I said.

"I do not like you, and your sort," she said.

"We are both from Earth, we are both in collars, we are the same now," I said. "Let us respect one another, or at least tolerate one another, if nothing else."

"You have avoided me," she said.

"I have been afraid. I am afraid. I want to conceal my identity. Fraternization with you would create suspicion. We might inadvertently speak English, or speak of things alien to Goreans."

"You think you are better than I," she said.

"No," I said.

"Yes!" she said.

"Forget such things," I said. "They are gone. We are the same now, as I said. Now there is no difference between us. Keep that in mind. Here we are a thousand times less than sluts. Here we are collared Gorean slaves."

"I am your superior," she said, "even as a worthless slave."

"Men will decide such things," I said, "in virtue of what they will pay for us."

"In the observatory," she said, "men paid more attention to me."

"You saw to that," I said.

"Beauty has power," she said.

"And its exercise can be gratifying," I said.

"And in many ways profitable," she said.

"You well understood the arithmetic of sex, the calculation of smiles and movements," I said. "In few businesses is the return so marvelously disproportional to the investment. Hint markedly and then feign misunderstanding; invite and then pretend resentment. Offer and withdraw, promise and deny. And accrue what you can, in goods, prestige, and power."

"I enjoyed myself," she said. "I found it amusing."

"You treated men like garbage," I said.

"They are garbage," she said.

"I recall that one turned away from you," I said. "One did not succumb to your charms, despite your flagrant efforts. In futility you displayed your blandishments. One held you in contempt."

"None," she said.

"Maxwell Holt," I said.

She turned white.

I did not understand that.

Surely that was in a distant past.

"I tormented him," she said.

"Perhaps he did not notice," I said.

"He desired me more than others, mightily so," she said. "I could tell."

"I do not recall that you added him to your conquests," I said.

She began to tremble.

"What is wrong," I asked.

"It is what I saw," she said. "I do not know what it means. I am frightened."

"What?" I said. "You had best speak quickly, because our deck lot may soon be returned to the hold."

"You know how the ships to our left and right sometimes pass ahead of us or slip behind us, and how they are sometimes closer to us and sometimes farther from us?"

"Of course," I said.

"One," she said, "that on our right, came quite close, and was no more than yards away."

"There is little danger in a calm sea," I said. "These vessels are extremely responsive to their helms. It is not that unusual. They occasionally approach one another closely. It facilitates ship-to-ship communication."

"It is what I saw," she said.

"What?" I asked.

"Him!" she said.

"Who?" I asked.

"On the other ship," she said, "from the observatory."

Instantly I was frightened.

Then I realized the absurdity of that.

"You are mistaken," I said, confidently.

"No!" she said.

"Yes," I said, "you are mistaken. Obviously mistaken. This is a different world. It is not like someone getting off an airplane, having flown from one country or state to another, and seeing someone you know. No one from Earth could be here."

"We are here," she said.

"And whom do you think you saw on the other ship?" I asked.

"He, he of whom we spoke," she said. "Holt, Maxwell Holt!"

"That is absurd," I said.

"No," she said.

"You must be mistaken," I said.

"No," she said.

"Someone who resembled him," I said.

"It was he," she said.

"It could be a relative," I said. "Genes persist. Consider family resemblances. Given the bringing of Earthlings to this world, one in his genetic line might have been brought here five hundred or a thousand years ago."

"It was he," she said.

I was beginning to be very afraid. If it was he, those who sought me, whom I had thought outwitted and astray, those whom I thought to have eluded, from whom I had thought myself at last safe, were no longer dependent on a vague description, or a name, or part of a name, but were now a thousand times more dangerous, for they might be abetted by one who could broaden and expedite their search, one who was not only somehow in the vicinity, but one who could recognize me at a glance, one who might even have photographs of me, to display to others."

"Did he see you?" I asked.

"No," she said.

"Good," I said.

Xanthe suddenly moaned.

"What is wrong now?" I asked.

"His accent," whispered Xanthe. "I thought little of it before. He had an accent, subtle, but an accent."

"There are many accents," I said, "Gorean and otherwise."

"I am afraid he is Gorean," said Xanthe.

"His name, 'Maxwell Holt,'" I said, "does not suggest that."

"Such may not be his true name," said Xanthe.

I supposed that that was more than possible. "I am sure it is," I said, reassuringly. But, I thought, such was not a typical Earth name. It seemed simple, blunt, and forceful. Might it not be the sort of name that a Gorean, one unfamiliar with Earth names, from the simple sound of it, might adopt as an alias or pseudonym?

"I am afraid he is Gorean," said Xanthe.

"It is unlikely," I said.

"He saw how I teased and taunted men, how I led them on and then refused them, how I fooled them and made sport of them, how I tried to do the same to him. He might even have realized I had had my hair dyed a false color."

"Let us fervently hope then," I said, "that he is not Gorean."

"Here I am a slave," said Xanthe. "I am helpless. I am in a collar. He could even buy me, own me!"

"Probably," I said, "you did not see Maxwell Holt. It was probably someone who looked like him. I am sure that there is nothing to worry about."

"He is following me, somehow," said Xanthe. "He wants me! I was displeasing. And now what if he should find me? Now I am a slave, in a collar!"

"Do not flatter yourself," I said. "If it is he, Maxwell Holt, he does not hunt you. It is I whom he seeks, as do others. You have no importance. You do not count. You are only an exploitative, pretentious, frivolous tart. It is I who hold the key to secrets I do not even understand. I know too much, far too much, and I do not even understand the portent of what I know."

"He seeks me, bitch!" she hissed.

"Doubtless," I said, "it was not he."

"It looked so like him," she said.

"Many people look alike," I said. "You saw someone briefly and at a distance. Perhaps he looked much like Maxwell Holt. That is surely possible. But the probability that it was truly he is miniscule. Surely you recognize that."

"I am not stupid," she said.

"You are not, and no one said you were," I said.

"I suppose it is improbable that it was he," she said, uncertainly.

"Extremely improbable," I said. "Think. Is it not possible you were mistaken?"

"Of course," she said, "—it is possible."

"The ships of the raiders," I said, "were foiled and left far behind in the delta. Forget them. The ship the fellow is on was not in the delta. It is a different ship. It is a ship of Brundisium, met with us at sea, taking over from the ships of Port Kar, to see us safely into Brundisium. Its mariners, amongst whom is the fellow you saw, would know nothing of us, personally. We are only cargo. Too, if the fellow you saw had any interest in you, or me, he would presumably have been more attentive, made inquiries, or taken some sort of action by now, say, devised a pretext for boarding, if only to confirm that you, or I, were aboard. How could one be otherwise sure of that? We are seldom in sight, being so much kept locked in the hold."

"I was frightened," she said. "Perhaps I saw only what I feared to see."

"So," I said, "it was not he."

"I think that you are right," she said. "It could not have been he. But it looked so much like him."

"Of course," I said.

At that point a bell rang sharply on the helm deck.

"Deck lot down," called a mariner. "Deck lot up!"

"A new deck lot," said Xanthe.

I turned about, and made my way to the opened hatch. I would lose no time. Dalliance can bring a stroke of the lash. Already some from our deck lot were at the hatch. I quickly took my place in the queue. I feared I had spent too much time in Xanthe's company, but then free men seldom pay much attention to loitering slaves. It is otherwise, I had been told, with free women. Xanthe soon joined the queue, some four slaves behind me. Temione was already below, in the hold. Luta was in a different deck lot, one earlier returned to the hold. There was a sudden crack of a whip and our entire queue reacted. Slave girls know well that sound. One whimpered. I do not think that anyone was struck. I heard no cry of pain.

The bell on the helm deck sounded again and we began to file down the stairs into the hold. A minute or two later, the bell rang again and the new deck lot climbed up the stairs and into the wind, and air, the spray, and sunlight.

I found a place at the side of the hold and sat down in the straw.

"Water, slave," called a voice, and Temione, from somewhere to the side, said, "Yes, Mistress."

When we reached Brundisium, I was sure that she would be again but one slave amongst others. New keepers would not be aware that she might have been found displeasing days ago, in the delta.

I remained disturbed by my conversation with Xanthe, the former Eileen Bennett. I think that I had convinced her that she had not seen Maxwell Holt on the flanking ship. But I feared that my arguments, persuasive as I knew them to be, had assuaged her apprehensions more than they had mine.

Yet he could not be on Gor.

My mind told me that.

Why then was I uneasy?

Then I smiled to myself.

How vain was the former Eileen Bennett! Could she actually think that Maxwell Holt might have come to Gor to find her! Had she no understanding of how inconsequential she was? I wished that I was as inconsequential as she. How little I would have had to worry about then, little more than the lash and the pleasing of Masters. How could she be concerned with her own fate when that of worlds might be at stake? But, of course, she would know nothing of that. If Maxwell Holt had come to Gor to seek a slave, it was not she, but another, one who was privy to secrets which even she herself did not understand. I feared that I would soon know whether Maxwell Holt, or others, were on Gor. If they were, I had no doubt as to their quarry, she whom they were seeking. I did not want to know secrets that men might kill to keep hidden.

The hold was close and crowded.

By noon tomorrow, as I understood it, we were to enter the harbor, or one of the harbors, of Brundisium, the greatest port on known Gor.

From Brundisium, as I understood it, we were to be shipped overland to Ar. This was to be done by a caravan of slave wagons.

No, Maxwell Holt could not be on Gor, surely not, but others were. I recalled a renegade tarnsman who had betrayed his fee givers, preferring to sell a slave in the Vosk Basin rather than deliver her to her death. How grateful I had been to be sold! But what of those betrayed fee givers? Might not they, or their factors, be seeking me even now? Had I not, here or there, discovered at least hints of an active interest in my apprehension, that of a barbarian, a portion of whose former barbarian name might have been something like 'Ag-nas?' Indeed, was not a terrible beast, dreadful to behold, somewhere, even now, seeking me? Then I tried to soothe myself. I had heard nothing of such things for weeks. Might I not then, by now, have eluded all pursuit? It seemed so. Then Xanthe had seen someone whom she had initially feared was Maxwell Holt, from the observatory. Had I not then found myself again enveloped in a storm of terror, until, by force of will and reason, I had calmed the wind and waters of fear which had raged about me? How foolish I had been, but how comprehensibly so!

As Xanthe had not seen Maxwell Holt, as she had been mistaken in the matter, he was not on Gor. Accordingly, I had no more to worry about now than I had had when I was first boarded on the ship. Indeed, I had grown more and more confident that I had had little, rationally, to fear after my sale in Victoria. I must now get a firmer grip on myself. The fact that most Goreans were taking me as Gorean was an advantage much in my favor. I did not think that Xanthe would betray me. She might not care for me, and she might be annoyed at my allowing myself to be construed as Gorean, especially as I was muchly successful in the effort, but I expected her to keep my secret, particularly as I had tried to make it clear to her that the matter, if trivial or absurd to her, was one of great importance to me.

The ship gently proceeded on its way.

The hold was quiet.

Tomorrow, I had heard, we should reach Brundisium.

And somewhere, far beyond Brundisium, perhaps weeks, perhaps months, lay Ar, spoken of as 'Glorious Ar.'

I was eager to see Ar.

What girl would not wish to wear her collar in such a city?

How silly was Xanthe, I thought, thinking that Maxwell Holt might have come to Gor in search of her. How vain could a woman be? What grandiose conceptions did she entertain as to her desirability, or as to the will and determination of some man to have her at his feet, as a Gorean has a slave, naked, in his chains and collar.

What man could so desire a woman, and, in particular, one as vain and petty as the exploitative little cheat, Xanthe, the former Eileen Bennett?

Alas, how naive I was at that time. I had less than an inkling then, naive woman, once of Earth that I was, of how unreservedly, determinably, violently, and mightily a man might desire a woman. Might not a woman shriek in terror, knowing that she was the object of such desire, that a man will be satisfied with nothing less than owning her, with nothing less than having her fully, uncompromisingly, in every way, as his rightless possession?

Then, if he tires of her, he can sell her.

CHAPTER FORTY

"So this is Brundisium," said Temione, with a stirring of links in the coffle chain about her neck, and a tiny a movement of her wrists behind her, fastened in slave bracelets.

"Where else can a fellow accept a friendly drink and then find oneself a hundred *pasangs* at sea?" asked a slave.

"I did not know it could be so vast and beautiful," said Temione.

"Or so vast and foul, so crowded and motley," said another slave. "Here is a world of strangers. Here mingle men, values, and customs, unbeknownst to one another, suspicious and wary. Commerce strides, greed at hand. Piracy lurks. Guard your purse. A thousand riches rest on the docks. Daggers rule in the alleys. Here find adventure and fortune, risk and peril, wealth and poverty, surfeit and hunger, and close enough to touch, beckoning, is broad, mysterious, gleaming Thassa, the Sea, nurse of storms and secrets."

"How crowded is the harbor," said Temione.

It seemed one could walk indefinitely, into the distance, stepping from ship to ship.

"This harbor," said a slave.

"This is no river port," said another. "From here one can voyage as far south as the jungles of Schendi, as far north as the ice floes of Torvaldsland."

"And west," said another, "to the Island Ubarates, even to the Farther Islands, and the World's End."

"Be careful in descending the plank to the dock," said a keeper. "Unpleasant things hide in the water."

"We will be housed tonight in the warehouse to the left," said Luta, whom I knew not only from the ship, but also, earlier, from the great pen at Victoria Minor and the sales at Victoria.

"The one with the blue-and-yellow roof?" I asked.

Luta looked at me, narrowly.

I was suddenly afraid. I should not have spoken. Few shields are as effective as silence.

"Of course," I said. "It is a joke."

Luta smiled.

I then suspected, what I later learned, that blue and yellow were the colors of the Slavers, regarded by some as an independent caste, by others as a subcaste of the Merchants.

"We are to be housed there tonight," said Luta. "Tomorrow we are to trek through the city to the Great Land Gate. There we will be housed, and then, later, the next morning, we will be transferred to wagons, to begin the journey overland."

"To Ar," I said.

"First, probably, to Torcadino," she said.

"The Masters are kind to impart to you such things," I said.

"They did not notice I was listening," she said.

I winced, pulling my head away, shutting my eyes against the thrown dirt.

"Filthy *kajirae*!" cried a woman.

"She-tarsks!" cried another.

"Oh!" said Temione, struck by a rock.

I had had little, if anything, to do with free women since discovering myself on Gor. I had, however, heard much of them. It seemed now as though free women had appeared from nowhere. Doubtless they had heard of the passing of a coffle of *kajirae*. They had then materialized from buildings, doorways, markets, and stalls about us, forming, in its way an improvised gantlet through which we must pass. We were coffled, chained together by the neck, and our hands were braceleted behind us.

"What is wrong with them?" asked Luta, stained from cast fruit or garbage. "Can they not see we are tunicked!"

"Keep moving," said a keeper.

"Man thieves!" cried a woman.

Xanthe smiled sweetly at one of the women, bundled in her robes of concealment. "You are all stinking bitches," she said, in English, pleasantly, "and you do well to hide your features under veils, as they would doubtless affright even a male pig or toad."

"Hear the barbarous tongue," laughed a woman.

"She does not even speak Gorean," said another.

"Speak Gorean," said another.

"What did you say?" demanded another woman, her switch raised.

"I said, Mistress," she said, in Gorean, "that you and your sisters are fine and noble, and are doubtless beautiful, as well."

At this point, the woman lowered her switch and began to berate another slave.

"Please, Ladies," said a keeper. "Back away. Let us pass. We will soon be beyond your sight. You will then be offended no longer."

I cried out in misery, stung on the leg by a cast stone.

"Do not damage the goods," said a keeper. "Do not injure the stock."

I tried to move forward, but, in the press, could not do so.

"Switches will not hurt them," said one of the women.

"They will do them good," said another.

We began to cry out in misery, reeling from a rain of supple leather.

"Where are the slavers, Master!" cried Temione. "How long must this last? Have we not endured enough? Have we not been bait long enough? Where are the slavers with their ropes, chains, and hoods to harvest this loot about us? Spring the trap, Masters. I beg that you spring the trap!"

The keepers regarded Temione with surprise.

The women then, looking about, wildly, exchanged terrified glances, and the gantlet dissipated, melted away, vanished, as quickly, indeed, even more quickly, than it had originally formed.

"Well done, slave," said a keeper, who then drew a hard candy from a wrapper in his wallet, and gave it to a grateful Temione.

I myself would not have dared to think of such a ruse.

What if it had been unsuccessful? What might have happened then?

Temione, of course, had once been a free woman, and not only a free woman, but, more impressively, a Gorean free woman.

"Should she not be punished for lying, Master?" asked a slave, one who had much tormented Temione on shipboard.

"Did you ask for permission to speak?" asked the keeper.

"No, Master, please, forgive me, Master!" said the slave, turning white.

"We shall allow both matters to pass," said the keeper, "canceling one another out. Now, let us continue on. Left foot as usual, then step. We are within a *pasang* of the holding near the Great Land Gate. Step!"

With a rustle of chain we continued on our way.

When we were being abused by the free women, few free men had paused to watch. Such things were not of great concern to them. Indeed, they tend to disapprove of such things, sometimes even intervening to prevent or lessen such abuse. Indeed, there is a saying that the one hope of the slave girl is the free man.

I had noticed, against a wall to our left, standing back, inconspicuous, one male figure who did observe. He was robed and hooded. I thought little of it at the time.

"What did you sell for in Victoria?" asked Temione.

"A silver tarsk, six," I said. That was one silver tarsk plus six tarsk-bits. That was substantially more than my earlier sale of sixty copper tarsks, plus twenty tarsk-bits, Brundisium, and somewhat more than the eighty copper tarsks the tarnsman had received for me near the Vosk from the agent of the House of Kleon.

"I sold for four silver tarsks," said Temione.

"And sales were depressed," I said, "as it was a buyers' market." That was because the slave holdings of the Lady Temione of Hammerfest had unexpectedly flooded the market.

I did suspect, of course, that the price which Temione brought on the block might have been influenced by the knowledge, of some, at least, that she was the former Lady Temione of Hammerfest. I wondered what she might have gone for if she had been unknown, if she had been no more than one slave amongst others. She was quite beautiful, of course. There was no gainsaying that.

"Usually," said Luta, "buyers' markets occur when a town or city falls. That throws many women on the market, fresh, branded merchandise."

"Men are always fighting," said another slave.

"They are quick to take offense," said another.

"They enjoy taking offense," said another.

"Sometimes," said Luta, "slavers instigate trouble, bad feelings, lies, rumors, and such, between towns or cities, in order to provoke wars, and thus more women become available."

"That is short-sighted," said a slave, "for it depresses prices."

"Not necessarily," said Temione. "Captives can be divided up and sent to other areas."

"Even to Cos and Tyros, or the Farther Islands, or even to the World's End," said another.

"Too," said another, "they could be held for the spring sales. It is commonly a sellers' market in the spring."

"It is late," said a slave.

"We are to be shipped tomorrow, in the morning," said another.

"Let us sleep now," said another.

"A Master," said Luta, and we stopped talking, knelt, and put our heads down.

"The wagons are ready," said a male voice. "Prepare for shackling."

CHAPTER FORTY-ONE

"We are at the crest," said Luta, twisting about, the chain on her shackling run under the horizontal metal bar that ran down the center of the wagon. "Thrust up the canvas, a little, no one is watching."

"Good," said Temione, turning about, and, with two hands, pushing the canvas up. A draft *tharlarion*, pulling the wagon behind ours, snorted.

"Ai!" cried a slave. "The line is endless!"

"Yes," said another.

"Look quickly, while you can," said Luta. "There must be thirty to forty wagons behind us."

"Put the canvas down," said Xanthe. "You could get us all whipped."

"Be silent, barbarian," said a slave.

"Are you afraid to be seen?" asked another.

"See ahead," said another slave, "there must be as many wagons before us."

I turned about, and, on my knees, pushed up the canvas near my place. Our Master, the slaver, Tenalian of Ar, had considerably added to his chain on our trek, rumored to terminate in Ar, Glorious Ar. He had added at least a hundred girls in Torcadino alone. It seemed clear that we were bound for Ar, as Tenalian was of that city, and we had been following, since Torcadino, the route of the Great Aqueduct, which extends from Torcadino and beyond, back, even to Venna, famed for its races, at the foot of the Voltai Range. Slave wagons can be crowded, or sparsely tenanted, so to speak, but, commonly, they house ten slaves, five to a side. Accordingly, if Tenalian's lengthy caravan consisted of, say, seventy wagons, they would be conveying some seven hundred slaves. Whereas this seemed to be a redoubtable number of wagons, particularly adding in supply wagons and wagons for the shifts of guards, I had been told that caravans exist which consist of as many as two to three thousand wagons. The point of large caravans is to seek safety in numbers. Few bandits, or even companies of brigands, have the resources to do more than harass caravans of that size. Such caravans are rarely those of a single merchant. Most often, dozens of merchants participate in such endeavors. Interestingly, there was nothing about the wagons in Tenalian's caravan to suggest that they might be transporting slaves. The usual slave wagon has, as I had found out, attending to conversations about me, a covering of blue-and-yellow canvas or silk, treated silk, as blue and yellow are the colors of the Slavers. This lack of identification had been distressing to some of the slaves, who felt not only uneasy at the omission of an attractive, expected appearance, but were annoyed by what they felt was a lack of due recognition. "In these wagons, so drab and brown," had said one slave, "one might as well transport *tur-pah, sa-tarna* or *suls*." I did not know what *tur-pah* was, but I was familiar with *sa-tarna*, and I had had a plenitude of experience, one far more extensive than I might have wished, with *suls*. Supposedly Tenalian, though I had no personal knowledge of this, had, within sight of the Great Land Gate at Brundisium, created a decoy caravan consisting of blue-and-yellow bedecked, but empty, slave wagons. They departed at noon on the same day that we had been discomfited by the free women in Brundisium. As for us, we found that we were not to be shipped forth from Brundisium the next morning, as we had thought, but that very night, under the cover of darkness. How surprised we had been! Also, although slaves are commonly transported naked, we were put in brown sacklike tunics, to be worn even in the wagons. "Why this garb?" had asked a slave. "Because," said a keeper, "you are all field slaves, good for nothing but the hoe and plow."

"There is an animal," I said, pointing, "there."

"Where?" asked a slave. "I do not see it."

"There," I said, pointing again, "far to the side of the wagon track, beyond the wagons, in the rocks."

"I do not see it," said the slave.

"There!" I said. "It moved!"

"I saw it!" said the slave.

"It is a *sleen*, a prairie *sleen*," said another slave, who had joined us, on our knees, looking out.

"I thought that *sleen* in the wild were nocturnal," I said.

"Commonly," said the first slave, "but it is not unusual for them to hunt when hungry."

"The wagons passing by, the bells and *tharlarion*, may have disturbed it," said the second slave, she who had joined us.

"I think it is large," I said.

"It is hard to tell at the distance," said the first slave.

"It is gone," I said.

"Back in the rocks," said the second slave.

"Do you think it is following the wagons?" I asked.

"I do not think so," said the first slave. "That is unlikely."

"I remember a domestic *sleen* from a camp, a long time ago," I said. "I think it was even larger."

"It probably was," said the first slave. "Domestic *sleen* are commonly larger and healthier than wild *sleen*."

There was a sudden striking, four times, loud, quick, impatient, of a coiled whip at the side of the wagon. "Get that canvas down," said a male voice.

Hastily we pulled the canvas down.

What difference could it make to the Masters if we peeped out for a minute or so? But Masters, it seemed, often liked to keep us ignorant, perhaps because it makes us more dependent, helpless, and vulnerable. Too, I suppose, it helps us to keep in mind that we are slaves. And who would feel it incumbent upon oneself to inform *verr* or *kaiila* of routes and destinations?

"I warned you," said Xanthe. "Your curiosity could get us all whipped."

"Silence, barbarian," said a slave.

"Let us slap her to silence," said another slave.

"Let her alone," I said.

"Do you take the part of a barbarian?" inquired a slave.

"She knows no better," I said.

"I need no help from you, pockface," said Xanthe.

"It is true," said a slave. "Barbarians are stupid."

"Surely not all of them," I said. "Those of the Green Caste think we are much alike, barbarians and Goreans, even belonging to the same species."

"Much like free women and slaves?" asked a slave.

"Something like that," I said.

"Let us beat the barbarian," said a slave.

"It is too hot," I said.

"It will be cooler in the evening," said a slave.

"Mark me, or cut me, even bruise me, without permission," said Xanthe, "and I shall invoke the might and wrath of Masters."

The wagon now tipped downward we began to descend the hill. Occasionally we could hear the driver applying the brake.

CHAPTER FORTY-TWO

The Yellow Moon was in the sky and the evening was warm.

Smoke hung about the camp.

There was a smell of roast *tarsk* in the air.

A soft, murmuring surf of conversation pervaded the area.

While it was still light, the center bars in the wagons had been unlocked, and lifted, and we, in our shackling, had slid along the bars and dropped to the grass. It was a welcome feeling, to be out of the wagons. One relished the fresh air and, to the extent our shackles permitted it, the movement. Too, despite the blankets in the wagons, many of us were sore and bruised, as the planks of the wagon bed were hard and the route uneven.

One slave, presumably hoping to complete the trek to Ar or Venna as soon as possible, had inquired the reason for the early stop, while an Ahn or so remained of light. I thought the reply she received was illuminating. "Because," she was told, "it must be clear to any who might observe, a flighted tarnsman, or such, that you are all field slaves, cheap, lowly slaves, as is clear from your sacking, in large numbers being moved south and east as temporary labor to assist in the *sa-tarna* harvests."

The camp was quite large, despite the double-wall of wagons that constituted its perimeter.

Here and there, blankets had been strewn about on the grass, usually about one fire or another.

"I see," said Xanthe, "that it is your left ankle alone which is set off by its ring. Your right ankle is free, its ring open, dangling on its chain."

"Am I to congratulate you on your perceptiveness?" I asked.

"I gather some Master thought that it was time your legs were split."

"One has little to say about such things," I said.

"One can be used quite well, even in close shackling," she said.

We were close-shackled in the wagons. In close shackling, one can move one's ankles only a few inches apart. In this way it is impossible to run or even walk normally. Indeed, it can be hard to stand. Whereas close shackling can be used for purposes of discipline, punishment, or mere instruction in one's condition, it is usually employed, as here, to hobble a slave, keeping her close about and discouraging thoughts of escape.

"As a *sleen* or *verr* might be used," she said.

"That is true," I said, "as you doubtless know."

"Perhaps you feel proud of your free ankle," she said.

"Masters decide how you will be used, if used," I said.

"I remember how proud you were in another place, so lofty and superior, looking down on we lesser folk. Now, in a different place, in a different way, you can be proud of your free right ankle. Now, again, swell with pride, she-tarsk."

"Thank you for speaking Gorean," I said.

"I can publicize your little secret, your great secret, any moment I wish," she said.

"I know that," I said, "please do not do so."

"Have no fear," she said.

"Thank you," I said.

"Arrogant she-tarsk," she said.

"I am not arrogant," I said. "I was not arrogant. We were differently stationed, that is all."

"I am much more attractive than you," she said.

"We are different," I said. "That is all."

"I sold for two silver tarsks," she said.

"Temione," I said, "sold for four."

"What did you sell for?" she asked.

"—A silver tarsk, six," I said.

She laughed.

"You are still close-shackled," I said. "My right ankle is free."

"I saw you," she said. "I watched. You kneel well, slave. You beg well. How superior I felt to you! How superior I am to you!"

"And, I take it, no one ordered you to his feet, slave?"

"She-urt!" she said.

"It behooves a slave to be a slave," I said.

"As you are!" she said.

"I gather that you know little or nothing of slave fires," I said, "how they rage and burn, how they put you at the amused, scornful mercy of Masters. Have your slave fires never been kindled? Have you never rolled, thrashed, moaned, and wept aloud with need?"

"Would that those of another place, one faraway, had seen you so," she said.

"Had I known myself then as I know myself now," I said, "I would have stripped myself in an instant and crawled to them, to kiss their shoes and beg to please them."

"You belong in a collar," she said.

"Yes," I said, "I do, and here on Gor, as I should be, I find myself collared, choicelessly, helplessly, rightfully."

"And you do not mind," she said.

"No," I said.

"And you love it!" she said.

"Yes," I said, "I love it!"

"You are an animal," she said.

"Of course," I said.

"I am not an animal," she said.

"Yet I see a collar on your neck," I said.

"That is a legal matter," she said. "It is trivial, and unimportant."

"Consider it trivial and unimportant," I said, "when you are again sold off the block. If nothing else, that should make the matter clear to you."

"I hate you," she said.

"Have you never longed for a Master?" I asked.

"No man can master me," she said.

"I think you know little," I said, "of the will and determination of men, of the nature and force of their desire."

"On the contrary," she said, "I have much enjoyed frustrating them and sporting with them. I found it amusing."

"Men of Earth," I said.

"Of course," she said.

"And now," I said, "you are in a Gorean collar."

She touched the collar lightly, fearfully.

"You cannot pretend that it is not there," I said. "It is there, locked on your neck. The petty, attractive, nasty tart is now collared. Hope then, if you wish, that you will never be so desired by a man that nothing will satisfy him short of having you at his feet, naked and in chains."

She looked at me, wildly.

"I see the thought has occurred to you," I said, "that one day you might find yourself so."

"No!" she said.

"And want yourself so," I said.

"No, no!" she said.

"Think, if you dare, of what it might be to belong to a Master, one you must obey and please."

"I shall think rather of exploiting men," she said, "for they are fools."

"Surely you can suspect the warmth, identity, and clarity, the wholeness, of belonging, of being owned?"

In the light, I could not well see her eyes.

"Have you never suspected the victory that lies in your defeat, the rapture of submission?" I asked.

"I will never submit," she said.

"Wait," I said, "until the hurricane of need casts you to the feet of a Master, and you beg to belong to him, wholly, and in every way, as the slave you have discovered yourself to be."

She turned abruptly, almost fell, and, as she could, given her shackling, hurried away between the wagons. In a moment she had been lost to sight.

The wagon I shared with her, Temione, Luta, and others was Wagon 311, the number chalked on the back and both sides of the conveyance. I could not read Gorean, but I could recognize its number well enough, knew its location, and, if necessary, could make inquiries. Sometimes Gorean slaves are not only disinclined to be helpful to barbarian slaves but enjoy frustrating and discomfiting them, but, as most Goreans took me to be Gorean, I did not anticipate any difficulties in such a matter.

I looked about the camp.

I had eaten well.

The fellow I had served had been pleased, and had shared his meal with me.

It was pleasant to share such food. To be sure, most privately owned slaves shared their Master's food, which, normally, they will have prepared. The Master will take the first bite, the first sip, and such, after which the slave, as permitted, will partake. The Master had been pleased. That is why he had shared his food with me. Naturally, I had hoped that he, if pleased, would share his meal with me. I had not, of course, 'earned' the meal or 'purchased' it with my service. And, most certainly, I had not 'bargained' for it. Does a dog or cat earn, purchase, or bargain for its food?

I wondered if Xanthe had been angry with me because a Master had shared his meal with me?

Or was she angry because I had been well ravished, because I, and not she, had been put to slave use?

Did she envy me slave ecstasy, slave orgasm?

Why would she deny to herself prolonged and inordinate pleasure? How could she do so?

Her slave fires, I gathered, had not yet been kindled.

Let her slave fires be kindled, let her be enwrapped in their flames. Then her games would be done; then the shoe would be on the other foot; then the tables would be turned. Let her beg then for the relief of her agonies, pleading for some surcease from the torments she had so often inflicted on others.

But perhaps she was just angry that I wore now a single shackle, that I could move about much as I wished, whereas she could scarcely stand upright, could scarcely move without falling?

I shook my left ankle a bit, and listened to the linkage of the short chain attached to the manacle which had been removed from my right ankle. I was not eager to be put again in close shackling, which is unpleasant, and there is always that danger in a camp filled with men coming and going. "Why are you not shackled, slave?" and then the manacle snapped again about my right ankle, and, again, the difficulty of moving. Too, when the signal for returning to our wagons sounded, I would be reshackled soon enough, the shackling going about the bar, it then locked in place, so I thought that I would go a bit beyond the wagons and the Masters. The evening was warm, inviting, and pleasant. I would not go far. It would be clear that I had no intention of escaping. Also, to where would one escape, if one were foolish enough to think of escaping? As far as I knew, we were somewhere in the midst of a vast, grassy wilderness, with no habitations within miles, unless it might be some palisaded peasant village.

I wondered why peasant villages were often palisaded.

Probably to protect against, or deter, bandits or hostile raids.

It did not occur to me at the moment that there might be other reasons.

I left the outer shell of the marshaled, arranged wagons behind me.

It was a cloudy night.

The Yellow Moon had now been joined by the White Moon in the sky.

In the gentle wind, blowing past the camp, away from it, I could smell, behind me, the odors of the camp.

I must have walked further than I had intended, because, when I turned, the campfires, outlining the wagons behind me, seemed far away.

I was sure that the signal to return to the wagons for the night, the striking of a wooden mallet on a suspended gong near the center of the camp, near the caravan master's wagon, might soon sound. Accordingly, I would lose no time in returning. When the gong rang again, the slaves were expected to be at the wagons, for their night's shackling. Tardiness was frowned upon, sometimes by the switch or whip.

I took a step toward the camp, and then stopped.

I feared, suddenly, that I might not be alone.

Before me, perhaps fifteen or twenty feet away, I sensed a darkness in the darkness, something that seemed darker than the dark, something long, and low, something alert, furtive, and alive. It was between me and the wagons. I moved a little, slowly, to the side, and it moved too, to the side, and then, quickly, suddenly, a yard closer. At the same time, borne on the breeze blowing away from the wagons and toward me, I detected a distinct odor, one unmistakable, one I had not forgotten, one I had encountered before, months ago, in a camp, faraway.

I stood still.

I wanted to scream but no sound came from my lips.

I wanted to scream but I could not.

The thing, its belly low, in the grass, took another step toward me, and, again, stopped.

I did not think that it was trained.

I did not think that anything like this was kept in the camp.

I was sure that, if I turned and ran, it would not hurry about me, and, snarling, and hissing, herd me back to the camp. Rather I suspected it would be on me in an instant and bite through the back of my neck.

We stood facing one another.

I was absolutely still.

It did not move, but I sensed that it was quivering with anticipation.

In the distance, at the wagons, I saw torches. Some men were coming from between the wagons and were making their way out, into the grass.

Intermittently, one or another would call out.

One or two of the torches were coming in my direction.

The torches seemed small, so far off.

I counted seconds. I wondered how many I could count before it sprang.

Then it seemed to be growing shorter and smaller, as though it was withdrawing into itself, as if it were coiling a spring, tighter and tighter.

I did not think it was aware of anything but me, and perhaps hunger, and perhaps the anticipation of a kill, the sinking of fangs into flesh, the taste of blood.

Then it charged, seeming to grow in dimension, fast, tearing at the turf, scrambling, lunging forward, in the darkness, clots of dirt and grass flung behind it, and it leaped.

CHAPTER FORTY-THREE

As it rushed toward me through the darkness, fully committed to its attack, I, miserable with terror, having anticipated the force and speed of its charge, flung myself to the ground, hoping to evade the brunt of its attack, hoping to live another second or so, and, as it pounced, I was in the grass, covering my head with my arms and hands. The beast was hurtling past, over me. I expected it to strike the grass behind me, scramble about, and then take me, prone, in the back, seizing me with its claws, and tearing at the back of my neck with its fangs.

But that did not happen.

Somewhere in midcareer it encountered an unexpected obstacle, something in the darkness which was large and alive, and perhaps as formidable as itself. The momentum of its leap, despite its force and speed, did not carry it several feet past my prone body as I had hoped, if my desperate tactic should prove successful. Rather its flight was arrested over my body, literally, almost as though it had smashed into a wall, one not anticipated, one not seen in the darkness, a wall with fangs and claws. Then two bodies were rolling behind me in the grass, in a frenzy of biting and snarling.

Two torches were approaching me, rapidly now, across the grass, coming from the wagons.

Perhaps it had been better were the approaching men not carrying torches. I shall never forget the horror of what I beheld.

The two torches stopped, some twenty feet away.

"Ai!" cried one of the men.

A gigantic, hirsute shape, now half upright, stood illuminated, the quivering body of the *sleen* clutched in its paws. It then, bent over, head down, sunk the fangs of its mighty jaws into the back of the neck of the *sleen*, and wrenched the head half from the body, and then, washed in a fountain of exploding blood, it raised its head and looked at me. Two large, round, bestial eyes, blazing like fire in the reflected light of the torches, regarded me. It was like gazing into a raging furnace where two round metal lids or plates had been slid to the side. A long tongue emerged and swept about the fangs, wiping blood away. It also made some sound, oddly bestial, but more than bestial. It seemed articulated. I could make nothing of it. The sound then, or brief succession of sounds, was repeated. This startled me. I thought this confounding. A creature could surely growl or snarl, but how odd it seemed that both emanations would be identical, or nearly so.

"Away!" cried the men, "away!" They brandished their torches, and, with them, poking and jabbing, threatened the monster.

But the beast did not seem to evince the anticipated fear of fire, presumably something unfamiliar and aversive to an animal.

Is not an animal, in the face of such surprising, unexpected, strong stimuli, not to withdraw?

Rather it seemed to regard the men with contempt, even amusement, and then it cast down the body of the *sleen*, at its feet, and backed away, snarling.

I then lost consciousness.

Perhaps a moment later I was slapped awake and pulled up to my knees.

"What is your wagon number?" asked one of the men.

"Three Hundred and Eleven," I said.

"Do not fear the beast," said the second man. "It is gone."

"What was it," asked the first man of the second.

"I do not know," said the second man.

"Some sort of two-legged *sleen*," asked the first man, "a monstrous, misborn *larl*?"

"I do not know," said the second man. "I never saw anything like it."

"We had best not tell the wagon master," said the first man.

"We have merely apprehended a strayed slave," suggested the second man.

"I was not a stray," I said, frightened, not even remembering to request permission to speak. "I just wanted to walk about a bit." I did not wish to risk being hamstrung.

The brief, strange sounds which had emanated from that fortuitous, fierce vision of the night recurred to me.

The loose shackle, dangling on its chain from my left ankle, was snapped about my right ankle. I was again close-shackled!

Two or three other men then, carrying torches, had joined us.

"What is going on?" asked one of the newcomers.

"A stupid slave, wandered from the wagons," said the first man. "Two *sleen* encountered one another. One was killed."

"Where is the other?" asked a newcomer.

"It left," said the second man.

"That is unusual," said a newcomer. "*Sleen* are tenacious."

"Probably," said the first man, "it was a chance encounter. Most likely the second *sleen* was not on a scent."

One of the newcomers went to the body of the dead *sleen*, lifting his torch. "This was not done by another *sleen*," he said, "by a *larl*, perhaps."

"That must be it," said the first man.

"We came upon the scene but now," said the second man.

I was pulled to my feet by the first man. I tried to keep my balance.

"Had the two men first forward with their torches," I wondered, "never seen such a thing? Did they truly see it only as some sort of savage animal? Did they not wonder as to its lack of caution or fear in the face of fire? Did they not wonder at the belts on its body, the iron rings on its left wrist? Was a beast emerged from its lair so accoutered? Did they refuse to see the marks of refinement or civilization on so fearsome a form?"

I was thrust toward the wagons and I caught myself from falling.

"Hurry, hasten, *harta*!" said the first man.

"Run!" snapped the second.

"I cannot run, Master," I wept. "I am hobbled. I can scarcely walk!"

His switch caught me twice across my calves. "*Harta*!" he said.

I hastened as I could, awkwardly. Before I reached the wagons, weeping, I had fallen four times, and had been switched at least a dozen times.

I had barely reached the wagons when the wooden mallet struck the gong near the center of the camp, by the caravan master's wagon. Shortly thereafter, *kajirae* should be at their assigned wagon. I did not think this would be difficult. When I had reached the wagons, the men had left me. I gathered that they had been satisfied that the missing slave had been recovered, and that they did not wish to pursue the matter of what had occurred outside the wagons further. I supposed that one must be judicious in what one reports or does not report. I wiped the tears from my eyes. My back and calves still stung.

I would have time to reach my wagon.

As I made my way to the wagon, I could not dismiss from memory the brief, odd set of guttural sounds which had emanated from the monster in the night. Aside from the terror of being in proximity to the monster, I was much upset by three things, the balance and spacing of the noises, unlike a simple expression of a visceral mood or excitement; the seeming repetition of the noises; and another thing which I could not place, or refused to place, or dared not place, something unwelcomely familiar. What could it be?

I, and the others, were easily at our wagon when the second gong sounded.

Shortly thereafter the center bar was lifted at the open end of the wagon box and we crawled into the wagon, our shackles about the bar, which was then dropped into its slot and locked in place.

We were thus accounted for and secured for the night.

It was sometime in the middle of the night that I awakened, suddenly. I realized what I had feared to suspect earlier. The noises emanating from the monster were words, vehicles of thought, and words, frighteningly enough, in Gorean. In English, there are many dialects, many accents. I had heard English spoken in more than one dialect which was initially unintelligible to me, until, after some familiarity, some adjustments, some alterations, and expectations, one could understand what had been little more before but a storm of noise. So, too, in Gorean, there are many dialects, or accents. It had suddenly come to me that the beast was addressing me in Gorean, its Gorean. It had asked a question. It had asked it twice. It was "Where is Ag-nas?" or "Where is Ag-nes?"

I felt frightened and ill, and I twisted about, and, on my knees, thrust up the canvas and stretched my neck out, over the edge of the wagon box, but, in the next few seconds, in the cool, night air, and having a chance to think, I recovered. I drew back in the wagon, put the canvas in order, and lay down.

Clearly the monster did not know that I was the former Agnes Morrison Atherton. Had it known it would not have asked. If it had saved me from the *sleen*, it could well have been because it thought that I might prove to be a valuable informant. Surely such creatures would not be likely to boldly enter a Gorean encampment, where it might meet a forest of spears or a rain of arrows. Too, if I had understood it, I would simply have denied that I was the former Agnes Morrison Atherton, and denied, further, knowing anything of such a person. Too, few would know my former identity. Xanthe knew but I did not think she would betray me. Happily, Masters commonly renamed their properties as they wished. Who would suspect of the slave, Mira, that she might once have been a Miss Agnes Morrison Atherton? Too, due to my Gorean, almost everyone took me, uncritically, to be a native Gorean. I reassured myself that little had changed. It was surely unsettling to encounter such a monster and learn that the search for the former Agnes Morrison Atherton was still in progress, but it seemed my enemies, those who sought to apprehend and destroy me, were no closer to their objective than they had been, perhaps several times before. I supposed it was natural that they might inquire into large aggregations of slaves, but I had survived the night's test, and my pursuers would presumably now look elsewhere. Once sold in Ar, or in some large city, it would be next to impossible to locate a particular slave. I was not in peril. Indeed, my life had been saved. Rather than be afraid I should now rejoice in my good fortune. I was still alive. Where might the former Miss Agnes Morrison Atherton be? Perhaps she had been sold in Brundisium, to be shipped to the Farther Islands, even to the World's End; perhaps she had been taken to the Barrens, or the jungles of the Ua, or even to the Lands of the Wagon People, or to far Turia.

How irrational it was for me to be afraid.

I was safe now.

I had nothing to fear.

CHAPTER FORTY-FOUR

I backed into a door on Emerald Street, my heart beating wildly.

A brawny, passing fellow, in the gray of the Metal Workers, scarcely noticed me.

Across the street, two free women, robed and veiled, were walking together, chatting, each followed by a female serving slave, bare-armed, gowned in silk.

I had not seen Xanthe, the former Eileen Bennett, since our arrival in Ar.

Ar is doubtless one city, but is it not, in its way, as many another *polis*, many cities? There is the colorful, soaring Ar, the Ar of lofty towers linked by graceful, arching bridges, and the Ar of crowded, wooden tenements, squalid *insulae*, ill-lit and foul, rampant with crime and susceptible to fire; there is the Ar of lovely parks, sparkling fountains, and broad boulevards, and the Ar of narrow streets and dark, crooked alleys, not to be traversed at night save by torches and with armed men. Bold, glorious, high-walled Ar, dismal, squalid, shabby Ar; Ar of palaces, theaters, stadiums, rich markets, elegant restaurants, lovely shopping streets, and Ar of basement brothels, dingy taverns, and secret markets where honor can be sold, poisons purchased, and assassins hired. Was Ar not noted for its heroes and patriots? Was she not known for her swindlers and cheats? Was she not noted for her noble and her base, her cheap and her generous, her sophisticated and her blunt; her tasteful and her crass? But one thing, it seemed, was shared by the diverse, variegated hundreds of thousands who populated this crowded, mighty city, a reverence for a Home Stone for which men, rich or poor, of whatever caste, of whatever ilk or stripe, would defend the gates and man the walls, a Home Stone for which men were willing to die. It was this that made Ar Ar. And yet it was rumored that here, even in Ar, there might be some for whom this was not true, that there were some in Ar, even here, to whom her Home Stone, so to speak, was not known. Perhaps it is so in all cities.

* * *

I was still in the collar of Tenalian of Ar.

I had not yet had my first sale in Ar. I, and several others, as a respite from our training, had been allowed out of the house, to enjoy the city before reporting back by what the Goreans called the Twelfth Ahn. The bar had not yet signified the Eleventh Ahn.

Xanthe had been approaching.

She had not seen me.

She, leashed, in a tiny tunic, of cheap *rep*-cloth, of the sort commonly inflicted on the lowest and most worthless of slaves, her hands fastened behind her, bound or braceleted, clearly frightened and miserable, not daring to look back, preceded her keeper or Master.

"Hurry, *harta*," he snapped.

She increased her pace, hurrying forward.

I saw that her keeper or Master carried a long switch.

I thrust myself back further in the doorway.

I shall never forget my first glimpse of Ar, from miles away, when we had come to the top of a hill.

It was morning.

There had been cries of delight coursing through the caravan.

The guards did not even bother worrying about the canvas. We thrust it, as we could, half way up the frame which supported it.

The colorful towers were ablaze with light.

"Have you ever seen anything so beautiful?" asked a slave.

"I did not know it was so large," said Luta.

"It is larger than it looks," said another slave. "It is far away."

"How soon will we be sold?" asked a slave.

"Not soon," said another. "We must be rested and refreshed."

"There will be measurements to be taken, finger and toe prints to be made, and papers to be prepared," said another slave.

"We will not be simply sold?" I asked.

"We are prize slaves," said another.

"Some of us," said Xanthe, looking at me.

"What will they want to know?" I asked.

"Pertinent things," said another, "whether you can play the *kalika* and sing, whether you can recite the 'Love Songs of Dina,' such things."

"Where is all this done?" I asked.

"In the House of Tenalian, of course," said a slave. "Where else?"

"I know nothing of the House of Tenalian," I said.

"It is the largest house on Ar's Street of Brands," said a slave.

"Tonight we will be chained there," said a slave.

"Or penned," said another.

"Is Tenalian there?" asked a slave.

"Probably," said another.

"He has been with the caravan," laughed a slave, "suitably disguised. Some of the guards, new guards, hired on at Brundisium, do not even know him."

"He is brave man," said a slave.

"Concern for one's stock, one's property, does not encourage diffidence or timidity in a Merchant," said a slave.

"How do you know Tenalian is with us?" asked a slave of the slave who had claimed that the Master was with the caravan.

"I saw him, several times," she said. "I recognized him from Victoria."

"Why did you not tell us?" asked a slave.

"I did not want my tongue cut out," she said.

"What sort of things will the Master wish to learn of us?" I asked.

"Mostly things which might affect your price," she said.

"What is wrong, Mira?" asked Luta.

"Nothing is wrong, is there, Mira?" asked Xanthe, smiling.

"No," I said, "nothing is wrong."

"I have heard of 'Purple Booth' sales," said Xanthe. "I think I will be sold from a Purple Booth."

"No," said a slave. "Those are private sales, in which a particular slave is offered to a particular customer."

"And she must expect to be asked to prove her slave worth before the sale is consummated," said another slave.

"I will be sold in the Curulean," said Temione, "from the central block."

"A slave sold there," said Luta, "commonly brings at least ten silver tarsks."

"I brought four silver tarsks in Victoria," said Temione, "in what was, as all agree, a buyers' market."

"What do you think you will bring, Pockface?" asked Xanthe.

"I do not know," I said.

"You have never sold for even two silver tarsks," said Xanthe, "have you?"

"Many slaves have never brought that much," I said.

"Kettle-and-mat girls," said a slave.

"Have you?" asked Xanthe.

"No," I said.

"The caravan moves," said a slave. "We descend. Look while you can, see the glory of Ar, for the guards will soon command us to put the canvas down."

"They have been kind," said a slave.

"They, too," said a slave, "wanted to look upon the beauty of Ar."

"They would not deny that even to slaves," said another.

I turned away from the street, and faced the door, as though I might have knocked, and was awaiting a response.

I sensed Xanthe and her keeper or Master pass me.

I then turned to look after them.

I had not really seen he who was conducting her because I had been so startled at seeing her on the street.

A few yards beyond my post in the doorway, he who was conducting Xanthe stopped. Perhaps something had slipped his mind. I feared he might turn around, or back, but he did not do so. He had snapped the leash twice. If the slave is moving, one snap signifies 'Stop.' If the slave is stopped, one snap signifies 'Proceed.' If the slave is moving and the leash is snapped twice, as he had done, that signifies that the slave should not only stop but kneel. If the slave is kneeling, one snap signifies that she should rise to her feet. A second snap then, if desired, would signal her to proceed. A simple tug on the leash to the right or left, has the slave change her direction. If the slave follows on the leash, she kneels when the Master stops, and rises, and follows, when he continues on his way. Commands also, of course, may be delivered verbally. When not leashed, the slave commonly heels the Master, a bit on the left, a pace or two behind, depending on the traffic, so to speak.

As the fellow conducting her had snapped the leash twice, Xanthe had immediately stopped and knelt. Whatever might have been the cause of his hesitation or dalliance, he now seemed ready to continue on his way. He looked down at her for a moment and then, with his long switch, struck her sharply, twice, across the calves. She whimpered. How it must have stung! He must have then said something to her, for she responded, earnestly. "No, Master! Thank you, Master! I beg you to do with me as you please, for I am your loving and helpless slave!" He then shook the leash once and she rose to her feet. He then snapped it again, that she should proceed, which she did, but, it seemed, she had not responded with sufficient promptitude, for he thrust her forward, and she stumbled, and struggled to maintain her feet. As she regained her balance, he gave her two more stripes, this time across the back of the thighs, and she hurried on, weeping.

As she had spoken of herself as his slave, I gathered that he who conducted her was her Master.

I had not seen his face, but something about him seemed familiar. This was not that surprising, as several of the guards on our long, overland trek from Brundisium to Ar had evinced interest in the slender, well-formed, dark-haired barbarian, Xanthe, the former Eileen Bennett.

She had referred to herself as his helpless and loving slave.

I recalled that she had vacuously, absurdly, denied her bondage, and had claimed that she would never submit to a man.

I supposed that many men would not be much interested in such anomalous asseverations, as long as they might use her as their plaything, in any way they pleased, and for as long as they wished.

But I had been startled when she had spoken, when she had identified herself as his helpless and loving slave. Could such words have escaped the former Eileen Bennett? Clearly, they had. And, more significantly, in the timber of her voice, there had been an undeniable, unmistakable quality of tone and sound. It was not only that of an abject, self-accepting, true slave, but of one who knew herself mastered, one who had met her master. I then shuddered, for I was suddenly sure, for no reason that I could clearly identify, that the man whom she had preceded, on her leash, he who had carried the long switch, was he whom I had known at the observatory as Maxwell Holt! I had not seen his face, but there was something familiar about his cut and carriage. And he had stopped briefly. Had he seen me? Did he know me? Then I tried to tell myself that it was not he, that it could not be he, but I was afraid that it was he, that somehow it must be he.

But he had not seen me.

I had been in the shadow of the doorway.

He could not have seen me.

There were a thousand reasons he might have stopped.

And did he not continue on his way, without turning about?

Ar was large, and populous, its many, many thousands unknown to one another.

Unreasoning fear had made me suspect it might be he.

It could not have been he.

I was pleased, however, that Xanthe, the former Eileen Bennett, had now come to grips with her sex and meaning, that she now knew herself a slave and the rightless property of a Master.

Though the bar had not yet sounded the Eleventh Ahn, and I needed not be back until the Twelfth Ahn, I decided to return to the house.

I no longer felt safe on the street.

CHAPTER FORTY-FIVE

"How is it, slave," asked the fellow in blue robes, in the curule chair before which I knelt, "that you do not know the name of Myron, the *polemarkos* of Temos?"

I put down my head, frightened.

"What are the names of the Farther Islands?" he asked.

"Forgive me, Master," I said. "I do not know."

"Everyone knows them," he said.

"Forgive me, Master," I said. "I do not."

"Perhaps you have forgotten," he suggested.

"Yes, Master," I said.

"Chios, Thera, and Pylos," he said. "Do you remember?"

"Yes, Master," I said.

"You are a liar, pretty collar-urt," he said. "They are Chios, Thera, and Daphna. Pylos is a town on Daphna."

"Yes, Master," I said, miserable.

"Do you know what is done on Gor to pretty little collar-urts who lie?"

"They are whipped," I said.

"Whip her," he said to my keeper.

A hand was put in my hair and I was pulled to my feet, bent over, my head held at his left thigh.

"When she is exhibited, hang the yellow placard about her neck," he said. Placards were used on the public shelves of Tenalian. The placards were of wood and were some six inches square, suspended at two edges by a loop of cord. Sales information was inscribed on the placards. Yellow placards were used for barbarians, red for native Gorean.

"Hold," he said.

The keeper turned to face him, my head held down.

"You are a barbarian," said the man in blue.

"Yes, Master," I whimpered.

"You could not fool me," he said. "I knew from the moment you spoke."

"Yes, Master," I said. I rather doubted that. Why then had he interrogated me further? But perhaps he had been suspicious, say, of some subtlety in my diction, and wished to confirm his suspicion.

"Were you free on your world?" he asked.

"Yes, Master," I said.

"Did you anticipate that you would one day be brought to this world and, suitably and appropriately, made a slave?" he asked.

"No, Master," I said.

"But you will try to be a good little slave, will you not?" he asked.

"Yes, Master," I said. I was not large, but I certainly was not little either.

"It would not be pleasant," he said, "to be thrown alive to leech plants or ravening *sleen*."

"No, Master," I said.

"Did you know," he asked, "that on your own world thousands of women are held in bondage, as secret slaves."

"No, Master," I said.

"Held so suitably and appropriately," he said.

"Yes Master," I said.

How many women, I wondered, had I unknowingly encountered on the streets, or in crowded stores, or in busy offices, or in libraries, parks, theaters, concert halls, or elsewhere, who were slaves? Did such women, upon returning to their dwellings, kneel and wait for their collars to be put on them by their Masters?

"Your Gorean is quite good," he said.

"Thank you, Master," I said.

I was sure that, had I known more of Gor, I might have succeeded in maintaining my pretense to be natively Gorean. But, then again, it is hard to know about such things.

He then made a small gesture, and I was hurried from his presence. Shortly thereafter, in a room strewn with straw, I was told to remove my tunic and present my wrists, crossed, for binding. I did so, and the rope was passed through an overhead ring. My hands were pulled high over my head, until only the tips of my toes could feel the floor, at which point the rope was secured to a hook at the side. Essentially then I was suspended, naked, before the keeper, who then uncoiled and shook free the blades of a whip.

"Forgive me," I begged.

"There will be plenty of time for that," he said, "after you have been whipped."

"The man, the clerk, the official, the functionary, in blue—," I said.

"The Scribe," he said.

"—did not specify a given number of strokes," I said.

"No," he said. "Ten blows are typical, but there could be more, or fewer."

"I beg fewer," I said.

"I have some discretion in the matter," he said.

"Fewer," I begged. "Master is handsome," I said.

"That will add a stroke," he said.

He then shook out again the blades of the five-stranded Gorean slave whip, designed for the instruction of female slaves. It is felt keenly but leaves no lasting mark.

"It is better not to lie," he said. "Free women may lie, but lying is not permitted to *kajirae*."

"Yes, Master," I said.

He then went behind me, and, as I dangled naked before him, gave me five measured strokes. I wept. My skin, my back, seemed aflame. I was a punished slave. I had been displeasing.

"Please do not whip me further, Master," I wept. "No more, please!"

It must stop. It must not go on. I could not stand it!

"You may choose, *kajira*," he said. "Five more strokes or putting 'liar' on your sales placard."

"Five more strokes," I wept. "Please, Master, five more strokes!"

"Good," he said.

"Who," I wondered, "would be so stupid as not to prefer five more strokes to being publicly certified a liar, a characterization which could well affect how one might be regarded and treated indefinitely. There was even a liar's penalty brand, though he did not mention it.

I endured five more strokes.

"That is ten," I wept. "May it not be enough, Master?"

"For some offenses," said he, "five strokes are enough, for example, a slight dalliance in complying with an order; for others, for your amusing, desperate little lie, ten would normally suffice."

"And I have received ten!" I said.

"But," said he, "did you not attempt to flatter me, with the intent of lightening your punishment?"

"Yes, Master," I said.

"Thus," he said, "you shall receive an additional stroke, the promised stroke."

"Ai!" I screamed in pain, suddenly, spasmodically, recoiling, in the ropes.

"You may thank me for your instruction," he said.

"Thank you, Master," I said, sobbing, "—for my instruction."

He then loosened the rope from its hook at the side of the room, and I sank to the floor, in the straw. He then removed the rope from my wrists. "Shall I put you supine?" he asked. "The straw will be kind to your back."

"Please do not," I said.

"You are afraid of me," he said. I was silent. I was afraid of him, and I did not want to excite him. To be sure, there are few attitudes, few positions, in which a collared, naked female slave is not exciting to a male. He then, to my surprise, flung me to my belly in the straw and jerked my wrists behind me where he tied them together with a part of the rope by which I had been suspended from the whipping ring. With another part of the rope, he crossed my ankles and tied them together, and then, with the free end of the rope, he drew me, twisting, through the straw, to the side of the room where he fastened my bound ankles up, a foot or so, from the floor. In this way, whether I was on my belly or back, I could not stand and was tethered in place.

"I am going to make notes for your sales placard," he said. "I shall be back shortly."

I did not think he was back so shortly.

He finally reentered the room, looked down on me, and grinned.

"I see you waited for me," he said. "Did you miss me?"

"What are you going to do with me?" I asked.

"You are a pretty little she-urt," he said, "a very pretty little liar."

"What are you going to do with me?" I asked. He would do with me, of course, what he pleased. I was *kajira*.

"You are from Earth," he said.

"Yes, Master," I said.

"Is it true," he asked, "that the women of Earth dominate their men?"

"Some, perhaps," I said.

"They should be brought to Gor," he said. "Did you dominate your man?"

"I had no man," I said.

"Here," he said, "you belong to men."

"Yes, Master," I said.

"Do you understand that?" he asked.

"Yes, Master," I said.

He then, to my relief, lowered my elevated ankles from the wall, and unbound them. My hands were still tied behind my back.

"You may now, woman of Earth," he said, "from your knees, and then belly, lick and kiss the feet of a Gorean Master."

"Yes, Master," I said.

I could not describe the thrill of what I was doing. How strong, and mighty, he seemed. How small and vulnerable, and mastered, I felt. I was dominated, and responded, globally, with a flood of feeling which informed me that I was where I belonged, and doing what I was meant to do.

After a time, he said, "You may desist."

"Yes, Master," I said.

"Do you still wonder what will be done with you?" he asked.

"No, Master," I said.

"I have two Ahn to spare," he said.

"I will try to be pleasing," I said.

"How is your back?" he asked.

My back apparently extended from the back of my neck to my ankles.

"Much better," I said.

The salves and ointments had done much to subdue the fires which still seemed to smolder beneath the skin.

He had been kind.

I think he had been pleased.

"I have not included, in my notes for your placard, that you are a liar," he said.

"Thank you, Master," I said.

"It was wise of you," he said, "in lieu of that characterization on your placard, to take the five lashes."

"I thought so," I said.

"But the next time you are tempted to lie," he said, "you might remember that there is a collar on your neck."

"Yes, Master," I said.

"You will be a pretty yellow-placard girl," he said.

I said nothing.

He had no way of understanding the terror which attended the yellow placard, which far exceeded a possible reference to the character of its wearer. In the house, in the pens, in the cages, and on the sales shelves of Tenalian, that signified that I was a barbarian. After my sale, of course, the placard would be removed, but what if, somehow, somewhere, during the sale, or in precincts pertinent to the sale, one who sought the former Agnes Morrison Atherton might note it and, perhaps coupling it with a description or likeness, be moved to investigate?

"Now," he said, "you may please me again."

"Yes, Master," I said.

CHAPTER FORTY-SIX

"Stand up straight, slave," said the Shelf Master. "You are not a slovenly free woman. You are in a collar. You are a plaything of men. Lift up your head. Let them get a look at you. Display your Master's goods, and display them well, or you will be well whipped."

I straightened my body, frightened, my eyes bright with tears.

My left ankle was chained to a metal ring set in the shelf. How helpless one is as a slave! I could move about a little but could not, of course, leave the shelf. The shelf backed against a wall which was equipped with a number of rings and chains. A few feet to my right, Luta was chained against the wall, her back to the wall, her wrists over her head. She was lovely. To my left, a few feet away, another slave was chained at the wall, sitting with her back against it. She was held in place by a neck collar. She could do little more than stand, to be examined. And other slaves were about, as well, on their chains. The placement of slaves on a shelf, incidentally, is seldom random or accidental. They are arranged in such a way, mixed in such a way, by appearance and chaining, that they present an attractive aspect, or view. When a slave is sold, or added to the shelf, others are often rearranged. This is best seen, of course, from the street. Similar considerations, dramatic, aesthetic, and such, may characterize the time and order in which slaves are brought to the block in auctions.

He pulled the small, wooden, yellow placard, on its cord, out from my neck, perused it, and then dropped it back, against my breasts.

"There is little to interest a buyer in you, other than what he can see by simply looking at you," he said.

I was not trained in slave dance; I knew few Gorean songs; I could play no instrument; I could not even string a *kalika*; I was ignorant of arranging flowers; I could not mix perfumes; wines were a mystery to me; I could not even read, let alone converse brilliantly on various periods in Gorean literature. I could not even arrange the pieces on a *kaissa* board correctly, if Masters were to ask me to prepare the board for play.

"There is little on the placard," said the shelf Master, "other than an adeptness in Gorean and that your slave fires are coming along nicely."

I was startled to hear the notation about slave fires. Could they rage more fiercely, more frequently, more profoundly than they did?

I had frequently knelt or bellied, pressing my lips to a Master's foot, begging for sex. How profound are a woman's needs, once a collar is on her neck! A slave, of course, may beg for sex. She is not a free woman. I think it is difficult for a free woman, with her sleeping, guarded needs, to understand how profound and overwhelming can be a slave's need for sex. Or are they, free women, truly so tepid, so minimal, so formal and inert? Do they not, sometimes, restless and weeping, thrashing in their beds, dare to suspect what it might be, to be naked and collared, at the feet of the Master of their dreams?

It is common, of course, to ignite slave fires in the belly of a slave. It amuses men, clearly, to make women their helpless, needful slaves. That gives them additional power over the property. Consider the free woman, so elevated and exalted, so superior and haughty, currently inert and seemingly smug in her frigidity, enslaved, transformed into a begging, groveling, chattel. Does this not amuse men? Is the bond of her needs not a thousand times more telling than chained limbs, a mark on her thigh, and a metal collar locked about her neck?

Consider the feelings of a former free woman, now a slave, who, to her misery, finds herself the property of a cruel, hated, scornful Master, perhaps even one whose suit for companionship she once, in her freedom, loftily rejected, one who now regards her suitably as no more than dirt and garbage, even as less than nothing. Then suppose that she is now the helpless victim of her raging slave fires. Consider the conflicts, the storms of feelings, within her. Now she crawls to his feet, hoping to be permitted to please him, begging, weeping, for his least caress.

Too, of course, economically, there is much to be said for the kindling of slave fires in a property. Economically, it increases the value of the merchandise.

Without warning, the Shelf Master touched me, firmly, decisively, as a slave may be touched. I cried out, startled. Then he jerked his hand away, before I could piteously grind my body against it.

"Put your hands behind your back," he said. "No, do not press forward."

I stood before him, my eyes glistening with tears.

"Barbarians," he said, "are still rare in the markets, but there are more now than heretofore. Some men prefer them. There is an exotic aspect about them. They respond nicely to the collar. They, of course, as females, were bred for it. They make good slaves. Perhaps there is little, or no, sex on their world. Could that be possible? It seems that men are reduced, and women are emptied, forlorn, and meaningless, lacking identity as women."

I was silent.

"The slaves are extracted from an artificial world, and introduced to a natural world, which they may at first fear," he said, "but soon they learn that it is their world, the world in which they have a natural place."

I dared not speak.

He then lifted his whip to my lips, and I pressed my lips to it, quickly kissing it and then licking it, and kissing it again. Slave girls are seldom, if ever, struck with the whip but they know that they are subject to it. The human being is a symbol-using animal, and rituals have their symbolic content. Rituals can be as simple as kneeling and standing, as collaring and marking. They can be as complex as modes of dress, speech, and behavior.

And they can be profoundly meaningful.

He drew the whip back, away from me.

"Keep your hands behind your back," he said.

He then turned away from me.

I was alone.

Some men were passing by. Occasionally one or another would pause near the shelf, standing on the street, perusing the merchandise.

I supposed that I could not well have maintained my posture of being Gorean indefinitely, but, with its loss, I felt far more endangered. And here, in this street market, my origin was trumpeted about by the yellow placard hung about my neck. Ar was a metropolis, and her streets and markets might be trodden by hundreds, perhaps thousands, of visitors, of diverse castes and backgrounds. This was no remote, unfrequented hamlet or obscure village. It was the crossroads of a hemisphere. Might not anyone who sought me, to find me, to kill me, simply pass by, and, curious, investigate and acquire me? I could be as easily purchased as a *tarsk* or *verr*. I was particularly miserable because, now, I was almost sure that Maxwell Holt, whom I had obliquely known at the observatory, was not only on Gor but, it seemed, in Ar herself. I was half sure that I had seen him, with Xanthe, on Emerald Street some days ago. He had doubtless been sent to Gor to silence me, or have me silenced. Why else might he be here? He could recognize me by sight. He might even have brought images of me to show interlocutors the nature of his quarry. Doubtless he hoped to utilize Xanthe in his search, as well. It had been a narrow thing on Emerald Street. My only hope was that Ar was large and that I might be soon sold, to disappear into a trackless urban jungle, or even out of the city. But I was conflicted. Could I have been mistaken on Emerald Street? Perhaps he with Xanthe on Emerald Street had not been Maxwell Holt. Perhaps my perception had been distorted by dread or fear? I knew such things could occur. Earth was far away. Passing amongst planets would invoke a technology far more complex and sophisticated than that involved in boarding an airplane in one country and deboarding in another. If Doctors Jameson, Archer, and Townsend wished to communicate with colleagues on Gor, presumably it could be done by a means far simpler than having recourse to a physical agent.

"Yes," I thought to myself, kneeling down and adjusting the small yellow placard on its cords slung about my neck, "you are in danger, but do not exaggerate the actual danger, which is negligible. Even were Maxwell Holt on Gor, which is unlikely, upon reflection, he did not see you on Emerald or elsewhere, and would have no idea of your whereabouts. Too, I should soon be sold and then, the yellow placard gone, I would be no more than another of Ar's thousands of female slaves. Indeed, buyers came to the markets of Ar from many municipalities. Indeed, whereas Ar was a *kajira*'s dream, with its sights and excitements, many cities might promise a similar venue with a greater security. In any event, I would go where I was taken. I hoped, of course, to be spared long hours and heavy labors. I had had my fill of that in the fields of the former Lady Temione of Hammerfest. But then no one came to the various markets of Tenalian of Ar for field slaves. Some of his stock was such that it might be displayed on the blocks of the Curulean itself, even on the central block itself."

My comforting reverie was suddenly interrupted. The Shelf Master said, sharply, "On your feet, *kajira*. Examination Position!"

I leapt to my feet, my feet widely spread, my head back, my eyes on the sky, my hands clasped behind the back of my head. There are various slave positions, familiar to all *kajirae*, which, upon command, are to be assumed immediately and unquestionly. One is drilled in them. One responds instantly, automatically, unthinkingly. Indeed, sometimes a female slave, trying to escape, attempting to pose as a free woman, even to robes and veils, is detected by no more than the utterance of such a command.

In the examination position a woman is not only exposed, but exposed with exquisite vulnerability. The spreading of her feet makes it difficult to change her position or protect herself, did she dare. The placement of her hands behind her head lifts her breasts nicely, and immobilizes her hands, locking them in place, lest she might be tempted to use them to obstruct an examiner's vision or interfere in any way with the examination. The position of the head, back, having her look upward, makes it difficult for her to follow the attention of the examiner, noting its nature, or to anticipate any action of his hands.

I heard a male laugh.

I did not understand this.

"Do not break position," said the Shelf Master.

Was I not worthy of this shelf?

"You may look," said the man who had laughed.

I screamed and tried to dart away, but, after but a stride, the shackle on my left ankle, its chain jerked taut, stopped me, sharply and brutally, and I fell to the shelf. Almost at the same time the whip of the Shelf Master fell upon me, again and again. Sobbing, I struggled to my feet and returned to Examination Position, except for the position of my head, from which attitude I had been relieved. When I did so, the Shelf Master lowered his whip.

"You are a pretty slave," said the man who had laughed. "I had thought, at the observatory, it would be so. I see you are marked with the common *kef*. That is appropriate, as you are only an Earth female. The collar on your neck, close-fitting and locked, is lovely, but then is not it so with any good-looking woman?"

"We will address the bleeding wound on her ankle," said the Shelf Master. "She is a stupid, foolish little *vulo*."

I looked at he who had laughed, he who had permitted me to change the position of my head. "Maxwell Holt!" I whispered.

His hand lashed out and he cuffed me twice, and, lip bleeding, tasting blood, I sank to my knees before him. "Forgive me," I begged. "Master! Master!"

I had, foolishly, in the stress of the moment, beside myself with misery and terror, addressed a free man by his name.

"She knows you," said the Shelf Master.

"And I her," said Maxwell Holt.

"What is your name, slave?" asked Maxwell Holt.

"Mira," I said, "if it pleases Master."

"I can give you a good price on her," said the Shelf Master.

I heard a jerking of the chain linking slave bracelets against a ring at the front of the shelf. "Do not buy her, Master!" cried a woman's voice. "She is not needed. She is too ugly for you! See the faults of her complexion! Do not buy her!"

It was Xanthe. One of her wrists had been braceleted and the other bracelet and its chain had been threaded through the ring, and then the free bracelet had been snapped shut about her other wrist, tethering her in place. In this way a Master's slave may be fastened in place, before the shelf, she on the street, while he inspects the merchandise.

"Were you on Emerald, some days past?" asked Maxwell Holt.

"But you did not then seize me," I said.

"I thought so," he said.

"It was I," I said.

"I glanced to the shelf," he said. "Lo, a slave looked familiar. I thought it might be you. The yellow placard caught my attention. I thought I would see."

"Do not buy her, Master!" cried Xanthe, jerking at the bracelets and ring.

How foolish was Xanthe. Did she not know that I was, for some reason I did not fully understand, an inestimable prize to be sought? Did I not know too much? Might I not, in no way that I fully understood, be somehow putting others at risk? Did she not realize that Maxwell Holt had been sent, even from far Earth, to effect my capture, sent for that, and nothing else? Did she not realize that she meant nothing to him, and that his interest in her, if any, was no more than incidental? Did she not realize that she lacked importance? Was that so hard to understand? Did she not realize that his quest was now ended, that he had achieved what he wanted, what he had come for, and that he would now buy me, and easily?

I had been caught. I was lost.

"You know my slave, Xanthe," he said. "She was Eileen Bennett on Earth."

"Yes, Master," I said.

"She tried to pull me away from the shelf," he said. "For some reason, she did not wish me to see you."

I was briefly suffused with gratitude. Xanthe and I had not been friends, either on Earth, or Gor, but she had accepted, and abetted, however reluctantly, however skeptically, my desire to conceal my barbarian origin.

"But now," said Maxwell Holt, "we have all renewed our acquaintance, though under somewhat different circumstances from the observatory."

"Yes, Master," I said, naked and collared, at his feet.

Xanthe, slave-tunicked, on the street, was braceleted at the edge of the shelf.

"I can let you have her for two silver tarsks, and five copper tarsks," said the Shelf Master.

I had never sold for that much before.

"Is such a price not high for such a slave?" asked Maxwell Holt.

"It is too high, Master!" called Xanthe.

"Not at all," said the Shelf Master to Maxwell Holt, ignoring Xanthe. "And do not forget, this is a Tenalian Shelf. Tenalian does not deal with kettle-and-mat girls."

"Is she hot and does she juice well?" asked Maxwell Holt.

"Read the placard," said the Shelf Master, lifting it for his perusal.

"I thought she might, once in a collar, where she belongs," said Maxwell Holt.

I began to weep, uncontrollably.

"What is wrong with her?" asked Maxwell Holt.

"Do not play with me, Master," I wept. "I am miserable enough. You have caught me. The hunt is done! I cannot escape! Please be merciful! Do not kill me! I will tell no secrets. I do not even know secrets! I know nothing! I do not even know why I am pursued! I beg my life!"

"I do not understand?" said Maxwell Holt.

"Master?" I said.

"Do not buy her, Master!" cried Xanthe, the former Eileen Bennett.

The Shelf Master poked me with his coiled whip. I then, on my knees before Maxwell Holt, my ankle bloody, kissed his bootlike sandals, and, head down, spoke as I had been told. "Buy me, Master," I said. "I beg to be purchased. I will try to be a good slave to you."

I then lost consciousness.

CHAPTER FORTY-SEVEN

I sat with my back against the wall of the alcove, tunicked, knees up, my left hand chained to the side, to my left, my right hand chained to the side, to my right. In this fashion, one cannot protect oneself from the attentions of others. I had been so positioned at the customer's request, while he quaffed another goblet, to await him. Supposedly he was to join me soon, but he had been hailed by some fellow, and better than an Ahn had passed.

Slaves, as animals, can wait; they are not free women.

I could not see back into the tavern for the leather curtain had been drawn, but not fastened.

The fur-lined alcove was illuminated by a tiny, vented *tharlarion*-oil lamp placed on a shelf to my right.

I could hear the music and the murmur of conversation.

What a vain fool I had been!

Maxwell Holt, as far as I could tell, knew little more of mysterious matters than I. Whereas I knew I was sought, and matters of moment, of some sort, were well afoot, his return to Gor, he a native of this lovely, perilous orb, had nothing to do with me, and much to do with Xanthe. For the first time, I was beginning to truly understand how fiercely a male can want a woman, and how completely, so completely that he would wish to own her wholly, each corpuscle of her body, each hair of her head, that he would be satisfied with nothing short of having her at his feet, in the full majesty of the law, stripped, and in his collar. His role at the observatory and that of perhaps others, as well, I gathered, had been rather in the nature of a forming a liaison of sorts between two worlds, for few of Earth spoke Gorean and few Goreans, other than slavers, spoke a language of Earth. While Eileen Bennett had been carrying on in the observatory, flirting and amusing herself, arousing, taunting, and tormenting males without satisfying them, she did not realize that she was doing so under the scrutiny of a native Gorean, one who looked upon her with amusement as little more than potential collar meat. Kurii, savage and technologically sophisticated, needed human agents to abet their schemes, and recruited such on both Earth and Gor. Many of the Gorean human agents, supplied with arms and spacecraft by the Kurii of the Steel

Worlds, were of the Slavers. In this way, the Kurii of their artificial worlds might obtain various supplies and goods from Earth and certain Goreans received the equipment and means whereby they might pursue ends of particular interest to themselves. In all this, I think that few humans had a clear understanding of the ultimate aims of the Kurii. In all such endeavors is there not a distinction between a public and a private politics? To be sure, I did not doubt but what some humans knew well, or shrewdly suspected, the final ends of Kurii, and were determined to act so as to occupy a secure and profitable station in what they expected would be two Kur worlds.

I was a *paga* girl at the Yellow Whip in Venna, several *pasangs* from Ar, famed for its *tharlarion* races.

I would have preferred a more private slavery.

How could I hide, a *paga* girl, put on the floor, half-naked, each night, at the mercy of any fellow who could afford the price of a drink?

I knew I was sought.

I knew I was in danger.

I heard hands fumbling at the leather curtain.

Some days ago, I had awakened, bound, hand and foot, in a closed, *tharlarion*-drawn wagon.

My left ankle was bandaged.

Blood had soaked through the bandage, but it was now dried.

What had happened since I had lost consciousness?

Where was Maxwell Holt?

Where was I being taken?

Why had I not been killed?

Was I to be killed?

Perhaps they wished to know how much I knew, or how much I understood of what I might know, or, more likely, had I imparted important or dangerous knowledge to others, and, if so, when, where, and to whom?

Lying in the wagon, on the boards, bound, I turned my body a bit, for my shoulder was sore.

I could see, through the canvas, ahead of me, imaged like shadows, that there were two figures on the wagon bench.

"May I speak, Masters?" I asked.

"She is awake," said one of the fellows on the bench.

"It is about time," said his fellow.

"Shall we let the *tasta* speak?" asked the driver.

A *tasta* is a common Gorean confection. It is sold at fairs, races, arena sports, in candy shops, by itinerant street vendors, and so on. It consists of a soft candy mounted on a stick.

"The road is long," said the other. "Can you sing, or recite?" he called back.

"Not well," I said.

"What do you want?" he asked, the driver's fellow, who, I took it, was the first of the two.

"Where is Maxwell Holt?" I asked.

"Who is Maxwell Holt?" he asked.

"I do not know what is going on," I said. "What has happened? Where are you taking me? Please be merciful. Whom do you serve? To whom do I belong? What is to be done with me?"

"Read your collar," said the driver's fellow.

I gathered that he thought that this was amusing.

"I cannot read," I said. "And even if I could, I could not read my collar without a mirror or some reflective surface."

"Are you insolent?" he asked.

"No, Master!" I said. "I must have fainted on the sales shelf, one of those of Tenalian of Ar. I know nothing."

"You proved yourself a skittish and worthless slave," said the driver's fellow. "You darted about. Were you trying to escape, manacled? Are you that stupid? You cut your ankle badly. You will be fortunate if you do not find yourself scarred. You might have harmed, or marred, your Master's property. That is not permitted. You are unreliable. You babbled nonsense. Were you mad, out of your senses, shaken, addled? Were you drunk? Had you stolen *ka-la-na*? Had merry Keepers filled you with diluted *paga* for their sport, for a joke on the Shelf Master? Then, as if all this were not enough, you collapsed, unconscious."

At this point the driver laughed.

"Forgive me, Masters," I said. "I was upset. I was frightened. Terribly frightened. I do not even know if I knew what I was doing. I could not help myself."

I was still shaken, and very frightened, but I was, thankfully, no longer panicked, no longer hysterical.

And I was still alive!

And it seemed possible that my present situation might not be related to the observatory and the secrets of worlds.

Did they, truly, know nothing of Maxwell Holt?

"Your Master," said the driver's fellow, "is Lycus the Fat, proprietor of the Yellow Whip in Venna. We were sent to Ar to shop for one or more *paga* slaves. Have you ever been a *paga* slave?"

"No, Master," I said.

"We were authorized to go as high as two silver tarsks," said the driver's fellow.

"That is a high price for a *paga* girl," said the driver.

"Too high," said the driver's fellow.

"You bought me to be a *paga* slave?" I asked, hopefully.

"Of course," said the driver's fellow. "What else?"

A laugh escaped me, inadvertently, one of sudden relief.

"Perhaps she is indeed addled," said the driver.

I felt tears in my eyes, of hope and gladness.

To be sure, the bondage of a *paga* girl is a rather public bondage. How can one hide, if one is sent regularly to the floor? Who knows who, or what, might visit a tavern? One can, of course, like most slaves, hope for a private Master, and even love.

"May I inquire," I asked, "what Masters paid for me?"

"What do you think?" asked the driver's fellow.

"Masters were authorized," I recalled, "to go as high as two silver tarsks."

"Only for a Curulean-level girl," said the driver.

"That is an auction house in Ar," I said.

"She is a barbarian," said the driver, apparently explaining my ignorance to his fellow.

"I know that, Master," I said. "Please tell me how much you paid for me."

"Vain slave," said the driver's fellow.

"Please," I said. "I have never sold before for as much as two silver tarsks."

"I believe you," said the driver, unnecessarily.

"The Shelf Master," I said, "was willing to let me go for a price of a two silver tarsks, five."

"That was before you spoiled the sale," said the driver.

"Surely I went for at least a silver tarsk," I said.

"We bought you for forty copper tarsks," said the driver's fellow, he who was seemingly first amongst the two.

I was silent.

As far as I knew, I had never sold for so little before.

I supposed that the driver and his fellow still had much of the two authorized silver tarsks, or so, left over. To be sure, such speculations are not appropriate for a *kajira*.

"I think Masters made a good buy," I said.

"Be careful," said the driver's fellow.

"Yes, Master," I said, warned.

"It is getting cloudy; it is going to rain," said the driver.

"I am in the tunic of the Yellow Whip?" I asked. It was brief, yellow, and bore black lettering which, I would later learn, spelled out the name and street of the tavern.

"Yes," said he who was first amongst the two, "and in the collar of Lycus the Fat, of Venna."

"In the tavern," I said, "I will not have to wear a placard signifying my barbarous origin, will I?"

"No," said the driver's fellow.

I was pleased. I was sure that I could pass as Gorean with most of those with whom I might come in contact.

"The wind is rising, I felt a drop of rain," said the driver's fellow.

"There is a rain cover, folded, under the bench," said the driver.

I could sense that it was cooler.

As the wagon was covered I had little to fear from wind or rain.

It might become colder, I supposed, uncomfortably so.

Perhaps they had a blanket they could give me.

"What have you been called?" asked the driver's fellow.

"Mira, if it pleases Masters," I said.

That name, whatever might have been its remote origin, clearly functioned as a Gorean name. I had met two other girls, both Gorean, who had worn that name.

It would probably have been better, had my name been changed, even several times, as that might make it more difficult to trace me.

At least I had not been given an obvious Earth name. Those names, incidentally, are normally taken to be slave names, presumably because most women brought from Earth to Gor are brought for the markets. Sometimes a natively Gorean *kajira* is given an Earth name as a punishment name, say, to demean her, or encourage her to improve her skills and services. Many Gorean *kajirae*, as you may have gathered, look down on *kajirae* of Earth origin. Are they not lowly barbarians, ignorant and untutored, who do not, initially, even speak the language? And might they not, in the helpless blossoming of their sexual needs, thriving piteously in their collars, prove rivals of a sort, for the attention of handsome Masters? And who can tell them from native Goreans presented naked on the block? Incidentally, I found this prejudice, the scorn for Earth *kajirae* by natively Gorean *kajirae* ironic, at the least, as all Goreans, as far as I knew, had an Earth origin, they or their ancestors seemingly having been brought somehow to Gor by some means.

"We are going to unbind you," said the driver's fellow. "Would that please you?"

"Very much, Master," I said.

I could hear the tapping of rain on the canvas.

"You must not then try to run away," said the driver.

"I will not try to run away, Master," I said.

"At least not for the first Ahn," said the driver.

"No, Master," I said.

He laughed.

Where would I run, tunicked, collared, and marked? I did not even know where I was, other than somewhere between Ar and Venna. There is no escape for the Gorean slave girl. She is a Gorean slave girl. I, once Agnes Morrison Atherton, was now a Gorean slave girl. There was no escape for me.

The rain was falling more heavily now.

I was grateful for the canvas.

The men on the wagon bench would have a rain cover. Even so, I did not envy them. Perhaps they could pull off the road and find shelter amongst some trees or perhaps under some bridge. I had felt the wagon wheels traversing more than one sort of surface.

The wagon was drawn to the side of the road by its middle-sized draft *tharlarion* and, to my surprise, the two men thrust up the forward canvas and, climbing over the board, joined me in the wagon. I supposed that wise, for the rain was becoming severe.

I sat up and pushed back against the side of the wagon.

"Belly," said the driver's fellow who, as noted, seemed to be first amongst them.

I went to my belly, and strong hands quickly undid the bonds on my wrists and ankles.

"Thank you, Master," I said.

He then turned me to my back.

"Master?" I said.

"*Sula!*" said he.

Almost before I realized it, I had spread my legs, and flung my hands to my sides, palms up.

I looked up at him. "Surely not, Master!" I said.

My tunic was then thrust up, to my waist, and I was brutally had, as may be done to a slave.

Might not a loving Master be kind to a slave?

But few things so thrilled me, or impressed my bondage upon me, as to be treated as what I was, and knew I was, and wanted to be, a rightless, meaningless animal, a ready appurtenance to a Master's desire, a convenience at hand by means of which he might satisfy his lust, however and whenever he might wish.

I knew there were such women, and that I, once Agnes Morrison Atherton, of Earth, was one such. I belonged in a collar.

"Ho," said the driver's fellow, clapping a hand to me, "she juices!"

"Please," I begged, "do not be done with me so soon. Touch me, again. I beg it!"

"Do you object?" he asked.

"No, Master!" I said, quickly.

"On your belly," said the driver.

I obeyed, frightened.

"Now, up on your knees, facing away from me," he said, "and put your head to the boards, and your hands, palms down, on either side of your head."

Tears burst from my eyes.

"Now the worthless she-tarsk is nicely positioned," said the driver.

I felt I wanted to cry out for mercy, for respect, for dignity! Did they think that I was an animal? "But, of course," I thought, "I am an animal, a domestic animal, a slave!"

The driver seized my hips, held me, and put me to his pleasure.

Then I lay on my belly, my hands beside my head, not satisfied, not daring to speak.

"I think Lycus will be pleased," said the driver's fellow.

"He may send us to Ar again," said the driver.

"With another two silver tarsks," said his fellow.

"Or three," speculated the driver.

"You will fit in well, *kajira*, amongst the tables, and in the alcoves," said the driver's fellow.

"May I not have more?" I asked.

The rain was drumming on the canvas.

"Remove your tunic," said the driver's fellow.

"Yes, Master," I said, delightedly.

The wind was whipping past.

Then he tied my hands behind my back and put a rope on my neck. He then lifted me over the wagon's end gate, and set me down on my feet, in the mud.

"Master?" I asked.

He tied the free end of the rope on my neck to the back of the wagon.

"Am I not to ride in the wagon?" I asked.

"We must be on our way," he said. "Surely you do not wish to be more comfortable, warmer and drier, than free men."

He then joined his fellow on the pelted wagon bench and, I assumed, sheltered with him under the rain cover.

Shortly thereafter he called to the *tharlarion*, flicked his long switch, and the wagon left the side of the road. I was then, on my rope, naked, in the rain and wind, following the trundling wagon, as it rolled over the flat, smooth stones of the road.

It was now dark.

I could barely detect, now and then, the high, dark form of the great aqueduct which, near the road, carries water from the Voltai range west, farther even than Torcadino.

About an hour or two later, half freezing, my hair sopped, half blinded by the driving rain, my body exhausted, my feet sore, I saw lights in the distance.

It was Venna.

* * *

I was sitting with my back against the wall of the alcove, tunicked, knees up, my left hand chained to the side, to my left, my right hand chained to the side, to my right. In this fashion, one cannot protect oneself from the attentions of others. I had been so positioned at the customer's request, while he quaffed another goblet, to await him. Supposedly he was to join me soon, but he had been hailed by some fellow, and better than an Ahn had passed.

It was late.

I heard hands fumbling at the leather curtain.

The curtain was then parted.

"Master?" I asked.

In the light of the tiny *tharlarion*-oil lamp, I recognized the fellow for whom I had been waiting.

It was clear that he, the patron, after better than half a night's carousing with friends, and then, apparently, later, with someone else, was in no condition to accomplish anything more demanding than collapsing into an unconscious stupor.

He slipped part way through the parted curtain and fell, half out of the alcove, on the polished wooden floor, and half within the alcove, on its thick furs.

"Master?" I asked, but expected no answer, nor did I receive one.

"Attenders," I called, softly. "Attenders!" These fellows were taverner's men. Some collected coin and made change, but others watched the doors and, when appropriate, kept order amongst the tables. One or two of the higher attenders functioned rather as floor managers, and were authorized to act on behalf of the proprietor himself in a number of matters. The slaves took care to please the high attenders, as slave discipline was largely in their hands. I did not even know if, this late, one of the high attenders would be available. I rather doubted it. Much of the business of the tavern was handled by the high attenders. Lycus, the proprietor, was seldom on the floor. Indeed, sometimes, it seemed he was absent for days.

"Be silent," said a voice.

The unconscious body of the patron was drawn back, outside the alcove.

"He can hold his *paga*," said the voice. "I should have used a spoonful of *tassa* powder."

Tassa powder is tasteless and is used by the Green Caste as a sedative. It was not unknown for slavers, and others, to rely on it, to render a woman unconscious, before her abduction. Thieves and swindlers, too, often found uses for the potion.

The newcomer then, crouching, entered the alcove, and tied the leather curtains shut behind him.

"Master is not an attender," I said.

"No," he said.

"It is late," I said.

"Do you not recognize me?" he asked.

"The light is poor," I said. "Master looks familiar; Master sounds familiar."

"You will recall one other than I better than I," he said. "Calla."

"Calla!" I said.

"She saw you," he said, "two days ago, on the street, when you and two others were wandering about, proclaiming the delights of the establishment of Lycus the Fat, soliciting patronage."

"I did not see her," I said. "She did not make herself known to me."

"She thought it unwise to do so," he said.

"Why?" I asked.

"I am Flavius," he said. "My Home Stone is that of Venna."

"You were amongst raiders, at the holding of the Lady Temione of Hammerfest."

"Yes," he said.

"And you claimed Calla for your own."

"Yes," he said. "And would have killed for her, and would still do so."

"Why did she not make herself known to me on the street?" I asked.

"She feared herself to be under surveillance," he said. "It seems known she knew you, and she suspects that there are parties who wish to reach you through her. Seemingly this goes back even to the vicinity of Hammerfest."

"Where is she?" I asked.

"On her chain, fastened to the foot of my couch," he said.

"Of course," I thought.

"I think her fears are groundless," I said.

"We shall hope so," he said. "But she overheard a wisp of conversation at the laundry troughs this morning. It seems a beast, belted, with rings on its left wrist, has been lurking about the *pomerium* of the city, one carrying a box which speaks, and the box promises a gold tarn disk, of double weight, for the return of a barbarian slave named Ag-nes, or such, to her Master."

I wondered if this were the same beast I had encountered earlier in the vicinity of Tenalian's camped caravan, that intending to wend its way toward Ar, the beast who had slain an attacking wild *sleen*. But that beast had had no rings or belts, no talking box through which it might speak, or perhaps by means of which it might be directed in its actions.

"I am afraid," I said.

"Vennan guardsmen are even now looking for the beast," said Flavius. "It cannot be allowed to haunt the *pomerium* or accost citizens and travelers. They are hunting for it now. It will be killed or captured, and, if captured, displayed, as an oddity, perhaps even being sent to Ar."

"Then I have little to fear," I said.

"There may be more than one such beast," said Flavius.

"The key to my manacles," I said, "is at the side of the alcove, out of my reach, by the cords, gags, and blindfolds."

He cuffed me.

"You will remain as you are," he said, "slave girl."

"Yes, Master," I said, stung. "Forgive me, Master."

I would remain tethered until it might please the free to relieve me of my constraints.

"Obviously," he said, "I come in the stead of Calla."

"You care for her," I said.

He looked at me, angrily. I feared I might be struck again. "She is a mere slave," he said. "Slaves are nothing."

"Yes, Master," I said.

"But much of this is moot," he said.

"I do not understand," I said.

"You are 'Mira,' are you not?" he asked.

"Yes," I said, "if it pleases Master."

"You are owned by Lycus the Fat," he said.

"Yes, Master," I said.

"What do you know of him?" he asked.

"Very little," I said. "I have seen him only twice."

"He owns three taverns," said Flavius, "one here in Venna, where he lives, the Yellow Whip, and two in Ar, the Red Whip, in the Metellan District, and the Purple Whip, in the Boulevard District."

"He must be rich," I said. I did not see what this might have to do with me. My chain, so to speak, was in Venna. It would be wonderful, of course, to wear one's collar in so great a city as Ar. And, too, where else could one be so inconspicuous?

"Given Calla's concern for you," he said. "I made inquiries."

"Master?" I said.

"Reports on you are excellent," he said.

I blushed, even in the dim light.

How could one help oneself in the arms of Gorean males?

Too, I did not wish to be whipped.

"I gathered from attenders," he said, "that you, and two others, perhaps those with whom you were when Calla saw you, are to be shipped to the Red Whip in Ar. If you do well, perhaps one or more of you might be elevated to the Purple Whip."

"Purple, is it not," I said, "is a high color, that of the robes of a Ubar?"

"Yes," he said, "and Purple-Whip girls sometimes entertain at Ubarial feasts."

He turned about and undid the straps on the leather curtains, and then faced me, again.

"I convey Calla's greetings to you," he said. "She wishes you well."

"I wish her well," I said.

He then withdrew.

Guardsmen would do away with, or seize, the prowling beast. I had no doubt it was mighty, but what could withstand the thrust of a dozen Gorean spears?

"Could it be true," I wondered, "that I might be sent to Ar?"

How pleased I was to have heard from Calla, even be it by means of another.

I pulled at the chains on my manacles, to my left and right, those holding my hands so far apart. and then sat back, again.

I was well held in place.

CHAPTER FORTY-EIGHT

"Serve him," said the tavern's man, pointing.

"Please, no!" I said, shrinking back.

"Let me serve him, Master," said another girl. "He is handsome!"

"He has requested this one," said the tavern's man, jabbing a thumb in my direction.

Then he scowled at me. "Must a command be repeated?" he asked.

"No, Master," I said, trembling.

Repetition of a command can be a cause for discipline.

I went to the *paga* vat, and the Vat Master dipped a goblet into the liquid, and handed it to me, beaded and dripping.

I then turned about and went to the low table at which the patron sat, cross-legged. I knelt, my head down. Perhaps he had not well seen me. Perhaps he had merely been intrigued by a form in the half darkness. Had I reminded him of someone? Surely he could not know me here.

I knelt at the table, head down.

The light was poor.

The Red Whip was in the shabby Metellan District.

"*Paga*, Master?" I whispered.

"Yes," he said.

I then pressed the goblet's rim to my belly, lifted it slowly to my lips, kissed it, softly, and then, my head down between my extended arms, proffered him the vessel.

He did not drink, but placed the goblet on the table.

"You did that well," he said.

"Thank you, Master," I said.

Surely he knew we were trained to do that, gracefully, slowly, seductively.

"But," said he, "when you kissed the goblet, you did not look at me, with the look of a hopeful, needful slave."

"Forgive me, Master," I said. "May a slave depart?"

"Of course," he said.

My heart leaped. He had not recognized me!

"But return," he said, "crawling, with two laces on your left wrist, and a whip in your teeth."

Tears sprang to my eyes, but I rose to my feet gracefully, backed away two steps, and then turned, and, a few yards later, went through the beaded curtain to the right of the *paga* vat and knelt before the tavern's man at the storing rack and, head down, extended my left wrist, about which he looped two laces, each about eighteen inches in length. I then went to all fours and lifted my head, and he placed a slave whip between my teeth, and dismissed me. Shortly thereafter I, on all fours, had returned to the patron's table.

He had not yet touched his *paga*.

I remained before the table, on all fours, laces on my left wrist, whip in my teeth, head down.

I hoped that, somehow, still, I might not have been recognized.

"Look up," he said. "I would have a good look at you."

I lifted my head, the whip between my teeth.

"You look well with a whip between your teeth," he said.

"Why are you crying, she-tarsk?" he asked.

I knew enough not to try to respond lest the whip fall. That could be a cause for discipline.

Now, of course, I knew he knew me, as I had feared before.

"You look well so," he said. "It is a long time since the observatory, is it not?"

I made a small, soft, single noise. When one is gagged, one such tiny noise signifies 'Yes,' and two such noises signify 'No.' Such signals may suffice, as well, if one is bearing a whip in one's teeth.

"Let me relieve you of that," he said, and, gently, removed the whip from between my teeth and placed it on the table, beside the filled, untouched *paga* goblet.

"May I speak?" I asked.

"After you have been prepared for our conversation," he said. "*Bara!*"

I placed myself prone on the polished floor, my head turned to the left, my wrists crossed behind my back, my ankles crossed, as well.

He trussed me with the casual efficiency of a Gorean Master. Thus, had I been uncertain of it before, I now knew Maxwell Holt was natively Gorean.

He then lifted me to my knees and faced me toward the table.

"How did Master find me?" I asked.

"Accidentally," he said, "by some graffiti in a *sul* market. It said, 'Ask for Mira at the Red Whip.'"

"There are several Miras," I said.

"Not at the Red Whip," he said.

"Not from the wall outside?" I said.

"No," he said.

Outside the gate there was a grooved display board into which panels might be inserted and from which they could be removed. Each panel contained the name of a girl. At one time, I had been told, likenesses had been included on the panel, but this practice had been abandoned, when complaints had been received, one of them involving a small riot, to the effect that the likenesses were often inaccurate, tending to err in the tavern's favor. Goreans, it seemed, tended to be less tolerant of misleading advertising, false claims, and such, than those of at least one other world. Had not Xanthe, the former Eileen Bennett of Earth, encountered certain difficulties having to do with such things?

"The Red Whip is a rather good tavern for the Metellan District," he said. "In many taverns in the district, slaves serve in camisks, and in others, nude, and, in some, nude and in chains."

"Tastes differ," I said.

"You are fetching in a slave tunic," he said, "far more so than in your severe, svelte attire in the observatory, so businesslike and professional."

"I am pleased, if Master is pleased," I said.

"You will note," he said, "that I am permitting you to retain it."

"Thank you," I said.

"As of now," he said.

"It is red, with black lettering, advertising the establishment," I said. "It is also light, brief, and without a nether closure. Other than that, there is little difference between it and nothing."

"You look well in a collar," he said.

"Thank you, Master," I said. "A slave is pleased, if Master is pleased."

"You belong in a collar," he said.

"I have learned that on this world," I said.

"But surely you suspected it on Earth," he said.

"Very much so, Master," I said.

"And it is now on your neck," he said.

"Locked, and I cannot remove it," I said.

"Excellent," he said.

"Master honors the Red Whip by his presence," I said. "Perhaps he seeks me?"

"Not really," he said. "But you had piqued my curiosity on the sales shelf of Tenalian."

"One of his shelves," I said. "I gather you were not hunting for me."

"No," he said, "but I thought I would introduce myself to you, for the sake of old times."

"I fear I behaved very badly," I said.

"I have not forgotten that," he said. "I wondered why you carried on in that fashion. You seemed terrified."

"I was terrified," I said.

"Why?" he asked.

"It was nothing," I said, "only the fears of a frightened slave."

"I saw the scratched reference to you in the *sul* market," he said. "Thus, as I was still curious, I thought I would look you up, and ask you about it."

"It had no meaning," I said. "It was not important."

"Let us establish that," he said.

"I am to be interrogated?" I asked.

"If you like," he said.

"You will learn nothing from me," I said.

"If you know something," he said, "I will learn it."

I understood little, and I knew nothing, really.

He then untied my ankles and wrists, and rewound the laces about my left wrist. He stood up, his *paga* goblet in his left hand and the whip in his right.

"To all fours," he said.

I assumed the commanded position.

"For my use of you," he said. "We will call you 'Agnes Morrison Atherton.'"

"Please, no," I said.

"Do not fret," he said. "It is no longer a free name. It is now a slave name, and a temporary one."

"I beg you, Master, no," I said.

He then pulled up the skirt of my tunic, and thrust it up, over my back, to my waist.

"Alcove Eleven appears to be unoccupied," he said. "Move, my collared Miss Atherton."

"Yes, Master," I wept.

"Oh!" I cried.

There was laughter from an adjoining table.

"Oh!" I cried again. "Oh!"

"Hurry," he said. "Hurry, Agnes, slave!"

Again and again I was stung by the whip.

At the curtain of Alcove Eleven he allowed me, now well humiliated, to rise and push the parts of the leather curtain to the sides. We then entered the alcove, and he had me tie the curtains shut from the inside. He then placed the *paga* goblet on a low shelf to the side, and, as I knelt, held the whip out to me. Unbidden, I licked it, and kissed it, acknowledging that I was a slave and subject to discipline.

I was pleased when he put it to the side.

"Now, my fine Miss Agnes Morrison Atherton," he said, "remove your garment."

I looked at him.

The observatory was far away.

"Strip," he said.

"Yes, Master," I said.

"Please, Master, be merciful!" I begged.

"Subside," he said, soothingly.

"No, not again!" I wept. "Not after so close, again!"

How cruel, he was, using my own body against me.

Well then did I understand how helpless and dependent a needful slave can be. Never before, to anything like this extent, did I understand the exquisite sexual tortures to which a vulnerable slave may be subjected.

Again and again I had been brought to the brink of ungovernable ecstasy, only to be denied the storm, the lightning, the wind and thunder, the clashing rocks, the shattering surf, the wild, shrieking relief, for which my body cried.

"Speak," said he, "*kajira*."

"What did it matter," I asked myself, "if this merciless Gorean brute learns of things not even I understand? He apparently did not come to Gor to kill me, or deliver me somewhere. Such things were paramount. Why should I not confide in him? How could it hurt? What difference might it make? Why, I asked myself, had he returned to Gor? Perhaps, I thought, wearying of Earth and its hypocrisies and pollutions, he had simply longed to return to his fresh, green, beloved, native world. But I sensed I knew him. There would surely be more than that in the matter. He was Gorean. I think he did not want Eileen Bennett, sent to the markets of Gor, to elude him. She, however shallow and unworthy, had caught his eye. He would see to it, if at all possible, that she would keep an appointment with his chain.

So, piteously, sobbing, begging, stuttering, half incoherently, I told him of the mysterious coordinates which I had uncovered, of my private investigations, of the discovery of two apparently secret artificial worlds emerging from the asteroid belt, and of the existence of a likely interplanetary intrigue, in which at least two worlds might figure.

"Please," I whispered to Maxwell Holt. "Please, now."

"I understand little of this," he said.

"Please, please," I begged.

"Very well," he said.

I cried out wildly, gladly, spasmodically, gratefully, clutching at him.

He covered my mouth, briefly, that I not more disturb the floor or the other alcoves.

Mercifully he stayed with me for a time.

He then undid the curtains, cast my tunic beyond the opening, to the floor of the tavern, chained me by the neck in the alcove, presumably that I could not follow him, and then drained the goblet of *paga*.

"I wish you well, Mira," he said.

"I wish you well, Master," I said.

He then left the alcove.

CHAPTER FORTY-NINE

"Ai!" I cried, leaping back, away from the bars.

"I told you not to approach it so closely," said the tavern's man.

"I thought it was asleep," I said.

"The brutes are clever," said the tavern's man.

That long, hairy arm, had reached out, suddenly, unexpectedly. Now I could see what I took to be frustration in the visage of the large, now-crouching beast. I could see the large, round eyes, a curved fang, moist, at the right side of its jaw.

I was shaken.

I had evaded its grasp.

It seemed displeased.

"You are standing," a man said.

"Forgive me, Master," I said, kneeling.

I looked at the thing in the cage.

It was clearly what I had learned to call a Kur.

"It was captured near Venna," said the tavern's man. "Lycus bought it, from the administrator of Venna, and had it carried here, to Ar, as an attraction, for the Metellan Menagerie."

"Better he had left it in Venna," said a slave.

I wondered for what reason, if any reason, Master Lycus might have purchased the beast and brought it to Ar. To be sure, I suspected he had a share in the Metellan Menagerie, which housed beasts and birds, a small zoo, so to speak.

"In Venna," I said, to no one in particular, "I heard it spoke through a talking box and accosted certain citizens, itinerant peddlers, local peasants, tradesmen, travelers, and such."

"Absurd," said a man.

"I have no knowledge of that," said another.

"Such stories are invented," said another man.

"Rumors have wings," said a man. "Fables fly farther and faster than tarns."

"This cannot be the same beast, if there were such a beast," said the tavern's man.

"Obviously this is a mindless, simple animal."

The beast hurled itself at the bars, rocking the stout cage.

Men drew back; some of the slaves screamed.

"Do not fear," said the first tavern's man. "That cage would hold a bull *kailiauk*."

The beast snarled, and then, throwing its head back, roared. Men and slaves shuddered.

A free woman screamed, through her veiling.

More of a crowd began to gather, outside the Red Whip.

Saliva ran from the beast's mouth. A long, dark tongue darted forth and then, curling, drew back, quickly, inside those massive jaws.

I thought it could take away the head of a man with one wrenching bite.

"One would almost think it had understood him," said a man.

Another fellow laughed at this speculation.

The Kur I had seen outside the camp of Tenalian had been belted and accoutered. It had had rings on its left wrist. It had borne no speaking box, but, I was sure, it had uttered noises intended to approximate Gorean phonemes. I did not know if this were the same beast or not. In any event, this beast was neither belted nor accoutered, and its left wrist bore no rings. I suspected such things might have been removed. The beast, so to speak, had been stripped. What was now within the cage appeared to be no more than an animal. I wondered if such things made a difference to it. Had it been, in its own eyes, reduced and humiliated?

I did not think it would have been pleased, if it had thought that to be the case.

"Master," I begged the nearest tavern's man, "I am not of Ar. I am from far away. What are such beasts? Tell me of them."

"They are rare," he said.

"Since the time of Decius Albus, who was trade advisor to the Ubar," said another man, "they are not allowed in the city, save as pets, exhibits, performing animals, and such."

"Some are thought to be clever," said the first man, "like trained *sleen*."

"Some were actually thought to be rational and involved in political intrigues," said a man.

"Ridiculous," said another.

"In any event," said the tavern's man, he to whom I had first addressed my question, "they are not allowed to roam freely in the city."

"Marlenus has seen to that," said a fellow.

"There are some outside the walls," said a man.

"Particularly in the vicinity of the Beast Caves," said another.

"Few go there," said a man.

"And some do not return," said another.

"What would Lycus want with such a thing?" asked a woman.

"An exhibit for the menagerie," said a man.

I wondered if that were true.

"The beast is somnolent," said another.

"I think it is going to go to sleep again," said another.

"Stick your hand in, between the bars," suggested another.

"This is bad for business," said one of the tavern's men. "People will be dismayed, or bored, or frightened, failing to think of *paga*, and the attractions of the tavern."

"Lycus has already arranged for it to be delivered to the menagerie," said his fellow.

"Girls!" said a tavern's man, clapping his hands sharply, "return to the tavern. Back inside with you!"

"Good," said a free woman. "Get these half-naked, shameless animals off the public streets, lest they soil the beauty of Ar."

"They make Ar far more beautiful," said a man.

"Beast!" she said. She then, with her switch began to strike about her, striking one girl after another.

I hurriedly arose, darted behind a free man and, like the others, hastened back into the tavern.

I was not struck.

I wondered about the beast.

I wondered about Master Lycus. What had he, a rich man, to do with some menagerie, and one in the Metellan District?

CHAPTER FIFTY

"She will be here soon," said a slave.

"That is my understanding," I said.

We were gathered together, inside the tavern, near the dancing oval.

We were often marshaled there before the day's business, to be inspected and addressed, sometimes to be informed, sometimes to be instructed, sometimes to be warned. Commonly we were filled in on matters of possible interest, many of which were not extracted from postings on the public boards. Was a trade delegation from distant Ti expected within the gates? Might a general from Corcyrus, with staff, be interested in reserving a private dining area? Watch for an influx of patrons following the afternoon tarn races, some of whom will be belligerent and disgruntled. A *kaissa* master from Tyros, a student of Centius of Cos, will play multiple boards following a discourse on the Turian Defense in the Garden of the Hinrabians. It is rumored that the captain of an outlawed free company, Rupert, of Hochburg, is in Ar, incognito. He has a jagged scar on the back of his left wrist. If you note such in a patron, convey this to a floor manager, and so on.

"Should she not be here by now?" asked the slave.

"I would have thought so," I said.

The management felt it important to keep us informed, as we might then the better please the patrons. On the other hand, we heard much, and shared much, which was not known even to the floor managers and high attenders. Indeed, it is thought by some that a *paga* slave may be much better informed even than a Ubar's spies or, more certainly, than the fellows who collect material for the public boards. As the saying has it, 'In the fumes of *paga*, what secrets are safe?'

It was shortly before the tenth Ahn, the Gorean noon. It was not yet time to open.

"*Kajirae*," said the tavern's man, "as you know, your beloved Master, Lycus of Venna, has purchased a new slave. She will soon be delivered."

"Good," said a slave. "I have been the last purchased for too long. I am tired of doing all the scum work."

That was an exaggeration. We all were given assignments. Yet, it was true that most of the low work was done by the newer buys. The earlier-bought girls, as they could, arranged that.

"No, my dear," said the tavern's man. "This is no ordinary new girl. She was purchased by your beloved Master from the central block of the Curulean, for seven silver tarsks."

"Ai," whispered a slave.

I, too, found this devastatingly impressive.

"That is because it was the Curulean," said a slave.

"Masters overpay at the Curulean," said a slave.

"That is because of the prestige of having a Curulean girl," said another.

"They are no better than we," said another.

"I sold for three silver tarsks in Venna," said a slave. "At the Curulean I would have gone for ten."

"I, as well," said another slave.

"She will seem all the more beautiful," said the tavern's man, annoyed, "when compared to all of you."

"What?" cried several of the slaves.

"It is simple," he said. "The homeliness of you she-tarsks will, by contrast, considerably enhance her charms."

"I cannot wait to see this paragon of beauty," said a slave.

"She will be no better than we," said another.

"No," said another. "We will be by far her superior."

"Any one of us," said another.

It is true that the Red Whip had a reputation for lovely *paga* slaves, and certainly so for the Metellan District. On the other hand, Master Lycus, I thought, need not apologize in any way for the quality of his tavern stock, either in Ar or, for that matter, in Venna. I doubted, incidentally, that the stock of his third tavern, The Purple Whip, was any better than that of the Yellow Whip or the Red Whip. It was, however, in the Boulevard District, not far from the Central Cylinder. Location and prestige can make themselves felt, particularly economically. The price of a drink at the Purple Whip was a full copper tarsk, not the usual tarsk-bit. Indeed, one could not even enter the Purple Whip without being charged a full copper tarsk as an entrance fee. This, and the high price of service, I supposed, helped to keep riffraff out. Thus, although the slaves might not be any better, it would be likely to be patronized by a more affluent clientele, and thus, I suppose, at least on the whole, by a more refined, higher-class clientele. Most likely that is what is essentially involved, self-esteem and status. But I cheerfully resign the mysteries of economics to those better suited to examine them.

"What is special about her?" asked a slave.

"Is she not marked and collared?" asked another.

"Wait until we get her away from the floor," said a slave.

"Let her eat the slave gruel we pour on her head," said a slave.

"Do not neglect to beat her for the soot, dirt, and grime we will smear on her body and tunic," said yet another.

"You must all be friends," said the tavern's man, patiently. "It is not her fault that she is so incredibly beautiful, far more so than you, that she was sold from the central block of the Curulean, while many of you never sold for even two silver tarsks. You must all welcome her, and help her feel at home."

"We will do that," said a slave, grimly.

Some other slaves laughed.

I did not envy the new slave.

"Be kind to her," said the tavern's man. "This will be new to her. She has never served in a tavern. She will be shy, and frightened."

I supposed that that was true.

"Ho!" cried a slave. "The wondrous prize is at hand!"

A keeper thrust a figure before him, through the tavern gate. The figure was enveloped, from her head down to the knees, in a body hood, a red body hood with black printing. The slaves crowded closer, toward the gate.

I did not know what might be the point of the body hood. Was it to protect the slave, being brought through the streets, from accosting, from unwanted attentions, from rude handling and pawing, or even from a mob's seizure and usage? I did not think so. Was it to keep the slave disoriented, so that, unhooded, she would not understand where she now was, that she would feel lost, dependent, and vulnerable? Was it so that she would not understand to what location she was being delivered? But would not a simple blindfold do as well?

"Take off the hood!" said one of the slaves.

"Is she so ugly?" asked another.

The figure in the hood shook, quite possibly with anger. As the figure could not see, and as its arms and hands were pinned within the hood, it could do little else.

"Why," I asked the nearest tavern's man, "is the slave so concealed?"

It did not seem likely that she had been stolen, and was now being so openly delivered to the Red Whip.

"To pique curiosity," said the tavern's man. "Note the trim ankles and the well-turned calves. Would not a fellow wish to see more? The writing on the hood says that she can be found this evening at the Red Whip."

"She will have attracted considerable attention," said another tavern's man. "We anticipate a good house tonight."

"Masters are clever," I said.

"Let us see the she-tarsk!" called a slave.

"We will be better than she," announced another slave.

"A receipt must be signed," said the keeper who had delivered the slave.

"It will be signed," said a tavern's man. "I can recognize the slave. I was present at her sale."

The keeper then began unbuckling the body hood.

Soon the hood was loose, and could be lifted away from what it had so amply concealed.

He then whipped it away.

"Temione!" I cried.

"A beauty," said a tavern's man.

"Marvelous!" said another.

"You know her," said a tavern's man, near me.

"Yes, Master!" I said.

"She is not so great," said a slave.

"Each of us is better," said another.

"Two tarsks at most for her," said another slave.

"Tonight, business will be brisk," said a tavern's man.

"Can she dance?" asked a tavern's man.

"Every woman can dance," said another.

"What place is this?" cried Temione.

"The Red Whip," said a tavern's man.

"On Dina Street, in the Metellan District," said another.

"A *paga* tavern!" cried Temione.

"That," said a tavern's man.

"In the Metellan District!" cried Temione.

"Yes," said another tavern's man.

"Remedy this mistake!" said Temione to the keeper.

"If all is in order, please sign this receipt," said the keeper to a tavern's man, a floor manager.

"All is not in order!" cried Temione.

The receipt was signed, and the keeper took his leave.

"This is a mistake!" cried Temione. "I sold for seven silver tarsks, from the central block at the Curulean! I am too good for a tavern!"

I wondered if, indeed, Lycus might have a disposition in mind for fair Temione which far exceeded the lot of a simple *paga* slave.

"I should be a display slave in the retinue of a Mintar or an Appanius of Ar," she said. "I should be the gem in a Ubar's Pleasure Garden! I should be put on the stage at the great theater of Publius!"

"Listen to the babbling of a homely *paga* girl," said a slave.

"Noble Masters made a mistake in buying that slave," said another.

"So plain a slave will reduce the reputation of the Red Whip," suggested another.

"Compared to me you are all mud *vulos*," said Temione.

"Urt, she-urt!" said a slave.

"From what *tharlarion* egg did you hatch?" inquired Temione, sudden tears in her eyes.

"Tear the hair from her head!" said a slave.

"Scratch her cheeks bloody," said another.

"Do not damage your new collar-sister," warned the floor manager who had signed the receipt.

Temione, apparently having understood enough, and having well realized where she was, sank to her knees, and covered her face, weeping.

"A frail little thing," said a slave.

"A weakling," said another.

"Give her to us," said a slave.

"She was free," I said.

"So were once we all," said a slave.

Most, I supposed, had fallen to victors, as claimed loot, taken in the frequent, bitter altercations amongst warring cities. Some, I supposed, had been acquired from raided villages; others had been seized at sea, or harvested from caravans and camps. Others may have been hunted down and acquired by slavers, or taken by sporting tarnsmen. Some were seized by creditors for debt. There were many ways in which a woman can come into the collar. As far as I knew, I was the only barbarian in the house. City pride was interesting. A woman who is celebrated and honored in one city, even viewed with awe, is looked upon as no more than rightful collar-meat in another.

"Let her alone," I said.

"Do not take her part," said a slave.

I felt sorry for the former Lady Temione of Hammerfest. Her bravado, vain and empty as it had been, had collapsed. Well now did she realize her situation, its perils and miseries. The stoutest stick can break; the most supple reed can snap.

"You called the slave's name," said the floor manager. "You know her?"

"From the Vosk Basin and the Delta," I said.

"Do not champion her," said the floor manager. "That will not go well with you, especially as you are a yellow-placard girl."

"I did not know you knew that," I said.

"It is on your papers," he said.

I wondered if that were why I seemed to have somewhat more than my share of disagreeable tasks when the tavern was closed.

"Take the new slave to the kitchen," he said. "See that she is fed."

"Tell her something of the tavern," said a tavern's man. "For her first month, her usage will require a full copper tarsk."

"Make certain she understands that if the customers are not fully pleased, she will be whipped."

"Yes, Master," I said.

"A full copper tarsk is a good deal of money," said another.

"Yes, Master," I said.

I was seldom whipped, but I had been whipped, twice, over no more than a tarsk-bit.

Some men, for one reason or another, it seemed, did not wish to be pleased. Perhaps things were not going well in their lives.

"Will the new slave be used in the suspended cage," asked a tavern's man of the floor manager.

"Not, at least, at first," said the floor manager.

I had heard of the 'suspended cage,' but, as of now, it did not even exist. A floor manager had apparently suggested it to Lycus, who had approved it. Supposedly it was to dangle some nine or ten feet above the ground, outside the tavern, to the right of the entrance as one would face the tavern. Such things had apparently been used elsewhere in Ar, and in certain other cities. It was a way, doubtless, of calling attention to the tavern, and suggesting the delights which putatively lay within.

The floor manager clapped his hands together, twice, sharply. "Ready yourselves," he said. "The bar for the tenth Ahn will ring any Ihn now."

The slaves melted away.

I went to Temione and lifted her to her feet.

Her eyes seemed vacant. Her cheeks were wet with tears.

"Come with me," I said. "I do not think you will be put on the floor until late, when the tavern is crowded."

"Mira?" she said.

"Yes," I said. "Come with me. We will talk. If you have work, I will help you with it."

"Where are you taking me?" she asked.

"Through the beaded curtain," I said, "to the kitchen."

"I am not a *paga* slave," she said.

"We are both *paga* slaves," I said.

CHAPTER FIFTY-ONE

"Have you been asked to report, to be fed to the beast?" asked the keeper.

"I trust not," I said.

"That is a joke," he said.

"A splendid one," I said. Actually, I could not really be expected to enjoy such humor.

"I asked Lycus for an assistant," he said, "a large peasant lass who could wrestle a draft *tharlarion* to the ground."

"We have none such at the Red Whip," I said.

"Why were you sent?" he asked.

"I think," I said, "because I am cheap, and thereby, presumably, the least valuable of his assets. I cost Master Lycus only forty copper tarsks."

"You are worth more than that," he said.

"I would hope so," I said. "The Shelf Master was willing to let me go for two silver tarsks, five."

"That might be a little high," said the keeper. "What happened?"

"I behaved badly," I said. "The sale went awry."

"I trust that you were whipped," he said.

"I was," I said.

"Well," he said, "here we do not need a five-tarsk beauty."

"Good," I said.

"Not that I would object to that," he said.

"No, Master," I said.

I did not tell him that there was another reason I had been sent to help with the menagerie. I was a barbarian.

I have girls to care for most of the animals, and the birds, and snakes, as well," he said. "But we need another, one to care for a certain beast."

"I think I know the one," I said.

"Some think it might be dangerous," he said.

"I suspect they are correct," I said.

"I do not wish to risk my slaves," he said.

"I understand," I said.

"There is no danger, if you are careful," he said.

"I will be careful," I assured him.

CHAPTER FIFTY-TWO

Several men moved about, below, on the street and near the two leaves of the tavern's gate. An occasional free woman, accompanied by a companion or escort, passed by. I did not think they were of high caste, or would seldom be so, as this was the Metellan District. Goreans do not always wear their caste colors. It was not a holiday. The sky was dark. It was near the Eighteenth Ahn. I could see lights in the windows of several of the nearby towers, sparkling against the night. Lamps, too, could be seen on certain of the graceful, narrow, arching, unrailed bridges which linked such towers, bridges which were often hundreds of feet above the streets. I feared to walk such bridges, but city Goreans, accustomed to them, apparently took them no more seriously, and worried no more about them, than did those of Earth their sidewalks. On those bridges without fixed lamps, I could occasionally see lamps moving, being borne by passersby. The narrow bridges can be easily defended, or destroyed, transforming each tower into, in effect, a keep, or isolated bastion or fortress, with its independent supplies. Just outside the tavern however, despite the Ahn, there was no lack of light, such furnished by four torches, two on each side of the entrance. Two slaves stood on the pavement below, one on each side of the gate, inviting customers within.

"Masters," they called, "patronize the Red Whip! Fine food and better *paga*. Rooms set aside for *kaissa* and stones. See our dancers. Hear our musicians. Our alcoves are plush and well furnished. Our eager, needful girls beg to be taught the meaning of their collars! Welcome, noble Masters. Are we and our sisters not of interest?"

I knelt in the high cage, slung perhaps some fifteen feet above the pavement. Occasionally I added my solicitations to those of the girls on the pavement below, those on either side of the entrance, especially when a tavern's man made his appearance. On the other hand, as I understood it, my role was largely in the nature of a unique poster or sign, a supposedly eye-catching, living advertisement. Happily, I was fully, if scantily, tunicked. I think the tunic was a concession to the sensibility of free women who frequented the street. Sometimes, interestingly, a free woman, found guilty of one crime or another, or perhaps of speaking disparagingly of an Administrator or

Ubar, is suspended nude in such a cage in a busy, public place. This seems to discourage crime, or even unwise flippancy, on the part of free women. The power of an Administrator is limited; that of a Ubar is not, save perhaps by revolution or the stroke of an assassin's knife. After her sentence as a free woman is satisfied, she is enslaved and sold out of the city. After such a scandal, that of lengthy, public exposure, what is left but to consign her to the collar?

I rose to my feet, carefully, and grasped the bars.

The cage is about six feet high, round, and has a width of some eighteen inches. The coloration suggests brass. The top is conical and has a ring at the top, into which a stout hook on thc chain is inserted.

When first put in the cage, in my turn, some days ago, as one of the girls used in this fashion, I became uneasy, even giddy, as the slightest movement could shift, rock, or turn the cage on its single, dangling chain.

I no longer suffered in this way.

One's inner ear eventually makes adjustments.

I considered the crowd below.

Then I thought of the beast in the menagerie, to whom I frequently attended, putting forth its food and water, cleaning the cage, and so on.

I think, by now, for better or for worse, we had grown accustomed to one another.

Twice he had thrown himself at the bars, trying to seize me, but I had been careful. As the keeper had suggested, there would be little or nothing to fear if I were careful. So I was careful, very careful. It was unnerving, however, knowing that it had tried to reach you, and might again. I was pleased the cage was stout. Could it not contain a bull *kailiauk*, whatever that might be? I did not blame the other girls, however, for so cheerfully relinquishing its care to another, to an unimportant slave from a nearby tavern. I would have been pleased to have returned the gesture had it been possible. As time passed, I grew more and more convinced that my charge was a simple, dangerous, ugly-tempered beast, no more. I did know that some such beasts bordered on, or were, rational. I recalled the animal Calla had warned me about. And I recalled the animal I had encountered outside Tenalian's camp on the caravan route to Ar. Doubtless there were degrees of intelligence, ranging from a tangle of genetically coded responses to something approximating the human mind.

I looked down, at the men, and the occasional free woman, who loitered near, or passed by.

The girl in the cage has little to do. She is expected, from time to time, however, to move about, to stand or kneel, or sit, to pose, to rise, to turn, to sway provocatively, to seem to beg for surcease, to plead for a caress, to assume a pathetic mien, or such.

My time in the cage this evening was almost over. Soon I would be put again on the floor or, depending on the house, allowed to sup and return to my cage.

I remembered that I had heard that monsters like the one in the menagerie were not allowed to roam freely in Ar, by order of the Ubar. On the other hand, they were allowed to be kept as pets, as performing animals, and such. I had seen one example of this sort of thing not far from the tavern, indeed, in the vicinity of the menagerie, but it had seemed cruel and had disturbed me. A small crowd, however, containing some street vendors, had apparently found it amusing, and its owner or keeper had had several tarsk-bits dropped in his cap. The monster had been as large as the one in the menagerie and it clearly resembled it. But it wore nothing like the wrist rings or belts alleged to have been worn by the beast near Venna with a talking box, which might have been the beast I now tended. I did not know. Had its foolish costume and quaint cap been removed, it would have been as unclothed as my charge in the menagerie. Its owner or keeper removed its leash, somewhat to the unease of some in the crowd, and tucked it in his belt. In this way, one supposes he was demonstrating how tame and harmless the beast was. I myself was not reassured. I sensed that, in any case, if some emergency should occur, the leash would be a frail object with which to attempt to control or manage so large, and possibly terrible, a beast. The owner or keeper then uttered commands and the beast responded promptly, squatting, leaping up, spinning about, lying down, rolling over, and so on. The owner or keeper then drew forth a small flute from his wallet and began to play tunes to which, clumsily, the beast appeared to dance. When he put away his flute, several tarsk-bits were deposited in his cap. He then removed the leash from his belt. "Here," he said to a child, "leash Bubu," much to the unease of the child's mother. "Go ahead," said a man, presumably the child's father. "There is nothing to fear." The beast bent down, docilely, and the child put the leash in place, and backed away into his mother's arms. Applause, a striking of the left shoulder with the palm of the right hand, ensued. A guardsman at hand politely tapped his spear blade on his shield. "One," said the owner or keeper, looking directly at me, "seems not to have enjoyed our little show." So noted, I instantly knelt. "Have you no tarsk-bit for us, fine lady?" he asked. This question was met with laughter. Slaves are seldom allowed to touch money, save in shopping, or such. "Perhaps you can run off to your Master," he said, "and fetch us back a tarsk-bit?" I was silent having no alternative but to absorb this ridicule. The beast, I was alarmed to see, was regarding me. "May I withdraw, Master?" I asked. The owner or keeper looked about, and, sensing the crowd's mood, said, "Yes, off with you, run!" I leapt up, turned, and hurried away, hearing laughter behind me.

Why had the beast looked at me, or had it only seemed to have looked at me? I had recently come from the menagerie. Had it sensed on me the odor of one of its kind, or perhaps even that of a particular one of its kind?

Below, looking down, I saw two guardsmen stop a fellow in a street robe, it of the gray of the metal workers. They had him push up the left sleeve of his robe. They then let him lower the sleeve and continue on his way. When this was occurring, those in the crowd had moved back, creating a small, circular clearing within which this action was taking place. When the fellow left, and the two guardsmen had moved on, much was the same as before.

I recalled a briefing, so to speak, within the tavern, some days ago, in which we had been informed that the captain of an outlawed free company, a Rupert of Hochburg, might be in Ar, incognito. Supposedly he had an irregular scar on the back of his left wrist. If we detected such a sign in a customer, we were to call it to the attention of a floor manager.

Much then was the same as before.

I was looking forward to the cage being lowered, and its curved gate opened. Another girl would then be enclosed within its limited precincts and lifted into place.

I noted a sudden freshness, or liveliness, in the solicitations of my collar-sisters below, on either side of the entrance. A tavern's man had emerged from the tavern. I made it a point not to look at him. "Enter noble Masters," I called to those below. "Sample the delights of the Red Whip! Sample the delights of the Red Whip!" I also put my hand and arm out between the bars. Shortly thereafter, happily, he returned inside.

I hoped, when released from the cage, and allowed to feed, that the Kitchen Master could be wheedled into dashing a swallow of *ka-la-na* into my watering pan. Even a captive free woman soon learns to be grateful for such things.

I think that it was something like twenty minutes later that I, upright, suddenly froze in the cage and grasped the bars so tightly that my hands hurt.

The bar for the first Ahn had not yet sounded.

I made not the least outcry or sound.

He had not looked upward. I was sure he had not seen me.

I had seen him, however, and not for the first time.

I had seen him before, long ago, in the field tent of Bazi Imports. It was not Master Philip, the Camp Master, or Backron, his deputy. It was the tall, short-bearded man in the reddish-brown tunic, the mysterious figure who had stood in the back and to the side, half in the shadows so inconspicuously, and yet seeming somehow to be the most important figure in the tent.

CHAPTER FIFTY-THREE

"I do not know," I said, "if you are inscrutable, or simply stupid. Perhaps it does not make much difference, not when you are in a cage. At least you understand that I will not put the meat pan in the slot under the bars unless you go to the opposite wall. To be sure, an *urt* could probably understand that."

I bent down, and picked up the end of the long towel, which the beast thrust through the bars.

"You want to play?" I said.

From that wide, fanged muzzle came a small noise.

"Again?" I said.

Another small noise escaped those massive jaws.

"I gather," I said, "we are now friends. I know a world where a kind of animal, one you do not know, enjoys the back-and-forth game, the 'I-tug-you-tug game.'"

The beast shook the towel, and looked at me.

"I assume," I said, "that you do not mind my calling you 'Cyrus.' I thought it would be nice to give you a name. That is an Earth name but we will keep it as our secret. It was the name of a king. A king is like a Ubar, only, I think, not as powerful. To be sure, power depends ultimately on those who support it. Few understand that, save perhaps those who wield power, and are afraid. What is a bandit without his thugs, a tyrant without his police, a king without his army? Only a man who must eat and sleep, a man who can easily be abandoned or done away with."

A little more of the towel was thrust through the bars, toward me.

"There is not much scenery in a cell," I said. "Even a mindless brute like you can grow bored. I know you did not ask to be here, but neither did I. Are there not worse things? Would you prefer to hop about at the bidding of a slimy little man; would you rather try to dance to so loathsome a piper's tune? I told you about that, when you growled and rushed about in the cage. Had you smelled the scent of that exploited, mocked beast? Surely not on me, for I was not in proximity to it. Perhaps from the outside, through the window, with a shift of the wind, for it was not far away."

Often, as one will, I spoke to the beast, rather, I suspect, to hear myself speak, to be able to say things to someone or something who could not hold me accountable, or punish me for it. Does not speech and expression ease the mind?

"Very well," I said. "We will play, but I must soon be back at the Red Whip. That is a *paga* tavern, but, of course, you, you poor, simple beast, know nothing of *paga* taverns."

It pulled on the towel a little, and I tugged back, outside the bars.

It was within the cage, not near the bars.

I was outside the bars, by a yard or so.

"I do not see what you find diverting in this game," I said. "But who am I to say what a beast enjoys? It is enough if it amuses you. I know you are far stronger than I. You could tear the towel from my grasp at any time you wish. Yet you play as you do, sweet, simple Cyrus. You note, of course, that I, even in tugging, hold the towel loosely. It would not do for me, surprised, clinging tenaciously to the towel, to be drawn forward and dashed against the bars and perhaps seized should you, in the game's excitement, suddenly, forcibly jerk the towel toward you. I am a human. I am too clever for that, and you are too dull to think of it."

We continued to play.

"I must soon leave," I said. "I will be soon due at the tavern."

I noticed, to my unease, that the beast had, over our time of play, bit by bit, come closer to the bars.

It was now at the bars.

To compensate, I moved back, further away.

Apparently this was not noted by the beast.

Or I did not think so.

"Only a little longer," I said to the beast.

I held to the towel, tugging, and it regrasped the towel, and tugged back. A little later, it changed its grip again, and, later, again.

Suddenly, I froze with fear, for I realized the length of towel on my side of the bars was being shortened, inch by inch, drawing me closer and closer to the bars.

I flung down the towel crying out and leaped stumbling back, as, with an ugly, fierce, snarling sound that dark, powerful, violent, hirsute form thrust itself suddenly against the bars and, its head turned to the side, pressed against the bars, reached for me with its two long, prehensile, clawed appendages. I had heard my tunic torn at the right shoulder. I backed away, further, shaken. I touched my right shoulder, and there was a streak of blood on my fingertips.

"You are not stupid," I said. "It was I who was the fool. Who are you, really? What are you, really? How much have you understood of what I have said? Anything? Can you speak in some way, if only by gestures?"

I put my fingertips to my tongue and tasted blood.

"I am a slave," I said. "I mean you no harm. Why should you attack me?"

It straightened up, as it could, in the cell. It could not stand fully erect. It seized the bars and I feared, for a moment, it might bend them apart.

It regarded me, balefully, and I heard a low-pitched, rumbling, growling sound emanating from that huge, supple, hirsute, muscular bulk.

I recognized that sound.

I had heard it before, at night, once, near a caravan camp on a route to Ar.

The phonemes were rough and ill-formed, but I had once made them out, and now did so again.

"Where is Ag-nas?" it said.

I turned about, screaming, and fled from the room, and the menagerie.

CHAPTER FIFTY-FOUR

"*Paga*, Master?" I inquired.

"That," he said, "and perhaps more."

I was kneeling before him.

His table was in the shadows, toward the side of the common dining-and-drinking area. A *kaissa* room, its door partly open, was nearby. Some who play the game like silence. In the *kaissa* rooms, the low tables were inlaid with the squares of the game.

"A tavern's man can list this evening's suppers," I said.

I did not think he recognized me. It had been, after all, a long time since the tent in the field camp of what was supposedly Bazi Imports.

I shivered.

"Is anything wrong?" he asked.

"I will fetch your *paga*," I said.

"You seem to know me," he said.

"I do not see how that could be," I said.

"Paths cross," he said.

"Many wear collars," I said.

"Yet not all are the same," he said.

"May I fetch Master's *paga* now?" I asked.

"Remain as you are, here, kneeling," he said, "but put your wrists, crossed, behind you."

I complied.

I was then as though a bound prisoner before him.

"Do we not know one another?" he asked.

"I do not think so," I said.

"You remind me much of another slave, one seen too briefly, too long ago," he said. "But that slave was stiff and awkward, in movement and speech, eager to please, of course, an authentic slave, but one knowing little how to display the slave she was and wished to be. You, on the other hand, are different. You speak suitably, and act appropriately, and naturally, without pretense or strain, without labor or contrivance. Further, you are beautifully exercised and well-figured. You have learned your collar, and its joys."

"Then we could not be the same," I said.

"Girls grow in the collar," he said. "Girls blossom in the collar."

"I fail to comprehend that of which Master speaks," I said.

"I have made inquiries," he said. "You were a yellow-placard girl, purchased off a street shelf stocked by Tenalian of Ar."

I was silent.

"Your Gorean," he said, "is quite good."

"Thank you, Master," I said.

"Were you once, in a field tent, far off, long ago, named 'Janet?'"

"I am Mira, if it pleases Master," I said.

"You are elusive, Mira," he said.

"I do not understand," I said.

Now I was sure he was playing with me.

"We have been searching for you," he said. "And not we alone."

"Surely you have in mind another," I said.

"You are trembling," he said.

"Dismiss me!" I begged.

"You were to be flown to Ar in a tarn basket," he said. "You were never delivered to the specified party. What happened?"

"I know nothing of this," I said.

"On another world," he said, "you were known as a Miss Agnes Morrison Atherton."

"No!" I said.

"Did you think I would not recognize you in the suspended cage, so lifted therein that that you might be perused by all with ease?"

"I did not think you saw me," I said.

"Yet," he said, "you saw me."

"I could not help it," I said.

"You were to be delivered to a predetermined location," he said. "You were not. What happened? The failure of this delivery much disconcerted us."

"The tarnsman," I said, "was kind. He did not wish to deliver me to those who might wish my death. He sold me, somewhere in the Vosk Basin."

"Kind," he said, "but with an eye to profit as well."

"I was afraid," I said.

"You are a fool," he said. "You would have been carried to safety."

I wondered if that were true.

"Now you are in greater danger," he said, "much greater danger."

"I feared," I said, "I was being delivered to my death."

"I am sure," he said, "that some wish to extinguish you. But others are much concerned to keep you alive."

"You seek another," I said. "Allow me to depart."

"You sensed that you were sought, and were in danger," he said. "That was true. My principal learned of this, and wished to know why. What is special or important about a new girl, merely another seized for the collar, another recently brought to the markets?"

"Let me alone," I said. "I know nothing of these things. Go away. Let me alone! Leave me be!"

"I would speak with you, slave," he said.

I leaped up, breaking position, spun about, and fled toward the gate of the tavern, but one of the tavern's men seized me. He wrenched me about, easily, and drew me across the floor by my upper left arm to the table from which I had run, where he put me to my knees. As soon as he did so, I put my hands as before, wrists crossed, behind my back, resuming the position I had broken without permission. Breaking position without permission can be a cause for discipline. I hoped I would not be beaten. I lowered my head.

"I apologize on behalf of the management and staff," said the tavern's man. "Sometimes a slave, dismayed, frightened, fearing a particular patron, bolts. I will bring a whip."

"No," said the patron. "A short cord will do."

"You are a fortunate *kajira*," said the tavern's man.

"Also," said the patron, "do not beat her later, not for her indiscretion. I deem it to have been sufficiently motivated."

I looked up.

"As Master wishes," said the tavern's man, turning about.

"You have caught me," I whispered. "I knew I must be caught, sooner or later. At least I feared so. But I know little or nothing. Please do not kill me, or have others kill me. I know little or nothing."

"It is not we who wish to kill you," he said.

Could I believe him? Did he want me to trust him, so that he could the more easily deal with me later, in a less public setting?

The tavern's man returned with a short cord and, as I knelt, the patron tied my ankles together, tightly.

"We will not dart away now, will we?" he asked.

"No, Master," I said.

The tavern's man withdrew.

"I know little more than you," said the patron, "and I suspect that my principal knows little more than I, but it seems serious matters are afoot. Let me speak generally for a moment. What do you know of Priest-Kings?"

"I understand them to be mythical creatures, fabled to be the gods of Gor. There is a caste, the Initiates, which claims to be favored by them, to be able to interpret their will, to intercede with them on behalf of humans, and so on."

"The Priest-Kings are large, splendid, powerful humanlike beings, are they not?"

"I understand them to be considered so," I said. "I suspect that they do not exist."

"Yet," he said, "there are the Sardar Mountains, and the high palisade which surrounds them, a palisade which, it seems, not even tarns can cross."

"If so," I said, "that suggests a technology unusual for this world."

"Technology is interesting," he said. "Perhaps you regard Gor as a primitive world."

"Of course," I said.

"Yet, in some ways, it would seem far more advanced than your Earth," he said.

"How is that?" I asked.

"For example, the Stabilization Serums," he said.

"What are they?" I asked.

I thought it best to feign ignorance. Was I not a barbarian? Might it not be wise to pretend to know less than one actually knew?

"Surely you received several injections before being marketed," he said.

"Yes," I said.

"What was their purpose?" he asked.

"I do not know," I said.

"I think you are lying," he said. "But I am not interested in having you whipped at the moment."

"Master?" I said.

"When effective, as they commonly are, they assure cellular replacement with pattern stability," he said.

"I do not understand," I said.

Who could believe such things?

Yet I feared I believed them.

"They prevent the onset of the drying, withering disease," he said.

"What is that?" I asked, uneasily.

Long ago, Xanthe, in one of the fields of the Lady Temione of Hammerfest, had spoken to me similarly.

"How old," he asked, "do you take most adult Goreans to be?"

"I have wondered about that," I said, "the women perhaps between fifteen and thirty, the men perhaps between twenty and thirty-five, and there seem to be very few, of either sex, who are, or appear to be, old."

"What would such injections be worth on Earth?" he asked.

"They would be priceless," I whispered.

"Here," he said, "all receive them, at least in areas accessible to the Green Caste."

"Even slaves," I said.

"Certainly," he said, "we wish them to retain their prime market value."

"Then such serums are really effective?" I said.

How long I had fought to retain my skepticism! How long I had attempted to dismiss such claims! How long I had sought for alternative explanations for disconcerting facts. Who could believe such things?

"Of course," he said.

His asseveration, that of a free person, presumably honest and informed, was prosaic, impersonal, simple, and blunt. I had no doubt that he believed what he said. This declaration was different from, and exceeded, the babble of slaves, the furtive speculations which might course through the fields, pens, kennels. and cages.

Suddenly, for the first time, a thousand small observations, suspicions, thoughts, and memories came together, ample and unified, making sense on but one hypothesis, one pointing to a truth that was no longer rationally deniable.

"I see," I said.

I was staggered.

A gradation is commonly encountered in such matters.

It is one thing to accept the possibility that an anomalous hypothesis, however surprising, might be true; it is another thing to accept that such a surprising hypothesis appears to be true; and it is a further thing to intellectually grant, at least provisionally, that it is true, but, beyond all these things, it is quite another to grasp its deep import, to absorb its impact as a fragment of reality, as real as the sun, rain, and trees. I forced myself to breathe slowly, and deeply. Surely it could not be true. But how else explain the paucity of elderly humans on Gor?

"What do you know of Kurii?" he asked.

"The Beast People?" I said.

"I doubt that they would care for that description," he said.

"I know that they, or some, exist," I said. "I know little of their nature, intentions, or projects. I was informed that one sought me, even in the Vosk Basin. I encountered one at night on the route to Ar. One was captured near Venna and sold to my Master, Lycus of Ar. I tend it now in the Metellan Menagerie, on Barr Street. I have seen another, the docile pet of a street entertainer. Doubtless there are others, but few now in Ar, given the prohibitions of the Ubar, Marlenus."

"Kurii," he said, "are rational, surely as much so as humans. They are a savage, ambitious, ruthless, proud form of life. It is rumored they think to oppose the might of Priest-Kings. It is rumored they want Gor."

"I know little of these things," I said.

"Let us suppose that such things are true," he said. "And let us suppose, further, that the power of Kurii is distributed amongst several artificial worlds. What is less known, or understood, is that Kurii have factions."

"For a form of life such as you describe," I said, "I do not find that surprising."

"Let us suppose," he said, "that at least two major factions of Kurii are represented on Gor. Let us call them, them, borrowing from racing factions, the Reds and the Blues. On Gor, of course, Kurii, of whatever faction, as are humans, are held subject to the enforceable, and enforced, laws of the Priest-Kings, dealing primarily with certain forms of technology, principally weaponry and communication. Such limitations do not apply, of course, to the Kurii on their own far worlds."

"Why do these supposed Priest-Kings limit the technology of humans and Kurii on Gor?" I asked.

"They do not wish to put their world at risk," he said. "What rational creature would permit dangerous devices, lethal chemicals, poisons, and such, to come into the hands of greedy, irresponsible children?"

"Why," I asked, "do the Priest-Kings, if capable, not take action against the far worlds of the Kurii?"

"Perhaps they are not capable," he said. "Perhaps they are uninformed, and are not cognizant of the danger. Surely there must be much that they do not know. Perhaps they do know, but, confident of their power, do not feel threatened. But perhaps, I think, most simply, they do not take action against Kurii because it is not their way. They value life and do not seek to kill. They do not wish to unleash the *sleen* of war."

"Kurii, I take it," I said. "Have no such reservations."

"No," he said. "In this way, they are much like humans. Indeed, Priest-Kings may view humans and Kurii as sister species, as resembling species, viewing both as short-sighted, emotionally primitive, ambitious, territorial, and belligerent."

"I understand little of this," I said.

"Yet clearly," he said, "you are somehow involved."

"I trust not," I said, "but if so, surely reluctantly, most unwillingly."

"One does not always welcome the roles into which one finds oneself cast," he said.

"Is my blood sought?" I said.

"I fear so," he said.

"I know nothing," I said. "Please be merciful. Please let me go."

"What secret lies covert on your former world, potent and undiscovered?" he asked.

"I do not know," I said.

"Some must know even if you do not," he said.

"I beg you then deal with them," I said.

"And with whom should I deal?" he asked. "And how am I to do that?" he asked. "Rent space in a public wagon, berth on a ship whose keel cleaves clouds and air, rent a tarn?"

"Forgive me, Master," I said.

He regarded me.

I feared he was displeased.

I trembled.

I dared not meet his eyes. He was a free man and I was a slave.

I knelt before him, collared, my ankles tied together, holding my hands, as instructed, behind my back, next to naked, clad only in the tiny tunic of a *paga* slave.

And how easy it would have been for him to reach out and, should he wish, pull that bit of cloth away.

Startled, I wanted him to tear it away.

He could do so if he wished, and I, a slave, had nothing to say about it. I had no recourse. I was at his mercy, wholly. He could do with me what he wished, wholly.

How different we were!

One free, one slave.

I wanted his strong hands on my body, handling it as the slave meat it was.

One free, one slave.

How mighty is the chasm on Gor which separates the free and the slave! Few people on Earth, I was sure, could even begin to imagine, conceive of, or understand, that distinction.

But I, once Agnes Morrison Atherton, now a Gorean slave girl, knew it well.

On Gor I had learned it swiftly.

On Gor, I realized how unimportant, how worthless, how meaningless I was.

I was a slave.

Dared I hope that he would free my ankles, take me to an alcove, and fittingly fling me to his feet?

"I know something of Earth, the decadent, barbarous world from which you derive," he said. "To be sure, I have never visited that threatened, wasted place, but I do have acquaintances, primarily of the Slavers, who are familiar with it. And I know one in particular who, though not of the Slavers, has had dealings with them. Perhaps you know he of whom I speak, Holt of Ar."

"No," I said.

"He knows you," he said.

"Maxwell Holt!" I said.

"Recently returned to Gor," he said.

"Master!" I said, startled.

"What is wrong" he asked.

"I am troubled," I said, suddenly.

"Speak," he said.

"In the *kaissa* room, to the side, where none are now playing, near the half-closed door, the lamp extinguished, in the shadows, I saw a figure move."

The patron did not turn about.

"Someone was there," I said. "I think he is gone now. He may have been observing us."

"Did you recognize him?" asked the patron.

"It was not easy to see," I said. "The figure was small and furtive. I think it was that of a street entertainer, one who performs with a pet Kur."

"I know whom you mean," he said. "Did he have his beast with him?"

"I do not think so," I said.

"He is too frequently in my vicinity," he said.

"His presence has meaning?" I asked.

"Let us hope not," he said.

Almost at the same time four guardsmen entered the tavern through the front entrance.

"No one is to leave the room," announced one of them, one whose helmet bore a crest of *sleen* hair.

There was an uneasy stir amongst the tables.

The patron swiftly thrust up his left sleeve, and, with his right hand, drew forth, from a sheath strapped about his left forearm, a small, curved, broad-bladed, wickedly sharp knife, the sort Goreans call a hook knife. I had seen three before, one in the camp of the so-called Bazi Imports, and two in the Yellow Whip in Venna, when two customers had had a falling out. Four tavern's men had intervened, with clubs.

I was much shaken with what I had seen, not only with the knife, but with the wrist which the thrust-up sleeve had revealed.

Then he pulled me about and slashed away the cords on my ankles.

"Your wrist!" I said.

"Get up," he said. "Find an empty *paga* goblet on an abandoned table. There are several such. Go to the *paga* vat as though to refill it.

You will stumble, cry out and fall. I shall depart the tavern through the rear entrance."

"There may be guardsmen at the rear entrance," I said.

"Then there will be death, too," he said, "at the rear entrance."

I considered screaming and fleeing away, and then turning and pointing back to the patron, crying out, "There he is, he whom you seek!" but I took a *paga* goblet from an adjacent table and, walking slowly, made my way toward the *paga* vat. In the midst of a thicket of tables close to the vat I struck my ankle against an empty, uncleared table, cried out, and fell rolling to the floor amidst a clatter of goblets and dishes. There was some consternation and much laughter. "Stupid, clumsy slave!" I heard. "Forgive me, Masters!" I cried. Clumsiness, as you may know, is not permitted to slaves. Almost instantly I felt several strokes of a switch on my arms and legs. "Forgive me, Masters!" I wept. There was more laughter. "Clean up this mess. Get back to work!" said a tavern's man. "Yes, Master. Yes, Master!" I said. Even when the switch had struck me I, on all fours, had looked to the beaded curtain leading from the floor to the kitchen, storage areas, and living quarters of the tavern. It hung complacently in place. It showed no sign of having been recently passed through. I then strove to gather up the residue of strewn paraphernalia about me. The Vat Master came to stand near me, looking about. "When you are finished here," he said, "return to the line of waiting slaves. Your customer left."

"Master?" I asked, looking toward the inert beaded curtain.

"By the front entrance," he said.

Shortly thereafter I joined the waiting slaves.

The guardsmen were busy examining the left wrist of one customer after another. After a time, they left.

"You are lucky you were not more beaten," said Temione.

"Yes," I said.

As Temione was quite beautiful and had sold for several silver tarsks at the Curulean, her usage for her first month at the Red Whip had cost patrons a full copper tarsk, rather than the traditional tarsk-bit. Now, however, the month over, her services cost the customer no more than the standard charge. Indeed, she was now in the waiting area, no different from the rest of us. Whereas this seeming reduction in status may at first have stung her vanity somewhat, this annoyance was far more than compensated for by a substantial reduction in the scorn and abuse to which many of her collar-sisters had been wont to subject her. This pleased me, as well, as my frequent efforts to protect her and share or lessen her labors had often resulted in my being exposed to similar unpleasantries.

"I would have beaten you more," said Temione.

"I do not doubt it," I said.

"The men go easy with you," said another slave.

"You are one of their favorites," said another slave.

"Different men have different favorites," I said.

The waiting line need not be a literal line. It is more of an area on the side of the *paga* vat, closer to the beaded curtain, where slaves wait to serve. When a customer enters, if he makes no selection but merely chooses a table or allows himself to be directed to one, the next girl 'in line' is sent to serve him. On the other hand, many customers like to inspect the unengaged slaves and make a personal choice. Also, of course, they can arrange with a tavern's man, either earlier or after arrival, that a particular girl be sent to their table.

I waited.

I recalled the irregular, ugly scarring on the patron's wrist. It may have been from a manacle.

I knew I was supposed to inform a floor manager if I noted such a characteristic in a patron, but I had not done so. I did not think I would have done so in any case. I did not know what might be the consequences of such an action. I did not think I would care to turn over a stranger to what might be a harsh justice or vengeance of Ar. That was a burden I did not care to bear. It is so much easier not to notice such things.

Why had he spoken to me of Priest-Kings and Kurii, and of factions amongst Kurii? What was the point of that? What might I have to do with such things?

I wondered if I had spared an enemy who would, when the opportunity presented itself, kill me, or deliver me to those who would do so.

One thing I knew.

I had been discovered.

I was terrified.

Did he mean me well or ill?

What, if any, was his relationship to Maxwell Holt, or 'Holt, of Ar?' Were they friends, colleagues, casual acquaintances, perhaps surprisingly met, allies, enemies, fellow outlaws, conspirators, or what? I did not know. That might mean much, or little, or perhaps nothing.

The patron had informed me he would exit through the rear of the tavern. He had not done so. Why would he have misled me? Or did a change in plan seem more promising? Perhaps he was taking no chances. Perhaps he did not trust me.

Did he think I would have betrayed him?

Would I, if I knew more, have betrayed him?

I did not know.

I was sure that the small figure seemingly observing us from the shadows of the *kaissa* room was the street entertainer, he who had performed with the large, docile pet.

What connection, if any, was there between them, between the patron and the entertainer?

Had the presence of the small man anything to do with the appearance of the guardsmen in the tavern, apparently looking for a man with a scarred left wrist?

He with the scarred wrist, I recalled, was supposedly Rupert of Hochburg, the captain of an outlawed free company.

I did not know what a free company was, or how and by whom, and for what, it might be outlawed.

I did know I had been discovered.

I was terrified.

What could I do? Where could I go? I was collared, marked, and, if clad, slave clad. At night I would be caged or chained.

I thought again of the Stabilization Serums.

They would not have much value, if one were to be soon hunted down and killed.

"Mira, you are next," said a tavern's man, pointing, "there, that table."

"Yes, Master," I said.

CHAPTER FIFTY-FIVE

"I am back," I said.

It seemed little more than a large heap of dried fur. I could not see its face or features.

"You must eat," I said. "It is important to the Masters. Too, I do not want you to die."

It stirred, uncurling itself, and the head and eyes, and jaws, became visible.

"Please get up and move away, to the far side of your cage," I said. I held the meat pan, with its slabs of raw tarsk. I would slip it through the slot and then turn away. I did not much care to see the beast tear at his food. "Please do this," I said, "as was done before. I know you must be hungry. Why have you not eaten? The girls of the Menagerie Master throw meat between the bars but you did not eat. You cast it back. The Menagerie Master fears you will die, that he will lose a prime beast. He petitioned for my return. I am now back. I am a slave and must obey the Masters. Forgive me for crying out before and running away, but I was frightened. You tried to seize me. I ran."

I had not run, of course, until it had addressed me. I had done that in terror without thinking, much as one might instinctively withdraw from a sudden unexpected sound or movement.

I think, now, upon reflection, I had given myself away.

Why would a slave, or anyone, have fled in misery and terror before a brief, simple succession of sounds emanating from a caged animal, unless those sounds had somehow touched a match to a waiting tinder or powder of terror?

Would not such a response to some utterance be unlikely or anomalous except in a particular organism to which such an utterance would be cataclysmically meaningful?

The heap of fur half slid itself, half thrust itself, back from the bars.

"That is enough," I said. "I will be careful."

From what I saw, and from what had been reported to me, I suspected that the beast must be considerably weakened, but I wished to take no unnecessary chances. Who knew how much power might still lurk within that large, seemingly passive, almost inert frame? Might not a last spasm of energy bring it to the bars?

I slid the pan into the cell.

"I know you are intelligent," I said. "I do not know how intelligent. Please forgive me for the way I acted and spoke, for I had been told that some of your kind are no more than simple beasts and I understood you to be no more. You were not belted, nor did you have rings on a wrist. I do not know how much you understand of what I say but I am sure my speech and actions are not entirely unintelligible to you."

The beast went to its water bowl, lifted it up and drained it in one draught.

"If your fasting was designed to have me returned to your purview," I said, "it was successful. Had you such an intention? But why would you wish me to care for you? Others could do it as well or better."

It moved slowly toward the food tray, as though it wished to make no unexpected or sudden move which might frighten me. I backed away from the bars, nonetheless.

Then it lifted a haunch of tarsk and slowly, watching me, began to feed, strip after slow strip.

"You are eating," I said. "The Masters will be pleased. Do not eat too much, or too quickly, not at first."

I watched.

Commonly it disturbed me to watch the beast feed. Usually I would turn away. Now, however, I was watching.

He was not feeding as before, tearing at the meat, almost pouncing upon it and attacking it, seemingly concerned to gorge as much down in as short a time as possible, lest he be interrupted, meanwhile looking sharply about, as if he feared that something, possibly as savage and terrible as himself, might suddenly appear from nowhere, or the darkness, and challenge him for spoils or the remains of a kill.

No, he fed slowly, almost carefully.

I wondered if he were trying to please me, or, at least, not disconcert or alarm me.

"I wonder if you are trying to please me or put me at my ease," I said. "I wonder if you think I am stupid. I am well aware that you are dangerous. Do you think I have forgotten how you lunged at me? Had you come an inch closer I might have lost an arm or shoulder. I fear humans may underestimate your kind, but, too, perhaps your kind might underestimate humans. Humans can be ruthless, too, and do what survival expects of them."

He then drew the feeding pan deeper into the cage, and thrust it to the side.

He then regarded me, closely, and emitted a succession of sounds, slow, patient, careful, measured, guttural sounds.

The hair on the back of my neck rose up.

"That is no simple ventilation of feeling or natural concomitant of frustration or emotion," I said. "You have a language, perhaps more than one language. I am sure of it. But I cannot understand it."

He then, to my astonishment, spun about and leaped into the air, following which display, or behavior, he crouched down, again regarding me, intently.

Was it pleased, or eager? Or was it suddenly mad? Or was this merely some sort of spontaneous displacement activity, a way of reducing tension, or diverting uneasiness and energy into harmless channels.

Such a movement seemed unaccountable. "This thing," I thought, "is very different from a human being."

I was afraid of him.

I backed away, a little further.

From that position, crouching, facing me, it would be easy to spring toward the bars.

It made sounds, heavy, slow, laborious.

I began to be afraid, terribly afraid that I might understand him. I was sure he was trying to utter selected Gorean phonemes.

"You ran," I understood him to say.

"I was afraid," I said.

"Why ran?" he said.

"I was afraid," I said.

"Why afraid?" he asked.

"I did not want to be caught and pulled in pieces through the bars and eaten," I said.

"You ran—you ran after safe," he said.

"I was still afraid," I said.

"Where is Ag-nas?" it asked.

"I cannot understand you," I said.

"I think you know where Ag-nas is," he said.

"I cannot understand you," I said. "If you are speaking a language, it is not one I understand."

He then tore off a strip of raw meat and held it out, toward the bars. The gesture seemed almost tender, almost one of apology, or regret, or reconciliation. I knew the importance and preciousness of food to an animal; it is living and life. Fearful natural selections had been involved over hundreds, perhaps thousands, of generations. I recalled how it had commonly fed, so warily, so rapidly. Even in civilization, even in an era of abundant food, anciently selected-for genes would whisper of fear and possible scarcity.

Cyrus, as I had named him, was the sort of animal which, no more than a wolf or tiger, would be likely to share food.

I, of course, did not accept the offering, did not approach the bars.

The beast put the bit of meat near the slot under the bars where I might take it, if I was pleased to do so.

He then withdrew, leaving the vicinity of the bars.

"I think," he said, "you are Ag-nas."

"I cannot understand you," I said.

He then, looking at me, begin to make gestures. He seemed to be outlining an object in space, seemingly rather cubical. Then, he seemed to place the object on the floor of the cage, as if it actually existed. He then bent over the nonexistent object, and seemed to be pressing switches or turning knobs.

I remembered hearing men speak of an object, or box, by means of which the Kur near Venna, prior to its capture, had supposedly been interrogating encountered humans.

Was this the same animal or another?

I was sure that Maxwell Holt, or whoever he might be, would know something of such things, of a mysterious box or such, or, at least, would know of some who might. The observatory on Earth, I was sure, had some role in the intrigues of two worlds.

"I am sorry," I said to the beast, "I do not know what you are doing. I do not understand you."

A low, warning snarl came from the beast.

I inadvertently touched the collar on my neck, which proclaimed me the property of Lycus of Venna. I trusted the beast did not know that *kajirae* were not permitted to lie.

The beast then pointed to the nonexistent box he had seemed to place on the cage floor, and twice, gently, meaningfully, patted the cage floor at its side, as if to say, "This, this."

"I must go," I said.

"I wish you well, Ag-nas," he said.

I remembered how the beast had lunged at me, so murderously, a few days ago. I was pleased it was well caged. I had little to fear while it was so housed.

I hurried from the room.

CHAPTER FIFTY-SIX

"Welcome to the Purple Whip," said Luta, brushing her dark hair back over her right shoulder. "I recall you from the great pen at Victoria Minor and from the Markets in Victoria."

"This is Temione," I said.

"You are both from the Red Whip," said Luta.

"Yes," I said.

"I recall Temione," said Luta. "She sold for four silver tarsks in Victoria."

"I brought seven silver tarsks in Ar," said Temione.

"The slaver, Tenalian, knows well what he is doing," said Luta.

"Why are we here?" I asked.

"Is it not obvious?" asked Luta. "This is a *paga* tavern."

"I think there is more to it," I said. I had been given to understand that it might take months for a girl to move from the Red Whip to the Purple Whip, if at all.

"I do not know," said Luta. "I think you are both Metellan girls."

"Not I," said Temione.

"I do know," said Luta, "that you were both personally requisitioned."

"But you do not know why, or by whom?" I asked.

"Strictly, of course," said Luta, "by Master Lycus."

"Lycus the Fat," said Temione.

"Beware, slave," said Luta.

"You know little of this?" I asked.

"Less than that," said Luta. "Girls seldom rise from the Red Whip to the Purple Whip. Commonly Master Lycus buys directly for the Purple Whip."

"I am not what you would call a 'Metellan girl,'" said Temione.

"You were at the Red Whip, on Dina Street," said Luta.

"How is it," asked Temione, "if the Purple Whip has such lofty standards, that you are here?"

"Doubtless because of my striking beauty," said Luta.

"And nothing else?" asked Temione.

I recalled that Luta, in the great pen at Victoria Minor, had been owned by the prestigious House of Ho-Turik. She seemed to have a knack for such things.

"It is no secret," she said. "In the streets I caught the eye of a floor manager."

"I suspect one carefully scouted," said Temione, "one accidentally brushed in passing, one to whose feet you then contritely cast yourself, weeping and begging for mercy."

"Something like that," smiled Luta.

"And doubtless there was an alley nearby?" said Temione.

"Something very much like that," said Luta.

"Anyone could do such a thing," said Temione.

"But try not to be beaten for it," said Luta. "That is the trick."

"You can understand my curiosity," I said.

"More so than I can satisfy it," said Luta, amiably.

"Someone must have approached Master Lycus," I said.

"I have only seen Lycus the Fat once," said Temione. "I doubt that he even knows me."

"Someone does," I said.

"I think," said Luta, "there must have been two requisitions, unrelated to one another."

"Why should you think that?" I asked.

"Because of the difference between you," she said.

"What difference?" I asked.

"Be serious, dear Mira, sweet Pock-Face," said Temione.

"She is a blonde," I said, "and I am a brunette."

"That is true," said Luta.

"Some customers prefer me to Temione," I said.

"What did you sell for?" asked Temione.

"I do not regard myself as your equal," I said.

"I have always admired your judgment," said Temione. "It is unclouded."

"I am beautiful," I said.

"Quite so," said Temione, "in an ordinary sort of way."

"In any event," said Luta, "you two are no longer at the Red Whip."

"I think that two different requisitions, two different Masters, are involved," said Temione.

"Quite possibly," said Luta.

"I am not sure of that," I said. "I think there is a connection."

"Why should you think that?" asked Temione.

"Because of the timing," I said.

"Coincidences exist," said Temione.

"That is true," I said. "I am probably wrong."

CHAPTER FIFTY-SEVEN

I stood just within the doorway of the Purple Whip.

There was a light rain falling outside.

There was no elevated cage to the left of the door as one faced the street. I gathered that that might be regarded as less than refined in the Boulevard District. The Purple Whip itself was on Proclus Street, just off the Avenue of the Central Cylinder. The Central Cylinder itself was a lofty sky-jarring, circular stronghold and palace. It was said to be a seat of governance and law in Ar, and the living quarters of the Ubar himself, a man named 'Marlenus.' Sometimes some of the girls at the Purple Whip served in the Central Cylinder, particularly at public dinners, banquets, feasts, entertainments, and such. There was no denying that The Purple Whip was well appointed and expensive. It was large and well-lamped. The floors were polished. The dancing sand was raked and sifted each night. Sometimes a missed coin would show up in the straining screens. Eight or ten musicians played, as opposed to the usual six, a *czehar* player, two flautists, two *kalika* players, and a fellow on the *kaska*, smaller than the common *tabor*. Whereas in a common *paga* tavern the tables are low and the fellows sit about cross-legged, in the Purple Whip the tables were higher and patrons were seated in curule chairs. Chairs on Gor, I gathered, commonly signified status. I was not sure that the food and drink served in the tavern was better than that served in numerous competing establishments but, if this were not so, the Purple Whip at least compensated by charging its customers considerably more. Whereas a larger price usually betokens a better buy, the connection falls short of being one of logic. Perhaps one pays much for location, privacy, décor, and ambiance. Such things, however, while undeniably pleasant, do little to assuage the pangs of hunger. A starving man may be forgiven for preferring a cheap pot filled with stew to an empty plate of gold.

"Move away, fellow," said one of the door guards to a loitering hawker, a rainproof cloth spread over his tray of pastries.

"And do not try to look within," warned another.

"But there are murals within by Ramos of Tor and Phineas of Ti," said the man.

"Is that true?" asked one of guards of the other.

"I do not know," said his colleague. "There are murals."

"I can buy my way in," said the vendor.

"Not as you are," said a guard. "Go home. Afford sandals. Buy fine raiment. Attend the baths. See the barber. Mend your manners. Improve your diction. Have yourself oiled and perfumed."

"A mural does not care how I am bedecked," said the hawker.

"Be on your way," said one of the guards.

The hawker then, whether annoyed or disconsolate, went on his way.

"Can you imagine the nerve of such a fellow?" said one of the guards to me.

"It is difficult to do so," I admitted. I had the sense that I had seen the hawker, or vendor, before. Why, I wondered, would he seek entrance while carrying a tray? Or did he merely seek to seem occupied with the guards? If so, why? On the other hand, I could not place him.

"He need only look at your tunic," said the guard, "to know that this is not a place for such as he."

"Surely," I said.

My tunic was of the best silk, purple in color, doubtless for the tavern's name, fashionably cut, and finely stitched. It was rather modest for a slave tunic, as well, as its hem fell almost, but not quite, to the knees.

"Perhaps we should be put in golden collars," I said.

"We cannot have slaves stolen for their collars," said the guard.

"That would not do," I admitted.

My attempt at humor had failed. But I reminded myself that he did not even understand the importance of the work of a Ramos of Tor or a Phineas of Ti, whoever they might be.

I did not much care for the Purple Whip.

Aside from décor, lavish furnishings, blatantly garish appointments, outrageous pricings, bold advertisements, dubious assertions, and pretentious claims, I saw little reason, on the whole, to rate it higher than the Yellow or Red Whip, nor, I suppose, any number of other taverns in the city or elsewhere. Some men, I supposed, will respect no merchant who does not rob them mercilessly, this assuring them that they are getting their money's worth, that quality is commensurate with cost. For example, the girls at the Purple Whip, on the whole, in my opinion, were no better than, or worse than, the girls elsewhere, but the house charged more for their services and their tunics were better sewn and of more expensive material. Is not a slave the same regardless of the expense of her tunic? Prestige, like power, is a heady stimulant. Too, I supposed, if one regards oneself as a superior person, it is natural to wish to consort, if at all, with similarly superior persons, though, hopefully not quite as superior. In any event, one wishes to protect oneself from the contaminations of the ignorant, rowdy, and boorish.

I wondered how many patrons of the Purple Whip, reclining in their curule chairs, appreciated, or even noticed, the work of Ramos of Tor or Phileas of Ti, whoever they might be.

Luta, in one of her many conversations with us, had assured Temione and me that the Purple Whip was a good place to catch a fine Master.

I was not sure of it.

She did warn us that the patrons of the Purple Whip were more likely to use the whip, or call for a tavern's man to use the whip, than patrons of most taverns. Perhaps that is to be expected of superior persons. I do not know.

It seemed clear that the presence of both Temione and myself in the Purple Whip was the result of two independent requisitions. Certainly Luta seemed to have thought so. I was still not convinced, however, that the two requisitions, whether separate or not, was a simple matter of coincidence.

Perhaps someone, or something, had some reason for wanting us both to be taken from the Metellan District, and placed in the Boulevard District, perhaps both to be more accessible to someone or something, or perhaps for us both, for some reason, to be more in the precincts of power, perhaps even to be nearer the Central Cylinder itself.

But this, it seemed, upon reflection, must be foolish.

I then, standing within the entrance of the Purple Whip, near the guards, the air damp, the rain still softly falling, smelled a strong animal odor, one which I soon understood to be that of wet fur.

"Be off, be away!" said one of the guards, waving his arm at the street entertainer with his pet Kur.

"Do not loiter here," said the other guard. "This is the place of the Purple Whip. Do not perform here. Take your odorous beast away."

"Yes, Masters," said the entertainer. "Forgive me, Masters."

"What a fool you are," said the other guard, "to be out in the rain. Who will watch you in this weather?"

"I depart, noble Masters," said the entertainer, turning about with a tug on the leash, but the beast did not stir.

The entertainer gave another short, impatient tug on the leash, but the beast growled in a way that was surely out of character for a tame, performing animal, and the entertainer instantly desisted.

"Take that thing away!" said a guard, stepping back, his hand clutched on the hilt of his belt knife.

"Come, Bubu, please come," said the entertainer.

The eyes of the beast were fixed on me.

"Go inside," said one of the guards to me.

"Yes, Master," I said, backing away.

As soon as I was inside, I recalled where I had seen the hawker before, he who had seemed to seek entrance to the Purple Whip. He had been one in the crowd, some days ago, when I had witnessed the entertainer's performance with his docile pet, not far from the Metellan Menagerie.

Odd, I thought, that I should see them this morning, that is, both of them, within so short a time.

CHAPTER FIFTY-EIGHT

"Master!" I cried, on Proclus Street, kneeling.

"Slave," said Holt of Ar, or Maxwell Holt, as I sometimes thought of him.

How natural, how appropriate, how necessary, it now seemed to me to kneel in the presence of the free. Once a free woman of Earth, now every cell of my body, every drop of my blood, was saturated with the rightfulness of my longed-for bondage. I would have been truly distressed, painfully uncomfortable, had I been commanded to stand in his presence. I belonged on my knees before him. He was free.

"Do not stop, Master," said Xanthe, the former Eileen Bennett. "Come away. Ignore her."

"Should she not be kneeling?" I asked.

"On your knees, slave," snapped Holt of Ar. "Put your head down."

"Yes, Master," said Xanthe.

"One must keep them in their place," said Holt to me.

"We want to be in our place," I said.

"You are bold to address me on the street," said Holt.

"Or elsewhere," said Xanthe, head down, kneeling.

"Forgive me, Master," I said, "but I desire, fervently, to speak with you, privately."

"Do not listen to her, Master," said Xanthe, careful to keep her head down. "She has designs on you. Do not permit her to seduce you. Let her machinations be fruitless. Do not be dazzled by the fashion and cut, the workmanship and quality, of a purple tunic. Put a field slave in a purple tunic and you still have no more than a field slave in a purple tunic."

"Be silent, slave," said Holt.

"I have hoped to see you about, in the city," I said. "I did not know how to reach you. I have looked often, and in many places, where I was permitted. I hoped you would have come again to the Red Whip, or that you would have learned that I was now at the Purple Whip, and would have come to see me there."

"Why should he have come to see you?" asked Xanthe.

"Let me speak privately with you," I begged.

"See!" said Xanthe. "She wants to be alone with you. Had she suitable wiles, I would be much afraid. As it is, I fear merely that your time will be wasted."

"Let me speak with you," I said.

"Privately?" he asked.

"Yes!"

"Beware, Master," said Xanthe.

"Please!" I said, desperately. Who knew when I might, if ever, see Maxwell Holt again? I wiped away a tear that had run down my right cheek.

"Is this so important?" asked Holt.

"Yes, Master!" I said.

"Do not be tricked by false tears," said Xanthe. "One can see buckets of them in the theater of Publius."

"We will tarry a moment," said Holt.

"A moment can undo a man," said Xanthe.

"You must admit," said Holt, "she is well curved.

"She is a *paga* girl," said Xanthe, "only that. They will do anything to obtain a private Master!"

"Perhaps I could afford a second slave," said Holt.

"Certainly not, Master," said Xanthe.

"Then it seems I would have to sell you," said Holt.

"Let me go away, somewhere to the side," said Xanthe, "where you can speak, and I cannot hear."

"If you wish," said Holt.

Xanthe then leapt up and hurried off to a point from which she might observe, and keenly, but, certainly, would be unable to hear.

"Beware, Master," she called.

"You came to see me in the Red Whip," I said.

"Earlier," he said, "I had been surprised to see you on one of Tenalian of Ar's slave shelves. As on Earth I had often thought that you should be a slave, I thought that I would take a closer look. You looked well on your chain, naked, marked, and collared."

"Thank you, Master," I said. But what woman would not look well, so exhibited?

"But I was startled and dismayed," he said, "with how you behaved, seemingly so distraught, so frightened, and such."

"I was afraid," I said, "because I thought you had pursued me to Gor, to find me and kill me, or deliver me to those who would kill me."

"I knew not what concerned you," he said. "But I had not forgotten your behavior. Why had you acted like that? I was curious. Your behavior bothered me. So, later, when I saw your name in graffiti, in a market, I thought I would inquire into the matter."

"And you did so," I said, "mercilessly, when I was piteously vulnerable and helpless."

"Why did you accost me just now, on the street?" he asked.

"Surely you were intrigued with the information you so cruelly forced from me?"

"Indeed," he said, "but I have been unable to confirm it, or even ascertain its import, if it should be true. I do not think it is even a rumor. And what does it matter if two spherical objects seem to have disengaged themselves from debris in the asteroid belt?"

"I do not know," I said. "But I am sure it is a matter of consequence, perhaps terrible consequence. Consider the secrecy."

"Certainly I knew nothing of it," he said.

"Few did," I said.

"Sometimes when one hears little or nothing of something, it is not because it is a secret. It may be merely that it is not deemed of interest or importance."

"You must have contacts," I said, "here on Gor."

"Human contacts," he said. "Most dismiss the story as unimportant, or as the result of a misunderstanding, or even the invention of a clever slave seeking to seem important."

"Why not the fantasy of a mad slave?" I said.

"That, too, was suggested," he said.

"I am not mad," I said.

"Nor do I think you such," he said. "But what is the purport of the matter?"

"I do not know," I said.

"I saw no point in contacting you again," he said. "Why did you wish to see me?"

"Master!" called Xanthe, plaintively from several yards off, where she waited, on her knees.

"I see I shall have to beat her," said Holt.

"Please do not do so, Master," I said. "She is forlorn. She fears to lose you. I think she loves you."

"What is the helpless, desperate love of a slave worth?" he asked.

"Much," I said, "to the slave. But perhaps, too, you care for her."

He drew back his hand to strike me, but, to my relief, lowered his hand.

"Love, for a slave?" he said.

"Forgive me, Master," I said.

How absurd was such a thought!

"Why did you think it important that you see me?" he asked.

"Do you know aught of the Metellan Menagerie?" I asked.

"Yes," he said. "It is on Barr Street."

"A beast, a Kur," I said, "was captured near Venna. My Master, Lycus of Venna, purchased it and had it brought to Ar and exhibited in the Metellan Menagerie."

"Why would he do that?" asked Holt.

"I do not know," I said, "but I, given the fear of several of the menagerie attendants and my supposed low worth as a slave, was assigned to care for it."

"And did you?" he asked.

"Yes," I said. "And that is why I wanted to speak to you. The beast I tend was captured near Venna. I think it must be the same which was reportedly accoutered and seeking, by some means, or device, to gather information as to my whereabouts. In my tending of it, I find it to be rational, and speeched, after a fashion. It tried to kill me."

"Are you sure?" he asked.

"I think so," I said.

"Perhaps it was only desperate and excited, and, completing its search, wanted only to seize and hold you, to speak with you."

"In any event," I said, "I fled."

"I understand," he said.

"It would not feed until I was restored as its keeper. It seemed desperate to communicate with me. I have reason to believe it understands Gorean, but it is almost impossible to understand its sorry attempts to make itself understood in Gorean. It tried, even, to communicate by signs."

"How so?" asked Holt.

Then, to the best of my memory, I imitated the movements of the beast.

"I do not think he was signing words," said Holt. "I think he was describing by gestures an object in space."

"I think you are right," I said. "Perhaps an object such as might have been taken from him after his capture."

"A translator," said Holt. "I have never seen one, but I have heard of them."

"It seems he may have had such a device near Venna," I said.

"Where is it now?" asked Holt.

"I do not know," I said. "I had hoped that you might have such a device, or have access to one."

"*Ela*, no," said Holt.

"It might be invaluable," I said.

"Possibly," he said.

"Surely the observatory has contact with the beasts," I said.

"Not directly," he said.

"I thought you might have personal contact with them," I said.

"I am still alive," he said.

"I have not seen the menagerie beast for several days," I said. "I was moved from the Red Whip to the Purple Whip, with another slave, a girl named Temione. It seems it will not do for Purple-Whip girls to tend to caged beasts, unless they be other female slaves."

"But would the beast not once more starve itself to force your return as its keeper?"

"Apparently not," I said.

"But you feared that," he said. "You were concerned about it."

"Yes," I said.

"It seems you should be pleased," said Holt. "Were you again within the purview of the beast, it might make another attempt on your life, assuming it had done so, perhaps one more successful."

"When it is caged, there is little to fear," I said.

"What if it were not caged?" he asked.

"Then I would be very much afraid," I said. "It now knows me as its quarry."

"Have you inquired after the beast, after your transfer to the Purple Whip?"

"Yes," I said. "I have been assured it is doing quite well. Were it not, as it is a valuable addition to the menagerie, I think I would have been returned to the Red Whip, which is much closer to the menagerie."

"Then it seems that all is well," he said.

"Yes," I said.

"You were lied to," he said.

"I do not understand," I said.

"Then you have not heard," he said.

"Heard what?" I asked.

"The beast," he said, "several days ago, perhaps about the time of your transfer to the Purple Whip, escaped."

"It cannot be," I said. "Not from the cage in which it was confined. That cage would hold an animal five times its size and ten times as powerful."

"Several of the bars seems to have been melted," he said. "And a large portion of the stone of the external wall appears to have been eaten away, presumably chemically."

"Goreans do not have such technology," I said.

"Someone does," said Holt.

"Or something," I said.

"Yes, or something," said Holt.

"Then the beast is loose," I said.

"Yes," said Holt.

"And will be hunting me," I said.

"Possibly," he said.

He then strode away and Xanthe leaped up, and heeled him.

I lost no time but, looking about, hastened back to the Purple Whip.

CHAPTER FIFTY-NINE

"What is that?" I had asked Luta.

"A warning bar," she said. "It is sounded when raiders cross the walls and are aflight in the city. There is little danger if you remain indoors. City tarnsmen will drive them away."

"I have heard it before, on other evenings," I said.

"This is spring," she said. "Spring is the optimum raiding season, as it is for the sales of *kajirae*."

"Doubtless there is a connection," I said.

"Certainly," she said.

"You know I am a barbarian," I said.

"I know it," she said, "a yellow-placard girl, but I was surprised to learn it."

"I still wonder at much on Gor," I said.

"Such as?" she said.

"I find it hard to believe," I said, "that raiding goes on."

"What is the problem if there is no sharing of Home Stones?" she asked.

"That women should be scouted, hunted, captured, and enslaved," I said.

"The coup," she said, "is to capture a free woman of an enemy city and make her a slave."

"Certainly the young men of Ar do not engage in such outrageous enterprises," I said.

"Of course they do," said Luta. "It is a common sport. Have not the women of the enemy always been amongst the spoils of the victors?"

Fittingly or not, I found myself thrilled, to be such that I could count as spoils or loot, that I was of such a kind that men would fight for me, that I was an object of desire, that I was coveted, that I was a prize of sorts, that men would risk their lives to bring me to their feet, and own me. I was wanted. I was special. How real it all was. What could be more real than that? I feared I had caught a glimpse of nature.

"The dancers will be dismissed shortly," said the Feast Master. "Retire to the vestibule. Prepare to serve. This is not your tavern, but a private supper chamber of the Ubar himself. Go now."

The large, bearded figure in a purple robe and golden sandals raised his hand, dismissively.

There was then a sharp clapping of hands by the Feast Master followed by a single stroke on a small metal gong.

The five dancers scurried from the floor and the musicians gathered up their instruments and took their leave.

"That is the noble Marlenus," Luta had informed us earlier, having indicated the large figure in the purple robe and golden sandals, "Ubar of Glorious Ar."

Power seemed to radiate from such a figure.

To look upon him was to see a leader of men, a wielder of power.

The purple of the tunics of the girls of the Purple Whip was clearly a different purple from that of the robe of the Ubar, but was doubtless intended to suggest it. In Ar, at least in theory, the 'Ubarial purple' is to be worn only by a Ubar.

Temione, after a glance from the serving vestibule at the dining couches, had begged not to be sent to the floor.

She had retired, recoiling, shaken, almost to the kitchen.

What was he doing here, a guest at a small private supper in the Central Cylinder, he, so far from the Vosk Basin, so far from Hammerfest?

"Please, no!" she had wept. "Not to him! Please, do not send me to him!"

"You are his personal slave for the evening," said one of the floor managers from the Purple Whip. "You have been specifically selected to serve him, following his request. Obey gladly. Smile. It is the will of the Master. Arrange your basket of fruit. Then, upon my signal, to the floor!"

"Do not let him see me as a slave," begged Temione.

"And as what else should he see you?" asked Luta. "He saw you sold in Victoria. Doubtless that much pleased him."

"How could he even know I was here?" said Temione.

"Perhaps it is because of him that you are here," speculated the floor manager. Some of the tavern's men were about, as well. The girls of the Purple Whip, as I have mentioned, occasionally served in the Central Cylinder. In this way, they freshened the occasions and assisted the house slaves.

On one of the dining couches was sprawled the huge, corpulent figure of Lycus of Venna. I had seen him no more than three times in the past months.

I was startled to note another guest, as well, the small entertainer. I did not understand how a mere street performer could be a guest at a small, private supper in the Central Cylinder, one attended even by the Ubar himself, Marlenus of Ar. Clearly the small, almost tiny, entertainer was other here than he appeared on the streets. Certainly his robes, if not his stature, now bespoke importance. There was no sign of his beast.

Besides the Ubar, Marlenus; Gordon, of Hammerfest; my Master, Lycus the Fat, or, better, Lycus of Venna; and the diminutive, putative entertainer, there were three or four others, whom I did not know. Two were later identified for me, Hermanus, currently first sword in the Taurentian Guard, the Palace Guard, and Marcus Rufus, First Captain of the City Guard of Ar.

I was soon, under the direction of Luta, serving *ka-la-na*.

The tables were arranged in such a way as to resemble a rectangle with one of the long sides open to facilitate serving. The dining couches on which the guests reclined were adjacent to the tables. Each of the guests, beyond his dining raiment, wore a fresh chaplet of *veminiums*.

As I served, a thought kept pressing toward me. Temione and I, unexpectedly and surprisingly, had been requisitioned to serve at the Purple Whip, presumably at the same time, or nearly at the same time, but, most likely, by different parties. But this did not preclude some deeper connection. Could both individuals be present here, this evening, in the same room, perhaps for the same purpose, considering us? It seemed likely that Gordon of Hammerfest might have had Temione requisitioned for the Purple Whip, there being ample reason for supposing that, but who, then, might have applied to Lycus of Venna to have me brought, too, to the Purple Whip, to so central, so prominent, so convenient, so exposed a location, even near the Central Cylinder itself?

"Remove your tunic, slave," said Gordon of Hammerfest to Temione, "and lie on your stomach by my couch. I am not sure I want you serving me. I do not think you are worthy of that honor. Perhaps I may use you to wipe my sandals or dry my hands."

Temione wept and assumed the position prescribed by Gordon.

"Dear Gordon," said huge Lycus, my Master, "if one slave is to be stripped, should not all serve so?"

"Customarily," said Gordon, "but let it not be so this evening. This evening, let only the lowest and most worthless of slaves be slave naked. Let it be only she beside my couch, the mat on which I wipe my feet, the napkin with which I dry my hands."

"Slaves," called the Feast Master, "continue the courses."

Marlenus, the Ubar, smote the table with an empty goblet. "More wine," he called.

I hurried to him, trembling. I could have reached out and touched the Ubar of Ar.

"What is wrong, girl?" he asked.

"Nothing, Master," I said.

Never before had I been so close to one who held such power.

"Do not drink," said the Feast Master, suddenly. "See the slave! She is frightened. She is agitated. She may know something of the wine. It may be poisoned!"

"No, Master!" I cried, stumbling back, almost dropping the decanter. Later, I was pleased that I had not dropped it. How suspicious that would have been!

"Surely a taster sampled the wine before it was served," said Marlenus.

"Who knows what might have been added later?" said the Feast Master.

"Use the slave at my feet," said Gordon, indicating Temione. "Let her drink. If she dies moments later, writhing in agony, the loss is negligible."

"Not quite," said Lycus.

"Send for Ennius, of the Green Caste," said he whom I would later learn was Hermanus, First Sword of the Taurentians. "He is a connoisseur, skilled in sampling wines and versed in detecting poisons, and he will have with him his kit of antidotes."

I would later be given to understand that a physician was normally within a Ubar's call, even in the field. Ennius, as it turned out, was one of the Ubar's personal physicians.

"Take all precautions," said Lycus, "but I think my slave was merely uneasy to find herself in such proximity to our mighty Ubar."

"Yes, Master!" I said.

"Do you like wine, girl?" inquired Marlenus.

"I have little taste for it," I said. Then I realized that that was not what should have been said. "I have not tasted wine since I was free," I said.

"She is a barbarian," said Lycus.

"Drink," said Marlenus, smiling, lifting the goblet to me.

"I am a slave, Master," I said, demurring.

"Drink," he said.

I took the goblet in both hands and drank deeply, almost draining it. Almost instantly it began to go to my head.

I did not think I had ever tasted so marvelous, so heady, a beverage.

I was vaguely aware that all eyes were upon me.

I realized, suddenly, uneasily, they were waiting to see if I was going to die.

"Retire to the vestibule and lie down," said the Feast Master. "Others will serve. You took too generous a draught. I expect that you will be good for little more tonight."

I steadied myself on one of the tables.

"Come along," said Luta. "I will help you to the vestibule."

Before the vestibule, I turned about, unsteadily, to view the room. Gordon of Hammerfest had pulled Temione up to her knees and was wiping his hands on her hair, presumably drying them of grease and juice.

"She is pretty, is she not?" asked heavy Lycus.

"What do you want for her?" asked Gordon.

"We can negotiate a price later," said Lycus.

Gordon then thrust Temione down again to her belly beside his couch. She lay there, a slave, humiliated and mastered.

"Here is Ennius," said a voice.

"He is not needed now," said another voice.

I saw the small, keen eyes of the entertainer on me.

I was afraid of him.

"Come along," said Luta.

I was led inside the vestibule, and, just inside, I lowered myself to the welcoming floor and lay down on my left shoulder, my legs drawn up. I knew myself a moment from passing out.

"I must congratulate you, sweet Mira," said Luta. "You are far more cunning than I thought. I did not expect such cleverness in you, particularly as you are a barbarian."

"What?" I said.

"Leading the Masters to suspect poison," she said, "and then gambling that you would be forced to drink from the suspected cup. What a brilliant way to inveigle yourself a draught of fine wine, from the stores of a Ubar no less. To be sure, it would not have been well for you if your throat had been instantly cut or if the wine had been truly poisoned."

All I wanted to do was to go to sleep.

Alcohol, I knew, was chemically an anesthetic.

Most Gorean wines are quite strong and they are usually served diluted, mixed with juice or water. I did not think, however, that the wine I had imbibed had been diluted.

Dimly, far off, I thought I heard the sounding of a warning bar.

Another raider or raiders must have been detected within the walls. Doubtless tarnsmen of Ar would drive them away. As Luta had said, there was little to fear if one remains indoors. Why I wondered, did free women, if what I had heard was true, sometimes wander the high bridges at night? Were they actually slaves put in the garb of free women to serve as Lure Girls, to trap raiders? If they were truly free women, as I had heard, why would they expose themselves to such risks? Did they, restless and unfulfilled beneath their burdensome robes, lonely and dissatisfied, weary of prescriptions and proprieties, hope to feel the capture ropes of raiders?

Did they, in their hearts, desire a Master?

Then, mercifully, I fell asleep.

"Wake up, *kajira*," I thought I heard. And then I knew I heard it. And my cheeks stung, being slapped several times in rapid succession. And I felt a kick on my thigh.

Confused, miserable, I struggled to my knees.

I shook my head to clear my vision. I did not know how long I had slept, but I sensed it might still be dark.

"Forgive me, Master," I said. Had I somehow been displeasing?

I was no longer in the vestibule but in a narrow hallway, near a heavy, bolted door. I could feel cool air beneath the door. I did not know if I were still in the lofty Central Cylinder or not. A *tharlarion*-oil lamp was in a niche on the wall, and I suspected that it had been recently placed there. I blinked my eyes against the light. It was much in my eyes. A small, even tiny, figure was facing me. I was illuminated, but I could not see its features, but, to my dread, I knew who it was.

"You are the slave, Mira," said the fellow, so small, but in fine raiment, he who had entertained on the streets with a pet Kur, and had somehow been amongst the guests at a Ubar's private supper.

"If it pleases, Master," I said.

Why had he beaten me? What had I done? What could he want of me?

I no longer felt the effects of the alcohol I had perforce consumed. I did not know if it had spent its force or if, in my misery and terror, I had been shocked into sobriety.

"You are a *paga* girl at the Purple Whip," he said, "and the slave of Lycus of Venna."

"Yes, Master," I said.

"We are going to talk," he said.

"I am a slave," I said.

"Where is Lucilius, Deputy to Agamemnon?" he asked.

"Forgive me, Master," I said, "but I do not know what you are talking about."

"A Kur was captured in the vicinity of Venna," he said. "It was later purchased by Lycus of Venna and brought to Ar, there to be placed as an exhibit in the menagerie, in the Metellan District, on Barr Street, an institution in which Lycus of Venna has an interest. While at the Red Whip you tended it. Why?"

"I was a low slave and thus," I said, "low and, I suppose, possibly hazardous, duties devolved upon me."

"You are a barbarian," he said.

"Yes, Master," I said.

"The Kur was searching for a barbarian slave near Venna," he said.

"There are many barbarians," I said.

"What do you know of a barbarian slave whose name when free was Agnes Morrison Atherton?" he asked.

"Nothing," I said.

"I think you are lying," he said. "I think you know of her."

"No, Master," I said.

"I think perhaps you are she," he said.

"No, Master!" I said.

"You fit the description," he said.

"I am sure many slaves would fit the description," I said.

"Barbarians?" he said.

"Some," I said.

"Inquiries were made," he said. "At one point, you fled from the cage of the Kur you attended in the menagerie. Why?"

"I was frightened," I said.

"It then refused food until you were reinstated as its attendant. Why was that?"

"I do not know," I said.

"Clearly, it suspected you were somehow important to it," he said. "I paid Lycus to have you elevated to the Purple Whip. My experiment proved successful. Almost immediately thereafter his cohorts risked much, given the laws of the Priest-Kings, to extract him from his cell in the menagerie. I think, thus, he believed you to be the barbarian, or a key to the barbarian, he sought."

"Surely not," I said. "My elevation, as you call it, to the Purple Whip and his escape is no more than a coincidence."

"That Kur, Lucilius, can speak Gorean," he said.

"It is only a beast," I said, "like your docile pet, Bubu."

"Surely you could understand him," he said.

"No," I said.

"You are intelligent," he said, "and your Gorean shows you have a good ear. In two or three days, perhaps less, accustoming yourself to the inevitable phonemic transformations, you could understand him easily, just as he could understand you."

I found myself muchly unsettled by this. When I had spoken to him, rambling on at my pleasure, as one might do with a dog or cat, he would have understood me as easily as a native Gorean might have done.

"There are rumblings in Ar," said the small man, "having to do with suspected intrigues of Kurii."

"I understand," I said, "that unattended Kurii are not allowed in the city."

"Rumors persist as to such intrigues," he said. "Men, some of importance, are interested in them, even the Ubar."

"I know nothing of such things," I said.

"When the Kur was captured near Venna, he carried a box, a translator," said the figure. "Where is it now?"

"I have no idea," I said.

"I will tell you about that box," he said. "It was brought to Ar with the Kur. It was held in the Red Whip."

"I did not know that," I said.

"Yet you assisted in its theft," he said.

"Surely not," I said.

"Do not lie to me," he said. "I observed you in the Red Whip. You were in converse with a man whom we suspect may have been Rupert of Hochburg, the captain of a free company outlawed in Ar. Who else would dare such a thing?"

"What thing?" I said.

"The theft of a translator," he said.

"I know nothing of this," I said.

"You created a diversion which allowed the theft."

"The customer wished to leave the tavern unobserved," I said. "I was commanded to distract investigating guardsmen. I obeyed. I thought he would leave by means of the rear exit, but he left by means of the front entrance."

"Because," said the small man, "his men had forced the rear entrance and were ransacking the private rooms of Lycus of Venna. They seized the box and fled into the night."

"I know nothing of this," I said.

"Did you expect Lycus to post the matter on the public boards?" he asked.

"Surely some would have spoken of it," I said.

"And risk losing their tongues?" asked the small man.

"I thought my action had to do with the departure of a customer," I said. "I knew of nothing else."

"You were a manipulated fool," he said.

"It was a coincidence, was it not," I said, "that the guardsmen had entered the tavern?"

"Hardly," he said. "They were to do so on the pretext of searching for Rupert of Hochburg, but were to await my signal to detain anyone who, in my opinion, would seem to be your contact."

"Why would you wish such a person detained?" I said.

"To be interrogated," he said, "in matters pertaining to Kurii."

"Why would guardsmen act on your behest?" I asked.

"You need not know," he said.

In this I saw the hand of the Ubar, or someone high in Ar, perhaps in the city guard.

"You did not know then about the robbery in progress," I said.

"I thought at first you were merely a clumsy slave," he said.

"I am not clumsy," I said.

"But vain," he said.

"A little, perhaps," I said. What woman, or man, after all, is not?

"Do you know the value of that box?" he asked.

"No," I said.

"It is invaluable," he said.

"How so?" I asked.

"It gives us a means by which to communicate with Kurii, interrogate them, bargain with them, influence them, and so on."

"There must be other such boxes," I said.

"Doubtless," he said. "But where?"

"Possession of such a box," I said, "might allow parties to enleague Kurii in their schemes or be enleagued with Kurii in their schemes."

"It would make possible, at the least," he said, "the solution of troubling mysteries. With such a box, men might more easily learn what is afoot with our hirsute friends. Something is stirring amongst them. Even the Ubar is curious, and apprehensive."

"I know nothing of these matters," I said.

"Perhaps more than you realize," he said. "Some suspect that you are the key to much."

I did not even know where I was, in this narrow corridor, somewhere, near a bolted door.

"It is suspected," he said, "that the engineer of the translator's theft was Rupert of Hochburg, known to be somewhere at large in the city. Was it not he by whom you were enlisted, perhaps unwittingly, in the theft?"

"I knew nothing of the theft," I said. "I knew only that a customer wished to elude guardsmen. I do not think he anticipated the appearance of the guardsmen."

"He was Rupert of Hochburg, was he not?"

"I do not know," I said. I thought it best to lie. If the stranger in the tavern were concerned to warn me, and possibly assist or protect me, I wished to assist him in any way I could, whether he might be the seemingly notorious Rupert of Hochburg or not.

"Did you see any unusual scarring on his left wrist?" asked the small man.

"I did not notice," I said.

"Perhaps then," he said, "it was not Rupert of Hochburg."

"It must be late," I said. "May I withdraw? I do not understand why I am here, wherever it is."

"You are still in the Central Cylinder," he said.

"I can give you little satisfaction," I said. "I know nothing. I will be missed at the Purple Whip."

"You will not be missed at the Purple Whip," he said.

"I do not understand," I said, alarmed.

"Remain as you are," he said.

I heard a warning bar struck again; it seemed far off. I recalled that there was little danger provided one remained indoors.

"Surely you know you have been sought for months," he said.

"No," I said. "Why should that be?"

"I am not fully informed," he said. "But I know that deep plans have been laid, plans which are not to be placed in jeopardy, plans with which interference is not to be brooked."

"I am party to no such plans," I said.

"Events proceed," he said.

"This has to do with factions amongst beasts?" I said.

"Clearly," said he.

"I am unfamiliar with beasts," I said.

"Some know you," he said.

"How is it," I asked, "that you, a street entertainer, with a dancing beast, are a guest at a Ubar's supper?"

"A Ubar," he said, "has need of a thousand eyes and ears. I am an informant, one of great value where Kurii are concerned. I know much of them. I listen and secrets speak to me. I have often astonished the Ubar with surprising intelligence."

"Unavailable to other informants?" I asked.

"Yes," he said.

"And how is this possible?" I asked.

"It is possible," he said. "That is all you need to know."

"What of Master Lycus and the noble Gordon, administrator of Hammerfest?" I asked.

"Each has an interest in these matters," he said. "Lycus purchased the Kur caught near Venna and, until recently, possessed a translator. Gordon is muchly concerned with Kur sightings in the Vosk Basin."

"Perhaps they, and the Ubar himself, desire to ally themselves with Kurii," I said.

"Many are the paths to power," said the small man.

"But are such paths not blocked by Priest-Kings?" I asked.

"But what if there were no Priest-Kings?" he said.

"You are bold to speak in this fashion before a mere slave," I said.

"But what if there were no mere slave?" he said.

"I do not understand you," I said.

"I fear you do," he said, "and well."

I began to shake. I could hardly speak.

"Who do you think I am?" I asked.

"She whom I seek," he said.

"Whom do you seek?" I said.

"A barbarian slave whose name when free was Agnes Morrison Atherton," he said.

"I am not she," I said. "Let me go. I will say nothing."

"I think you are she," he said.

"No!" I said.

"You might be she," he said, "and that is enough. If you are not she, we merely continue our search."

"Suppose I am she," I said. "In any case, a murder would be impractical, even a disappearance. The situation is sensitive. If I am truly of some importance, questions would be asked. If some seek me to do away with me, I think others seek me to save me, if only temporarily and for their own purposes. Beware of them. If you are formidable, so, too, are they. An inquiry would be made. It would be much better for me to remain silent. Too, you are in no danger. I cannot reveal a secret I do not even possess."

"You would promise to remain silent?" he said.

"Yes, Master!" I said.

"Marvelous," he smiled. "I must take that up with my principal. I am sure my principal would be eager to risk a matter of great moment, one bearing on the future of two worlds, on the word of a slave."

"Two worlds?" I said.

"Two," he said.

"It would be difficult to conceal wounds or marks on my body," I said.

I heard the bar sound again.

Enemy tarnsmen must be abroad in the city.

"You were drunk," he said. "You were asleep in the vestibule. Many know this. You awakened. You staggered drunkenly, stumblingly, about. You somehow found your way out of the cylinder and onto a high bridge. Then, in your stupor, you fell to the pavement, far below."

"I will not go out onto a bridge," I said. "I have never been on one. They are narrow. They have no rails. I am terrified of such bridges. I will not go on them. You cannot make me do so!"

"You will be carried out, onto the bridge," he said, "and then, after a time, perhaps from its highest arching point, flung to the ground below."

"No!" I said, leaping up. "I may not be strong, but I am not weak. You might find me more than a match. You are not large. You are small for a grown man, far too small. I suspect that you will have scarcely the strength of a child, and I will be desperate. You will have no easy time of it, if you can manage it at all. And I will cling to you. We could fall together. Let me alone, and go away. I will not reveal your role in this business, whatever it might be. I will remain silent."

"It is not I who will carry you," he said. He then turned about. "Here, Bubu," he whispered.

From about a turn in the corridor emerged his pet Kur, crouched down, shoulders hunched, knuckles on the floor. Its eyes blazed in the light of the small *tharlarion*-oil lamp. Its lips drew back from its fangs. This grimace was weirdly like a smile.

I screamed and turned about, throwing back the bolts on the door. I flung it open, and stood in the doorway, frozen with fear.

I should not have looked down.

I heard the small man laugh.

I went to my hands and knees.

The air was fresh and cool. It was still dark, save for the light of two moons. The night, I supposed, was beautiful. Let others enjoy it, as they might. Towers were about, some with windows lit; too, I could see bridges, some closer, some far away, some of which had a mounted lamp at both ends.

I could not move.

I must move!

I crawled a yard onto the bridge.

I must not look down.

"How do you like the bridge, *kajira*?" asked the small man. "They are beautiful, are they not, the bridges? Goreans can run on them, though most are too wise to do so. Perhaps you will try to stand and do so. But beware that you do not fall. It is far to the ground. Bubu, incidentally, can manage them quite well. We sometimes entertain on the bridges. You should see him dance on the bridge. Good, you are now on your feet, if unsteadily. Walk a little farther on. Good. Put your arms out, if you wish. Excellent, that will help you to keep your balance. Keep going. If you wish to soon end this, remain where you are. Bubu can carry you farther. You will then be in no danger until he flings you from the bridge. If you wish to run, if you can do so, that is fine, too. Bubu does not mind. He can outrun even a fleet human. I think I will now return to the supper, for the final sweets and liqueurs."

The small man then stepped aside and let the Kur onto the bridge. He then entered the corridor and closed the door.

This left me alone on the bridge, with the Kur.

Again, from somewhere, sounded the warning bar. Raiders had been detected in the city. Doubtless local tarnsmen would soon drive them away.

I hoped not too soon.

I wondered if any raider would have the courage to ply his perilous trade in the vicinity of Ar's Central Cylinder itself.

I hoped so.

I was not free and robed, but might I not still be deemed worthy of a raider's capture rope?

The bar had told me that one or more raiders were about.

Let one see me!

Trying to keep to the absolute center of the arching bridge, I began to climb.

CHAPTER SIXTY

The Kur was in no hurry to close with me.

No sense of urgency drove him, as it did me.

I suspected it did not even know the meaning of the sounding of the bars.

I had the sense it enjoyed the sport, coming closer to me, until some yards away, and then letting me increase the distance between us. But each time now, it seemed he did not let me increase the distance as much as before. I was reminded of the towel game which the caged Kur had played with me, in which he, almost imperceptibly, would shorten his grip on the towel, bringing me closer and closer to the bars. I had wondered sometimes if the beast, in lunging toward me, was actually trying to kill me or merely terrify me, to make me more frightened and voluble. I did not know. Or had it been a test of sorts? If so, to what end? He had then asked his question, "Where is Ag-nas?" I had then, though safe, away from the bars, screamed and fled. Surely that would have been a surprising and anomalous reaction to the question unless, perhaps, it had been addressed to the actual Agnes, who, distraught and miserable, had suddenly feared herself discovered.

I looked wildly back.

It was perhaps twenty yards behind me.

It was not moving.

"Go back!" I cried. "Go back! Leave me alone!"

It took a sudden move forward, a yard or two, and stopped, abruptly. I almost lost my balance.

"It is playing," I thought. "It is enjoying itself. Then, when it wearies of the sport, it will attack, seize me, and finish the matter."

I doubted that anyone had heard me cry out.

I faced it, struggling for breath.

The door at the far end of the bridge was unlit.

Who would unbolt and open a door when the bars had sounded? Might it not be a raider's trick, utilizing a female's voice, to gain access to one of those keeplike towers?

If I should dart toward that far door, I was sure the beast would be upon me almost instantly. I did not think I could reach the door.

If I could reach the door, I would be trapped against it.

My most reasonable hope, slim as it was, was to be on the bridge, visible, exposed, and conspicuous, vulnerable, a tempting morsel to be noted by a cruising raider.

But if raiders were about, where were they?

I wondered if the bars had been sounded by mistake.

Perhaps there were no raiders?

Perhaps raiders had been driven away?

Perhaps no raider would have the courage, or be so foolish, as to be aflight over the Boulevard District, over central Ar, in the vicinity of the Central Cylinder itself. But then, I thought, why not? Would that not be an indubitable manifestation of courage, a splendid demonstration of contempt for a hated enemy? How better to challenge, upbraid, and insult a foe? Are not men, some men, particularly younger men, fresher, greener men, fond of such gestures? Do such acts not enliven feasts, not make good telling about campfires? My heart leaped when I saw, outlined against the White Moon, a soaring tarn. But it was far off. Indeed, it might not be a raider, at all, but the mount of one of the tarn guards of Ar. Even if a raider might come near enough to see me in the moonlight on the bridge, he might not be interested in risking a strike on a slave. Did not the 'game' prize free women? Are not slaves easily obtained? One can buy them in hundreds of markets, sometimes cheaply. Might not a slave be a Lure Girl, trying to entice a raider into danger? Indeed, might not a putative free woman be a slave in disguise, utilized by Masters to trap and serve a raider similarly? And would a raider look for a genuine free woman on a bridge in the Boulevard District? Commonly, I had heard, free women, daring for whatever reason to risk the tarnsman's capture loop, did so on lonelier bridges or roofs in remote areas, that being socially safer. A free woman suspected of such an act, courting the collar, so to speak, is likely to be denounced and ostracized by her scandalized peers. A safer way to attain such an end is to take dangerous journeys, stay in unsavory inns, hostels, or caravansaries, or, even, intrude boldly into a *paga* tavern, particularly unveiled, in which precincts, of course, free women are not permitted.

The beast approached more closely.

I was on the apex of the curve of the bridge.

It expected me, I was sure, to break and run toward the far door.

Certainly I would not wait for him.

I set myself to run toward the far door.

Almost at the same time a gigantic figure, a spread-winged tarn with helmeted rider, soared past, some fifteen feet over my head.

I was startled, and, I think, so too, was the beast. It looked wildly after the huge, soaring figure. I think it had anticipated nothing of the sort. Even now I do not think he considered the possibility that his quarry might be snatched from him. Who or what would come between a Kur and its prey?

"Come back!" I cried after the bird and rider. "See me! I am here! Come back! Come back, you unseeing, stupid urt!"

But scarcely had I denounced the winged apparition than two more tarns with riders swept past, with spear pennons and shields bearing the sign of Ar.

Clearly they were pursuing the other tarn and rider.

"Coward! Coward!" I called after the original figure. "Come back, you coward!"

It was at that moment that the capture rope snapped about my waist, and I was torn from the surface of the bridge, and found myself swinging wildly, dizzily amongst the towers and bridges of the city. As I spun about, dangling, I saw the Kur, behind and below me, on the bridge, seemingly flying away from me, reaching upward with extended paws. A moment later, fading away in the distance, I heard, faintly, a savage cry of frustration and rage.

CHAPTER SIXTY-ONE

I was sitting in a grove, my knees up and my back against a tarn saddle.

It was morning.

I suppose it is a simple strategy but it seems to be one which is often successful.

Some raiders appear to threaten, or attack, say, a caravan. Engaged by guards they seem to flee. If all goes as planned, the guards, exhilarated at their presumed success, and perhaps eager to distinguish themselves or secure trophies, pursue. This exposes the caravan, shortly thereafter, after a calculated interval, to attack by other raiders, generally coming in from an opposite direction. In my case, the first tarn and rider had drawn guards after him, and the second raider, his way then clear, his flight then uncontested, had made the strike.

"Are you comfortable?" he asked.

"As comfortable as I can be," I said, "bound hand and foot."

My ankles were bound together and my hands were tied behind my back.

"May I be clothed, Master?" I asked.

"We strip our captures," he said. "In that fashion, they know they are captures."

"Yes, Master," I said.

"Surely you do not object," he said. "As a slave, you must be accustomed to being naked, slave naked, before men."

"Yes, Master," I said.

"What is your name, pretty animal?" he asked.

"Mira," I said, "if it pleases Master."

"A good name for a slave," he said.

I thought so. It was a simple, lovely name and, like Lita, Tula, Lana, Dina, and such, it was relatively common. That was an advantage. It would be harder to trace a particular slave with that name. I had chosen it months ago, pretending that it had been put on me, choosing to conceal my identity, after my theft by raiders near Victoria Minor, the Lesser Victoria.

"Thank you, Master," I said.

"May I inquire your Home Stone?" I asked.

"No," he said.

"Forgive me," I said.

I moved a little in my bonds.

"Master regards me," I noted.

"She-sleen," he said.

"I trust not," I said.

"You are not a free woman," he said.

"Master is disappointed?" I said.

"Not really," he said.

I had been well used last night by him and his fellow.

"You are a *paga* slave," he said.

"Yes, Master," I said.

"Your tunic," he said, "in length, material, and cut, was unusual for a *paga* slave."

"The Purple Whip," I said, "is prestigious and expensive."

"I despise such establishments," he said.

"Many do," I said.

"And others prize them," he said.

"Some do," I said.

"Were you not ashamed to serve in such a place?"

"We do not choose where we will wear our collars," I said.

"Doubtless you thought yourself superior, serving in such a place."

"No, Master," I said.

"*Paga* taverns," he said, "are usually at street level."

"Some of us were serving at a private supper," I said.

"What were you doing on a bridge, at the third Ahn?"

"I was accidentally locked out when the alarm sounded," I said.

"I find that hard to believe," he said.

"How so?" I asked.

"When an alarm sounds," he said, "commonly free women go indoors and slaves are secured."

"What might Master find easier to believe?" I asked.

"You were trying to escape," he said.

"There is no escape for the female slave," I said. "We are tunicked, marked, and collared."

"Eluding a particular Master," he said.

"Are we not commonly caught and returned to our Masters?" I asked.

"Stolen property is not always returned to its rightful owner," he said. "That is seldom the point of stealing it. I suspect that you have been stolen before."

"Doubtless, as many slaves," I said.

"You were seeking the capture loop," he said. "You were alone at night, knowing that raiders were over the city, conspicuous on a high bridge, a location ideally suited to a tarn strike."

"Am I now to be whipped?" I said.

"It is early," he said. "It will not be dark for some Ahn. We have some wine, bread, and cheese. You will be unbound. You can arrange a small repast. Too, water must be carried for the tarns. There is a stream nearby."

"Are you not afraid I will run away?" I asked.

"We will shackle your ankles," he said. "You will scarcely be able to move. Then you will not be able to run away, will you?"

"No, Master," I said.

I was then unbound and shackled.

They lifted me to my feet. It was hard to stand.

"May I be given my tunic?" I asked.

"No," he said. "We like you the way you are."

"Yes, Master," I said.

Late in the afternoon, I was unshackled.

Soon I was on my back, writhing, under their least touch.

"She is lively," said one of them.

"More," I begged, "more!"

I was on Gor.

It had been done to me.

I was helpless as a woman. I could not help myself. Indeed, my slave fires had been aroused, shortly after my first collaring. I had been given no choice. Masters had seen to it. I now, as doubtless thousands of other Gorean slave girls, needed Masters and was helplessly, desperately, dependent on them.

"The tarns are saddled," said one of my captors.

The other snapped his fingers. "Here, Mira," he said. "I won the toss. You will be tied on your back over the saddle apron. In that way, if I wish, I can while away the time caressing you. Mira!"

I was kneeling down, my head to the grass.

"Please, please, Masters," I begged.

"There is time," said he who had not won the toss.

"Do you beg to please us again?" asked he who had won the toss.

"I am in a collar," I said.

"You love your collar, do you not?" asked he who had won the toss.

"Yes Master," I said. "I love my collar."

"Very well," said he who had won the toss.

"Thank you, Master," I whispered.

CHAPTER SIXTY-TWO

"There is the Sardar!" cried a man.

I heard others cry out, similarly.

I had been told that the Sardar mountains were black, and encircled by a high palisade.

Supposedly the Priest-Kings of Gor, the mysterious gods of this world, held their courts within those mountains. Do not many cultures populate their worlds with such fanciful creatures? It was said that not even tarns could fly over those mountains, but would become disoriented and uncontrollable. I found that unlikely, but it added an element of interest to the mythology of the area.

In Gorean, as I expect is clear, the expression 'Sardar' is used to refer either to the Priest-Kings or, by association, to the realm of the Priest-Kings, the Black Mountains, the meaning being determined by context.

The coffle was long.

I did not know how long.

We had been marched since early morning.

We were now stopped.

"It is the third day of the fair," said a man.

There are four great fairs on the known Gorean world, associated the solstices and equinoxes. The largest, and best-known, of these fairs is that of the Spring equinox, which date begins the Gorean year, En'Kara, the First Turning, or, more fully, En'Kara-Lar Torvis, the First Turning of Lar Torvis, or the 'Central Fire.' Similar expressions exist for the other equinox and the solstices, understood as the Second Turning, and the First and Second Resting of the Central Fire. The more common Gorean expression for the sun, though not when referring to time, is Tor-tu-Gor, or 'Light Upon the Home Stone.'

I was hooded.

Few things can make a woman feel more helpless and vulnerable, more prisoner, more slave, or more owned, than being hooded or blindfolded. We are not much aware of our environment, and of who or what is about. Where are we being taken? What is to be done with us? Are we being looked at? Will we be unexpectedly touched, or switched or lashed? We can be at the mercy even of children, who sometimes enjoy tormenting us, pelting us with pebbles and poking or striking us with sticks. Sometimes, to the amusement of Masters, we are put at their mercy, and they are used to control and herd us. At our least reluctance or demur we are subject to the lash.

I was naked.

This, too, adds to the sense of unimportance and vulnerability.

Does this not take note, too, of the chasm separating the free and the slave, the lofty citizen with his legal standing and Home Stone and the meaningless, vendible animal?

In the coffle, in my place, I was chained by the neck.

How could one be chained more effectively?

My hands were braceleted behind my back.

How helpless then was one, how defenseless, how slave, so much at the mercy of others!

How then could one fend away even the least of touches, had one the foolishness or the courage to attempt to do so?

Resistance is not permitted.

One is a slave.

I did not know how long the coffle was, as it had been added to, twice, just this morning. Smaller coffles were being linked, to form larger ones. This had begun yesterday.

I recalled that Luta had said that Spring was the optimum raiding season, as it was for the sales of *kajirae*.

I supposed that that was to be expected.

I was utterly helpless.

Gorean Masters know well how to keep slaves. What a delicious pleasure it is to be mastered, well mastered.

As I had soon learned, the two riders who had captured me in Ar, whose shields and accouterments bore no identificatory devices, were not entirely independent of others. There was originally a large group which divided itself into several smaller groups, and each smaller group was itself divided into groups of two to four riders. To simplify, the large group, call it 'A,' was divided into 'B' groups, each of which was divided into small 'C' groups, consisting of two to four riders. After the individuals of the 'C' group had tried their 'chain luck' here and there, for a time, they returned to their 'B'-group position, pooling their catches, and, eventually, the 'B' groups returned to the 'A' location, once again pooling their catches. In this way an enormous amount of territory can be hunted, and the 'A' camp, in particular, at the closure of the raiding, can provide the raiders with a large, relatively secure holding area.

Most of us had been landed by tarn four days ago, at the 'A' camp, often as many as ten in each basket, and had since been marched overland to this point.

"See the jewels on the slaver's necklace," said a man.

"Those *vulos* will market well," said a man.

"Even hooded, they will prove prizes," said a fellow.

"Fear not," said a man. "Only beauties are buckled in the hoods of Treve."

"Those of Treve know their business," said another.

"What is all this talk of Treve?" laughed a man. "I see no insignia, no pennons, no designs on shields, nothing to hint of Treve."

"How true," laughed another. "Yet that luscious, soft, well-curved loot speaks of the eye and skill of Treve."

Treve, I gathered, was some formidable polity.

"Be patient, *tastas*," called a man. "You will soon be hoisted on your sticks."

"Help! Help!" cried a woman's voice. "This is all a terrible mistake. I am a free woman! I am a free woman!"

I heard laughter.

"Where is your clothing?" called a man.

"Why are you collared?" asked a man.

"Is that not a brand on your thigh?" asked another.

"Please, please!" she screamed.

Then I started, for I heard the sudden sound of a whip, and a woman's cry of misery.

"On your knees, slave," said a man, "where you belong!"

"I am a free woman!" cried the voice. "I cannot be whipped!"

"Are you addressing me?" asked a male voice.

"Yes!" she cried.

"You did not say 'Master,'" he said.

"I cannot be whipped, Master!" she wailed.

"She said 'Master,'" said a fellow. "She must be a slave."

"No!" she cried.

"Whip her, whip her well," said a cold, unfeeling female voice, presumably that of a free woman. Slaves fear free women. Slaves depend on men, desperately, to protect them from free women.

A rain of leather began, accompanied by shrieks of pain, but was soon ended.

Then there was only the sobbing, whimpering voice of a beaten slave repeating, over and over, the word 'Masters.'

"She is learning her collar," said a fellow.

"I wish to see the exhibits," said the free woman.

"This way," said a man, presumably her escort or companion. "See the tapestries from Telnus, the rugs from Tor."

"Excellent," she said.

"What collars on this coffle?" asked a fellow.

"Those of Ho-Turik," said a man. The House of Ho-Turik was a major house with branches in several cities. It was expected that it would have a strong presence at the fair of En'Kara. It did its own buying and selling, but, often, too, on a commission basis, handled the stock of others, particularly when the principal preferred to remain anonymous.

"I sense the tarns of Treve," said a man.

"Guard your tongue, friend," said another. "Men of Ar may be about."

Whereas the great fairs are understood to be truce grounds, on which bloodshed is prohibited, tensions can exist. It is not unusual for the rivers of hatred to flow beneath the surface. Too, he who comes to the fairgrounds is likely, eventually, to wish to leave them.

"The pilgrimages are doing well this spring," said a man.

"I have heard so," said another.

Each Gorean, at least once in his life, is expected to undertake the pilgrimage to the Sardar Mountains. In this way, I gather, he acknowledges, reverences, honors, and celebrates the majesty and importance of the Priest-Kings, or Sardar. The Sardar Mountains, thus, are, in Gorean, the Mountains of the Priest-Kings. A common libation on Gor is to spill a drop of wine, and say 'Ta-Sardar-Gor,' '*to the Priest-Kings of Gor*.'

"Four caravans were raided," said a man, "two by the Black Slavers of Schendi."

"Will they sell here?" asked a man.

"Some," said another, "but they enjoy taking their white catches back to Schendi, even to the jungles of the Ua."

"Doubtless they soon learn to serve their black Masters well," said a man.

"What slave does not learn to serve her Master well?" said another.

"Four raids are not many," said a fellow.

"It is still early," said another.

How many women, I wondered, undertaking the pilgrimage to the Sardar Mountains, expect to see them from a sales block.

It is well, incidentally, for villages, towns, and cities organizing pilgrimages to the Sardar, to handle matters themselves, if possible, or make certain they deal only with reputable, trustworthy companies. Economy can be costly. More than once, a cheap pilgrimage has been delivered by design into the hands of slavers.

"The Holding Pens of Ho-Turik are ready," said a voice. "The barrels are filled with water. The gruel in the troughs needs only moistening."

"Are the posters up?" asked a voice.

"On their stakes, for days," he was told.

"The lads called the sales this morning, and will again tomorrow morning," said a man.

"When do the sales begin?" asked a man.

"The first batch tomorrow, at the tenth Ahn," said a fellow.

"They will continue until dark, and then under torches," said another man.

"When does the House of Ho-Turik set up its exhibition cages?" asked a man.

"By the ninth Ahn," said a man. "That gives prospective bidders a suitable opportunity to review the stock, neither too short nor too long."

"There are at least fourteen markets on the grounds," said a man.

"That of Ho-Turik is said to be one of the best," remarked a fellow.

"I hear he has brought in Alexis of Teletus as auctioneer," said a man.

"He is expensive," said one of the bystanders.

"He can anger and insult bidders," said a fellow.

"He can also squeeze every tarsk-bit out of a sale," said another.

"It will take days to complete the sales," observed one of the men in attendance."

"Most slaves are not even auctioned," said a man. "They are sold off slave shelves or from market tents."

"Will you attend the *kaissa* matches?" asked a man.

"Is Scormus of Ar playing?" asked someone.

"I think not," said a man.

"I think then I will not attend the matches," said the man.

"I prefer the song and poetry contests," said a gruff voice.

"The plays," said another.

"The city competitions," said another.

"I for the Pyrrhic dances," said another.

"*Tarsk* and *verr, vulos* and *bosk*, will be exhibited," said a man. "Prizes will be awarded."

"Leave that for the Ox on which the Home Stone rests," said another. This was a reference to the Peasantry.

"I am starved," said a man. "Who is for the Pavilion of Kal-Da?"

"I," said more than one, and it seemed, shortly thereafter, the group had disbanded.

I had heard that the pens were ready, but the coffle had not yet moved. It was then that I, hooded, chained, and helpless, heard it, not yards away, what I had heard before and did not care to hear again, the merrily piped tune to which, in the vicinity of the Metellan Menagerie, the Kur in its silly hat and costume, had danced.

"The cart for hoods has arrived," said a man, presumably an officer of the coffle guard.

"Unhood the slaves," said another, presumably he, too, an officer.

"No!" I thought. "Not now! Leave the hoods in place!"

In misery I realized that it all made sense. The small entertainer would have shrewdly conjectured what had occurred. I had been snatched from the Kur's grasp by a marauding tarnsman. It was unlikely, at this time of year, given buyers, prices, and such, that a captor's choice of where to deliver his prize would range indifferently amongst a thousand possible markets. Rather, the several markets of En'Kara, in the shadow of the Sardar, while not a necessary destination, would be a likely destination. If one, at this time of year, were searching for a randomly stolen slave, one whose origin and background would be of no interest to the captor, where better to begin that search than at the fair of En'Kara?

I winced against the blinding sunlight, freed from the darkness of the hood.

"What tarnsmen," I asked myself, "would risk taking their mounts over the high walls of Ar, intruding into one of the most dangerous skies on Gor? The ignorant, the naive, the foolish, surely, or proven, tried, inveterate enemies of Ar, enemies with insolent skill, proud of their daring, stirred by the gambles of war, confident of the strength, agility, and speed of their mounts, tarnsmen perhaps such as those of alluded-to Treve? And did it not seem to be an open secret that Treve would choose to reach the markets of En'Kara by means of the House of Ho-Turik, so great a house and, when appropriate, so discreet a house?"

I tried to turn about, but it was futile to do so, so I turned back.

The small man was looking at me, smiling.

Behind him, to the side, crouching down, on its leash, incongruous in the colorful costume and hat, was the Kur. It seemed to me somehow objectionable to impose such indignities on a natural, simple animal, or was it so natural and simple? It seemed larger than before, perhaps because it was closer to me.

It was looking at me.

I was sure it recognized me.

A *sleen* could have done the same.

It uttered a soft, almost inaudible growl.

I wondered if it, this particular beast, was intelligent, and, if so, to what extent. I was sure it could understand simple commands. That seemed clear from the bridge. On the other hand, I had no doubt but what the beast I had tended in the menagerie was not only intelligent, but rational. I suspected it could even be adept with a translator. Could the beast of the mountebank or street entertainer be similarly intelligent, even rational? I did not know. If so, might it not feel humiliated or resentful, even angry, to leap about and dance at the bidding of the small man, its master or owner, whose belonging or pet it was.

Hoods were being removed from the slaves. A red-haired slave girl was pushing a small cart back down the line, into which the guard was tossing the hoods.

The entertainer lifted his purse, on its belt strings, and shook it. It was heavy. I was sure it held enough coins, even if only of copper and silver, to buy several slaves.

He then approached me and, as he was then before me, I knelt down, the chain on my neck, immediately, without thought.

He bent down and put his thin lips to my ear.

"By tomorrow night," he whispered, "I will own you."

I did not respond.

"It will not do, of course," he whispered, pleasantly, "to kill you on the fairgrounds. Blood is not to be shed at the fair. That is not permitted. One must be careful of such things. But we will take you from the fair and soon find a secluded, appropriate spot. There Bubu, whom you so disappointed on the bridge, will tie you upside down from a tree limb, bite open your throat, and suck out your blood. Then he will dismember you, feed for a time, and leave what is left for the *jards* and *urts*."

"Ho, small noble Master," said a guard, "be pleased to deny yourself the pleasure of conversing with a pretty slave until you own her."

"Yes, Master," said the small entertainer. "Of course, Master. Forgive me, Master."

He then, with a tug on the Kur's leash, turned away, and left. The beast cast me a last glance and then meekly followed his small master.

"Get up," said the guard to me. "He has left."

I struggled to my feet. I was shaking. I could hardly stand.

"Are you all right?" he asked.

"Yes, Master," I said.

The coffle was apparently now ready to move, presumably to some pen where we would be relieved of the common chain and our slave bracelets.

Looking about I saw a tall fellow in the garb of a cloth worker. Something about him seemed familiar.

He turned away.

I assumed that I did not know him.

How could I know him?

But, moments later, I realized that I had seen him before, once near the Metellan Menagerie on Barr Street and once before the Purple Whip itself. But now he held no tray of pastries.

CHAPTER SIXTY-THREE

It is a simple tie. A long leather strap is used. With one end of the strap my hands had been tied behind me. Thc rest of the strap had then been lifted up behind me, wound three times about my throat and knotted in place. The remaining free end of the strap, some seven or eight feet in length, serves as a leash, but is also long enough to be used to strike me without compromising its utility as a leash. In this way, a single strap serves as a binding, tethering device, a leash, and, if one wishes, a disciplinary device.

"This is the tent," he said.

Through the canvas, I could see a light inside.

"Kneel here," he said, indicating a position some fifteen feet from the tent, near a heavy, half-sunken stone block in which an iron ring had been fixed. This was far more primitive than the slave rings which, in Gorean towns and cities, are often found in public places, usually attached to walls, or stanchions, providing a convenient means for securing slaves while masters go about their business. In many Gorean buildings, slaves, as other animals, are not allowed.

I knelt down where indicated, and he bent down and tied the long end of the strap about the ring in the stone.

I was thus held in place.

Only a few minutes before I had been lying down, naked, wrapped in a slave blanket, in one of the holding pens allotted to the House of Ho-Turik.

I was frightened and miserable.

I could not begin to sleep.

I had no way of preventing my purchase by the small entertainer, unless he were outbid, and I was sure that he had enough coins to purchase perhaps twenty or more slaves of my market value. I could not conceive of him being outbid. He had been frank with me, and had seemed to be pleased to be so. Once outside the fairgrounds I understood him to seek some secluded spot, and there surrender me to the mercies of his pet.

When the guards passed by, I would pretend to be asleep. I was supposed to be asleep, and I had no desire to be punished for not being so.

But then, later, one guard did not pass by.

Had he marked my position earlier?

I felt the nudge of his sandal on my right thigh.

The lamp he held was over me. It was half shuttered.

Its light dimly illuminated a circle of only three or four feet.

"Master?" I said.

"Mira?" he said.

"Yes, Master, if it pleases Master," I said, rising to my knees.

"You are to accompany me, and be silent," he said.

I had followed him to a small side gate of the pen. At the gate he had put me in the single-strap, back-tether-and-leash tie. He had then responded to the gateman's challenge with what must have been the evening's password. Shortly thereafter, in the light of the Yellow Moon, we were threading our way amongst several of the fair's permanent buildings, interspersed with dozens of tents.

We had come to a particular tent, little different from the others, save that a lamp was lit therein.

"Kneel here," he had said.

I was now on my knees, naked, bound, fastened by the leash to the ring fixed in the half-sunken stone block.

My keeper, he who had brought me to the place of this tent, went to the opening of the tent, but was stopped from entering by a hand placed against his chest. He then took a step backward. Thusly, prohibited from entry, he would be unaware of who, or what, might be within the tent. I then saw the fellow, a tall man, he who had denied the other entrance, place coins in his extended palm. Following this transaction, the man from the door of the tent approached me, and snapped a collar about my neck, and he who had received the payment, with a key, removed the collar of the House of Ho-Turik. In this way, there was not one moment in which I was not in at least one collar. Following his removal of the collar of the House of Ho-Turik from my neck, he who had brought me to the tent disappeared into the darkness, presumably to return to the pen or its vicinity.

In the light of the Yellow Moon, I recognized the tall man, he who had prevented the keeper from entering the tent, but I gave no indication of this. Nor did he manifest any sign that he knew me. I had seen him before, seemingly a street vendor, near the Metellan Menagerie when the small man had been performing with his beast. He had been one in the crowd. It was also he who, with his tray of pastries, had been near the entryway to the Purple Whip, when the small entertainer had been about, perhaps following me or watching me. Too, of course, I had seen him this morning, near the coffle, in the garb of a cloth worker, when the entertainer had spoken to me.

The tall man then removed a scarf from his wallet and wrapped it about my head, blindfolding me. He then undid the strap from the stone. He shook it once and I rose to my feet. Then, responding to a slight tug on the leash, I followed him to the tent. There, taking me by the upper right arm, and brushing aside the canvas, he guided me within.

I was on a carpet.

"Kneel," he said.

I knelt.

CHAPTER SIXTY-FOUR

I knelt on the carpet in the tent, blindfolded, naked and bound. I could now feel the leash between my breasts. It had been taken behind me, and under my body, and used to lash my ankles together. Thus, I could not rise.

No one spoke.

I sensed I was being looked at, even studied.

I assumed they were men. I hoped they were pleased with what they saw. One hopes that Masters will find one pleasing. Things proceed so much better then; things flow so much more easily then. I pulled a little at my wrists, bound together behind my back. It is flattering to be desired. We hope to be desired. We want to be desired. What woman does not want to be desired? Even women who hate men wish to be attractive to them. Does this not tell us something about women, about nature? The radical sexual dimorphism in the human species suggests not an identity of, but a complementarity of, the sexes. This complementarity is clear even in the case of the free man and the free woman, but it is indubitably, most pronounceably obvious, most unmistakably and most dramatically visible, in the dichotomy of Master and slave.

"You are Mira," said a voice.

"If it pleases, Master," I said. I thought that I had heard the voice before, but I could not place it.

"Consider yourself a stolen slave," said the voice.

"I am a stolen slave," I said. I was more than happy to be a purchased slave, a stolen slave, anything, to escape the waiting clutches of the small entertainer and his comically attired, dancing, but terrible, beast.

But before whom was I kneeling?

There was a pause.

"Should I not protect the tent from the outside?" asked a voice.

From his position in the tent, I knew the voice to be that of the tall man, he who had placed coins in the palm of the keeper, he who had locked a collar about my throat before the keeper had removed that of the House of Ho-Turik.

"Do so, Desmond," said the voice.

I sensed that he who had been addressed as Desmond had moved to the flaps of the tent's opening.

"Are you prepared to kill?" asked the voice.

"Of course," said he who had been addressed as Desmond. He then departed from the tent.

I was uneasy.

Clearly those of the tent were serious about their business, whatever it might be.

"You are a barbarian, are you not?" asked the voice.

"Yes, Master," I said. I wished to conceal as much about myself as possible, but, since my salc as a yellow-placard girl, I assumed my Earth origin could no longer be plausibly denied. Whoever those in the tent might be, they might well know at least that much about me.

"Your name when free, pretty Mira," said the voice, "was 'Ag-nes-mor-iss-on-ath-er-ton,' was it not?"

I stiffened with fear. "No, Master," I said. "But I have been confused with such a person, perhaps because I resemble her in some way."

"You are not she?" said the voice.

"No, Master," I said.

"You are sure?" he asked.

"Yes, Master." I said. It seemed to me that my best hope for survival on this world was to convince those who found me of such interest, for no reason I clearly understood, that I was not she whom they sought. I gathered that not even the small entertainer with his dancing beast was fully convinced of my identity. He was willing, however, clearly, to have me killed on the mere suspicion that I might be the person he sought. If I were not, as I recalled, he would merely continue his search.

"What was your name when free?" asked the voice.

I suppose that this question should have been anticipated, but I had not done so. Why was it not sufficient merely to deny that I was the person they sought?

I cast about wildly for a moment, panic-stricken, my mind blank, and then blurted out the first name that came to mind, certainly an obvious Earth name, even one familiar, that of a former fellow worker at the observatory and, later, a chain sister. "Eileen Bennett!" I said.

"It is fortunate," said the voice, "that you are not the barbarian sought."

"Yes, Master," I said, relieved.

"Shall I tell you about her?" he asked.

"Please do," I said.

"You have some sense of Kurii, do you not?" he asked.

"I have heard certain beasts so spoken of," I said.

"Some believe," he said, "they are interested in seizing and ruling Gor."

"I have heard something of that," I said.

"There are factions amongst them," he said. "Of greatest interest to us, at present, are two such factions, those of, as we speak of them, as we cannot pronounce their true names, Agamemnon and Pompilius. Most Kurii inhabit steel worlds, far away in space. Agamemnon was supplanted on one such world and exiled to Gor. His adherents are mainly in the vicinity of Ar. His command center, or headquarters, if you like, is located in what are sometimes called the Beast Caves. Pompilius reigns within, and remains within, one of the larger steel worlds. His adherents on Gor, on the other hand, are of late, from whatever region on Gor, withdrawing to the Vosk Basin, far from both Ar and the Sardar. This seems to us noteworthy. Further, it was learned by Kur spies planted within the forces of Pompilius on Gor that a barbarian woman sent routinely to Gor to be enslaved was, against all precedent, to be hunted down and killed. Why would that be? The faction of Agamemnon, with which I am, in my way, affiliated, is urgently concerned to locate and interrogate that woman. We suspect that she, somehow, is a key to the plans of Pompilius, the success of whose ambitions would seem to require the elimination of both the faction of Agamemnon and the masters and guardians of Gor, the Priest-Kings."

"Surely Priest-Kings do not exist," I said.

"Perhaps not," he said, "but there is clearly power and mystery within the palisade of the Sardar."

I would have given much for the removal of the blindfold. Tiny signals, sounds and stirrings, had suggested to me that there were more in the tent than myself and he who spoke to me.

"It is said," he said, "that Pompilius has the cunning of the *sleen* and ambitions which soar higher than the tarn can fly. It is also known that Kurii in the steel worlds have a serious technology, one capable of interplanetary space flight and powerful enough to shatter worlds, as seems to have been the case with their original, natural world. Now, suppose, as a game of thought, that Priest-Kings do exist, and defend Gor from Kurii, and were then eliminated.

Then, with the laws of the Priest-Kings no longer enforced, nothing would stand between Pompilius and the ownership of Gor, death rays against arrows, flames and poisons against knives and spears, other than perhaps some limited resources at the disposal of some other despised, hated faction of Kurii, say, that of Agamemnon."

"I know little of all this," I said.

"Then you are not the elusive slave in question," he said, "whose life we have striven to save, that she might shed light on these dark matters?"

"No, Master," I said.

"Very well," he said. "You will now be returned to the pen, that you may be purchased tomorrow by the highest bidder."

"Please, no, Master!" I cried. "Keep me! Give me away! Sell me elsewhere. Anything!"

"You fear to be purchased by Tiskias?" he asked.

"I know no Tiskias," I said.

"Perhaps you know his colleague, Bubu?" he said.

"Keep me, sell me, anything," I said. "Do not let me fall into such hands!"

"Why not?" he asked.

"Because I am she whom you seek!" I cried.

"You denied that," he said.

"I lied!"

"You are lying now," he said, "to save your life."

I could not rise or run, my ankles tied together with the leash drawn back and under my body.

"No," I said, "I am she! I match the description!"

"The description is vague," he said. "Many slaves might match the description."

"I am she!" I said. "I know little or nothing! But I am she!"

"I have seldom seen," he said, "a pretty slave more in need of a whipping."

"Forgive me, Master," I said. "Please do not whip me. It hurts, terribly."

"Remove the blindfold," he said.

So there was, now clearly, at least one more person in the tent.

The scarf, the blindfold, removed, I shut my eyes for a moment against the light of the tiny tent lamp. Then, eyes half shut, for a moment, I opened them.

"Yes," said he who had spoken with me.

It was he whom I now recognized as short-bearded Rupert of Hochburg, the captain of a free company, a man outlawed in Ar. I had noticed him when I was locked in the suspended slave cage outside the Red Whip. Later, in the tavern, he had spoken with me. After that, commanded, I had created a diversion during which time he had taken a swift, surreptitious exit from the premises.

The person who had, from behind, removed my blindfold, put it in his belt.

"So," he said, "your name, when free, was 'Eileen Bennett.' I have a slave, one who has learned well how to crawl about my feet, who would be interested in hearing that."

"Forgive me, Master," I said.

Maxwell Holt, or Holt of Ar, then resumed his position, sitting down, cross-legged, beside Rupert of Hochburg.

Beside him, on his left, was a small, rectangular box, some eight inches by six inches, by six inches, on the front of which were certain switches and knobs. I had no doubt that it was the translator which had originally been carried by the Kur in the vicinity of Venna, had been purchased by Lycus of Venna, and had later been stolen from his tavern.

The third person in the tent was not known to me. His robes were substantially yellow, suggesting the habiliments of the Builders, one of the five high castes of Gor. The other allegedly high castes are the White Caste, that of the Initiates; the Blue Caste, that of the Scribes; the Green Caste, that of the Physicians; and the Red Caste, that of the Warriors. Certain aspects of the caste system seem to be in dispute, or at least are devoid of universal agreement. One such unclear matter involves whether or not the White and Yellow Caste, or the White and Gold Caste, that of the Merchants, is or is not a high caste. Another has to do with whether or not the slavers is an independent caste or a subcaste of the Merchants.

"I have been apprised, slave," said Rupert, "by my friend, Holt of Ar, who once rode with my company, of certain matters."

I was silent.

"It seems that in an alcove of the *paga* tavern, the Red Whip, you were interviewed."

"If it may be called that," I said.

"You spoke, as I understand it," he said, "of various things, in particular, of two spherical objects, possibly artificial, emerging from amongst space debris, objects the existence of which, for some reason, was to be kept secret. That I think is important. You had also gathered, or surmised, as I understand it, that these objects might have some bearing on, or figure in, some plan or strategy the outcome of which might affect the fate of one or more worlds. You can, accordingly, understand our interest in this matter. Further, the fact that the faction of Pompilius wished to ensure the secrecy of this business by eliminating a possible informant, a mere slave, adds to the fear that something momentous is afoot."

"I know little more than I said, or has been reported to you," I said.

The man in the largely yellow habiliments then spoke. "The sphericity of the two objects informs us that the objects in question are artificial, the result of intelligent engineering. Their noted location also speaks of the work of Kurii. Normally Kurii conceal their habitats. That suggests the objects are not habitats." He then regarded me. "Given the calculations and measurements with which you were familiar, I speculate that you deemed the objects to be hollow, or largely so, and quite possibly under intelligent control."

"Yes, Master," I said.

"The two objects moved together," he said.

"Seemingly so," I said.

"We may then infer that both objects are part of a single plan or scheme. Did you, in any inquiries in which you might have engaged, or in any documents to which you had access, establish or detect a direction, trajectory, or destination for the two objects of interest?"

"No, Master," I said.

"Where are the objects now?"

"I have no idea," I said.

"You have designed instruments," said Rupert. "Can you not examine the sky and seek them?"

"The sky is large, the sky is wide," he said. "I doubt that the objects are large enough to trouble the orbits of planets."

"I am uneasy, noble Temicus," said Rupert.

"I, too, my friend," said the fellow largely in yellow.

"I fear matters may be underway," said Rupert. "The quarrel may be in the guide, the arrow at the string, the repast prepared, the racing *tharlarion* poised at the ribbon."

"Perhaps," said Holt of Ar, "the spherical objects have withdrawn into the remote debris."

"Unlikely," said Temicus, the fellow largely in yellow.

"Surely the Priest-Kings must be advised of these things," said Holt of Ar.

"And how will one do that?" asked Temicus.

"Who amongst us has quaffed *paga* with a Priest-King?" asked Rupert.

"Some would petition the holy caste, the pure caste, the pale caste, the White Caste," said Holt, bitterly. "Do they not have the ear of Priest-Kings? Are they not in favor with Priest-Kings? Can they not, for a coin, intercede on behalf of a suppliant, that the maiden's heart be swayed, that victory will be his in a lottery, that his foe will stumble and the marked stones will fall propitiously?"

"Little is to be expected," said Rupert, "of those who purify themselves with mathematics, and eschew women and beans."

"Who knows the ways of Priest-Kings, let alone their will?" asked

Temicus. "Who has heard the voice of a Priest-King? Who has seen his footprint? Who has touched his cloak?"

"Some," said Rupert, "think there is nothing within the palisade but stones and cold."

"I fear they may be right," said Temicus.

"Even if Priest-Kings once existed," said Holt, "they may no longer do so. They might have perished, by disease or internal war, leaving certain works behind them, functioning but unsupervised."

"That is possible," said Rupert.

"It seems," said Holt, "we know much and nothing. We do not even understand the purport, if any, of what we know. We are lost. We are helpless. Something momentous is amongst us, something we do not understand. We have stumbled upon a secret, a secret we cannot unravel, a secret to protect which some are prepared to kill."

"It is interesting," said Rupert, "that there were two spheres and not one, or, say, three or more. Why two?"

"A thousand reasons," said Temicus. "Who knows?"

"What is the point of the spheres?" asked Rupert.

"There are several possibilities," said Temicus. "Without a precise investigation being made, they might easily be confused, almost indefinitely, with natural objects. Thus they might constitute a secret or camouflaged delivery system intent on bringing Gorean Kurii supplies, even weapons. They might even have in mind facilitating the establishment of a new Kur enclave on Gor, say, in the Vosk basin where sightings of Kurii have much increased in the past months."

"Particularly if the Kurii are of the faction of Pompilius," said Holt.

"More likely," said Rupert, "their role would be ancillary to Kur ambitions on Gor, say, serving as reconnaissance spheres, or communication posts, hopefully beyond the range of the laws of Priest-Kings."

"Perhaps we should be more generous or benign in our speculations," said Temicus. "Perhaps the spheres are experimental laboratories conducting research on zero-gravity phenomena, or observatories scanning the night for new worlds. Some Kurii, not unlike some humans, must tend to be curious and seek truths not so much for their political and economic coin as for the joys of discovery, the ecstasy of knowing, the rapture of learning."

"Yes," said Rupert, "as the *sleen* delightedly sniffs flowers and the *larl* thrills to sunsets."

Suddenly something encountered long ago occurred to me, something to which, at the time, I had given little thought or attention, something which had seemed pointless, incidental, and meaningless in the context wherein I had found it, something which I had forgotten about for months and recalled only now, while the men were speculating about the possible significance of the two spheres. It was a single, neat, lightly penciled word in the margin of a table of calculations, one amongst those fateful documents into which I innocently, wisely or not, without permission or authorization, had dared look. It was so unimportant to me, that I had not even copied it into my own notes.

"*Tunguska!*" I cried.

The men looked at me, startled.

"Forgive me, Masters," I said, frightened. "May I speak?"

"Serious matters are afoot, slave," said Temicus, sternly.

"Forgive me, Masters," I said. "May I speak? I beg to speak!"

"It is seldom," said Holt, "that slaves so lightly risk the lash."

"Who owns this slave?" asked Temicus, annoyed.

"Her collar says Bazi Imports," said Rupert. "I will assume responsibility for her leash."

"It seems, dear colleagues," said Holt, "that we are at an impasse. Thus, though she is a mere slave, no more than a purchasable animal, let us let her speak. If we are not satisfied, it is easy enough to put her under the leather, and well."

"You may speak," said Rupert.

"Do Goreans know aught of Tunguska?" I asked.

"No," said Rupert.

"I do not know the word," said Temicus.

"Who is Tunguska?" asked Holt. "What is his Home Stone?"

"It is not the name of a person," I said.

"It is a barbarian thing?" asked Rupert.

"Yes, Master," I said.

"Speak," said Rupert.

"Even on my original world, Terra, statistically, few know of Tunguska, or what is sometimes called the Tunguska Happening or Event," I said. "It was a meteorological phenomenon of astounding dimensions. I heard of it only obliquely, as an oddity. Master Holt of Ar has a slave, Xanthe, who may be better informed."

That seemed likely to me, as the former Eileen Bennett had been a reference librarian, and, moreover, one in an observatory.

"The happening occurred in early Summer of the year one thousand, nine hundred, and eight in Earth chronology, in a remote, heavily forested area in Earth's northern hemisphere. There was a blue light in the sky, almost as bright as Tor-tu-Gor, and then it seemed the sky grew red and was afire, and then some force struck down, and, for better than a thousand *pasangs* in every direction, trees were felled, blasted in a radial pattern to the ground save for those left standing at the center but stripped of branches and leaves."

"The force struck vertically," said Temicus.

"What was the cause of this phenomenon?" asked Rupert.

"There are many theories," I said. "One commonly favored is the bursting of a stony body succumbing to heat and pressure, thus leaving no crater."

"Do you know more of this?" asked Temicus.

"I am not even sure of all that I have said," I said. "I know little of the matter. I heard of it long ago. I may even be misremembering things. I do recall that the occurrence was denominated the largest, fiercest impact event in historical times on Earth."

"How can it be an impact event," asked Holt, "if there is no crater?"

"Much is obscure," I said.

"Released energy," said Temicus, "a bursting force, a shock wave."

"The word 'Tunguska,'" said Rupert, "appeared in the documents which you, perhaps unwisely, perused?"

"Yes, Master," I said, "only once as far as I know, and without emphasis or integration in the text. I think the name was derived from a river in the vicinity."

"Perhaps," said Rupert, "Kurii were involved in the event, testing a weapon, exploring possibilities."

"I would suppose not," I said.

"Kurii are familiar with both Terra and Gor," said Holt.

"And what nature might do, might not technology imitate, or even modify, say, in range and penetration?" mused Temicus.

"How large was the stony body conjectured in the Tunguska incident?" asked Rupert.

"Opinions differ," I said. "But not that large. Perhaps a hundred and eighty feet or so in diameter."

"And the two artificial bodies?" asked Rupert.

"Considerably larger," I said.

"One," said Temicus, "for the Sardar, and the other for the Beast Caves, headquarters of the adherents of Agamemnon."

"Consider the range," said Holt. "A blow to the Beast Caves must engulf and destroy Ar, as well. My Home Stone is that of Ar!"

"I think," said Rupert, shuddering, "we have laid the secret bare."

"And have thereby much endangered our lives," said Temicus.

"Two strokes," said Rupert. "Hammers from the clouds. Bludgeons from the sky."

"Unanticipated," said Temicus.

"Again," said Holt, "I submit that Priest-Kings must be warned."

"And who," asked Temicus, "will do so, and how, again, might it be done?"

"It can be death to penetrate the Sardar," said Rupert.

"Priest Kings may not exist," said Temicus.

"Something exists," said Rupert.

"The Initiates are of no help," said Holt. "They are pretentious, pompous, lying, hypocritical, useless frauds."

"This may all be nonsense," said Temicus, "a story invented by a conniving slave seeking attention, desiring to avoid the lash."

"No, Masters!" I exclaimed.

"No," said Rupert. "She has tried to be helpful. It will not be necessary to beat her. Certainly not now, and for this."

I sank back in my bonds, gratefully.

"But later perhaps," said Rupert, "lest she begin to think of herself as important."

"What has she done," asked Temicus, "other than present us with an insoluble, tragic dilemma? Either we continue to bask in ignorance or recognize and bemoan our helplessness."

"Dear noble Temicus," said Rupert, "do not rush to embrace defeat. Taking comfort in resignation is no substitute for the sweat and agony of battle, its fears and glories, even a battle one knows one will lose."

"Speak for your own caste," smiled Temicus. "There are ways other than those of the scarlet cloak."

"I know of one to whom the Priest-Kings, if they exist, would listen," said Rupert, "one who does not shudder before their laws, one who is the master of forbidden devices, one who would not fear to use them, if only to call attention to their existence."

"Agamemnon," said Holt.

"I have dealt with his agent," said Rupert.

"Beware of Kurii," said Temicus.

"We do not know the power of the artificial worlds," said Holt. "Might they not tilt the axis of Gor, rendering it uninhabitable, or even dislodge Gor from its orbit?"

"They would not do so intentionally," said Rupert. "The adherents of Pompilius want merely the Priest-Kings and their Kur foes gone, thereby putting Gor at their uncontested mercy. They do not wish to damage or destroy the game's desiderated prize."

"A single move may lead to a multitude of unforeseen continuations," said Temicus. "One loosens a stone. Who knows where it might roll? One kindles a fire. Who knows how and where it might burn?"

"There are doubtless many adherents of Pompilius on Gor," said Holt. "Surely he would not choose to risk them."

"Commanders differ," said Rupert, "in the assessment of acceptable losses."

"But he would not wish to risk the prize itself," said Holt.

"Not knowingly," said Rupert.

"Let us withdraw," said Temicus. "We must eschew knowledge of this secret. It is not wise to know too much."

"It is less wise to know too little," said Rupert.

"Let the Sardar and the Beast Caves, and Ar, go," said Temicus.

"My Home Stone is of Ar," said Holt.

"This war is not ours," said Temicus.

"The next one would be," said Rupert.

"This very night," said Holt, "let us begin the journey to the Beast Caves."

"For what purpose?" asked Temicus. "They are far. The journey would be long, arduous, and contested. Even if we could reach them, we would have no way of accessing them. And, if we could access them, we would have no way to make our mission known."

"There, dear Temicus," said Rupert, "you are mistaken. Behold. Next to our colleague, the noble Holt of Ar, you see a small, strange box. The use of such a box, perhaps the same box, for all I know, was communicated to me by an adherent of Agamemnon months ago, near Venna. By its means, we can speak to Kurii and Kurii to us."

"I do not know how to make the box do this," said Holt.

"We can test its workings," said Rupert.

"How did you come by this box?" asked Temicus.

"I have it on loan, so to speak, from Lycus of Venna," said Rupert.

"Lycus the Fat?" said Temicus.

"Some know him so," said Rupert.

"Is he of the faction of Pompilius or that of Agamemnon?" asked Temicus.

"I did not ask," said Rupert.

I recalled the private supper in the Central Cylinder. At that supper, the Ubar himself, Marlenus of Ar, had presided. The small entertainer had been in attendance. So, too, interestingly, had been Gordon, the Administrator of Hammerfest, an Oligarch of the Vosk, a man well known in, and powerful in, the Basin of the mighty Vosk. I also knew that he was secretly Einar, the Sleen of the Vosk, a notorious river pirate. Lycus of Venna, proprietor of the Purple Whip, had also been present. Two others were Hermanus, first sword in the Taurentian Guard, which is the Palace Guard, and Marcus Rufus, who was First Captain of the City Guard of Ar. Three or four others I did not know, but supposed them to be individuals of importance. I suspected that the meeting, if only implicitly, had had much to do with Kurii and the politics of Ar.

"The artificial worlds may even now be on their way to their targets," said Holt.

"The gradual withdrawal of adherents of Pompilius into the Vosk Basin suggests that," said Rupert. "But we do not know."

"Am I to gather," said Temicus, "that you are thinking seriously of attempting to intervene in matters so hazardous and so far beyond your ken?"

"We are giving it some thought," said Rupert.

"I take it that you are aware that Kurii, of whatever faction, are extremely dangerous."

"I do not contest that," said Rupert.

"They are extremely territorial," said Temicus. "In essaying the Beast Caves, I fear you are as likely to be attacked and killed by adherents of Agamemnon as by those of Pompilius."

"It is a rare enterprise of moment which does not entail risk," said Rupert.

"Are all members of the Scarlet Caste mad?" asked Temicus.

"Not all," said Rupert.

"You know, of course," said Temicus, "if you are truly intent on embarking on this sorry, mad scheme, the first thing you should do is return the slave to the pen, so that she may be in the exhibition cage by noon. Tiskias will doubtless check the cage. Seeing her in the cage, he will be content to wait until evening to buy her. That will give you a start of several Ahn."

I looked wildly, plaintively, to Master Rupert.

"That is what we should do, of course," said Rupert, "but it is not what we will do."

"I did not think so," said Temicus.

"I find her flanks of interest," said Master Rupert.

"I feared so," said Temicus.

"I have a better," said Holt.

"It is true," said Temicus, wearily. "Slaves are to be exploited and put to slave use, not slain."

"I knew you would see it so," said Rupert. He then rose up, and called, softly, "Desmond."

The flaps of the tent parted, and Desmond entered.

"How were things outside?" asked Rupert.

"Quiet, Captain," said Desmond. "But it is near dawn."

"We are leaving," said Rupert. "Unbind the slave, and fetch her a tunic, one of Bazi Imports."

"I had one ready," said Desmond, reaching into his wallet.

"It is, I trust," said Rupert, "quite short."

"Certainly," said Desmond.

"She is a pretty animal," said Rupert. "I want her legs well displayed."

"Of course," said Desmond.

Tears had begun to run down my cheeks. "Thank you, Master," I said, "for my life, and clothing."

"For even the tunic of a slave?" he asked.

"Yes Master," I said. "Yes, Master!"

"Why?" he asked.

"Because I am a slave, Master," I said. "I am a slave!"

Rupert turned to Temicus. "We are leaving," he said.

"I, too," said Temicus.

"How so?" asked Rupert.

"Surely," he said, "you do not think that madness is confined to those of the Scarlet Caste."

"You dare mix in the matters of worlds?" asked Master Rupert.

"I am vain," said Master Temicus. "I find it pleasant to find myself of importance. Besides, someone must look after you."

Desmond, meanwhile, had begun to relieve me of my bonds.

CHAPTER SIXTY-FIVE

There were six in our party, four persons and two animals. One of these persons was short-bearded Rupert of Hochburg, the captain of an outlawed free company, now disbanded, who stirred me profoundly in the way a slave cannot help being stirred, but who paid me little attention other than to keep me well aware that I was in a collar; he knew I was a slave and he treated me as such; his company, it seemed, as many others, had fallen on hard times. In this was largely seen the gold and hand of Marlenus of Ar, who resented, and perhaps feared, the existence of free companies. How can one control them? How can one threaten their walls when they have no walls? They have no Home Stone to seize. They can move about. Where will they next appear, and with what prospects in mind? In any event, many Ubars and Administrators, particularly minor ones, proved unwilling to risk incurring the displeasure of the Ubar of Ar by having recourse to mercenary companies. Thus, in their frequent squabbles and small wars they were tending to depend, for the most part at least, on their own forces, such as they might be. No longer might the tide of battle be turned from the outside. One supposes that there is something to be said for that, but it bodes ill for free companies. On an individual basis, of course, mercenaries would continue to seek employment. Certainly, catapult engineers and authorities on fortification and siege works continued to be in demand. A second person in our party was Holt of Ar, whom I had known as Maxwell Holt in the observatory, and who had apparently once ridden in Rupert of Hochburg's company. A third person was Temicus of Argentum, a Builder, known to Rupert, met in Venna, at the Yellow Whip, and perhaps enlisted there. The fourth person was Desmond of Hochburg, who had been lieutenant to Rupert in the latter's former company. The two animals were Xanthe, the former Eileen Bennett, and myself, Mira, the former Agnes Morrison Atherton.

It was evening.

The men, other than Desmond, who was elsewhere, sat cross-legged about the remains of what had been a small, banked fire.

Xanthe was curled up near Maxwell Holt, Holt of Ar, who occasionally, idly, touched her hair.

I was kneeling to the side, neglected, in the darkness. Neither Xanthe nor myself was bound, chained, or tethered. We could easily, in the days past, have sped away. But neither of us had done so. I do not think we even considered it. Were the men so sure of us? Why should they be so sure of us?

"I have little doubt," said Temicus, "the free companies will blossom again."

"Not if Marlenus frowns upon them," said Holt.

"What if the free companies, in their hundreds, should join against Ar?" asked Temicus. "Such a league might well threaten Ar."

"Mercenaries," said Rupert, "fight for pay, not for glory, not for Home Stones. Where pay is scarce, so, too, will be free companies."

"Still," insisted Temicus.

"Enleaguing is not the way of free companies," said Holt.

"It could become so," said Temicus. "Then let Ar fear."

"It is expensive to field a free company," said Rupert. "What mercenary will come to a table lacking the bread of gold?"

"One hoping to own cities where such bread is baked," said Temicus.

"There is no leader," said Rupert. "No one for whom the tarn feather could be carried from camp to camp."

"I know one for whom that might be done," said Temicus.

"It is not the way of free companies," said Holt.

"An end achieved they could disperse later," said Temicus.

"One who has ridden the first tarn," said Rupert, "will seldom be content to ride the second."

"Then," said Temicus, "let chaos and fragmentation rule."

"More likely," said Rupert, "you would have a sky ruled by Ar."

"I prefer fragmentation and chaos," said Temicus.

"Marlenus is not Ar and Ar is not Marlenus," said Holt. "My Home Stone is that of Ar, not that of Marlenus. Besides, Ar has less than two thousand tarnsmen."

"Let us not concern ourselves with the fate of free companies, or Ar," said Rupert. "I suspect that our business is elsewhere, and may concern the fate of worlds."

"I hear a sound," said Holt.

"I hear nothing," said Temicus.

It was quiet and then there were two clicks from the darkness, and then one.

"Are knives sheathed?" asked a voice.

"For you it is so," said Rupert. "What have you learned from Rarir?"

Tall Desmond emerged from between the trees, and took his place, cross-legged, with the men.

Gorean men commonly sit cross-legged, and Gorean women, both free and slave, kneel. The free woman, of course, kneels fully clothed, her knees together. Some Gorean free women, I had heard, called Panther Girls, sit cross-legged. These commonly move in small, free-roving bands in remote, uninhabited areas.

"My sojourn in Rarir," said Desmond, "was productive. The great fair is coming to a close, and the roads are rich with memories and pilgrims, with peddlers and tradesmen. I met several men and some women from Rarir itself, some with exhibited animals, woven goods, and produce."

"Does the Peace of the Fair hold on the roads?" asked Holt.

"Seemingly, for the most part," said Desmond.

"I take it," said Rupert, "you delved for information discreetly, while ostensibly being concerned with matters frivolous and topical."

"In the course of seeming banter and reminiscence," said Desmond, "remarking on the pleasures and sights of the fair, I remarked on the oddity of an entertainer and his dancing beast."

"I would have given much," said Temicus, "to have witnessed the consternation and horror of Tiskias visiting the exhibition cage and failing to find therein a particular slave of interest."

"Reality is often indifferent or careless where plans are concerned," said Holt, "even those most seemingly assured and most carefully made."

"I speculate," said Temicus, "that Tiskias is entitled to a measure of uneasiness, having failed a principal such as Pompilius."

"Several of the men and women of Rarir," said Desmond, "recalled the entertainer and his beast, Bubu. He had been much about, gathering in coin, and then, one morning, suddenly, he was seen no more."

"I think we know the morning," said Temicus.

"The present whereabouts of Tiskias and his Kur pet," said Rupert, "are unknown?"

"Yes," said Desmond. "After the 'fateful morning,' no one recalls seeing him at the fair, or at the gates, or on the roads."

"He took flight," said Holt of Ar.

"Unlikely," said Rupert. "He could be tracked down and killed."

"There is more," said Desmond. "Gangs of men were hired, supposedly by the Board of the Fair, to watch the Sardar palisade in the vicinity of the Fair, to report any entry or attempted entry into the Sardar Mountains."

"That is not the doing of the Board of the Fair," said Holt of Ar.

"Who but the despairing and suicidal would attempt such an entry?" asked Temicus.

"The hiring of such men," said Holt, "even for a brief time, tells us that the resources at the disposal of Tiskias are considerable."

"I gather," said Temicus, "as Desmond is silent on the matter, that Tiskias did not hire fellows to search for the missing slave."

"No," said Desmond.

"Why not?" asked Temicus.

"Doing so," said Rupert, "would be unwise. The missing slave was not his. Instigating such a search would raise questions. Why should an entertainer be interested in finding a slave who does not even belong to him? A secret is best kept when it is not known to exist."

"How, friend Rupert, do you assess the situation?" asked Temicus.

"Let us consider the matter from the point of view of our friend, Tiskias," said Rupert. "He may well know nothing of the two spheres. Also, he will most likely assume that the sought slave does not understand the full implications of what she knows. But perhaps she knows enough to prove dangerous. He knows she is missing from the pen of Ho-Turik, but probably little else. He cannot be sure that she is other than a stolen slave. Thus, her theft might have nothing to do with matters of moment. In particular, he may not know of us, and our part in her disappearance. Perhaps she is in Brundisium or the Farther Islands by now."

"He knows of the theft of the translator," said Holt.

"Which might have nothing to do with larger matters," suggested Rupert.

"We will continue, will we not, as hitherto?" asked Temicus, "watching the sky for tarns, traveling overland, avoiding frequented roads?"

"Yes," said Rupert.

"He, or his principal," said Temicus, "may anticipate our attempt to make contact with the faction of Agamemnon."

"The Beast Caves," said Holt.

"As unlikely as that possibility might be, I am sure it has not been overlooked," said Rupert.

Temicus laughed.

"What is wrong?" asked Holt.

"Gor is wide," said Temicus, "and much of it has not been explored. We have a world in which to hide, and we intend to seek the Beast Caves."

"We will approach Ar and the Beast Caves surreptitiously, indirectly," said Rupert. "We will not march in on the Viktel Aria with pennons flying, drums beating, and trumpets blaring."

"Good," said Temicus. "You have set my mind at ease."

"Courage is measured by what one does," said Rupert, "not by what one feels."

"I am glad to hear it," said Temicus.

The men then decided to retire. Master Holt was given the first watch. I do not think that this pleased Xanthe.

CHAPTER SIXTY-SIX

I summoned the courage to kneel before him, in the grass.

"Master," I asked, "may I speak?" Speech is a joy to a woman. How precious is the opportunity to speak! How frustrating it is to wish to speak and be denied permission to do so. Few things so remind her of her bondage as the curb on her speech which may be imposed by the free.

"Yes," said Rupert of Hochburg.

"I understand myself to be a stolen slave," I said. I did know, of course, that the keeper on the En'Kara fairgrounds had received some coins for my delivery to the tent of Rupert of Hochburg. And I knew that my collar and tunic were those of Bazi Imports.

"That is correct," he said. "You are a stolen slave. I do hold your leash, of course. It is appropriate that someone should do so."

That expression, the 'leash expression,' denoted that he was my understood keeper.

"To whom do I belong?" I asked.

"You recognize, of course," he said, "that you are clearly and obviously, and indisputably, a slave?"

"Yes, Master," I said. There was no doubt about that, legal or practical.

Did he think that I, as a barbarian, might be ignorant of that?

Did I not know what I was?

"At the moment then," he said, "you are an unclaimed slave."

"I am not sure I understand that status," I said.

"You can be claimed," he said, "by any free person."

"By a stranger, a passer-by, a child?" I asked.

"Yes," he said.

"I," I said, "the former Agnes Morrison Atherton of Terra, would be your slave."

"What?" he asked.

"I, the former Agnes Morrison Atherton of Terra, now a slave girl on Gor, beg to be your slave."

"I wager," he said, "you did not, when a fine, lofty, free woman on Terra, anticipate that you would one day find yourself a branded, collared slave girl on Gor, begging a man to own you."

"No, Master," I said. What joy it gave me to address him as 'Master!' Had I not, even on Earth, when free, dreamed of a Master, such a Master?

"Why me?" he asked.

"Must I respond?" I asked.

"No," he said.

How could I tell him that he had so deeply stirred me, even in the tent of Philip, at a supposed camp connected with Bazi Imports, so long ago? I had never forgotten him. How I had thrilled in his bonds at the Red Whip! How eager I was to obey him! Then I had been brought naked, bound, leashed, and blindfolded to his camp at the Fair! Had he not noted me about him, putting myself subtly so often in his vicinity. There are many ways a woman can beg a man for a collar. Had he not seen the loose, simple bondage knot I had tied in my hair twice in the last few days?

He looked down on me. I was small, kneeling before him.

I looked up, tearfully.

"Claim me," I begged. "Please claim me! I beg to be claimed!"

He reached down, and took my hair in his left hand, lifting my head. He then cuffed me thrice, first with the palm of his right hand, and then with the back of his right hand, and then, again, with the palm of his right hand.

There was no doubt that the blows were administered to a slave.

I tasted blood about my lips.

He then released me. "You are mine," he said.

I threw myself to my belly before him and covered his feet gratefully with kisses.

"You seem to have been too frequently in my vicinity," he observed, stepping back.

I could not deny that.

One does one's best in such matters.

"Perhaps you have grown too sure of your tunic," he said.

"No, Master," I said. A slave should never be too complacent in the matter of clothing. She must discard it at a gesture or a word.

"Return to your work," he said.

I sprang up, and hurried away.

"I have a Master!" I told Xanthe.

"I have had one for a long time," said Xanthe. "And stay away from him, or I will claw you to pieces!"

We then, tears in our eyes, embraced one another, lovingly, joyfully, two slaves.

CHAPTER SIXTY-SEVEN

"Do not touch that container!" said Rupert of Hochburg.

I drew my hand back, quickly.

I had not touched it. I had only been curious. I had seen it, and its companion container, more than once, both of glass or something much like glass.

"Nor the other!" he said.

I stepped back, and knelt, having been addressed.

"Curiosity is not becoming in a *kajira*," he said.

"Yes, Master," I said.

"Do you wish to be whipped?" he asked.

"No, Master!" I said.

"Not even Temicus, who is of the Builders, understands the nature of the contents of those vessels," said Rupert.

"I gather then," I said, "that the contents are not water, or not purely water." I had seen no color in the fluid.

"No," he said, "the contents are not water or purely water."

"Neither container is full," I said.

"And that," he said, "leads you to suspect that both containers might have been opened at least once previously.

"Yes, Master," I said.

"It seems you do wish to be whipped," he said.

"No, Master," I said. "Forgive me, Master."

"I do not understand the nature of the fluids in those bottles," he said, "but I know how to make use of them."

"A *kajira* is curious to know more," I said.

"Stay away from the containers," he said. "Both are extremely dangerous."

"They are poison?" I asked.

"Not as you would commonly think of poison," he said.

"I do not understand," I said.

"They are strangely carnivorous," he said.

"Carnivorous fluids?" I said.

"Of a sort," he said.

"Like the *larl*, like the *sleen*?" I said.

"In a way," he said.

"Master is generous to a slave," I said.

"I tell you this much to warn you," he said. "Let it be enough. If you should open and misuse the contents of either one of those vessels, you need not fear a whipping. There would not be enough left of you to whip."

"I think," I said, "those fluids are not of Gor."

"Perhaps not," he said.

"May I inquire," I asked, "how it is that Master possesses such fluids."

"No," he said.

"Would not the possession of such fluids violate the laws of Priest-Kings?" I asked.

"I do not know," he said.

"Are they fluids of Priest-Kings?" I asked.

"No," he said.

"Then of another form of life," I said.

"Possibly," he said.

"I would think so," I said.

"Curiosity," he said, "is not becoming in a *kajira*."

"Yes, Master," I said. "Forgive me, Master."

CHAPTER SIXTY-EIGHT

"The skies seem clear," I said.

"More so than yesterday," said Xanthe.

"That is," I said, "because tarnsmen of Ar patrol these skies."

I returned my attention to the road.

"Xanthe," I said.

"Yes?" she said.

"Have you been rifling about with the food stores?" I asked.

"No," she said. "But I intended to ask you about it."

"It is not my doing," I said.

"The pilfering is minor," she said, "but real."

"I noticed it," I said. "This morning and yesterday morning."

"I, too," she said. "Are you sure that you are not responsible?"

"Quite," I said.

It was not unusual that both Xanthe and I would have noticed this, as we cooked and distributed the food.

"What about you?" I asked.

"It was not I," she said. "And it was not an animal. Animals are not neat about such things, nor do they rearrange matters so it is less obvious that something is missing."

"I assure you it was not I," I said.

"You are good at lying," she said.

"Not about things like that," I said.

"Somebody has been into the stores," said Xanthe.

"Ruling one another out," I said, "I think we both know who is responsible."

"Temicus," said Xanthe. "He is large of appetite and has nimble fingers."

"You could ask him about it," I said.

"You ask him," she said.

"I do not want the back of my legs switched," I said.

"Nor do I," she said.

The *tharlarion* wagon to which Xanthe and I were tethered had stopped.

Masters Rupert and Temicus were interrogating a peddler. Such fellows, coming and going as they do, are often well informed. Holt of Ar was well in advance of the wagon, and Desmond of Hochburg trailed the wagon by several hundred yards. In this fashion Holt could inform us of possible difficulties which might lie ahead, and Desmond, as a rear guard, so to speak, might alert us to any signs of pursuit.

Traffic had picked up on the road, presumably because we were nearing Ar.

Happily, both Xanthe and I, by our respective Masters, Rupert of Hochburg and Holt of Ar, had been granted a standing permission to speak. This made things much easier in communicating with the Masters. Both of us were grateful for this permission. It could, of course, be revoked at any time, by as little as a word.

In the first days out from the Fair we had traveled overland and avoided roads, particularly well-traversed roads. As the number of days grew greater, however, and pursuit seemed less likely, we began to frequent more popular routes. The primary motivation for this, I was sure, was to save time. We knew little more except that the artificial worlds had emerged from space debris. Had they begun their journey to Gor? Were they on their way to their targets? We did not know. Had they retreated into the space debris? Had the mission been canceled, or delayed; perhaps having to do with political differences in the court of Pompilius, or engineering refinements introduced to make their mission even more precise or destructive? Temicus speculated that their strike might be delayed until those of the faction of Pompilius had fully withdrawn to predetermined locations, perhaps in the Vosk Basin. We did not know.

As we waited for Masters Rupert and Temicus to finish with the peddler, a Peasant approached, coming across the field to the road. I gathered he had approached to better scrutinize the two slaves tethered to the wagon. Slaves are accustomed to being regarded, and in detail. Are they not splendid animals? Are they not a form of attractive, even exciting, livestock?

The Peasant stopped at the edge of the road, and leaned on his hoe.

"You are well-curved," he said.

"Thank you, Master," we said.

"What are your collars?" he asked.

"We cannot read," said Xanthe.

"I cannot either," he said.

"Yes, Master," said Xanthe.

"Reading is for Scribes," he said.

"Yes, Master," said Xanthe.

"Surely your Masters have enlightened you," he said.

"Master?" asked Xanthe.

"As to your collars," he said.

"They are Bazi collars," said Xanthe. "Collars of Bazi Imports."

"I do not know that group," said the Peasant. "I did, once in Ar, sip a Bazi tea."

"I trust you enjoyed it," said Xanthe.

"I did," he said.

"There are hundreds of blends," said Xanthe.

That did not surprise me, but I could not vouch for that. Xanthe projected the image of an extremely well-informed slave, particularly when she could not be found out. It was one of her more annoying, or endearing, characteristics.

"You are First Girl?" said the Peasant to Xanthe.

"Not at all," I said. "There is no First Girl here."

"There must be a First Girl," he said.

"No, Master," I said.

"There should be a First Girl," he said.

"There are only two of us," I said. "Masters saw no need for a First Girl."

"Interesting," he said.

"If there were to be a First Girl," said Xanthe, "it would be I."

I certainly did not see any warrant for that remark. I did suppose that, if the opportunity arose, Xanthe, if possible, would be quick to arrogate that position to herself. As my position at the observatory had surely been superior to hers, higher and more prestigious than hers, I did not doubt that she, as female to female, would have enjoyed finding herself over me, having power over me, being able to order me about, and such.

"Why is that?" asked the Peasant.

"As I am far more beautiful than she," said Xanthe.

"I do not think so," I said.

"You would both look well in chains," said the Peasant. "And the most beautiful is seldom made First Girl. It often pleases Masters to keep the most beautiful girl subordinate, to better humble her, and to please the less beautiful."

"Oh?" said Xanthe. "Then I would probably not be First Girl."

"Neither of us is First Girl," I said.

"Why are you tethered as you are," asked the Peasant, "tied by the neck to the back of the wagon, your hands tied behind your backs?"

"It pleased Masters," said Xanthe.

"It helps us to remember that we are slaves," I said.

"Then you were not Panther Girls," said the Peasant.

"Panther Girls?" said Xanthe.

"Yes," said the Peasant.

"No," said Xanthe.

"May I inquire why you ask?" I said.

"Panther Girls are about," he said.

"Not in this area," I said, incredulously. From what I had heard of Panther Girls, their bands were almost always found in sparsely inhabited areas, forests and jungles, and such, which made sense as their bands, at least according to report, tended to be largely formed by haters of men, haters of their own womanhood, rejecters of society because of its restrictions and conventions, girls fleeing unwanted companionships, women fleeing enslavement for debts, female thieves sought by guardsmen, and so on. Most towns and cities viewed them as female outlaws, and, as female outlaws, subject to seizure and enslavement. It was said that, collared and mastered, they, as other women, made excellent slaves.

"I know it is rare," said the Peasant. "But we do not bother them, and they do not bother us. They are furtive, and move mostly at night."

"Have you seen any?" asked Xanthe.

"I have spoken with more than one," he said.

"What are they doing this close to Ar, this far from the wilderness?" I asked.

"Pursuit, and vengeance," said the Peasant. "They are seeking one of their own, a deserter, a fugitive, one who fled the band."

"A thief, who made off with the band's gold," said Xanthe.

"Perhaps," said the Peasant. "I do not know."

"What will they do with the fugitive if they find her?" I asked.

"I fear it will be unpleasant," said the Peasant. "They intend to strip her, bind her hand and foot, and throw her to leech plants."

I had never, to my knowledge, seen leech plants, but I was familiar with the dangers involved. These plants commonly grew in thick patches. I did not understand the chemical and thermal reactions involved, but the plant, aside from its normal processes of photosynthesis, by means of hollow thorns, could strike like a snake, and then rapidly suck in blood, filling bladderlike pods. Normally one can tear oneself away from such plants, even uprooting them, but, of course, this would be impractical if one were lying helpless amongst them.

I shuddered. "I fear for her," I said.

"I, too," said Xanthe, shivering.

"And well you might, *kajirae*," said the Peasant.

"*Tal*," said Rupert of Hochburg, coming back to the wagon, Temicus at his side.

"*Tal*," said the Peasant, lifting his hoe in greeting.

"*Tal*," said Temicus.

"*Tal*," said the Peasant.

"What do you think of our stock?" asked Rupert.

"Pretty enough," said the Peasant. "They could do to pour swill in the *tarsk* pens, but they are too light for the plow, even if yoked together."

The men then wished one another well and parted.

"We will camp nearby," said Rupert of Hochburg. "We have learned that the gates of Ar are being watched."

"We anticipated it would be so," said Temicus. He looked up. I followed the movement of his head.

"Do not notice the tarnsman," said Rupert. "Let us not be concerned with him, and let him not be concerned with us."

"We will approach Ar by way of Venna," said Temicus. "We will go east and circle back."

"If our presence, or our mission, is suspected," said Rupert, "we are in considerable danger."

"Let us hope," said Temicus, "that the absence of the slave, Mira, will be understood as no more than a common slave theft, and that it has nothing to do with the plots and plans of Kurii."

"I suspect," said Rupert, "that they think that likely, but, even so, they cannot afford to neglect the possibility that her disappearance might pose some threat to their machinations."

"I do not think the Beast Caves will be easy to approach, let alone access," said Temicus.

"It is my hope," said Rupert, "it will not be necessary to do so."

"How so?" asked Temicus, pleased.

"I think we have an ally," said Rupert.

"I do not understand," said Temicus.

"Just protect the translating device concealed in the wagon," said Rupert. "Our lives may depend on it."

At this point, as we were paused, Desmond of Hochburg, who had been following our group, joined us. Similarly, a bit later, Holt of Ar, who had been preceding our group, made his way back to the wagon, joining us, as well.

Xanthe put her head down.

"I have news from down the road," said Holt of Ar. "Gordon, Administrator of Hammerfest, a town on the Vosk, is raising men in the vicinity of Ar."

"What for?" asked Rupert.

"It is not known," said Holt.

"Is he involved in the disputes of Kur factions?" asked Temicus.

"I do not know," said Holt of Ar.

We soon, as it was now late in the afternoon, drew the wagon away from the road and into a nearby grove of trees. In this way, for all practical purposes, it was concealed. Shortly thereafter, the small draft *tharlarion* unharnessed and hobbled, the camp was made and

Xanthe and I prepared an evening meal. As it grew dark, we could hear the occasional traffic on the road, voices, sometimes singing, occasional wagon bells, which road, tomorrow, would join the Viktel Aria, the Victory of Ar. The first watch would be taken by Desmond of Hochburg.

"Master," I whispered, well after midnight, lying in my blanket near the feet of Rupert of Hochburg.

"Yes?" he said.

"The noble Gordon of Hammerfest," I said, "he who, following the report of Master Holt, is raising men in Ar, is also the famed river pirate, Einar, the Sleen of the Vosk."

"I know," said Rupert of Hochburg. "Go to sleep."

"Yes, Master," I said.

I had scarcely closed my eyes, when, some yards away in the darkness, I heard a stirring and scuffle.

I sat up, abruptly.

"Master!" I said.

"It is nothing," he said. "Go to sleep."

"Yes, Master," I said.

CHAPTER SIXTY-NINE

We had finished our breakfast when Desmond rose up and left us, drawing back amongst the trees.

"Here," he said, a few moments later, returning to the camp.

"What have you there?" inquired Temicus.

I suspect he had little doubt what it was.

"Let us see," said Desmond.

He put the object down. Several lengths of rope tied a blanket snugly about the object. He undid the knots and jerked the ropes upward, spilling the hitherto concealed object onto the grass.

"Good," said Rupert of Hochburg.

The young woman, on her back, bound hand and foot, and gagged, looked wildly from one face to another.

Xanthe and I exchanged glances. The mystery of the missing supplies had been solved.

The captive's hair was short and rudely cut, as though shaped with a knife, or edged stone. It was brown. Her eyes, too, were brown. There was a necklace of beads about her neck, and an armlet of beads on her upper left arm. Her garment, brief, like a tunic, was of tan hide.

"An attractive catch," said Holt of Ar.

"She is not so much, Master," said Xanthe.

I feared Xanthe was risking her permission to speak with such a remark, but nothing came of it.

"Would you like to speak?" asked Rupert.

The captive shook her head, negatively.

"Would you like to be able to speak?" asked Rupert.

She shook her head, affirmatively.

Rupert nodded to Desmond, and Desmond undid the gag and put it to the side. The captive then watched while Rupert himself undid the bonds on her ankles.

Her ankles freed, she struggled to her feet, but the right hand of Desmond closed about her right ankle and he pulled her feet from beneath her, sprawling her to the grass. She struggled to a sitting position, cross-legged, and glared at Rupert, Holt, and Temicus. She pulled at the thongs holding her wrists behind her back, fiercely, briefly, and then desisted, realizing herself helpless, utterly so.

Desmond lifted her up under the arms and then with a foot, swept her legs back and then knelt her on the grass.

"You may think yourself a man, or wish yourself a man," said Rupert, "but you are not a man. You are a female. You are much more attractive kneeling. Even the free women of the high cities kneel."

Both Xanthe and I, somewhat in the background, were kneeling.

"Much better," said Temicus.

Her knees were clenched together.

"Of what hide is your tunic?" asked Rupert.

"She does not choose to respond," said Holt.

"That is the right of a free woman," said Rupert. "It is the hide of a forest panther, probably from the northern woods."

"What shall we do with her?" asked Temicus.

"We will tie her to a tree by the side of the road," said Rupert, "and leave her there."

"No!" said the captive, quickly. "They would find me. They would kill me!"

"She speaks," noted Temicus.

"Yes," she said, "my tunic is of the hide of the forest panther, from the high woods, the great woods, far to the north."

"You are a thief," said Desmond. "You stole from us."

"I took little," she said. "I wanted to live."

"We would have shared our food with you," said Rupert.

"But you stole," said Desmond.

"I was afraid to ask," she said. "A woman has much to fear from men, if not within the aegis of her Home Stone."

"What was your Home Stone?" asked Temicus.

"It was that of Laura," she said.

That is in the north, I think on the Laurius River. I had once heard someone speak of it. Too, it may be near Holmesk, another town on the river, but on its southern bank.

"But you abandoned it," said Temicus.

"Who are you, and what are you doing here, and whom do you think places you at so dire a risk, and for what?" asked Rupert. "Your garb suggests that you are, or were, of some band of what many call 'Panther Girls.'"

"I am Philippina, once of Laura," she said. "I am, or was, a Panther Girl, of the band of Wanda the Mighty."

"Wanda the Mighty sounds formidable," said Holt. "How many hundreds are in her band?"

"Her band now numbers eleven girls," she said.

"That does not sound excessively mighty," said Holt.

"I think she hoped to recruit many more and control the northern forests, and become rich by limiting access to nautical timber."

"A bold, if naive, ambition," said Temicus.

"Cos, Tyros, Port Kar, Brundisium, and other maritime powers would have little patience with such pretentions," said Holt. "They would sweep the forests with *sleen* and have the arrogant she-tarsks in chains within a week."

"Free women," said Temicus, "sometimes have inflated views of their importance and less than realistic notions of their prospects."

"For some reason you are a fugitive from your small band," said Rupert.

"Yes," she said.

"And they are pursuing you and hunting you," said Temicus.

"Yes," she said.

"To kill you," said Temicus.

"Yes," she said.

"And what was your crime?" asked Holt. "Did you steal meat, weapons, coins?"

"No," she said.

"What was it?" asked Temicus.

"I need not speak," she said. "I am a free woman. I am too ashamed to confess my crime."

"It was so serious?" said Temicus.

"Yes," she said.

"So serious you dare not admit it?" asked Temicus.

"Yes," she said.

"You had a moment of weakness?" asked Rupert.

"I fear it was more than a moment," she said.

"And they did not just cast you out?" said Temicus.

"No," she said. "They wanted to kill me."

"It was so unforgiveable," said Temicus.

"It seems so," she said. "Wanda and some others feared my weakness, if unpunished, might spread, might infect others, and bring about the end of the band, the ruination of our entire ideology."

"And this terrified them?" said Holt.

"Seemingly," she said.

"Your crime is common," said Temicus.

"And it is not a crime," said Rupert of Hochburg.

"I have said nothing!" she cried.

"You need not do so," said Rupert of Hochburg. "But you will be happier, if you confess it openly, clearly, and fully."

"Surely not," she said.

"Untie her," said Rupert of Hochburg.

Desmond removed the bonds which fastened her small wrists behind her back. The captive, unsure, remained on her knees.

Rupert of Hochburg then drew his knife, and the captive shrank back. With one small movement of the blade he cut the beaded necklace from her throat, and, with another, removed the armlet from her upper left arm.

"What are you doing?" she asked.

"A slave does not need such things," he said.

"I am not a slave!" she said.

"Stop! Stop!" she said, but Desmond held her in place, on her knees.

"Slaves," said Rupert of Hochburg, "are not clad in the proud dignity of noble hide, but in cloth, if at all."

"She is attractive," said Holt of Ar.

"But not so much so," said Xanthe.

Desmond forced the captive's head down, held it there for a few seconds, and then, his hand in her hair, pulled it up again. Her eyes were wild with wonder and tears.

Her head had been held down, before men.

"*Tal*, slave," said Rupert.

"I am not a slave," she said.

"You will grow used to being naked," said Rupert. "Slaves need not be clothed."

"I am not a slave," she said.

"Excellent slave curves," said Temicus.

"I am not a slave!" she said.

"She lacks only the collar and mark," said Desmond.

"You are a slave, in your heart," said Rupert.

"No!" she said.

"Your needs were much upon you," said Rupert.

"I cried out my needs in my sleep," she said. "I could not help it. I was beaten awake by my outraged sisters. I was confronted. I confessed the power and constancy of obsessive thoughts, the recurrent, insistent pleading of a deep, secret self."

"Do not be alarmed or disturbed," said Rupert. "Health and truth need not be denounced or denied."

"It was against the ideology of the pack," she said.

"The hereditary coils are older and deeper than ideology," said Rupert.

She put down her head and covered her eyes with her hands, weeping uncontrollably, her body shaking.

"Cry," said Rupert. "It will do you good."

"I wanted a Master!" she wept.

"It is natural for a slave to want a Master," said Rupert.

I suspected I knew a world where many slaves longed for their Masters.

"I do not understand," said Temicus, "the fierce torrent of abuse to which you were subjected. I do not understand why, for such a simple, natural thing, you would be driven from the pack, even pursued to be caught and slain."

"An ideology was questioned," said Rupert. "A belief system was threatened."

"Let the *urt* who lacks the pack odor beware," said Holt. "It will be torn to pieces."

"We must be on our way," said Desmond.

"Take me with you!" said the captive.

"With thoughts such as yours, we cannot well take you with us as a free woman," said Rupert.

"What are you going to do with me?" she said.

"Nothing," said Rupert.

"You cannot leave me behind, naked," she said.

"You are mistaken," said Rupert. "Nothing would be easier."

"Perhaps you are reluctant to take me with you," she said.

"Perhaps," said Rupert.

"Why is that?" asked Temicus. "Why should we be reluctant, other than for the bother of it, to take you with us?"

"The band," she said. "It could be dangerous for you if they found me in your company."

"Not with their small numbers and so close to Ar," said Desmond. "They must know that they themselves are in jeopardy of apprehension."

"Let us take her along with us, and hope to meet them," said Holt. "We could sell her to them."

I trusted that this was a jest.

"No!" she cried.

"For a tarsk-bit and a slice of cheese," said Holt.

So it was a jest.

"No, please!" she said. "Do not!"

The captive, clearly, was less sure of that than I.

"Tell Desmond and Holt," said Rupert.

"Yesterday afternoon," said Temicus, "the captain and I interrogated a peddler on the road. We learned various items of interest, among them that tarn patrols of Ar, to their surprise, had detected a small group of apparent Panther Girls approaching Ar. This was reported to the Ubar who called it to the attention of a friend, Tenalian of Ar, the slaver, who promptly dispatched several men to welcome the group to the vicinity of Ar."

"Accordingly," said Rupert, "I think it likely that your ambitious, bloodthirsty little band will soon be exchanging their panther skins for chains and collars, if they have not already done so."

"Perhaps," said Temicus to the captive, "you would enjoy seeing your Wanda the Mighty being auctioned off to the highest bidder."

"It is interesting," said Holt, "that Panther Girls would risk coming this far south."

"They must have been excessively zealous to apprehend and kill our fair captive," said Temicus.

"Am I fair?" asked the captive.

"Yes," said Temicus.

"Only moderately so," said Xanthe.

"Sometimes," said Rupert, "men do not understand their true motivations. They may think that they are doing things for one reason, but, unbeknownst to themselves, they are doing it for another reason."

"I do not understand," said Temicus.

"Why," asked Rupert, "do some women walk the lonely bridges late at a night, take perilous ventures to dangerous areas, stop at remote inns and hostels, dare to enter taverns despite explicit prohibitions?"

"Courting the collar," said Temicus.

"Possibly," said Rupert.

"I shall harness the *tharlarion*," said Holt. "I viewed the road earlier. It is well traveled. I think we will have no difficulty blending in and traveling unnoticed."

"Things will become more dangerous," said Desmond, "the closer we come to Ar and the Beast Caves."

"Beast Caves?" said the captive.

"That," said Rupert, "is why we will circle about, via Venna, and approach Ar not from the west but the east."

The captive rose to her feet.

She was permitted to do so.

"That stratagem may be anticipated," said Temicus.

"Let them anticipate a thousand stratagems," said Rupert. "Their resources are limited, and they can guard against few. They will doubtless marshal themselves against the most likely, particularly if they deem us oblivious of their possible intervention."

"Too," said Desmond, "Kurii commonly shun a public presence."

"Perhaps they will buy allies," said Temicus.

"Kurii?" said the captive.

"Plant seeds of gold," said Temicus. "Harvest swords of steel."

"I know nothing of Beast Caves," said the captive. "What are Kurii?"

"Do not concern yourself," said Rupert.

"Are they hirsute like *larls*?" she asked. "Can they see in the dark like *sleen*? Are they large and long-armed, and frightening in appearance? Do their eyes sometimes blaze in moonlight or in the light of fires? Do they sometimes walk upright, and sometimes leap and hurry on all fours? Is the tongue long and dark, the ears wide and pointed? Are the hands armed with retractable claws? Are the jaws wide, massive, and fanged?"

"You have seen a Kur!" snapped Rupert.

"I have seen such a thing," she said. "Several times."

"As you followed us, to hide and steal food," said Rupert.

"It followed me," she said. "But it did not attack me or seize me. Sometimes it did come close. I was terrified."

"It was not following you," said Rupert. "It was following us."

"That is your ally, your colleague," said Temicus.

"It could as easily be our enemy," said Rupert.

"The *tharlarion* is harnessed," said Holt, returning. "Let us be on our way."

"Take me with you!" begged the captive.

"No," said Rupert.

"At least give me some clothing," she begged.

"No," said Rupert. "You will do quite well as you are."

"I will follow you," she said.

"If you attempt to do so," said Rupert, "you will be tied, hand and foot, and left at the side of the road."

"As I am?" she said. "Stripped?"

"Yes," said Rupert.

"How dare you do such a thing?" she said.

"Are you a free woman?" he asked.

"Certainly," she said.

"Then," he said, "that is how I dare do such a thing."

"No!" she said.

"We share no Home Stone," he said.

Rupert turned away from her, and, the camp broken, we prepared to move to the road.

"Wait!" cried the captive, falling to her knees, stretching out her arms.

Rupert, and the rest of us, turned back, to face her.

"I am not a free woman!" she cried. "I am a slave! I am a slave! I cried out my need for a Master, even in the northern forest. I have known this in my heart for years! I lacked the courage to admit it! But why should I not tell the truth? Is deceit not prohibited to the female slave?"

"Do you beg the collar of a slave?" asked Rupert.

"Yes!" she said.

"Why?" he asked.

"Because I am a slave," she said. "I know I am a slave! I want to be a slave! I beg to be a slave!"

"Are you prepared to pronounce yourself slave?" he asked.

"Yes!" she said.

"Beware," he said. "Once that is done, it is done. That word, once uttered, cannot be revoked, changed or altered. Once it is uttered, you are a slave, legally, with no power whatsoever to alter, qualify, or change your condition."

"I understand," she said.

"You will then be an animal, a domestic animal, subject to marking and collaring, to chains and the whip, to being sold or given away. Men may, at their pleasure, treat you as the sex animal you will then be and do with you as they please. They may even, if they wish, kindle slave fires in your belly, at the mercy of which you will then be."

"They burn already," she wept.

"Speak," he said.

"I am a slave," she said.

"It is done," he said.

"I am now a slave, truly," she said. "I am a slave."

"But no more than an unclaimed slave," said Rupert. "You may now be tied, hand and foot, and left beside the road, naked, as an unclaimed slave."

"No, Master!" she cried. "No, Master!"

"Does anyone want this slave?" he asked.

The slave then leapt to her feet, ran to Desmond, and fell to her knees before him, grasping him at the knees, and looking up at him, piteously. "Please claim me!" she wept. "Were you not the first to bind me and make me helpless? As you tied me, did it not occur to you to keep me for yourself? I think more than once you had noticed me take my tiny share of your stores. Surely you must have considered putting bracelets on me and taking me to an iron. Did you fail to notice that I invariably waited until it was your watch before I indulged in my modest raids? I think now I must have been putting myself before you, exhibiting a quarry only too eager to fall into your trap. Oh, I fought fiercely enough to retain my freedom last night, but I knew only too well, and gratefully, that my strength was as nothing to yours, and that my most strenuous and arduous struggles would happily be in vain."

"I have had my eye on this prize for some time, even when she was no more than a free woman," said Desmond. "I trust that there is no objection."

"None at all," said Rupert.

Desmond looked down at the slave. "You are mine," he said.

"Yes, Master!" she cried and threw herself to her belly, kissing her Master's feet.

Xanthe and I broke into tears of joy.

"We are to the road," said Rupert to Desmond. "Try to catch up with us by noon."

"Yes, Captain," said Desmond.

CHAPTER SEVENTY

It was night,

There had been much rain of late.

Dry tinder was scarce.

I had been dispatched to a nearby caravanserai with a tarsk-bit to purchase a 'fire package,' which consists of a spark striker, tinder, and 'black stones.' To guests at the caravanserai these packages are included in the rental fee, and supplied as a convenience for use in the cooking pits.

I hurried through the darkness, hoping that my passage would not be noticed. A few minutes ago, I had been returning to our small night camp just west of Venna, with the 'fire package' when I stopped, abruptly.

My group, Masters Rupert, Holt, Temicus, and Desmond, and the slaves Xanthe and Philippina, the latter name now on her as a slave name, was not alone.

They stood in the center of a circle of Panther Girls, eleven Panther Girls, several of whom had bows drawn and arrows to the string. These must have been nearby on the road from which they had departed suddenly to encircle our camp.

The weapons of the men had been put to the side.

They were now unarmed.

"Surrender the free woman, Philippina, who grievously shamed my band," said a large, strapping woman clad in tan hide, and ornamented with beads and claws. "We must do justice upon her."

"Justice means different things to different people," said Rupert. "And just as falsity often wears the mask of truth, so, too, diverse agendas can hide under golden words, such as 'right' and 'justice.'"

"Surrender her," said the large woman, who seemed to be the leader of the Panther Girls.

She, I assumed, was Wanda, called the Mighty.

I suspected she would prove attractive to few men.

As nearly as I could tell, some sort of stand-off was taking place.

"Unbend your bows," said Rupert.

"But keep your arrows to the string," said the woman.

"As I understand it," said Rupert, "you are looking for a free woman, Philippina."

"Yes," she said.

"There are no free women here," said Rupert.

"There she is!" announced the woman, pointing at Philippina, who was kneeling and trembling at the thigh of Desmond.

"That is no free woman," said Rupert. "That is a slave."

"My slave," said Desmond.

"Where is her collar?" asked Wanda.

"You see the cloth I have knotted about her throat," said Desmond. "It serves as her badge of servitude. We will, when convenient, soon I trust, have her fitted with a proper collar."

"At least, I see," said Wanda, "she is stripped, stripped as a slave, that she is slave naked."

"That is not unusual for a slave," said Rupert.

"There is no mark on her," said Wanda.

"That lack will be soon remedied," said Rupert. "In the meantime, let her fair thigh anticipate the kiss of the hissing iron."

"How do I know she is a slave," said Wanda.

"Because I have told you," said Rupert, coldly.

A moment of fear appeared on Wanda's features, but she recovered promptly. "Are you a slave?" she asked Philippina.

"Yes, Mistress," said Philippina.

"What do you want for the worthless animal?" asked Wanda.

"She is not for sale," said Desmond.

"What would you offer," asked Rupert.

"A tarsk-bit," said Wanda.

"Obviously you are a woman," said Rupert. "I am a man, and, as I regard the slave, I deem her worth far more. Consider the ankles, the calves, the thighs, the belly and shoulders, the throat, the loveliness of the features."

"What do you want her for?" asked Desmond.

"Her crime within my band was heinous," said Wanda. "We have found a large expanse of leech plants nearby. We will bind her, hand and foot, and cast her, as she is, naked, to the plants."

"They would suck the blood out of her in two Ehn," said Rupert.

"What crime could be so heinous as to justify so hideous a fate?" asked Desmond.

"That need not concern you," said Wanda.

"Let us see the color of your coins," said Rupert. "There are few Streets of Coins in the northern forests."

"Behold," she said. She took a small, brown leather sack from her belt, and spilled several coins into the palm of her hand, which, smiling, she promptly replaced in the bag.

"Gold!" said Temicus.

"Tarn disks of Ar," said Wanda.

"How is it," asked Rupert, "that a woman from the north, roving and clad in hide, has gold, and the gold of Ar?"

"They are in fee," said Holt.

"Clearly," said Rupert.

"There is more in this than the seeking of a slave," said Desmond.

"You realize, do you not," asked Wanda, "that you are all our prisoners?"

"And you realize, do you not," said Rupert, "that you are sought by the men of the slaver, Tenalian of Ar?"

"We eluded them," said Wanda. "The woodcraft of the men of the cities is no match for ours. Too, we are now beyond the aegis of Ar."

"What do you want with us?" asked Rupert.

"We want nothing of you, personally," she said. "But our principal wishes you detained."

"For what reason?" asked Rupert.

"I think he wishes to interrogate you," she said. "Are you thieves? Is this a matter having to do with missing coin?"

"Perhaps," said Rupert. "Who is your principal?"

"When matters deal with gold," she said, "names need not be looked into."

"I suspect he was a small man," said Rupert.

"Yes," said Wanda.

"And he was accompanied by a large, fearsome beast?" said Desmond.

"I saw no such beast," she said.

"It saw you," said Desmond.

The scene was illuminated by the White Moon.

A light rain began to fall.

I slipped back, further into the shadows. I gathered that nothing was likely to take place immediately. The Panther Girls were waiting with their prisoners for the arrival of Tiskias, who was enleagued with the Kur faction of Pompilius. That gave me some time, how much I did not know. I knew that Philippina was in mortal danger from the Panther Girls. But what of the others? Would Tiskias, after he had satisfied himself with respect to what the prisoners knew, and whom they might have been in contact with, pay the Panther Girls to do away with the prisoners? I feared that that was likely. I remember the lonely bridge that night in Ar. But, would the Panther Girls do such a thing? I had never heard of Panther Girls, like mercenaries or assassins, killing for pay. Who knew what might occur? I also wondered if the men were willing to risk an escape or an overthrow of their captors. They were unarmed, of course, and significantly outnumbered, eleven to four. Would they nonetheless resist, and, if so, when, or were they waiting for something, and, if so, what? They would realize, of course, that I had not yet returned from my errand at the caravanserai. I wanted to go for help, but to whom could I apply, a lone slave? The caravanserai guards, suspecting a trick, would not be likely to abandon the precincts of the caravanserai. There were guardsmen in Venna, of course, but such guardsmen, like many guardsmen, were unlikely to see their jurisdiction as extending much beyond the *pomerium* of their own town or city.

Then a thought came to me, and I sped away, back toward Venna.

CHAPTER SEVENTY-ONE

"It is not far now, Masters," I said.

Flavius of Venna, the raider, the Master of my friend, Calla, lifted his hand, and the men with him, some fifteen men, moved more warily through the trees at the side of the road. Some carried bows. Others, bearing shields, now unsheathed their swords.

I did not think much action would be involved as I was sure that the Panther Girls would not knowingly engage a larger number of well-armed and presumably formidable males. If they had time to appraise the odds, I expected them to fade away amongst the trees. Yet, I knew there could be danger.

"Dear Calla," I said, "you should have remained in Venna."

"Nonsense," she said.

I had hurried to Venna and soon, as the location of the holding of Flavius turned out to be well-known, I was drawing on the bell rope to announce my presence. The watchman demanded I leave, and, given my reluctance to do so, was preparing, stick in hand, to drive me away when I began to cry out, "Calla! Calla!"

"Be silent!" he said. "Do not stir the household!"

Happily, Calla soon appeared behind him and welcomed me with an embrace and kiss.

I had not seen her in Venna, but she had apparently seen me in the streets, some weeks ago, and her Master, Flavius, had contacted me on her behalf when I was serving in the Yellow Whip.

"How pleased I am to see you," she had said.

"*Tal*," I had said. "I, too, am pleased."

Flavius soon made his appearance at the gate.

It took but a moment for me to explain the hunt for Philippina and the straits in which my party found itself. I did not touch on deeper matters, pertaining to Tiskias, Kurii, and war.

"You must help them, Master," begged Calla.

"They are planning to kill an innocent slave?" asked Flavius.

"Yes," I said.

"We march," he said.

It was still dark, save for the light of the White Moon.

Flavius lifted his hand again, and he, and those with him, stopped.

"Slave," he said.

"Yes, Master," I said.

"I think," he said, "that the best thing to do is for you to enter the camp alone and announce our presence."

"You do not intend to rush upon them?" I asked.

"I would like to eliminate, or at least reduce, bloodshed," he said. "If we charge forth, even with surprise in our favor, fighting is likely to ensue. In such a case some Panther Girls and perhaps some members of your own party, in particular, the slave, Philippina, might be in jeopardy. Victory would be won easily but possibly at a price we would not wish to pay. Not all battles are won by fighting."

"Let me go," said Calla.

"No," I said, "I will go."

I crept to the edge of the camp.

Things seemed much as before, save that most of the two parties were resting, reclining or sitting, save for two Panther Girls who were on watch. I saw no sign of Tiskias or the beast which often accompanied him. I gathered that he had not yet arrived. Philippina, frightened, her eyes open, was in the arms of Desmond.

"Hold, noble Masters and Mistresses," I called.

The bows of the two Panther Girls on guard bent.

Arrows were leveled in my direction.

"Do not fire!" I called.

I hoped it was difficult to see me in the darkness and trees by the side of the camp.

The camp, with my utterance, came alive. Any who might have slept were now awake. Most, I assumed, as quiescent as they might have been, had not been asleep.

All now, even the slaves, were on their feet.

"Do not fire," I repeated, muchly aware of the genuine possibility that arrows might be loosed in my direction.

"Step forth!" ordered Wanda.

I stepped forth, however unwillingly, from the trees, my hands in sight.

"She is unarmed," said one of the Panther Girls.

"And nearly unclothed," said another.

I wore as much as they, save for some ornaments. To be sure, my garment was of cloth and theirs was of skin.

"It is a slave," said another.

"Do not waste an arrow on her," said Wanda. "A knife will do."

I did not turn and run. I was not being brave. My legs were trembling. I felt I might fall. Too, might not three or four arrows, before I could manage two or three steps, find their marks in my back?

"Where have you been?" asked Rupert of Hochburg, sternly. "You are late."

"Forgive me, Master," I said.

"As you can see," he said, "we have guests."

"Yes, Master," I said.

"Are they not free?" he asked.

"Yes, Master," I said.

"Why are you standing?" he asked.

I immediately knelt.

"We sent her for a fire package, from the caravanserai," he said.

"Dry wood is scarce," said Wanda. "There has been much rain."

"The rain is good for leech plants," said a Panther Girl.

Philippina shuddered. Desmond held her closer.

"Where is the fire package?" asked Rupert.

"At hand," I said.

"Fetch it," he said.

"Stay where you are," said Wanda. "You think to send her for help."

"You are clever," said Rupert. "It is as though you discerned a subtle intent."

"It was transparent," she said.

"It seems to have taken you some time to return from the caravanserai," said Rupert.

"She was lost," said a Panther Girl, "wandering about in the woods."

"She is stupid," said another.

"She is a slave," said another.

"So stupid a slave that she entered the camp and put herself at our mercy," said another.

"Why," asked Rupert, "did it take you so long to return from the caravanserai?"

"Master?" I said.

"I think," he said, "you occupied your time productively, as in seeking help."

"Now it is you who are clever," said Wanda. "Will you not now suggest that we withdraw while there is still time, abandon the slave, Philippina, and frustrate our principal who wishes to speak with you?"

"Yes," said Rupert, "that sums it up, nicely."

Wanda laughed, as did some of her band, but not all.

"Will your slave be clever enough to play along with your game. I doubt it."

"Why," asked Rupert, "do you think the slave returned to the camp?"

"That is interesting," said Wanda. "I speculate that she may be more clever than we surmised. I speculate that she returned to the camp earlier, noted your predicament, waited an Ahn or so, and then made herself known, as having alerted guardsmen to our presence, that to alarm us, and hurry us on our way."

"You credit her with brilliance, bravery, and innovation?" said Rupert.

"If so, reluctantly," said Wanda.

"It is well known that slaves can be useful," said Rupert, "and not merely while writhing about in the furs."

"Have I permission to interrogate your pet animal?" asked Wanda.

"Surely," said Rupert.

"Slave," said Wanda.

"Mistress?" I said.

"I gather that you are prepared to abet the scheme of your Master, pretending to have summoned help for your party."

"I need not pretend, Mistress," I said.

"Do you maintain that you were successful in summoning help?"

"Yes, Mistress," I said.

"You are a liar," she said.

"No, Mistress," I said.

"Where is this help?" asked Wanda.

"Near," I said. "About."

"Let them now show themselves," said Wanda.

"They may not wish to do so, now," I said.

"But they stand ready, out there in the darkness, amongst the trees, to rush upon us," said Wanda.

"I trust so," I said.

"You are a stupid slave," said Wanda.

"I trust not," I said.

"Do you know how I know that you are lying?" asked Wanda.

"Forgive me, Mistress," I said, "but I am not lying."

"The night is dark, the road is lonely," said Wanda. "The closest guardsmen are those of the caravanserai or Venna. No others are within reach. The guards of the caravanserai will not abandon the caravanserai to the possible attack of thieves and brigands. The guardsmen of Venna will not abandon their posts. Too, they have no jurisdiction beyond the *pomerium* of Venna, and do not concern themselves with the safety of the road. Thus, there are no armsmen available to recruit, either from the caravanserai or Venna. And even if there were, the solicitations of a loose slave importuning men in the night would be scorned. In any event, no action would be taken until morning or, more likely, noon, by which time we expect to have left the vicinity."

"It seems then," I said, "that Mistress has little to fear."

"Let us be off," said one of the Panther Girls to Wanda.

"Do not become the victim of a pathetically obvious hoax," said Wanda.

"Let us seize the she-tarsk, Philippina," said another Panther Girl, "bind her, and give her to the nearby leech plants, and then, most quickly, be on our way."

"We will not receive the second sack of gold," said Wanda, "if we do not dally until our prisoners are turned over to the mercy of our principal."

"I am afraid," said a Panther Girl.

"Greed for gold has brought more than one of our kind to the collar," said another.

"Be firm," chided Wanda, angrily. "The wood is dark but empty. I have explained how there are no guardsmen to be feared."

"There are armsmen other than guardsmen," I said.

"Not for a hundred *pasangs*," said Wanda.

"Within yards," I said.

"I advise you to withdraw in peace," said Rupert. "Too, you may have yet to reckon with the men of Tenalian, the slaver."

"They have lost our trail," said Wanda.

"A trail once lost may be found again," said Rupert. "Forget your fee giver, your principal. One sack of gold is better than no sacks of gold."

"You are afraid," said Wanda.

"Of course," said Rupert.

"We will wait," said Wanda.

"As you wish," said Rupert.

"What of the traitress, Philippina?" asked a Panther Girl of Wanda, her leader.

"Very well," said Wanda. "Let us have that matter done with." She designated two of her band. "Seize the weak and treacherous Philippina. Bind her hand and foot, and give her to the nearby leech plants."

"No!" shrieked Philippina. Desmond then stood between her and the two designated to deal with her.

"Bows ready, arrows to the string," said Wanda. "Cut down any who dare to interfere!"

"Enough!" cried Rupert of Hochburg, in a terrible voice, which struck me with terror, like a knife of ice. "Come forth! Fair loot awaits. Pluck what fruit you will!"

Flavius, and his men, several with shields lowered, others with bows lifted, emerged from the shadows, and woods, moving silently, rapidly, menacingly toward the camp. It was difficult in the light to determine their numbers, but there seemed no mistaking their intent.

At the same time, as the men were almost upon them, but feet away, the Panther Girls, startled and dismayed, taken unawares, many of whom had apparently been already in a pitch of apprehension, broke and ran, crying out and screaming, in their haste disencumbering themselves of their bows which they had no time to lift and arm.

"Hold!" cried Rupert. "Leave them for the nets of Tenalian! They must be near. Word of this was on the road."

From yards away we heard cries of fear and consternation.

There were also, in several cases, shrieks of pain and a thrashing of bodies.

"Leech plants!" cried Maxwell Holt, Holt of Ar.

"They have been guided, herded, into them," said Temicus.

That was not difficult, I came to understand; a channel seems open and the quarry, attempting to evade the hunters, is guided into the waiting trap.

"Go, Mira, Xanthe," said Rupert of Hochburg, gesturing in the direction in which the Panther Girls had fled, "your sisters may need care; you may be needed."

He had the mercy to exempt Philippina from this instruction, I think not only in her best interest but in that of the Panther Girls, as well. In any event, she, sobbing, inarticulate, shaking with gladness, was held safe in Desmond's arms.

In moments, Xanthe and I had come to the point where the flight of the Panther girls had had been diverted and stopped.

It was beginning to become light.

Xanthe and I screamed at the horror of what we had come upon.

Before the Panther Girls realized what was happening they had plunged into a dense carpet of leech plants. Such plants, with their hollow thorns and pods, are commonly quiescent, little different from other forms of plant life, innocently sustained by the chemistry of photosynthesis, but this quiescence is abruptly and terribly superseded when something warm and living is sensed near or stirs amongst them. This stimulus triggers a hideous flurry of reactions in which the plant rears up, almost as though conscious, the hollow thorns striking out like the fangs of angry snakes, and blood is sucked rapidly through the hollow thorns into the then-swelling pods. The Panther Girls still within the patch seemed to be wading to their knees in writhing snakes. They were screaming in pain and terror, trying to force the plants from their bodies. The air, aside from the cries of the women, was filled with the frenzied rustling of the plants, and a mélange of popping and sucking sounds as the plants struggled to fill the distending chambers of their pods. I had stopped, half falling, at the edge of the leech plants. I looked down. Tendrils were reaching out, creeping, rustling, toward my ankles.

I cried out in misery, and sprang back. The tendrils stretched toward me, as though straining to reach me. But, the plant rooted, they could not reach me. Xanthe cried out in pain, a thorn anchoring itself in her calf. There was blood around the puncture. She tore the entire plant from the ground with two hands, and, crying out in terror and disgust, flung it yards away.

As long as one is not helpless amongst leech plants, perhaps bound or having fallen and being somehow unable to regain one's feet, leech plants commonly pose no mortal threat to humans or large animals. On the other hand, obviously the scales tip if one who could free oneself is not permitted to do so.

"Mercy! Mercy!" begged Panther Girls.

Some seven girls, including Wanda, were within the patch, at its periphery. Their legs and lower bodies were covered with blood, and leaves, and clinging vinelike growths, amongst which were penetrating thorns and throbbing pods. Slavers stood about the patch with poles and the butts of spears preventing the Panther Girls from making their way out of the living terrain of misery in which they found themselves trapped and tangled.

Four Panther Girls were lying outside the thick, agitated growths. They were trembling and shaken. It seems they had been permitted outside the range of the leech plants, or, perhaps, clinging to poles or spear hafts, had been dragged from the clutches of the violent patch. Some had uprooted growths still anchored to their bodies by thorns, leading from wounds to swollen, sacklike pods. The hands of the four Panther Girls were thonged behind their backs, and they were attached to one another by a long leather strap which was knotted about the neck of each in turn and then carried to the next. One of the slavers, noting the arrival of Xanthe and myself, gestured with his pole to the four bound Panther Girls and said, "Clean them, tend them, comfort them."

Xanthe and I hurried to the bound Panther Girls, two of whom seemed in shock. We pulled the thorns from their legs and thighs and discarded the attached pods, tendrils, and leaves.

"We are slaves," sobbed one of our charges, which utterance I did not understand at the time. Given the recent rains, Xanthe and I had no difficulty in finding wet leaves and grass with which to wipe away the plant stains and blood which coated their lower bodies. "Thank you," whimpered one of the Panther Girls. This surprised me. Surely she realized that I was a slave. "Lie still, rest," said Xanthe to another. "Yes, Mistress," whispered the Panther Girl. This, too, surprised me. Meanwhile, nearby, the other Panther girls, including their leader, Wanda, scarcely now in danger of being deemed the Mighty, were struggling amongst the leech plants and continuing to beg for mercy.

Xanthe rose up. "They will die amongst the leech plants," she said. "The blood will be drawn from their bodies. They will weaken. They will fall. It is only a matter of time."

"We must intercede with the Masters!" I said.

"I fear to do so," said Xanthe.

"I, too," I said, "but what choice have we?"

Xanthe and I ran to the writhing leech plants and flung ourselves to our knees, adding our petitions to those of the encircled, suffering Panther Girls.

"Please have mercy, Masters!" we wept.

"Be silent!" said one of the men. "They are free women!"

"Mercy, mercy!" cried Xanthe and myself, adding our desperate solicitations to those of the entrapped, besieged Panther Girls.

"You must be barbarians," said one of the slavers, thrusting a Panther Girl back with the butt of a spear. "Can you not see they are free women?"

"Release them," I begged.

"Let them emerge from the plants!" wept Xanthe.

"Do you wish to join them?" asked one of the men, angrily.

"No, Master!" I cried, in horror.

"No, no, Master!" said Xanthe, aghast.

One of the slavers, one who had been watching from the side, strode forward and seized Xanthe by the upper arm. Only too obviously he was ready to fling her out, into the plants.

"No!" I screamed.

Then I, too, was seized and held from the back, my arms pinned behind me, and I felt myself being forced toward the plants.

"No, please, no, Master," I screamed.

But both Xanthe and I were flung to the ground, to our knees, before the leech plants, at the very edge of the patch.

I saw one of the plants lift itself up, perhaps a foot, and turn to face me.

I scrambled back, but was stopped, against the knees of one of the men.

"Understand," said the man, "these are free women. Free women are exalted, distinguished, and noble. In the sacking of a city, they have the same right as men to be slaughtered in the streets. They are entitled, as are men, to die a free and honorable death. Would you deny to them such a privilege?"

"Free women are priceless," said another man. "Thus they have no value. They are not meaningless slaves, commodities whose disposition is subjcct to the movements, stresses, and strains of the market. They are not persons, but properties. As properties, they have value. As domestic animals, they have value. What rational person discards objects of value? One keeps even so little as a tarsk-bit. One does not cast it into the sea. One does not kill the mounts of the enemy but adds them to one's own stable. One does not destroy loot but keeps it for oneself."

"I confess myself a slave!" cried one of the beleaguered Panther Girls. "Let me leave the thorns and vines that I may kneel and kiss your feet as the slave I am!"

"I am a slave!" cried another Panther Girl.

"I, too," cried another.

As one Panther Girl after another acknowledged herself a slave, she was permitted to exit the swirling, hungering plants. Two who had fallen in the midst of the plants, clutching at poles, were pulled, tendrils whipping about their bodies, from the eager foliage.

"Lie on your bellies, wrists crossed behind you," ordered a man.

The surrendered slaves, the former proud Panther Girls, prostrate and prone, then had their hands thonged tightly behind them, and were lifted and carried, weeping and shuddering, to be placed beside the four earlier, as I now understood, submitted slaves.

"I am a slave!" cried Wanda, lastly, and, vomiting and shuddering, bleeding, was allowed to wade free of the leech plants, dragging behind her a thick train of encircling tendrils and vines. Shortly thereafter she, bound, was placed with the others, and added to the leather coffle rope.

Xanthe and I, then, at a gesture of one of the men, hurried to care for the new additions to, so to speak, the 'slaver's necklace.'

A few minutes later, the eleven former Panther Girls were aligned, knelt in a row, heads down, hands tied behind them, linked together by the neck.

"Tenalian will be pleased," said one of the men.

Some of the former Panther Girls were weeping, some, it seemed, interestingly enough, with tears of gladness.

"They led us a merry chase," said one of the men.

"Sooner or later we would have come up with them," said another.

"It was helpful," said one of the men, "that they contacted peasants, inquiring after the traitress they sought."

"Then," said another, "we needed only, by means of travelers, peddlers, peasants, and such, to trace women who seemed to answer to the description of their quarry. Thus we could hunt them as they hunted her."

"You may now return to your Masters," said one of the slavers to Xanthe and myself.

"Yes, Master, thank you, Master," we said.

How pleased we would be to leave!

"Wait!" he said.

"Master?" we asked.

"This is for your Master," he said. He handed me a small dark sack. There was no mistaking the feel of the sack, or the sound of metal within it. "This," he said, "was taken from the former leader of the Panther Girls. It contains several coins of gold. Its owner, soon to be collared, has no need of it. Inadvertently though it may have been done, your party held the Panther Girls nicely in place, giving us the time to arrive, position ourselves, and effect their capture, speedily und easily. Do not demur. Tenalian himself would approve."

I had, of course, no intention of demurring.

Commonly, slave girls may not touch money without permission. They cannot, of course, own money. It is they themselves who are owned.

"I thank you on behalf of my Master," I said.

In my hands, I, a slave girl, held enough coinage, I had no doubt, to purchase a dozen or more slaves, perhaps even a tarn.

The fellow seemed to think little of the money.

I supposed that when one had much money, and someone else's money, in particular, it was easy to think little of money.

On the way back to our camp, Xanthe and I turned back, once, to see the former Panther Girls on their feet. They were aligned in a column, apparently being readied for a march, presumably back to Ar, as in Ar lay the headquarters of the house of Tenalian.

"Look," said Xanthe.

"I see," I said.

The ornaments of the former Panther Girls were being removed. Following that, the brief skins they had worn were being cut away, one by one. It is common for slaves, incidentally, to be marched naked in coffle, unless in areas where free women might be offended. Too, slaves are commonly clothed, if clothed, not in the dignity of skins but in the simplicities of cloth, ranging from silk to common *rep*-cloth.

"I do not think that Wanda, the Picayune or Diminutive, is likely to be found attractive to many men," said Xanthe.

"She will appeal to some, who see beauty so," I said. "Besides, I gather that she might do well with the hoe and plow."

When we returned to the camp, we found that the fire package I had purchased with my Master's tarsk-bit at the caravanserai had been located where I had left it at the edge of the camp, and put to use. Xanthe and I helped Philippina with the breakfast.

It was a pleasant repast as Flavius and his men, and Calla, joined us.

My Master, as I had expected he would, gave the gold to Flavius.

Thus he and his men unexpectedly profited from the good turn they had done us.

"The rain is over," said Philippina. "The sun is shining."

"Good," I said.

"You and Xanthe were gone for a time," she said.

"We were attending to Panther Girls," I said. "They were distraught and muchly afflicted. Many were in pain. We had to draw thorns from their flesh. They were in terror and misery. Blood had been lost."

"I gather then," she said, "that you do not know what has occurred."

"No," I said. "What has occurred?"

CHAPTER SEVENTY-TWO

I knelt beside my Master, Rupert of Hochburg, and licked and kissed the scarring on his left wrist.

"Master was once injured," I said, "and grievously."

"It was done," he said, "by a manacle, and being dragged behind a saddle *tharlarion* as a trophy of war."

"It was long ago," I said.

"It is amongst many things I owe to Ar," he said.

"Glorious Ar," I said.

"Yes," he said. "Glorious Ar."

"Do you care to speak of this?" I asked.

"If you wish," he said.

"Muchly so," I said.

"I was a wanderer, who would see the world," he said. "I was far from Hochburg. My sword was for hire."

"Master was a mercenary," I said.

"But one who would choose his principal with care," he said.

"I knew it would be so," I said.

"You have heard of Marlenus of Ar," he said.

"I was once close enough to reach out and touch him," I said.

"You are aware of his reservations concerning free companies?" he said.

"He prefers to stand alone on the mountain of power," I said. "And he fears an enleaguing of free companies."

"A pointless fear," he said, "as each is independent, vain, jealous. proud, and suspicious of the other."

"Go on," I said.

"It was before I formed my own company," he said. "There was a village under the aegis of Ar, Tall Tree, west of the Great Swamp. Supposedly they wished to recruit mercenaries to protect themselves from roving bandits. It was, however, a hoax, designed to rid the local area of free swords. I and others were seized and forced into impressed labor, primarily on the roads."

"How did you obtain your freedom?" I asked.

"That has much to do with our present situation," he said.

"I do not understand," I said.

"Long before I had heard of Tall Tree," he said, "I had once come upon a wounded beast who had been sorely beset by hunters."

"A Kur?" I said.

"Yes," he said, "but I did not know that at the time. I knew only that it seemed manlike and was alone and dying. At the time I thought it no more than a simple beast of some sort. It did not even occur to me that it might be rational."

"I do not think it is unusual," I said, "for men to attack and try to kill what seems to them other, different, frightening, and strange."

"I bound up its wounds as I could," he said. "I found it food. I brought it water. I stayed with it and watched it for some days. Then, as it seemed to be recovering its strength, I left. I never thought to see it again."

"Later," I said, "the beast saw you, somehow, chained, laboring with others on the road."

"With its help," he said, "I, and the others, were freed. They formed the nucleus of my first free company. The first thing we did was burn the village of Tall Tree."

"And thus became an outlawed free company."

"Inevitably," he said.

"It was you," I said, "who freed the captive Kur at the menagerie on Barr Street in the Metellan District?"

"Yes," he said, "with fluids which had been earlier supplied for use if a need should arise."

"You had been recruited by the beast," I said.

"Kurii often recruit humans," he said. "Consider Tiskias."

"This was done by means of the translator?" I said.

"Of course," he said.

"Which you later recovered from the Red Whip."

"It was most likely the same one."

"Was the Kur you dealt with the same as that you tended to so long ago?" I asked.

"No," he said.

"Are you sure?" I asked.

"Yes," he said.

"One *verr* looks much like another," I said. "One *tarsk* looks much like another."

"They were quite different," he said, "and perhaps it is just as well."

"Why is that?" I asked.

"The Kur who freed us bit through the throats of a dozen guards," he said.

"But your experience with the first Kur," I said, "undoubtedly made you more open to dealing with that form of life."

"I owed my liberty to the first Kur," he said.

"And thus, in a sense," I said, "you are repaying that debt by abetting the work of another Kur."

"You are a barbarian," he said. "The matter touches on honor. Can you understand that?"

"I think so," I said.

"Good," he said.

"But," I said, "you choose your principals with care."

"I think I have done so," he said.

We were then quiet for a time.

"When I was an unclaimed slave and you claimed me, why did you cuff me?" I asked.

"That you might better realize that you are a slave," he said.

"When Master Desmond claimed Philippina," I said, "he did not cuff her."

"She is not a barbarian," he said. "She is Gorean. She knows what is involved."

"I am well aware that I am a slave, Master," I said, "a slave, and only a slave."

"Often," he said, "a slave is whipped after her claiming."

"Whipping hurts," I said. "I do not want to be whipped. I am afraid of being whipped. I will try to do my best, to avoid the lash."

"See that you do," he said.

"Yes, Master," I said.

"Good," he said.

"I do not object, however," I said, "to the 'whip of the furs.'"

"Few slaves do," he said. "Remove your tunic."

"Yes, Master," I said.

CHAPTER SEVENTY-THREE

One morning, several days ago, eleven Panther Girls had been captured by slavers of Ar, slavers of the House of Tenalian. In the course of their capture they had been driven into, or diverted into, a morass of leech plants, resulting in considerable pain and suffering. Xanthe and I, commanded, had been dispatched to tend to them, cleaning their bodies and cleansing their wounds. In our absence, a lad of the Peasants had arrived at our camp, bearing a flat, rectangular board on which, scratched, as by a spike or claw, were the following provocative but problematic words:

"Beware of friends who are not friends."

Below these words was scratched an arrow, which, presumably, had pointed to our camp. This board, with its transcribed words, had been placed near the peasant lad who had soon noticed it. He could not read but he had no difficulty in recognizing letters and he naturally assumed a message of some sort was implicit in the letters. As the arrow pointed to our camp, not far off the Venna Road, he brought it to the attention of the camp, comprehending that this was most likely the intention of the writer and doubtless hoping to receive some reward for his trouble. The message was not read aloud in his presence. He was delivered a tarsk-bit and was happily on his way. As he was near an important road, he had probably seen, and even handled, coins before. In this way, he was likely to differ from many of his peers in more remote locations. Outside of towns and cities most commerce on Gor is managed by barter. Near towns and cities, of course, markets are familiar and practical.

After breakfast, and the departure of Flavius, his men, and Calla, Rupert read the message once more to the entire camp.

"Beware of friends who are not friends."

"Of course," said Temicus, "but is the problem not how to tell which friends are not friends?"

"Patience," said Rupert of Hochburg. "A warning is a warning. It may prove of value."

"And who is our mysterious correspondent?" asked Temicus.

"Our ally," said Rupert.

"Why does he not show himself?" asked Temicus.

"If you were he," said Rupert, "you, too, at least in this area, would prefer to remain in the shadows."

We were now some twenty or so *pasangs* from Ar.

It was toward evening.

Given the traffic, Holt and Desmond were with the wagon. They were walking beside it, one on each side. Rupert and Temicus were on the wagon bench, the reins in the hands of Temicus. The slaves, Xanthe, Philippina, and myself, were in the wagon, resting on canvas amongst packs and supplies. The canvas had been removed from the overhead hoops. Thieves, bandits, brigands, and such, I had been told, were likely to be more intrigued with closed wagons than open wagons. As our wagon was open, it seemed we had little to hide and thus, presumably, we transported little of value. Yet I could have reached out and touched the packing tied about the translator which had been removed from the Red Whip in Ar.

A number of men mounted on swift saddle *tharlarion* thundered by.

"Who are those men with badges sewn on the shoulders of their scarlet cloaks?" I asked Rupert of Hochburg, my Master.

"We are close to Ar," said Rupert. "They are road guards. They are on patrol."

"Now we have less to fear from bandits," I said.

"From common bandits," said Rupert.

As the wagon trundled on, I, warm, bemused, and smiling to myself, curling on the canvas, recalled my claiming by Rupert of Hochburg. In particular, I recalled the sharp, authoritative cuffing to which I had been subjected. That had surprised me. I did not think that I had displeased him. Certainly I had not intended to displease him. Was that commonly done, such a cuffing? I doubted it. Days later, as Philippina had not been struck by Desmond in her claiming, I had queried my Master about the difference between us in this matter. I had not been fully satisfied with his answer, particularly after reflection. I had suspected that a deeper reason might lie behind my cuffing, but I did not dare suggest it. I did not doubt that the cuffing was intended to be instructive, particularly as he knew me to be a barbarian, but I suspected that there was more to it. Gorean Masters tend to be firm and leave their properties in little doubt as to their bondage, but they are seldom cruel, no more than a typical Master of Earth would be cruel to a dog or horse. On the other hand, it seems that many Gorean males, where slaves are concerned, either fear love, or are embarrassed by, or are disconcerted by, its prospect. A Gorean male suspected of something so absurd as tenderness or affection toward a slave is likely to be teased by, and ridiculed by, his peers. He could become the butt of humor, and even a laughing stock. Stories might circulate, graffiti might show up on walls and at fountains, and so on. How embarrassing that would be! How could a free male, with all his status, power, and glory, fall so low as to care for a mere slave? And, naturally, free women would be aghast at the very thought. Accordingly, that there might be such a thing as love Masters and love slaves not only exceeds the pale of propriety but its very thought defies credibility. Thus, I suspected that my cuffing had had more to do with Rupert of Hochburg than the former Miss Agnes Morrison Atherton, once of Earth. Might he not be, in a way, reassuring himself against a feared weakness, and trying to convince himself, by cuffing me, of the absurdity which might attend on caring for a lowly slave? But then I told myself not to make much of little, or of nothing. Perhaps it meant nothing. Perhaps I meant nothing. Tears came to my eyes. I knew I loved my Master, deeply and hopelessly, with the whole love of a vulnerable, rightless, helpless slave. I dared not tell him. Would I be whipped? Would I be sold, traded, or given away? Could he care for me, if only a little?

I heard voices, ahead.

I rose up, and looked forward.

"More soldiers, guardsmen," I said. "Of Ar. See the cloaks. But these are afoot."

There was much traffic on the road, much of it, I supposed, from Ar and to Ar.

"Please be kind enough to draw off the road and stay your beast," we heard. The speaker threw his cloak back. This freed the sword at his left thigh. His helmet was trimmed with what I supposed to be *sleen* hair.

Temicus pulled the wagon to the side, off the road.

"You are road guards of Ar," said Rupert.

"Yes," said the speaker.

"And how may we serve the glory of Ar?" asked Rupert.

There were some thirty of the newcomers, far more than our men might comfortably deal with, if need be, weapon to weapon, sword to sword.

"Hail, welcome and worthy travelers," said the man in the helmet, that with the crest of apparent *sleen* hair, he whom I took to be the leader of the newcomers. I will refer to him hereafter, for the sake of convenience, as the 'officer.' I did not much care for his looks. He seemed pleasant enough. I wondered if he wore his cloak with ease.

"*Tal*," said Rupert. "How is it that we, out of many others, are honored by the attention of noble guardsmen of Ar? We are humble tradesmen bound for great Ar, doubtless the house of your Home Stone. Have we inadvertently committed some fault of which we might be as yet unaware?"

"Not at all, noble tradesman," said the officer. "I bring you happy tidings."

"Of what sort?" asked Rupert. "Inform me, that I might rejoice."

"It is well known," said the officer, "that there are occasionally found small groups of free women who forsake their role in society, flee away to the forests and jungles, and disport themselves shamelessly. They scoff at civility and taxes. They have robbed granaries and stolen supplies. They have waylaid travelers and looted small caravans. They have captured and sold both men and women. They live by their own laws and hunt and fish as they please. They are no more than vermin, nuisances, and bandits."

"I have heard such things," said Rupert.

"Recently," said the officer, "one such band was reported between Ar and Venna."

"Surprising," said Rupert.

"Dreadful," said Temicus.

"What has this to do with us?" asked Rupert.

"The group was apprehended," said the officer.

"May all law-abiding citizens rejoice," said Temicus.

"Their members will soon ascend the sales block," said the officer.

"Thus their worth as females, if any, will be discovered," said Temicus.

"May we proceed?" asked Rupert.

"Slavers of the House of Tenalian of Ar effected the capture of the miscreants," said the officer, "but they were abetted in their work by a small party of travelers."

"Bold fellows," said Temicus.

"And you, your party," said the officer, triumphantly, "was that small, brave group of travelers!"

"You are mistaken," said Rupert.

"Your modesty becomes you," said the officer, "but you must not seek to evade your meed of glory, that due to you for your achievement."

"It was not us," said Rupert.

"You have been identified," said the officer.

"By whom?" asked Rupert.

"A reliable witness," said the officer.

"With your permission," said Rupert, "we will decline the honor and be on our way."

"Tenalian has spoken to the Ubar," said the officer, "and the Ubar himself wishes to commend you in a private audience in the Central Cylinder."

"I see," said Rupert.

"As we are afoot, the afternoon spent, and Ar *pasangs* away," said the officer, "let us camp nearby and proceed in the morning."

"Splendid," said Rupert.

"We have brought with us," said the officer, "the constituents of what we trust will be an agreeable collation."

"Including wine?" asked Temicus.

"Of course," said the officer.

"Welcome news," said Temicus.

"Please follow us," said the officer. "A campsite has been prepared. Given the retiring of Tor-tu-Gor, seeing to his rest, fires will be lit and conviviality may reign. In the meantime, refresh yourselves, rest, and look forward to a humble but hardy soldiers' meal. Perhaps your comely slaves may cook for us and do the serving."

"I am delighted to apply them so," said Rupert.

"After the alarms to the east, Panther Girls, and such," said Temicus, "it is well to be amongst friends."

"It is so," said the officer. "Be at ease. You are amongst friends."

"True friends," said Rupert.

"True friends," said the officer.

A few minutes later the wagon had been drawn well away from the road, and the *tharlarion* unhitched.

"Master," I said. "I am afraid."

"How so?" asked Rupert.

"I do not think our escort means us well."

"You are correct," he said.

"I fear they are not genuine," I said.

"They are not," he said. "This far from Ar, road guards are mounted. These men are afoot. Too, their talk of Marlenus and Tenalian, and an audience in the Central Cylinder, and such, is twaddle. The apprehension of a handful of Panther Girls near Venna is of little interest to high authorities in Ar. Certainly it would not justify sending troops to meet us or an audience in the Central Cylinder.

"They spoke of a witness," I said.

"It must be Tiskias," he said. "Who else would know us?"

"They must be in his hire," I said.

"Did you not notice the wallet slung at our host's belt?" asked Rupert.

"No," I said.

"It was identical with the one carried by Wanda, the leader of the Panther Girls," said Rupert.

"The newcomers profess friendship," I said.

"Another indication of their inauthenticity," said Rupert. "Disciplined soldiers do their duty. They are civil and efficient. They do not make friends like jolly fellows well met on the road."

"I have noticed," I said, "that members of our escort are scattered about, in such a way as to encircle the camp."

"I suggested to Holt and Desmond that they might attempt to depart the camp," said Rupert. "They were both turned back, politely, to be sure."

"For we are all friends," I said.

"True friends," said Rupert.

"We are prisoners," I said.

"Guests," said Rupert.

"It is getting dark," I said. "Our hosts' surveillance will increase."

"And it will become less easy to mark small differences," he said.

"Master?" I said.

"Did you know," he asked, "that barbarian slaves are chosen in part for intelligence?"

"No," I said, "but, in any event, I was not scouted by, and selected by, slavers."

"Do not be too sure," he said.

"I do not understand," I said.

"Those who employed you on your former world," he said, "may have had some such disposition of you in mind," he said.

"I do not think so," I said.

"Surely they were not unaware of your charms," he said. "Surely, being men, they must have speculated on what you might bring on a sales block, how you might look, stripped, kneeling, collared, and marked."

"I trust not," I said.

"In any event," he said, "I assure you that you are the sort of catch that Gorean slavers prize, beautiful, slave hot, and highly intelligent."

"A slave is flattered," I said, "but I do not understand the purpose or relevance of this conversation."

"It has both purpose and relevance," he said. "Our hosts plan a supper. You, Xanthe, and Philippina will prepare it. Wine will be served. There are some thirty of them, and seven of us, four men and three slaves. I do not know if the slaves will be allowed to drink or not. The bottles of wine will differ, possibly by location, but, more likely, as to marking. A certain number of the bottles, the larger number, will be intended by the hosts for themselves, and a smaller number of bottles will be intended for us. Our hosts, of course, will control the distribution of the wine."

"We will change the markings on the bottles," I said, "or exchange the contents, as we can, so that we are served the wine intended for them and they are served the wine intended for us."

"Precisely," said Rupert of Hochburg, "and may good fortune attend your efforts."

"There," said Rupert of Hochburg. "That will do."

He had just snapped the manacle about the left ankle of the unconscious officer.

"How long will they remain unconscious?" I asked.

"I do not know," he said. "Probably several Ahn."

The men who had intercepted us on the Venna Road, leading to Ar, were chained together, one to another, the chain encircling a large tree. The chaining had been extracted from the stores of those who had sought to detain us. Undoubtedly the chains had been intended for us, or us and an even larger company, had we been joined by others. Their weapons had been broken or cast aside, in the woods.

"Are they not in danger," I asked, "tethered helplessly in the woods, lacking food and water?"

"Not at all," he said. "They can call out, and be heard on the road. If not, Tiskias, and others, will investigate, and discover them."

"Was it necessary," I asked, uneasily, "that we removed their clothing, all of it?"

"Why do you ask?" he said.

"I think they will be incensed," I said. "They will be rife with fury. They will seek prompt, dire vengeance."

"Excellent," he said. "Men flung about by the storms of their emotions make desirable enemies. They are reckless, intemperate, and short-sighted. They see no further than their hate. They are easily bested, easily killed. Patient steel, careful steel, precise steel has little to fear from frenzied steel."

"I take it," I said, "that we are now forth to the Beast Caves."

"Caution is advised," said Rupert. "The Beast Caves will be watched. We must tread with care."

"What are we to do?" I asked.

"Test the ground," he said. "Reconnoiter."

"Enemies," I said, "will expect us to approach the Beast Caves directly."

"That is why," said Rupert, "we will enter Ar and learn what we can before taking action."

"The gates of Ar will be watched," I said.

"We will not enter Ar as the party they hope to detect," he said. "We will pass the gates, one or another, variously, individually, or in small groups, and later reassemble within."

"Time may be short," I said. "The forces of Pompilius may have completed their retreat to a place of safety. The spheres may even now be in motion."

"It is possible," he said.

"Master is troubled," I said.

"It is my fear," he said, "that we may be unable to reach the Beast Caves."

"Now that we have been discovered," I said, "I think that is quite possible."

"Even likely," he said.

"What then?" I asked.

"We must then hope that the Beast Caves can reach us."

"I do not understand," I said.

"Do not forget our ally," he said.

CHAPTER SEVENTY-FOUR

"At least," said Holt, "we have reached Ar."

"Is this place safe?" asked Temicus.

"For us," said Rupert, "no place is safe."

We were in one of six one-floored, common-walled, stone-sided storage facilities in Ar's largest warehouse district, that near the Gate of the Wagons. It was not the closest gate to the Beast Caves. That would be the Gate of the Urts. We surmised that that gate might be more carefully watched than the others. We had planned to avoid it. But even by the Gate of the Urts, the Beast Caves were some three *pasangs* beyond the *pomerium* of Ar, and through open, largely desolate terrain, a sober indication that few humans cared to approach them.

"There is no rear exit," said Desmond.

"Now," said Rupert.

"Two exits may be covered as well as one," said Holt.

"The walls are of stone," said Rupert. "Our private gate is stout. If necessary, we could hold it against a much larger number."

The layout of the building in one section of which lay our informal, provisional headquarters was, as one might guess from the text, low, flat and rectangular. A main entrance or gate opened onto a long, horizontal corridor off which lay six compartments, each with its own door or gate.

"I would still prefer a rear exit," said Temicus.

"See the harnessing and saddlery," said Rupert. "It is more secure given walls of stone and a single door."

"I had us in mind," said Temicus, "not harnessing and saddlery."

"Two doors can be watched as well as one," said Holt.

"But where there is no door," said Rupert, "one does not watch."

I was sure that this cryptic contribution to the conversation did not much allay the uneasiness of Temicus, but at that very moment an unusual knock was heard at our private door, off the long horizontal corridor.

"Two knocks, followed by three, repeated twice," said Holt.

"A signal agreed upon, long ago, near Venna, should it be deemed appropriate," said Rupert.

"He whom you spoke of as your ally?" said Temicus.

"The same," said Rupert.

"A Kur," said Desmond, shuddering.

"Ready the translation box," said Rupert.

Holt of Ar immediately went to the packs and undid the wrapping on the translation device.

I did not think he knew much of the device, nor how to operate it, but the Kur outside, it at the door, if it were a Kur, would presumably be familiar with the controls. I hoped its operation might be as obvious and simple as switching a light on and off. I did fear that it might require some sort of code to allow it to be used.

"You are sure," asked Temicus of Rupert, "that what is at the door is Kur?"

"Reasonably so," said Rupert. "The signal."

"Signals can be stolen," said Temicus.

"Would you care to try to steal a signal from a Kur?" asked Rupert.

"How do you know it is friendly?" asked Temicus.

"I do not know that," said Rupert.

"If you open the door and a Kur bursts in amongst us," said Temicus, "we might all be slaughtered within the Ehn."

"Unsheathe your weapons then," said Rupert. "Kurii shed blood, and their hearts are as averse to steel as ours."

Temicus, Desmond, and Holt readied their weapons. From this, I gathered they were less assured of the nature of our visitor than Rupert of Hochburg, my Master.

The knock was repeated, more insistently.

"With all due respect, Captain," said Holt, "Kurii, of late, are rare in Ar."

"Publicly," said Rupert.

I thought of Bubu, the pet, or confederate, of Tiskias.

"How could a Kur follow us, in mighty Ar, without being noted, with no alarm being raised?" asked Desmond.

"Perhaps," said Rupert, "it was seen, but, for some reason, say, a regard for one's personal safety, an apprehension that the beast, discovered, might turn on them, the alarm would not be raised."

"The night is dark," said Rupert. "Shadows, even with the moons, are dismal, jagged, and long. Cloaks, too, can conceal much. Too, in many places, in this area, aside from the wagon routes, roofs are accessible and streets are narrow."

"I watched with care, with heightened senses," said Holt. "I saw no sign of a Kur."

"Perhaps it did not wish you to do so," said Rupert.

"Who will open the door?" asked Desmond.

"Surely a slave," said Temicus.

"I will open it," I said.

As my Master was leader of the group, it seemed to me that it should be his slave who attended to the task.

"Do so," said Rupert of Hochburg.

"Yes, Master," I said.

I saw that he was pleased with me.

I had done the right thing.

A slave wants muchly to gain the approval of her Master. She lives to please him. He is all to her. He is her Master.

I slid back the bolts on the door, and, with some effort, swung the heavy door inward.

Before the threshold, crouched back on its haunches, was a large Kur. It looked at the armed men, and, behind them, at Xanthe and Philippina, standing back, the swords of our Masters between them and the door.

"Sheath your swords," said Rupert.

The men did so, however reluctantly.

The beast entered the room, with an agility that seemed anomalous in so large a body.

I thought it might be the Kur whom I had tended at the menagerie in the Metellan District, but I was not sure. Within limits, I found it occasionally difficult to distinguish one Kur from another. Interestingly, I later learned that many Kurii sometimes find it difficult to tell one human female from another and one human male from another. Is that the same human female I saw yesterday? Is that the same human male I saw five days ago, and so on. One supposes that, for a time, the members of one species use a large, simple template for recognizing members of another species. Humans can recognize flamingos, lions, and zebras, but is that the same flamingo, lion, or zebra as one saw this morning, or earlier this afternoon, or a week ago? Happily, with more experience, these broad templates become more and more refined until, in many cases, one can easily distinguish one member of a species from another, much as the average human being can easily tell one human being from another.

My Master gestured to the door, so I swung it shut, slowly, given its weight, and then slid the heavy bolts in place.

Our guest growled and pointed at the translation device which Maxwell Holt, or Holt of Ar, had removed from its packing. The device seemed small in the large paws, or hands, of the beast, but the digits, six to each paw or hand, moving quickly, nimbly, enabled the device. I do not know the capacities of the device but it could move promptly and, I trust, accurately, back and forth between Gorean and at least one of the languages of the Kurii. As nearly as I could tell, aside from volume, there were no adjustments on the device for nuancing speech, for example, conveying intonation contours or tones of voice. The tenderest declaration of love and the screamed utterance of a dire threat were rendered by the machine with the same lack of either interest or passion. In what follows, and elsewhere, when and where a translation device is in use, I will generally ignore its contribution to a discourse which, without it, could not have taken place.

"How is it," asked the Kur, "that I was greeted with unclothed steel?"

"Who knows," asked Rupert, "what fist knocks on a closed door."

"I am Lucilius, deputy to Agamemnon, Eleventh Face of the Nameless One," spoke the Kur.

"*Tal*," said my Master, "I am Rupert of Hochburg."

"We meet again," said the Kur.

"It is so," said Rupert.

"Are we well met?" asked the Kur.

"I trust so," said Rupert, "for you and I, in our way, have traveled far and endured much. Before we begin, however, may I speak openly of these matters, for there are some here who may know less than is appropriate for them, some who should be allowed to withdraw from our project if they wish, while there is time to do so."

"There may be no time now," said the Kur.

"Even were it so, Captain," said Holt of Ar, "I am with you."

"I, too," said Desmond.

"And I," said Temicus.

"Speak then," said Lucilius. "Let all be informed, even slaves. But do not speak too much at length, no more than is necessary. I may have been followed."

"The noble Lucilius, I, and others," said Rupert of Hochburg, "addressed ourselves to what originally seemed no more than an unimportant mystery, why Kurii and others, now recognized as minions of Pompilius, a Kur commander, from a far world, should wish to hunt down, acquire, and eliminate a particular woman, a mere slave. Our curiosity was aroused. Might she hold some key to matters of moment? Thus, two parties sought the slave, one to remove her, and one to inquire into her importance. As you know, we have found the slave and ascertained the nature of the knowledge she bore, that two spheres were constructed, spheres which might be intended to be employed as impact weaponry. What else would comport with the ambitions of Pompilius? The two likely targets of these spheres would be first, the Sardar, to destroy Priest-Kings and render Gor vulnerable to the invasion and attack of a ruthless, determined, technologically sophisticated enemy, and secondly, the Beast Caves, headquarters of the faction of Agamemnon, the foe of Pompilius."

"It might be added," said the Kur, "that a blow directed at what you are prone to denominate as the 'Beast Caves,' a blow comparable to that which could destroy the domain of the Priest-Kings, would presumably, in this area, not only destroy the 'Beast Caves' but would be likely to level the walls and towers of Ar itself."

"No!" protested Holt.

"Ar is the house of his Home Stone," said Rupert.

"Are these mighty stones catapulted from space?" asked Temicus.

"Mira!" snapped Rupert.

"More like immense, hollow, guided worlds or spheres," I said.

"My spies," said Lucilius, "inform me that the stones, as they think of them, have at last been sighted, that they hurtle even now, swiftly and silently, toward the Sardar and the High Lair of Agamemnon."

"How much time have we?" asked Rupert.

"A day, perhaps two, perhaps three," said Lucilius. "Who knows? Perhaps only Ahn."

"We must contact the Beast Caves," said Desmond.

"That will not be easy," said Lucilius. "Hirelings of an operative, a sycophant, of Pompilius, one named Tiskias, block approaches to the High Lair."

"Do they not realize the dangers to which they themselves are exposed?" asked Holt.

"Presumably not," said Rupert. "Doubtless most see their role as merely one of denying access to a dreaded area. Even Tiskias may be ignorant of his own peril. He may know of the 'stones,' so to speak, but have no idea of what would be the width and force of their impact. His Kur colleague may be similarly uninformed."

"I doubt that," said Lucilius. "He is Kur. Kurii prize glory."

"He would sacrifice himself, as well as possibly hundreds of uninformed others?" asked Rupert.

"For glory," said Lucilius.

"If forces we are unequipped to deal with, forces we cannot penetrate, seal off the entrances to this 'High Lair,' how can we reach Agamemnon?" asked Temicus.

"I feared this impasse," said Rupert. "It is for this reason that I have hoped that somehow, if we could not reach Agamemnon, that Agamemnon, or a colleague, or messenger, could reach us. Thus we are in desperate need of the wisdom and counsel of the noble Lucilius."

"There is a possibility," said Lucilius. "Agamemnon and his cohorts in the High Lair will undoubtedly be aware of the anomalous activity in their vicinity. They will wish to investigate it, and understand it. On the other hand, as Kurii on Gor, Kurii subject to the weapon and communication laws of the Priest-Kings, they cannot simply throw a switch and burn or blast away, like lightning decimating a flock of *verr*, large numbers of armed men crowded about in the vicinity of the High Lair. Similarly, how would the double-bladed axes of a handful of Kurii fare against hundreds of loosed quarrels and cast spears? Indeed, mighty as a Kur is, it can be hunted down, and killed or captured, even exhibited, as if it were merely a wild, dangerous animal. I can vouch for the experience."

"What is this possibility to which you allude, noble Lucilius?" inquired Rupert.

"Let me speak to you of the bodies of Agamemnon," said Lucilius.

"Speak," said Rupert.

"The brain," said Lucilius, "is the centrality of the organism; it not only thinks, reasons, and decides, but it sees, hears, smells, feels, and tastes; a pain seemingly felt in a paw is actually felt in the brain and extradited to the paw where it seems to exist; for example, a pain may seem to be felt in a paw when the paw no longer exists; a suitably stimulated brain, isolated from an organism, would have experiences indistinguishable from those of the same brain imbedded in an organism."

"These are strange sayings," said Temicus.

"There was once a mighty Kur," said Lucilius, "a Kur amongst Kurii. It stood high in the rings. It was a great leader. Thousands would hasten to proclaim its name and lay their axes at its feet. You could not understand or pronounce his name. To refer to him, Goreans gave him a high, proud name, that of an ancient king, from legends of Earth, Agamemnon. Ring by ring, kill by kill, step by step, he climbed to a throne, one which no one, for countless revolutions, dared dispute with him. His thoughts were long and his studies deep. He cultivated industry, commerce, and science. He was brilliant and savage, subtle in diplomacy and ruthless in battle. He could be as adamant as a rod of steel, as supple as a reed bending in the wind. He mocked the past, noting how it had thoughtlessly forged an accidental, foolish present, and then he gripped the anvil of the present that on it he might forge a future to his liking. Was he not the greatest of all the people? But how could the ambitious and envious endure such a being, so mighty, so fearful and strange? Is it not the dream of the *urt* that there shall be no *larls*? Do not the small resent the large; do not the insignificant object to the significant, the magnificent? Do not the little want all to be little. Do not their rulers, who are not themselves little, pretend to be little, that the hypocritical farce on which their power depends may continue unabated? Truth is uncomfortable; it is thus not surprising that it would be shunned. The great Agamemnon was fallen upon, his body lacerated and torn from the bones, but the mighty brain, filled with blood, lived. Skilled men of science removed it from the remnants of its body, kept it alive in solution, and eventually equipped it with sensors and controls by means of which it could communicate and initiate signals to external housings, metal housings which commonly were tooled to resemble animals."

"What was the fate of the would-be assassins?" asked Rupert of Hochburg. "I gather that they did not manage to seize their steel world for themselves."

"It was a festival of blood," said Lucilius. "None survived the Ehn."

"What has all this," asked Temicus, "to do with our problem?"

"A Kur amongst men cannot help but be noticed," said Lucilius, "and, possibly, in many situations, attacked. But what if a Kur did not seem a Kur?"

"How can a Kur not seem a Kur?" asked Temicus.

"If we cannot reach the High Lair," said Lucilius, "it is my hope that the High Lair can reach us."

"I do not understand," said Temicus.

"He speaks of a body, unlike that of a Kur," said Rupert, "a shape or form within which is somehow ensconced the brain of a Kur."

"It is Agamemnon," said Lucilius. "The body is indifferent."

"I had hoped some recourse might be found," said Rupert.

"I have been gone for months," said Lucilius. "I know little of what now transpires in the High Lair. The last body of Agamemnon, that of a giant mechanical tarn, was destroyed in a forest near Samnium. It is my hope that he has now a new body, one which might awe our enemies while we alert him to the danger of the hurtling spheres."

"Let us make haste," said my Master. "We must act before it is too late."

At this very moment there were shouts outside our bolted door, and spear butts smote the beams, and then there began the blows of axes.

"It is too late," said Temicus.

CHAPTER SEVENTY-FIVE

"I feared I was followed," said Lucilius.

"What can follow a Kur?" asked Desmond.

"A *sleen*," said Lucilius, "—or another Kur."

"Blades forth!" said Holt. "Let us prove ourselves worthy of our Home Stones!"

"Recall," said Temicus, drawing his sword, "I lamented the folly of a single door."

"Your point was well taken," said Rupert, turning toward the packs unloaded earlier from the wagon.

"We are trapped," said Temicus.

"Not at all," said Rupert.

Axes were now splintering away the sturdy beams of the door.

"There is only one door," said Temicus.

"Now," said Rupert.

"I do not understand," said Temicus.

"We shall make another," said Rupert.

"I gather," said Lucilius, "that, despite the danger, you retained the residue of the fluids used in Ar to melt the bars and dissolve the stones of my prison."

"You were wise to furnish me with such materials near Venna before you were captured."

"I did so," said Lucilius, "anticipating that a need for them might arise."

"What are you talking about?" asked Temicus.

Rupert turned to Holt. "How long do you think the door will hold?" he asked.

"Perhaps ten Ehn," said Holt.

"I think so," said Rupert. "That will give us a start of some ten Ehn."

"Are you mad?" asked Temicus.

"Stand back!" said Rupert.

He held one of the two bottles against which I had earlier been warned. It was less than a third full.

"Back away, back away!" I told Xanthe and Philippina.

The bottle, cast with great force, shattered against the rear wall of the room. For a moment the fluid clung to the wall, and it might have been no more than innocent water dashed against stone, but, a moment later, in the midst of what seemed a blazing white fire, the wall began to shudder and ripple. "Look away!" said Rupert. A moment later the room seemed filled with a throbbing, blinding light. I threw my hands before my eyes. I could hear a hissing, grating sound. Then the light was gone. We looked to the wall.

"Not enough!" said Rupert.

"No," said Lucilius, and tore saddles and harnessing from a high rack at the side of the room. He broke the rack apart, and then began, with a stout shelf, to punch at the wall. Meanwhile axes struck again and again, frenziedly, at the door.

Suddenly the wall seemed to shower down in tiny, disklike plates and the plates, a moment later, began to dissolve before our eyes.

Lucilius, shaken with agitation, cast the broken, splintered shelf to the side and uttered some violent explosive noise. "Let us take our leave," came from the translation device, in quiet, unaccented syllables.

To my surprise our Masters ordered us through the wall first. Could Holt care so much for Xanthe, or Desmond for Philippina? Did they not realize we were slaves? If they did, would they not soon remind us of that unmistakable salient fact?

We bent down and were soon in the cool air of the night. I conjectured that a larger aperture would have been occasioned by more of the fluid. We were soon joined by the men, and Lucilius.

"It seems you did not put us in a trap," said Temicus to Rupert.

"I began to fear I might have done so," said Rupert.

"The fluids are useful," said Lucilius. "On the steel worlds they are often used in grenades."

"Follow me," he then said, "on, toward the High Lair. We must hope the mercenaries will stand confused, even in consternation at what may have emerged from what they dare to think of as the Beast Caves."

"Proceed," said Rupert. "I will join you shortly."

"We have little time," said Lucilius.

"I will gain us some more time," said Rupert.

"How is that?" asked Lucilius.

"I shall drag some racks and goods from the outside before the opening in the wall, to conceal it. Those who crash into the room, intent on a fray and slaughter, will find an empty room. How can this be? What anomaly is this? Where did the defenders go? How can it be explained? Let them shudder in the face of the inexplicable and uncanny. They may run screaming, back into the street."

"This mystery would be soon solved by a Kur," said Lucilius.

"Perhaps no Kur was involved, but only, say, Tiskias," said Rupert.

"Unlikely," said Lucilius.

"I conjecture," said Rupert, "that a Kur, few of which are about, knowing his importance to the plans of his principal, Pompilius, and that he would be a prime target for desperate defenders, would be unlikely to risk himself in the storming of a bitterly defended room. He may even have left the vicinity, leaving the matter to his underlings, content to await a report. Too, I think that one may presume that many Kurii in the faction of Pompilius would have little or no reason to suppose that such sophisticated means of demolition as that of the unusual fluids were at our disposal. They would at least first hazard other hypotheses to explain the strange report of their minions, most likely that their minions were confused, mistaken, or lying. In any event, I think we will have gained a few more Ehn."

"Join us as soon as possible," said Lucilius.

"I will do so," said Rupert.

"We may have to force a gate," said Lucilius.

"The captain has the gold of Tiskias," said Desmond, "that which his hirelings were kind enough to place at our disposal."

"Loyal gatesmen of Ar," said Holt, "cannot be bribed."

"What about disloyal gatesmen?" said Temicus.

"Gatesmen of Ar cannot be bribed," said Holt.

"You might be surprised," said Temicus, "not that your civic pride does not do you credit."

"Beware," said Holt.

"In any event," said Temicus, "the experiment is easily arranged."

"The key to opening a gate need not be either steel or gold," said Rupert.

"What else?" asked Holt.

"The metal of cunning," said Rupert.

CHAPTER SEVENTY-SIX

"Stride bravely, show no fear," said Rupert.

"We are now well beyond the gate," said Desmond.

"Thanks to the captain," said Holt.

The slaves bore all packs and burdens as was appropriate.

Our party had been detained at the Gate of the Urts, the nearest gate in Ar to the Beast Caves, by six guardsmen and an officer. Some putative loiterers, too, were about. I suspected that, given the hour, at least one or more of them were detailed by Tiskias, on behalf of the faction of Pompilius, to observe traffic at the gate. We would have avoided that gate had our station in the warehouse not been discovered and attacked, had matters seemed less urgent.

Lucilius had switched off the translator, suspended now on a cord about his neck, as we had neared the gate.

"Hold!" had said the officer. "The gate is closed. What is that with you, so well cloaked?"

Rupert flung the cloak aside, and Lucilius reared up, growling, regarding the guardsmen balefully.

"Aii!" cried more than one of the guardsmen, freeing their weapons.

"This animal," said Rupert, "haunts our streets, rifles our garbage, and frightens our children. Such beasts are now, as you know, unwelcome in Ar, certainly if loose. I and my fellows, steel at the ready, wish to conduct it outside the walls."

"Why is it not bound?" asked the officer.

"It does not wish to be bound," said Rupert. "Would you care to bind it?"

"I think it enough," said the officer, "if it allows itself to be peaceably escorted out of the city."

"Are such things rational?" asked one of the fellows near the gate, perhaps an innocent loiterer.

"I have heard," said another, "that some such beasts, given lengthy, intensive training, as in carnivals and circuses, appear marvelously to simulate intelligence."

"Be fair to the poor beast," said the officer. "Surely it is intelligent, certainly as much so as a *sleen* or a *larl*, perhaps even more so."

I was pleased that the translation device had been turned off.

"I should like to get this beast beyond the gate before morning," said Rupert.

"So you can return to your beds," said a bystander.

"Surely," said Rupert.

"Morning is soon enough," said the officer.

"I do not think so," said Rupert. "It will grow hungry and restless toward morning. Unpleasantries might occur."

"Be pleased to get it outside the city," said Temicus.

"We can wait, however inconvenient and possibly dangerous it might be," said Rupert, "but we do so under protest and you must accept full responsibility for any untoward or fearful incidents which might occur."

The officer gestured to his men and they opened the gate.

"Pass," he said.

"Good," said Rupert. "It is a wise decision. You are a fine officer. May Ar be proud of its guardsmen."

"Do not leave it at the gate," said the officer. "Get it well beyond the *pomerium*, and farther."

"We will do so," said Rupert.

"Some *pasangs* to the south and east," said a bystander, "are said to be caves of a sort, frequented by such beasts."

"Be thanked," said Rupert. "We shall search them out."

"Do not approach them too closely," said the officer. "Not all these ugly brutes are tame or satisfactorily domesticated."

"We will be careful," said Rupert.

"What is that around the neck of the beast?" asked the officer.

"I do not know," said Rupert. "It must be something it picked up while examining garbage. Perhaps he thinks it is an ornament. He seems fond of it. I do not think I would inquire into the matter further."

"Why are slaves with you?" asked the officer.

"They were with us when we came on the beast," said Rupert. "We decided to hasten it to the gate. We did not wish them to try to reach our *insula* alone, through dangerous streets at a late Ahn."

"I wish you well," said the officer.

"I wish you well," said Rupert.

We then made our way through the Gate of the Urts, and turned east, and soon left the walls of Ar behind us.

Lucilius snapped on the translator.

"I am going ahead," he said. "You will be less suspect and safer if I am not with you. Look for an oddity. It is likely to resemble an animal of metal. Presumably its makeup will incorporate a translator.

Hopefully it will be a body of Agamemnon. Communicate with it, warn it."

"Wait!" said Rupert.

But Lucilius had slipped away, into the darkness.

We continued on our way.

"What are we looking for?" asked Temicus.

"Most profoundly," said Rupert, "the Beast Caves, but, as they may be closed to us by armed men, some sort of emissary to which, or artifact by means of which, we can deliver our warning to Agamemnon and his faction without entering the Beast Caves."

"Perhaps," said Holt, "we can encounter what Lucilius referred to as a body of Agamemnon."

"That seems to be his hope," said Rupert.

"It may not be in place, or be ready, or may not exist," said Desmond.

"True," said Rupert.

"Our prospects," said Temicus, "do not shine brightly."

"We must try," said Rupert. "Should we fail, it is ruin to Priest-Kings and catastrophe to the Beast Caves and Ar."

"The Priest-Kings," said Desmond, "protect us from Kurii. Without the Priest-Kings, Gor falls to Kurii."

"And Terra, as well, if they choose to have it," said Holt.

"Hold!" said a voice from the darkness.

We stopped short.

"Turn back," said the voice. "Danger lies ahead."

"What sort of danger?" asked Rupert.

"Wicked beasts," said the voice, "wild, unpredictable, violent, and terrible."

"Splendidly done," said Rupert. "Your commander has instructed you well. Were we ordinary wayfarers, common travelers, or such, we would retire or amend our route. On the other hand, we are well aware of what is afoot, the commander's desire to restrict movement in this area, in effect, to close it off."

"Temporarily," said the voice.

"Let us hope so," said Rupert.

"Turn back," said the voice.

"We dare not disobey the commander," said Rupert. "He wishes to be informed of matters in Ar, in particular, if there is awareness in Ar of his actions outside the *pomerium*, and, if so, of how they are viewed."

"You do not need three slaves for that," said the voice.

"The slaves are to content and pacify the men," said Rupert.

"Leave one here," said the voice.

"We have too few to do that," said Rupert, who then, boldly, saying no more, and asking no leave, marched forth, we following him, through the darkness, on our way toward the Beast Caves. It was an anxious moment for all of us, but there was no attempt to stop us. Not one weapon was unhoused.

A bit later, however, Rupert called a halt. His breathing was quick, deep, and irregular. I was then more afraid than I had been before. What we had done had apparently, in his view, been more dangerous than I had hitherto understood.

"We are alive," said Holt.

"Things may not go as smoothly next time," said Rupert. "Keep your weapons loose in their scabbards."

Shortly thereafter, calmed, and wary, we continued on our way.

Xanthe, Philippina, and I, burdened, brought up the rear.

Something like an hour later, we saw lanterns, and some torches, ahead.

"We must be in the vicinity of the Beast Caves," said Holt.

"Surely you have been here before," said Temicus.

"No," said Holt.

"But you know of this place," said Temicus.

"One knows certain things," said Holt.

"I saw a post a bit back," said Desmond. "It was surmounted by a double-bladed ax head."

"That is a warning," said Holt.

"Then we are near the Beast Caves," said Temicus.

"The soldiers, ahead, seem in no military order," said Holt.

"I doubt that they are soldiers," said Rupert, "more likely riffraff, hastily recruited thugs and ruffians."

"What are they doing," asked Desmond.

"I do not know," said Rupert.

"There are several of them," said Temicus.

"A hundred, easily," said Holt.

"I see no sign of either Lucilius, or Tiskias," said Desmond.

"That may be just as well," said Rupert.

"Nor an emissary nor a contrivance of metal," said Desmond.

"We must have been seen by now," said Temicus.

"Of course," said Holt.

"We have not been challenged," said Temicus.

"Interesting," said Rupert.

"Are things not going too easily?" said Temicus.

"Far too easily," said Rupert.

"Let us withdraw," said Temicus.

"That would attract attention," said Rupert.

"What shall we do?" asked Temicus.

"When in doubt, go forward," said Rupert.

We then advanced toward the mercenaries. As far as I could tell, they took no note of us. As we approached, it became evident that they were gathered about something the nature of which, because of their bodies, was difficult to make out. I did see, in one moment, with a sudden frisson, as some men shifted, the reflection of torchlight on metal. The object, as we came closer, became more clear. It was reasonably large and heavy. It seemed to have a flat base and a globular body. Its height would come roughly to a man's waist. If it could move, it must be by means of low wheels or rollers set in the base. I did not know how long it had been in its present position. Given the interest and curiosity of the men gathered about it I thought it might have recently arrived at its present position. I wondered if it might have emerged from its housing, the Beast Caves, or wherever, about the same time as we were approaching.

"It is a heavy metal hemisphere," said Temicus.

"Consider the enveloping plating," said Rupert. "It is like a hood, or cap, or shell, on the hemisphere. What does it look like to you?"

"In its way," said Temicus, "save for its large size, a common creature of the rivers or mashes."

"A form of life," said Rupert.

"An ordinary, six-legged, shelled, river globe," said Temicus.

"Some mercenaries are formed behind us," whispered Holt.

"You men ahead," said Rupert sharply, with authority, "move to the side. Stay away from the object. Do you not know what it is? Do you think it is some mere inert artifact of steel?"

"We do not know what it is," said a man.

I am sure we did not know what it was either.

The fellows who had gathered about the metal hemisphere drew to the sides. It is interesting how an authoritative voice often induces compliance, particularly in an unclear or ambiguous situation. Surely they did not know my Master, nor was he in any obvious position of authority, certainly not in their ragged band.

We followed Rupert of Hochburg as he neared the object.

I guessed that the rounded, caplike hood on the object might rotate up and back, opening the hemisphere. This made me uneasy.

"There are scratches on this beautiful metal globe," said Rupert, sternly. "Who has dared to do this?"

"Forgive us, noble officer," said a man.

"It came out of the darkness," said another.

"We attacked it," said another, "with swords, spear blades, and knives."

"We were afraid," said a man.

"We meant no harm," said another.

"We could not harm it, we could not stop it," said a man.

"It is stopped now," said Rupert.

"Do not touch it," said another man. "It sizzles like water poured on a scalding plate; it crackles and sparks like a stirred fire; it, without arms and hands hisses and flings men who touch it yards to the side."

This had to be some form of shock, I was sure.

"Of course," said Rupert, as if this was naturally to be expected in such cases. Actually, I supposed that he knew no more of such things than the others.

"Move away, step away," ordered Rupert, with definition and assurance, as if, in their modest force, he was a duly instituted officer of considerable rank, one to whom it never occurred that he might be questioned, let alone disobeyed.

"Where is Tiskias?" whispered a man.

"This goes beyond the craven Tiskias," said Rupert.

This declaration took the mercenaries aback, as doubtless it was the gold of Tiskias which had brought them together. I supposed that it was only in a recently formed assemblage of undisciplined thugs with no clearly understood purpose and no clearly established chain of command, that so a bold a hoax as that of my Master might prove successful, if only for a short time. I trusted that Tiskias would not make an appearance, which would be most inopportune at this moment. I wondered where he might be. Too, I wished that Lucilius might be safely at hand. Who but he would understand how to deal with the mysterious metal hemisphere?

"Give way, back away, clear the area," commanded Rupert. "Farther, farther!"

It is not clear whether the matter had to do with an unwillingness to risk disobedience to a possibly authentic authority or the result of some unfortunate experiences with the hemisphere, but the mercenaries complied. They drew well away from the hemisphere, but, I noted, in such a way as to keep us in the center of a now considerably enlarged circle. I supposed that one or more portals to the Beast Caves, or the High Lair as Lucilius termed it, lay some distance behind the hemisphere, which seemingly had come forth to meet us, perhaps a hundred yards or more.

Rupert approached the hemisphere.

This was done with the semblance of a confidence I doubted he felt.

He bent down.

I expected him to address it, but quietly, certainly to no degree which would carry to the encircling mercenaries.

Our party gathered about him, closely.

Doubtless we all wanted to hear, but, too, I think we, particularly the slaves, surrounded as we were, wanted the comfort and reassurance of proximity.

Xanthe, Philippina, and I exchanged glances.

Our strength was slight. We were unarmed. We were scarcely clothed. That, as the free will have it, increases one's sense of difference and minimality, of helplessness and vulnerability. Too, we were collared. Well we knew the meaning of that. We were no more than vendible, purchasable domestic animals. We were totally dependent on the free for food, for clothing, if any, even for the opportunity to speak. We were slaves. We were owned. The free were our Masters.

My Master straightened up and looked about.

I could sense his uneasiness. What was he to do, how was he to act?

Given my background I might have anticipated something like a two-way radio or camera arrangement to be involved, but his Gorean background would not encompass such possibilities.

But then I shuddered.

What if this hemisphere were not a communication device, but actually a Kur, Agamemnon, housed in a crafted body?

"Shall we proceed?" asked Rupert of Hochburg.

"Yes," said Desmond.

"By all means," said Holt of Ar.

"There is little else to do," said Temicus, "unless it be to await a rain of spears."

My Master regarded us, the slaves.

"I do not know what will occur," he said. "Put down your packs."

Gratefully, I put my pack down, which I had borne since Ar. My shoulders were sore. Similarly, since Ar, Xanthe had borne the pack of Holt of Ar, and Philippina had borne that of Desmond of Hochburg. We had taken turns in adding the pack of Temicus to that of our Masters. This, incidentally, our bearing of burdens, while tactically intelligent, had nothing in particular to do with freeing the limbs of Masters for the use of weapons, or such. It would not have occurred, in any case, to the men, Goreans, to think of relieving us of these burdens, onerous as they might be. We were slaves. They were free.

Rupert bent a bit, again, toward the hemisphere.

"Can you hear me?" he whispered.

"Yes," came from the hemisphere.

There was a long silence.

I suppose that we all were startled, even frightened, to hear this response, any response, from the hemisphere.

Could it be the body of a Kur?

What Gorean would expect to hear a voice emanate from a metal object?

Xanthe and I regarded one another.

Our Terran background not only enlarged but guided our interpretation of what might be occurring.

Our natural suspicions led us away from the hypothesis of a living brain somehow inhabiting, perceiving through, and controlling an artificial body, a possibility which, although we knew it was theoretically feasible, seemed less likely than that of a contrivance incorporating a speaker and cameras, which device or contrivance was well within the compass of contemporary Terran science, let alone that of Kurii.

There was of course, the possibility that we might, after all, be dealing with an artificial body housing an active brain.

That was alarming.

It spoke of a technology currently only dreamed of in Terran science.

I wished that Lucilius might be present. I did not doubt but what he would have been able, almost instantly, to attest or disprove the authenticity of the device about which we were uneasily gathered.

"Mysteries abound," came from the device. "Communications from without have been disrupted. Denizens of the High Lair are threatened. I, armored, have emerged from the High Lair to investigate. Who are you and what is going on?"

"I am Rupert of Hochburg," said my Master. "I and my party, Holt of Ar, Desmond of Hochburg, and Temicus of Venna, are unknown to you. We are friends. We wish you well. Forces of an enemy, one spoken of as Pompilius, wish to keep Agamemnon and those of the High Lair from learning of a murderous plot drawn against them."

I had expected that a translator would be incorporated in either a communication device or an artificial body. But these interactions were all in Gorean. Would a Kur, I wondered, be conversant in Gorean? Could it either speak Gorean or understand Gorean? Also, this interchange between my Master and his interlocutor, whatever or whoever it might be, was quite different in nature and tone from what I would have expected were a translation device involved. It seemed natural. There seemed nothing artificial or mechanical about it.

I began to be more and more afraid.

My fears were not lessened as I realized that the Masters and Philippina had no knowledge whatsoever of electronic surveillance devices, radios, cameras, or such. They did not know what to expect or not to expect. Intelligent, even as brilliant as they might be, they had no inkling of what they might be dealing with. Everything to them was awesome and magical. And then I realized that I, too, might be at a loss, and naive, as well. How did I know that the hemisphere was not in its way a Kur? Might not a sophisticated Kur technology exist which far transcended the primitive capabilities of a familiar translation device? Surely such would be within the compass of a science whose capabilities could produce brain-controlled artificial bodies, which I had learned could and had existed.

"This is concerning," came from the hemisphere. "What is the nature of this murderous plot."

"A striking down from the sky of a great body, a flying, falling stone or such," said Rupert.

"Do not fear," came from the device. "There is no danger. In the High Lair all is safe."

"If the stone strikes," said Rupert, "I think there will be no High Lair, or Ar."

"On what might your story be based," came from the hemisphere.

"A slave was being sought, presumably to eliminate her. Why? What did she know? We, too, hunted the slave, but to learn from her. Eventually we apprehended her. She little understood what she knew but the import of what she knew, matched with other knowledge, soon became clear. We have come to warn Agamemnon and his cohorts."

"All this is based on a slave?" came from the hemisphere.

"Substantially," said Rupert.

"Dismiss it," came from the device.

"A slave can hear, a slave can see, a slave can think," said Rupert.

"Dismiss it," came from the device.

"Why do men venture to seal off the High Lair?" asked Rupert.

"Some vagary, temporary, dealing with the politics of Ar," came from the device.

"These men about," said Rupert, "armed and dangerous, are not posted here at the behest of Ar."

"There is no danger," came from the device.

"At least," said Rupert, "convey our words, our fears, our warnings, to Agamemnon."

"I am Agamemnon," came from the device.

This announcement took us aback.

I looked at Xanthe. I think that neither of us could have spoken, even with our standing permission to speak.

We were looking on Agamemnon.

Were we looking on Agamemnon?

"Do not think me ungrateful," came from the device. "I would thank you. Please let me see those who would be my benefactors."

There was a whirring sound and the shell-like casing of the hemisphere rotated up and back some inches, revealing a row of six glowing orbs.

"That is better," came from the hemisphere. "Do not draw back, my friends. I apologize for my present body. It was at hand. I have had several better. To look upon me now you would not suppose that I was once quite handsome, with keen eyes and a glistening coat, with the strength of a dozen of my fellows. I stood high in the rings. None stood higher. Lovely females, well clawed and fanged, crawled to me to be seeded. Please stand before me, the better to be seen, to receive my thanks. Have the slaves stand to the side. This does not concern them."

It seemed odd to me that Agamemnon, a Kur, would wish to arrange things so, placing the men before him together, and being solicitous to have slaves elsewhere, perhaps safely elsewhere. Slaves, of course, did have value, as other domestic animals.

Might not a photographer arrange a picture so, attending to a desirable grouping, and keeping extraneous matters to the side?

There was another mechanical sound and the two circular openings, each about four inches in diameter, appeared below the row of glowing orbs.

I bent down wildly, and, crying out, tore open my Masters' pack, which I had borne from Ar, and seized up the remaining bottle of clear liquid therein.

"Stop!" cried Rupert, in horror.

From the two circular openings emerged two nozzles.

I did not even open the bottle but dashed it forthwith on the surface.

"Fool!" cried Rupert.

A sudden, unexpected, horrible reaction bubbled and hissed and the entire surface of the hemisphere began to crackle and spark. The machine spun about as though looking for me. I could not move. The two nozzles were starting to train themselves on me, when the machine, with a strange noise, rotated up and back, and two torrents of flame, each a hundred feet in height, stabbed the night with two swords of fire, towering swords which might have been seen even from the walls of Ar. The mercenaries were screaming and running. From within the disturbed, reeling machine came the beginning of a long curse, which then flattened out and was lost in a fading whine. Rivulets of ropes of color and noise then began to encircle the hemisphere, and, a moment later, the metal of the machine began to burst apart and then melt into hissing droplets.

The figure of Lucilius suddenly emerged from the darkness, armed now with a large double-bladed ax.

The translator, on its cord, swung wildly about his neck. A noise of violent, snarling rage came from his cavernous, fanged maw and the translator said, quietly, "You have killed Agamemnon."

He lifted the great ax.

My Master, sword drawn, stood between me and Lucilius.

The remains of the machine like a drench of molten metal were spread over the seared grass.

Mercenaries had fled.

Lucilius took a menacing step forward.

"Do not harm her," said Rupert.

"I spun about and ran toward the Beast Caves.

CHAPTER SEVENTY-SEVEN

I do not know now why I ran toward the Beast Caves.

I suspect that it was an unthinking, primitive reaction, to avoid the outraged Kur, Lucilius, and the mighty ax he wielded.

I had no trouble reaching one of the caves, like a wide, descending, dark, metal tunnel. I stopped, gasping, looking about. Lucilius, stayed perhaps by the intervention of my Master, was nowhere in sight. I saw no men of Tiskias. They had broken and fled upon the unexpected, seemingly inexplicable, uncanny destruction of the hemisphere, with its glowing, crackling, hissing, and melting, its unexpected noises, some of which suggested Gorean, and the two discharged spumes of towering fire. I had thus easily passed where their lines had been.

I doubted very much, despite Lucilius' wild asseveration to the contrary, that I had somehow wrought the destruction of Agamemnon. There had been no obvious intermediation by means of a translation device between the hemisphere and Rupert; the reactions of the hemisphere seemed inappropriately disinterested with respect to the sealing off of the Beast Caves and the warnings of Rupert; the hemisphere seemed oddly concerned to separate and position the Masters and slaves, as if it had different dispositions in mind for them, say, bringing one party into a line of fire while keeping the other out of harm's reach; lastly, the projection of the fire tubes clearly suggested a hostile intent, incomprehensible in a grateful, if skeptical, subject. What point could Agamemnon have in murdering those hoping to warn him of impending danger?

I looked to the left and right.

In the moonlight and shadows, I could see dark shapes to the sides, the riffraff of Tiskias, forming, hesitating, beginning to edge back toward the opening of the cave. In moments, perhaps emboldened by quiet and darkness, some might place themselves between me and the entrance of the cave before which I stood. Were I to run to one side or the other, I feared I might be apprehended or slain. Were I to retreat I feared meeting the ax of Lucilius, or putting my Master at risk from the same instrument. How had he, my master, dared hold his place between me, a cheap slave, and so dreadful an adversary? Was he mad? Had he no understanding of what he faced? Might not one blow of that huge, weighty weapon, like a sweeping scythe through *sa-tarna*, cut through not one but two or three men?

"Seize her!" I heard, a voice in the darkness, just yards away.

An entrance to the Beast Caves lay before me.

In moments it would be closed by armed men.

Had this not been a hope of my master, of Desmond, of Temicus, and, indeed, of Lucilius, to reach this portal?

With a cry of misery, alone, terrified, I ran through the opening.

I heard more than one cry of dismay behind me. I fled further down the broad, descending metal flooring. I heard the clatter of bootlike sandals behind me for a moment but then they stopped. I did not think the men of Tiskias would follow me. Their role had been to seal off the Beast Caves, certainly to prevent entry into them, not invade their dark precincts.

Some yards within the tunnel, where it leveled off, I stopped, and put myself against the cool, metal side of the tunnel, looking back toward the entrance.

I could barely see it.

I heard cries of anger and frustration.

I think there was the reflection of one or two torches on the metal.

"Come back, *kajira*!" I heard. "Come back!"

"Fear the beasts!"

"They feed on humans!"

"You will be killed."

"You will be eaten!"

"They will tear your flesh! They will drink your blood."

"Come back, *kajira*, or we will cut you to pieces!"

"Come back, *kajira*, we will not hurt you."

"Hurry back, *kajira*, and we will try to keep the beasts from coming out."

I turned about, and, feeling my way, touching the side of the metal tunnel, made my way deeper into the darkness.

Kurii, I had heard, had excellent night vision. It was said that they, like the *sleen* or *larl*, could see in a light in which a human being could not, in a light which, for a human being, would be indistinguishable from an impenetrable darkness. I did not know if this were true or not.

I, feeling my way, went deeper into the tunnel.

I was many times tempted to turn back, but what was to be encountered if I returned, the men of Tiskias, perhaps even the ax of Lucilius?

I continued on.

I was not sure how far I had gone.

Then I stopped.

Suddenly I was afraid, seeming to sense, somehow, that I was not alone. I froze in place. Had I heard something, something perhaps below the level of conscious awareness? What might I have heard, a breath, a body's changing of position on the metal flooring, a movement somewhere to the side? I waited. I listened. Then I told myself I had heard nothing. I was frightened. It was my imagination.

Then, suddenly, I did hear something.

It was a tiny noise.

It sounded like a soft scratch on the metal flooring.

What could make such a sound?

Then from the darkness to my left I heard a soft growl.

I was not alone!

I also recalled the likely source of the tiny sound I had heard. I had heard such a sound often enough when I had tended Lucilius in the heavy, steel-floored cage in the menagerie on Barr Street in the Metellan District.

It was the trace of a clawed foot on a metal surface.

When the growl, a noise in the darkness, was repeated, I fled away from the sound, reaching out into blackness, until I felt the smoothed, curved surface of another side of the tunnel. I then moved away from the sound.

I was frightened, and miserable.

I began to cry.

I assumed that that growl had emanated from a Kur, but I did not know that. What if it had been from a *sleen* prowling in the tunnel, or perhaps guarding it on behalf of the beasts? I had never seen a *larl*, but I knew they were quite large, and I did not think they would be likely to feel comfortable in the confines of the tunnel, either as intruders from the wild or as released guard animals. I did not know it at the time but wild *sleen* were extremely rare in the area and *larls* even more so.

Again I heard the growl and, crying out softly, in misery, I fled away, again, reaching out once more, in a moment or two, for a wall or solid surface.

I felt helpless and vulnerable, as a slave might in a blindfold or hood. Another growl led me to change my way again.

I realized suddenly something which should have been obvious. Whereas I was clumsy, and in consternation, weeping, and distraught, feeling my way about in the darkness, the beast presumably labored under no such handicap. I suspected that it might easily behold me.

After I fled away from another growl I realized I was being herded amongst branching tunnels.

For all I knew I was being driven through a maze.

What, I wondered, might be the intention or plan of the beast? Toward what was I being driven?

I knew nothing of these tunnels.

I must now be deep within them.

What if there were a chasm or ledge to which I was being herded? Might this not be a trap of sorts? What if one were to plunge unwittingly into a pool of carnivorous *tharlarion* or fall hundreds of feet into dark, cold, rushing waters or onto rocks and bones?

"Noble Master," I wept. "Be merciful to a poor slave. Have you a translation device? If so, please use it. Can you speak to me, or try to speak to me? Can you understand what I am saying? I mean you neither disparagement nor harm. I am a poor slave, only that. Forgive me if I am unwelcome here." I addressed the beast in the darkness. I spoke to it in Gorean. I even, desperately, foolishly, spoke to it in English.

What, I wondered, if the source of those growls was not a Kur, but a *sleen*? What if no rational thing knew I was in the tunnels?

What could become of me?

Feeling the curved wall, I continued my journey in the darkness.

I think I lost my sense of time.

The beast, now, I was sure, was closer to me. I sensed its breathing. Then I felt a clawed paw touch my arm, and I fainted.

I awakened, I know not how much later, abruptly, startled, frightened, to the sharp snap of a whip.

That is a sound well known to a slave girl.

It had not touched me.

I gritted my eyelids against the light, which, while not objectively bright, stung my eyes.

Paws pulled me up to my knees, and a paw fastened itself in my hair and pulled my head up and back.

I blinked against the light.

The huge head and maw of a Kur were close to my face.

Those jaws might close easily about my head. I felt that my head could be easily wrenched from my body.

It took me a moment to realize that he was reading my collar.

The Kur said something in Kur, but to whom, or what, I did not know.

There were five or six Kurii in the oblong, high-ceilinged room.

There was a high, wide, flat-topped pillar or pedestal some feet before me.

One of the Kurii, he with the whip, bent over, approached me, shuffling, and held the whip against my lips.

I kissed it, licked it, and kissed it again.

I was not a free woman. I was a slave, as I wanted to be.

He returned to his place.

He touched a point toward the back of the pillar or pedestal.

It was my hope that this somehow activated a translation device.

"May I speak?" I asked.

Relievedly, I heard my Gorean translated into Kur.

I could not see the device but I supposed it was somehow imbedded in the pillar.

"No," was the mechanistic response.

I bit my lip in frustration.

In what follows I shall, for the sake of simplicity and convenience, recount exchanges and interactions as though they might have been in a single language, say, Gorean, and not as they were actually produced by means of a translation device. Needless to say, my utterances and those of my respondents and interlocutors were delivered in a natural voice, so to speak, and the device's equivalents were invariably rendered as dispassionately, and as neutrally, as the ticking of a clock. And, naturally, the comments, exchanges, and such amongst the Kurii themselves were similarly registered, this making their discourse intelligible to me.

"What is it?" asked one of the Kurii, regarding me.

"It is a human, of the type female," he was told.

"There are many humans on Gor," he was told.

"Which of the four sexes is female?" asked the Kur.

"There are only two sexes amongst humans," said a Kur.

"Remarkable," said the other.

"It is like a pet, a drink bringer, a groomer," said a Kur.

"But it has a cloth on its body, and it seems to have a language," said the Kur.

"Are you a groomer?" I was asked.

"I do not think so," I said. "I do not know what a groomer is."

"See," said one of the Kurii.

"Your sort commonly enters the High Lair only roped or leashed," said a Kur.

"I did not know," I said.

"They are given as gifts to humans we wish to enlist in our service," said a Kur. "Some male humans prefer them to bits of metal."

"Interesting," said a Kur.

"Human females are not allowed clothing in the High Lair," said a Kur.

"I did not know," I said.

"So?" said a Kur.

"Master?" I asked.

"Remove your clothing, instantly," said another Kur.

"Yes, Master," I said.

"There, now," said the Kur who seemed to know less of the locale than the others, "that is more like a groomer."

"She cannot remove the metal circlet on her neck," said a Kur. "Merchant law prescribes it. It is locked on her neck. It helps to identify and keep track of the smooth little beasts. It also helps the little beasts keep in mind that they are properties, that they are owned."

"Note as well the brand," said another.

"Why did you hold the whip to her face?" asked he who seemed less familiar with Gor and its ways.

"You saw her press her lips to it and lick it," said a Kur.

"Of course," said the other.

"It is a ritual," said a Kur. "Thus she acknowledges that she is owned and subject to discipline."

"Interesting," said the other.

"She is a slave," said a Kur.

"Like our chain females?" said the other.

"Precisely," said the Kur.

Of course, the collar was a sign that I was owned. What else could it be? Are not owned animals, such as I, often collared? And surely there was no mistaking the brand. How, more clearly, could I be marked as property? Yet, in a sense, at least in my case, were not such things externals, little more than visible tokens of an inward profundity. I am one of those women who need and want slavery. I want to be owned by a fine, strong man, who will keep me as his property, his belonging, and slave. I wish to have no choice but to submit and love. It is my joy to love and serve. Masters will have it so. It excites, thrills, fulfills, and pleases me, as nothing else. I am a born slave. I suspected it on Earth. I learned it on Gor.

"May I speak, Masters?" I begged.

"No," I was told.

"I miss the grooming pets," said the Kur who seemed less informed than the others.

"One learns to do without them," said a Kur.

"Much here is primitive and savage," said a Kur.

"One can do much with combs," said another."

Desperate, I cried out, "Lucilius!"

This exclamation startled the Kurii gathered about the base of the high pedestal.

"She spoke without permission," said a Kur.

"Lash her," said another.

"Kill her," said a third.

"Eat her," said a fourth.

"No," said one of the Kurii. Then he turned toward me. "What of Lucilius?" he said.

"What do you know of Lucilius?" asked another.

"I did not enter the High Lair lightly," I said. "I come as an emissary of the noble Lucilius, bearing a message from him to the mighty Agamemnon."

"Absurd," said a Kur.

"Lucilius is missing," said another.

"He has been missing," said another.

"Where is Lucilius?" asked another.

"Outside," I said. "Denied entry to the High Lair by dozens of swords and spears."

"Men have been about the entrance," said a Kur. "We could burn them from our path in a moment, but that would violate the laws of Priest-Kings and possibly invite retaliation. That was forbidden by Agamemnon."

"Let me speak to the great Agamemnon," I begged.

"He is Agamemnon," said a Kur. "You are a beast."

"I speak not on behalf of myself but of the noble Lucilius," I said.

"Lucilius is second to Agamemnon," said a Kur.

"Give us your message and we, if we deem it of sufficient interest or importance, will convey it to Lord Agamemnon, the Eleventh Face of the Nameless One," said a Kur.

"There is no time," I said. "Danger is imminent. It may be too late already. And Lord Agamemnon may wish to question me himself, to clarify matters, and form his own judgment of my credibility."

"Awaken him," said a Kur.

I began to tremble.

I half expected, in spite of what I had been told, that another Kur might appear, perhaps from a side entrance, perhaps one larger and more savage, if possible, than those before me. I knew nothing of artificial bodies. I recalled the hemisphere which I had destroyed outside the Beast Caves. Supposedly it bore some resemblance to a familiar, six-legged globular river creature, save that it was much larger. Lucilius, I recalled, had assumed it was a body of Agamemnon, this motivating his murderous charge toward me with a brandished ax. By now I trusted it had become clear that it was not a body of Agamemnon. Certainly I hoped it had not been such.

I had stripped myself, earlier, as commanded. I had done this without the least demur, instantly and obediently. Female slaves on Gor are not to dally in responding to commands. Repetition of a command can be cause for discipline. Also, I had done so, as I had been taught, gracefully, even before the beasts. The female slave is to be the loveliest of women, in appearance, demeanor, movement, expression, attitude, and diction. She is to be the sort of woman that a man wants to own, and completely, as a slave is owned. As I waited, I wanted to reach out and clutch the tiny, handful of cloth that was my tunic. But I did not dare do so. A slave delights to be naked before her owner, in the privacy of his domicile, but it is a rare slave who desires to be exposed before strangers. Is it not enough to have been exhibited wholly on a block or sales shelf? To be sure she is well aware that her Master may command her naked whenever, wherever, and however he might wish, a command with which she must instantly comply. This is sometimes done at parties at which she serves, on occasions when Masters are comparing slaves, and so on. Masters are often protective of, and jealous of, their slaves, but the slave knows that if her Master consigns her to another, she must do her best to serve the other, and as a slave, or expect the whip.

As negligible as my tunic was, I felt vulnerable without it.

I waited, on my knees, naked, a slave.

One of the Kurii went to the back of the pillar.

I gathered that there was a control panel of some sort there. In any event, as nearly as I could tell, he was manipulating switches and twisting dials.

I was reassured, at least a bit, to learn that Agamemnon had been sleeping. He was then still alive. Then he could not have been ensconced in the hemispherical body I had destroyed, unless, of course, the Kurii in this strange, high-ceilinged, almost-bare room, were naive or misinformed. I did know that it was not unusual for the location of leaders to be concealed, and often changed, as a precaution against capture and assassination.

There was a humming sound and two changes took place where the pillar was concerned. First, the broad, circular, flat top began to rise, bringing into view a now-elevated flat surface on which was mounted a transparent container, rather like a large bell jar, which had hitherto been concealed within the pillar. A variety of tubes and wires led into sockets on the container and other tubes and coated wires, or cords, within the container, led from these sockets into a large, dark buoyant object within the container. In this way, the jar could be moved from one place to another, rather as a machine might be moved about and plugged into diverse feeds, power sources, and such. Secondly, various panels on the front of the pillar opened, like curved doors revealing various boxes, diaphragms, speakers, lenses, and such. Apparently, several of the external tubes, wires, and such, socketed at points on the jar above, led, by means of the pillar, down into the paraphernalia revealed by the open doors. In this way there could be a seamless passage, between, say, a box to the jar and, within the jar, from that point to the large, dark, buoyant object in the jar, and, similarly, a route from the buoyant object down, eventually to, say, the box.

Some of the lenses revealed by the opened, curved doors moved, turning toward me.

Something somewhere, I was sure, was regarding me.

Might not a camera be involved?

Might not then something somewhere be looking at me, watching me, even now, perhaps something in another room, even miles away?

Then I began to recall snatches of conversation, disjointed remarks, things half heard, absurdities to be cast aside, things dismissed as too impossible to believe.

What was the nature of the dark, buoyant object?

Suddenly it took on, in my imagination, dark in its fluid world, the cast of something menacing, something minacious, something grossly improbable but awesomely threatening.

"Hail, Agamemnon," said a Kur.

"Hail Agamemnon," said the others.

Fighting the recognition, unwilling to accept what must be the case, I realized that the dark, floating object must be a brain, a living brain, a center of sensation and consciousness, something that could feel, something that could hunger and hate, something that could command and plan, something which, consequent on its embodiment, might fell trees and shatter stones, might swim with *tharlarion* and fly with tarns, might lead armies and parley with Ubars.

I shuddered.

Even were it disembodied, I sensed that I was in the presence of a considerable force, something dreadfully alien, a dangerous and terrible being, something ruthless and remorseless, a mighty personality.

Surely it deserved to be destroyed.

I felt myself under the scrutiny of the lenses.

They seemed to adjust themselves.

Perhaps I was being brought more into focus.

I felt like leaping up and running, but I knew I could not escape the Kurii in the room, and I would be lost in the darkness of the tunnels.

I looked up at the container or jar at the height of the pillar, so far above me.

"May I speak, Master?" I asked.

"Yes," said a voice.

Then, half hysterically, wildly, unable to control myself, words tumbling out, I blurted forth, as I could, the story of my adventures and fears, what I knew, and what I thought I knew. I spoke of the observatory, of imaging and space, of engineering and unusually crafted celestial bodies, of secrets and intrigue, of war and civil strife, of factions, of the flights and terrors of a pursued slave, of her apprehension by Rupert of Hochburg, and his alliance with Lucilius, a high Kur, and muchly I spoke of danger, dangers to a world, to the

Sardar, to the Beast Caves and Ar, the dangers of hurtling bodies, like swift, descending, massive hammers, dangers imminent and devastating in their consequences.

CHAPTER SEVENTY-EIGHT

I had been hurried through the darkness, sometimes stumbling, responsive to the leash, my hands thonged behind me.

One of the two Kurii who had conducted me now removed his leash from my throat. He did not free my hands.

Now, perhaps a hundred yards before me, I could see, at the end of an incline, the opening.

The Kurii then left me.

We had had no translation device. They could not understand me. I could not understand them.

It was daylight outside.

I sensed men about the entrance.

I did not know their nature.

Happily, I had been permitted, in the oblong chamber, to don my tunic.

I supposed, in the opinion of many, particularly free women, there is little difference between a slave tunic and stark nudity, but, in the opinion of the slave, there is a great deal of difference. Even a rag can be precious to a slave girl. To be sure, a rag conceals little of what may be concealed beneath it, and the rag, of course, can be easily torn away, stripping the slave. Men will have it so. We are slaves.

I decided to make my way toward the opening.

My guides had left me.

I did not dare go back.

I did not know what lay before me.

Whereas new slaves are often upset to the point of tears to be exhibited in a slave tunic, most slaves, unashamed of their bodies, and reveling in their sex and desirability, are more than happy to have such a tunic. What garment can do more to proclaim their condition and enhance their charms? And have they not sometimes sensed the ill-concealed envy and fury of free women, their competitors for men, denied the freedom, excitement, and joy of such a bit of covering. The paucity of clothing, intended to demean and humiliate, often, contrarywise, augments and celebrates.

How much depends on context and culture, on background, on expectations and familiarities!

As a free woman of Earth I would have been dismayed, even terrified, to be seen as I was, so scantily clad, and collared. How came I so? What could it possibly mean? Would not the men of Earth be scandalized, would they not avert their eyes, would they not rush to cover me? How different the men of Gor! They would point to the ground, where I was to kneel before them. They would inquire the name of my Master.

What would the sweet men of Earth make of a collar on my neck? Would they even understand it? How easily they would note and never question a collar on the neck of an animal. Why then should it be so incomprehensible on the neck of a woman? Might it not there, as well, designate a beast, an animal, a property, an object, something owned? Could they even understand that? Men of Gor understand it. And what of an exquisite flank bearing clearly a lovely, tasteful mark, a brand? Might not that have its meaning, as well?

Clearly the men of Earth, or many of them, and those of Gor are different. But perhaps there are some men of Earth who are not that different from the men of Gor, and, indeed, if the truth might be known, perhaps not different at all.

Slaves long for their Masters.

And might not a Master consider accepting a kneeling, begging slave, if she pleases him?

"Mira, Mira!" cried a voice.

A slave was running toward me.

"Here," I cried. "Here!"

I broke into a run, as I could, my hands tied behind me, toward the opening.

In a moment I was embraced, held, and kissed.

"Mira!" she said.

"Temione!" I said.

"It was said that you had fled into the tunnel," she said, "before the entrance was once more sealed. We thought you lost, torn to pieces, eaten! How have you fared? What has been done to you?"

"Beware," I said. "Dangerous men are outside, near the opening of the tunnel."

"Yes," she said, "dangerous men, but not those I think you mean."

"What are you doing here?" I asked. "How can you be here?"

"Gordon of Hammerfest, my Master," she said, "was recruiting men for action in the Vosk basin, but Marlenus, the Ubar, learning of mysterious doings at the Beast Caves, the sealing off of the caves, the prohibition of beasts to come and go, advised Gordon, my Master, to investigate, as a private party, one not acting officially in the name of the state of Ar. He would do so. We arrived in the darkness, apparently not long after your reported flight into the tunnel."

"War ensued," I said.

"Not really," she said. "The men of my Master are not garbage from the alleys of Ar. They are highly trained swords, whose skills are costly. Resistance never formed. Villains and scoundrels commonly have little stomach for the swallowing of steel, lawful or otherwise."

"The entrances to the caves are not yet freed?" I said.

"Soon perhaps," she said, "but not now. Much remains politically unclear."

"How will I recognize the men of your Master?" I asked.

"They are uniformed," said Temione. "But even were they not, they have the carriage and mien of warriors, not brigands."

"Still then," I said, "no one is permitted to enter the tunnels."

"Not even your party, which made itself known to us, four men and two slaves," she said. "Swords were unsheathed, but wisdom prevailed. They were too few to fight their way through a thicket of arms."

"They wished to follow me?" I said, in awe.

"Yes," she said, "oddly, as you are a slave."

"How are you here?" I asked.

"I heard that something was detected within the tunnel," she said. "I thought it might be a sign of you. I hurried to investigate."

"You did not have permission," I said.

"I had not been denied permission," she said.

"That is not quite the same thing," I said. "You risk a lashing."

"I will hurry gladly to the ring or post if it be his will."

"You have been mastered," I said.

"When I was free," she said, "I only suspected the joy of being mastered, of being an object, a property, of being owned, of being wholly subject to the will of another. Now, I have no choice, but I want no choice. I wonder and marvel at his strength. I am dominated, totally, and love it. I am joyful in my collar. I would not trade it for the world."

"You are so much his slave," I said.

"That and more," she said.

"I am bound, untie me," I said.

"That is not for me to do," she said.

"Hurry," I said.

"No," she said.

"Do it now," I said.

"No," she said.

"Now!" I said.

"It would be easy enough for me to pull away your tunic," she said.

"What?" I said.

"Face the opening, and walk toward it, humbly, with your head down," she said.

"I do not understand," I said.

"You are my prisoner," she said. "I am going to present you to my Master."

"Do not be absurd," I said.

Her hand seized my tunic at the shoulder.

"Do not!" I said.

"Will it be stripped, or clad?" she asked.

"Clad!" I begged.

"You may now, head down, humbly, walk toward the entrance," she said.

"Temione!" I protested.

"Move," she said, giving me a push, so much so that I stumbled and almost fell.

I straightened up, regaining my balance.

"Move, barbarian slave," she said.

"Yes, Mistress," I said, very much annoyed.

"Excellent, sweet Mira," she laughed. "Perhaps men will one day be pleased with you. Who knows? You might even sell for as much as two silver tarsks."

I threw myself to the feet of Rupert of Hochburg, putting down my head, and kissing his bootlike sandal.

I was weeping.

I was once again at the feet of my Master.

The knife of Temicus slashed away the thongs on my wrists.

"Desist, report," said Rupert.

"Master and others tried to find me," I said, half disbelievingly, half grateful.

"Kneel up," said my Master.

I straightened my body.

With his right, shod foot, he thrust me angrily to the ground. I looked up at him, frightened, miserable.

"Worthless slave," said he, "must a command be repeated?"

I again knelt.

"No, Master," I wept.

"Did you see Agamemnon?" he asked.

"I do not know," I said.

"How can that be?" he asked.

"I saw a column, a pillar," I said. "The pillar changed, opening in various ways. There were many tubes and wires, and boxes, and things like small windows of glass. On the height of the pillar, there arose a transparent container. In this container, floating in fluid, there was some object, one I could not see well."

"This is not helpful," said Temicus.

"She was not slain, nor eaten, but returned to the opening of the cave," said Maxwell Holt, Holt of Ar. "Something must have been done. Something must have been accomplished."

"Not necessarily," said Temicus. "She may just have been ejected from the tunnel as an unwelcome intruder or visitor. This close to Ar, Kurii might be reluctant to kill casually or at will. It is unlikely they think they could do so with total impunity. They are already feared and hated by many in Ar. A spark might ignite a conflagration that would course through the Beast Caves with fire and steel. Besides, they might think she had some value. One seldom discards objects of possible value."

"You saw beasts?" asked Rupert.

"Several," I said.

"But not Agamemnon?"

"I am confused," I said.

"No machines in the likeness of animals," asked Rupert, "in the likeness of *tharlarion, tarsks,* tarns, even enlarged versions of river globes?"

"No," I said.

"Would that Lucilius had tarried," said Temicus.

I was relieved that he was not present. I recalled how he had lunged toward me in the fullness of Kur fury, his ax raised. Had my Master not thrust himself between me and the maddened Kur, I had little doubt but what that moment would have been my last. The great ax would not have long remained cold and unstained.

Why had my Master placed himself in such jeopardy? More than once modest sums had taken me from the block.

"Was there communication?" asked my Master.

"Very much so," I said. "A single communication device, a translator, was utilized."

"Excellent," said Temicus.

"What occurred?" inquired Rupert.

I then broke down, spewing forth a half incoherent babble, recounting, as I could, what I had endeavored to communicate to the largely impassive, seemingly skeptical, beasts, a tale of my adventures, suspicions, encounters, and fears, at least as they bore on the possible jeopardies to which the Beast Caves and the Sardar might be exposed.

"And what response," asked Desmond, "greeted so unusual and improbable a demonstration?"

"I was allowed to replace my tunic, was bound, and was conducted to the opening of the tunnel," I said.

"So little?" asked Maxwell Holt.

"I am sure it was more than enough," said Rupert. "I have full confidence in the slave. She is a woman of intelligence and judgment as well as one of more important aspects, those of being a stimulating, exciting slab of needful collar meat. Her confusion, uncertainty, and terror are understandable. She was stressed. She was at risk. She knew not what might occur. Might she not be set upon and eaten? The situation of the interview was harrowing. Many subtleties of tone and inuendo are obscured by the translation device, on both sides. And Kurii might well in such an affair affect the demeanor of stones, keeping feelings and views to themselves."

"Thank you, Master," I said.

He frowned.

"Forgive me, Master," I said.

I feared I had displeased him. How vulnerable and helpless are slaves!

"We may take it," said Rupert, "that the gist of the situation has been conveyed, that our message has been delivered, that our work here is finished."

"I would not be too sure of that," said Temicus.

"The matter is done," said Rupert.

"The slave said nothing of Agamemnon," said Maxwell Holt. "Does he know? Has he been informed?"

"Lucilius would be the best judge of that," said Temicus.

"Surely the other Kurii could communicate with Agamemnon," said Desmond.

"If he is about," said Holt of Ar.

"Our message may have been delivered too late," said Temicus.

"We have done our best," said Rupert.

"So, let us suppose," said Temicus, "that Agamemnon has been informed. What can he do? We could not penetrate the Sardar. How can he? How can he, or anyone, or anything, fend away hurtling stones."

"We have done all we can," said Rupert.

"Kurii of the faction of Pompilius are said to threaten the Vosk," said Desmond.

"That is not our concern," said Rupert.

"I fear," said Temicus, "that those of the Beast Caves may yet need the services of men."

"For what?" asked Rupert.

"Lucilius might know," said Temicus.

"He has withdrawn," said Rupert.

"Why, now?" asked Temicus.

"Who knows?" said Rupert.

"What of Tiskias and his Kur ally?" asked Desmond.

"We must be on our guard," said Rupert.

"May I speak?" I asked.

"Yes," said Rupert.

"I am afraid of Lucilius," I said. "He may come back. He thought I killed Agamemnon. He may want to kill me."

"He no longer thinks you killed Agamemnon," said Maxwell Holt. "The hemisphere you destroyed was not a body of Agamemnon. Its ruin bore no traces of organic material, tissue, blood, or such. This was made clear to the noble Lucilius. It was a simple contrivance, available even to Earth technology, containing a microphone and speaker, a camera, and weaponry trainable and dischargeable by signals at a distance."

"Made by Tiskias?" I said.

"Utilized by him," said Holt.

"Captain," said Desmond, "I suggest, as our work seems done here, that we slip away to a place of greater safety."

"From the bodies, the stones?" said Rupert.

"For you," said Desmond. "I fear for you in this vicinity. We are within *pasangs* of the *pomerium* of Ar. You are wanted in Ar."

"We will leave tonight," said my Master.

I bent over and kissed him on the side of the knee. I hoped I would not be cuffed away.

"Later," he said.

CHAPTER SEVENTY-NINE

"Do not look at blazing Tor-tu-Gor!" said Temicus. "It does not wish it! It will burn your eyes away!"

"It is shrinking!" cried a man.

"It is being eaten!" cried another.

We were some four *pasangs* from the Gate of the Urts, returning to Ar from the Beast Caves.

"Call to the Priest-Kings!" cried a man.

"Will they hear us?" moaned a man.

"Hear the bars sound from the great temple in Ar!" cried a man.

"Other bars, too," said a man. "The city is in alarm."

"The Initiates will save us!" said a man.

"They must!" cried another.

"Let them be about their business," cried another. "Let them lose no time intoning the sacred chants, nor casting their spells."

"Do not fear," said Temicus. "Such things have happened before. Old records attest it. It is like tides and currents, as natural as wind and rain. It is the interposition of a moon, daring to cross the path of mighty Tor-tu-Gor."

"Good," said a man. "Then we need not pay Initiates to save us."

Our party was closely formed on the road, four men, Rupert and Desmond of Hochburg, Holt of Ar, Temicus of Venna, and three slaves, Xanthe, Philippina, and myself. I could have reached out and touched my Master.

"There was nothing of this on the public boards," said Holt of Ar.

"There seldom is," said Temicus.

"I saw no moons," said Holt.

"There were none," said Temicus, of the Builders.

"Why then did you speak as you did?" asked Holt.

"Panic solves few problems," said Temicus. "Do you wish to share the road with men mad with fear, who may go wild and do sudden, and terrible things?"

"Then it is not natural," said Rupert.

"I am sure it is natural," said Temicus, "in its way, as natural as the flight of the quarrel the thrust of a sword, the blow of an ax."

We watched, some in awe, some in fear, the gradual obscuring of the fiery disk of Tor-tu-Gor, Light Upon the Home Stone.

"Darkness!" wept Philippina.

"How can there be darkness at the Tenth Ahn?" asked a man.

"The world ends," said someone.

"It is not total darkness," said Temicus.

"Tor-tu-Gor has turned black," said a man.

"Tor-tu-Gor is safe," said Temicus. "It is at ease, and undisturbed. The blackness you see is another body, one between us and Tor-tu-Gor."

"Tor-tu-Gor is gone!" wept a man.

"Be patient, wait," said Temicus.

A cry of joy rose from better than a dozen throats as a rim of fire, a glimmer and then a blaze, became visible.

"Tor-tu-Gor returns!" they cried.

"It never left," muttered Temicus.

I was definitely uneasy.

I was sure that we had looked upon one of the two large, hollow steel balls, or artificial moons, or worlds, I had detected long ago at the observatory. It was now hard to detect in the bright sky but it was there, somewhere between us and the common star that gave warmth, light, and health to both Earth and Gor. I suspected that it had held itself, waiting and poised, to an orbit for months, but had now, for some reason, broken that orbit. Had it waited until Kurii of the faction of Pompilius had now occupied predetermined positions, perhaps in the valley of the Vosk? Had some diplomatic or political difficulty on some remote steel world finally been resolved, clearing the way for bringing a plan to fruition? Or had some unanticipated technical difficulties been at last addressed and repaired. Or was it merely following some program which had been devised and set in motion years ago and had never been altered, and it was only a coincidence that an aspect of this program had been activated at this time? I did not think the latter likely. I was sure that something had changed, but I knew not what. Then I realized what must have taken place. A plot had been discovered, and it had been deemed necessary to proceed without delay, lest the plot be somehow foiled. In this way, the orbiting mallets, or bombs, or missiles, had been freed of their orbits and directed to begin their long descent, their path, presumably taking a matter of days, to their targets. This may have occurred when it was ascertained that I had been located by representatives of the faction of Agamemnon, or perhaps somewhat later, when such representatives, despairing of contacting the Sardar, were enroute to the Beast Caves, presumably to warn Agamemnon of the approaching peril from the sky.

The predator prefers to make his move in his own time, but, if the prey is alerted, he must change his plans.

"Tor-tu-Gor was not in danger?" said Philippina.

"It is quite safe," said Temicus.

"Something came between Tor-tu-Gor and us?" she asked.

"An object," said Temicus.

"I have heard Tor-tu-Gor is large," said Philippina.

"Quite large," said Temicus.

"Then the object must be as large or larger," she said.

"Not at all," said Temicus. "It is a matter of distances, illusions, and perspectives. Tor-tu-Gor seems small because it is far away. The Central Cylinder in Ar is larger than a copper tarsk, but if you hold a copper tarsk before your eye it seems larger than the Central Cylinder."

"Then the object may be smaller than Tor-tu-Gor?"

"Much smaller, doubtless thousands of times smaller."

"Then there is little to fear," she said.

"I fear," said Temicus, "there is much to fear."

"Should we not hasten away?" asked Philippina.

"I doubt there is time," said Demond, grimly.

"One such object," said Rupert, "could destroy the Sardar, and another, the Beast Caves, Ar, and everything in their vicinity."

"The object is gone," said Philippina.

"It is there," said Temicus. "You saw it because it was blocking Tor-tu-Gor; now, no longer doing so, it is hard to see, lost in the light of Tor-tu-Gor."

I hoped that the object might be destroyed by its descent into and through the fiery abrasion of the atmosphere, but I almost instantly realized how weak and forlorn was such a hope. A technology capable of conceiving and constructing such an object would make certain that it could achieve the end for which it was designed.

"I think it will soon reappear," said Rupert.

"Discarding its shield of light," said Temicus, "like a pellet in the sky, hard to see, then increasingly growing larger."

"Let us run," said Philippina.

"Do so, if you wish," said Desmond.

But she sank to her knees beside her Master.

Interestingly, those about us, villagers, men of Ar, lower Merchants, some with carts and wagons, moving about, coming and going, seeing to their business, now no longer concerned themselves with a frightening sky. Conversation was about. Men called to their animals. A slave stole a *tospit*. The sky was a placid blue; the breeze was soft, the day warm.

"There!" said Xanthe, pointing. "No! It is a bird!"

"I wonder," said Temicus, "how much longer we have to live."

"Things seem pleasant and quiet," said Holt, of Ar.

"Perhaps," said Desmond, "there is no danger. Perhaps the object is off course. Perhaps it will pass the world, or plunge into the sea, or fall to earth harmlessly, and exhaust itself, doing no more than discomforting some rude wilderness."

Might that not be possible?

How could simple beasts like Kurii design a weapon which might be the envy of human engineers, even those of Earth, fertile and practiced in the design of weapons of mass effect?

"*Ela*!" moaned Rupert.

"Yes, there," said Temicus.

"Where?" asked Philippina.

"There," said Temicus, pointing.

"It is so tiny," said Philippina.

"It is not tiny," said Temicus. "It is far away."

"It is only a speck," she said.

"Wait," said Temicus. "Your speck may cover half the sky."

"I assume it approaches," said Holt, of Ar, looking upward.

"That will become clear," said Temicus.

"How fast does it approach?" asked Rupert.

"I do not know," said Temicus. "The further it comes, the faster it comes."

"It is falling," said Desmond.

"One could think of it that way," said Temicus.

"The further it falls, the faster it falls," said Desmond.

"Consider the speed, the force, the impact," muttered Rupert.

"Might it not dislodge Gor from its orbit, might it not alter the axis of the planet?" asked Holt.

"No," said Temicus. "That would do the ambitions and plans of our friends no good. It is their intention to own a world, not destroy it."

"I fear for Ar," said Holt.

"Well you might," said Temicus.

"Ar is a rich prize," said Holt. "Surely it is better to seize than destroy such a prize."

"Its misfortune," said Temicus, "is to be in the vicinity of the Beast Caves."

"We do not know the range of the impact," said Rupert. "Perhaps Ar will be spared."

"Lucilius did not think so," said Temicus.

"Lucilius could be mistaken!" said Holt, angrily.

"Of course," said Temicus, absently, affably.

Holt seized the hilt of his sword, but Rupert gently placed his hand on Holt's hand, staying the draw.

"How much time do we have?" asked Rupert.

"I would think," said Temicus, "until late afternoon."

"The object is larger now," said Philippina.

"Yes," said Desmond, her Master.

My Master, Rupert of Hochburg, his party, and its properties, had drawn to the side of the road.

"I have some bread, cheese, and olives," said Temicus.

"Good," said Rupert.

Xanthe and I excused ourselves, and Philippina ate little.

From time to time, others, passing by, looked up, and some even pointed to the speck in the sky, and then continued on.

"At times like these," said Temicus, "I suppose it is customary to contemplate missed pleasures, squandered opportunities, and such."

"I would not know," said Holt.

"I saw her on a block in Market of Semris," said Temicus, "but I failed to bid on her."

"Doubtless several others failed to do so, as well," said Holt.

"I never saw her again," said Temicus.

"There are some slaves that many men have never seen at all," said Holt.

"What was her name?" asked Desmond.

"Luta," said Temicus.

"That narrows it down," said Holt. "That is one of the most common of slave names."

Xanthe and I, of course, and Temione, too, knew a Luta, from the Purple Whip. Indeed, I had known one even from the Great Pen in Victoria Minor.

From a few yards away, there was a sudden cry of wonder. "Look!" cried a man, pointing upward. He was joined by some few others. I could also see, up and down the road, closer and farther, other men, with wagons and carts, paused as well. "It is a cloud," cried one. "It does not seem a cloud," said another. "It must be," insisted the first. "It is in the sky."

"It is a bird with unseen wings," said a man.

"A ball of gray hail," said another.

"But there is but one such ball," said another.

"There is no storm. Tor-tu-Gor shines. The sky is clear, and blue."

"A child's kite," insisted another.

"It is a stone cast from a catapult of Priest-Kings," suggested another.

Here and there I heard the snort or bellow of an uneasy *tharlarion*.

"How much time have we?" asked Rupert.

"Not much," said Temicus. "It increases in speed by the Ihn."

"One can see it grow larger as we watch," said Desmond.

Philippina screamed but was not chastised by her Master.

"How large is it?" asked Desmond.

"I do not know," said Temicus, shading his eyes. "Perhaps a *pasang* in diameter. It will seem to fill the sky, and then there will be the impact. It will shake the world."

"Unsheathe your swords," said Rupert. Holt and Desmond did do.

I did not understand this at the time. Did he expect to fend away the stroke of a mountain, the blow of a world? Later I learned that Warriors do not care to die with their swords sheathed.

There was a mighty and enlarging shadow.

By now, in these terrible seconds, the imminent peril became clear to the crowds on the road, and there were cries of terror and misery, moans of despair, and curses. I saw one man raising his fist against the sky; another gathered a child to his breast. A *tharlarion*, bellowing, dragged a wagon wildly to the side. Some men stood where they were, as if frozen in place. Others broke and ran, as if they could elude the fate falling from the sky. I fell to my knees, beside my Master, and covered my head with my hands. "Do you wish to die now?" asked Rupert, softly. I sensed his blade at my neck. "No, no, Master!" I cried. "Let us die together."

I looked up, in agony. A great metal ball seemed to fill the sky. I could see the curved plating, the welded seams on its surface, the glint of steel. It seemed then for a moment as if it might be night.

I waited for the blow, the mighty impact that might rattle a planet to its core.

"Something is wrong," said Temicus. "Something is acting on the sphere. Surely its target was the Beast Caves, but here it is closer to Ar."

I waited for the crash which, unlike the Tunguska Event, might leave a crater *pasangs* wide and a thousand feet deep.

There were cries of wonder from the men about.

"You may sheath your swords," said Rupert.

The gigantic ball, like a metal world, seemed arrested in space.

"It is trembling," said Holt of Ar.

"Forces war," said Temicus.

I tried to conceive the titanic powers in action. Nothing in my background, as scientifically respectable as it had been, had prepared me for what I saw, perhaps a hundred yards over my head. What force could have matched the silent, rushing, descending fury of a plunging world? What could withstand, what could mitigate, what could resist the force of gravity? And then, shuddering, I realized what must be the case. I had witnessed the effects of a knowledge and technology I had never dreamed possible. A giant had been turned against itself. Gravity had been utilized against gravity. "How could this be?" I asked myself. "Who, or what, could manage such a thing?"

Had the Kurii of the Beast Caves such power?

I became uneasy. The ground felt less solid under my feet. I feared almost as though I might be in water. If I were to push away from the ground, I felt I might hover, or float, and then settle down to the ground again.

Temicus bent down, tore up a handful of grass and then, inverting his palm, released it. We looked at one another. It floated downward but with unexpected slowness.

Some about us spoke in hushed tones.

I was apparently not the only one who felt the world had changed.

Slowly the large metal ball began to rise higher in the air.

As it did so, the disturbingly, seemingly anomalous alteration in the nature of the world faded and then disappeared. I do not think this was so much connected with the gravitational pull of the sphere itself, lessening with distance, as with the retreating location of those forces independently acting on the sphere.

"Look!" said Xanthe, pointing upward.

The sphere was now seemingly arrested in its ascent. I guessed that it might be four or five miles above. It looked like a cold, gray moon.

"It is stopped," whispered Philippina.

"Something is changing," said Xanthe.

"What?" I asked.

"Look!" said Xanthe.

"I see," I said.

The aspect of the sphere, suspended in space, some miles above, was beginning to change.

This was occurring gradually.

Philippina wiped sweat from her brow. "It is getting hotter," she said.

"Yes," said Desmond, squinting upward.

The cold gray color of the vast, hollow metal ball was turning into a dull red.

"Behold," said Temicus. "Few have looked into the smithy of the Priest-Kings, few have beheld their forge."

Xanthe and I exchanged glances.

"How natural," I thought, "to cast words at a mystery. One makes use of what limited concepts one has at one's disposal, and tries to force reality to submit to them. May reality be patient with science."

The men removed their cloaks and tied them about their waists.

The slaves pulled their tunics away from their warm, moist skin.

"The red grows more fierce," said Philippina.

"Like the iron with which you will soon be marked," said her Master.

"The ball should soon be white hot," said Holt.

"Let us run!" said Philippina.

"Where?" asked Desmond.

"What are the Priest-Kings doing?" asked Rupert.

"They are softening the round metal stone," said Temicus. "They are preparing to destroy it."

"There is danger," said Desmond. "What if the metal melts, turns into a scalding liquid, and drenches the plain? It would be like a lake of lava pouring from the clouds."

"Not a drop need be feared," said Temicus.

"How so?" asked Desmond.

"Because the extended open palm of the hand of the Priest-Kings is between us and so molten a deluge," said Temicus.

"Are you sure of that?" asked Holt of Ar.

"Not completely," said Temicus.

"It grows dismayingly hot," said Rupert.

"I think the discomfort will be tolerable and brief," said Temicus.

"Do you know that?" asked Holt.

"Actually not," said Temicus.

"I fear the grass will soon begin to burn," said Holt.

"Not at all," said Temicus.

"How do you know?" asked Holt.

"I don't," said Temicus.

The metal sphere was now ignited to a white heat. It first had seemed like a small, cold, gray moon; then it had seemed like a glowing red ball; now it seemed like a young, mutant offspring of Tor-tu-Gor, a fierce newborn, blazing and white.

Suddenly air seemed to be sucked upward.

"It is growing smaller!" cried Philippina. "It is moving! It is going away!"

"Ever more swiftly," said Desmond.

I spoke to no one, not even Xanthe. I was muchly shaken. The descent of the falling sphere had been arrested. It had then been somehow taken skyward, and held in place. Now, it was climbing, actually, in a sense, falling, upward, away, at an ever-increasing speed. Such effects would require the control and manipulation of gravity. This spoke of a technology almost inconceivable to me. It was far beyond anything of which the most advanced sciences of Earth were capable. Had I not witnessed the effects of such a technology, I would have dismissed the notion as absurd. With such a technology, the existence of even a planet could be masked. With such a technology, one might even employ one's own planet as a comfortable, convenient spaceship, perhaps seeking out younger, fresher, more nourishing stars. And, with such a technology, one might dismantle and destroy worlds.

"The metal ball is gone," said Philippina.

"It is just farther away," said Temicus.

I suspected that the last of the sphere's protection to enable its descent had been abraded away by the fiery scouring atmosphere of its unusual flight, or fall, upward. When that was completed, the sphere, earlier so violently heated, I supposed, would be so worn, weakened, stressed and fatigued that a renewed descent, should it take place, would pose little danger to the surface of Gor.

"It is growing dark," said Desmond.

"We will camp to the side, and proceed to Ar in the morning," said Rupert.

"Good," said Temicus. "I am hungry. Let us have supper."

"You are always ready to eat," said Holt.

"Thus, it is only to be expected that I am ready now," said Temicus.

"I am hungry, Master," said Xanthe to Holt of Ar.

"You did not eat before," said Holt.

"That was before," said Xanthe, "and neither did Mira."

Xanthe was a great believer in the safety of numbers.

"You neglected your share," said Holt. "You gave it up. That is not my fault."

"I was merely postponing it," said Xanthe.

"I do not recall your asking permission for such a postponement," said Holt.

"Perhaps it slipped Master's mind," said Xanthe.

"Perhaps a whipping for you slipped my mind," said Holt.

"I now recollect," said Xanthe, "that I forgot to request such a permission."

"A solution is simple," said Rupert. "Masters, if they wish, may share their meal with their slave."

"Excellent," said Temicus. "As I have no slave, I shall have twice as much to eat."

"I trust," said Xanthe to Maxwell Holt, Holt of Ar, "that Master will arrange for himself an ample repast, one both nourishing and generous."

"I ate earlier," said Holt, "and am less hungry now."

"But you must eat, Master," said Xanthe. "It is important for you to keep up your strength."

"You are right," said Holt. "I must force myself to eat."

"But not too much," said Xanthe.

"Give me the extra food," said Temicus.

"Do you not think, slave," said Holt to Xanthe, "that Master Temicus eats too much?"

"I dare not contradict Master," said Xanthe.

"What then shall we do with the extra food?" asked Holt.

"May I help?" I asked.

"No!" said Xanthe.

"You might give it to your slave," I said.

"Yes!" said Xanthe. "That is an excellent suggestion. Mira, for a slave, is quite intelligent."

"Putting a collar on a woman," I said, "does not diminish her intelligence. If anything, it enhances it. Certainly it improves her value."

"If you own an animal," said Rupert, "you should take care of it."

"One does not want it to get fat," said Holt.

"I am in little danger of that, Master," said Xanthe.

"It is a great pleasure to own a beautiful woman," said Holt, "to have absolute power over her."

"Quite so," said Rupert, glancing at me. I quickly put down my head, submissively. I was his slave. How excited and pleased I was to be on Gor, and in my place in nature, a place in which Gorean Masters would see me kept.

"*Tal*, little beast," said Holt to Xanthe.

"*Tal*, Master," said Xanthe.

"What are you?"

"A slave," she said, "a property, a domestic animal."

"To whom do you belong?" he asked.

"To you, Master," she said.

"Are you hungry?" he asked.

"Very much so, Master," she said.

"Get on your knees," he said.

Swiftly Xanthe went to her knees before him.

"Do you beg to be fed?" he asked.

"Yes, Master," she said. "I beg to be fed."

"Very well," said Holt. "We shall see if Temicus has left anything for the rest of us."

"Fear not," said Temicus. "I have restrained myself."

"That is easier to do when the provender is simple and plain," said Holt.

"Quite so," said Temicus.

"Slave," said Rupert.

"Master?" I said.

"Are you hungry?" he asked.

"Very much so, Master," I said. I then went to my knees before him, lifted my head, and said, "I beg to be fed."

"Very well," said Rupert, who then went to Temicus, who was laying out the supplies.

* * *

"Look," I said, breathlessly.

I lay beside my Master on my back, my head at his waist, looking up.

"I see," he said, on his back, looking up.

"It is like a golden rain," I said.

"Lovely," he said.

"It is like the stars are falling," I said.

"I trust," he said, "they will not crush the earth."

"There is little or nothing to fear," I said.

"They are the remnants of the great metal globe, are they not?" he said.

"Yes," I said. "And they blaze with heat and fire, rushing through the air, only to burn away and disappear far above."

"It is strange," said Rupert. "By men were the Beast Caves saved."

"How strange, Master?" I asked.

"Little kindness exists between Kurii and humankind."

"Yet once," I said, "a man, a Warrior, cared for an injured, wounded Kur."

"And once," said he, "a Kur rescued a man from chains and onerous labors."

"Even in the vast tides of war," I said, "I think there are sometimes small countercurrents and eddies, when one sees a mortal foe as a needful brother."

"But beasts and men," said Rupert.

"I think it is the beasts who see us as beasts," I said.

"One repays a favor," said Rupert.

"Some do, some do not!" I said.

"What was Agamemnon like?" he asked.

"I do not know," I said. "I did not see him."

"Perhaps you did," he said.

"I am not aware of having done so," I said.

"You saw no mechanical bodies, perhaps resembling the large, metal river globe by which means Tiskias sought to deceive us?"

"No," I said.

"No metal, reticulated, serpents, no gigantic spiders of steel, no iron-clawed *tharlarion*?"

"No," I said.

"You saw live Kurii?"

"Yes," I said. "Perhaps one of them was Agamemnon."

"Unlikely," he said. "You saw a pillar, you heard an artificially produced voice."

"Yes," I said.

"Surmounting the large pillar," he said, "was a transparent tank or jar, containing a liquid, in which could be seen a buoyant, dark object, possibly restless or reactive?"

"Something dark, floating," I said.

"I think," he said, "you looked upon Agamemnon, cunning and fierce, one of the mightiest and most dangerous of all the Kurii."

"Surely not," I said.

"Not then ensconced in a formidable body."

"I do not know," I said.

"I think," said Rupert, "you are one of the few who have been permitted to look upon Agamemnon, the living brain of Agamemnon, unbodied, unhoused, lacking an emplacement in an artificial body. He was, I gather, between bodies. Or perhaps the Beast Caves now lack resources. Perhaps their shops are impoverished; perhaps they are now short of the means and materials necessary to construct a new and viable body. Wars are wont to impose grievous limitations on possibility. In the exigencies and harrows of war, the hopes of both beasts and men must often accept curtailment and restraint."

"I have recounted what I saw," I said. "I am unclear as to its meaning."

"Surely you have been puzzled as to how Agamemnon could pause the giant metal globe in its swift flight, control it, and thrust it away?"

"Yes," I said.

"He could not do so," said Rupert. "That is beyond the power of the Beast Caves."

"We saw it done," I said.

"But not by the Kurii of the Beast Caves, not by Kurii disengaged from the technology of the Steel Worlds."

"By Priest-Kings then?" I said. I shuddered. "They exist?"

"Something exists," he said.

"We could not penetrate the Sardar," I said.

"That is why we gambled," he said, "why we crossed hundreds of *pasangs*, enduring both privation and peril, to reach the Beast Caves."

"But you said the Beast Caves lacked the power to achieve what our senses assure us we saw."

"They do," he said. "But those who lack the power to touch and move worlds might possess the power to address those who can. Even a child might tug at the mantle of a Ubar."

"It seems it was done," I said.

"Somehow," he said.

I did not speak, but I knew a world where such feats were commonplace, words crossing oceans and circling continents.

Here on Gor, of course, such technologies were denied to humans. It seemed the Sardar saw to that. What rational form of life would allow infants to amuse themselves with matches and dynamite? But what Kur, already in possession of a formidable technology, would deny himself the least enhancement of his personal power, unless for diplomatic or prudential reasons? It did not seem to me at all impossible then that some private channel of communication might exist, or have lain ready for employment in a case of emergency, between, say, the Beast Caves and the Sardar.

"What of the Sardar?" I asked.

"Do not concern yourself," he said.

"The Sardar is then safe," I said.

"Certainly," said Rupert. "It would have taken action before, or much at the same time, as it took action locally."

"I was very frightened," I said, "in the steel tunnels."

"That is understandable," he said. "It is seldom that a *vulo* looks forward to supper with a *sleen*, or a *verr* to dinner with a *larl*, as they may find themselves on the menu."

"I am not brave," I said. "I just did not know what to do."

"You warned Agamemnon," he said, "and Agamemnon warned the Sardar, and thus both the Sardar and the Beast Caves, enemies for once enleagued, were saved."

"One thing happened after another," I said.

"You take no credit?" he said.

"I am happy," I said. "I am pleased."

"You did well," he said.

"I hope to have done so," I said.

"Perhaps you now think well of yourself," he said.

"No, Master," I said.

"Perhaps you are now proud?" he said.

"No, Master," I said.

"Perhaps you are now arrogant and wayward?" he said.

"I am not proud," I said. "I am not wayward. I cannot be such things. I am collared."

"Perhaps you should be rewarded," he said.

"Master?" I said.

"Perhaps I should free you," he said.

"No, Master," I said. "Please do not free me. Keep me!"

"Do not fear," he said. "You are pretty. I would not free you. If I wish to rid myself of you, I would sell you."

"Do not sell me!" I begged. "I am your slave. I want to be your slave, wholly and only your slave."

"I will do what I wish," he said.

"Of course," I said, "for you are Master. You can do anything you want with me. I am helpless! I am vulnerable. You own me! I am a slave. I am utterly dependent! I am totally at your mercy! But do not sell me!"

"You want a Master?" he said.

"Yes," I said, "I need a Master, and I want a Master! I do not want to be one of those tragic slaves who have no Master."

"Are there such?" he asked.

"Yes," I said, "on a world I know."

"Have no fear," he said. "You belong in a collar and will be kept in one."

He put his hand in my hair, and shook my head, gently, fondly.

I thrust myself closer to him.

"I will try to be pleasing to my Master," I said.

"You will be given no choice," he said.

"I want none," I said. "Lash me if I am not satisfactory."

"I will," he said.

There was a moaning and whimpering, and a gasping, to the side.

"Xanthe," he said, "is being put to use."

"She writhes well," I said.

"How far," I thought, "is Xanthe now from her games in the observatory."

"Master Holt imperiously derives much pleasure from her collared helplessness," I said.

"Of course," he said. "But let her know, as well, her own pleasures, as intense and inordinate as they may be, those of a subdued and conquered woman, those now of a mere ravished slave."

"She is so helpless," I said.

"She is a slave," he said.

"Thus she must endure whatever ecstasies her Master chooses to impose upon her," I said.

"That is appropriate," he said. "Her neck is in a collar."

"It pleases you, does it not," I asked, "to drive us mad with pleasure."

"Oh!" I cried. "Ohh!"

"You juice quickly," he said.

"Please do not stop!" I said. "More! Please more!"

"Rest," he said.

"I hope to do so," I said.

"Even the day rests," he said, "drawing over itself the blanket of the night."

"Yes, Master," I said.

I kissed his thigh.

"We are safe now," I said.

"I think so," he said.

"Our work is done," I said. "The plot of the faction of Pompilius has been foiled. The Sardar and the Beast Caves have been saved. The men of Tiskias have been scattered. We are victorious."

"There are large wars and small wars," said Rupert. "They are won and lost in different places at different times. Many an ost has coiled in the goblet of victory. Beware the foe who advances to surrender, sword in hand."

"The spheres have been destroyed," I said.

"But not those who cast them forth," he said. "The fate of the arrow does not decree the fate of the bow."

"Surely the security of the Sardar will now be heightened," I said.

"Undoubtedly," he said.

"Be then, dear Master, at ease," I said.

"Let not the celebration of the *larl*'s defeat blind one to the ost at one's ankle."

"I do not understand," I said. "What is there now to fear?"

"Vengeance," he said. "It is the solace of the defeated."

"I trust my Master's wisdom, his judgment, his keenness, and his sword," I said.

"We will leave early in the morning," he said, "enter Ar through the Gate of the Urts, read the public boards, gather supplies, spend the night, and leave through the Great Gate, to recruit in Venna."

"I would avoid Ar," I said.

"Where but in Ar," he asked, "can a dozen accents pass unquestioned, hear the news of a hundred cities, and be invisible in crowds?"

"Is Ar not dangerous for you?" I asked.

"I do not intend to pound on the gate of the Central Cylinder," he said.

CHAPTER EIGHTY

"I hear the drumming, the pounding, on a *tabor*, or *kaska*," said Xanthe.

"On more than one *kaska*," said Philippina. "It is a street performer. Let us look!"

"Dare we do so?" asked Xanthe. "The Masters have not yet returned."

"See the slave rings," said Philippina. "The shackles are open, the keys are in their niches. We have not been chained in place. Let us go look."

Public slave rings are a convenience in many Gorean cities, certainly in Ar. In many establishments, shops and such, and certainly in temples, slaves, as animals, are not permitted. One simply chains the slave in place, takes the key, and goes about one's business. When one is finished, one returns, frees the slave, and leaves the key in its niche. The *kaska* is much like the *tabor*, only smaller. Sometimes a player handles three or more linked *kaskas*.

"We were not given permission to stir," said Xanthe.

"Nor were we forbidden to stir," said Philippina.

"Your Master, Master Desmond," said Xanthe, "is permissive."

"Not at all," protested Philippina. "He is not weak. He keeps me well in my collar, surely as much as you and Mira are kept in yours."

"I am not eager to be lashed," I said.

"Nor I," said Xanthe.

We, Xanthe and I, women once of Earth, now well knew ourselves as no more than Gorean slaves.

"See, a little crowd is gathering," said Philippina. "Hurry."

"I would like to see," I said.

"I, too," said Xanthe.

"We can be back before the Masters emerge from the emporium," said Philippina. "There is no danger."

"Mira?" said Xanthe.

"All right!" I said. Certainly I was eager to see what was attracting some passersby.

We then, I, with Xanthe, and Philippina, excited and curious, hurried about the corner and rushed to a tiny square at the side of a fountain. The crowd was small and ragged, and we went to an opening through which we could see, but, suddenly, we held up shortly. I think that the three of us instantly regretted our decision to leave the side street. Philippina whimpered, and stepped back. The pounding on the *kaskas* became more intense. Xanthe and I could not move. The small crowd seemed to be uncertain as to how it should view the performance. There was an uneasy laugh from a man. The Kur fixed us with the nail of his gaze. The corner of its mouth wrinkled slightly, and one fang, bright with saliva, came into view over the dark moist lips. Then it swiftly turned its gaze away from us. Was it pretending not to havc seen us? It wore wide, polished double belts with accouterments. One foot held the end of a long leash pressed to the pavement. The pounding on the linked *kaskas* now began again, and a small human figure, decked out in a silly hat, jingling with bells, and an outlandish, baggy costume of red, yellow, and blue stripes began to dance again, cavorting and prancing about, on its leash. "It is Tiskias and his beast Bubu," I thought, "but now it is Bubu who is the Master and Tiskias who is the dancing pet." It was no wonder the small crowd seemed uncertain as to how to view the performance. It had not expected nor was it certain how to respond to what it saw. "See," said a man to his friend, "how clever! It is almost as if the man was the animal and the beast the Master."

"One would almost think it so," said his friend. The performance ended with a flourish of the *kaskas*, following which the Kur hooked the linked *kaskas* on one of his belts, picked up the leash, and pointed to the fountain, at which point Tiskias hurried to the fountain, fell to all fours, put down his head, and drank from the lowest tier of the two-tiered fountain, which tier is reserved for slaves and other animals.

"See," said the man. "Yes," said his friend, "clever." The Kur then jerked on the leash, pulling Tiskias abruptly up and back from the fountain, and Tiskias pulled off his hat and, the hat jingling, held it to one or another of the members of the small audience which was swiftly, uneasily, melting away. A man behind me tossed a tarsk-bit into the proffered hat, and Tiskias hurried to another. I had glimpsed the eyes of Tiskias. They seemed filled with terror and misery. I did not even think he recognized me, or cared if he had. I gathered that he had displeased an adherent of the faction of the Kur, Pompilius. The Kur, with Tiskias on his leash, then left the small square.

"Well, well done, pretty slaves," said the voice of the man behind me, he who had placed the tarsk-bit in the cap of Tiskias. We recognized the voice. We all fell to our knees, not daring to look back. "The Kur recognized you," said Rupert of Hochburg. "He did not even have to search for you. You sought him out and presented yourself to him, as a gift, a gift of golden stupidity. You are all stupid. None of you are worth more than a tarsk-bit, at best."

Tears sprang to my eyes. I felt crushed.

"How is it," asked Desmond of Hochburg, "that I find you here, where you were not left?"

"We meant no harm, Master," said Philippina. "We heard the *kaskas*, and wanted to hurry off and see."

"Were you given permission to do so?" asked Desmond.

"No, Master," sobbed Philippina. "Forgive me, Master."

"I am displeased," said Maxwell Holt, Holt of Ar.

Xanthe, I think, could not speak. Her small shoulders shook. It is not a light thing for a Gorean slave to displease her Master. I do not think she was afraid, so much as upset.

"We did not disobey," whispered Philippina. "We were not commanded to remain where we were."

"You should have known enough to stay where you were," said Desmond.

"Had I a slave," said Temicus, who had now joined us, "she would have known enough to stay where she was."

"Perhaps not," said Holt.

"Who was the leader in this small exercise?" asked Rupert. "Who instigated this action?"

Philippina caught her breath.

"We are all guilty," I said. "We departed together."

"Whip us," said Xanthe.

"It is partly our fault," said Desmond. "Slaves are foolish. We should have chained them in place."

"That is what slave rings are for," said Holt.

"No," said Rupert. "They should have known better."

"I have displeased my Master," said Xanthe. "I beg to be punished."

"We have been seen," said Rupert. "We have been discovered. Our lives are now in jeopardy, more so than even before. In such a case what could be the good of administering a taste of the leather? This is not equivalent to breaking a plate or spilling wine, or dallying the least bit in obedience."

"The slaves have disappointed us," said Desmond. "They know that. Let that be their punishment."

Philippina broke into sobs.

Suddenly it seemed to me that the world had ended in a torrent of misery and shame.

I had disappointed the Master I loved.

I turned about and put down my head and pressed my lips to

the bootlike sandals of Rupert of Hochburg. "Whip me," I begged, "please whip me. I beg to be punished. I beg to be whipped. Please, Master, whip me. Do not do nothing. Do not let it go. Please whip me, as the worthless slave I am!"

Faraway then was a woman of Earth.

I was then only a Gorean slave at the feet of her Master.

But his bootlike sandal merely thrust me away, angrily, to my side, on the pavement.

I sobbed. I had displeased my Master. I was worthless, less than dirt beneath his boot. How far I was then from Earth, from the observatory, from a wanton, cluttered, confused, artificial, unnatural, far civilization.

I was only a marked, collared slave.

"Ar has become trebly dangerous," said Rupert. "Shadows, darkness, and lonely places are no longer our allies. We must now seek light, crowds, and noise. A Kur can emerge from a doorway or drop from a roof and flood an alley with blood."

"Excellent," said Temicus. "Openness. Public places. A Kur is neither immortal nor invulnerable."

I knew that Kurii, as mighty and terrible as they were, wisely avoided villages and inhabited areas.

Certainly Lucilius had done so.

He had disappeared in the vicinity of the Beast Caves.

We had heard nothing more of him.

"Yes," said Temicus. "Kurii are also in jeopardy."

It was true.

No heart welcomed the greeting of a triple-finned, metal quarrel, or that of a long shaft sped from a peasant bow, whether it be that of a human or a Kur.

But were there not spies or officers, or informants, about who might carry tales of us to authorities, even to the Central Cylinder?

Impalement, I conjectured, where one's enemy is the weight of one's own body, would be an unusually unpleasant way to die.

"Slaves," said Rupert of Hochburg, "what is done is done. The marked stones have fallen from the cup. The fountain is nigh. Crawl to it. Wipe away your foolish tears, clean yourselves, and drink. We must soon be off."

I and the other slaves, on all fours, made our way to the fountain, and washed and drank, making certain we confined our ablutions to, and satisfied our thirsts from, the lower level of the fountain.

At the same time, a watchman, with a leashed *sleen*, satisfied their thirst, each from his appropriate level.

A free woman, with a pitcher, waited until the fountain was clear before approaching it.

I suspected that the *sleen* was trained to attack anyone that the watchman might designate. In the vicinity of such a watchman, or guardsman, few thefts occur.

"Let us now repair to our quarters and don festive garments," said Rupert of Hochburg. "Tonight we shall revel in the hospitality of the Purple Whip."

On the way from the small square, I thought I glimpsed Temione. But when I looked again the street behind us was empty, or seemed so.

CHAPTER EIGHTY-ONE

"Why did Master summon me to his table?" asked Luta, airily.

"Be silent," said Temicus. "Kneel down, facing away from me, and place your hands, wrists crossed, behind your back. Perhaps I will permit you to retain your tunic."

A moment later Luta's small wrists were thonged tightly behind her. Temicus then moved her about by the shoulders so that she faced the low table about which he, Rupert, Desmond, and Holt sat cross-legged.

"Put your head down now," said Temicus, "and kiss the table."

Luta, annoyed, complied.

I, Xanthe, and Philippina knelt rather behind and to the left of our respective Masters. They had not yet ordered. I trusted that they would share their meal with us, in one way or another, perhaps by putting a plate down beside the table, from which we might feed without the use of our hands, or by feeding us by hand. We were very hungry. We might have to beg prettily to be fed. It was earlier in the afternoon that we had hurried off to see a street performance which it would have been far better not to have seen. In doing so, our presence in Ar had been noted by a Kur, an adherent of the faction of Pompilius whose machinations to do away with Priest-Kings and the cohorts of the Kur, Agamemnon, had been sorely thwarted. I thought we would be fed. I hoped we would be fed.

"Keep your head down," Temicus warned Luta. "Your forehead is to be kept in contact with the table."

"May I speak?" asked Luta.

"If you wish," said Temicus.

"I do so wish," she said.

"Very well," said Temicus.

"I am high in the Purple Whip," she said. "I am not a common *paga* girl, as were two of the slaves with you. I am consigned to serve more elevated patrons. Your raiment, while gaudily festive, is cheap and I see no rings on your fingers. I conjecture, too, that your wallets are thin and light. I am surprised that you were allowed entrance. This is, after all, the Purple Whip, a tavern designed to appeal to a particular custom, that of the notable and well-to-do. If I am not mistaken, even the tunics of your slaves can boast of no material more august than common *rep*-cloth."

I had wondered about our facile admission to the tavern. Despite our unprepossessing appearance we had been instantly, unquestioningly, ushered within. It was almost as though our appearance had been anticipated, almost as though the guards might have been watching for us, almost as though certain preparations might have been made for our arrival.

"The anomaly to which you allude," said Rupert, "the ease of our passing through the gates of the Purple Whip, without even the substantial bribe I was prepared to offer, did not escape me."

"Yet you entered," said Desmond.

"Of course," said Rupert, "the light is good; there are numerous patrons about; we are armed and wary; and we did not accept the services of the first slave who approached our table."

"There is more," said Desmond.

"Curiosity," said Rupert. "When a door unexpectedly opens, who is not curious as to what lies on the other side?"

"It may be a trap," said Maxwell Holt, Holt of Ar.

"But what sort of trap?" asked Rupert. "Are you not curious? A welcome or threatening trap, a benevolent or perilous trap?"

"The Kur and Tiskias would not have had time to lay such a trap," said Temicus.

"Others might have," said Holt.

"But how could they know we would repair to the Purple Whip?" asked Desmond.

"We may have been overheard," said Temicus. "We made no attempt to conceal our intentions."

"We were followed," said Rupert. "Surely you noted the lovely slave of Gordon of Hammerfest following us."

"Temione," I said.

"I think this has to do with an important man, Lycus the Fat," said Rupert.

"He is a confidant of the Ubar," I said. "He was at a private party in the personal quarters of the Ubar, a supper at which I, Xanthe, Temione, and others served."

"So was Tiskias," said Xanthe.

"I take it," said Desmond, "Lycus is a patriot of Ar."

"He is of Venna," said Holt.

"I suspect," said Rupert, "he is a patriot of Lycus, a patriot of the winning side."

"It is easy to be on the winning side," said Holt. "All that is necessary is to choose your side after the battle."

"May I leave?" asked Luta.

"Stay as you are," said Temicus, "kneeling, bound, bent over, your forehead in contact with the table."

"I gather you do not wish me to serve you," said Luta.

"I would not say that," said Temicus.

"Do I know you?" she asked.

"I have seen you, here and there, from time to time," he said.

"I do not recall Master," she said.

"That is not necessary," he said. "I recall you."

"You were overcome with my beauty," she said.

"Not really," he said. "You are short, and a bit plump."

"Oh?" she said.

"But you are well-curved and have nice ankles," he said. "And you are exciting, in a petty, luscious way. It is easy to imagine you naked, in my collar, in my arms."

"May I leave?" she asked.

"Are you hot?" he asked.

"I am bound and helpless, and my head is down," she said. "Please do not speak so."

"It is easy enough to determine the matter," he said. "Shall I touch you?"

"No!" she said.

"Excellent," he said. "You have told me what I wished to know."

"You could not afford me," she said. "I once sold for three silver tarsks."

"That is too high," he said. "You are not worth that much."

"May I take your order to the Vat Master?" she asked.

"I do not think so," he said. "I have waited long enough to have you as you are now."

"Summon others then," she said.

"Perhaps I shall give it some thought," he said.

"If the slaves of the Purple Whip, who are amongst the most beauteous slaves in Ar, do not please you, have some of the other slaves, say, those here at the table, fetch your *paga* or carry your orders to the Vat Master, or to any of the tavern's men. Two here, I know, Mira and Xanthe. They are familiar with such duties, and more."

"We, Xanthe and I, are ready," I said, "if Masters wish it."

"We are going to order expensively and lavishly," said Rupert.

"How is that?" I asked.

"We are hungry," he said.

From my former experiences at the Purple Whip, where I had served as a *paga* girl, I was more than well aware of the establishment's prices.

"Even to order modestly, Master," I said, "would in this place strain your resources."

"Expensively and lavishly," said Rupert.

"How can that be?" I asked.

"What curbs exist where food is free?" he said.

"I do not understand," I said.

"Is it not clear?" he asked. "We are the honored guests of our host, of Lycus of Venna, of Lycus the Fat."

"What is going on?" asked Luta.

"Keep your head down, where it is," said Temicus.

She obeyed, somewhat angrily.

CHAPTER EIGHTY-TWO

We could see Venna in the distance.

To our right, rearing above us, stark against the blue sky and white clouds, was the great Vennan aqueduct, bringing water not only to Ar, *pasangs* behind us, but to far Torcadino, and cities and towns yet farther away.

Beyond Venna, ahead of us, we could see the foothills of the rugged, massive Voltai Range, called by some the 'keel of the world,' many of whose peaks are covered by snow throughout the year.

On each side of our small caravan, consisting of only three wagons, were some twenty assigned soldiers, ten on a side, of the newly formed Vosk Guard, commissioned by Marlenus of Ar, delegated by its commander, Gordon of Hammerfest, to accompany us to Venna. The balance of the Vosk Guard was still in training on the grounds of the Yard of Spears, a large martial park north of Ar, before its projected deployment in the Vosk Basin. Our escort, the contingent of the Vosk Guard assigned to us, was to return to Ar once we were safely within the walls of Venna.

The Vosk Guard itself had been ostensibly commissioned by the Ubar to protect trade between Ar and the river ports of the Vosk, but it seemed far more likely that its real purpose was to deal with a possible threat posed by numbers of Kurii in the Vosk area who had been identified as adherents of the faction of Pompilius, a faction feared by Ar. Indeed, later, it was thought that that faction was responsible for, or associated with, the recently, narrowly averted 'attack of the Plunging World,' which attack had threatened the very existence of Ar itself. As the Priest-Kings, thanks to the warning of Agamemnon, had foiled the plot of Pompilius, the 'attack of the Plunging Worlds,' their laws, and the powers essential to enforcing them, remained in effect. Thus, Kurii of the faction of Pompilius could not now, in virtue of a superior technology, simply impose their will on a vulnerable world, even wiping out or driving into hiding, should they wish, anything human or Kur which might dare to oppose their views and policies. Both human and Kur must now be comparable in their paraphernalia of adjudication, wit to wit, cunning to cunning, steel to steel. What Kur, as what man, need not fear the thrust of a spear, the stroke of a knife, the slash of a sword, the sudden flight of a quarrel or arrow? The irony of an unusual alliance, too, was not lost on me, that of the Vosk Guard and the Vosk League. Einar, the Sleen of the Vosk, the pirate, and Gordon of Hammerfest, Administrator of Hammerfest and commander of the Vosk Guard, were secretly one and the same person. How odd then that the forces commanded by he who was perhaps currently the greatest pirate on the Vosk were united with those of the Vosk League, which was charged with policing the Vosk. I knew, of course, that several individuals, both slave and free, important and unimportant, knew the supposedly secret identity of Gordon of Hammerfest. What is secret in one tier of society may be public knowledge in another. Such arrangements, as I understand it, are neither unprecedented nor unfamiliar in the corridors of power.

Xanthe, Philippina, and I rode in the back of the third wagon, the last wagon of our small caravan. Desmond was on the wagon bench. Luta, sweating and weary, stripped, her hands braceleted behind her, followed our wagon, closely. She had little choice in the matter for her neck chain, fastened to the rear of the wagon box, was only about five feet long. Her new Master, Temicus of Venna, who was driving the second of the three wagons had deemed her behaviors and attitudes, those manifested some two days ago in the Purple Whip, to have been somewhat less than wholly pleasing. Luta, at the time of course, had given no thought to the possibility that she might sometime find herself in his collar. That had been her mistake. A property should always keep in mind the possibility that it might become the property of someone, and completely.

Rupert of Hochburg was driving the first wagon, and Maxwell Holt, Holt of Ar, was seated on the wagon bench beside him.

"Mistresses," begged Luta.

"Are you addressing us?" asked Xanthe.

"Yes, Mistresses," said Luta.

"Surely you understand," said Xanthe, "that both myself and Mira, plain as she is, with a somewhat blemished countenance, and such, are barbarians."

"Please, Mistresses," wept Luta. "I am exhausted. My legs grow weak. If I fall and am dragged, I may be scarred."

"Are not native-born Goreans far superior in all respects to mere barbarians?" inquired Xanthe.

"No, no!" said Luta. "All human Goreans trace their origins to Terra. That is in the Second Knowledge. We are all the same form of life."

"Interesting," said Xanthe.

"Please be kind, and help me into the wagon," gasped Luta.

"Were you once free?" asked Xanthe.

"Yes, Mistress," said Luta.

"But now your pretty neck is in a collar," said Xanthe.

"Yes, Mistress," said Luta.

"You are a human female, are you not?" said Xanthe.

"Yes, Mistress," said Luta.

"Then," said Xanthe, "you are slave stock, the same as myself and Mira."

"Yes, Mistress," said Luta.

I had known myself a slave, even on Earth. I was thrilled to be a slave. I wanted to belong, to obey, to serve and love. I wanted men to be Masters so that I could be a slave. I was well aware of the radical sexual and psychological dimorphism in the human species. I did not want to pretend that the sexes were indistinguishable. I did not wish the sexes to be reduced to socially programmed antagonists. Did not all animals have a nature? Why then should human beings be different?

"Please, please help me into the wagon before I fall, Mistresses," said Luta.

"Let us help her," I said to Xanthe.

"She is a low slave, not even clothed," said Xanthe.

"Even so," I said.

"A slave," said Xanthe, "is to be docile, deferential, and submissive."

"I am such!" said Luta.

"And she must authentically, without the least subterfuge or reservation, endeavor to be pleasing, wholly pleasing," said Xanthe.

"I will, I will!" said Luta.

"Walk closer, backwards," I told Luta. "We will try to lift you into the wagon."

Luta, turning about, and, half falling, pushed against the back of the wagon and Xanthe and I, at the same time, reaching down, one on each side, seizing an arm, managed to lift and pull her into the wagon.

I thought that she might pass out from exhaustion.

Xanthe held her half up, sitting, and I filled a small cup with water from a bota, extracted from the supplies in the wagon, and lifted it to her lips.

"Another, and another, Mistresses," begged Luta.

"You need not call us 'Mistress,'" I said.

"Water," she whispered.

"One more now," I said, "perhaps more later."

"Does he know?" she asked.

"Does who know what?" I asked.

"Does my Master know that I am in the wagon?" she said. "I am afraid."

"Do not fear," said Xanthe. "We are not risking a lashing."

"He gave Xanthe instructions for your keeping," I said.

"Which I interpreted liberally," said Xanthe.

"You let me enter the wagon early?" said Luta.

"Actually," said Xanthe, "I made it a point to interpret his instructions liberally in the opposite direction. I added several *pasangs* to his suggestion."

"I did not know that," I said.

"You did not ask," said Xanthe.

"Why did you do that?" asked Luta.

"I found you annoying," said Xanthe, "long ago, and recently, as well, at the Purple Whip."

"Are you 'First Girl?'" asked Luta.

"There is no First Girl," I said.

"The position is then open," said Luta.

"Not to you," said Xanthe.

"Perhaps I can see about that," said Luta.

"Would you like to be returned to the road?" asked Xanthe.

"No!" said Luta.

I put aside the bota and put the small cup back in its box.

"I am naked," said Luta.

"For now," I said, "I will cover you with a bit of wagon canvas. Later, amongst the supplies, is some *rep*-cloth, thread and needles. I am sure that we can fashion you a ta-teera or tunic."

"If your Master allows you clothing," said Xanthe.

If a slave girl wishes to have a thread with which to cover her nudity, she must earn that thread.

Sometimes a new slave pretends indifference in this matter but, sooner or later, broken to her Master's will, and realizing she is now irremediably a slave, and no more, she throws herself weeping and kissing to her Master's feet begging for the bit of cloth which she had hitherto scorned as no more than a mark of shame and degradation.

But what woman, too, is not concerned with what she wears?

And what woman, too, does not wish to be exhibited in all her attractiveness and desirability?

And what woman, or man, is not familiar with the exciting garmenture of a female slave?

"Have no fear," said Luta. "I have no doubt my Master, for his pleasure and for that of others, will clothe me suitably. Who would not envy him such a property as I? I will be exhibited as a trophy slave."

"Quite possibly," I said.

"I doubt it," said Xanthe.

"Is he weak?" asked Luta.

"I do not think he has given it any thought, one way or another," I said.

"He is that strong?" asked Luta.

"I think so," I said.

As a Gorean, Temicus would assume, without question or cavil, that there was no antagonism or conflict between nature and society. A natural civilization is a civilization at peace with nature.

"What is his caste?" asked Luta.

"The Builders," I said.

"A high caste!" she said, delighted. "My Master is of high caste! Lycus the Fat, my former Master, he of Venna, was very rich, but he was not of high caste."

"My Master is also of high caste," said Xanthe. "He is of the Scarlet Caste, that of the Warriors."

"That caste," said Luta, "is a high caste only because the other castes are afraid to deny it that status. It is like the *larl* proclaiming himself the Ubar of beasts. Who is so unwise as to dispute the matter?"

It seemed to me that those who defended and policed worlds, who supported and protected civilizations, who had much to do with what survived and what did not, with what rose and what fell, deserved to be a high caste. To be sure, who would dare stand between the *larl* and the fruits of his hunt?

"It would be easy enough to roll you off the back of the wagon," said Xanthe.

"Would you please be so kind as to adjust the canvas about my body?" asked Luta.

"Certainly," I said.

"Thank you," she said.

"It is nothing," I said.

"I am sore and weary," she said. "I want to rest."

"Do so," I said.

She lay back, and, in a moment, with a small sound of chain, she was asleep.

"Into this private room, Masters," had said the tavern's man. "The noble Lycus, of Venna, my noble employer, has been waiting to speak with you."

Although I had served in the Purple Whip, I had never been in this part of the tavern, a private area not easily accessed from the floor or kitchen. Xanthe, Philippina, and I had followed our Masters, as we had not been forbidden to do. Temicus had pulled Luta to her feet and thrust her, her hands still bound behind her, before him. I suspect she would have much preferred to be with us, discreetly in the background. This part of the tavern, I supposed, was seldom accessed by floor girls.

One feels uneasy in such a situation.

"Masters," said the tavern's man, holding aside the heavy curtain.

Rupert entered the room pleasantly and promptly, as though it might have been in the holding of a well-known and trusted friend. Holt, Desmond, and Temicus, he with one hand on the upper arm of the bound Luta, entered more warily, more circumspectly. We followed the Masters. Inside, we knelt in the background. There, in a moment, Luta, still bound, joined us.

"I trust that you fed well," said Lycus of Venna, sitting cross-legged behind a low, jewel-inset table, on a colorful, deeply piled rug, which I was later informed was most likely derived from the bazaars of Tor, a city at the edge of a vast desert called the Tahari.

"Very well," said Rupert. "The hospitality and service of Lycus of Venna is legendary not only in Ar but throughout her entire hegemony."

"I am pleased that the meager offerings of my humble establishment have found favor in the eyes of so astute a critic," said Lycus. "Please be seated."

The men then sat down, cross-legged, facing their host.

I had the impression that Lycus was not particularly familiar with Luta. She was doubtless better known to one or another of the tavern's men. I recalled that when I was serving in his taverns, the Yellow Whip in Venna and the Red Whip and Purple Whip in Ar, I had scarcely ever caught a glimpse of him.

"We have been watching for your esteemed party in Ar," said Lycus.

"Given the ease of our admission at the gate," said Rupert, "almost a welcome, I suspected it might be so."

"It is convenient, pleasant, and apt," said Lycus, "that you saw fit to honor us with your presence this evening. We were intending to seek you out and issue a subtle, private invitation to visit, certainly before you left the city. Imagine then our relief and gratification, when, to our delight, you arrived at our very portal."

"The pleasure is all ours," said Rupert.

Maxwell Holt, Holt of Ar, loosened his sword a bit in its dark sheath.

"Why an invitation, why a private invitation?" asked Rupert.

"Surely you can conjecture," said Lycus.

"It has to do with recent events in the vicinity of the Beast Caves," said Rupert.

"Of course," said Lycus. "Your party thwarted a threat which might have leveled the walls and towers of Ar, a threat which might have murdered a population."

"I suppose," said Rupert, "the gates are being watched."

"I suspect so," said Lycus.

"You are interviewing us as an agent, on behalf of a principal," said Rupert.

"Possibly," said Lycus, his belly lying half over the edge of thc small table before him.

"We were followed this afternoon," said Rupert, "by a slave, one recognized as one owned by Gordon, the Administrator of Hammerfest, and the recently appointed commandant of the newly formed Vosk Guard."

"You have been followed from the time of the Beast Caves," said Lycus.

"By Gordon of Hammerfest," said Rupert, "he active on the behest of another."

"Rumor would have it so," said Lycus.

"I suspect," said Rupert, "you and the commandant have a common principal."

"It is quite likely," said Lycus.

"A principal who would find it politically inadvisable, given certain earlier declarations, events, and positions, to involve himself publicly in this business."

"Exactly," said Lycus. "And now you can understand, given the delicacy of the matter, the importance of discretion."

"You may inform the Ubar," said Rupert, "that one whom he decreed an outlaw and one whose blood he sought, graciously accepts his thanks for saving his city and his people."

"Your gracious acknowledgement of his gratitude will be conveyed through clandestine channels into the relevant quarters," said Lycus.

"And you may also tell him," said Rupert, "that I intend to recruit, and once more form a company, a free company, a roving company whose steel is pledged to no particular Ubar, Home Stone, or city, a company that will not bow to the highest bidder but will consider with care the uses to which its steel might be put."

"I do not think we need tell him that," said Lycus.

"He might not care to hear it," said Rupert.

"That is a plausible conjecture," said Lycus.

"I wish you well," said Rupert, rising.

"Oh, stay a moment, noble Master," said Lycus.

Holt's hand went to the hilt of his sword.

Lycus reached within his robe, drew forth a small, heavy, wax-sealed leather sack, and dropped it on the table.

Philippina gasped, and Desmond scowled in her direction, and she quickly put down her head.

"Words are but puffs of air," said Lycus. "Surely the gratitude of a Ubar is weightier than that."

"The Ubar is generous," said Rupert.

"The sack contains a hundred gold tarns," said Lycus, "twenty-five for each of the valiant four who saved Ar."

"The Ubar is indeed grateful," said Rupert.

"All Ar is grateful," said Lycus, "though few know to whom they are grateful."

The purse was sealed with a patch of wax, on which was imprinted some design. It was a single letter. I was later told that the wax had probably been imprinted with the Ubar's own medallion, that of mighty Ar.

Rupert bent down, lifted the purse up, and slipped it in his blouse.

"Do you not wish to count the gold?" asked Lycus.

"Marlenus and I are both of the Scarlet Caste," said Rupert.

"Forgive me," said Lycus.

Thus, I took it, there would be no checking of the contents of the sack. Honor, it seemed, as in so many transactions on Gor, was involved.

Too, I supposed, one does not lightly suspect, doubt, or insult a Ubar.

Would it not be embarrassing, if not dangerous, to do so?

Too, a Ubar is not some cunning, ragged peddler doling out tarsk-bits.

"We are free to leave the city, I take it," said Rupert.

"Certainly, now," said Lycus. "What is your destination?"

"Venna," said Rupert.

"I shall furnish you with three wagons and supplies," said Lycus. "And the Ubar will have Gordon of Hammerfest furnish you with a contingent of the Vosk Guard, to get you safely to Venna."

"You and the Ubar are generous," said Rupert.

"It is nothing," said Lycus.

He then rose ponderously to his feet.

"I wish you well," he said.

The two men grasped wrists, at which point Desmond, Holt, and Temicus, rose, too. We, the slaves, would remain on our knees until the men were prepared to leave the room.

"Why is that one slave bound?" asked Lycus, noting Luta.

"She is one of yours," said Temicus. "I found her of interest. I am prepared to buy her, particularly in the light of what I have just seen."

"She is yours," said Lycus.

"Master!" protested Luta.

"My thanks, noble Master," said Temicus.

Lycus looked about. "As you take your leave," he said, "take others, too, should they please you."

I was immediately frightened, as, I am sure, were Xanthe and Philippina. Most girls prefer to be the single slave of a single Master. We did not want to compete for the caresses of a Master. Too, what if we were less than fully pleasing? We could be sold or given away on a whim. I was shaken and frightened. I well knew then that I, kneeling and collared, helpless and vulnerable, was a slave.

"You are generous, indeed," said Rupert.

"I am alive," said Lycus, "and the Red Whip and the Purple Whip have not been ground to dust."

"One slave, particularly one so charming, is more than enough," said Rupert.

Temicus reached down, seized Luta by the upper arm, and jerked her to her feet. "On your feet, slave," he said, and thrust her stumbling through the portal and into the hall.

Shortly thereafter the Masters had left the room, and we had risen to our feet, and had followed them.

"She is awakening," I said to Xanthe and Philippina.

"Please adjust the canvas about me," said Luta. "How long have I slept?"

I rearranged the canvas.

"Perhaps half an Ahn," said Philippina. "I heard the tenth bar from Venna, but have not heard the eleventh."

The tenth Ahn was the Gorean noon. The day was divided into twenty Ahn.

"The wagon has stopped," said Luta.

That was perhaps why she had awakened.

"All three have stopped," said Philippina, "and the supply wagon of our escort has, as well."

"What for?" asked Luta.

Philippina was standing in the wagon, shading her eyes.

"I think a party from Venna is meeting us," said Philippina. "Perhaps they wish to accord us an official welcome."

"Unlikely," said Xanthe.

"Perhaps they are suspicious and wish an accounting of our presence and intentions," said Philippina.

"Nonsense," said Xanthe. "Venna is a cosmopolitan town, accustomed to visitors, accommodating and welcoming."

"Accommodating for a price and welcoming of coin," said Luta.

"Of course," said Xanthe.

"Perhaps they are well-disposed merchants who wish to warn us of high gate fees and recommend lodgings outside the walls."

"You spent too long in the forest," said Xanthe.

"What Philippina said is not impossible," I said. "This is the season of races, and lodging might be in short supply."

Venna was noted for her *tharlarion* races.

"A Master approaches, Master Temicus," said Philippina, kneeling.

Xanthe and I went to our knees, too, as was suitable for a female slave before a free person.

Luta, too, went to her knees, this inadvertently dislodging the canvas I had placed about her.

"We will be proceeding shortly," said Temicus.

The slaves in our party, that of Rupert of Hochburg, Holt of Ar, Desmond of Hochburg, and Temicus of Venna, had been granted a standing permission to speak, a privilege for which we were grateful but also one which, we understood, might be instantly revoked and was not to be abused.

"I am unclothed, Master," said Luta.

"May I inquire as to the delay?" I asked.

"A body of men from Venna has come forth to meet us," said Temicus. "Lodging has been set aside for us within the walls."

"Splendid," said Xanthe.

"Who knows what one might encounter on the road, even one as well-traveled as the Venna Road from Ar," said Philippina.

A caravan of three wagons was large enough to attract attention and small enough to encourage predation.

We did have gold with us, of course, that given to us by Marlenus, Ubar of Ar, delivered to us through the auspices of Lycus of Venna, at the tavern of the Purple Whip in Ar. Our escort, assigned to us from the Vosk Guard, was to return to Ar once we were safely ensconced within the walls of Venna.

"I have not yet been given clothing, Master," said Luta.

"Will we reach Venna by nightfall?" asked Xanthe.

"Easily," said Philippina.

"Clearly word of our arrival has preceded us," said Xanthe.

"Clearly," said Temicus.

"Perhaps it is an oversight," said Luta, "that I have not yet been given clothing."

"We thought it would be permissible to bring Luta within the wagon," I said. "She was miserable and worn. We feared she might fall, and be injured."

"Would you like clothing?" Temicus asked Luta.

"Yes, Master," she said.

"Why?" asked Temicus.

"'Why?'" asked Luta.

"Yes," said Temicus.

"For the sake of my beloved Master," she said, "of the noble and high caste of Builders. I would not like strangers to think that my Master was too poor to clothe a slave."

"I appreciate your concern," he said. "But let me allay your fears. You and I both know that I could afford to clothe a slave, and that is what is important. Surely you agree. Thus we need not concern ourselves with the views of strangers."

"It will be nice to be within the walls of Venna," said Xanthe.

"Think, too," said Philippina, "of the emporiums, the markets, the sights and shopping."

"We will not be entering Venna," said Temicus. "Certainly not immediately."

"I do not understand," said Xanthe.

"What?" said Philippina.

"Master?" said Luta.

"Few would know of our approach," said Temicus. "But a racing *tharlarion* from Ar could easily reach Venna before us. If Marlenus or Lycus in Ar had intended such an arrangement, designated, sheltered, lodging, we, or our escort, would have been apprised of it, probably in Ar. Those who halted our wagons are not a delegation, as they claimed, from the city. Such things are not the custom in Venna. She is not so accommodating. Too, I am of Venna, and their badges of office were spurious. It was clearly an artifice to trick us into accepting a vulnerable location where, perhaps hemmed in, pinned against a wall, we might be done away with, probably at night."

"We thought to be safe within walls," said Xanthe.

"Walls for one," said Temicus, "can be a shield, but for another a trap, and cage."

"You pretended to take their offer seriously," I said.

"Of course," said Temicus.

"I thought the war was done," I said.

"It is," said Temicus, "but the taste of defeat can be bitter and sometimes one hopes to wash it away with the wine of revenge."

He then reached into his wallet and removed a pair of keys, and relieved Luta of her neck chain and the slave bracelets which held her hands behind her back.

He then turned about, but then he turned back again.

"Master?" I said.

"Obtain or fashion a tunic for the slave, Luta," he said. "Make certain that it is exquisitely short. Leave her in no doubt that she is a slave."

"Yes, Master," I said.

I could have assured him that none of us, Xanthe, Philippina, or myself, owned, mastered, marked, and collared, had the least doubt that we were slaves.

That is what our Masters, in their uncompromising, ruthless possessiveness and masculinity, wanted us to be, helpless, vulnerable slaves, wholly owned women, totally dependent on them.

How happy I was to be what I was!

Their will would be imposed upon us.

We would have nothing to say.

We were collared.

We were grateful.

CHAPTER EIGHTY-THREE

I awakened, uneasy.

"Do you sense it?" I asked, lying beside him, my Master.

"Yes," he said.

"What is it?" I asked.

There seemed a trembling of the earth.

"*Tharlarion!*" he said.

We sprang up.

Almost at the same moment, one of the guards, from the escort furnished by Gordon of Hammerfest, from the Vosk Guard, stuck the alarm bar.

"Shelter behind a wagon!" said Rupert.

I hurried to the nearest wagon, in the light of the White Moon.

The ground, now, was clearly shaking.

It was difficult to stand upright. I held to the wagon. I heard a woman scream, possibly Philippina, maybe Luta.

The alarm bar was deafening, struck savagely, again and again.

In the camp there was turmoil, men rushing about, shouting and cursing, slaves screaming.

Then there seemed a churning of the ground, a thunder in the night, a wildness beneath the moon, and huge bodies were everywhere, and the wagon to which I clung was buffeted yards from its place, to a splintering of wood, amidst the bellow of hurrying beasts.

This afternoon we had not entered Venna. The Masters' suspicions had been aroused by the party fraudulently representing itself as welcoming Vennan officials, proffering inexpensive, convenient quarters in the city. Those quarters, as inquiries had later made clear, would have proved to be little more than a narrow, wall-rimmed *cul-de-sac*, which one might almost have speculated had been designed with an ambush or trap in mind. Beyond that, given the height of the racing season, housing was scarce, as well as dear, and there seemed no practical way to accommodate a party of our size in a single venue. Accordingly, we had camped outside the walls, as had several other groups, both larger and smaller than ours.

I was half choking in the dust.

The beasts had now gone.

It was rather dark now, the moon behind clouds.

"Are you all right?" inquired Rupert.

"Yes, Master," I said, wiping dust from my face.

The wagon behind which I had hidden was askew, on its side, yards away, two wheels torn away.

"They must have turned five dozen *tharlarion*, or more, out of the stables," said Rupert.

The stampede then, to which we had been subjected, was no accident, no startling of milling, quiescent animals, but the result of an organized, deliberate act.

"Go to the center of the camp," he said, "get within the forming shield wall, join the other slaves, and the injured."

"Master?" I said.

I wanted to remain with him.

"Hurry," he said.

"Master!" I protested.

"The attack will come shortly," he said. "Armed men, to profit from the advantage of disruption, to fall upon the demoralized and confused."

It seemed I could not move.

"But," he laughed, frightening me, "they will be little more than recruited malcontents, ruffians, and brigands. Should they dare to engage, they will find themselves up against not shattered and bewildered men but picked men, impatient and steel-eager, furnished by Gordon of Hammerfest."

"You welcome them, intruders?" I said, frightened.

"I would only they were worthy foes," he said. "There is little glory in the extermination of *urts*."

"Is not a shield wall defensive?" I asked.

Cloud cover, as I had noted earlier, had obscured much of the illumination of the moon.

"Let them address it," he said. "That is our expectation. It is one side of a two-sided trap. Have you not received a command?"

"Yes, Master!" I said. "Forgive me, Master!"

I turned about, and fled toward the center of the camp. I hoped not to be beaten. In a moment I had slipped between the shields of two men of our escort. Philippina, Xanthe, and Luta were already within the shields. Two or three men lay supine within the enclosure, being tended to by the fellows who had driven, or tended to, the escort's supply wagon. I looked out, as I could, over and between shields. I saw no sign of my Master, nor of Maxwell Holt, Holt of Ar, Desmond of Hochburg, or Temicus of Venna.

Only seconds later I heard a shouting, which was perhaps intended to be a war cry, and a number of bodies appeared out of the darkness and began to flail about with swords and axes, striking disabled wagons and cutting at boxes and bundles.

A moment later the attackers seemed to become somewhat confused. I speculated that they had expected to fall upon a handful of disorganized and unsuspecting caravan's men, and then, to their surprise, they had encountered no one. A moment after this, they had discerned the sturdy shield wall. I gathered they had not expected resistance, let alone to discover clear evidence of an organized, prepared defense. The reckless way in which the camp had been entered led me to suppose that their principal, presumably Tiskias, had not been at pains to inform them of the exact nature of their foe. Had he been more clear on the matter, perhaps his efforts at recruitment would have been less rewarding. He had doubtless hoped that a sudden attack, one not anticipated, following closely on the damage and confusion inflicted by stampeding *tharlarion*, would accomplish whatever results he was hoping to bring about.

"There are shields," said a man.

"Throw down your weapons!" said one of the attackers.

"Surrender and you may be spared," said another.

But these demands were met with no response from the men of our escort.

I was not certain of the number of the attackers, but I knew they would be a number ample enough, in the judgment of Tiskias, or a confederate, to overwhelm our modest escort. The shieldsmen of our escort remained inert, their shields ringing the slaves, the injured, and those attending to their needs. This quiescence doubtless emboldened the attackers for, while none of them threw themselves against the shield wall, several poked at it with thrusting spears and jabbing swords.

"Break your formation!" cried an attacker. "Advance and meet us, blade to blade, steel to steel! Now! Craven cowards!"

But most of our assailants held back. They did not seem eager to pit their metal against a set defense, one they had apparently not anticipated and did not care to deal with. Some may have departed already in the darkness.

The shieldsmen did not respond to the provocations of the intruders.

They were firm.

They might have been of stone.

Three or four of the attackers seemed far more desperate or aggressive than their fellows. "At them!" cried one. "Do you fear stable boys, petty merchants, peddlers, wagoners, *tharlarion* tenders? Fight! Attack! Attack!"

"Be cautious," said one of the attackers. "We face a set rank. We were promised dismayed, routed men, frightened and running. I do not see them. These are not such."

"Gold awaits the ending of our task," said an attacker, one of the louder and closer of our foes. "Gold unearned is gold unpaid! Attack! Break the wall!"

One man backed away. "What good," he asked, "does gold do the dead?"

An attacker then, one of the more prominent of our foes, perhaps a leader, in frustration and rage, drove his sword into the back of the fellow who had spoken. "Very little," he said, "as you now well know." Then he called out to others. "Attack! Break the shield wall!"

"Break it yourself!" said one of the attackers, turning to face the man, his sword ready, he now on guard, prepared to defend himself.

He who had mortally struck his fellow did not engage the man facing him. How quickly odds can change.

Rather, he backed away and called out, "A full copper tarsk, of Brundisium, for each man's head brought to the fee giver! Slaves to be sold and coins distributed!"

In the distance, I saw some torches, apparently lit from other camps nearby.

A voice then rang out, that of my Master. "The trap has been sprung," it cried. "Pin the *urts* against the shield wall, and slay them to a man!"

"Who is there?" cried a foe.

"Ten dozen men at arms, thirsting for blood," cried my Master.

"No!" cried one of our attackers.

"Who are you?" cried a foe, looking about, wildly.

"Where are they?" asked another.

"At your throats," said Rupert.

"Speak," cried an attacker. "Identify yourself!"

"Guardsmen of Venna," cried Rupert, "intent upon cleansing away scum whose very presence offends the Home Stone. We have waited long to trick you out of the city, luring you out with the promise of gold, to where you may be dealt with expeditiously."

"No!" cried more than one man.

"You lie!" cried another.

"You who thought to encircle are encircled," said Rupert. "Not one man will escape."

Surely our forces were too thin to warrant such a threat. Who of our party could be outside the shield wall but my Master and his fellows, Holt of Ar, Desmond of Hochburg, and portly Temicus of Venna?

"You are not guardsmen!" cried an attacker.

"You are netted," called Rupert, calmly. "Did you truly expect us to search for, find, and hunt down every brigand, thief, and cutthroat, one by one, in the city? Such an effort would be difficult and lengthy. Better our ruse of having so many of you gather yourselves together, after which we had merely to lure you outside the city with the promise of gold. Too, who would care to bloody the streets of lovely Venna and thereby discomfort thousands of visitors come happily for the races, visitors on whom you doubtless hoped to prey?"

"Guardsmen would not have permitted us to release *tharlarion* and drive them through the camp!" said an intruder, surely more to his fellows than to that voice from the darkness.

"That," called Rupert, "was our Master stroke, to assure you of an easy victory, the slaughtering of a distraught, confused foe, and to put you off your guard."

"Mercy!" cried an intruder.

"Beware," cried an intruder. "We are many, you are few!"

"It is we who are many, and you who are few," said Rupert.

I was not clear, in the darkness, the moon muchly obscured, how many foes might be about.

"How many are you?" cried an intruder.

"Enough for our mission!" called Rupert, "to see that not one of you sees the dawn."

"Torches approach," said an attacker, wildly looking about.

To be sure, torches were nearing, doubtless to investigate this commotion in the night.

"Our support," said Rupert, "but we deem it unnecessary."

"Let us make away," said one of the intruders to his fellows.

"Yes!" said another.

"Cast down your weapons and your wallets!" cried Rupert.

"Our wallets?" said a man.

"That you may hope to buy your lives," said Rupert.

"Who are you, truly, make yourself known!" cried a man.

"There is little in my wallet!" cried another.

"I am sure that it will be more than you are worth," said Rupert, from the darkness.

"You are not guardsmen," cried one of the intruders. "You are brigands, merely brigands!"

"If so, ones far more clever than you," said Rupert.

"You want Venna to yourselves!" said an intruder.

"Who would not?" asked Rupert.

"That is theft!" cried an intruder.

"If it is acceptable for you to rob Publius," said Rupert, "it is acceptable for Publius to rob you. That is made clear by parity of reasoning."

"Tarsk!" cried an intruder.

"We will fight, rather than be slaughtered like *verr*," said an intruder.

"Fighting assures that you will be slaughtered like *verr*," said Rupert. "On the other hand, the time of the races is a happy time in Venna. Let not the shadow of slaughter darken the sun of good cheer. Mercy tempts us. Cast down your weapons and purses. The gates of Venna will be closed against you, but you may beg on the roads and happy men are generous."

"Thank you, Masters!" cried a man, throwing down his sword and cutting his purse free, to fall at his feet.

He then sped away into the darkness.

"Fool!" cried others, but, one by one, others followed his example.

"Are you guardsmen or villains?" cried an attacker.

"Neither," said Rupert.

"What are you?" the voice demanded.

"What you fear most," said Rupert. "Honest men, who are armed."

Shortly thereafter the attackers, coinless and weaponless, disappeared into the night.

The shield wall opened, I and the others emerged.

The men were gathered about.

"It was hard to see," I said.

"It is getting light now," said my Master.

"I see only two bodies," said Maxwell Holt, Holt of Ar.

"One," said Rupert, "is that of he who had urged his fellows to caution, who was wary, who was diffident of addressing himself to the shield wall, he who perished from a thrust to the back. The second, I think, is that of the man who had delivered that thrust to the back of his fellow."

"He bled from the heart," said Desmond of Hochburg.

"It seems a sword was utilized before it was cast down," said Rupert. "Put it with the other discarded weapons."

"I expect he understood who administered that thrust," said Temicus.

"Most likely he was informed by the assailant," said Rupert.

"You did well, Captain," said Holt.

"Fortune was our fellow," said Rupert. "We knew not their numbers."

"Nor they ours," said Holt.

"It was important to avoid an engagement," said Rupert, "even were numbers aligned. Darkness neutralizes skill. In a blind helmet, a champion might fall to a novice, a *larl* to a *tarsk*."

I did not understand this allusion at the time. I was later given to understand that it referred to an arena sport, one outlawed some years ago, in which antagonists were unable to see one another.

"Too," said Holt, "one is sometimes reluctant to stain one's blade with unworthy blood."

"I think," said Rupert, "things turned out well."

"I would not wish to be our small friend, Tiskias," said Temicus. "Many will regard him as the craftsman of their misfortune, either by intent or inadvertence."

"At the least," said Desmond, "one suspects he was not fully candid about the possible risks his hirelings might face."

"The edge of morning is upon us," said Temicus. "How shall we now occupy ourselves?"

"I am weary," said Rupert. "Did you sleep well?"

"Not at all," said Temicus.

"Nor I," said Rupert.

"Perhaps then," said Temicus, "we might consider a nap before breakfast."

"An excellent suggestion," said Rupert. "See that a guard is set."

"I will do that," said Temicus.

"Master," I whispered.

"What?" he asked.

"I have not been caressed in four days," I said.

A slave is sometimes deprived of sex for days before her sale. Let them whine and moan, and scratch at their cages. How beggingly piteous are they then when exhibited nude on the block.

"You are uneasy, restless, needful?" he said.

"Very much so," I said.

"A free woman," he said, "may go weeks without being needful."

"I am not a free woman," I said.

Did he not know what men had done to me? They had, as it had amused them, callously and without my consent, kindled the slave fires which smolder within the belly of any woman. It had been done to us. We were no longer free. We were now helpless. We were now the prisoners and victims of our needs. Surely it is that, more than a brand or collar, more than a degrading rag or unbreakable chains, which made us their slaves, the slaves of men. What free woman can begin to understand our needs, our torments and passions, those of the helpless, vulnerable female slave?

"Earlier," he said, "you dallied in compliance, not hurrying immediately to conceal yourself within the shield wall."

"I wanted to be with you," I said.

"I wanted you to survive," he said.

"Surely Master does not care for a mere slave?"

"You have value," he said, "perhaps as much as a silver tarsk."

"I sold for a silver tarsk six in Victoria," I said.

"Beware," he said.

"Forgive me," I said.

"You dallied," he said.

"Am I to be beaten?" I asked.

"No," he said.

"What are you going to do with me?" I asked.

"We must rest," he said.

"Yes, Master," I said.

"I am going to tie your neck to my ankle," he said. "It will help you to know your place."

"Yes, Master," I said.

Later, struck suddenly with fatigue, worn and weary from the night, I licked and kissed his ankle and fell asleep.

I had not realized how tired we were.

Who would care to embark upon a banquet while fighting sleep? So, too, a Gorean Master prefers that his senses be fresh, alive, alert, and keen before putting his properties to use, before setting himself to enjoy the 'feast of the furs.'

Who am I to dispute such a matter?

CHAPTER EIGHTY-FOUR

We stood back, observing the flights, like clouds of angry hornets, and thrilled to the snapping and pounding, the ripping penetration of wood, canvas and straw.

"Fetch the arrows," said Temicus.

Philippina, Xanthe, Luta, and I ran lightly to the targets, drew forth the numerous missiles, and brought them back to the racks and stands from which new archers would extract them. Holt of Ar and Desmond of Hochburg made notations on their marking boards.

The bows were short bows, of wood, horn, and sinew. Such bows have considerable striking power and can easily clear a saddle. They are rare in the north, but are popular with the *kaiila*-riding wagon peoples of the south. We were unable to bend them.

The targets were now set at the 'third distance,' which I estimated would be something like ninety yards.

"My fellows are the best," said Xanthe.

"If so," I said, "that has very little to do with your skill in bringing back arrows."

"It has a great deal to do with it, dear Pockface," said Xanthe. "The finest archers insist on using my targets, that they may watch me return their arrows."

"This morning," I said, "it was Philippina's targets which almost had their centers torn out."

"Since this morning," said Xanthe, "the fellows have had longer to look us over."

"If you observe carefully," said Luta, "my fellows are the best."

I thought that my fellows were the best, but I did not see fit to press the matter.

Shortly after reaching Venna, my Master had begun the recruitment of a free company. His high officers were Desmond of Hochburg, Holt of Ar, and Temicus of Venna. We were now, several days later, in a temporary recruiting and training camp east of Venna, nestled amongst the foothills of the Red, or Voltai, Mountains. The Voltai Range has a reddish hue, presumably attesting to large amounts of ferrous oxide in its composition.

"Keep to the side, away, out of the line of fire," said Temicus.

There are numerous 'free companies' on Gor. A 'free company' is one which is independent of established polities. Men with diverse Home Stones, or no Home Stones, even betrayed Home Stones, may serve in such a company. Free companies may be large or small, ranging from hundreds of men, such as that of a Dietrich of Tarnburg, to a dozen or so men. The average size of a free company is between a hundred to three hundred men. Each free company has a captain or leader. Some free companies are careful in the commissions they undertake, considering justice, right, and honor, but others are less so. For example, many free companies are known to let parties bid for their steel, which is then put at the service of the party with the deepest purse. Occasionally, in a dispute, as gold appears or disappears, a company may switch sides. This however, is rare, as so egregious a shift in putative loyalties invariably taints a company's reputation. Similarly, a free company's disappearance in the middle of the night, when beleaguered or hard-pressed, when tides turn or auspices prove unpromising, does little to enhance a reputation or encourage the investments of future clients. Some free companies are little more than assemblages of uniformed brigands. A man may die for his Home Stone, but few, if the option exists, will die for their pay.

"Ai!" I screamed, spinning to the side. I sank to my knees, vomiting in the grass. The point of the quarrel had been diverted by my collar. I recollected only the sense of a flash, a jagged, swift scratching, maybe a spark. Then I was prone in the grass, clutching at the grass. I could not speak. I was shuddering.

"What is wrong with her?" said a man.

"An accident, a mistaken arrow!" said a man.

"Who fired that arrow?" cried Temicus, in fury.

"That was no arrow!" said a man. "I saw it carom away. Too short, too heavy, for an arrow!"

"What happened?" said another.

"A loose shaft," said a man.

"Who would fire on a slave?" said one man, incredulously.

Xanthe, Luta, and Philippina rushed to my side.

"A mad, stupid accident," speculated a man.

"Who fired?" asked a fellow.

"Who knows?" said a man.

"Some fool," said another.

"There!" cried a man.

"One flees!" said another fellow, pointing I suppose.

"He has no bow!" said a man.

"After him!" cried Temicus.

Desmond and Holt, I learned later, were already in pursuit of the fugitive.

"He discarded the weapon," I heard.

"Are you all right?" begged Xanthe.

"I think so," I whispered.

"He will not escape," said Luta. "He is pursued even now."

"It is some kind of terrible mistake," said Philippina.

"I was not watching," said Xanthe. "Did you disobey Master Temicus? Did you stray into the line of fire?"

"No," I said. "No!"

"I do not see how such a thing could happen," said Philippina.

"It was some sort of accident," said Xanthe.

"Men of skill do not loose wayward shafts," said Luta.

"Look!" cried a man. "A tarn, aflight!"

"He escapes!" said a man.

"Bring him down, arrows to bows!" cried a man.

"Some fire," said a man.

Bow strings snapped and hummed.

"Consider the tarn's flight, altering and darting!" said a man.

"He will be out of range in a moment," said a man.

"He knows the tarn," said another.

Shafts vainly streaked the sky.

"He is out of range," said another.

"Call the captain," said a man.

"He is at the edge of the camp, negotiating with suppliers," said a man.

"Bring him here," said Temicus.

"Officers return," said a fellow.

Xanthe helped me to my knees.

I saw Desmond and Holt approaching. Holt was carrying a crossbow. It seemed to me large and heavy. I think I could not have held it level or steadied its aim. I could see why it might have been flung aside lest it impede a flight.

Shortly thereafter Desmond and Holt were before us. In their presence, the slaves, all, went to their knees.

Holt cast down the crossbow angrily.

"Clearly this was no accident," said a man.

"He had a tarn, tethered and waiting," said Desmond.

"A hireling," said a man.

"One considerably skilled," said Holt.

"Who would kill a slave?" asked a man.

"One hired to do so," said another.

"A crossbow," said a man. "There are none in camp."

"Their rate of fire is too slow," said another.

The crossbow, of course, has its advantages. It can remain cocked, so to speak, the quarrel patient in its guide. Too, rightfully or wrongly, it is generally thought that less time, skill, and experience is required to employ it effectively.

"The captain," said a man.

The fellow, or fellows, who had gone to fetch him would have apprised him of what had occurred.

He knelt on one knee beside me and took me into his arms. He held me for a moment, closely, and then, as though embarrassed, thrust me back, away, and rose up.

"The archer escaped," said Holt.

"By tarn," said Desmond.

"Men come and go, seeking fee," said Temicus. "He must have carried the bow in his pack, in parts, disassembled, and then assembled it once in camp."

"Cunning," said a fellow.

"From whence did he fire?" asked Rupert.

"I think from there, by the rise," said a man, gesturing.

"Well over the third distance," said Rupert.

"A fine marksman," said a man.

"An excellent shot," said another.

"One pays high for such skill," said another.

"He failed of his target," said a man.

"Not really," said a fellow. "The quarrel was turned aside by the slave's collar."

"She may have moved," said another.

Kneeling, I again felt sick.

"Where is the quarrel?" asked Rupert.

"Somewhere over there," said a man. "I saw it. It caromed off the slave's collar for forty or fifty paces."

This gave me some sense of the force of the flight.

If it had struck the collar directly, I wondered if my neck would have been broken.

"Fetch it," said Rupert.

Shortly thereafter, a man found the quarrel in the grass and returned it to Rupert.

"Aii!" whispered a man.

"As I thought," said Rupert, "the quarrel is black."

"The Black Caste," said a man.

"The Assassins," said another.

"They are expensive," said another.

"I do not understand," said a man. "One does not kill slaves. One buys and sells them. One owns and enjoys them."

"What human would fee an Assassin for so strange and ugly a deed?" asked a man.

"Perhaps nothing human," said Rupert. He then turned to me. "Are you all right?" he asked.

"Yes, Master," I said. "I felt sick, but now I am better. I am now all right."

"What do you know of Assassins?" he asked.

"Very little," I said.

"Your assailant was an Assassin," he said. "He will have taken fee."

"Master?" I asked.

"He will try again," said Rupert.

CHAPTER EIGHTY-FIVE

I awakened, screaming.

"What is wrong?" said Rupert, casting aside covers, sitting up, abruptly.

"Nothing," I said. "Forgive me, Master. It was a dream."

He was now on his feet, at the tent entrance, looking about, sword in hand.

"Lantern!" he called.

One was soon brought to him.

It was still dark.

A soft rain was falling outside.

"It was only a dream," I said. "Forgive me, Master."

He lifted the lamp.

He looked at me, strangely. I did not understand this.

"Only a dream," I said.

"Speak," he said. "What was the dream?"

"It is unimportant, Master," I said.

"Speak, slave," he said.

"I dreamed I awakened," I said, "and left the tent, I knew not why. I dreamed I walked away from the tent, and out, into the field of training. I stopped, at the line of fire, from which men discharge their bows. It was dark. I could see little or nothing. I felt wet grass about my ankles, and, here and there, mud beneath my feet. I was alone, puzzled and apprehensive, and then, to my considerable uneasiness, I felt I was then not alone. 'Who is there?' I called. There was no answer. I was afraid. I called again. 'Is anyone there?' Then, moments later, in the darkness, my senses were regaled with a subtle atmosphere of unfamiliar aromas, some pleasing, some not so, most neither really pleasing nor displeasing, rather only unfamiliar. It was like an articulated fog of scent, ripples emerging and then drifting away. It was scent, true, but, oddly, it seemed almost calculated, designed, somehow almost mathematical, in its waves, times, successions, and arrangements, and then, frightening me, I heard the spaced, mechanistic emissions of a translator, much like the ones with which we are familiar, like the one carried by our ally, the Kur, Lucilius.

"'You are the slave, Mira,' it said.

"I immediately knelt in the grass and mud. 'Yes, Master,' I said.

"'The Mother lives,' came from the device. 'The Nest is inviolate.'

"'I do not understand,' I said.

"'You need not,' I heard.

"The voice seemed to come from before me, some feet before me, but well above me. But I knew of no platforms on the field of training.

"'There are proportions,' came from the device. 'There are alignments. The scale is awry. One pan rises; another declines. There is only one weight on the scale. There must be two weights on the scale. The weights must be equal. The scale must balance.'

"'I do not understand,' I said.

"'You acted once, and things were not as before. Now know this. We, too, will act, but once, once and only once, and things will be again as before. The scale will then be balanced.'

"'Who are you? What are you?' I begged. 'I understand nothing of this!'

"Then I heard no more," I said to my Master. "I stood there. I sensed I was now alone. The translator was silent. A breeze in the damp air wafted away the unusual odors I had earlier experienced. Then I awakened wildly, here in the tent, terrified, at your side, discovering, to my relief, that it was only a dream. I fear I cried out. Forgive me, Master."

"That is all?" asked Rupert.

"Yes, Master," I said.

"Perhaps you dreamed of a Kur," he said, "possibly of our confederate, Lucilius."

"I do not think so," I said.

"What then?" he asked.

"I do not know," I said.

"'The scale must be balanced,'" mused Rupert.

"I understand nothing," I said.

"It was all a dream," he said.

"Clearly," I said. "Happily, thankfully."

"You are frightened," he said. "You are putting things from your mind."

"Master?" I asked.

"Clean your feet," he said. "They are muddy."

The rain continued to fall softly, pelting the canvas of the tent.

CHAPTER EIGHTY-SIX

She was on her knees, chained hand and foot. "I have no clothing!" she wept.

"You have your collar," I reminded her.

Men like to see us on our knees, perhaps because we belong there.

"What is that garment you wear," she said. "You are scarcely clothed!"

"It is a slave tunic," I said. "I am a slave."

"You are collared!" she exclaimed.

"Fittingly," I said, "as are you."

"It is like you are an animal!" she said.

"I am an animal," I said, "a domestic animal, a slave, as are you."

"I am not a slave!" she said.

"This is Gor," I said. "Here you are a slave and only a slave. Even now the iron is heating which will mark your thigh. There will be no mistaking that mark."

"Gor does not exist!" she said.

"This is Gor," I said. "And you are a slave."

"I cannot even understand the language they speak here," she said.

"You will learn it," I said, "quickly and well. It is the language of your Masters. It is Gorean."

"I must escape!" she said.

"There is no escape for the Gorean slave girl," I said, "and you are a Gorean slave girl."

"Why am I chained?" she wept.

"Guess," I said.

"Never!" she wept.

"Surely you have dreamed of a Master," I said, "one to whose feet you would beg to crawl, one who would buy you and own you as only a female slave can be owned, one who could ruthlessly and pitilessly, without thought or consideration, subject you to unbelievable and overwhelming pleasures, and then, should it be his wish, simply despise you and thrust you aside."

"I would be degraded," she said.

"Of course," I said, "and appropriately. You are a slave."

"I am ashamed of such thoughts," she said. "I try desperately to put them from me."

"But they are persistent, are they not?" I said.

"Yes," she wept. Yes!"

"Why is that?" I asked.

"I do not know," she said.

"I think you do," I said. I then turned away from her. As far as I knew she had no name. Do animals have names, and slaves are animals. But she would probably be given a name. Names are useful in referring to an animal, summoning them, commanding them, and such. They are also useful in distinguishing one animal from another.

She was one of fifteen girls, shipped from Brundisium to Venna, by way of Ar. She was the only one whose thigh had not yet been seared, the only one not yet marked.

My Master, Rupert of Hochburg, had, over the past few weeks, formed, organized, and disciplined a hundred and fifty men, these to form the nucleus of his free company. And, as is well known, Gorean warriors want their slaves. It was thus that the fifteen girls had been purchased. It is common on Gor, incidentally, that armies, mercenary forces, free companies, even prowling bands of marauders, have their slaves. A wise commander is attentive to the needs of his men. To the extent possible, he wants to furnish them with amenities beyond their basic pay, good drink, good food, and lovely, helpless, needful slaves. Some men will enlist their swords only in units which they find satisfactory in such respects. This is quite different from units which are patriotically formed in the service of, or in the name of, particular Home Stones. In such units, men will cheerfully undergo privations and hardships and do battle under conditions which the average mercenary would find not only unsatisfactory but wholly unacceptable. Few men will die for their pay, but many, without thought, will risk their lives for their Home Stone. The nearest thing to loyalty to a city, town, or village, understood in terms of loyalty to a Home Stone, is, interestingly, loyalty to a leader. Some men, for better or for worse, can, and do, inspire others, sometimes, frighteningly, even peoples. I find this mysterious, but indisputable. Some can communicate a vision and foretell a supposed future, turning disconsolate and confused crowds into determined armies. This surprising loyalty to a remote and charismatic leader can produce a fanaticism which may prove to be a prelude to disaster. He who marches blindly may be led singing over cliffs or into the sea. But far less harrowing and on a much more modest scale, and far more typical and piecemeal, is the occasional loyalty to a personal captain or commander, one who is a fellow in arms, one whom men trust and esteem, whom they wish to please and obey, one from whom they find a word of commendation more valuable than gold. Unfortunately, these leaders are not always vessels of honor or paragons of virtue. They may be pirates or bandit chieftains, ambitious, avaricious, and ruthless. Others may be, at least to their lights, worthy, stalwart, and noble. In either case, mercenary companies, and such, usually take on the character of their commander, be it alarming or reassuring, cruel or kindly, base or noble.

"Why have you wandered off?" asked Rupert of Hochburg, less than pleased.

I immediately knelt.

Briefly the thought passed through my mind as to how my life had changed since Earth. I supposed that that was because I had just been speaking with a new slave, a lovely, kneeling, naked, chained, English-speaking slave who could not yet even speak or understand Gorean, whose fair thigh had not, as yet, even been marked. She, as I, had not even known that Gor was real, let alone that we would one day find ourselves beached on her planetary shores, let alone that we, on this fresh, unspoiled, beautiful world, would find ourselves routinely marketed and owned. How our lives had changed! So I, now, once Miss Agnes Morrison Atherton, of Earth, young and, I think, attractive, educated and sophisticated, once so prim and reticent, once so proper and formal, once so shy and timid, was now on another world, on my knees before a man.

I looked, up, frightened.

On this world I was a slave.

How significant it was that I should be on my knees!

He was my Master.

I belonged to him, as much as a belt or sandal.

"Have I done wrong, Master?" I asked.

"Han-leel," he said, "has called your dereliction to my attention."

Han-leel was at hand.

I did not care for Han-leel. He was too much about. He was a spearman, burly and narrow-eyed. His skills were formidable. He hailed, as I understood it, from Brundisium. Certainly he knew much of that port. He had much impressed Rupert, and had already been appointed a minor officer. He spoke little. He kept much to himself. He had few friends.

"I did not wander off," I said, defensively. "I stayed within the camp."

Suddenly there was a crack and I was on my side in the grass, my cheek and mouth burning. I tasted blood from my lip. For a moment there had been a flash of darkness torn with flakes of light. I struggled to my knees and licked and, fearfully, kissed the extended hand that had struck me. "Forgive me, Master," I begged. How I had erred! A slave is to be mindful of her tone and diction. She is not to make excuses. She is to obey and be pleasing. What I had said, and perhaps even more so my tone of voice, had suggested sharpness, disagreement, self-defense, perhaps even implicit reproach. What a fool I had been! I hoped I would not be whipped.

"The camp is large," said Rupert, "and the newly purchased slaves are at the perimeter, to be held there until they are to be thrown to the men."

Since the attack on my life, assuming I had been the intended target of the black quarrel, Rupert had been, or seemed to have been, perhaps to his embarrassment, and certainly to the amusement of several of his men, solicitous of my safety. "She might be worth two silver tarsks," he had explained to more than one fellow. I wondered if I might, actually, bring so much as two silver tarsks. It was flattering to think so. Too, I wondered if my Master might be solicitous of my welfare, other than in some simple economic regard. Why should he be embarrassed if such should be the case? Was it truly so amusing, absurd or unconscionable that a Master might care for a mere slave, if only a little? I hoped that that needed not be so. Indeed, I wondered if Rupert, my Master, despite Gorean *mores*, customs, and proprieties, might care for me, if only that little. Why not? Do the men of Earth not care, at least a little, for their dogs and horses? As for my part, owned and collared, subject to his word and whip, I bore to Rupert of Hochburg, my Master, the deepest, most profound, and most helpless of all loves, that of a slave for her Master. How vulnerable I was, and how terrified I was, that he might put me from him, that he might tire of me, that he might give me away or sell me! How easily that could be done! I was a slave!

I realize now that I had been waiting all my life for a Master. Then I had been brought to Gor, and thrown to my knees before men.

It is not unusual, incidentally, for a slave to fall in love with her Master. It is hard for a slave to be owned by a strong, attractive, dominating man, to kneel before him, to wear his chains and collar, to obey him, promptly and unquestioningly, to be subject at all times to his grasp and lips, to depend on him for all things, even a thread to wear or a bite to eat, to have the deepest needs of her belly and heart stirred, and not, eventually, willingly, readily, and eagerly, beggingly, yield gratefully to him the ready, waiting, genetically coded submissiveness of her femaleness. She is then in her natural place, is at last fulfilled, and can be finally whole in her body, mind, and heart.

"Shall I take her aside, strip her, and lay the whip well to her nakedness?" asked Han-leel.

"No," said Rupert.

"I trust that you are not concerned for her," said Han-leel.

"She has coin value," said Rupert.

"Others more so," said Han-leel. "Consider the blemishes on her countenance."

"They are minor," said Rupert. "Few notice them. And few slaves are perfect."

"Men speak," said Han-leel. "Discipline may suffer."

"I am aware of that," said Rupert.

"I do not understand your interest in the slave," said Han-leel.

"Yet she is of interest," said Rupert, "at least to someone."

"How so?" asked Han-leel.

"Some days ago," said Rupert, "before you enlisted in the company, an attempt was made on her life."

"I heard something of that," said Han-leel, "an arrow."

"A quarrel," said Rupert.

"An attempt on her life?" said Han-leel. "That is absurd. Slaves are for work and pleasure, not for killing. Who on Gor can be safer than a slave? They are plunder, not persons. She could not have been the intended target."

"Perhaps not," said Rupert.

"Certainly not," said Han-leel.

"The men talk?" asked Rupert.

"Too much so," said Han-leel.

"Blades must be sharp, and arrows fletched," said Rupert. "Men tire of training, and wish to act. Discipline must be strict. I have already posted our availability in Venna, Ar, Torcadino, Brundisium, and elsewhere."

"Excellent," said Han-leel.

"I cannot afford the distractions of a slave," said Rupert.

"Certainly not," said Han-leel.

"Yet I want her watched, and protected."

"More so than other slaves?" asked Han-leel.

"I fear she may be at risk," said Rupert.

"Surely not," said Han-leel. "Who has designs on a slave, other than perhaps stealing her?"

"I want her safe," said Rupert.

"Chain her to a post in the center of the camp," said Han-leel.

"I want her watched," said Rupert, "someone to keep an eye on her."

"I would not waste a man on such a task," said Han-leel.

"The guard must be wary, sober, skilled at arms, and trustworthy," said Rupert. "He must have some authority, enough to be respected and taken seriously, but not enough to draw attention to his activities, thus, most probably, a lesser officer."

"Several would be suitable," said Han-leel.

"I have one in mind," said Rupert.

"I pity him," said Han-leel.

"Do you like the slave?" asked Rupert.

"No," said Han-leel. "She is lovely and well-curved, but she is a barbarian. Who would wish to neck-leash a barbarian? I am Gorean. It would be demeaning."

I listened to this conversation with mounting dismay.

"I appoint you," said Rupert. "Your disclination for the post confirms my judgment. It speaks to your independence and objectivity. Uncontaminated by personal interest or desire, you will discharge your duties straightforwardly and professionally."

"Surely there is some post in which I might better serve," said Han-leel.

"The company needs at least ten men who can ride the bipedalian *tharlarion*, and at least five who know the tarn, useful for scouting and reconnaissance," said Rupert. "Have you such skills?"

"*Ela*," said Han-leel, "I know the heavy spear, the stabbing sword, the broad shield, and the long march, but I know neither the saddle of the light *tharlarion* nor the reins of the mighty tarn."

"You will then content yourself with, and will well discharge, the duty to which you have been assigned," said Rupert.

"I dare object, if not protest," said Han-leel.

"Your reluctance becomes your pride as a soldier," said Rupert. "Your obedience becomes your authenticity as a soldier."

"Recently the slave proved less than perfectly pleasing," said Han-leel. "Have I whip-rule over her?"

"Yes," said Rupert, who then, to my unease, departed.

Han-leel then put his bootlike sandal against my left forearm and thrust me to the side. I caught my balance on my knees and hands, so that I was on all fours.

"On your belly, barbarian tarsk," said Han-leel.

I went prone.

He put his hand in my hair, and twisted and jerked it, pulling my head up and back. It hurt. He then thrust my head back down, roughly.

"On your back, worthless slave," he said.

I rolled quickly to my back.

I looked up at him, frightened.

He unbuckled his belt, looped it, and thrust it to my lips. My lips were still sore, where I had been cuffed. Immediately, desperately, I began to lick and kiss the leather.

Then he said, "First obeisance position!"

I went to my knees, my head down between my hands, their palms pressed to the ground, on either side of my head.

How right this posture was for me, a slave!

I was thrilled to obey.

I had no choice.

I wanted no choice.

Those who have worn the collar will understand this.

"You are contemptible, are you not?" he said.

"Yes, Master," I said.

"You are despicable, are you not?" he said.

"Yes, Master," I wept.

"You may now, barbarian tarsk, worthless slave," he said, "show respect to the free."

"Yes Master," I wept.

I then fearfully, fervently, with lips and tongue, tears coursing down my cheeks, addressed myself to his feet.

After a time, he stepped away from me.

I kept my head down, in first obeisance position.

"Now," said he, "go to all fours, and on all fours, you will fetch a leash, which you will bring to me, it held between your teeth. In this exercise, you are not to speak or use your hands. As you hold your head, and expose your throat, whimpering, it will be clear that you are begging the leash."

A few minutes later, I returned to him, on all fours, and lifted my head to him, proffering the leash, held between my teeth.

He took it, and it was snapped about my throat.

It was seven or eight feet long, long enough to double as a slave lash. I trusted that its harsh inducement or remonstrance would not be deemed necessary.

I looked up, and whimpered.

"Yes," he said. "You may speak."

"I do not request an explanation, nor, as a slave, am I entitled to one," I said, "but I am puzzled."

"Do not be so," he said. "You are leashed and on all fours that I may keep you at hand. You will not be wandering off, or scampering off, eluding my sight."

"You are not pleased with your assignment," I said, "being responsible for a mere slave."

"I am a soldier, a spearman," he said, "not a keeper or herdsman. It is beneath my dignity to look after you."

"But you will do so," I said.

"I must," he said.

"You are angry," I said.

"Of course," he said. "It is not only that this task to which I have been set is beneath me, but that it is unnecessary. Slave girls are marked and collared. They are even distinctively garmented, in such a way as to make clear their condition and status. There is no escape for them. There is no need for watching them, setting guards over them, and such."

"A speeding quarrel," I said, "was deflected by my collar."

"Clearly," said he, "the quarrel was not meant for you, but for some fellow near you, perhaps even the captain."

I supposed that that might be true.

"Yes, Master," I said.

At that point, there was a long, sobbing scream of pain from the periphery of the camp, where the new slaves were being kept, before casting them before the Masters, for perusal and selection, before the evening meal.

I recalled the iron which had been heating.

I supposed that it had been applied to the new girl, she to whom I had been speaking, she whom alone had not yet been branded. If that is the case, I surmised that she, now, her fair thigh clearly and indelibly marked, had a much better understanding of what she was.

CHAPTER EIGHTY-SEVEN

"Are you an obedient slave?" asked Han-leel.

"It is my hope to be pleasing," I said.

"I fear that time grows short," he said.

I did not understand his remark. It was true that there had been much stirring in the camp in the last few days.

I did not understand what might be occurring.

"I wish information," said Han-leel.

To me that seemed an odd remark.

"I am only a slave," I said.

"Much is afoot of late," he said.

"It seems so," I said.

"Would you like a sweet?" he asked.

"Surely," I said.

He placed a hard candy in my mouth.

From my knees, I looked up at him, gratefully.

Such things, easily accessed by free women, are much prized by slaves.

"You may rise," he said.

"Thank you, Master," I said.

"I have whip-rule over you," he said, "but I have not been permitted your slave use."

"I have no say in such things," I said.

I was pleased that he had not been accorded my slave use. I feared and detested him.

"I have been kind to you, have I not?" he asked.

"After the first Ahn," I said, "five days ago, Master has been surprisingly gentle with me. Certainly he has not tormented me or subjected me to wanton cruelty."

"I have even," he said, "occasionally let you stand up and move about, upright, as I now permit you."

"Yes, Master," I said.

He commonly kept me on all fours, and, when we went about, on a leash. I gathered that this was to simplify and ease my custody. How much easier this made it to have me in view and at hand! My sister slaves found this durance imposed on me amusing. Xanthe, in particular, neglected few opportunities to divert herself at my expense. In the observatory, my status and condition had been much higher than hers. She now clearly enjoyed seeing me, a rival of sorts, I suppose, so leashed and on all fours. I had been far higher than her; now I was exhibited as much lower than she, one wholly inferior in status and position.

"You are grateful, are you not?" he asked.

"Very much so," I said.

"And this is not the first candy I have given you," he said.

"Master has been generous," I said.

Twice before he had given me a candy.

"Your Master, the noble Rupert of Hochburg, has been much occupied of late," he said. "Messengers go back and forth. Action brews."

"I fear so," I said.

"I have your custody by day," he said, "but after supper I return you to the tent of your Master."

"Yes, Master," I said.

"Does he chain you in the tent?" he asked.

"Seldom," I said.

"Does he sleep you at his waist, or feet?" he asked.

"Variously," I said. "Sometimes at his shoulder."

"Does he speak in his sleep?" he asked.

"Not to my knowledge," I said.

"A thousand marches might be planned, a thousand actions considered," he said.

"I do not understand," I said.

"The burdens of office can be weighty and grievous," he said. "Command, like the bridge of a knife ship, the top of a mountain, the watchful tower of a border outpost, can be lonely. It is not unusual for a challenged and harried man to unburden himself, even to the corner of a tent, to a shadow, to a lit candle, to a glowing brasier, or a pet *sleen*."

"Or a slave?" I asked.

"Precisely," he said.

"I suspect, Master," I said, "that this conversation is best not continued."

"Slaves, about and not noticed, unseen, so to speak, coming and going, serving, are often better informed than legates, ambassadors, and diplomats."

"My Master does not discuss logistical or tactical matters in my presence," I said.

"Natural questions, subtle inquiries, might be made," he said.

"Curiosity is not becoming in a *kajira*," I said.

"Information can be valuable," he said.

"If information is to be sold," I said, "it must have a buyer?"

"Perhaps a buyer exists," he said.

"My Master does not discuss logistical or tactical matters in my presence," I said, again.

"You are not to repeat or share this conversation," he said.

"I understand," I said.

"Get again on all fours," he said.

"Yes, Master," I said.

CHAPTER EIGHTY-EIGHT

I sensed a fumbling with cords, over my head.

There seemed a sudden flush of fresh air.

I had the vague understanding that my head was now freed.

I knew not where I was, or what had happened.

My cheeks stung, again and again.

"Wake up!" I heard, dimly, as though from faraway. "Awake!"

Thrice more I was slapped.

The sweat on my head, and hair, seemed suddenly cold.

I awakened, wholly, suddenly, wildly.

I could barely move my body.

My legs were closely together, extended. I could hardly move them. My arms were at my sides, down. I could not lift them or draw them upward.

I tried to scream but little sound escaped the packing strapped in my mouth.

I remembered Han-leel kneeling me and binding my wrists behind my body. He had then bent me back, by the hair. I could see the sky. He then forced the spout of a bota between my teeth and filled my oral cavity with some fluid, presumably water, with a taste of *larma*. Held as I was, I could not expel the fluid. At last I must breathe and must swallow the fluid. I recalled a similar experience early in my bondage when I had been forced to imbibe slave wine, which fluid assures keepers and Masters that a slave will not conceive. The effects of slave wine can be removed by the administration of another fluid, called a 'releaser.' As the Gorean slave is a domestic animal, her breeding is supervised by, and controlled by, keepers and Masters, as is the case with other domestic animals, *kaiila, tarsks*, and such.

Shortly after I had swallowed a mouthful of the fluid blocking my breathing, I had lost consciousness. I assumed the active ingredient in the drink forced upon me was *tassa* powder, a tasteless sedative often employed by slavers. As my loss of consciousness was almost instantaneous, I had little doubt but what the dosage had been selected with celerity in mind. He would lose little time in leaving the camp.

My wrists were no longer tied, but I could scarcely move in the tight confines of the slave sack. The sack itself was of black leather, but it itself, as I soon became aware, had been inserted into a larger sack, a coarser, loosely woven, brown sack, a sack of the sort in which peasants commonly carry field produce, most often *suls*.

He had hurried me, upright, moving on my leash, which was still on me, behind a shed at the edge of the camp. Doubtless he had ascertained that this was not observed. He now wore the habiliments of a peasant, not so different from those who came and went supplying the camp. The slave sack, the larger, coarser sack, and his disguise must have been waiting for him by, or in, the shed.

There was a trumpet's note in the distance. It was long, and piercing.

"That is the first call, that of assembly," said Han-leel, bending over me.

My eyes must have been wide, wide with terror, over the gag.

"Let us slip you free of these sacks," said Han-leel. "We need them no longer. They have done their work."

He thrust his hands, with some effort, into the slave sack, down, past my shoulders, and caught me under the arms, and then, bit by bit, holding and pulling, freed me from the sack. The air felt cold after my confinement in the heat and tightness of the sack. I was placed on my stomach in the grass and he pulled up my ankles and, with the leash, turning it so the ring was at the back, and it could dangle behind me, bound them together. He then lifted me to my knees, facing him. My hands were free, but I could not rise for the binding of my ankles.

"Do not touch the gag," he said. "It is a lock gag, and you cannot free yourself from it. I shall remove it shortly."

I lowered my hands.

"*Nadu*," he snapped.

Instantly, automatically, without the least hesitation or thought, I went to *nadu*, as best I could with my bound ankles, back straight, head up, knees split, the palms of my hands down on my thighs.

"You look well, Earth woman," said he, "as a collared Gorean slave."

How did he know, I wondered, even from the first, that I was from Earth, that I was a barbarian? Perhaps it was better known in the camp than I suspected.

Then he thrust his bootlike sandal between my already widened knees and forced them even further apart.

He then looked down upon me, pleased.

I knelt before him in full *nadu*. How vulnerable, how helpless, how ready, how prepared, how slave is a woman kneeling in *nadu* before a man! Does she not then know that she is a woman? Does she not then know what she is for?

I whimpered piteously. I could do no more, for the gag.

"I shall remove the gag," he said. "Know, however, that you are far from the camp and, if you scream, no one will hear you. And know, too, if you try nonetheless to scream, I will cut your throat instantly, and your scream will be no more than a breaking rush of blood from your throat."

He then went behind me and unlocked the gag, which he then, with its loathsome packing, dropped to the grass beside the discarded sacks.

"Master!" I wept.

He slapped my head twice, sharply, from side to side.

"Forgive me, Master," I said. "May I speak?"

"Certainly," he said.

"I understand nothing of this," I said. "What is going on? What are you doing? Let me go! Return me to my Master! You are my guard! You are to protect me! Who are you? What are you?"

"Perhaps," said he, "I found your lineaments of interest and am stealing you. Perhaps I want you for myself. Perhaps I want you for another. Perhaps I intend to sell you. Perhaps, given my suspicion that the captain may be fond of you, however farcical is such a supposition, I am thinking of holding you for ransom."

"Which of these is it?" I begged.

At that point there was a second note of the trumpet, drifting to us from far away.

"That is the second call," said Han-leel, "that for forming columns and preparing for the march."

"Which is it?" I begged. "What do you want of me? What do you want me for? I am of little worth. Let me go!"

"Do not break position," he said. "And do not attempt, should I leave you for a moment, to undo the binding on your ankles. You would find it difficult to do and you could not manage it before my return. It is convenient, incidentally, to bind a woman's ankles together, even when her hands are free. So trussed, she may use her hands to feed herself, and such. She is, of course, commonly under observation, and is forbidden to tamper with or undo the ankle-binding. She is thus well secured, and well knows herself so, to her frustration, even though her hands are free."

"You have an errand?" I asked.

"In a way," he said. "There are customs, proprieties, and such."

Should he depart, I would do my best to free my ankles of the knotted leash.

"Return me to my Master," I said. "You cannot get away with whatever it is that you intend. I will be missed. You will be missed. There will be inquiries, searches. I will be rescued. You will be caught."

"We will not be missed for some time," he said. "Supposedly you were taken to the rear of the march, where you will follow the march, as is fitting for slaves, guards, and baggage."

"You will be pursued," I said. "You cannot escape."

"I can depart in safety, at any time," he said. "I have a tarn nearby, waiting."

"You are a spearman," I said. "You do not know the tarn, you do not even know the bipedalian *tharlarion*."

"I am skilled in the management of both," he said.

"You lied to my Master," I said.

"It suited my purposes to do so," he said. "Your Master is a truthful and honorable man. Such men, of course, simple fools, commonly take it for granted that others are similarly truthful and honorable. That is a not unprecedented failing of such men. Trust invites exploitation and betrayal. It smooths the road for falsehood and deceit. Without trust and truth in others it would be difficult for dark designs to prosper."

"Civilization requires trust and truth," I said. "Otherwise, civilization would be impossible."

"That is very true," he said. "Without trust and truth, civilization would collapse into a bloody chaos overnight. Certainly I would not care to live in such a civilization. I would flee from it as soon as possible. No one celebrates an orderly civilization more zealously than I."

"But you make exceptions for yourselves," I said.

"We find it profitable to do so," he said.

"What if everyone did as you do?" I said.

"But they do not," he said. "Happily, we remain a minority, a tiny minority. Else we could not exist."

"Master is not honorable," I said.

"But I appear honorable," he said. "That is what is important. That is all that is necessary."

"You were clever," I said. "You were seen frequently in my vicinity. Thus my Master might think of us together. You called his attention to my being at the periphery of the camp. This indicated vigilance and a concern for his interests. Burdened by the responsibility of command and distracted by the various pressures of office, and possibly concerned for my safety, given the earlier affair of the quarrel, might not my Master welcome the thought of assigning my temporary custody to a strong, reliable, attentive retainer, this freeing his mind for matters of greater importance? And then, on his horizon, appeared you, as though from nowhere, a suitable candidate for that role, a fine soldier, limited as to the posts which he might otherwise occupy, say, that of the tarnsman or that of a rider of the light *tharlarion*. And then, most egregiously clever of all, you pretended disinterest in so humble and servile a role, feigning reluctance to be so assigned, this confirming in my Master his assurance as to your independence and objectivity. How better could my Master have been put at ease?"

"Do not forget," said he, "my waiting to act until my movements would be less likely to be noticed in the bustle of breaking camp."

"Why have you abducted me?" I asked. "Is it for information, information for which someone might well pay?"

"Have you such information?" he asked.

"No," I said.

"I believe you," he said. "The captain and his high officers are discreet. Secrets are well kept. Even the crumbs of golden discourse are well concealed. They do not fall from the table to be snatched up by gossiping slaves, let alone by strangers and spies."

"What information is sought and who would pay its price?" I asked.

"Information as to ventures in the Vosk basin," he said. "A campaign is planned. Its nature and scope are unclear. Tarns will fly, ships will weigh anchor, and men will march."

"Who will pay for this information?" I asked.

"A small man," said he, "with a heavy purse."

"Tiskias," I said. "But he acts on behalf of another."

"I did not ask his name," said Han-leel. "I did bite his gold."

"I know nothing," I said. "I can be of no help to you."

"I believe you," he said.

"Then you have not seized me for information," I said, "even were it to be extracted by torture?"

"No," he said.

"And I am not being stolen for ransom, marketing or slave use?" I said.

"No," he said.

"Then for what reason," I asked, "have I been taken from the camp and brought to this place?"

Then, once more, was heard the distant trumpet.

"That is the third note," said Han-leel. "The march has begun."

"Why, Master," I begged, "was I taken from the camp? Why have I been brought to this place?"

"I will return shortly," he said.

CHAPTER EIGHTY-NINE

As soon as he had turned his back I spun about and began to tear at the leash strap knotted about my ankles.

How fiercely tight were the knots!

Tears of frustration burst from my eyes.

He had said he had a tarn nearby.

Too soon he returned.

He was helmeted.

I turned to face him. My weight was on my knees and hands, my fingers clutching at the grass.

In the Y-shaped aperture of the helmet I could see little of his forehead or features.

"*Tal*," said he, "pretty *kajira*."

"What are you going to do with me?" I asked.

Slowly he removed the helmet, and put it beside him, at his feet.

"There are customs," he said, "proprieties."

On his forehead, inked there, was a tiny dagger.

I did not understand that.

"I have ascended the nine steps of blood," he said. "I am of the Black Court of Brundisium."

"I do not understand," I said. "I understand nothing. Why have you put the image of a dagger on your forehead?"

"It is the sign of one of the Black Caste, when he is hunting," he said. "It warns others not to interfere with his hunt."

"I do not understand," I said.

"I will be quick," he said.

"I am a slave," I said, "only a slave!"

"I have taken fee," he said.

"You are he of the black quarrel!" I said.

"Yes," he said.

"I escaped," I said. "My collar turned aside the quarrel."

"The distance was considerable," he said. "A muscular tremor, a sporadic puff of wind, might have diverted the quarrel."

"Do not kill me!" I said.

"I have taken fee," he said.

"I have not injured you," I said.

"No," he said. "Do not mistake matters. In this there is nothing personal. I am merely a subsidized instrument."

"I am a slave," I said, "only a property, only goods. What you contemplate is wrong."

"Gold, not right," he said, "will have its say."

"Who hired you?" I asked.

"The small man," he said.

"No," I said, "another, one who did not show himself, one behind the small man!"

"Perhaps," he said. "That is not my concern."

"There must be a motive," I said.

"There is," he said. "It seems you once, not so long ago, rendered deep and labored plans awry."

"Surely my collar protects me," I said.

"Once it did," he said, "oddly, from a speeding quarrel. Do not expect it to do so again. Do not be dismayed. I will be quick."

He slipped a dagger from its sheath.

I cast a glance of misery at the encircling, narrow windings of the leash strap about my ankles, turned about, and, bound as I was, began to scratch and pull myself away.

Behind me I heard him laugh.

What a fool I was!

I could not hope to elude him.

I had gone no more than a handful of yards before I turned about, again. "Mercy!" I cried. "I beg mercy!"

He had not even moved from his position. The removed helmet, with its Y-like aperture, so simple and in appearance so menacing, was on the grass, at his feet.

I threw back my head and screamed in misery, a wild, desperate scream.

Perhaps he was ten yards away.

I was on my knees and hands.

He took a step toward me.

"Stop!" I cried. "Stop!"

Something in my cry arrested his progress.

Clearly it was not a plea to be spared, not a cry for mercy. It was more in the nature of a horrified warning.

"Behind you!" I cried. "It is there. It approaches! Turn, look, see it!"

He stopped, stock still, but he did not turn about.

Doubtless his training had taught him to regard such claims or outbursts as a ploy of sorts, commonly a vain, pathetic one, initiated by a foe hoping to distract him, perhaps to escape or attack, but I posed no danger to him. And I could not run. He remained still, clearly puzzled.

Was it an animal? But the *sleen* commonly hunts by night; there were no *larls* this close to Venna. I was not missed. Men of the camp were on the march. Might not a peasant or stranger have strayed into the vicinity? If so, would such intervene or dare to interfere?

Did not Han-leel wear the image of the black dagger on his forehead?

"Look!" I cried. "Run!"

Had I, in my fear for my life, gone insane? Had I, somehow, out of stress and fear, conjured up some monstrosity? Was I subject to some hallucination? Had I conjured up something, anything, to interpose between me and an unsheathed knife? But this seemed no comforting delusion, no welcome, if imaginary, deliverance, summoned up to help me deny a terrible, inevitable doom. Rather I bore alone the sight of a terror I found more dreadful than the knife of Han-leel.

"Run!" I cried. "Run!"

In the beginning, I had taken it as no more than a bit of fog, or cloud, oddly low, some few feet wide, moving toward us. Then it spread itself like a hand, widely, reaching out, a hand with taloned fingers.

Han-leel, curious, annoyed, wary, turned about, knife ready.

He uttered a wild cry of alarm.

The hand began to close about him, like a closing fist. He slashed and stabbed at it wildly but it seemed his blade encountered no substance, no resistance; it was as if he rained blows on mist or fog, as if he sought vainly to draw blood from the air.

Then it was as though the fog or cloud hardened and he was clutched in some uncanny fist, real or imaginary; he could scarcely move; the knife fell from his limp hand; I heard the cracking of bones; blood burst from his mouth and eyes, and then, weirdly, the fist and its clutched prey began to glow, and then, a moment later, there was a crackling and a roaring burst of flame, and then the flame faded, and I saw only ashes and blackened grass.

I think I then lost consciousness.

I awakened to the voice of my Master. Behind him was Xanthe.

My ankles had been freed of the leash strap and the leash itself was discarded, to the side.

"Why are you here?" he asked. "What are you doing here? Where is Han-leel? What has gone on here? What happened?"

I did my best, my words tumbling forth half incoherently, to recount what had been done and what I had seen.

"Xanthe," he said, "missed you at the rear of the column. She saw no sign of either you or Han-leel. She was concerned. She begged for an investigation. She was permitted by a wagon guard to hurry forward and call the matter to my attention."

"I did not care for Han-leel," said Xanthe. "I did not trust him."

"She was more perceptive than I," said my Master. "We learned from a camp guard, at the time of the second trumpet call, that a peasant had been noted earlier outside the perimeter of the camp, burdened with a sack of *suls*. The direction he had gone was made known to us."

"Some Ehn ago," said Xanthe, "we saw a brief blast of flame. We sought its source. We found you here, on the grass, unconscious."

"Han-leel," I said, "was an assassin."

"I wager no simple assassin," said Rupert.

"No," I said, "he was of the Black Caste. It was he who had loosed the black quarrel earlier."

"Undoubtedly," said Rupert.

"He said something about the Black Court of Brundisium," I said.

"I have heard of it," said Rupert. "It is one of the most famous, largest, and most feared, holdings of the Black Caste. It is no wonder that Han-leel seemed to know much of Brundisium."

"Why would he want to kill me?" I asked.

"I am sure he had nothing against you," said Rupert. "He did not even know you. He had simply taken fee."

"Tiskias had hired him," I said.

"On behalf of his Kur companion," said Rupert. "The mind, the force, the hatred, is that of the Kur. Tiskias is no more than a convenience, an operative."

"Han-leel had his escape planned," I said, "as in the matter of the quarrel. There is a tarn nearby."

"We will find it," said Rupert. He then turned to Xanthe. "Attend upon her," he said.

"Yes, Master," said Xanthe.

He then left me, shaken, on the grass.

"Thank you," I said to Xanthe, "for your concern, for all that you have done."

"It is nothing," she said. "We are collar-sisters."

After a time, Rupert returned to us. "I have found the tarn," he said. "I have two men who know the tarn. I will send one back for it." He carried the removed helmet of Han-leel, and the fallen knife. He dropped them to the grass. "Where the flame burst," he said, "there is little left. The earth is scorched. Some pebbles seem to have melted away into droplets. They are cold now. Perhaps ashes were blown away."

I made as though to struggle to my knees.

"Remain as you are," he said.

I did not know if I could stand.

"Do you believe in Priest-Kings?" asked Rupert.

"I do not know about such things," I said. "I do not know what I would believe, even if I believed in them."

"Initiates, those of the White Caste," he said, "claim not only that Priest-Kings exist but that they, the Initiates, are favored by them, can influence them, intervene with them, and so on. Such claims, when taken seriously by others, can prove profitable. Personally, I suspect that Initiates know no more, or less, of Priest-Kings than wood-workers or tarn-keepers, than Ubars or button peddlers."

"I saw a frightening thing," I said.

"Have you ever heard of the Flame Death?" he asked.

"No," I said.

"What occurred here," he said, "must be it, or something much like it."

"I would not know," I said.

"There are anomalies in the vicinity of the Sardar Mountains," said Rupert. "They are well authenticated, for example, the inability of tarns to wing-tread its sky."

"As I understand it," I said, "the beasts, the Kurii, are at war with something, something powerful, and wish to overcome it, that they may invade and seize Gor. Their foe, whatever it may be, must be very powerful. Surely some mighty power averted the crashing down of the metal spheres upon the Beast Caves near Ar, and, I gather, on the Sardar itself."

"That is clear," said Rupert. "But effects are one thing and causes another. One effect may, in theory, have many, and different, causes. Might not what we attribute to Priest-Kings be explained in a thousand other ways? Might we not have effects whose etiology we do not understand, and perhaps cannot understand?"

"Has anyone ever seen a Priest-King?" I asked.

"Not that I know of," he said.

"What are they like?" I asked.

"Supposedly," he said, "they are like large, powerful, glorious human beings."

"I see," I said.

"But what if *larls*, *sleen*, and osts had Priest-Kings?" said Rupert. "Would not the Priest-Kings of the *larls* have the sharpest teeth, those of the *sleen* the most marvelous of tracking skills, those of the osts the shiniest of scales, the most deadly of venoms?"

"Are there not tiers of knowledge on Gor?" I asked.

"Yes," he said. "Not all knowledge needs be imparted to everyone. Let knowledge be given only to those for whom it is fit. Who would teach the bow to the *tarsk*, the sword to the giant *urt*?"

"There are, are there not," I asked, "what are called the laws of the Priest-Kings?"

"Yes," he said, "laws whose breach is not accepted, the breach of which may be attended by fearful consequences, even by the Flame Death."

"The sort of thing which destroyed Han-leel?" I asked.

"It would seem, at least, to be similar," he said.

"And perhaps similarly caused?" I said.

"To me that seems likely," he said.

"Did Han-leel then not break the laws of Priest-Kings?" I asked.

"I do not think so," he said.

"Why then," I asked, "the horror which seized and destroyed him?"

"It is thought," he said, "and I think it may be true, that the Priest-Kings, if they exist, and whoever or whatever they may be, if existing, intervene in the affairs of men only to enforce their laws. Other than that they leave human beings alone, leaving us free to do as we wish, to love and kill, to injure and heal, to trust and betray, to swindle and cheat or labor after honesty and fairness, to proclaim falsehood or seek truth."

"How then the fate of Han-leel?" I asked.

"I think," he said, "proportion and reciprocation."

"I do not understand," I said.

"I think," he said, "the scales must be balanced. I think that a human being, a mere slave, once somehow intervened in the affairs of Priest-Kings. How shocking and bitter must be such a thing, so dreadful an anomaly, to Priest-Kings. Their view of seemliness and reality must have been threatened. Their world seemed shaken. Must not harmony be restored?"

"I understand very little of this," I said.

"Must not a debt be repaid, even a shocking and unwelcome debt?"

"What are you saying?" I asked.

"One act saved Priest-Kings," he said. "Another act saved a slave. All is now even. All is as before. The scales are balanced. Do not think that Priest-Kings would act twice in your favor."

"I think I see," I said.

I tried to struggle to my feet, but fell.

My Master then picked me up, and carried me. Later I could walk. Xanthe followed behind. Toward evening we caught up with the march, at its first camp.

CHAPTER NINETY

I lay at my Master's feet, content.

This was the night of the third day of the march. We had reached Venna, and now we were camped between Venna and Ar, some *pasangs* west of Venna.

How kind was my Master!

He had caressed me, taking me out of myself, turning me into a gasping, begging, spasmodic slave. How owned, how helpless, how mastered, a woman can feel! Then he had seized me, holding me to him, and exploded within me, and I had been had, as only a slave can be had. How mighty were the men of Gor! What could an Earth woman be, but a slave at their feet? Yet those men were of Earth origin, surely of a species identical to that I had known on my former world. How then could the differences be accounted for?

I lay at his feet, and feared I might be unworthy to wear a Gorean slave collar. I had not been scouted on Earth, perhaps for weeks, watched and noted, reviewed, considered, and then selected by skilled, professional slavers for shipping to, and marketing on, Gor. Was I intelligent enough, and beautiful enough, to be sold naked from a Gorean slave block? In an observatory on Earth I had stumbled on a perilous secret, having to do with interplanetary politics, intrigue, and war. Even though I had little understood the nature or importance of my discovery, it must have aroused concern amongst those more privy to its meaning. What was to be done with me? Surely they must be rid of me. I realized that I might have been killed. But was there not a simpler, more obvious, perhaps more amusing, solution to this small problem? So I was sent to Gor, to share the fate, I supposed, of most women sent to Gor, to be made a slave. Perhaps those who arranged for my conveyance to Gor were even accorded, as a joke, a token coin or two. Would that then not have been my first sale? So I learned to be naked in public, as the animal I now was; so I was marked and collared, so I was enslaved. No longer was I Agnes Morrison Atherton, a person; I was now an object, a domestic beast, a property, marketable goods.

Was I, I wondered, so inferior to the carefully scouted, appraised, and selected Earth girls brought to Gor by professional slavers? I did not really think so. Certainly Masters thought me acceptable barbarian slave meat, indistinguishable from others. Might I not, as a possibility, if noted, have been as carefully studied and selected as others? I thought so. And what of Xanthe? Presumably she had not been a quarry of slavers, noted, trailed, examined, and hunted over a period of days or weeks. Presumably she had done nothing more amiss than neglecting to lock a cabinet drawer, to be sure, not just any cabinet drawer. Presumably she, having displeased Doctors Jameson, Archer, and Townsend, had preceded me to the chains of Gor. Certainly she was lovely enough to please even the most discriminating and meticulous of slavers. No one would find anything surprising or puzzling at finding her in an exhibition cage or on a sales block. But then, I wondered, was it so anomalous that Xanthe, the former Eileen Bennett, had been hired at the observatory, or even that I had been employed there, though in a junior position? Surely sexual attractiveness, when a woman seeks admission to a school, a program, a position, or such, need not always be a handicap. Too, was it not possible, that the women hired at the observatory, or some of them, might have been selected with an eventual, particular disposition in mind, the markets of Gor? I found this speculation both plausible and comforting. Perhaps, after all, I was worthy of what I most wanted and loved, a Gorean slave collar. In any event, I had frequently seen the eyes of men upon me, regarding me, and relishing me, as the Gorean slave I was.

And so, I lay content at the feet of my Master.

I wanted him to awake, and put me again to slave use, even ruthless, uncompromising slave use, but I dared not disturb his rest. Had I done so, surely I would have been at least cuffed, and possibly whipped.

I regarded myself as educated and intelligent. And certainly I knew much from Earth, thousands of things which a native of Gor, even of the Scribes or Builders, would know little or nothing. On the other hand, I had met few, if any, Goreans who seemed to me slow or dull in mind. Whoever or whatever had brought humans to Gor, and perhaps other species, perhaps beginning over thousands of years ago, had been selective in their efforts. It was almost as if it might have been stocking a terrarium with varied and interesting specimens of life, perhaps for observation or study, or even for aesthetic reasons, rather as one might situate an aquarium of interesting tropical fish in an office. For example, I sensed that the raw intelligence of my Master was far greater than mine. Indeed, I took pride and comfort in that fact. A slave belongs on her knees. She must look up to a Master.

Whereas I knew I was a natural slave, and loved being a slave, and could only be fulfilled at a Master's feet, I sometimes shuddered with terror, understanding how abjectly and utterly helpless I was. I, like other slaves, was owned, wholly. I was subject to the whip. I could be chained or beaten. I must obey, unquestioningly and immediately. I could change hands at a word. My greatest fear was that my Master might tire of me and sell me or give me away. He could do with me as he wished. I was a slave.

At that point, I heard a voice, soft, but urgent, from outside the tent.

"Captain, Captain!"

It was the voice of Temicus, portly officer in the company, he of the Builders.

Rupert of Hochburg rolled over and was instantly on his feet, drawing a robe about himself.

"Enter," he said.

I pulled the furs up, about me.

Temicus pushed aside the tent flap and entered, bearing a lantern. He spoke softly, quickly.

"Good news, Captain," he said. "Lucilius, our Kur ally, adherent of Agamemnon, foe of remote Pompilius, is heard from. He is at last making contact. Moreover, he has captured our common enemy, Tiskias!"

"Excellent," said Rupert.

"It will be amusing," said Temicus, "to see him cast naked to leech plants, be fed to *sleen*, or squirm on the impaling spear."

"Soiled impaling spears, and bloodless or half-devoured bodies are of little use, compared to information and exacted service," said my Master. "Bring them to the tent."

"Lucilius is Kur," said Temicus. "He is reluctant to enter the camp. He is wary of excited men and bright, broad-bladed spears."

"Where is he?" asked Rupert.

"At the edge of the camp, safe, concealed in darkness," said Temicus. "He was challenged by guards. He did not know the night's password, of course. He wishes to see you, alone."

"Why alone?" asked Rupert.

"I do not know," said Temicus. "I assume he wishes to impart information, doubtless of a secret or confidential nature."

"Where is he?" asked Rupert.

"At Post Eight," said Temicus.

This was one of the posts toward the rear of the camp. The number of posts obviously depends on the size of the camp, but our camp had fifteen posts, including the 'Roving Post.' Imagine a rectangle whose longer sides are, say, on the north and south, and whose narrower sides, or ends, are west and east. The first post is the northwest post, from which point the remaining situation or location posts are counted as the Gorean chronometer measures, clockwise for the Goreans, but what those of Earth would consider counterclockwise, 1, 2, and 3 moving 'south,' 4 through 7 moving 'east,' 8 through 10 moving 'north,' and 11 through 14, moving 'west.' The 'Roving Post' patrols the location or situation posts, and may also circulate within the camp. Its movements are sometimes determined by a simple random-selection device, a marked wooden disk equipped with a metal needle, which may be spun with a flick of a finger.

"Do not go alone, Master," I begged, not even begging permission to speak.

"I shall overlook your lapse," said Rupert, frowning.

"Forgive me, Master," I said. "But I am afraid." Surely sometimes rituals or proprieties must be held in abeyance. Circumstances vary; urgencies take priority.

"Do not be afraid," he said.

"Take spearmen with you, at least two," I begged.

"Lucilius is our ally, our colleague and friend," said Rupert. "He is long overdue. I must have his report. The capture of Tiskias, in itself, is a prize."

"How is Lucilius communicating?" I asked.

"By his device," said Temicus, "as would be expected. Few Kurii can approximate the sounds of Gorean."

"Be patient with me, Master," I begged. "Demand first the surrender of the prisoner, Tiskias."

"Why?" asked my Master.

"Need we keep Lucilius waiting?" asked Temicus. "It will be light soon. He may be at risk."

"Perhaps you will speak of secret things," I said, "which it would not be meet for Tiskias to hear."

"That is possible," said Temicus.

"You are a shrewd little she-sleen," said Rupert. "You are not concerned about secret things. You have something else in mind. Why do you attempt to mislead me?"

"I am afraid," I said.

Rupert turned to Temicus. "Inform Lucilius," he said, "that I shall attend him shortly. In the meantime, have him give over the prisoner."

"Yes, Captain," said Temicus, shrugging.

Rupert then clothed himself and girded on a sword. I took the opportunity to don my tunic, pulling it down, over my head.

"Why are you fussing with your hair," asked Rupert.

"A slave wishes to reflect well on her Master," I said.

"You are a vain little she-urt," he said.

"Though we are in collars, we are women," I said.

Shortly thereafter Temicus returned, clearly puzzled. "Lucilius is reluctant to surrender the prisoner," he said.

"Why?" asked Rupert.

"He said," said Temicus, "he wants to present him as a trophy to Agamemnon at the Beast Caves."

"I feared such," I said.

"Speak, slave," said Rupert. "I do not wish to keep Lucilius waiting."

"If it is Lucilius," I said.

"Speak further," said he.

"The vocalizations of beasts, processed through the translation device, are indistinguishable, one from the other," I said. "In Gorean they will sound the same."

"So?" asked Temicus.

"Thus, Master," I said, "from mere sounds we do not know who is putting the translator to use. Further, without greater familiarity with Kurii, perhaps close association with them, many of us cannot easily discriminate one beast from another, even in good light. And now the beast which has made itself known at Post Eight is in poor light, even darkness."

"But, foolish slave," said Temicus, "the beast must be Lucilius, for he has captured Tiskias and brought him a prisoner to our camp. No enemy would do so."

"But he is unwilling to surrender him to us," I said. "Tiskias is important to that Kur which is of the faction of Pompilius. He needs him to deal with humans and carry out his plans."

"He merely wishes, as he made clear," said Temicus, "the glory of conveying the wretch, Tiskias, to the Beast Caves near Ar, perhaps to be eaten slowly at some victory banquet."

"Dear Temicus," said Rupert, "inform Lucilius that if Tiskias is not given into our custody, I shall not meet with him."

"Surely, Captain," said Temicus, "you are not going to take the apprehensions of a frightened slave seriously."

"No Tiskias in custody," said Rupert, "no meeting."

"As you wish, Captain," said Temicus. "Perhaps he will kill Tiskias instantly. Few predators are eager to relinquish their prey." He then brushed aside the tent flap and, lantern in hand, prepared to make his way back into the night. Then he turned back for a moment. "My captain is clever," he said. "I see it now. If the Kur, however reluctantly, gives Tiskias to us, that will prove it is Lucilius, for the enemy Kur would not surrender so important an ally, so valuable an accomplice."

"We shall see," said Rupert.

Temicus then dropped the tent flap. He paused outside. We could see the lantern light through the cloth. He then left.

CHAPTER NINETY-ONE

"Captain," said Temicus, "Lucilius has turned over the prisoner, Tiskias, to us."

"Good," said Rupert of Hochburg.

"So great a sacrifice would be made by no Kur enleagued with the faction of Pompilius," said Temicus.

"Consider *kaissa*," said Rupert. "It is not unusual to sacrifice one piece for a piece of greater value."

I knew little of *kaissa*. I knew not the pieces nor their moves. I found the game complex and bewildering. Slaves are seldom allowed to touch the pieces or the board. It is said it is not for slaves. It is too fine and beautiful. Sometimes men play the game for hours, lost in its intricacies, while slaves, tormented by their needs, are warned to silence.

"Lucilius wishes to speak with you alone, at Post Eight," said Temicus.

"Where is Tiskias?" asked Rupert.

"In the center of the camp," said Temicus, "chained to a post."

"How did he react to his entry into the camp," asked Rupert.

"In abject terror," said Temicus. "He had to be dragged into the camp, weeping and whining."

"Interesting," said Rupert. "One supposes he would feel safer with us than in the custody of a Kur."

"Lucilius is waiting," said Temicus. "It will soon be light."

"Inform him that I shall meet with him presently," said Rupert.

"I will do so," said Temicus.

"But first," said Rupert. "I wish to pay my respects to his notable capture, whom he kindly brought to our camp, our small friend, Tiskias."

"Yes, Captain," said Temicus.

My Master then turned to me. "Heel me," he said.

"Yes, Master," I said.

I loved heeling him, as the slave I was. I was happy and proud to heel him. He was my Master.

"The slave!" cried Tiskias, rising wildly, with a rattle of chain.

He was chained hand and foot, to a heavy post, sunk in the earth, in the center of the camp.

He backed against the post, his face white, his eyes wide.

"You are startled," said Rupert.

"No, no," said Tiskias, struggling with himself. "Why should I be startled?"

"Perhaps because you thought the slave done away with," said Rupert.

"I know nothing of such things," said Tiskias.

"Perhaps because you thought an Assassin successful in completing his part of an understanding, one you arranged at the behest of a Kur."

"No!" he said.

"The Assassin was unsuccessful," said Rupert. "The slave lives."

"Excellent," said Tiskias. "Slaves are not to be killed, but to be worked, enjoyed, and used."

"The Assassin's name was Han-leel," said Rupert. "You do not know of him, of course."

"No," said Tiskias.

"If you did know of him," said Rupert, "you need concern yourself with him no longer.""I understand," said Tiskias.

"How were you captured by Lucilius, he of the faction of Agamemnon?" asked Rupert.

"Lucilius surprised me and my pet Kur, Bubu, at our camp, south of Venna," said Tiskias. "He and Bubu fought, biting and tearing, but Bubu was no match for mighty Lucilius. Bubu fled, scurrying away, having had his fill of war. I was deserted by my pet. He proved craven. He was seen no more. I, too, fled, but the keen senses of Lucilius set him immediately on my trail. I was soon apprehended, roped, and led, a forlorn prisoner, to your camp. No longer have you anything to fear, either from the cowardly Bubu or from my own modest cunning. The schemes of Pompilius have come to naught on the fair shores of Gor. All is done. All is lost. We are defeated. There is nothing left."

"Not even the hope of a last, desperate act of vengeance?" asked Rupert.

"Certainly not, noble Master," said Tiskias.

"Lucilius," said Rupert, "he who drove away your Bubu and brought you to our camp, wishes to speak with me, privately. Do you know the ground or purport of his request?"

"*Ela,*" said Tiskias, "I do not, Master. I am no more now than an ignorant, woeful captive. Why should the great Lucilius confide in me?"

"I think," said Rupert, "as the war is done and you have been delivered to us, it will not now be necessary to meet with the noble Lucilius."

"Oh, no, Master!" said Tiskias. "I am sure that the noble Lucilius has many important secrets to share with you, perhaps pertaining to the intrusions and machinations of Kurii in the Vosk Basin. That would be urgent. You must see him, and soon, for dawn grows near and he might find himself at risk."

"Very well," said Rupert. "I now go to meet with the noble Lucilius."

"Splendid," said Tiskias. "But go alone, alone!"

"Of course," said Rupert.

My Master spoke briefly with Temicus after leaving Tiskias.

He then took his way toward Post Eight.

I followed him, unbidden, not heeling him, but some yards behind him, through the dark camp. If he heard me, or was aware of this, he did not turn about, to confront me, or chastise me, perhaps cuffing me for my boldness.

Some fifty yards from the perimeter of the camp, in the vicinity of Post Eight, he stopped, but did not turn about.

"You may approach," he said, softly.

I hurried forward and knelt before him. "Do not go further alone, Master," I begged. "Summon spearmen."

"Would you have me show such disrespect to the entreaty of the noble Lucilius," he asked, "that I come alone?"

"Who knows the nature of a beast in the darkness?" I said.

"Who, indeed?" he said.

"Let me precede Master," I said. "You saw the response of Tiskias when he saw me, his surprise, if not consternation. Let me then be shown to the beast, and judge of its reaction. If it, like Tiskias, thinks the Assassin has successfully completed his dark work, it should be similarly taken aback, startled, or discomfited. Lucilius, on the other hand, knowing nothing of the business of the Assassin, would be likely to do no more than warn me away, for the sake of security."

"Of course," he said.

"'Of course?'" I asked.

"Why else," he asked, "do you think I have permitted you to follow me?"

"Master intended to use me as a test?"

"You should do very nicely," he said.

We shortly thereafter arrived at Post Eight. One of the guards there carried a lantern. "The beast is out there, in the darkness," he said, pointing.

"What is darkness to us," said Rupert, "is unlikely to be darkness for the beast. They have excellent night vision."

"It wants the lantern either shuttered or extinguished," said a second guard.

"Give it to me," said Rupert. He then shuttered the lantern. He then turned to me. "Stay behind me," he said. "Conceal yourself as best you can. I do not want you to be seen clearly, until at once, suddenly. I will tell you to step into view and I will unshutter the lantern."

But we had scarcely taken ten steps beyond Post Eight when we heard the evenly spaced, mechanically produced sounds of a translator. It was almost like a metronome, save that the sounds were clearly an approximation to Gorean phonemes.

"Friend Rupert, he of Hochburg, why have you kept me waiting? Surely I am not to be a mark for flighted arrows or cast spears. Men often think little of attacking what appears to them unusual, different or strange. Do I mean so little to you that you would risk me? Why do you bring the slave, Mira, with you? What I have to impart is not for the ears of a slave. There is little time. Come forth, alone."

"Forgive me, Lucilius, noble colleague," said Rupert. "Give me a moment, to lead the slave away, to place her in the custody of guards, that she be clearly located beyond the scope of our discourse."

Almost simultaneously with my Master's words, we heard their translation into Kur.

"Time is short," then came from the translator. "I am not pleased."

"A moment," said Rupert.

He then drew me a pace or two toward Post Eight.

"Hold, Master," I begged.

"The matter is done," said Rupert. "We must not place Lucilius in more jeopardy than we have already done. He has already surrendered Tiskias to us, which presumably no Kur of the faction of Pompilius would do, and he has expressed no surprise or amazement at the sight of you, only impatience, even annoyance, that your presence might compromise his plans."

"The device conceals emotion," I said.

"No hint of disturbance or surprise occurred explicitly in the words of the device," said Rupert.

"That is true, Master," I acknowledged.

"There is always risk," said Rupert. "But time is short and one must act."

"There is another test," I said. "Permit it to me."

"What test is that?" asked Rupert.

"It has to do with something known only to Lucilius and I," I said.

Rupert looked down at me. "There is little time," he said. "Tor-tu-Gor will soon awaken."

"Hurry!" came from the translator.

I leapt up, unbidden, and ran toward the darkness, within which I sensed a large, dark, crouching shape.

"*Tal*, Master Lucilius," I cried. "It is I, Mira, who tended you in the menagerie, on Barr Street, in the Metellan District in Ar!"

"Go away," came from the translator.

"Surely you remember me!" I cried. "I convey my greetings to you!"

"Leave, depart," came from the translator. The sound had clearly been turned higher.

"Do you not remember me?" I asked. "I am overjoyed to greet you. Are we not fond of one another? Are we not friends?"

"Yes, dear Mira," came from the translator, its volume now clearly reduced. "Yes, we are friends, dear friends, but go away now. I must speak with your Master."

"I could not pronounce your name in Kur," I said. "I gave you a name I could say. What was it, dear friend?"

"I could not put it in the translator," came from the translator.

"We had no translator," I said. "Say it, say it, dear friend."

"You know I cannot speak Gorean," came from the translator.

"You tried, dear friend," I said. "Try it! I will recognize it!"

"Noble Rupert, he of Hochburg," came from the translator, "send this babbling, foolish, interfering slave away."

"What was the name?" demanded Rupert, unshuttering the lantern. He lifted it high in his left hand, and drew his sword with his right.

I screamed.

In the light of the lifted lantern, suddenly emerged from the darkness, was a gigantic, fearful shape, shaggy, wide, like a boulder of fur, crouching, ready to spring. Its eyes in that broad head were like disks of blazing copper, reflecting the flame of the lantern. A translation device dangled from its neck. It snarled, and spread its jaws, white, large, moist, curved, sharp fangs taking up the light. It had mighty arms and short, thick legs. In its hands, or paws, was clutched a huge, long-handled, double-bladed ax.

It tensed, lifting up the ax, but then, suddenly, it stopped, and looked about, angrily, wildly, ears lifted, nostrils wide.

It uttered a howl of fury, turned suddenly about, and disappeared into the darkness.

I became aware of men crowded about us. I could distinguish Holt of Ar, Desmond of Hochburg, and Temicus, of Venna, each with a readied, lowered spear. And there were others, as well, similarly armed. These were guards from Post Eight and the men of the 'Roving Post.' I then understood what must have been the purport of the short conversation between Rupert and Temicus which had taken place earlier, in the camp, not far from the post to which Tiskias had been chained.

I knelt quickly, unnoticed, surrounded by free men.

"Come back!" called Rupert. "It is death to follow it into the darkness. The night is its element, as it is that of the *sleen*."

Reluctantly Holt and Desmond, with their spears, and some others, returned to the pool of light about my Master.

I was pleased that I had knelt. I was shaken. I did not think I could have stood.

"I was a fool," said Temicus. "I did not realize what was occurring. I thought that the beast was Lucilius. You might have been killed."

"Many would have thought it Lucilius," said Rupert. "Who would have thought that a Kur, let alone an enemy Kur, would dare approach an armed camp? The Kur well represented himself as Lucilius. You had no reason to doubt that it was Lucilius, and every reason to suppose that it was. He even brought a valuable prisoner to the camp, not one likely to be surrendered willingly. But he agreed to surrender that prisoner, even if reluctantly. He evinced no detectible surprise at learning that the slave was alive. Too, the communication he wished to impart was alleged to be urgent, and there was presumably no more than a pathetic particle of time in which to deliver it. Soon, the presence of a Kur in the vicinity of the camp would be noted, this very likely putting the Kur at risk, and, at the least, would establish its whereabouts and the likelihood that a certain message, a message whose contents might well be surmised by an enemy, had been delivered. In war it is often useful to keep both what one knows and what one does not know from the enemy. All that you did was intelligent, plausible, and rationally justified."

"And wrong," said Temicus, bitterly.

"One casts the stones," said Rupert. "They fall as they may. One awaits the outcome."

"The beast intended to kill you," said Temicus.

"Undoubtedly," said Rupert. "It doubtless thought the slave had been done away with, and I was to be next."

"Vengeance," said Temicus, "against the two most principal in warning Agamemnon, who, in turn, warned the Sardar."

"I think so," said Rupert.

"Do you think the beast knew that the slave was still alive?" asked Temicus.

"I do not think so," said Rupert, "but he may have considered that possibility. Who knows the possibilities of which a beast might take account, who knows the *kaissa* of which a beast is capable?"

"He gave no sign of surprise or consternation?" said Temicus.

"Not that I know of," said Rupert, "but there was both darkness and the imperturbable habits of the translator."

"At least we have Tiskias," said Temicus. "Perhaps the Kur will attempt to retrieve him."

"Or kill him," said Rupert.

"How so?" asked Temicus.

"He is now in custody," said Rupert. "Who knows what he might say, do, or reveal."

"Tor-tu-Gor awakens," said Temicus looking to the east.

Rupert extinguished the lantern.

"Let us now return to the routines of the camp," said Rupert.

I knew little or nothing of the plans of the Masters. It seemed clear that we were on the way to Ar, and, from hence, might proceed, by one route or another, to the waters of the long, wide, and mighty Vosk, in the vast basin of which Kurii had been assembling, presumably of the faction of distant Pompilius.

Most of the men, all dismissed, had now taken their leave, filing away.

Rupert looked down upon me.

"Master?" I said.

He did not seem pleased. I was uneasy. Had I not served him well? Had I not foiled the scheme of the Kur? Had I not exposed its charade? Had I not penetrated its disguise and then ripped it away?

"I did not know the secret name of Lucilius," he said.

"It was not really secret," I said. "I did not think it was important. I did not think to tell you."

"What was it?" he asked.

"'Cyrus,'" I said. "It is the name of an ancient king on Terra."

"Your test was simple, intelligent, clever, unanticipated, and effective," he said.

"Thank you, Master," I said.

"The time was short," he said, "but I had decided that your test was excellent, and that I would utilize it."

"I did not know," I said.

"Instead," he said, "you broke position. You leaped up without permission, rushed forth, and addressed yourself to the beast. You usurped my prerogative. It was mine to take that risk. You might have been killed."

Then he stopped, abruptly, as though he might have said too much. He thrust his sword into its scabbard, with an angry crack.

I shuddered. I thought of the crack of a slave whip.

"You placed an article of my property in jeopardy," he said. "That was wrong, intolerably wrong. Had you been given permission to do that? You had no right to do that. Would you cast your Master's coins away, irretrievably? It was unconscionable for you to do what you did."

"I did not know that Master intended to act," I said. "Even had I known I would have done what I did."

"Why?" he asked.

"To protect my Master, to keep him out of danger," I said.

"I see," he said, angrily.

"Is Master displeased?" I said.

"Sorely," he said. "What is on your neck?"

"A slave collar," I said.

"To whom do you belong?" he asked.

"To you, Master," I said.

"You are insolent, refractory, and recalcitrant," he said.

"No, Master!" I said.

"Do you contradict me?" he asked.

"I must," I said. "I am a slave. I am not permitted to lie."

"I find you muchly displeasing," he said.

"Forgive me," I begged. "I gather that I behaved badly. I knew no better. I meant neither disrespect nor harm. I am an ignorant slave. I did not think. Punish me! I beg to be whipped!"

"I ban you from my tent," he said. "At night you will be chained with the public slaves."

"Please, no, Master!" I begged.

"It is said," he said.

"I do not understand," I said.

"You are indeed an ignorant slave," he said.

"Was what I did really so wrong?" I said. "If so, punish me. Whip me! I beg to be whipped!"

"I see no point in wasting the tutelage of the leather on you," he said. "There is little point in whipping a stupid slave."

"I am not stupid," I said.

"No," he said, angrily. "That is true. You are not. And that made your foolish, presumptuous act more heinous."

"What is to be done with me?" I said. "What are you going to do with me?"

"Sell you, in Ar," he said, turning away.

"No!" I cried. "No, no, Master!"

Tears burst from my eyes. I clutched at the collar on my neck. I tried to tear it away. I was unable to do so.

Then I threw up in the grass.

CHAPTER NINETY-TWO

She moved her ankle, stirring the chain.

She was the girl from Earth, with whom I had once spoken, shortly before her marking, one of the fifteen who had been purchased for the use of the soldiers.

"You are restless," I said.

"What has become of me?" she asked. "I want the feel of ropes. I want to be braceleted. I want to kneel and beg. I want to lick and kiss. I want to be pleasing! I am so different from what I was!"

"Try to speak in Gorean," I said. "If the Masters discover us speaking in English we may be beaten."

"I must have someone to speak to," she said. "I do not know what is going on in my body!"

"Nor in your mind, or heart," I said.

"I want to be owned!" she whispered.

"You are," I said.

"But I want it," she said. "Is that not wrong?"

"No," I said, "not if you are a woman, not if you are a slave."

She twisted to the side, sobbing.

"Have the Masters given you a name?" I asked.

"Rika," she said.

"That is a lovely name," I said. "I knew a slave in a distant camp, long ago, who had that name."

"But it is a slave name is it not?" she asked.

"Yes," I said.

"I should hate it!" she said.

"Why?" I asked.

"But I love it!" she said. "It makes me feel slave, so slave."

"You are a slave," I said.

"I must resist these feelings," she said.

"Why?" I asked.

"It is to be done," she said. "I do not know why. Perhaps because they are disapproved by society."

"By a society," I suggested. "Societies differ."

"I have been taught what to think," she said.

"Better you had learned to think," I said.

"Surely that is dangerous," she said.

"Certainly," I said. "Thought entails risk. It permits a thousand birds to fly, a thousand snakes to crawl. Is that not why it is prohibited by a thousand competitive, contradictory tyrannies?"

"I fear I have been conditioned to hold certain views," she said.

"Perhaps then," I said, "you are already an unwitting slave, whose collar cannot be seen, the slave of your conditioning. It is difficult to escape from a prison you do not know exists. The first step to escape is to see the prison."

"You must understand," she said, "the voices to which I am expected to respond, prescribe conformity and obedience."

"Would they not," I asked, "had they their way, discourage you from listening to another voice?"

"What voice?" she asked.

"Your own," I said.

"I do not know what to think," she said.

"We know men and women," I said, "by what they do and what they are. Can one then not know societies and cultures by what they do and what they are? Is the culture from which you derive really the better for its scorning of nature, its lies and hypocrisies, its divisions and hatreds? Perhaps, but perhaps not. Are life consequences to be deemed irrelevant to such questions? Perhaps it is not wrong to weigh unhappiness and pain, or joys and fulfillment, in the scales of life"

"Masters approach," she whispered, suddenly.

"Gorean," I said, "Gorean."

Four soldiers passed by.

They took no note of two slaves, kneeling, their heads bowed.

"It pleased me," she said, "to kneel and bow my head."

"It seemed right to do so?" I said.

"Yes," she said.

"You are a slave," I said.

"I confess, Mira," she said, "openly, without embarrassment, I have sexual needs, and they torment me. On Gor, I have found myself. Here, I find myself deeply and irremediably sexual, sometimes painfully so."

"The Masters," I said, "as is their wont, have kindled your slave fires. They enjoy doing such things. How can you prevent or resist them? You are a slave. You are helpless. They are now a part of you."

"They put me so much at their mercy," she said.

"Doubtless," I said, "that was their intention."

"They are cruel," she said.

"They want us that way," I said, "needful, and begging. Who cares for the feelings of a slave?"

"On Earth," she said, "I was taught that men were the enemy."

"Here," I said, "they are the Masters."

"On Earth," she said, "I was nothing. I had no identity. I had no meaning."

"That is behind you," I said. "Here you are something, something well understood and very real, something precise and exact. Here you have a clear and well understood identity. Here you have a role, a function, and meaning. Here you are an essential component in a rich and complex society. Here your place is assured. Here you know how to speak, behave, and act. Here you have your collar and brand, these testifying that men want you, have found you sexually desirable, and worth owning. Here, too, you have a distinctive garb, if permitted clothing, a garb which conceals few of your charms and leaves no doubt as to your status, that of property, that of the domestic animal."

At that point, the camp bell sounded.

"I must help attend to the tables," I said.

"When will they permit me to serve?" she asked.

"I think soon," I said. "Work on your Gorean."

"Help me, more," she begged.

"Your fourteen chain sisters are Gorean," I said. "Plead for their help."

"They will not help me," she said.

"Because you are a barbarian?" I said.

"Yes," she said.

"I will speak to Master Temicus," I said. "One sight of his whip and, I assure you, they will become diligent, eager tutors."

"Do you know the archer, Ho-Rak?" she asked.

"By sight and name," I said, "by little else. I understand he is adept. Do you like him?"

"Is he not handsome?" she asked.

"I suppose so," I said, "in a rough way. Would you like his hand on your leash?"

That was a way of asking her if she might want him for a Master.

"I saw him looking at me," she said. "I covered my breasts with my hands, for they were bared, and smiled at him."

"What did he do?" I asked.

"He gestured that I should remove my hands from my breasts."

"And did you?" I asked.

"Instantly," she said.

"Good," I said. "That probably saved you a cuffing."

"I hope I am attractive," she said.

"Have no fear," I said. "You would not have been brought to Gor were you not."

"I hope he likes me," she said.

"You smiled?" I said.

"Yes," she said.

"Don't worry," I said. "A smile over a slave collar is unusually fetching."

"I hope to soon attend the tables," she said.

"You can then hurry about, seeing that he is well served," I said. "Indeed, with some fortune, he may let you kneel under the table at his knee, and be fed by hand."

"I hope that will be the case," she said.

"And well you might," I said. "The Masters are not fed on slave gruel."

"I hope he will use me in night sport," she said.

"You may have to compete for him," I said.

"I will do so," she said, "shamelessly, as a slave."

"Good," I said.

"But I am a barbarian," she said.

"Some men like barbarians," I said. "They find them exotic. Too, they are often starved for sex on Earth, beg well, and are more than grateful to find themselves ravished again and again on Gor as the worthless slaves they now are."

"I want a private Master," she said.

"That is not unusual," I said. "It is a common dream of city slaves, camp slaves, brothel slaves, tavern slaves, and such. Perhaps someday you may be given or sold to the Master of your dreams."

"You have a private Master," she said.

"He shuns me," I said. "I was displeasing. I failed him. I am denied his tent, his arms, his caresses. I am to be sold, in Ar."

"You are crying," she said.

"No," I said. "I am not."

"You are," she said.

I rose to my feet. "I must give attendance at the tables," I said.

CHAPTER NINETY-THREE

"Why are your hands braceleted behind your back?" asked Temione.

We were camped west of Venna, a few *pasangs* from Ar. Gordon of Hammerfest, commander of the newly formed Vosk Guard, had sent a delegation to meet the company of Rupert of Hochburg, and certain other units from in and around Venna, marching to join the forces of the Vosk Guard before it embarked on its campaign to counter Kur incursions in the Vosk basin. Temione had been assigned to accompany the delegation as a baggage slave. In such a way a Gorean Master can remind a woman, no matter how beautiful and intelligent she may be, to keep in mind that she is now no more than a slave.

"I suppose," I said, "that I not be tempted to run."

It is, of course, hard to run with one's hands braceleted behind one's back, or, for that matter, before one's body. It is clumsy and awkward to do so. Too, of course, it is difficult to use one's hands, feed oneself, steal a garment of the free, and such. Also, a back-braceleted slave is more likely to be noted, as that tends to make her more conspicuous, particularly in an area where slaves are normally untethered and free to rove about.

"Surely you are not tempted to run?" asked Temione.

"I ran once," I said. "I was soon recaptured."

"Surely you know there is no escape for us," she said, "the brand, the collar, and so on. Almost certainly you would be caught and punished, perhaps severely. You might even be seized as a loose slave and find yourself immersed in a far more rigorous and unpleasant bondage."

"I am miserable," I said.

"Why?" she asked.

"I am to be sold," I said.

"You were displeasing?" she asked. "You are a failed slave?"

"I fear so," I said.

"Then," she said, "you have lost status. You must kneel before me, and address me as Mistress."

"Yes, Mistress," I said, kneeling.

"There is nothing personal in this," she said.

"I understand," I said, "Mistress."

I knew there could be hierarchies, even amongst slaves. The most obvious example of that was the office of 'First Girl.' Too, of course, the distinction between the native-born Gorean slave and the barbarian slave was familiar.

"Incidentally, Sweet Pockface," she said, "I made numerous inquiries pertaining to the young men of the Voltai who supposedly glide about on kitelike wings. No one has ever heard of them."

"I just made that up," I said, "to give you enough courage to risk an escape from the Ul's lair."

"You saved my life," she said.

"Our lives," I said.

"You may break position," she said, "and you no longer need to address me as Mistress."

"Thank you," I said.

"I do not know why I believed that," she said.

"You were desperate, terribly desperate," I said.

"I must have been," she said, "to believe so preposterous a lie."

"On Terra," I said, "individuals do build such devices and do such things."

"How stupid you must think me," she said. "Get back on your knees."

"Yes, Mistress," I said.

CHAPTER NINETY-FOUR

"That one!" said a harsh voice.

The keeper turned to me.

"You!" said the keeper.

I hurried to him, knelt, and lowered my head.

I was tense, listening carefully. I was prepared to respond instantly. Twice I had felt the switch, once from him, and once from another keeper.

"Look up," he said.

I looked up.

The back of his right hand faced me. His thumb was folded back, into the palm. The four fingers were extended and pointed downward. He made a quick, sharp gesture toward the ground.

Instantly I went to all fours.

I then, following him was led to the bars.

The holding cage was large. It was circular, and had a diameter of some thirty yards. It had a barred flooring, but that was a foot or so below the concealing sand. Its barred ceiling was some eight feet above the sand. There must have been a hundred girls in the cage. We were all naked. It was one of four such holding cages. The vertical bars were some seven inches apart. The lateral bars were some eighteen inches apart. Each cage had two gates. Normally a girl was introduced into the cage through one gate, the entrance gate, so to speak, and removed from it by means of another gate, which one might think of as the exit gate. I no longer wore the collar of Rupert of Hochburg. I had been placed in a simple cage collar bearing the sign of Tenalian of Ar and the Gorean letter 'Delka,' a simple equilateral triangle, which was, as I had been given to understand, the fourth letter in the Gorean alphabet. That done, the collar of Rupert of Hochburg had been removed. Thus, there was no moment when I was not collared. I was housed in Delka cage, one of the aforementioned four cages. Technically, as it was explained to me, I was still the property of Rupert of Hochburg. I was slated to be sold in Ar four days from now, my sales price to be divided in some proportion between the house of Tenalian and Rupert of Hochburg. This procedure is occasionally used, by agreement, the house acting, in effect, as the seller's agent. It may be used, too, when the house has overextended its capital and wishes to conserve its resources. The usual arrangement is that the house owns what it sells.

"Is this the one?" asked the keeper. Two fellows stood outside the bars. From their garmenture, I could not determine their caste.

I did not care for their appearance.

"Yes," said the taller of the two men outside the bars. He was half-shaven.

"Be certain," said the shorter man, short-bearded and muscular.

"She was pointed out to us, yesterday, in the processing," said the taller fellow, whom I took to be first amongst the two.

"What is your name?" asked the shorter fellow.

"Whatever pleases Master," I said.

"By what name have you been called?" he asked, unpleasantly.

"Mira," I said, quickly, "if it pleases Master." It is not pleasant to feel the lash.

"See?" said the taller fellow.

"It would not do to be mistaken," said the shorter man.

"There is no mistake," said the first.

I did not understand what was occurring. Who would have pointed me out, and for what reason? If someone was interested in me, they could wait until I was entered into an exhibition cage, within the walls, or, even, put on the sales block. Who might be interested in me, that is, particularly, more than in many others? Certainly I was no Temione, or even a Xanthe.

"You have the paper?" asked the keeper.

"Here," said the taller man, handing a piece of stamped paper through the bars to the keeper.

The keeper perused the slip.

"This is not a running slave," he said. "This is a housed slave, a boarded slave, due as most in Delka cage to be sold four days from now at the close of the passage hand. We have some running slaves in Ba-ta cage. If you are interested in serious catch sport, we even have two bred racers in Ba-ta, recently brought in from the stables in Venna. You would need a saddle *tharlarion* to net them. They often return to us unnetted. You pay a copper tarsk for the game, and, if you win, you get five copper tarsks."

"The paper," said the half-shaven, taller man, "does not specify a running slave, only a slave to be run."

"This one," said the keeper, "if you are interested in a good game, is a poor choice. She is miserable, and frequently cries. She eats little and stays muchly to herself. We are thinking of possibly postponing her sale until after the passage hand. If she does not improve before then, we may have to whip-sell her."

I shuddered.

Certainly I would try to exhibit well, regardless of my rejection and my Master's scorn, despite my having been found wanting and having been put aside, despite the lassitude and sorrow, the emptiness and cold, which seemed to threaten to engulf me.

"This is the one we want," said the taller man.

"Go capture a free woman, and strip her and run her," said the keeper. "If she wins, she keeps her freedom; if she loses, she gets the collar. Even a free woman, striving desperately to keep her freedom, as is the case with some, fearing the collar, will give you a better game."

"This is the one we want," said the taller man.

"Surely you can understand," said the second man, he with the short beard, "why we might be interested in running this one. Consider her flanks, her figure."

"We have a private wager, a catch bet," said the taller man. "A silver tarsk."

"So much?" whistled the keeper. "Many girls do not sell for that."

"We wish to make certain that at least one of us catches her," said the taller man. "Thus, we do not want a skilled, practiced running slave."

"I see," said the keeper.

"I will win," said the shorter man.

"No, I," said the taller, half-shaven man.

"You said someone pointed her out to you," said the keeper.

"A mutual friend," said the taller man, "suggesting she might make a suitable quarry."

"I see," said the keeper.

I was pleased to hear this, for I deemed then the matter had little or nothing to do with me personally.

"Fit her with a running tunic," said the shorter man. "We want it clear she is a sport slave. We do not wish to provoke an inquiry or attract undue attention, particularly on the part of a guardsman."

"That would disrupt, if not spoil, the game," said the taller man.

"Clearly," said the keeper.

He then received a copper tarsk from the taller man, and handed him back the slip of stamped paper.

"She is to be back by the Twentieth Ahn," said the keeper.

"We understand," said the taller man.

"Slave," said the keeper.

"Master?" I said.

"Should you manage to elude capture, surprising as that might seem, you are to make your way back here by morning. At night you can see the tarn beacons on the walls of Ar; by day you can see the walls themselves, and the roads will be clear."

"Yes, Master," I said.

"Avoid the swamp forest south of Ar," he said. "It is dangerous, particularly at night."

"I understand," I said.

"And I would not run her in that vicinity either," said the keeper.

"We would not think of doing so," said the shorter man.

"You understand," said the keeper, "the copper tarsk does not entitle you to any slave use of the quarry."

"Of course," said the taller man.

"Accepted," said the shorter man.

I then realized that, if caught, I would doubtless be well used before being returned to Delka cage.

My thoughts began to race.

What if, despite the likelihood, I managed to elude my pursuers? Why should I not dally, or even try to escape? Might that not be an amusing affront to the arrogance of the house of Tenalian? Did they really expect every slave to come back, begging for her bowl of gruel? Whereas I would expect to be punished, perhaps severely, for my action, I did not think I would be hamstrung. Technically, I still belonged to Rupert of Hochburg until my sale. Surely, neither he nor the house of Tenalian would want me to be crippled before being put on the block. Indeed, while he, as most Goreans, thought little of disciplining a slave whose behavior required correction or whose character needed improvement, or even to remind her that she was a slave, he, as most Goreans, would never seriously hurt one, no more than they would any other vulnerable domestic animal. I suspected that most Gorean Masters, though few would admit it, regarded slaves as treasures to be cherished, not objects to be abused.

I knew Rupert of Hochburg regarded me as intelligent. I did not want to disappoint him in that particular. If I tried to escape, would he not think me stupid? Surely I knew that there was no escape for the Gorean slave girl. That was clear. One might do little more, if eluding one Master, than fall into the hands of another, and, most likely, it would result in a closer, harsher slavery, given that one had run. Indeed, where on Gor was there to escape to? Thus, I decided I would, if I managed to elude my hunters, return to the cage. What other choice had I, other than stupidity or indulging a doomed transitory vanity?

A few minutes later I was in a runner's tunic. It was white, which, I supposed, was to make it easier to descry me in the dark. I was warned that it was not to be removed, presumably, I supposed, because that might be thought to provide me with some unfair advantage. To be sure, I expected to be caught long before it became dark. There was also some writing on the tunic which, I gathered, identified it as a runner's tunic. It was also slit at the sides. This made it a garment in which it was easier to run. Perhaps that should have been accounted a mistake, as well, as it might have been thought to supply me with some advantage, however small. But, in any event, the tunic was as it was, so designed, so cut. Of course, too, so fashioned, it made it easier for Masters to brush it aside.

A bit later, the exit gate of Delka cage had been opened and I joined the two fellows outside the bars.

"Good sport, good hunting," called the keeper after us.

Neither the taller man nor the shorter man responded.

"Follow us, *kajira*," said the taller man.

"Yes, Master," I said.

After we had left the cage well behind, the men took a turn.

I was uneasy.

"May I speak, Masters?" I asked.

"No," said the taller man.

I followed behind.

We were moving south.

CHAPTER NINETY-FIVE

"Am I to be run here?" I asked.

I received no answer.

It was late afternoon.

The ground was spongy. Mixed scents assailed my nostrils, those of a rich, moist, lush, thriving growth, of thousands of large, exotic flowers, and the dark, pervasive smell of layers of decaying, rotting vegetation. Insects were about. Small bright birds darted past. I heard, far off, an occasional splash. Here and there, there were high, broad-leaved trees. I could see loops of vine dangling amongst branches.

"Masters are clever," I said. "We have come to the swamp forest, which is it is unwise to enter. Thus my flight will be limited on one side, as if by a wall. Nonetheless, I will try to give you good sport. What start will you give me? How much time will you give me, before you begin your pursuit? I will try not to favor either of you, as that would not be in the spirit of the game."

"Put your hands behind you, wrists crossed," said the taller man.

"Masters?" I asked, puzzled, but I obeyed.

My wrists were tied behind my back.

"I do not understand," I said.

A leash collar was put about my neck. Then a leash was attached to the collar.

"Masters?" I asked.

"Few are about," said the taller man. "This area is avoided by most. If you scream, you will not he heard."

"Sometimes *tharlarion*, wild *tharlarion*, emerge from the forest, at night," said the shorter man.

"Even *sleen* are rare here," said the taller man.

I threw back my head in terror and loosed a long wild, miserable, quavering scream.

"You are correct," said the taller man. "You are not to be run. We are not interested in a game of girl catch. The girl in which we have an interest has already been caught. She is already well in hand, bound and leashed."

"No," said the shorter, muscular man. "Do not scream again.

There is no one to hear you, but one beast or another might come to investigate. That might prove unpleasant and cost us time."

"Who are you and what do you want?" I asked.

"Who we are is unimportant," said the taller man, "and what we want is our pay."

"Sixteen copper tarsks," said the shorter.

"Then you do not leash me for yourselves," I said, "but for another."

"Possibly," said the shorter man.

"Who?" I asked. "One who saw me west of Venna, one who saw me at the house of Tenalian, one who saw me conveyed to the country cages?"

"Let us uncover the raft, poles, and lanterns," said the taller man. "We have little time to waste. It will be easier to follow the trail of the tufted wands in the light."

"Beware, noble Masters," I said. "I am to be back by the Twentieth Ahn, and certainly by noon tomorrow."

"That is a long time from now," said the shorter man.

"It gives us time to vanish at our leisure," said the taller man. "By then, we can be far, and anywhere."

"A search will be made," I said.

"One both foolish and futile," said the shorter man.

"They will not know where to look," said the taller man.

"To no one will it occur that we might have broached the swamp forest," said the other. "Only mad men would suppose that."

And perhaps, I thought, only mad men would enter the swamp forest.

"It is not unknown for men to enter the swamp forest and never be seen again," said the taller man.

"Yet," I said, "you would dare to do so?"

"Briefly, and cautiously," said the half-shaven, taller man.

"Some," said the short-bearded, muscular man, "know the swamp forest, its quarters and trails, the times, habits, and natures of its denizens, its dry, high, secret places, its clearings and holdings, the camps of its rebels and bandits."

"And such men might be mistrustful, fierce, secretive, dangerous, and territorial?" I said.

"It is true that not everyone who enters the forest and fails to return has fallen to its serpents, wild *tarsks*, and *tharlarion*," said the taller fellow.

"But yet you will risk the forest?" I said.

"We are armed, expected, and the trail is marked," said the shorter man.

"You are keeping a rendezvous," I said.

"Yes," said he whom I took to be the first of the two.

"Who wants me?" I asked. "To whom am I being taken?"

"Here is the raft," said the shorter man, wading in a foot or so of water.

Some vines and leaves were then cast aside. There were two poles with the raft, two spears, and two lanterns. There was also a box which contained a miscellany of objects, such as tools, pans, bowls, cordage, and chains. There were also two large botas, filled, I supposed, with water, some round, flat loaves of bread, and a sack of meal.

The shorter, muscular man then lifted me in his arms and put me, sitting, towards the center of the raft, on a mat, leashed, my hands bound behind my back. He then crossed my ankles and, with the free end of the leash, bound them together.

"Stay toward the center of the raft," he said. "There are unpleasant things in the water."

Each of the men then took a pole and began to propel the raft through the water, slowly and smoothly.

A small yellow bird flashed by.

Sometime the men had to bend down, to avoid being entangled in descended loops of vine.

At other times they had to use the poles to brush aside vegetation.

Far off, I heard the bellowing snort of a *tharlarion*.

"There, to the right," said the taller man, "is the seventh tufted wand."

Time went by and it grew dark. The two lanterns were lit.

"Masters!" I cried, when a large body suddenly surfaced and rolled, glistening, in the water, its scales reflecting the lanternlight, not a yard away.

"It is harmless," said the taller man.

"Not all are," said the shorter man.

I conjectured that it was somewhere in the vicinity of the Twentieth Ahn, the Gorean midnight, when we saw a speck of light far off in the darkness, far off in the distance.

"There it is," said the taller man.

"I see it," said his companion.

They began to pole slowly toward the light.

"Masters," I begged. "Please, Masters! I understand nothing! What are you doing? Where are you taking me?"

The taller of the two men turned toward me.

I saw his face, reddish and dark, in the lantern light.

"To the small man," he said.

CHAPTER NINETY-SIX

"Tiskias!" I wept.

"Master Tiskias," he said.

"How can you be here?" I asked. Had I not last seen him in chains, fastened to a post in a camp west of Venna? Should he not be in custody? How was it that he was no longer a helpless prisoner, at the mercy of Rupert of Hochburg?

The poles thrust down and the raft was poled up the sloping beach. I heard, and felt, the gravel under the roped logs.

I struggled to a kneeling position, my ankles bound and my wrists tied behind my back. Few slaves willingly court the risk of a beating.

There was no mistaking the small figure of Tiskias on the beach. He was flanked by two men in motley garb, which might, I supposed, in daylight, blend in with the dense and variegated growth in the swamp. One of these men held a lantern, the other a spear. Both were bearded and hooded. Both wore swords and knives. I saw only these two men flanking Tiskias. I saw nothing of a Kur.

The fellow holding the lantern, our landing effected, put it down on a rocky shelf to his right.

"You escaped the men of Rupert of Hochburg," I said.

"Without difficulty," said Tiskias.

"How can that be?" I asked, frightened. I feared that the Kur of the faction of Pompilius, a dark bloodthirsty shape in the darkness, intent on the rescue of his colleague, might have infiltrated or stormed the camp, tearing away limbs and opening the throats of any who might stand in his way. But Tiskias would have been chained. Might the Kur then, with its bulk and power, its feet in perhaps bloody dirt, have literally torn the post to which Tiskias was held from the ground, or, with his mighty grasp, have ripped his chains from the wood?

"Are you surprised?" asked Tiskias.

"Yes," I said.

"Do not conjecture risk and slaughter," said Tiskias, "nor think my hirsute friend so simple as to emplace himself in the midst of darting spears. Things can be managed far more deftly and safely with fewer and more convenient means."

"I do not understand," I said.

"That, charming *kajira*," he said, "is because you are stupid. More gates have been opened by gold than thundering rams and raging fire. The clink of silver can drown out the blasting of trumpets and the beating of drums. A beleaguered garrison has more to fear from an opened purse than scaling ladders and siege towers."

"No one would betray Rupert of Hochburg," I said. "His men would die first."

"You know little of the ways of the world, my naive, lovely, collared beast," said Tiskias. "Honor is no more than a wisp of fog, a puff of air. A copper tarsk is more real. It has more substance, more weight and solidity."

"I do not believe you," I said.

"Of what account is what a slave believes?" said Tiskias.

"Who freed you of the holding post?" I asked. "Who was bribed to undo your locks and smuggle you from an armed camp?"

"One of many," said Tiskias, "who would put gold before duty, advantage before honor."

"Not from the camp of Rupert of Hochburg!" I said.

"One who still stands high in that camp," said Tiskias, "one ready to betray again when opportune."

"Who?" I demanded.

"One at the elbow of power, well placed in the company of Rupert of Hochburg," he said. "Holt of Ar."

"I do not believe it!" I cried. "It cannot be!"

"Who but one so high, so trusted, so well fixed," asked Tiskias, "could manage so delicate and perilous a matter?"

I was kneeling before him, on the simple mat stretched over the rough logs of the raft, shaken, miserable, and helpless. Tears coursed down my cheeks.

"Has the house of your dreams collapsed?" he asked. "Do your illusions fade? Does the earth tremble? Awaken, naive child, and glimpse the rocks of fact, shiver in the cold, bitter wind of reality, weep at the touch of the claws of truth."

"You are a liar!" I exclaimed.

Weeping, at that wild, furious instant, I had not cared if I were beaten or not.

And then, a moment later, the enormity of my utterance gripped me, and I was much afraid.

"No," he said to the men about. "She is distraught. Do not beat her. What she has lived by has perished. Her world has fallen to ruin. That is far more painful than the hasty kiss of an angry lash."

Suddenly a wild, irresistible thought seized me.

I almost laughed with joy.

I put my head down. I did not want the men to see, to suspect. No longer did the earth shake. Might not the bitterness and sorrow which had gripped me be groundless and unreal? Was I not more sure of the loyalty of Holt of Ar to the Scarlet Codes, the ways of the Warriors, and to Rupert of Hochburg, his captain, than I was of the convictions of Tiskias, who doubtless saw the world less as it was than as he believed it to be? Could not betrayal be as much of an illusion as loyalty? Might not the dishonorable be as blind to honor as the honorable might be to dishonor? Who knew the nature of the rocks of fact? Who best recorded the subtle or sweeping currents of reality? Need the touch of truth draw blood? Might it not as easily soothe wounds and dispel darkness?

Let Holt of Ar be loyal. And I was clearly in the presence of Tiskias, the minion of a mighty Kur, of the faction of Pompilius, some remote lord of intrigue, war, and battle. How could this be? Were chains easily broken or spears unavailing? I did not think so. Might not a putative, deceitful escape have been engineered? What would be the object of such a subterfuge? Presumably to follow Tiskias in the hope of being led to a foe far more dangerous and determined than he, a foe which seemed relentless, even to the point of madness, in his intention to wreak vengeance on those who had brought to naught the plan of his remote lord, Pompilius. That Kur, the ally of mere Tiskias, must be first in the thoughts of Rupert of Hochburg. Surely meeting with, and dealing with, that foe must have been paramount in his reasoning.

I lifted my head.

"Thank you, Master," I said, "for not having me beaten, for your patience, your understanding, and mercy."

"You did not realize what you were saying," he said, almost kindly.

"I should have said," I said, "that I hoped that Master might be mistaken."

"But your foolish hope would have been dashed," he said, "for I am not mistaken."

"I do not see Master's mighty ally, the Kur," I said.

"Rejoice that you do not," he said.

"May I inquire as to his whereabouts?" I asked.

"My pet is near," he said.

"I did not know he was your pet," I said.

"I am Master," said Tiskias.

"I have done your pet no wrong," I said, uneasily. "Why should I fear his appearance?"

"You played a role, however unwittingly or unwillingly, in games far beyond your ken," he said. "You, a dupe, utilized by one far more important than you, the uncaring, troublesome villain Rupert of Hochburg, effective agent of the Kur faction of Agamemnon, brought to ruin a costly, secret, carefully laid plot which, if successful, would have dethroned Priest-Kings and enthroned the mighty Kur, Pompilius, whose powerful, sophisticated weaponry might then have been employed however he wished, as Master of Gor."

"I beg mercy," I said.

"My pet would not stand for it," he said.

"Are you not Master?" I asked.

"I am," said Tiskias. "But my pet can become surly and unpleasant, and one wishes him to be content."

"I am a slave," I said. "I do not think that I am important enough to deserve the wrath of so mighty and formidable a figure. Why should so awesome a personage waste his wrath on so unworthy and trivial a subject?"

"It is not of my doing," said Tiskias. "You are not unattractive. I would spare you."

"What does he want of me?" I asked.

"He intends to take his time with you," said Tiskias, "to eat you, bit by bit, and drink your blood, sip by sip."

"I am only a slave," I said.

"This does not really have to do with you," said Tiskias. "It has everything to do with Rupert of Hochburg. He will be captured. Then he will be tied helplessly and forced to observe the Kur's casual feeding. It is an excellent way of torturing him, do you not agree?"

"He would be unmoved," I said. "He would laugh contemptuously. I am only a slave."

"Does he not care for you?" asked Tiskias.

"No," I said. "I was found unsatisfactory as a slave. I was displeasing. Remember, he consigned me to the house of Tenalian, to be sold."

"But are you not still his property?" asked Tiskias.

"Until my sale," I said.

"Then he will be forced to see his property destroyed, slowly, little by little, before his eyes," said Tiskias. "Is that not a fine insult? Is it not well calculated to frustrate and outrage his sense of self, propriety, and honor?"

"And what then of him?" I asked.

"He will be accorded the same lamentable fate, two or three days later," said Tiskias, "in order that he may have time to suitably savor the impending eventuality and the Kur have time to regain his appetite."

The Kur, I gathered, like many animals, need not feed daily.

"But you have not yet captured Rupert of Hochburg," I said.

"Let me explain our plan," said Tiskias. "It is simple and flawless. You have been removed from the Delka cage. You will not have returned. This will be brought to the attention of Rupert of Hochburg. He will pursue you, if only to regain his property before its sale."

"He will bring men," I said.

"Few," said Tiskias. "Do not forget. He will expect to deal with two only, only two slave thieves."

"But many more will wait to ensnare him," I said.

"Better than fifty brigands, men familiar with the forest, men well aware of its ugly and perilous ways," said Tiskias.

"His free company contains more than two hundred men," I said. Why should Tiskias not worry about numbers?

"Closer to a hundred and fifty," he said.

"Even so few would outmatch your fifty or so brigands," I said.

"No commander in his right mind would lead a free company into the swamp forest," said Tiskias, "and certainly not in pursuit of two slave thieves."

"Your plan," I said, "is less flawless than you conjecture. It is lacking. My Master will not know where I am. Where should he look? And surely he will not suppose that two slave thieves would be so foolish as to venture into the swamp forest, putting at risk both their own lives and that of their capture."

"A false trail has been arranged," said Tiskias. "Rupert of Hochburg will note it and, following it, will be led into an ambush."

Again I felt miserable.

The scheme of Tiskias, or that of his ally, the Kur of the faction of Pompilius, was well contrived. My Master, unsuspecting, intent on recovering his property, wresting it back from two thieves, would be led into a trap.

"All should be concluded by tomorrow evening," said Tiskias.

I shuddered.

I pulled at the thongs encircling my wrists. I was helpless.

How could I warn my Master?

I was bound!

There was no escape!

"We have delivered the slave," said the taller, half-shaven man, he who was first of the two who had taken me from Delka cage. "Give us eight copper tarsks, the second half of our pay."

"Better in the morning," said Tiskias. "It would be foolish to address yourself to the forest in darkness, with only the light of lanterns. It would be difficult to discern the tufted wands."

"Too," growled one of the two men in motley garb flanking Tiskias, he who had earlier held the lantern, "the stirring of the water with the poles and the movement of the light of lanterns over the water might provoke the interest of hungry friends."

"Pay us now," said the taller man to Tiskias. "We will leave at first light."

Might not, I wondered, the lantern here on this small bar, or island, prove similarly attractive? To be sure, it was well above the water and lodged on a rocky shelf. Its flame would do little to suggest life and movement.

"In the morning," suggested Tiskias.

"Now," said the taller man, the tone of his voice edged with impatience.

"Of course," said Tiskias.

"He is reluctant to open his purse before us," said the muscular, short-bearded man.

"We could open it for him," said one of the fellows who had been flanking Tiskias, he who had lifted the lantern, signaling us in.

"Stop," cried Tiskias, for the hand of the fellow who had held the lantern pulled the purse away from the belt of Tiskias and cut its strings.

"There is more than copper here," said he who now held the purse.

I heard the clink of metal disks.

"Give it back," said Tiskias.

"He gave us only sixteen copper tarsks," said the short-bearded man.

"He gave us only eight, four apiece," said the fellow in motley garb who held a spear.

I wondered why he carried the spear about.

"A mere oversight," said Tiskias, "easily remedied. It will be eight for each of you, my brave and loyal friends."

"Let us cut his throat now and share his purse's contents equally," said the taller, half-shaven man, he who, with his fellow, had taken me from Delka cage. "We will then have more and none will know."

"The body is easily disposed of in the swamp," said his shorter fellow.

"My noble friends," said Tiskias, "your jests are ill-timed and lack taste. Were I to take them seriously, I would call to your attention the existence of gold of which you know nothing, which much exceeds the miserable coins now in my purse, gold which might easily be yours with little expenditure of either time or effort, but gold to which, however, I have no immediate personal access."

"One coin that exists," said the fellow who had originally lifted the lantern, "is worth more than a hundred which do not."

"But less than a hundred which do exist," said Tiskias.

"Let us kill him now and depart in the morning," said the tall, unshaven man."

"And how many of you will be alive in the morning to depart," asked Tiskias, "two, or only one?"

The men looked uneasily at one another.

"I also propose two further thoughts for you to ponder," said Tiskias. "First, some fifty men or so lie in wait to intercept Rupert of Hochburg tomorrow. They will not be pleased, after having done their work, that they are to receive no recompense. They will look into the matter, and, I am sure, several will know where to look. Second, I have a colleague, dark and strong, not human, mighty and fierce, who can trail like the *sleen* and feed with the zest of the starving *larl*."

"I do not understand," said the fellow who had held the lantern.

"One of the mighty beasts, the Kurii," said Tiskias, "a Kur."

"Kurii do not exist," said one of the two fellows in motley garb, he with the spear.

"They do," whispered the short-bearded man, he who had helped pole the raft to this small island in the swamp. "Two years ago, I saw one in Ar."

"I have my spear," said the man.

"Beware shadows in the darkness," said Tiskias, "claws and fangs that can strike in the night."

"I am unafraid," said the man with the spear.

"Perhaps the Kur is watching us, even now," said Tiskias.

"It would know nothing," said the man who had held the lantern.

"It can hear a whisper at fifty paces," said Tiskias.

"If he is about," said the fellow with the spear, "let him show himself."

"The Kur," said Tiskias, "seldom shows himself to strangers, or prey."

"You perceived the nature of our mirth well," said the taller, half-shaven man, looking about, and moving a bit farther from the light of the resting lantern.

"We are well met," said his friend, "and amongst fellows well met there thrives trust and accord."

"It never occurred to me that you were not jesting," said Tiskias, smiling and, at the same time, feeling within his robes, high on the left side. A moment later he withdrew his hand, seemingly satisfied.

"It will surprise the keepers at Delka cage that the slave is not returned by midnight as she is neither a trained nor bred runner," said the half-shaven man, "but it will be assumed she somehow managed to elude her hunters. In that case they will expect her to find her way back by noon tomorrow at the latest. When she does not, Rupert of Hochburg will be notified and a pursuit will be underway. As a plain, clear trail has been prepared for him, he, unsuspecting and eager to retrieve the slave, should reach the forest by the Twelfth Ahn and, shortly thereafter, perish in the trap which has been laid for him."

"If all goes well," said his short-bearded fellow.

"Fear not," said Tiskias, "it will."

I struggled again, futilely, in my bonds. I must somehow escape to warn my Master! I did have one hope, that he would care so little for me that he would not risk an entry into the swamp forest to recover me. Surely I was not all that valuable. The most that I had ever sold for was a silver tarsk six. Would a rational fellow imperil his life for a silver tarsk six? But this surcease of my anxiety was woefully temporary. He was no peddler, no merchant, but one who knew, and one who was entitled to, the scarlet cloak. Might not honor or pride prove to be his downfall? Principle, however wayward and misguided, might take precedence over calculation and caution. Let him choose chagrin and resignation. In the face of fearful odds, who would not sheath his sword and turn away? One, I feared, one who wore the scarlet cloak.

I must have my limbs free.

I wore the collar of a Gorean slave.

Did this not, even if only in a small way, testify to desirability?

Might I not, in my collar, have a device, tool, asset, or weapon which might be turned to my account? Certainly not every female captive is enslaved. Sometimes, and often to their humiliation and fury, they are turned loose, naked, by raiders as failing to be of sufficient 'block interest.' One of the reasons given for the Robes of Concealment, other than modesty, show, and vanity, distinguishing free women from slaves, and such, is to discourage the capture of free women. That is understandable. Being keenly disappointed is not much recompense for a fellow's having put his life at risk. In the case of the slave, the raider, tarnsman, or such, can pretty much see what he is getting.

I decided I would call out to my captors.

If I could get my limbs free, I might find an opportunity, particularly in the darkness, to wade away from this small island and make my way to the fields beyond the swamp, sometime before morning. I was afraid, as had been the two men who had taken me from Delka cage, to enter the swamp, but I was desperate enough to venture amongst its perils, and even more, to warn my Master of the dangers awaiting him.

I would remind my captors of my presence.

Were they not males?

And were they not Gorean males?

And was I not a slave, well aware of the meaning of my collar? My freedom was far behind me. I now well knew that I was an object, a property, vendible, purchasable goods, that which could be, and was, owned, a possession, a domestic beast, a toy if men pleased, collar meat, a morsel for masters, something which, whether I wished it or not, could be brought to helpless, yielding, begging ecstasy by the whim or touch of a Master.

Though I feared and loathed the men, I knew that I, a slave, would be helpless in their arms. I had been made so. I could not help myself. We are so helpless, collared! Many times I had heard of a slave crawling to the feet of a hated Master begging pathetically even for his most brutal, contemptuously scornful caress. Were not women often starved for sex for days before their sale that their needs might be manifested all the more piteously on the block? Did not men make us the way they wanted us?

I turned to the men, bound, my lips parted, but then, in the lantern light, drew back, frightened.

The two fellows who had poled the raft were regarding me, and, behind them, were the two fellows in motley garb who had flanked Tiskias as we had reached the small island, he who had lifted the lantern, and he who still clutched the spear.

"It is some Ahn before light," said the taller, half-shaven man, "and Rupert of Hochburg and his party will not fall into the ambush until tomorrow, presumably in the late afternoon. How shall we entertain ourselves until we receive word of his downfall?"

The other men, save Tiskias, laughed. Tiskias seemed uneasy. I suspected he regarded himself as in jeopardy, and not merely from the denizens of the swamp.

"Our small friend is well-provisioned," said the fellow with the spear.

"Yes," said Tiskias quickly. "Wines, pastries, and cheese."

"We have food," said the short-bearded man.

"And you will share it with us?" asked he who had tended the lantern.

"If you like," said the taller man.

"I think not," said the fellow who had managed the lantern.

"Let suspicion not darken fellowship," said Tiskias. "I am happy to share my supplies, and, if you like, will partake first of each bite or sip."

"He has done so for us, for three days," said the fellow with the spear.

"None the less," said the taller man.

"Very well," said he who had tended the lantern. Then he said the words I had feared he would say and had hoped he would say. "Fetch the slave."

The fellow with the spear thrust it point down, deeply, into the sand and made his way to the tethered raft. He unbound my hands and freed my ankles of the leash strap. He lifted me to my feet, and I stood unsteadily on the mat on the raft. It did not help that the raft moved slightly in the water.

"What of the leash?" asked he who before whom I now stood. "It is a lock leash."

"Leave her in it," said the taller man. "I have the key. She cannot remove it."

There are many things which can be done with a slave leash. It is not simply a leading tether or holding tether. One may use it to bind a slave in many effective, cunning ways. For example, a slave may be tied on her knees her head held down by the strap run under her body and back, tying her ankles together; the strap might be used to tie her hands close to the collar; the collar might be turned and her hands tied back, over and behind her head, which lifts her breasts nicely; the strap might be passed back between her legs and her wrists tied high up, tightly behind her, and so on.

I was led onto the island.

Before the men I knelt.

"You will prepare, lay out, and serve a small supper," said the taller man. "I and my friend will be fed from our own supplies. Our new friends will partake of provisions already on the island. Our host, the noble Tiskias, will show them to you. There is to be no cooking. I gather that it is dangerous enough to have one lantern lit."

"Some eyes doubtless watch it now," said he who had put aside the spear. I then thought I understood the reason for the spear.

Who knew what lurked in the swamp?

"There are some excellent wines," said Tiskias. "I call them to your attention. I will sample each before it is served. Will that be acceptable?"

"What wines?" asked the taller man.

"We have some even from the Ta grapes of many-terraced Cos," said Tiskias.

"You will drink first?" said the taller man.

"Certainly," said Tiskias.

"It is acceptable," said the taller man.

"Have the slave stand up," said he who had tended the lantern.

"Stand," said the taller man.

I stood up, as a slave, not meeting a Master's eyes, my body soft, and alive.

"Are you a free woman?" asked he who had tended the lantern.

"No, Master!" I said, frightened.

He put his hand under the leash collar on my metal collar, light, encircling my throat closely, impossible even to think of slipping.

"You understand the meaning of this?" he asked.

"Yes, Master," I said.

"What are you for?" he asked.

"To serve and please the free," I said.

"You are not unattractive," he said.

"Thank you, Master," I said. "A slave is pleased if she is found pleasing."

"What manner of garment is it which so scarcely conceals this slave?" asked he who had tended the lantern.

"A runner's tunic," said the taller man. "We pretended to rent her for a hunt."

"I prefer to run slaves naked," said he who had tended the lantern. "They are then in little doubt that they are quarry. So run, too, they are conscious of their vulnerability, and, too, aware of the inevitable end of the hunt, they are frightened, helpless, and miserable. Then, when one catches them, it is pleasant to bind them, hand and foot, as the caught, helpless prey they are."

"The runner's tunic," said the taller, half-shaven man, "makes it clear that they are legitimate prey. Otherwise, complications might occur. Matters might prove socially, even legally, awkward."

"You understand what you are to do?" asked he who had managed the lantern, setting it in its place.

"Yes, Master," I said. "I am to prepare and serve a small supper."

He of the lantern turned toward the half-shaven man. "Do you mind?" he asked.

"Not at all," said the partially shaven man.

The running tunic was then torn away.

I stood before the men, the leash strap dangling between my breasts.

"Turn slowly before us," said the fellow of the lantern, "and then face me, again."

I obeyed.

"Excellent," said the fellow of the lantern.

"Indeed," said his fellow.

I was frightened, of course, but other emotions swept through me, and about me, as well. It is difficult to make clear to those who have not worn the collar how real, how deep, how exciting, how fulfilling, how meaningful this was!

I, so exhibited, felt one with myself and nature.

Here, on Gor, I knew what I was, what I wanted to be, and what I had no choice but to be. Here I was real, more real than I had ever been on Earth. Here I knew how to act, speak, live, and be, and, indeed, what alternatives would be permitted me?

I was a form of life, the slave, which was an essential, familiar, valued part of this world, a form of life which was understood in, accepted by, and important to, this world.

In this society my position was accepted, assured, and secure.

In this society, chattel and property, I was an ingredient.

In this society, marked and collared, I was prized and desired. I was wanted.

What woman does not wish to be bought and owned? What woman does not want to kneel naked at the feet of her Master?

"Put me on the block," I thought. "I am ready! Let men bid for me!"

How far from the trivialities, conventions, hypocrisies, and pretenses of Earth I was! Here I, collared, was real, so real, so excited, so alive!

I was overwhelmed.

Now, on Gor, I, an unclothed woman, would serve clothed men.

How deep, profound, and right this seemed to me. Was this not how it should be?

If men were not the Masters, who were the Masters? What if men should choose to reassert their mastery? Might that not be done, even if bit by bit, over time? Would that not eventually return a species to a healthier, more natural order? Would we not then become more docile, more fulfilled, more attractive, more desirable?

"After supper," said he who had tended the lantern, "we will cast stones for the order of her usage."

"Agreed," said the half-shaven man and his colleague, the broader, more muscular, shorter, short-bearded man.

The fellow who had tended the lantern then turned to me.

"Get to work," he said.

"Yes, Master," I said.

"Goblet!" muttered the short-bearded man, he who had assisted in extracting me from Delka cage, thrusting his goblet toward me.

He, it seemed to me, alone of all the others, had drunk too much.

Would that the others had imbibed similarly, but they had not. In particular, the half-shaven man and he who had tended the lantern seemed suspicious and wary. I suspected that each might fear the knife of the other, and perhaps before morning.

And Tiskias, doubtless, felt ill at ease with both factions.

I was sure that if I had darted away my leash would have been in the hands of one or the other of the men before I could have splashed five or six yards from the island.

Who knows what then might have been done with me?

I, a slave girl, would have been foolish and displeasing.

But I must warn my Master!

I needed an opportunity.

I needed a diversion.

I had endeavored to create one.

I wished I had access to *tassa* powder or some similar sedative. The men drugged, I might then have waded away from the island with ease. But, alas, the men, with the exception of the short-bearded man, had remained alert and abstemious.

I saw no sign of the Kur with whom Tiskias was a confederate. At first I conjectured he might be with the ambush party, waiting to intercept Rupert of Hochburg and any men he might have with him, but I later dismissed this speculation on the grounds that he would be unlikely to interact with humans without the presence and aid of Tiskias. Lucilius, too, he of the faction of Agamemnon, who had been of such help to us, similarly tended to avoid human interactions. Men are often ready to kill what seems different or dangerous to them. In the case of the Kur, this human penchant may be less irrational than it might otherwise seem.

I took the goblet, filled it from the nearest bottle, and handed it to the short-bearded man.

He reached for it, missed it, grasped at it again, and then, spilling a bit of the fluid, centered the goblet before himself, carefully, intently, and then drank it down in a single draught.

Amongst the items in Tiskias' pantry crate, were several strips of dried *tarsk* meat and some packages of diverse cheeses. Utilizing these ingredients, plus some spices, I had rolled a number of '*tarsk* cakes.' These, when cooked and combined with the flat wedges of the typical Gorean bread, can be quite tasty. We refrained from cooking, however, because we did not wish to attract the attention of creatures which might be lurking in the water. In any event, before and during the meal, as I could, when the men were not noticing, I had cast some of these small, rolled balls of dried *tarsk* strips and cheese into the water, and then on the shore.

I noted that the fellow in motley garb who had tended the lamp was looking at me.

I approached him, and knelt.

"More wine, Master?" I asked. He and the half-shaven man were the two whom I most feared.

He stood up, grasped my leash strap, and, not releasing it, put it on the ground and pinned it in place, putting his heavy, bootlike sandal on it.

"Master?" I asked, apprehensively.

He then began to draw on the strap which in a moment or two brought my face to the dirt at his feet. My cheek was on the ground.

"Lick and kiss," he said.

I put my mouth to his high, rugged sandal.

"Better," he said, "more lengthily, more humbly, more reverently, more tenderly, more gratefully."

I began to weep, but dared not desist.

I continued my ministrations, a slave at the foot of a free man, hoping to please him.

"Stop," he said.

I trembled at his foot.

He stepped away from me.

"Your wine service was slovenly," he said.

"The other Master," I said, "was drunk. He did not care. He was not thinking! He did not mind! He wanted his drink, soon. See? He is asleep now!"

There was little doubt about that.

"Punishment position," he said.

Instantly I knelt with my head to the ground, my wrists crossed beneath my body as though bound, the bow of my back exposed to the stroke of the lash.

"Beg punishment," he said.

"I beg punishment," I said, though that would be the last thing in which, under the circumstances, I was interested.

The slave girl is subject to the whip, and she knows this, but she is seldom, if ever, whipped. Similarly she will do much to avoid the stroke of the whip. The whip hurts. There are few occasions on which a slave wishes to be whipped. One of these is when a slave feels she has failed or disappointed a beloved Master and, contrite and miserable, wishes to make amends. Another is when she wishes to be reminded that she is a slave. For many slaves, their harshest punishment is merely to be overlooked or ignored by their Master. Punishment may be physical or psychological, and it is often both. The humiliation of punishment is often more lasting and grievous than the smarting of a few blows. This is particularly the case when discipline is implemented before other slaves, this suggesting that the punished slave is a lacking slave, that she is an inadequate or inferior slave, that she is dull, incompetent, or stupid. Who but an ignorant or slow slave would require the whip to correct her behavior?

He cast aside the now-doubled leash strap, and sat down, cross-legged, some feet back from the fire.

"Serve me," he said.

I lifted my head, slightly.

"Am I not to be whipped?" I asked.

"Do you wish to be whipped?" he asked.

"No, Master," I said.

"We shall see how you serve," he said.

"Yes, Master!" I said.

I sprang up and fetched a half-emptied vessel of Market-of-Semris ruby *ka-la-na*. The Cosian wines were gone.

I poured a goblet to the second ring.

As noted earlier, the shorter, muscular man, he who had assisted his half-shaven colleague in removing me from Delka cage was asleep. By now, Tiskias, too, had fallen asleep, the effect, possibly, of having been forced to sample the contents of several newly opened bottles and at least two-leather-stopped botas.

Two fellows other than the man who had ordered me to serve him were clearly awake, the taller, half shaven man who had helped pole the raft and the fellow in motley garb who had driven the blade of his spear like a post into the island.

I approached the fellow who had tended the lantern, he who had ordered me to serve him.

I knelt, holding the goblet in two hands. The two-handed grip is common. If both hands are on the goblet, one is not holding a knife or pellet of poison.

"Hold," said the taller, half-shaven man. "Is it not time to cast stones?"

"Is it not?" said the fellow in motley garb who had handled the spear.

"Are you white silk?" asked he before whom I knelt.

"No, Master," I said. "I was scarcely marked and collared before I was thrown to keeper's feet and red-silked."

They had lost no time before attending to this triviality.

"Nonetheless," said the half-shaven man, "let us cast stones."

"Soon," said he before whom I knelt.

"Might I not," I wondered, "have them at one another's throat and escape while they were adjudicating the order of my usage?"

But, it seemed, that was not to be.

Perhaps there were understandings amongst gamblers.

In any event, it seemed that stones would rule the day, or approaching morning. Would it have been different, I wondered, had I been white silk?

Presumably not, I speculated.

"You may serve," said he before whom I knelt.

"It is a great honor for a slave to be permitted to serve a free man," I said.

I knew this was true. To understand it, one must understand the enormous chasm which separates the free and slave on Gor. The slave is not a person; she is rightless; she is goods, a purchasable object, livestock, a domestic animal suitably sold naked from a sales block. On Gor, I had learned that the free were incredibly, enormously different from myself. Sometimes I trembled in their presence. Sometimes I could barely speak. Automatically, without thought, naturally, rightfully, I went to my knees before them. Slaves were not commensurate with the free. They are other from one another. This was a given social reality, unquestioned and unchallenged. I had not been more than two or three days on Gor before I had not only understood and accepted, but wholly internalized, this distinction. I had discovered who I was, and what I should be, a slave. It was incontrovertible. It was real, like mountains and rivers, like the ground and the sky. I had become a marked, collared domestic animal, and one who knew that she belonged at the feet of the free.

"You may serve me," he said.

"Thank you, Master," I said.

I was thrilled to use the word 'Master.' How clearly, in the use of that simple word, was manifested and acknowledged the fact that I was not free, but something owned, a belonging. I wondered if there were men on Earth who so desired a woman, who so wanted her, so profoundly, so intensely and fiercely, that nothing less would satisfy them than having her at their feet, a naked, collared slave. And I wondered, too, if there were not women on Earth, needful, ready, eager, and passionate, perhaps lonely and deprived, perhaps neglected and overlooked, perhaps disappointed with prescribed, recommended, emasculated, reduced males, who might not hope one day to be noticed, claimed, and collared.

I pressed the edge of the metal goblet, filled to the second ring, against my lower belly. I then lifted the goblet, with two hands, and, over the lifted rim, as a slave, regarded he who had tended the lantern. I then kissed my side of the goblet, as a slave, and then put my head down between my lifted, extended arms, proffering him the drink.

He had scarcely sipped the wine when the taller, half-shaven man called out, "The stones, bring the stones!"

He who had tended the lantern finished his drink, rather abruptly, lay the goblet to the side, and rose to his feet.

The taller man then began to prod his colleague, the shorter, more muscular man, with his feet. "Wake up!" he said. "Be awake!"

The second fellow in motley garb, he whose spear was upright, to the side, fetched forth a small wooden box. He shook it, and I heard the clatter of the housed gambling stones. He seemed, in the lantern light, as much a denizen of the swamp as any serpent, fish, bird or *tharlarion* in the vicinity.

As the men gathered together to cast the stones to determine the order of my usage I rose to my feet and made my way to the shore of the island. When the men had not been looking, I had rolled some of the prepared food balls into the water there, and placed three or four on the beach, hoping to lure some creature onto the island, which, I hoped, would create a diversion of which I might take advantage.

Apparently this stratagem had been unsuccessful.

Some yards behind me, near the lantern, I heard the stones being shaken in the box, from which receptacle they would be scattered to the ground.

Time was short.

It would soon be light.

It would then be impossible to escape.

I was afraid to enter into the water of the swamp forest, here or elsewhere, but if I were to move much about, or pass the men, I would be noticed.

I looked back at the gamblers.

"My throw," I heard the taller man snarl.

I wrapped the leash strap several times about my throat and fitted the free end under the other coils. I did not want the strap to be loose where it might be seized or tangled in brush or debris.

It also occurred to me that I might pick up one or another of the food balls I had left on the shore. Might they not give me needed strength in the swamp?

It would be easy enough to wash them in the water.

As it was still dark and the lantern was yards behind me, it was difficult to see. I bent down, feeling about.

I thought I knew, very closely, where I had cast the food balls.

Then I stood up, frightened.

They were gone!

There was a furrow of dirt at my foot.

Something narrow had moved there.

What happened then remains a blur, a sudden chill, a water-shedding, bursting forth in my memory.

Something had been in the water, large, floating, and almost motionless, perhaps watching. It may have been attracted to the light of the lantern, like something different or alive in the night. But yet the flickering was unlike moving. How long had it been there? I did not know. I conjectured it might have only recently arrived. Perhaps it had nothing to do with the lantern. Perhaps it had merely been following a smaller object, something narrow, something which had found one or more of the food balls in the water, something which had then followed their trail onto the island, something which I might have lifted in two hands. Or was its patience at an end? Did it fear it might lose its quarry? Or was it unrelated to some small scavenger in the night? Perhaps it was my presence, so near the water's edge, like a *tabuk* or *verr* come to drink, which decided the matter? I do not know.

In any event, with a sudden snort and bellow, a lengthy, gigantic shape burst forth from the water, scrambling up the beach, propelled by short, thick, stubby legs. I screamed. Almost at my feet a small body scuttled past. And, almost at the same time, the snout of the thick-scaled beast, startled, jerked slightly to my right. It, in its rush, struck and abraded my right leg. The body was still wet from the water, and, oddly, from its rough, scoring passage, I had the sensation that my leg was bleeding and the water scalding.

"*Tharlarion!*" cried one of the men.

"Kill it!" said another.

"Drive it away!" begged Tiskias, who, I gathered, had awakened with the commencement of the gambling. I did not think the others would permit him to join in the gaming.

The fellow in motley garb who had been armed with the spear, the presence of which now seemed not only explicable but more than well justified to me, seized it and worked it up and out of the dirt.

The small object which had scurried past my foot, had darted to the side, and disappeared in the darkness.

The large, short-legged *tharlarion* was some yards up the beach. It was still, now, save for an occasional small motion of its heavy tail. Its hunt, it seemed, had been frustrated. Such beasts, for a short distance, can outrun a man, but it is hard for them, given their weight and inertia, to make sharp turns. Thus, evolution has selected for erratic flight patterns in their likely prey species. Thus, the common swamp *tharlarion* tends to fare better when its presence is not suspected by the prey animal, when it is immobile, as it may remain for hours, or its approach is unnoticed.

The fellow with the spear was now shouting at the *tharlarion* and prodding and striking it with the butt of his spear. It is not easy to penetrate the thickness of its overlapping scales. Too, most wild animals tend to find noise aversive. *Larls* and *sleen*, for example, will commonly withdraw from beaters, even women and children, crying out and beating on pots and pans. The taller man, the half-shaven man and his colleague, the shorter, short-bearded, muscular man, had doubly armed themselves, a knife in one hand, a sword in the other. He who had tended the lantern now had the lantern, lifted from its rocky shelf, in one hand and a sword in the other. Tiskias cowered in the background, his right hand slipped within his robe, up, near the left shoulder.

"Turn it about, turn it back," said the man from whose left hand dangled the lantern. The fellow with the spear jabbed at the *tharlarion* with the butt of the spear. It raised its massive head with that long, heavy snout lined with thick, pointed teeth and hissed like oil being poured into flames. "Go, go!" screamed the men, with the exception of Tiskias who, his hand still within his robes, near his left shoulder, apparently clutching something, backed away, to the side.

The *tharlarion* then, still hissing, still threatening the men, its huge tail thrashing, began to back away toward the water.

"Good, good!" shouted he with the lantern.

"Away, oaf!" cried the taller, half-shaven man. "Nothing for you here, monstrous dolt! Go! Go!"

He and his shorter fellow kicked dirt at the retreating *tharlarion.*

As the attention of the men, including Tiskias, was centered on the angry, still dangerous, and certainly annoyed, *tharlarion,* I sped away, to the side, past the men. I feared to enter the water near the point from which the *tharlarion* had emerged. The lantern light and the location of Tiskias were soon behind me.

At the opposite shore of the tiny island my nerve failed me.

To my misery and shame I dared not enter the water.

Did I not know what might lurk within it?

I crouched down, concealing myself in a stand of fleshy, broad-leafed shrubbery, some of the roots of which trailed in the water.

I could see the lantern approaching.

"The slave!" I heard. "Find her!"

"Let her go," said a man. "She has served her purpose, to lead Rupert of Hochburg into an inescapable trap."

"No!" screamed Tiskias. "After her!"

"Leave her to the swamp," said another.

"No!" cried Tiskias. "Catch her!"

"Catch her yourself!" said a man. I think it was he who had wielded the spear. "If you think I am going to pursue a slave at night in the swamp, you are mad."

"My colleague wants her," wailed Tiskias.

"Let him catch her himself," he said.

"For such insolence," said Tiskias, "your head could be torn from your body."

"I think not," said he of the spear.

"Morning will be soon enough," said he whom I took to be the half-shaven man.

The lantern was now nearby, lifted in the hand of he who had commonly tended it. "She is not a fool," he said. "She knows the danger. She is still on the island."

I crouched even lower in the shrubbery. Tears stung my eyes. How right he was. What a coward I was!

But who would choose to be seized in the jaws of a *tharlarion*, to be held under water until one drowned, and then be eaten?

The island was tiny.

Even a cursory search would soon uncover me.

I considered my Master, innocently, unwittingly, having been tricked, following a false trail with perhaps two or three companions, a trail that would expose him to the ambush of perhaps half a hundred or more men.

I was terrified, but knew what I must do.

A moment later I felt the warm, sluggish water of the swamp swirling about my body.

CHAPTER NINETY-SEVEN

I remember little of my flight through the swamp, a nightmare of shadows and feelings, of miseries and alarms, ending in a moment of terror.

I had thrust myself into the water and begun wading, away from the island, out from the island. I hoped, soon, however, despite the danger, to circle about and put myself back on the line of tufted wands, to find my way back to where, at the edge of the swamp, the raft had originally been hidden.

I stumbled about, wading in the darkness, sometimes slipping and falling, in various depths of water. Despite what I had heard on the island I feared pursuit, and certainly pursuit as soon as it was light. I wanted to find the island to orient myself in the swamp, but I did not want to come too close to it as I did not wish to risk discovery. Most often the water was to my knees or waist. Sometimes my progress was arrested as I tried to force my way through, or evade, thick tangles of swamp growth. More than once I changed my direction, sensing, or seeming to sense, a shape in the darkness. Once, too, something had touched my leg. I had stifled a scream and fled blindly away. Always, naively as it turned out, I was confident that I knew where I was, at least with respect to the vicinity of the island camp of Tiskias. Once I feared I had actually come upon it, but there were no signs of habitation or use there. Then I realized that there were probably innumerable islands or bars of that sort in the vastness of the forest.

Shortly thereafter, in the darkness, to my misery, I realized I was lost.

I knew the swamp forest was large but I had no idea how large it was or, now, where I was within it. From one location, one might leave the forest within hours, from another, it might take days.

I felt about in the darkness, in the water to my waist.

I felt nothing.

I felt lost in darkness and space.

I was terribly afraid.

I began to fear I was losing my mind.

Were there voices in the swamp?

"Tal. I am Nar. May I be of service?"

"No!" I screamed. "Go away!"

I tried to thrust back time.

I could not do so.

I was confused.

I was frightened.

Was I losing my mind?

How much stress and fear can a human mind take, before it bends and breaks, before it crumbles and shatters?

I could not be here.

Should I not be on Earth?

Was this not a dream?

Was I not Agnes Morrison Atherton, educated and sophisticated, shy and reserved, so formal, correct, and untouchable?

Was I not a person? Was I not free?

"No," I said. "Do not lie. Do not deceive yourself. This is not a dream. You are not a person. You can be bought and sold. You are a property, a domestic animal. You are not free. You are a slave. Are you not collared? Beware your thoughts, slave. Do you wish to be punished, and as the slave you are?"

Surely I had never expected to be a collared slave on another world, let alone one so pristine, fresh, beautiful, and perilous.

But I had been put in a collar, and on such a world.

On such a world I had learned what I was, what I had long suspected I was, even on Earth.

I belonged in a collar.

Now, how could I warn my beloved Master, he who had set me aside, he whom I had so displeased, he who was so disgusted with me?

How could I save my beloved Master, he who was so disappointed with me, he who scorned me, he whose loathing I so richly deserved?

Tears of helpless frustration came to my eyes.

I sensed a stirring in the water. I remained absolutely still.

I feared that, at any moment, the jaws of some *tharlarion* would close on my leg and pull me down, under the water.

I knew it must soon be light.

I knew the orientation of the swamp to Ar. Ar would be to the north. In an hour or so, there would be at least the hint of the kindly, friendly, warming, glimmering rays of Tor-tu-Gor on the horizon.

Rather than wandering further about then, aimlessly, forlornly, in the swamp, perhaps with each step lengthening the distance to Ar, or, quite possibly, given the likely subtle difference between the stride of the right and left legs, unwittingly describing large circles, I decided I would wait until morning.

I must now, as soon as possible, the decision made, get out of the water, finding dry land, a bar or island, on which to wait in comparative safety until light.

I had not wandered far before I encountered some tendrils or roots in the water by means of which, in the darkness, clutching them, holding them, guiding myself by them, I came to a shrubbery of fleshy, broad-leafed undergrowth, half in the water. I was reminded of the growths in which I had earlier concealed myself on the small island before entering the water. I then crawled ashore. I did not want to remain near the water, fearing what it might contain or conceal, so I crawled some yards up the shallow beach.

I was sure it would soon be light.

My Master was not expected before late afternoon.

Hopefully, before that time, I might manage to intercept him, and warn him of the danger threatening him, a danger he did not anticipate, one of which he would know nothing.

I lay down on the slope leading up from the beach.

I was tired, very tired.

I had been hours in the swamp, wading about, lost and confused, half mad with fear, not knowing if each step might be my last.

It would soon be light.

I was afraid for my life. I was afraid for my Master's life.

I was afraid to re-enter the swamp, but I knew that I would do so.

I was very tired.

It would soon be light.

It would not hurt to close my eyes.

I awakened with a start.

It was light.

Tor-tu-Gor blazed over the swamp, almost overhead.

I leaped to my feet, dismayed.

Too long I had slept.

I looked about, wildly.

Then I was more afraid than ever. I saw a lantern, unlit, on its rocky shelf. That shelf was familiar. To the left of the shelf, a small clearing was no more than some few yards before me. In the clearing, as though dropped or discarded, I saw a small wooden box. Some gambling stones were near it, in the dirt, apparently tumbled from it.

In my confusion in the night, searching for a small bar or island on which to escape the swamp and wait until morning, I had inadvertently returned to the same island from which I had earlier fled.

My consternation was acute.

I remained absolutely still, every sense alive.

But I saw no sign of life on the island.

Then, from behind, a heavy hand was placed over my mouth and I was pulled back, tightly, suddenly, forcibly, against a leather jacket and the large metal buckle on a transverse-slung sword belt.

CHAPTER NINETY-EIGHT

I could not see who held me.

I was held in place, tightly.

I was helpless.

After a time, I stopped my futile struggles.

Docility in a slave is commonly accepted as her acknowledgement of her capture, that she is now under male control. Free women, of course, who are not slave trained, do not always understand this. They will sometimes pretend to complaisance, only to embark on a new act of escape or resistance. This deceit is seldom tolerated by a captor. The perpetrator then is commonly knife stripped to avoid poisoned needles which might be concealed in her robes. Incidentally, Goreans distinguish between 'face-stripping' and 'body-stripping.' Interestingly, at least from the Earth point of view, Goreans regard face-stripping as a far more serious matter than body-stripping, presumably because bodies, however lovely, seem more alike and are less expressive than faces. Surely a woman's individuality, specialness, uniqueness, beauty, and identity are more marvelously manifested in her face than her body. This Gorean notion also, I suspect, influences their frequently encountered view that most Earth women are shameless, and begging for the collar. There is no denying, at any rate, that the naked, or bared, faces of most women of Earth, is a boon for slavers, rendering their work far easier than might otherwise be the case. On Gor, of course, slaves are not permitted facial veiling. Who would consider veiling a domestic animal? The bared face of the slave thus, rather like the distinctive garmenture of the slave, further distinguishes her from free women, particularly those of the high castes. Free men, of course, seldom object to the bared faces of women, free or slave, no more than to scrutinizing and appraising other such delights. Returning to the case of the free woman who might insincerely or fraudulently signify docility or surrender and then betray or retract that signification, little need be said. The least that is likely to be done to her is to fully strip her, tie her hands with her own hair behind the back of her neck, and beat her. Soon she is kneeling at the boots of the men, endeavoring to make amends. She has learned that men are not to be trifled with.

As soon as I stopped struggling, the large, firm hand was removed from my mouth and I was released.

I stood, shuddering.

I knew enough not to scream.

The wild thought clawed at me to betray the indulgence I had been accorded, my release, and dart to the side, to try to dive again into the swamp. Fortunately, I did not yield to this temptation. I knew men, and I was not a naive free woman. I would have been instantly taken in hand, and forced to accept the consequences of my indiscretion. The promptings of hysteria are seldom a wise or useful guide to action.

Too, after the first moment of abject terror, I realized that my captor was unlikely to be either one of the two slave thieves who had delivered me to Tiskias or either of the two fellows in motley garb who had been with him on the island. None of these had worn leather or had had the belt of their sword sheath worn over the shoulder. The danger of the waist belt is that its attached sheath, loose and empty, might be seized in the confusion and tumult of battle. Warriors, accordingly, commonly wear either the simple over the shoulder sheath or the 'across the body over the shoulder' sheath. In both of these arrangements the belt and sheath may be easily discarded and thus will not constitute a possible liability. If interaction with enemies is likely to be immediate the simple over the shoulder belt tends to be preferred. In normal circumstances, the 'across the body over the shoulder' belt is standard. The buckle I had felt against my back indicated the across the body over the shoulder arrangement. Any of these three arrangements, of course, the scabbard-to-the waist arrangement or the two 'over the shoulder' arrangements, might be used by any swordsman. In either of the two latter arrangements, the over-the-shoulder arrangements, it is easy to grasp the sheath and draw the weapon, after which the belt and sheath, if one wishes, may be discarded. When the scabbard is anchored to or near the waist belt, the one-hand draw is practical.

Standing, half in shock, I knew enough to realize little more than the fact that I had fallen into the hands of neither the two brigands who had brought me to Tiskias or the two fellows who had been with him on the island. I did not know, of course, the identity of my captor or captors, other than that he or they would be enleagued with Tiskias. I knew that from his, or their, presence on the island to which I had inadvertently returned. They must be fellow brigands. Perhaps, even, they had been recruited from the larger group waiting to ambush my Master, to assist in the search for a fugitive slave. But why, I wondered, would they risk men in the swamp to pursue a mere slave? Then I recalled that I seemed to be of importance to the Kur whom I associated with Tiskias, who claimed it as his pet. It seemed it wanted vengeance for a plot foiled, that it wanted the blood of a slave and that of her Master, Rupert of Hochburg.

I saw no point in running, certainly not at present.

Then I shivered.

How distraught, how shaken, I was!

I was on my feet!

Did I know nothing?

Was I not in a collar, a Gorean collar!

I swiftly knelt, head down, facing away from my captor. I shuddered, fearing to be beaten.

"It is about time," said a voice.

I spun about on my knees, looking up, wildly. "Master!" I cried. I began to laugh and cry. I put my head down, shaking with emotion, my lips to his boot.

CHAPTER NINETY-NINE

"Keep your voice low," said Rupert of Hochburg.

"Beware, Master," I said, softly. "Enemies may be about, Tiskias, and at least four confederates."

"Perhaps one far worse," he said.

"Yes, Master," I said.

"How is it that you are here?" he asked, seemingly genuinely puzzled at my presence.

"How is it that Master is here?" I asked, bewildered.

"Speak," he said.

"Two slave thieves, on the pretext of renting a sport runner, removed me from Master Tenalian's Delka cage in his compound outside Ar, and delivered me to this island, into the hands of Tiskias of Venna."

"Why would they do that?" he asked.

"To ensnare Master," I said. "If I were not again in custody in Delka cage by noon today, you were to be notified. It was then anticipated that you, and some others, would follow the thieves to recover me."

"I see," he said.

"—If only to protect your investment and subject the thieves to the unpleasant consequences of their action," I said.

"I understand," he said.

"It was all a stratagem," I said. "A false trail, presumably an obvious one, has been laid down, which you were expected to follow, a trail ending in a trap where you, and any few with you, as you were pursuing only two thieves, would be easily and summarily dealt with."

"And I," he said, "am expected to follow that trail, which is allegedly obvious, and I am to assume that two professional slave thieves were so inadept as to leave such a trail?"

"I fear so," I said.

"And when is all this supposed to take place?" he asked.

"Presumably the ambush is to take place today, most likely in the late afternoon."

"You are filthy," he said.

"I spent much of the night in the swamp," I said.

"Where is the Delka tunic?" he asked.

"It was removed in Delka cage," I said, "and I was issued a runner's tunic. That tunic, the runner's tunic, was torn away last night that I might prepare and serve supper suitably, as a nude slave."

"Excellent," he said.

The removal of clothing helps us to keep in mind that we are not free women but slaves.

"You are in a lock leash," he said.

"It is leather," I said. "It can be cut away with a knife."

Some lock leashes are of metal and chain.

"Why were you wandering about in the swamp?" he asked. "That is dangerous, even in the light."

"I wanted to warn you of the trap," I said.

"You would risk your life to do so?" he asked.

"You are my Master," I said. "You are in great danger. Why did you put your life at risk to recover me?"

"I did not," he said. "I thought you were still in Delka cage."

"Of course," I said, bitterly. Did I not know I was a slave? "Master must be startled to find me here," I said.

"I am," he said, "as, I gather, you are to find me here."

"How is it that Master is here?" I asked. "Surely it is dangerous. Where are Tiskias, and his four confederates."

"I know the location of two," he said, "but of only two, two on whom you might not care to look."

"I do not understand," I said.

"Distilled, concentrated ost venom," he said, "administered by the scratch of poisoned needles."

"There are some fifty cohorts or so in the swamp," I said, "waiting to ambush you."

"We shall hope to disappoint them," he said.

"So Master's presence here," I said, "has nothing to do with me?"

"No," he said.

"So then it has to do with Tiskias," I said.

"And more so with another," he said.

"Of late," I said, "I have seen little or nothing of the other."

"We let Tiskias believe he contrived an escape from our custody by means of bribing an officer," he said. "Tiskias, given his character, found nothing dubious or out of the ordinary in this. Is not everything for sale, at one price or another? Holt of Ar was cooperative. Then we monitored the movements of Tiskias, certain that he would attempt, sooner or later, to make contact with his allied Kur. It is the Kur we most fear and wish to encounter. Monitoring the movements of Tiskias, we were led to the swamp forest. Late last night we struck.

To our surprise, the island seemed muchly deserted. We found the bodies of two fellows who had met a most unpleasant death, fellows in variegated garb. Other than that, there was only Tiskias, who was easily taken into custody. We found no others."

"There were two," I said. "There was a raft."

"It was gone," he said.

"There was no sign of a beast, a Kur?" I said.

"No," he said.

"What might have accounted for their departure?" I asked.

"I do not know," he said.

"Are you alone?" I asked.

"No," he said. "I have Holt of Ar and Desmond of Hochburg with me. Temicus, of the Builders, is with the company."

"With you are only two?" I said.

"In the scales of war," he said, "brigands are weighed with copper, warriors with richer metals."

"Tiskias must know why the slave thieves departed," I said.

"Probably," he said.

From somewhere, carrying over the swamp, there came a long, wild, horrid cry, which abruptly ended. A minute or two later, there was another such cry which, too, ended abruptly.

CHAPTER ONE HUNDRED

"You cannot do this!" cried Tiskias. "You cannot leave me here like this!"

"You are mistaken," said Rupert of Hochburg.

"Untie me!" begged Tiskias.

"I suspect," said Rupert of Hochburg, "that your charming pet understands by now that you were so clumsy as to have allowed your movements to be traced, the outcome of which is that you have spoiled his plan to do away with a warrior and a slave, and have brought him himself into the vicinity of enemies and pursuers."

"I was betrayed by the knave, Holt of Ar," he said. "I gave him gold to free me of chains and conduct me from your camp."

"Which he did," said my Master. "Surely you do not expect your money to be refunded."

"I was followed!" said Tiskias.

"I am sure your friend is aware of that," said Rupert. "Perhaps he will overlook the matter."

"Why am I bound like this?" asked Tiskias. His hands were tied behind his back and his neck was roped to a stake, one of several in the small square. He was on his feet.

"So that you might move about, try to pull away, cry out, and the better evince anxiety and terror," said Rupert.

"I do not understand," said Tiskias.

"Surely you are aware that such movements and sounds intrigue and stimulate a predator."

"Free me," he begged.

"Recall, if you will, the antics of a bleating, terrified *verr* staked out for the apprehension of a prowling *sleen* or *larl*," said Rupert.

"I am not a *verr*!" cried Tiskias. "I am a free man!"

"Quite so," said Rupert. "But you are also bait."

"There is a slave behind you," cried Tiskias. "She is a beast. Stake her out for any passing predator! She can be easily replaced, perhaps even with copper."

"At the moment," said Rupert, "your life is not worth a tarsk bit. Thus, at the moment, she is worth several times what you are worth."

"Let me go!" whined Tiskias.

"Shall we gag him?" asked Holt of Ar.

"No, let him squeal and bleat," said Rupert.

"He could then warn the Kur," said Holt.

"The Kur needs no warning," said Rupert. "It understands the nature of bait."

"It will then be wary," said Holt of Ar.

"Of course," said Rupert.

"What shall we do now, Captain?" said Desmond of Hochburg.

"We shall retire now, to wait within a nearby hut," said Rupert.

"As a hunter concealed by a blind," said Holt.

"Surely," said Rupert.

The plot devised by Tiskias and his putative pet, the Kur of the faction of Pompilius, had failed of its purpose. Prior even to its inception, the movements of, and the whereabouts of, Tiskias had fallen within the cognizance of Rupert of Hochburg. Some five days ago Tiskias, who was familiar with the haunts and habits of the Kur of the faction of Pompilius, had made his first brief contact with his fellow. This was reported to Rupert by the scouts appointed to follow and report on Tiskias. Two contacts later, it appeared that Tiskias and the Kur had joined forces, and, for some reason, had established a headquarters of a sort in the large swamp forest south of Ar. Rupert, of course, knew nothing of their plans to entrap him, by luring him into the forest to recover a stolen slave. Had the plot been successful, the Kur, in one brilliant move, would have wrought his vengeance on both a warrior and a slave. As soon as it had become clear that Tiskias and the Kur had joined one another, establishing a camp in the swamp forest, Rupert, with two cohorts, Holt of Ar and Desmond of Hochburg, had dismissed their scouts, availed themselves of hunting spears, and prepared to close personally with the foe. Their attack on the camp, in which they had approached it from three sides at the same time, took place sometime after I had fled the camp and had found myself lost and disoriented in the swamp.

What Rupert and his two fellows found, following their surprise attack on the camp, were two bodies, each clothed in motley garb, and Tiskias. The features of the two contorted bodes were drawn with pain and horror. Their skin, too, was dried and discolored, with an orangish hue, and cracked, as though it might have been exposed to the blaze of some inner fire. There was no sign of a Kur, though the deep claw prints of such a beast were discovered in the vicinity of a lantern.

Tiskias, stunned and shocked at the sudden, unexpected arrival of Rupert and his fellows, was easily disarmed and subdued. Bewildered and dismayed, babbling, roped, at sword point, he had presented a voluble account of what had occurred.

The two fellows of the swamp, those in motley garb, and two brigands from Ar, each pair wary of the other, had begun to exchange views and discuss options. Two considerations seemed paramount. First, a coin in the purse was likely to prove preferable to two or three not in the purse, and certainly to several which might not even exist. Second, the men were reluctant to have anything to do with what might prove to be an unpredictable, dangerous, possibly irrational beast, a Kur. The fellows in motley garb, prior to that night, had not even known that Kurii existed, and had, one supposes, not been pleased to learn that they shared their world with so large, cunning, and dangerous a life form. Of the slave thieves, only one had actually seen a Kur, some two years before, in Ar, and, apparently, he was not eager to see one again. The two fellows in motley garb were more prone to action than the pair of slave thieves, possibly because they better knew the forest and might the more easily disappear within it. Accordingly, the fellows in motley garb challenged Tiskias for his gold, whether it should be on his person or concealed locally, perhaps buried in a nearby sack or jar. While this interrogation was taking place, the slave thieves stood aside, waiting to assess the outcome of the matter, and, presumably, share in, or dispute, the proceeds. Tiskias' protests, as one might suppose, however eloquent or well-reasoned, were unavailing, and he soon realized that he was in immediate danger of torture or death, or both, torture to obtain information as to hidden gold, and death to eliminate a witness, thereby in theory foiling pursuit by a possibly avenging Kur. Too, of course, from the point of view of the fellows in motley garb and the slave thieves, there was something of an urgency in this matter, as the ally of Tiskias, the Kur, might at any time make its appearance.

"Desist!" had cried Tiskias. "Be content! Be patient! All will be well! You must wait! Wealth is on its way! I aver it so."

"Gold, now," had insisted one of the men in motley garb, drawing his belt knife.

"Intervene!" Tiskias had begged the two brigands from Ar. "Protect me! Become rich!"

Neither had moved.

"Relinquish your coin," said one. "Reveal where it is hidden," said the other.

"Save me!" had begged Tiskias.

"Be done with whining," said he closest to Tiskias, he who had drawn his belt knife. "We are one, and are adamantly so resolved."

"Perhaps he cannot understand our demands," said the other fellow in motley garb. "Write them on his face and body, in large script, in letters of blood."

"That is unnecessary," said Tiskias. "I am eager to accede, and am gratefully so!"

"Remember," said he with the knife, "we want more than what was in your purse. You are a clever fellow. You will have gold hidden about the camp."

"There was little enough even in my purse," said Tiskias. "There is none elsewhere."

"It seems," said he with the knife, "your death will be prolonged and unpleasant."

"No!" cried Tiskias, and, wildly, seemingly hysterically, seized a handful of coins which had been concealed within his robes and cast them over the heads of the two fellows in motley garb in such a way that the coins fell to the ground between them and the two slave thieves. The fellows in motley garb, crying out, spun about angrily and they and the slave thieves, the latter facing forward, rushed to retrieve the coins. This diversion accomplished, Tiskias reached high within his robes at the left shoulder, opened a sheaf of poisoned needles such as free women sometimes carry about themselves, and fell on the forest brigands whose backs were turned and the slave thieves, all of whom were looking down, scrambling to seize the coins.

For a moment the forest brigands, intent on the coins, did not even understand what was happening. They might not even have attended to the sudden stinging about their backs and necks. The two slave thieves, on the other hand, facing the charging Tiskias, could not help but be aware, if only on the upper edge of their vision, of the form rushing toward them. Lifting their heads, they instantly realized their jeopardy, leapt up, drew their weapons and warned Tiskias back.

One of the men in motley garb, he who had drawn his knife threatening Tiskias, stood up, unsteadily. "The coins are moving," he said. "They shrink in size, they dissolve, they disappear."

"You are dying, fool," said one of the slave thieves. "You have been struck by the ost of the free woman."

The other fellow in motley garb struggled to his feet.

Tiskias had withdrawn some yards. He still gripped needles.

"Slay the little tarsk while you can," said one of the slave thieves. "You have only moments in which to do so."

He himself made no move to approach Tiskias.

The fellow who had drawn the knife took a step toward Tiskias.

"Dear friends," said Tiskias. "Perhaps you would prefer to live. If I am slain, how can I prepare the antidote for you?"

"The antidote!" cried the fellow who had drawn the knife. "Give me the antidote, now, quickly, or die!"

"Give me a moment, and I shall prepare it," called Tiskias.

"Kill him now, instantly," said one of the slave thieves. "He dallies. He plays for time. There is no antidote for the bite of the free woman's ost."

"It will take only an Ehn," called Tiskias.

The fellow who had struggled to his feet, somewhat behind the other, suddenly clutched at his throat, spun about and fell writhing to the ground.

The fellow who had drawn the knife took another step toward Tiskias and then he, too, lost his footing and fell to the ground.

"Perhaps," said Tiskias to the slave thieves, "you might withdraw. The aftereffects of the free woman's ost are difficult to watch. They could turn the stomach of a *tharlarion*."

"Surely we have time enough to cut out your dishonest, cowardly heart," said one of the slave thieves.

"You must not begrudge me the efficacy of so practical and convenient a weapon," said Tiskias. "Why should such a utility be confined to free women?"

"Craven tarsk," snarled one of the slave thieves.

"I trust that we, as friends, will not be reduced to the futility of denouncing one another?" said Tiskias.

"Poison is a woman's weapon," said one of the slave thieves.

"Venom itself draws no such distinction," said Tiskias. "It bestows itself without prejudice, rejecting no one, being free to all."

"To employ so subtle and lethal a weapon is dishonorable," said the other slave thief.

"With what authority does one such as you speak of honor?" asked Tiskias.

"Our swords will speak for us, and as they please," said a slave thief.

"Fear the ruined bodies before you, between us, at your very feet," said Tiskias. "Be away! Dread the contagion. It spreads more swiftly than the Bazi plague. Even now it reaches out for you."

"Let us flee!" said one of the slave thieves.

"Stay where you are," said the other. "He takes us for ignorant dullards. There is no contagion with the ost of the free woman. The poison is without effect until it swims in your blood. Otherwise, it would be universally outlawed."

"I discover, regrettably," said Tiskias, "that you are well informed."

"Your ruse is transparent and ineffectual," said the slave thief. "Prepare to die."

"Who will approach me first?" asked Tiskias.

"How speak you so?" asked a slave thief. "What does it matter?"

"It matters not to me," said Tiskias. "But it might matter to he who first approaches me, for he shall surely die, and perhaps his fellow a moment after."

"How is this?" asked a slave thief.

"These needles I grasp," said Tiskias, "can be hurled, rather like the famed, dreaded darts of Anango, except that each, unlike its Anango brothers, carries its cargo of poison."

The slave thieves hesitated, each glancing to the other.

"I can cast these needles well before your steel can touch me," said Tiskias, "and at so close a distance I cannot miss."

There was silence.

"If I may," said Tiskias, "I propose a compromise which might prove acceptable to all parties. You give me my life and I give you yours. And I enrich the arrangement thusly. Pick up the gold which now lies strewn about. It means much more to you than it does to me, as I can have it replenished elsewhere, at another time."

"What of the gold hidden on the island?" asked one of the slave thieves.

"There is no such gold," said Tiskias.

"How do I know that is true?" asked a slave thief.

"You do not," said Tiskias.

"We are two, and you are one," said the slave thief. "One of us may sleep whilst the other watches. When you sleep you are at our mercy."

"If you wish, charge now," said Tiskias. "I think the odds are well in my favor."

"We can wait," said one of the slave thieves.

"I do not think so," had said Tiskias. "I am expecting my loyal pet, Bubu, to arrive at any moment. He is somewhat overdue already."

The two slave thieves then looked about. The swamp was lush about them. All appeared peaceful.

They then gathered up the coins, freed their raft of its tether, and poled away from the island.

It seems that shortly thereafter, the Kur made its appearance, was given an account of doings on the island, and then addressed himself once more to the swamp. That is why he was not on the island when Rupert of Hochburg, and his two fellows, Holt of Ar and Desmond of Hochburg, converged on the island from three sides. Tiskias fell into their hands, but the Kur, their primary objective, much to their disappointment, did not. Later, in examining the island, toward noon, Rupert had discovered, and grasped, a slave.

It was now late afternoon.

Peeping through a crack in the wall of the small hut, one could see the bound, tethered Tiskias, stripped to an underrobe, at the stake.

The margins of the large swamp, naturally, like those of other natural features, hills, meadows, lakes, and such, are irregular. As the swamp might intrude into the land, so, too, the land can intrude into the swamp. In any event, our makeshift camp was on what might be thought of as a small peninsula of land thrust into the swamp. It was surrounded on three sides by water. On this small peninsula were the remains of a small, abandoned peasant village, possibly once a seasonal village, an ancillary village, one most likely associated with a larger village somewhere else, the smaller village to be tenanted at various times, depending on fishing, hunting, particular sowings and reapings, and so on.

I was now clothed, though as a slave.

The Masters had been kind.

I had been permitted to fashion a garment from some pieces of sacking found in one of the small huts of the abandoned village. A small, sharp stick well served as an awl, and lengths of twisted cloth run through the holes functioned nicely as thread. In the end I had improvised something which might be likened to a ta-teera, though an actual ta-teera, designed to seem to the casual observer little more than a degrading slave rag, would be likely to be far more artfully, skillfully, and cunningly designed. Things are not always what they seem. Rupert of Hochburg, had demanded that the improvised garment I was fashioning be longer and more ample than a typical slave garment, apparently in order that he, and his fellows, would not become uneasy. It does not take long for a slave to learn that she is not powerless. She soon becomes aware of the effect she might have on a virile male. I was still in the lock leash, the coils of its strap wound about my throat.

"By now," I said, "had things proceeded according to the plan of Tiskias and his allied Kur, you would have all been killed or captured."

"Possibly not," said Rupert. "If the trail laid for us to follow, that leading into a trap, was as clear as you suggested, our suspicions would have been aroused. In war, that which seems a boon must always be suspected. Competent enemies seldom give gifts to foes."

"Perhaps," I said, "they were incompetent, or, more likely, thought that your desire to recover your stolen property would be so intense that you might put caution aside."

"Why might they think that?" he asked.

"Forgive me, Master," I said. "It was a foolish suggestion."

Indeed, how foolish it was!

Tiskias and the Kur thought, for some reason, I was sure, that I, though a mere slave, might mean much to Rupert of Hochburg, that he might even care for me, that he might be desperate to recover me.

Certainly some men so desired their slaves that they would risk their lives in such ventures. Might not Ubars undertake wars for their recovery, braving armies and risking fleets? Might not lesser men cross burning deserts and trek freezing trails, wade amongst sharks and enter the dens of ferocious beasts? "But how little," I thought bitterly, "did I mean to Rupert of Hochburg!" I had fallen from favor, if ever I had been in favor. He now despised me. He would rid himself of me. I was scheduled to be sold in Ar. To be sure, even if I meant little or nothing to him, I was property and a principle might be involved. Is one to rob with impunity from those who know the ways of steel? And who better knows such ways than those who have earned, and wear, the scarlet cloak?

"It is best to overestimate an enemy," said Rupert of Hochburg. "If one is in error, one is merely embarrassed. One might even be pleasantly surprised. If one underestimates an enemy, and one is mistaken, one may be dead."

"Fifty or more men," I said, "lie in wait for you even now. What happens when you do not appear?"

"They will wait for a time," said Rupert. "Perhaps we are late, or have been detained. Perhaps we are so inane as to have missed the fraudulent trail, despite its embarrassing conspicuousness. Then, annoyed and desolate, they will cast about, searching for their elusive prey. In any event, I think our business here will be soon complete, certainly well before they appear on any horizon of ours."

"It was hard to look upon the two bodies on the island," I said.

"They may have been brigands or felons," said Rupert, "but they were men, and thought of men as men think of men. They commonly think no further than clubs and blades. But poison in a vial can be as deadly as steel in a scabbard."

"Poison is dishonorable?" I said.

"It is generally frowned upon by men," said Rupert. "Its use is foresworn even by those of the Black Caste. Perhaps it is too much like the ost, small, unseen, furtive, unsuspected, difficult to guard against, suddenly striking."

"It is dishonorable," I said.

"For men," he said, "at least inappropriate."

"They prefer meeting," I said, "sword to sword, spear to spear."

"Much depends on the caste," he said. "Those of the Black Caste do not eschew the patient bow, the crossbow."

"But the Scarlet Caste?" I said.

"Sword to sword, spear to spear," he said.

"There were two slave thieves," I said. "They escaped."

"Apparently they did not wish to risk the cast dart, the needle in flight," he said.

"You disposed of the poisoned needles," I said.

"Certainly," he said. "They were crushed and drained. I would not care to step on one, even booted. The needle neither knows nor cares if its scratch is by accident or intent. The results are the same."

"The slave thieves feared, too," I said, "the arrival of the cohort of Master Tiskias, the Kur."

"With justification I suspect," said Rupert. "Ironically it was he, the Kur, whom we most desperately wished to meet. Neither you nor I will be secure until he is dealt with."

"The Kur fled," I said.

"I do not think so," he said. "If I thought that, I would not have staked out our small friend, Tiskias."

"It must be terrible to be staked out as is Master Tiskias," I said, "to know that one is bait, helpless bait."

"Perhaps not," said Rupert. "The Kur may spare him, for further employment."

"I do not think Master Tiskias was looking forward to safety and liberation," I said. "To me, he seemed terrified."

"Doubtless he knows his friend better than we," said Rupert.

"I am pleased you did not meet the beast," I said.

"It must be done sooner or later," he said. "The battle will be joined. I wish merely to choose the time and the terrain."

"That is why you have staked out Master Tiskias," I said.

"Of course," he said.

"I am afraid," I said.

"We are all afraid," he said.

"I think it likely," I said, "that the Kur was absent from the camp when you attacked because it was in pursuit of the two slave thieves who had betrayed him and Master Tiskias."

"And made off with Kur gold," he said.

"Yes," I said.

"I think that is more than likely," he said. "Tiskias affirmed as much."

"We heard two screams this morning," I said, "far off in the swamp."

"The Kur was finishing its hunt," said Rupert.

"The thieves then are dead?" I said.

"Yes," he said. "I arranged our path from the swamp, as well as I could, to cross the point from which we had heard the screams, hoping to encounter the Kur, presumably feeding."

I felt sick.

"You saw nothing of the thieves?" he said.

"No," I said.

"The body of the one and the arm of the other?" he said.

"No," I said.

"I saw no reason to call such things to your attention," he said. "As I recall, you were reluctant even to look upon the discolored, contorted bodies of the swamp brigands on the island."

"Had there been feeding?" I asked.

"Some," he said.

I shuddered.

"It is the way of the carnivore," said Rupert. "It is the way of wind to blow, of fire to burn, of rain to fall, of the carnivore to feed."

"It hunts us," I said.

"And we it," he said.

"Did you see anything of the Kur?" I asked.

"No," he said.

"Perhaps he is gone," I said.

"The most dangerous of enemies," he said, "is the one you cannot see."

"You think he is about," I said.

"Surely," he said.

"Out there somewhere," I said, "watching?"

"I am sure of it," he said.

"I fear the beast is intelligent," I said.

"I think it highly so," said Rupert.

"If he sees Master Tiskias staked out, he will anticipate a trap," I said.

"Of course," said Rupert. "That is expected. We are not dealing with a *sleen* or *larl* in the wild. But obvious bait is nonetheless bait, authentic bait. We challenge him as a noble foe. We appeal to his vanity. We call him from the shadows into the light. We set forth the field of battle, open, frank, and clear, and invite him to appear upon it. We set forth a prize and dare him to claim it. I know Kurii. Such beasts covet glory. What Kur could resist such an opportunity; what Kur could reject such an offer?"

"He may not care to face three men armed with hunting spears," I said.

"He does not expect to do so," said Rupert.

"I do not understand," I said.

"I had myself accompanied by my colleagues, Holt of Ar and Desmond of Hochburg," he said, "lest I must deal with numbers of men."

"Master?" I asked.

"This other war is between myself and the Kur," he said.

"I do not understand," I said.

"It is I whom he most sorely blames for the ruin of the plot of Pompilius," he said.

"And I?" I said.

"And you, as well," he said. "Do not fear. He has not forgotten you."

"You are three," I said, "and he is one."

"I am one, and he is one," said Rupert.

"Be three," I said. "It will be difficult enough to overcome him, even with three."

"No," said Rupert of Hochburg.

"Has this to do with honor?" I asked.

"Of course," he said.

"I hate honor," I said.

"Captain," said Holt of Ar, backing away from the crack in the wall of the half-ruined hut through which he had been watching the clearing, with its stakes, including that to which Tiskias was tethered.

"Yes?" said Rupert.

"The Kur," said Maxwell Holt, Holt of Ar.

CHAPTER ONE HUNDRED AND ONE

"There," said Holt of Ar, "on the far side of the square."

"I see," said Rupert.

"He seems to be waiting," said Holt of Ar.

"He is waiting," said Rupert.

Desmond of Hochburg reached for the spear he had left leaning against the wall.

"No," said Rupert.

"One man cannot well stand against a Kur," said Holt of Ar.

"One man can try," said Rupert.

"He has not yet attacked Tiskias," said Holt of Ar.

"Tiskias is not important," said Rupert. "He can be eaten or spared."

"He is now on his knees, his head to the dirt," said Holt of Ar.

"I would not rely on the mercy of a Kur," said Desmond, "nor on that of a shark or nest of *urts*."

"But the Kur can think beyond the satisfaction of a kill," said Holt. "He has need of Tiskias."

"Tiskias has failed him," said Rupert.

I shuddered.

"The path of Tiskias is the path that led to the Kur's discovery," said Rupert. "Too, Tiskias failed to subdue or control the ardor and greed of his hirelings, and surrendered the Kur's gold to them. Such things are unlikely to be overlooked by our large friend."

"Is Tiskias not essential to his doings with men?" asked Holt.

"One comparable to Tiskias might be," said Rupert. "But a replacement for Tiskias, purchased by means of a translator and the clink of gold, can be recruited from a thousand road camps, from a hundred taverns in Brundisium or Torcadino, from dozens of alleys in Venna or Ar."

"But he has not advanced to kill Tiskias," said Holt.

"I think," said Rupert, "he wishes to allow Tiskias time to anticipate his end, the fastening of claws in his flesh and the tearing of fangs at his body."

"Let Desmond and I abet you," said Holt. "Three may be a match for the Kur."

I wondered if that were true.

"My thanks," said Rupert. "But even did I not deem your assistance improper, it would be impractical. The Kur would simply fade back into the swamp to brood and await his next opportunity. All would be but postponed. Let us finish matters this afternoon."

I looked up, from my knees, from the dirt floor of the ruined hut. The back wall was largely missing.

"May I speak Master!" I begged.

"No," he said.

"Listen to her, Captain," said Holt.

"To the babbling of a slave?" asked Rupert.

"Do not fight the Kur alone," said Desmond.

"I am resolved to do so," said Rupert.

"You court death," said Holt.

"I offer her a flower," he said. "It is up to her to accept it or reject it."

"I protest, Captain," said Holt.

"I, too," said Desmond.

"Your well-intentioned protests are noted and will now be ignored," said Rupert.

"How can you keep us from intervening?" asked Holt of Ar.

"Easily," said Rupert. "You are forbidden to interfere."

"No!" wept Holt.

"You were too long on the Slave World, the Dismal World," said Rupert. "Have you become a stranger to Gorean discipline?"

I saw tears in the eyes of Holt and Desmond. "How strange for men to weep," I thought. How little I knew then of Warriors, of their blood and their depth. There are tears of rage, tears of irrevocable loss, tears of joy. How naive I was to suppose that those who draw the sword and string the bow should prove immune to the storms of the heart.

"Leave, beloved friends," said Rupert. "I must attempt this alone. Honor will have it so. Would that matters were otherwise. Would that this was a different war, with a different foe, with a different cause. Then, if I were to die, what better than to do so in battle, in the company of such friends. But this is the war that it is, which I must wage alone, and the foe it is, whom I must face alone."

"You must allow us to come later and strive for reprisal," said Holt.

"No," said Rupert, "not if the terrain is honest and the fight fair."

"Discipline," said Desmond, "was never meant to be so stressed."

"Were it not capable of enduring such torment," said Rupert, "it would not be discipline."

"I beg to speak!" I cried.

"Men are in discourse," said Rupert. "You will be quiet, slave."

How I wanted to cry out and beg him to flee!

"When I approach my waiting foe," said Rupert, regarding Holt and Desmond, "you are to take your leave, expeditiously and discreetly. Do so through the back of the hut. You are then unlikely to be observed. You are to move quickly. And take this meaningless slave with you, and, if you care for me, guard her with your lives."

I was startled that he spoke so.

And I was amazed that neither Holt of Ar nor Desmond of Hochburg seemed surprised. Neither protested nor in the least demurred at accepting this baffling charge. I then, shuddering, began to glimpse what it might be, to be the slave of a Gorean male. We are nothing, and yet so much. We kneel; we kiss; we obey instantly and unquestioningly; we are clothed, if clothed, for his pleasure; we are subject to his whip; we may be bought and sold; we are owned, wholly, as much as a boot or cup, but he would place his life in jeopardy to protect us; he would die for us. Could a mere slave mean so much to a man? Could there be an explanation for this, that a Master would himself be unwilling to acknowledge? A free woman with whom one shares a Home Stone, of course, is to be routinely defended to the death, for proprieties are involved, expectations, even obligations and duties, but what of a slave? What possibly could explain a man's willingness to die for a slave, worth perhaps only a handful of copper coins? A slave, I dared not pursue this inquiry, even privately. Then I realized that the edges of the mystery on which I had inadvertently encroached, would have had nothing to do with my own situation. I had displeased my Master; I had disappointed him. I was no longer in his favor. I was held in contempt. I was to be sold. The coin or two I might bring would, if nothing else, be put to the treasury of his beloved free company.

"I think, dear Captain," said Holt, "the slave would prefer to stay with you."

I nodded, desperately, looking up, tears in my eyes.

"What she wants means nothing," said Rupert. "She is a slave. Take her with you. Go, now, begone!"

Holt of Ar and Desmond of Hochburg looked at one another.

"Go," said Rupert. "I wish a moment to compose myself."

"On your feet, slave," said Holt of Ar. "Be with us."

"You cannot leave him!" I cried.

"We leave the hut," said Holt. "Leave your Master to his thoughts."

Desmond of Hochburg seized my arm.

I wondered what thoughts might occupy one who goes forth to battle, a battle he does not expect to survive.

Does he recall a mother, and a childhood? Does he recall being invested with the scarlet cloak? Does he recall his first battle? Or do stray, random thoughts occur, meaningless thoughts, a rainy morning, clouds, wind, snow, the crack of lighting, wet grass about his ankles, a *sleen* seen at dusk, its movement like the flow of water, files of armed men approaching, the sound of drums, a flower on which he once avoided treading?

Then Rupert of Hochburg shook himself, grasped a hunting spear, and departed the hut.

I was dragged from the hut, through its ruined back.

A moment later, from a higher ground, I saw Rupert of Hochburg walking toward the Kur, the hunting spear across his shoulders.

I saw the Kur rise up, to its full height, a large double-bladed ax in its right paw.

Then, my arm in the custody of Desmond of Hochburg, I was again drawn, weeping, perhaps fifty yards from the huts, back into the grass, out from the small peninsula that protruded into the swamp. Then he released my arm.

"Master?" I said.

He and Holt of Ar regarded me.

"I do not understand," I said. "Am I not now to be led away, leashed or bound?"

"You are in our charge," said Holt of Ar. "Were you to attempt to escape, a most foolish act, we would have no choice but to attempt to recapture you."

"Yes, Masters!" I cried, and spun about, racing back toward the huts.

CHAPTER ONE HUNDRED AND TWO

I cried out with misery.

Rupert of Hochburg was on one knee, bleeding, grasping the sundered shaft of his hunting spear. The blade of the spear and a yard of its haft had been struck away, and might have been anywhere, lost in the grass or amongst the huts.

Tiskias, in an underrobe, his hands tied behind his back, was on his knees, beside the stake to which he had been tethered by the throat.

"Kill him, great and noble Master!" cried Tiskias to the Kur. "Do not play. Be done with it! Then free me! You need me! I can speak to men for you! I am brave! I am clever! I am loyal! Hail Pompilius! Hail Pompilius, wonder and paragon of the glorious Kurii!"

These words rattled toward the translation device slung on its chain about the Kur's massive throat. The device then iterated a succession of bestial sounds which, doubtless, rendered Tiskias' utterances intelligible to the Kur.

I shall henceforth, for convenience, recount what occurred in the small square as if the discourse took place in a single language rather than in two languages, Gorean and Kur. The emanations of the translator, designed as it was, were delivered in a carefully timed, dispassionate, mechanistic monotone, which, naturally, considerably contrasted with the often violent, intense, and rushed phonemes of Gorean and Kur submitted to it for processing.

"Cease your pandering blather," the Kur to Tiskias. "And fear not. I do not regard you as a food object."

"Thank you, Master!" cried Tiskias, gratefully, shedding tears of joy.

"You would turn my stomach," said the Kur. "I shall leave you tethered for some passing, ignorant *sleen*, or, better, for dying of thirst in your bonds."

"No, Master!" wept Tiskias.

"That is a lengthy and most unpleasant death," said the Kur.

"No, no, Master!" cried Tiskias.

"When I feed here," said the Kur, "it will be first on the heart of the Warrior."

"Come and take it, Beast," said Rupert, casting down his sundered spear, staggering to his feet, drawing his sword.

It was then that Rupert, angrily, became aware of me, and of Holt and Desmond, who had come up close behind me.

"What are you doing here?" he hissed, back over his shoulder.

"Fleeing from custody," I said. "I am an unruly, foolish, slave. I am running away. I am escaping, but I fear I am now caught. Tie me. Bind me helplessly. Punish me!"

"Get away, run!" snarled Rupert.

"I cannot," I said. "I am now captured."

"Go!" he roared.

"I am disobedient," I said.

"And you, noble Holt of Ar, and noble Desmond of Hochburg," he cried in fury, "what are you doing here?"

"Pursuing an escaped slave, Captain," said Holt of Ar.

"Do not interfere," begged Rupert. He was weak. I feared he would fall.

"My ax welcomes you, you fools," came from the translator. "Its blade is scarcely moistened. You will quench its thirst."

"They will not interfere," said Rupert.

"Their spears suggest otherwise," said the Kur.

"Cast away your spears," said Rupert, angrily.

"No, Captain!" cried Maxwell Holt, Holt of Ar.

"Never, beloved Captain!" said Desmond of Hochburg.

"Now!" cried Rupert. "This war is mine, not yours."

"Keep your weapons!" I cried, but each hunting spear had been hurled to the side.

Tears blazed in the eyes of Holt and Desmond.

"Behold, a human female," said the Kur. "How different they are from you, and how easy it is to tell them from the male of your species, even for one of the high race, the Kurii. And how deprived is the human species, having only two sexes. The Kurii have four sexes. But note, is there not a slender metal band closely encircling her throat. Such a band is well placed. It cannot be slipped as might a cuff from a wrist or a manacle from an ankle. It is on her, closely and well. Too, perhaps it is locked. If that is so, she cannot remove it. If that is so, she must be the least and most worthless of human females, the slave."

"How true that is in one sense," I thought, "in some legal or institutional sense, and how false in another. What could be the most essential and irreducible of human females, the most real of human females, the most treasured of human females, but the slave, the complement of the most fulfilled and splendid, the most virile and masculine, of males, the Master? Did he not understand that there are men who so desire a woman, so intensely and mightily, so fiercely and passionately, that they will be content with nothing less than owning her, with nothing less than having her and keeping her as their slave? On Gor I met such men and on Gor I found myself, to my excitement and joy, a collared chattel."

"But did she not speak without permission?" asked the Kur. "Has your belt or whip nothing to say about that?"

"Ignore the slave," said Rupert. "She is no concern of ours."

"You are mistaken, dear foe," said the Kur. "She is very much a concern of ours, or, at least, of mine. Now I need not search her out. Indeed, I marvel at this happy coincidence, that she should be here. This will save me time. I had feared that she would have been hidden away somewhere. Now all is convenient and tidy. Now all is well and in order."

"Run!" hissed Rupert. "I will try to cover your withdrawal."

"I cannot run," I said. "I have been captured."

"Get her from here," said Rupert to Holt and Desmond.

I knelt down.

"I fear," said Holt, "she is a recalcitrant slave. She may do contest concerning her departure."

"Some slaves," said Desmond, "prefer to stay with their Master."

"Pull her to her feet," said Rupert. "Carry her."

"I might seize her hair and escort her away, in leading position," said Holt.

For a grown woman, to be put in leading position is indescribably humiliating. One is grasped by the hair and is bent over, one's head held at the left thigh of the keeper. One is then conducted about in that position. This is an amusing joke to other slaves, of course. And the least resistance may be met with the application of excruciating pain. Being treated in this fashion well reminds a free woman that she is a woman, and a slave that she is a slave.

"Get her out of here," snarled Rupert.

"If necessary," said Desmond, "I could unwrap the leash from her neck, and drag her forcibly away. That could be done quickly."

"Get her away, now, swiftly, to safety, tarsks," hissed Rupert.

"There is no hurry," said the Kur. "From here, she can be trailed easily."

I leaped to my feet, and ran to the spear discarded by Desmond of Hochburg.

But I could not lift it from the ground, for Desmond of Hochburg's booted foot was upon it, pressing it tightly to the ground.

"Stop!" said Holt of Ar, startled.

"That is a weapon," said Desmond of Hochburg. "Do not touch it! You are a slave! Do you wish to be slain? Do you wish your hands to be cut away?"

"Then, Master," I cried, "lift it and use it to defend your captain, my Master!"

"Would that we could!" said Holt of Ar.

"You can!" I cried.

"Run, leave!" snapped Rupert of Hochburg. "I will not be dishonored. Do not disgrace me!"

I straightened my body. Tears ran from my eyes. I was helpless.

"In any event," said Holt, "you could not manage the weapon. For you, it is large, long, clumsy, and weighty. You could not cast it. I doubt that you could thrust it with the force necessary to penetrate to the heart of a man, let alone to that of a Kur."

"Seize up your weapons," I said to Holt and Desmond. "Wield them. Fight for the life of your captain. You see he is weak. He bleeds. Fight!"

"Do so," said the Kur. "I can slay three as easily as one. Indeed, I prefer that you do so. Your intervention, however, should be only with the permission of he whom I face, in which case he, by such a permission, forfeits his honor and grovels for his life."

"I accord no such permission," said Rupert of Hochburg, weakly, but tensely. "And if I did, and so abjured my honor, and our foe should feel uneasy or threatened, he need only withdraw, and conclude this matter at his own discretion, later, when he pleases."

"Fight for him!" I cried to Holt and Desmond.

"We cannot," said Holt of Ar, tears in his eyes.

"Protect her, defend her with your very lives," said Rupert of Hochburg.

I did not understand this. I was a slave.

Perhaps it had something to do with honor, something that I did not understand.

"We will do so," said Holt of Ar.

"Spear to ax," said Desmond of Hochburg.

"Surely," said the Kur, "you show no solicitation for an object. You can buy a hundred such as she in a thousand markets."

"We choose as we do, and spend our coin as we please," said Rupert.

"Is she not a domestic animal?" asked the Kur.

"A particularly lovely one," said Rupert.

I was startled. Tears sprang anew to my eyes.

"She is clothed, if scarcely," said the Kur. "Why permit clothing to animals?"

"We do what we wish with them," said Rupert, "clothing them or not."

"Interesting," said the Kur.

"Kill him, Master!" cried Tiskias, bound and tethered to the post. "Then free me. I am loyal, and needed!"

"Be silent," said the Kur.

"Do battle," said Rupert.

"Are you ready," asked the Kur.

"I am ready," said Rupert.

"I shall kill you first," said the Kur, "and then your minions, and then the slave. They cannot escape."

Rupert was silent.

I feared he might fall.

"I dedicate this victory," said the Kur, "to the glory of my sovereign lord, Pompilius, the Mighty, Master of Six worlds, he whom you have so grievously offended."

"It is customary to achieve a victory before dedicating it," said Rupert.

I knelt down a bit behind Rupert, and to his left, facing the Kur. If one rises, then one is in heeling position. One commonly heels to the left, as most Masters are right-handed. One is then unlikely to block or encumber his weapon hand.

"I wait," said Rupert.

"You will not wait long," said the Kur. "I have played with you until now, amusing myself, a mere cut here, a mere cut there, and yet already you can scarcely stand. I give you a moment to anticipate my blow. It lurks in my ax. Will it split you from the head to the belt, or divide you from belly to back?"

"You had best strike quickly," said Rupert, "if you wish me to be sensible of your stroke. Things begin to go black."

"Master!" I wept.

"Have you not gone?" asked Rupert.

"No, Master," I said.

"Go, run," he said.

"I remain," I said.

"Worthless, disobedient beast!" he said, tottering.

"Yes, Master," I said.

"Noble Holt, noble Desmond," he said, "gather up your spears, turn your backs, and walk slowly away. Remember me, in the bright afternoon light, with clouds in the sky and wind in the grass, standing, facing the foe. Remember me so, as you left me."

"Yes, Captain," they said.

"No!" I said. "Stay! Fight!"

"Barbarian fool," said Rupert. "How little you know of codes and deeds."

Holt and Desmond turned away, and began, slowly, sorrowfully, to depart.

"Go with them," said Rupert.

"Please, no," I said.

"Will you disobey my last command?" he asked.

"No, Master," I said.

I rose to my feet, weeping, turned away, and began to follow Holt of Ar and Desmond of Hochburg. They were some yards before me. I had taken only a few steps when, in sorrow, I turned back.

Rupert of Hochburg had collapsed in the grass.

The Kur, ax lifted, was approaching him.

I screamed wildly, and pointed, back toward the steaming swamp forest.

CHAPTER ONE HUNDRED AND THREE

Emerged from the shadows and greenery of the dark swamp forest, wading, every step making it seem larger, some vines and leaves tangled about its legs and waist, grasping a sharpened, postlike branch, was a huge, half-bent-over, hirsute figure.

My startled, inadvertent scream had instantly alerted the Kur threatening Rupert of Hochburg. He spun about, crouching down, every sense wild with attention, ears lifted and turned, two paws grasping his gigantic double-bladed ax.

As quickly as I could, I ran back to the fallen Rupert of Hochburg.

I seized him and began to kiss him madly, wantonly, without permission.

He must be alive!

His eyes opened, partly, dully.

He was alive!

I half lifted him, turning his body.

In the first moment I had seen the figure emerging from the forest I had thought nothing but 'Kur,' another representative of that fearsome form of life, perhaps even a compatriot or ally of the cunning, dreadful giant advancing on Rupert of Hochburg. But surely Kurii were rare in this vicinity, and the Kur form of life is not one to be found happily or naturally inhabiting so inhospitable an environment as a serpent-infested, *tharlarion*-ridden swamp forest. So what might a Kur be doing here, spending time in so unlikely a vicinity?

Surely it had some purpose.

And might not that purpose have to do with intrigues, with factions, with the politics of worlds, with another Kur?

About the neck of the newcomer, he bearing the sharpened postlike branch, as I could now see, slung not on a chain, as was the case with the other, but on its cord about his neck, was a translation device.

Rupert shut his eyes and opened them, trying to brush my hand away from his face.

"What?" he asked.

"Another Kur, Master," I said. "It has a translator. I think it must be Lucilius, or Cyrus as I denominated him, of the faction of Agamemnon."

As easy as it doubtless was for these beasts to tell one another apart, it was often difficult for a human being to do so without some time and familiarity.

The newcomer approached more closely.

The Kur near us, who had fought with Rupert, angrily, abruptly, switched off his translator. In this way he avoided what might have produced a confusing redundancy of vocalizations.

"Yes," I said. "It is Lucilius!"

Lucilius left his device activated.

With a surge of strength which must have cost him much, Rupert struggled to a half-seated position.

"Do not interfere," he called to Lucilius. "The enemy has won."

"He has not won until you are dead," said Lucilius.

"The war is mine!" said Rupert.

"You must wait your turn," said Lucilius. "My war has priority."

"Yes!" I cried. "Yes!"

Holt of Ar and Desmond of Hochburg, having heard my scream, had turned about and, bearing their spears, hurried back to where the Kur and Rupert of Hochburg had done contest.

"Go away," said the Kur to Lucilius. "I have business to attend to here. It will take but a moment."

"I, too, have business here," said Lucilius, "and my business is one earlier, and of a previous standing."

"Throw down your stick and go away," said the Kur. "I might spare you."

"You are generous, and I am flattered by your indulgence," said Lucilius, "but I choose to remain."

"A branch is nothing compared to an ax," said the Kur.

"I would agree with you," said Lucilius, "but you must grant that much depends on the skill with which each implement is wielded."

"Go away," said the Kur.

"I have sought you," said Lucilius. "How ironic, and yet so plausible, that I should find you by means of following the traces of a human."

"I grow impatient," said the Kur. "Turn about and flee before I shut the gate of your escape."

"I see a human, weakened and bleeding," said Lucilius. "Of what importance has a lowly human for one such as you, so formidable and richly pelted?"

"He, and his fellows, and the she-beast with them," said the Kur, "ignored the will of, and bent awry, the designs of, my lord, Pompilius the Mighty, Lord of Six Worlds."

"And thus you would give them to the mercy of your ax?" asked Lucilius.

"To the justice of my ax," said the Kur.

"The occasion is past, the matter is done," said Lucilius. "To proceed further would be a pointless act of petty vengeance."

"Call it what you will," said the Kur. "My ax is thirsty."

"Your entitlement to seek blood in this matter, as I understand it," said Lucilius, "is to act in such a way as to please your lord, Pompilius."

"And myself," said the Kur.

"Then," said Lucilius, "by parity of reasoning, you must accord me a similar entitlement, one to act in such a way as to please my lord, and myself."

"Who is your lord?" asked the Kur.

"Agamemnon, the Eleventh Face of the Nameless One," said Lucilius, "whom your lord, Pompilius, sought foully to slay in the environs of the city of Ar."

"I have no wish to kill you," said the Kur. "Change your belt."

"It is interesting," said Lucilius, "how the same act can seem both good and bad, how the same act can seem both criminal and righteous. Much depends on perspective; much depends on one's view."

"I must kill these humans," said the Kur.

"And I," said Lucilius, "at this time, in this place, in my name, and in the name of my lord, a grateful Agamemnon, must defend them to the death."

"Let not Kur fight Kur," said the Kur. "An unspoiled and fertile world waits to be claimed and seized."

"In another time, and in another place," said Lucilius, "we might have worn the same belt. We do not do so now."

"The rings?" asked the Kur.

"The rings," said Lucilius.

"Be it so," said the Kur. "I stand in the rings."

"I, too," said Lucilius.

"Kill him, Master!" cried Tiskias. "He has only a stick. Then free me. I am dependable! I am loyal!"

But I fear neither Kur attended to his pleading.

Each, for moments, tense, not moving, regarded the other.

"For glory," said the Kur.

"For glory," said Lucilius.

With a sudden cry of rage, the Kur, ax raised, flung himself toward Lucilius. The heavy double-blade struck down at Lucilius but Lucilius, grasping his branch, it like the trunk of a small tree, with two uplifted hands, interposed it as a barrier between the blade of the Kur's ax and his head. The haft of the Kur's ax was mighty but no mightier than the postlike branch which had so abruptly arrested its violent descent. How Lucilius must have been shaken! How his arms must have ached and his hands stung! Then he spun his branch diagonally, thrusting the ax by its shaft, to the side. The two implements seemed interlocked. Inches of bark were slowly scraped from the branch of Lucilius. He then, suddenly, drew back the branch and the Kur, off balance, spilled and stumbled to the side, and received a heavy blow at the side of his head. I saw blood springing out of the fur. The Kur struggled up, lost his footing, regained it, and then, bent over, faced Lucilius, who did not press his advantage. The Kur wavered. His ax fell to the ground. Such a blow as he had sustained, I thought, might have broken the neck of a bull.

"A splendid stroke, noble stranger!" cried Tiskias. "Kill the monster! He has threatened and demeaned me. I hate him. Kill him! Free me, and I will serve you! I am dependable and loyal. You need a human confrere. I can skillfully and marvelously abet the designs of my betters. Let me ease your dealings and promote your ends with men!"

"Your staff appears, then disappears, then appears, and strikes," said the Kur.

"Yield," said Lucilius.

"I yield," said the Kur.

I cried out with gladness.

Rupert, sword in hand, struggled to his feet, wavering.

The Kur lowered his ax.

"Ring Brother?" asked Lucilius.

"Ring Brother," said the Kur.

"Kill the murderous, lawless brute, noble stranger!" called Tiskias.

Lucilius lowered the scraped, heavy, postlike branch he carried. At the same moment the Kur seized up his ax, inverted it, and plunged the handle into the belly of Lucilius.

I screamed in misery.

"Well done, Master!" cried Tiskias. "A brilliant stroke! We are victorious!"

Lucilius staggered backward, the translation device jerking on its cord about his neck.

The thrust of the ax handle had been one of terrible force. I thought it might have broken a stone wall or shattered the handle itself.

"I cry acclaim for my Master!" cried Tiskias.

I steadied Rupert, fearing he would fall. He pushed me aside, standing uneasily.

The Kur now grasped his ax with two hands, one hand at the center of the handle, the other closer to the blades. In this way both handle and blades might be employed variously. He did not attempt a frenzied charge, as he had initially done. Certainly Lucilius was now being taken seriously as an antagonist.

Lucilius was bleeding about the belly and, twice, he vomited into the grass.

"That was not well done," said Lucilius, half choking, blood running from his fanged mouth. "You spoke yielding. Your heart is not worth eating."

"Depart," said the Kur. "Withdraw."

"I see you fear me," said Lucilius.

"We bestride a fair world," said the Kur. "Here, on this ground, let Kur not kill Kur."

"You betrayed your yielding," said Lucilius. "You have stained the rings."

"That I might the longer, and the better and more, serve my lord, Pompilius, the Mighty, of the Six Worlds," said the Kur.

"You have dishonored your lord," said Lucilius.

"Victory, at any cost," said the Kur.

"Success may be achieved at any cost," said Lucilius, "but not victory."

"Let us engage," said the Kur.

"I am ready," said Lucilius.

"Ring brother?" asked the Kur.

"No," said Lucilius.

"For glory?" asked the Kur.

"No," said Lucilius. "This is now no more than a squabble betwixt *urts*."

There then began a duel of sorts, two able combatants participating, a formidable ax against a weighty staff. Sometimes neither contestant moved, and I could have screamed, waiting for something to occur. Then there would be a tentative exchanging of feints and blows, and sometimes, unexpectedly, suddenly, even after a stillness, there would be flashes of action like two storms, blasting with lightning, each, in its striking conflagration, hurling itself upon the other.

Then I cried out with horror, for Lucilius' staff, rather than blocking the blow of the Kur's ax, either by striking it aside or stopping it with his branch below the double-blade, exposed it to the blade itself and the branch, wrenched and cloven, burst apart, splintering and divided. How he had misjudged the position of the ax! Or had he judged it with perfection? In that very instant, that of the blade slashing apart the post-like branch, Lucilius stepped to the side and seized the briefly encumbered ax behind the descended blade, and the two Kurii, biting and snarling, were rolling on the grass, struggling for control of the ax. In the tumult of that violence, in the rapid transitions of position, I sometimes could not tell the combatants apart.

Holt of Ar and Desmond of Hochburg approached, their spears raised.

"Do not interfere!" said Rupert of Hochburg, on his feet, sword in hand, bleeding, shaking his head, apparently trying to clear his head or vision. I did not know if he really knew, or could see, what was occurring.

I tried to touch him.

I was afraid he would fall. He thrust me away, angrily.

The ax, behind its head, was grasped by the Kur, but he was in no position to wield it. It had apparently been surrendered by Lucilius in order to obtain a different advantage. Lucilius' hands were twisted in the chain by means of which the Kur's translator had been slung about its neck. The chain was twisted tighter and tighter, deeper and deeper, about and into the Kur's neck. Thc ax, unwielded, slipped aside, into the grass. I could no longer see the links of the chain, which were buried in the fur of the Kur's neck. A look of recognition, of bulging terror, appeared in its eyes. Then its head fell to the side. No motion appeared in that great, savage chest.

"It is dead," breathed Holt of Ar.

"It looked upon life, with might and power," said Desmond of Hochburg, lowering his spear. "Now it looks no more."

Lucilius slowly, painfully, disentangled the six digits of his clenched hands from the chain about the throat of the Kur. He then struggled unsteadily to his feet.

"You are injured," said Holt of Ar. "You are wounded, you have lost blood, you are bleeding, you have been torn and bitten."

Slowly, Lucilius lifted his head and looked at Tiskias, whose hands were tied behind his back, who was tethered by the neck to the post in the small village square.

"Congratulations on your glorious victory, noble stranger," cried Tiskias. "My heart leaps with joy. How I trembled for you and your cause! How I feared that you might fall and your cause fail! But you live! And your cause, whatever it might be, is vindicated. Your dreadful, loathsome foe, whom I much hated, as I had fervently hoped, has succumbed. You will require a dependable, trustworthy, loyal ally, clever and astute, to aid you in your dealings with men. Think of me. Free me, and permit me to be of service."

Suddenly there was a scratching and hiss, a tearing through grass, a blur of sound and movement behind us, a scrambling, a rushing forward, and then, suddenly, abruptly, a hideous, whining, gasping, choking, coughing cry.

We spun about; looming over us, we in its shadow, was a gigantic, upright form, that of a tottering Kur, its ax uplifted, with a sword penetrating to the hilt in its heart. Rupert of Hochburg drew out his sword, and the monster fell.

"Master!" I cried.

"When a foe seems dead," said Rupert of Hochburg, "he is not always dead. It is well to make sure of such things."

"Captain!" said Holt of Ar.

"Doubtless it recognized that it was on the point of expiring," said Rupert. "Then it, in a last moment of life, feigned death and held its breath."

"Brilliant," said Holt.

"Sometimes effective," said Rupert.

"We turned away," said Desmond.

"You turned away," said Rupert.

"We might have been all killed," said Holt.

"Had one not watched," said Rupert.

"I am reminded of the twenty-third maxim," said Desmond.

"Not all who lie amongst the dead are dead," said Rupert.

"Your sword did its work well," said Holt.

"Little skill was involved," said Rupert. "The beast's attention was on you. I do not think he even saw me. He rushed forward, grasping the ax, his arms high, his chest exposed. A novice, not yet granted the scarlet cloak, could have done as much, as well."

"I think not," said Holt of Ar.

"Masters," called Tiskias, from the stake to which he was tethered. "What of me?"

"Ponder your just desserts," said Desmond.

"Where is Lucilius?" asked Rupert.

"Near," said Holt of Ar.

Lucilius had staggered apart. He was crouched down, some yards away. His body seemed to shake with emotion.

Rupert of Hochburg sank to one knee, cleaned the blade of his sword on the grass, and slipped it into his sheath.

"Lie down, Master," I said. "You have lost much blood. You are weak. Rest now."

I did not think he could rise to his feet unassisted. He steadied himself, putting one hand, palm down, on the grass.

"Please, Master," I said.

"Holt, Desmond," he said. "Conduct me to our colleague. He is distressed."

Holt and Desmond regarded one another and then went to my Master, and, lifting him to his feet, and supporting him, and half carrying him, helped him to the side of Lucilius.

"The business is done, friend," said Rupert. "You have done well."

"Let Tor-tu-Gor flee and look no more on this day," said Lucilius.

"What is wrong?" asked Rupert.

"I am twice shamed," said Lucilius.

"How so?" asked Rupert.

"He was unworthy to stand in the rings," said Lucilius. "He stained them. He was no Ring Brother. He betrayed his belt. He shamed the High Race."

"Treachery and deceit are not confined to humans," said Rupert.

"I will not eat his heart," said Lucilius. "It would not nourish and enflame me. It would sicken and poison me."

"Rejoice," said Holt. "You won. You were victorious."

"As an *urt* is victorious, not a Kur," said Lucilius. "I was not victorious as a Kur, only successful as might be an *urt*. What satisfaction, what glory redounds to the boot that steps on an *urt*, breaking its back?"

"Sometimes, disconsolate friend," said Rupert. "Honor does not always bedeck itself in the same raiment."

Lucilius lifted his head.

"Honor might be diversly conceived," said Rupert.

"I do not understand," came from Lucilius' translator.

"Consider that some may view it as a higher honor, even a greater honor, to sacrifice all things, even honor itself, as once conceived, in the name of a yet higher honor, a higher thing, properly or improperly conceived."

"What higher thing?" asked Lucilius.

"You would die, would you not," asked Rupert, "for your lord, Agamemnon, the Eleventh Face of the Nameless One?"

"Assuredly," said Lucilius.

"And so might another," said Rupert, "for another, perhaps Pompilius, of the Six Worlds."

"He is a heartless, foul tyrant," said Lucilius.

"Such have often been loved," said Rupert.

"I do not understand what you are saying," said Lucilius.

"Only that honor may be diversely conceived," said Rupert.

"When honor grapples with honor which is to win?" asked Lucilius.

"That which you choose," said Rupert.

"But one might choose mistakenly," said Lucilius.

"Of course," said Rupert.

"I think," said Lucilius, "you speak not of honor but of love."

"Perhaps they are entangled," said Rupert.

"Disparate are love and honor," said Lucilius.

"Consider only," said Rupert, "that not all might see them so."

"We can dispose of the body in the swamp," said Holt of Ar.

Lucilius seemed lost in thought. He was silent, like a living stone.

"I will help," said Desmond.

"No," said Lucilius. "We will burn the body."

"It is growing late," said Desmond. "Such a fire would mark our position for others."

"For various others," said Rupert.

"Should we not depart this place?" I asked.

"Later," said Rupert.

"Then rest, Masters," I begged. "You are both weak and tired."

"Dear Lucilius," said Rupert. "You spoke of being twice shamed."

"I am Kur," said Lucilius. "And yet you, a mere human, saved my life moments ago from a charging foe. Thus, I am shamed."

"Be not so, friend," said Rupert, "for you, an Ahn ago, emerging from the forest, saved the lives of three men and a slave. Our debt to you is thus far more grievous than yours to us."

"I must be about what I must do," said Lucilius.

"What are you going to do?" asked Desmond.

"I am going to gather wood," said Lucilius. "A pyre must be built."

It was early in the morning.

"It is too late," said Desmond. "Men approach, an armed host."

The pyre had been lit last night, and it had blazed for better than an hour. Its light must have been visible for *pasangs*. Rupert, though sore, weary, and weak, had resisted the pleadings, demands, and remonstrances of Lucilius, begging him to leave. He had refused to do so, and Holt and Desmond, despite what might have been their misgivings, would do nothing other than remain with their captain.

Earlier, in the half-darkness of an early dusk, Holt and Desmond had dragged the body of the Kur, foot by foot, log by log, branch by branch, to the top of the pyre.

Before they had begun their task, I had shuddered to view the body. Its chest had been torn open.

"Perhaps," I thought, "honor might not always bedeck itself in the same raiment. Perhaps, like truth and justice, like propriety and impropriety, it could be diversely, honestly conceived. Honor, commonly so clear, might not always be so clear. When honor grapples with honor, how is the match to be adjudicated, and who shall adjudicate?"

"Should not Tiskias be tied alive and placed on the pyre?" had asked Desmond of Hochburg.

"No," had said Lucilius. "It is unseeming to mix the ashes of an *urt* with those of a *larl*."

"Are the ashes not to be gathered," had asked Rupert of Hochburg, "enfolded in silk, and placed in a vessel?"

"No," had said Lucilius. "It is not the Kur way. They are to be given to the wind and rain, the temperatures and seasons, that they may be scattered on the fertile ground and lie amongst the blades of living grass."

"We have been seen, Captain," said Holt of Ar.

"We may have time to withdraw into the swamp forest," said Desmond of Hochburg.

"You may do so if you wish," said Rupert, "but I myself would prefer to partake of a fine breakfast."

"Look!" said Holt of Ar. "There is no mistaking that portly form!"

"Temicus!" cried Desmond, and rushed forth to meet and embrace that favored, high officer in the free company of Rupert of Hochburg.

"Master," I cried, joyfully.

"You have occasionally of late spoken without permission," he said.

"Forgive me, Master!" I said.

"Make yourself presentable," he said.

"Master?" I asked.

"Tie your garment in more tightly," he said, "and shorten it, considerably."

"Yes, Master," I said.

CHAPTER ONE HUNDRED AND FOUR

There is little to tell now, at least of these things.

We are camped near Ar, and will soon be marching overland to the Vosk Basin. There we will investigate claims of an increased Kur presence in that area. The free company of Rupert of Hochburg will join two other forces similarly engaged, the newly formed Vosk Guard under the command of Gordon of Hammerfest and the free company of Flavius of Venna. Our efforts are intended to supply the Vosk League, which is essentially a river navy, with land forces capable of locating, and dealing with, Kur encroachments in the basin. If necessary, town levies may be raised, as well. It is rumored that this project is being largely underwritten by Marlenus, Ubar of Ar, presumably to keep the Vosk free for trade, and to ensure a continued flourishing of the vast Vosk Basin's agriculture, but, some suspect, to bring more territory under the aegis of Glorious Ar. I suppose that a given project might have more than one motivation, just as a given action might have various, and sometimes unexpected, consequences.

It may be recalled that Tiskias, and his principal, the Kur, had plotted the entrapment of Rupert of Hochburg and his party, if any, in the swamp forest, as they were supposedly following a false trail hoping to recover a stolen slave. Some fifty men were supposedly hired to spring this trap. Naturally, when Rupert and any with him failed to keep this appointment with doom, the putatively ambushing party was forced to search for their prey elsewhere. The blaze of the Kur's pyre, fierce in the night, could not escape their attention. Thus, they would investigate it in the hope of discovering their hitherto elusive quarry. Unfortunately for them, as Rupert had anticipated, his free company, waiting on the margin of the swamp forest, which he wanted to keep free of the swamp forest, marked it as well. The free company soon intercepted the assemblage of murderous thugs, learned their intent, and presented them with a proposal which, on the whole, was much in their best interest. They were to immediately surrender their arms and valuables, and disband, or be slaughtered on the spot. As the assemblage of thugs was outnumbered some three or so to one by professional soldiers, they thought the better of stupidity and complied with the arrangements suggested to them. The life of a brigand, like that of his law-abiding counterpart, is not always an easy lot. All trades doubtless have their exigencies and hazards.

Tiskias, for better or for worse, properly or not, was turned loose to beg on the roads. No one, it seemed, was willing to have his blood on their sword. Tiskias, rather than committing suicide at the shame of this, as some seem to have expected, found it acceptable, even agreeable. Before leaving the camp, he requested that he might be given the translation device which had been removed from the throat of the slain Kur, but this had been refused to him. Rupert of Hochburg feared it might fall into the wrong hands, for example, into those of Tiskias. And, who knew who else might market his services to Kurii by means of so unusual, sophisticated, and valuable a device? Too, might it not prove to be of use in the Vosk basin? Interestingly, its utility proved illusory. The translators issued to agents of the Six Worlds, as it was later discovered, were responsive to a coding which needed to be reset after a time period corresponding to several rotations of one of those six worlds, perhaps that regarded as the most important. If the code was not reset by that time, the device, following a warning, would self-destruct. The point of this feature was presumably to limit the use of the such devices, at least over time, to authorized personnel. All we knew of this, initially, was an explosion which blasted apart one of the supply wagons attached to the company, scattering flaming scraps of wood and hot debris over a considerable area. After this, some members of the company expressed regret that the device had not, after all, been given to Tiskias, who, presumably, as a human, and a certain type of human, would not know of, or would have been entrusted with, the code in question. In any event, I have little doubt but what Tiskias, quick-thinking and clever, skilled in chicanery, duplicity, and deceit, will thrive on the roads amongst most Goreans, who tend to be frank, trusting, generous fellows. On the other hand, they do not care to be deceived. One who pretends to be blind may have his eyes burned away with red-hot irons, one who pretends to be crippled may have a leg removed with a wood saw, and so on.

Soon we will break camp and the three companies, those of Gordon of Hammerfest, Flavius of Venna, and Rupert of Hochburg, will begin the trek to the Vosk. As these companies are composed largely of warriors and men-at-arms, several of whom are entitled to the scarlet cloak, they will be accompanied by slaves. Such men are fond of their slaves and do not wish to be without them. Free women, of course, are not to be placed in jeopardy. They share a Home Stone and are precious. Too, they could be killed as free citizens, whereas slaves, commonly, would be spared as loot. It is not unusual, of course, for slaves, bought and sold, lost and stolen, won and lost, acquired and discarded, to find themselves, like *kaiila* and other domestic animals, with new Masters.

As we had approached Ar, on our way back with the company from the swamp forest, I had grown more and more uneasy that I would be returned to the Delka cage of the holdings of Tenalian of Ar, for imminent sale in the metropolis. Had I not failed to be pleasing to my Master? Had he not determined to rid himself of me?

How helpless I was!

How little I could do!

I knew nothing of the games of free women, games they may play with impunity, pretending disinterest, distaste or even contempt, casting about coy glances and smiles, hinting at favors never to be bestowed, fluttering and teasing with veils, permitting supposedly inadvertent glimpses of a well-turned ankle, and so on. How little that has to do with a girl in a collar and tunic, who at a snap of the fingers or a click of the tongue must afford a man the most consequential and inordinate of pleasures.

I was the most lascivious and shameless of women, the most helpless, distressed, and needful. The man was everything; I was nothing. He was Master; I was slave. How different this was, save from my dreams, from when I had been a free woman on Earth! Who could have dreamed I could become such? Was this needful, squirming, groveling woman, her neck encircled with a light but momentous collar, her left flank seared with a small but incredibly significant mark, she who had once been the sophisticated, educated, refined Miss Agnes Morrison Atherton? Where was her pride, her dignity? They were gone, evaporated, vanished, lost, discarded, forbidden. In my belly aroused slave fires raged. My skin was a tissue of flame. Every inch of me screamed with wanting and hunger.

I put myself to the feet of my Master, pressing my lips to them. "Be merciful, Master!" I wept. "Keep me! Do not sell me! Keep me! Please keep me! I love you! I love you!"

"Remove your garment," he said.

I tore it away and looked up at him, from my knees.

"I do not find you entirely unsatisfactory," he said, "slave."

"Please do not sell me," I said. "I will try to be a better slave."

"What gave you the idea that I was going to sell you?" he asked. "To be sure, I could do that at any time."

"When the enemy Kur came to the camp one night, pretending to be Lucilius," I said, "bringing Tiskias with him as his supposed prisoner, I did much without permission. I was flagrant in my lack of propriety. I hurried forward and discovered that he was not Lucilius, as he knew not the name 'Cyrus,' which I had given to Lucilius in his captivity. You were furious with me. I had displeased you. You set me from you. Your tent was closed to me. You would not let me share your furs. You later consigned me to Tenalian of Ar, to be sold in Ar."

"It was by means of your stratagem, improper though it might have been," he said, "that not only did we realize that the Kur in the darkness was not Lucilius, but that it, by its very presence, made it clear that the matter of the descending worlds was not over, that vengeance was to be sought, that we were both in mortal danger. Accordingly, I pretended displeasure and, to protect you, separated you from me. The Kur must not find us together. I even went to the lengths of having you caged near Ar, presumably to be soon sold, while I, and others, took steps to pursue the Kur, even to the extent of allowing Tiskias to think he had escaped our custody."

"I knew nothing of this," I said, smarting with the memory. "I suspected nothing of this."

"It seems I dissembled well," he said.

"Quite well," I said, annoyed.

"Do you object?" he asked.

"I am in a collar," I said. "It would be unwise for me to object."

"You were to be kept safe, until all was resolved," he said.

"Yet I was rented from the Delka cage," I said.

"That was the doing of Tiskias and his ally," he said. "We knew nothing of it, nor did we anticipate it. Tiskias and his ally were supposedly in hiding, somewhere in the swamp forest. We knew little of their resources, and nothing of their hirelings."

"I might have been better concealed, more closely guarded," I said.

"That would have defeated the point of the entire deception," he said. "It would have put you in the light of a thousand lanterns."

"I see," I said.

"You are highly intelligent," he said. "You would have instantly suspected the truth."

"Master flatters me," I said.

"The intelligence of a slave," he said, "like that of any other animal, is one of the things that considerably enhances her value. Men will pay highly for it. Who wants a stupid slave? How marvelous it is to have a highly intelligent woman at one's feet, in your collar, naked and in chains, she fully aware that she is helpless, that she is fully and utterly owned."

I dared not tell him how thrilling it was to be such a woman, helpless at the feet of her Master.

"You could have informed me," I said, "that your disdain and coldness were mockeries, no more than a pretense."

"You would have given yourself away, a hundred times, in a hundred ways."

I feared that that might be true.

"A secret not known to exist," he said, "is a secret easy to keep."

"Yet," I said, "it seems that some thought that I might matter to you, that you might risk much, even your life, to recover me."

"A mere slave?" he said, scornfully.

"Some seemed to think so," I said. "Could they have penetrated a facade of feigned indifference. Some, it seemed, may have seen things in you of which you yourself were unaware."

"Absurd," he said, angrily.

"Often," I said, "one can see in another what that person does not see in himself. May not the deepest of secrets be those we withhold from ourselves?"

"I knew nothing of the slave theft," he said. "And any who could have conceived of such a plan, founded on the premise that I might care for a mere slave and put myself in jeopardy on her behalf, were grossly misinformed."

"Yes, Master," I said.

"To be sure," he said, "there would be a principle involved. One does not care, for example, to have even a boot or goblet stolen from one."

"That is true, Master," I said.

"Perhaps," he said, "I am not as skillful an actor as I thought."

"Perhaps not," I said.

"I will not, thus, consider a career upon the stage," he said.

"Keep to the sword," I said.

"Would you care to be lashed?" he asked.

"No, Master," I said.

The slaves in and about the camp may be divided into personal slaves and public slaves. The collars of the personal slaves identify the Master; those of the public slaves identify the company. For example, I no longer wore the collar of Bazi Imports, a public collar. My present collar read, I am told, 'I am the slave of Rupert of Hochburg.' The collar of the lovely Rika, on the other hand, a barbarian slave acquired in Venna a few days ago, a public slave, reads simply, as I understand it, 'I am a slave of the company of Rupert of Hochburg.' Slaves generally prefer a private Master. For example, Rika's attentions to the archer, Ho-Rak, putting herself frequently, presumably inadvertently, before him, surprisingly managing to serve him at the tables, all by accident, of course, and such, suggest that she would not object to a name collar which would identify her as his property. She, in her tiny, single garment, the simple, scandalously brief tunic allotted to her, that garment which proclaimed, irrefutably and unmistakably, to herself and to all others, that she was a slave, only a slave, desperately needed, and wanted, a Master. How fully aware is the slave, even the new slave, of her needs and her sex! How precious it is to have a Master, her own Master! More than once I had seen her literally kneel before him and put her head down, casting her hair about his feet. A free woman may not behave so, but a slave may do so. Presumably, as a free woman on Earth, it had never occurred to her that she might one day find herself doing so, hoping to be found pleasing. But then, on Earth, she was not a slave. Being branded and fastened in a metal collar effects changes in a woman's behavior, freeing herself to be the slave she was born to be, and wants to be.

Temicus of Venna seems pleased with clever, sometimes annoying, Luta, and Desmond of Hochburg with his gentle, loving Philippina, once a Panther Girl of the Northern Forests, once mercilessly hunted by her sisters for the weakness, even in her freedom, of wanting a Master.

"Master!" I begged Rupert of Hochburg.

My needs were much on me.

"It will soon be time for the evening meal," he said. "Rise up. Go to the cooking fires. Petition to be made useful."

"No, please Master," I said.

"On your feet," he said. "Hurry, slave."

"Yes, Master," I wept, hurrying from his presence.

A short time thereafter I was carrying food and drink to the tables.

I sometimes remembered Eileen Bennett, who had been charged with the care of the observatory library on Earth, her flirtations, games, teasings, and smiles. How angry she had made me! Had I been jealous of her? I trusted not. I hoped not. She had much amused herself with the younger males at the observatory with her posings, turnings, and comments, often witty and provocative, sometimes arch and demeaning. She had seen men as hapless playthings, as objects to be assorted and arranged into patterns of her own choosing, as arranged, fawning retainers and courtiers, this one vying with that one, this one trying to outdo that one, each more eager to impress her than his fellows, all manipulable weaklings, eager to please her, so anxious to curry her favor. One of the young men, the quiet, unusual Maxwell Holt, had seemed immune to her charms. Each stratagem and wile had failed to have its effect. Had her carefully marshaled artillery failed her? What wall could remain impervious to so well-planned and brilliantly executed a cannonade? Every provocation and enticement fell short. How frustrating for her! How inert and dull must be such a fellow! Yet how his eye followed her. Had she been so looked upon before, so differently, as if each movement, each syllable, was noted, and would be remembered? Did it occur to her that he might be conjecturing her price in copper or silver, or considering how she might look, being sold naked off a block, as a slave or, say, how she might look, purchased, naked and collared, in chains, at his feet?

In any event, the former Eileen Bennett, now the *kajira*, Xanthe, the property of Holt of Ar, was surely one of the most beautiful and pleasing slaves in the camp. Her Master had seen to it that she had learned her collar quickly and well.

It does not take an intelligent woman long to do so.

She, too, this evening was serving at the tables.

She had told me that the following small ritual is occasionally enacted between herself and her Master. She approaches him in the morning on all fours, head down, the whip between her teeth. She stops before him and lifts her head. He removes the whip from between her teeth. She then says, "Whip me if I do not please you today." He says, "I will." After that, she requests permission to clothe herself, which permission may or may not be granted. Their day then begins. There are many rituals between slaves and Masters.

I have mentioned that one of the contingents readying itself for the trek to the Vosk Basin is that of Flavius of Venna. Doubtless he will be recalled from the raid on the holdings of the lady Temione of Hammerfest, now in the collar of her Master, Gordon of Hammerfest, captain of the newly formed Vosk Guard. I mention this in particular because of his slave, Calla, whose acquaintance I have now happily been able to renew, and from whose kindnesses I had once muchly profited.

This morning, Lucilius, Kur of the faction of Agamemnon, took his leave of the camp. I was present when he bade farewell to my Master, Rupert of Hochburg, and certain officers, amongst them, Temicus of Venna, Holt of Ar, and Desmond of Hochburg.

"The Priest-Kings continue to rule in the Sardar," said Rupert.

"And their laws lurk in the clouds," said Lucilius.

"Would you have it otherwise?" asked Rupert.

"Were it not for the Priest-Kings," said Lucilius, "Gor would be a Kur world."

"Cannot Kurii be content to share a world?" asked Rupert.

"It is not the Kur way," said Lucilius.

"I trust," said Rupert, "that we part as friends."

"We do," said Lucilius, "and may we never meet as enemies."

"How could that be?" asked Rupert.

"I am Kur; you are human," said Lucilius.

"Even so," said Rupert.

"Causes divide even brothers," said Lucilius.

"I hope," said Rupert, "never to raise my sword against you."

"And I hope," said Lucilius, "never to lift my ax against you."

"I wish you well," said Rupert.

"I wish you well," said Lucilius, who then took his leave from the camp.

Temione, the former Lady Temione of Hammerfest, once rich and powerful, once a prospective oligarch of the Vosk, now the slave of Gordon of Hammerfest, still does not believe that men might glide about on artificial wings on Terra. I have tried to convince her that my improvisation in the delta, by means of which we saved our lives, was an adoption of a Terran invention and practice, but she remains adamantly opposed to the claim. Such things could not obtain on Terra, as it is a primitive, backward, uncivilized, barbarian world. Her current position is that my original claim, to assuage her apprehensions, that such things were familiar in the Voltai, was not the lie I later confessed it to be, but a fact. At this point, her difficulty seems pretty much limited to the fact that few in the Voltai seem to have heard of such things. That problem is easily solved, however, by the likely infrequency of the practice and the vast extent of the Voltai range. Indeed, perhaps somewhere in the Voltai, young men do engage in such unusual and risky sports. Thus, for all I know, she may be right.

I was serving at the common tables. So, too, amongst others, were the slaves of the high officers, amongst them Luta, slave of Temicus of Venna; Philippina, slave of Desmond of Hochburg; and, as noted, Xanthe, slave of Holt of Ar. In this way, we were given to understand that we, despite being the properties of high officers, were naught but slaves amongst slaves. This was supposed to reduce our sense of status, and diminish the likelihood of invidious comparisons amongst us and other slaves. There was already enough of that between the public and private slaves, or, in our case, between the company slaves and the privately owned slaves. This arrangement was also thought to be in the best interest of morale amongst the men, they being served, amongst others, by the slaves of the officers.

"I am hungry," said Xanthe.

"I, too," I said.

The slaves were not yet permitted to partake of the food and drink they served. Even in a private dwelling where standing permissions as to speech and eating are likely to exist, the Master will commonly take the first bite.

"I hope that we shall soon be permitted to crawl to the feet of our Masters," said Xanthe.

"I trust so," I said.

I wondered if she, when a free woman on Earth, had ever thought of crawling to the feet of a Master. I wondered, too, if, had she known the true nature of Maxwell Holt, whom she tried so frequently to provoke, taunt, and diminish, she would have fled from him in terror or, upon reflection, knelt before him and begged his collar.

The officers, as of yet, had not joined the tables. The message involved in this seems to be that the first concern of the officers is the care and welfare of their troops. They will see the men cared for before they themselves eat and drink. This also, of course, helps to demarcate the difference between the officers and the men. The officers are concerned for the men but they are not chums of the men. Discipline is more than important; it is essential. The order of a friend might be questioned or discussed; the order of a superior is to be obeyed. The distinction between the officers and the lower ranks is sharp and inviolate. There was a sudden loud, warning utterance from someone amongst the tables. The men instantly stood, as one, and the slaves instantly knelt, as one. The officers were at hand. They had arrived together, this betokening their unity and solidarity. They seated themselves at the special tables reserved for them. Once they were seated, another command was uttered, and the men returned to their places and their meal, and the slaves rose up and continued serving.

I noted that Rika, the new barbarian slave, purchased some days ago in Venna, knelt under a table at the knees of Ho-Rak, the archer. She lifted her head and was being fed, bit by bit, from his hand.

It seemed that it was at his knees that she had chosen to kneel.

She had not known such men on Earth.

She was grateful to be fed.

Sometime later, the slaves of the officers, having brought food and drink to their Masters, were permitted to take their place below the tables, at the feet of their Masters. There we would be fed by hand. If aught else were to be desired, we could be dispatched to fetch it.

"Master," I whispered to him.

"Be silent, slave," he said. "Men are speaking."

"Yes Master," I said. "Forgive me, Master."

I remained crouched down, kneeling.

I should have known more than to interrupt the men while they were speaking.

From time to time, almost absentmindedly, Rupert of Hochburg, would hold a bit of food beneath the table and I would reach up and take it delicately in my teeth. I would then press my left cheek against his knee, or kiss it softly. Xanthe and Philippina were to my left and right, as Holt of Ar and Desmond of Hochburg conferred with my Master. Second to my left was Luta, the slave of Temicus of Venna. Sometimes bowls were set down under the table from which we might feed, refraining from using our hands. And sometimes we were fed at the slave trough, where, too, we were refused the use of our hands. Privately, of course, we often fed from dishes and drinking bowls, much as the Masters themselves. This was expeditious and convenient. Much depends of course, on the will of the Master.

The men spoke of many matters, but of nothing that might not be common knowledge. It is said that a careless word, an indiscreet utterance, is like a feather borne by the wind. Who knows where it may settle or pause? Have not drunken soldiers published secrets? Have not battles been lost in taverns? It is said that to confide a secret to a slave is to inscribe it on the public boards.

"The order of march is public and clear," said Rupert of Hochburg. "The Vosk Guard leads; the center is held by the free company of Flavius of Venna; and we will bring up the rear."

"And little else is to be public and clear," said Holt of Ar.

"Precisely," said Rupert.

"Speculation will be rampant," said Temicus.

"The more so the better," said Rupert.

"We may have spies already within our ranks," said Holt of Ar.

"More likely in those of the Vosk Guard," said Rupert. "Our high captain is Gordon of Hammerfest."

"The serpent who wishes to steal eggs is not to be found far from the nest," said Temicus.

"Our men know little of the object of our march or of what is intended in a projected campaign," said Holt of Ar.

"That is acceptable," said Rupert. "They are soldiers."

"When men learn, desertions may thin the ranks," said Desmond.

"Ours less so than others," said Rupert. "We have recruited with care."

"Rumors suggest a fearsome foe," said Temicus.

"Even a short foe can cast a long shadow," said Rupert. "And a foe unseen is often feared over a foe seen. And the driven steel and the flighted quarrel do not inquire into the fearsomeness of their targets. They ask no questions of such things."

Crouching under the table, my needs were much on me. How could a free woman even imagine the needs of a slave girl? What the Masters have done to us! How we were at their mercy! Let the free woman thrash in her bed and sob her needs to her pillow! She does not even have a collar on her neck! I heard Xanthe moan at the knees of Holt of Ar. Doubtless in the observatory she had not anticipated that she would ever be so. Others, too, I suspected, deprived beneath the tables, chained to their stakes, caged, fastened at the foot of couches, miserable and tormented, wept, yearned, and suffered. Sometimes slavers deprive a slave of sex for two or three days, even four or five days, before her sale, that she will present herself all the more piteously before the buyers, begging to be purchased.

"Tomorrow," said Rupert. "We march."

The tables were now being cleared. Some men were drifting away to their tents. Others remained at the tables, conversing, some playing stones. I heard a *kalika* being strung.

"It is time for the public slaves to be staked out on the grass for usage," said Holt of Ar.

Rupert made a sign to a spearman and he, gesturing to a pair of others, set about their work.

"We will need more slaves for the men," said Holt.

"They are easily acquired," said Temicus. "The cages are full this time of year. You need not frequent cities and towns. You can find some in any caravanserai, at any roadside inn, at any crossroads."

"We are looking for quality merchandise," said Rupert. "A company is noted for not only the livery of its slaves but for that which the livery bedecks. The excellence of its slaves is important to the image of a company. Lovely slaves, as do other badges of prestige, such as uniforms and imposing arms and gear, suggest the success, affluence, and viability, of a company."

"And, implicitly," said Desmond of Hochburg, "the prowess of our men and the formidableness of our steel, that we can take, have, and keep such goods."

"Certainly," said Rupert.

"What of barbarians?" asked Temicus.

My attention was immediately aroused.

"To be taken seriously," said Rupert. "One must honor the skills of the slavers who somehow bring such cattle to our markets. Commonly their taste is shrewd and their judgment flawless. They must have thousands amongst whom they can choose, as they deem fit, the most intelligent, beautiful, and passionate, the most helpless, vulnerable, and needful, the sorts whose necks most obviously belong in collars."

"I understand," said Desmond, "that there are no free women on Terra, the Slave World."

"No," said Holt of Ar, "that is not exactly it. Rather, say that the women of the Slave World have no Home Stones."

"But if they have no Home Stones, they must be slaves."

"No," said Holt.

"Why then is it called the Slave World?" asked Desmond.

"I think for two reasons," said Holt. "First, because it is so rich in beautiful, needful women so easily brought to our markets."

"And how is it," asked Desmond, "that they can be so easily acquired?"

"As they are not owned, not properties, they are not guarded, not protected, not chained or caged," said Holt.

"I see," said Desmond, "and what is the second reason that some call Terra the Slave World?"

"Because," said Holt, "there are so many of that world, male and female, who do what they are told and think what they are told to think, who value comfort and security over self-reliance and freedom. They live in a kind of zoo whose bars they fail to see."

"I am told," said Desmond, "that most women of that world do not veil themselves, but keep their faces as naked as those of slaves."

"That is true," said Holt, "but it is a cultural thing, a matter of custom."

"A splendid boon, what good fortune for the slavers," said Temicus.

"Indubitably," said Holt.

"Many women of the slave world then are free?" asked Desmond.

"Legally," said Holt.

"Interesting," said Desmond.

"Not as Gorean women are free, of course," said Holt. "Their freedom is a lesser thing, something little noted, something scarcely considered. Their freedom, such as it is, lacks the importance and status, the dignity and momentousness, of a Gorean woman's freedom. Where all are free, freedom means little or nothing. It lacks significance."

"Barbarians sell well," said Desmond.

"Presumably they will sell less well when there are more of them in the markets," said Temicus.

"I think there is more to it than that," said Holt.

"They are different," said Temicus. "They have a touch of the exotic. Most give themselves away almost instantly, with their delightful accents."

I, I was sure, was not one of those.

I took another bit of meat gratefully, delicately, from the hand of my Master.

"And more to it than that," said Rupert. "They make excellent slaves. They steam, oil, and gush helplessly and profusely. One would think they had never had sex."

"The slave world," said Holt, "is hard to understand. It substitutes prescriptions, cultural imperatives, and instilled conventions for biology. Nature is to be overlooked or condemned. Artifice is to be proclaimed and promoted. Men are supposed to be like women and women are supposed to be like men. Confusion and distress ensue. Guilt is encouraged, even cultivated, with its inevitable attendants, anxiety, paralysis, dejection, and depression. An unnatural minority invents new goods and bads, to profit thereby, weaponizing language to enhance their fortunes. Their sickness poses as health. They denounce difference. Those suspected of nonconformity are disparaged, marginalized, excluded, silenced, or ruined. The pack odor, the nest odor, is required of all. All must be as one, act as one, and think as one."

"I do not see how such stupidity, control, and mental immobility can exist," said Temicus.

"With sufficient resources," said Holt, "it can be manufactured and enforced."

"Rigidity," said Temicus, "is intellectual suicide. Without difference, options are constricted. What if conditions change or new challenges arise? To follow a road leading to stagnation and doom is not courage but lunacy. What if conformities split? Are they then to eat one another, or die, tearing at one another's throat? The animal which cannot adapt consigns its bones to the clay of history."

"Little is to be gained by pondering the tragedies of distant, unimportant worlds," said Desmond.

"We were concerned," said Temicus, "with the problem of acquiring new slaves for the company."

"And we were, as I recall," said Desmond, "speaking of barbarians."

"For many of them," said Holt, "slavery is a liberation, a liberation into the freedom of nature, into the freedom of their deepest self."

"The 'freedom of the collar,'" said Rupert.

"If you like," said Holt. "For the first time, they become aware of certain truths, truths long suspected but societally denied to them."

"Many have waited years for their collars," said Desmond.

"Are not all free women but slaves without collars?" asked Temicus.

"Beware of saying such to a Gorean free woman," said Desmond.

"Even such, once collared," said Temicus, "squirm well."

The men then rose from their benches, each to go his own way.

Luta and Philippina, and Xanthe and myself, and others, then emerged from beneath the tables. What had been left on the plates of the Masters, and what might be left in their goblets, was ours for the taking, and might be accessed as we wished. Often the Masters left some of their provender behind for us, and, sometimes, even a swallow or so of *ka-la-na*. I did not care for *paga*, a swallow of which was like a liquid fire scoring and burning in my throat, a burning which would be soon followed by an unsteadiness of equilibrium and a reeling of senses. I did savor the *ka-la-na* he had left behind. As the meal was a barrack meal, so to speak, the *ka-la-na* was cheap.

It was also somewhat more diluted than would be common in a residential supper, say, perhaps one part wine to four or five of water, as opposed to one part wine to two or three of water. Gorean wines tend to be very strong and are seldom drunk unmixed. Most homes will have a ceramic *crater* in which wine and water will be mixed. The proportions are usually agreed on by the hosts and guests prior to the meal. Few but young men intent on a night of rowdy license leave the mixing *crater* in its cabinet. When such spill out onto the streets, singing and shouting, streets are emptied and doors locked.

Shortly thereafter, we finished clearing, and gathered, washed, and stored the paraphernalia from the officers' tables. I then looked about. From where I stood, I could see the upright spear with its pennon in the distance, marking the command tent. In that tent, plans were laid, spies and informants were dispatched and questioned, prisoners were interrogated, officers were briefed, and orders issued. The private tents of the high officers were scattered throughout the camp. Their tents bore no special insignia nor any other marks of identification. They were indistinguishable from the tents of the men. These features of anonymity and location were a precaution against a raid hoping to suddenly and unexpectedly deprive an enemy of its leadership. The company's own men, of course, were familiar with these arrangements. Two similar precautions were, first, the similarity of the uniforms of officers and men, difficult to tell apart at a distance and the occasional minimizing of military protocols, such as subordinates removing their helmets before officers. There was no point in assisting enemy marksmen to discriminate judiciously amongst their targets.

I began to make my way from the tables toward the tents. I supposed that there must be several differences between natively Gorean slaves and barbarian slaves, just as there were between natively Gorean men and the men of Earth, but I saw the differences as being primarily, if not entirely, cultural. If there were physiological or intellectual differences, they would not be differences pertaining to species or even varieties within a species. They would be traced to the particular samples of humans brought to Gor, whether long ago in some distant past by, say, Priest-Kings, or more recently by slavers, or others. Such samples would not be representative of Earth humans as a whole, but of particular groups of Earth humans, say, the healthiest, the more intelligent, and so on. And who knew, actually, how these selections were made? Who knew the criteria which might have been employed? Some criteria might seem obvious, health, and such, but others might be less so. Perhaps criteria might vary over time, responding to needs felt, or even the vagaries of fashion. And under all, is there not the dichotomy of men and women, the abrasions of reality, and a human nature that has been selected for over thousands of years in the light of those abrasions? Evolution asks no more questions than thunder and the sea. It disdains nothing; it prizes nothing. It draws no distinction between the hero and the crocodile, between the saint and the termite. It chisels life and death, extinction and survival, and does not notice.

I did not ask to be brought to this world.

I did not ask to be marked and collared.

Yet I would beg not to be taken from this world. I would miss the joy of its air, the purity of its water, the glory of its cloud-bestrewn, vast, salubrious sky, its meadows of flowers, its flowing rivers and rugged mountains, the green of its enormous fields of flowing, bending grass. Earth might once have been so. What has happened to Earth? I guess it has no Home Stone.

The simplest and most common of beasts will not soil its own nest or lair.

What then of those who do so?

On my way to the tents, I walked amongst the staked-out slaves, the company slaves, the public slaves, of the camp, supine, their wrists and ankles widely spread.

It was true that there were now too few of them for the men. More could doubtless be acquired on the trek to the Vosk Basin or in the Basin itself. Victoria on the Vosk, for example, was a major center for slave dealing.

Most of the slaves, by now, had been well handled, but, tethered spreadeagled as they were, several were still thrashing in an agony of need. Some moaned, softly, the hunger of their bellies unassuaged, the passions forced upon them unalleviated, in the grip of which they were choiceless, deprived and unrequited. The men had been too quick with them. They were, after all, only slaves. It is commonly much different with private slaves, or even slaves in a tavern or brothel. It is not unknown for private slaves, who may, of course, be used as abruptly and casually as a public slave, to be enjoyed generously and at length, tenderly and attentively, again and again, not only for a morning or a night, but for a day or more.

"Please, Mistress," begged one. "You are upright, you are abroad, you are tunicked. Beg the Masters to return. My slave fires have been ignited, but not quenched. The stakes to which I am fastened are firm. My wrists and ankles are cruelly parted. I am spread for use. I strain in the ropes. I am helpless. Every inch of my body is alive and pleading. Beg the Masters to return and be merciful!"

"I may not do so," I said. "You know that. In such matters, the slave must plead directly with the Masters. You should have pleaded with them."

"I did!" she said.

"With what result?" I asked.

"A cuffing," she said.

"Perhaps you now know better that you are a slave," I said.

"Please beg for me," she wept.

"I may not," I said. "It is forbidden. Too, I have no wish to be put at the post and lashed."

"Mistress!"

"The Masters do as they please," I said. "You will be released after a time."

"To be chained in the mud!" she said.

"Such things encourage a girl to strive to be a better slave," I said.

She twisted as she could, pulling against the stakes. She was quite helpless.

I heard a noise to the side.

I became apprehensive.

"Were you permitted to speak?" I asked the slave. "Had you permission to accost a passer-by?"

I saw fear in her body.

"What is going on here?" said a male voice.

I knelt immediately, head down.

"Nothing, Master," I said.

"Did this slave betray her tethering, and speak to you?" he asked.

"She had no choice," I said, "for I addressed her."

"And for what reason?" he asked.

"She was distraught," I said. "I inquired into the cause and nature of her distress."

"And what was this cause and nature?" he asked. "You hesitate," he said.

"She is hungry," I said.

"She is a public slave," he said. "We feed them before we stake them out."

"Her hunger," I said, "is not that of the stomach. It is that of the belly."

"She is comely," he said, regarding the slave.

"Very much so," I said.

"You may speak the saying of the evening," he said to the slave.

"I am a slave, Master," she said. "Take pity on me."

"What is your name?" he asked.

"Rika, if it pleases Master," she said.

"I have seen you about," he said.

"Forgive me, Master," she said.

"Do you know my name?" he asked.

"It is Ho-Rak, of the contingent of archers," she said.

"How is it that you know my name?" he asked.

"I inquired," she said.

"You are bold," he said.

"I was curious," she said.

"Curiosity is not becoming in a *kajira*," he said.

"Forgive me, Master," she said.

"Why were you curious?" he asked.

"I am in a collar," she said. "I am a vendible object. Master is strong and handsome."

"You find me attractive?" he asked.

"Tremblingly so," she said.

"You were near me, under the table, hoping for scraps, at supper, were you not?" he asked.

"Yes, Master," she said.

"Intentionally?" he said.

"I fear so," she said.

"I thought it might be you," he said. "You have been much about."

"Paths cross," she said.

"You are a barbarian, are you not?" he asked.

"Yes, Master," she said. "Please do not beat me or despise me for my world of origin."

"I do not," he said. "There are women and there are men."

"I come from a world where society wishes to deny slaves to Masters and Masters to slaves."

"Why would they wish to do that, if slaves are slaves and Masters Masters?"

"I do not know," she said.

"I suppose," said he, "customs and cultures can take different turns, some natural, others not, some healthy, satisfying, and fulfilling, and others not."

"I am a born slave," she said. "All my life I have yearned for a Master. Now, at last, here, I have found myself on a world where I am a slave, in full undeniable legality, a collar on my neck."

"I could double my time on the range," he said, "had I a girl to fetch and return my arrows."

"Master clearly needs such a girl," she said.

"Do you think you might prove acceptable?" he asked.

"Try me!" she said.

"Perhaps," I said, "Master might consider assuaging the needs of her belly."

"She is already primed," he said. "I can soon bring her again to the brink."

"And then the rolling thunder, the blasts of lightning, and the crying out and begging," I said.

"It is pleasant to see a slave so helpless, so ravished, and so mine," he said.

"Afterwards," I said, "perhaps Master will be kind enough to stay with her for a time, to hold her, to talk with her."

"She is not a free woman," he said.

"Nonetheless," I said.

"Perhaps," he said.

"I must not linger," I said. "My Master will be expecting me."

"Is it true," he asked, "that the slave kept her silence, until you first addressed her."

"That is what I said," I said.

He looked at me.

"I think you are a liar," he said.

"Yes, Master," I said. "Forgive me, Master."

"I need a girl to fetch arrows," he said.

"I am sure she will do very nicely," I said.

He gestured that I might rise from where I knelt on the grass.

I stood.

"Go," he said.

"Yes, Master," I said.

"Wait," he said.

I turned about.

"I wish you well," he said.

"I wish you well," I said.

I then hurried away.

"Yes!" I heard Rika cry. "Yes, yes, Master!"

Outside the tent, indistinguishable from so many others, I hesitated.

I held the tent flap, and moved it slightly, twice.

"Mira is at hand," I said. "May she approach her Master?"

"She may enter," said Rupert of Hochburg.

I entered the tent and knelt, in the light of a small *tharlarion*-oil lamp. My master was sitting cross-legged on a tent carpet. Across his knees was spread a map. He put the map to the side, next to some notes, a marking stick, and a small, adjustable calipers, used to measure *pasangs*. The distance a company and its supply train can move in a day varies with the nature of the terrain and the condition of the men and wagons. Under ideal conditions, as on the Viktel Aria, or Ar's Triumph, a day's march, I am told, would be expected to cover forty *pasangs*.

"You dallied, did you not?" he asked.

"Masters ignite slave fires!" I said.

He seemed puzzled.

What had this to do with my possible dalliance?

"Surely you do not object," he said.

"It makes us so helpless and needful," I said, "so much yours!"

"They exist in every woman," he said. "We do no more than remove impediments to their raging."

"You give us no choice!" I said.

"No," he said.

"Why!" I said.

"It pleases us," he said. "We like you on your knees, begging."

I clutched my fists.

"I am collared!" I said.

"You are perceptive," he said.

"Like an animal!" I said.

"You are an animal, a slave," he said.

"I was a free woman on Terra!" I said.

"Now," he said, "you are less than nothing. You are a slave girl, on Gor."

"I love it," I wept.

"You are a female, in your place," he said.

I sobbed.

"Is that all?" I begged.

"Is that not enough?" he asked.

"Do I mean so little to you?" I asked.

"You are a slave," he said.

"On Terra," I said, "I was denied my deepest self."

"We often fault Terra," said Rupert, "for the poisoning of its food, the fouling of its water, the contamination of its air, for the greed, exploitation, and stupidity in virtue of which an innocent, defenseless world is desecrated, but we do not fault her for her women. Many, like yourself, are attractive. They grace our markets. They, with their deprivations, their hunger for Masters, their readiness for, and need for, chains, are a splendid addition to our slave stock."

"We are owned," I said, "we are properties, belongings, possessions!"

"Of course," he said. "You are slaves."

"You do not respect us," I said.

"No," he said. "But rest easy. You are abundantly and significantly regarded otherwise, in ways more suitable to your nature, and mine."

"As animals you can put to your pleasure, as animals who must obey!"

"Certainly," he said.

I wept.

"What is wrong?" he asked.

"But I want to be owned," I said. "I want to be a possession. I want a Master. I want to kneel, to kiss, and obey!"

"What you want is of no interest," he said. "You are a slave."

"You can whip me, and put me up for sale," I said.

"If I wish," he said.

"I am choiceless," I said. "I am so helpless."

"As I recall," he said, "you came late to the tent. You dallied."

"I lingered," I said, "to comfort a distraught slave."

"One staked out?" he said.

"Yes," I said.

"Her slave fires burned unassuaged?" he said.

"Yes," I said.

"What is that to you?" he asked.

"I sorrowed for her," I said. "I, too, have known such deprivation."

"Do you complain?" he asked.

"I dare not," I said.

"What occurred?" he asked.

"A nearby Master consented to caress her," I said.

"Tethered as she was?" he asked.

"Yes," I said.

"And how did matters turn out?" he asked.

"Well, I think," I said. "I heard her cry out with joy. I think, bound and helpless, she leaped in the cords."

"We march in the morning," he said.

"I know," I said.

"Gordon of Hammerfest, Oligarch of the Vosk, commander of the Vosk Guard, will be first to take to the road. Second will be the company of Flavius of Venna. We shall guard the rear."

"That is the most dangerous, is it not?" I asked. "For the enemy may attack the rear, to isolate the column, cutting off retreat?"

"Then to harass the flanks at leisure, intermittently, while opening a road before the vanguard," he said.

"To draw the column forward, attenuating it, making it more vulnerable, lengthening and hastening its marches," I said.

"Presumably," he said.

"And how shall these things be met?" I asked.

"We will not divide our forces," he said. "We will ignore insults and provocations. A *larl* does not pursue *urts*. I doubt that a wise enemy would care to risk a major engagement this far from the Vosk. Should he do so, we will meet him shield to shield, spear to spear."

"I gather," I said, "that Kurii converge on the Vosk."

"Surely there is evidence that more Kurii have been of late noted in the Vosk Basin," he said, "but I think their numbers are likely to be limited, to perhaps a few hundred at most. I anticipate that their ventures in the Vosk Basin will be mounted largely in terms of mercenaries, presumably from the maritime ubarates, Cos and Tyros, and the Farther Islands. Surely such forces will see the hand of a grasping, far-reaching Marlenus of Ar in this whole enterprise. Thus, in the hope of evening scores, for their expulsion from Ar, and gaining territory on the continent, they will be more than willing to accept Kur gold to be used against Ar."

"The character of the noble Gordon of Hammerfest," I said, tentatively, "is problematic."

"How so?" asked Rupert.

"May I speak?" I asked.

"Yes," he said.

"Freely?" I asked.

"Surely," he said.

"The noble Gordon of Hammerfest," I said, "is not only the Administrator of Hammerfest, an Oligarch of the Vosk, and the Commander of the Vosk Guard, but a dreaded pirate, Einar, Sleen of the Vosk."

"Many know that," said Rupert. "The secret, if not open, is ill-concealed."

"How can this be managed?" I asked.

"Do not think the law is keenly observant, objective, or impartial," said Rupert. "Those who make the law have ends in mind. Too, when the law proves inconvenient, it can be overlooked."

"Surely not," I said.

"Do not be naive," he said.

"The law," I said, "is the same for all."

"Scarcely," he said.

"Are not all equal under the law?" I asked.

"No," he said.

"I hear that with dismay," I said.

"Law is made to further the interests of the powerful, not that of the many, not those of the weak," he said.

"Surely sometimes," I said, "law can confound and frustrate the powerful, and bring them to an accounting and ruin."

"When used to advance the interests of elements even more powerful," he said. "Law is a weapon not unfamiliar to warring giants."

"Giants?" I asked.

"The blade of the law is heavy," he said. "Who but a giant can lift it?"

"Surely Hammerfest must look into such matters," I said.

"Is it in its interests to do so?" he asked. "Einar does not raid and despoil Hammerfest. If anything, he enriches it."

"Can the people of Hammerfest be ignorant of this deceit and hypocrisy?" I asked.

"Doubtless some," he said. "But it can be difficult for an observer to distinguish between one's being ignorant and one's pretending to be ignorant. Also, few will search for an object they do not care to find."

"I suppose," I said, "that enemies, unaware of the identity of Gordon of Hammerfest and Einar, the Sleen of the Vosk, might fear both, to our advantage."

"Even if informed," said Rupert, "they would find two forces pitted against them, the ground forces of the Vosk Guard, commanded by Gordon of Hammerfest, and, on the Vosk itself, the fleet of Einar, the Sleen of the Vosk."

"I am uneasy," I said, "that a pirate might be enlisted in a proper cause."

"And how do you delineate a cause as proper?" he asked. "It is not unusual for warring adherents to regard their causes as proper, even vehemently so, despite their incompatibility."

"I understood," I said, "that Master would risk the blood, fortune, and treasure of his company only in a cause he deemed proper."

"That commitment," he said, "does not preclude me from recognizing that my enemy may be as convinced of the propriety of his cause, as I am of mine."

"And how do you know that your cause is the most proper?" I asked.

"I do not know," he said.

"I am distressed," I said.

"Some see such matters as adjudicated in the court of blood and steel," he said. "They accept the verdict of history."

"The defeated may disagree," I said.

"Reality does not notice," he said.

"At least," I said, "a pirate like Einar, Sleen of the Vosk, is not to be enlisted in a cause which we, ourselves, take to be proper."

"What if he believes our cause is proper?" he said. "Why then, should his sword remain in its sheath? Why then should he not be allowed to fight on its behalf?"

"What if he does not believe in causes?" I asked. "What if he is a simple mercenary unconcerned with such matters, collecting his pay, and leaving them to others?"

"You know little of war," he said.

"Nor do I care much to do so," I said.

"Hazard reigns," he said. "Death watches, waiting for its opportunity. One hopes to disappoint it. One hopes to scorn it. Each sword, each soldier is precious. One is less concerned with character than with vigilance and skill. A villain who will protect you is to be preferred to a friend who will fail you. Be less concerned with motives than deeds. Who is so much a fool as to question the nature of a sword that honestly serves us, on which much might depend? Why question what is of use? Rather, rejoice."

"I think it is rare that Masters discuss these matters with slaves," I said.

"There are slaves," he said,"—and slaves."

"And we are all in collars," I said.

"Where we want them," he said. "If you are uneasy or disturbed that I have spoken of these things with a slave, consider that I have discussed them only with myself, the presence of a slave being accidental."

"The lamp burns low," I said.

"Replenish it," he said.

This done, I returned to my knees.

The evening was warm.

Momentarily there was a soft wind, registered in the canvas of the tent.

A guard, far off, making his rounds, called out that the night was quiet.

There was little to suggest that tomorrow a camp would be broken and a march begun, to distant, unfamiliar fields, for whatever reasons, concealed or unconcealed, to encounter a foe of unknown numbers, resources, resolve, and skill.

"I fear war," I said.

"Do not repudiate your fear," he said. "It is justified."

"I fear Kurii," I said.

"As well you might," he said. "They are savage and merciless, and will expect those properties in their cohorts."

"I fear you," I said.

"How so?" he asked.

"Your sort of man frightens me," I said.

"Why?" he asked.

"You are of the Warriors," I said.

"It is my caste," he said.

"Why are you of the Warriors?" I asked.

"I was born to the caste," he said. "I have been trained in the work of the caste, from childhood with wooden swords and shields of woven reeds to the award of the scarlet cape."

"The happenstance of birth need not determine all," I said. "Surely some put aside the sword and lay down the spear."

"Some," he said.

"Do so," I said.

"Do you know what you are saying?" he asked.

"You need not be the servant of custom, the slave of duty, the victim of honor," I said.

"I am none of those things," he said.

"Why then are there such men as you?" I asked.

"I do not know," he said. "It may have to do with life."

"I do not understand," I said.

"It is a way of being alive," he said, "a way of feeling life, and knowing life."

"I do not understand," I said.

"I think," he said, "life is sharpest, and keenest, at the edge of a sword."

"I do not understand," I said.

He looked away.

"Master is troubled?" I said.

"To what do we march tomorrow?" he asked. "Who knows what is concealed in the cruel, gigantic, cunning mind of Marlenus of Ar? Who knows the resources and power of remote Pompilius? Or of Agamemnon, at the very edge of Ar? Who knows what might occur, suddenly, unexpectedly? Who knows the unforeseen consequences that might accompany the shortest step? A dislodged pebble unleashes an avalanche. A *larl* might crouch in the darkness. An ost might lie curled at one's ankle. Intrigues abound. Does that which is public mask that which is private? Who can fathom the subtleties of factions? Are there spies amongst us? I fear so. Perhaps some in Ar, perhaps some in the Vosk guard."

"You have some reason for fearing such?" I asked.

"Why, by the supply captains of Ar, have we been denied outriders and tarnsmen?" he asked.

"I did not know that," I said.

"It is allegedly an economy," he said.

"I think a foolish one," I said.

"I will hire such from my own funds," he said. "I will not march blind. I will have my flankers, my outriders, and my eyes in the sky."

"Alert Gordon of Hammerfest and Flavius of Venna," I said.

"I have done so," he said.

"Withdraw from the project," I said.

"We march tomorrow," he said.

I drew back on my knees, frightened.

"Yes, Master," I said.

He turned to regard me.

"You are a meaningless slave," he said. "You have heard nothing. I spoke to myself, and you were not present."

"Yes, Master," I said.

"It is several Ahn before morning," he said.

"I replenished the lamp," I said.

"Are you content?" he asked.

"Very much so," I said.

"Danger portends," he said. "You need not accompany the march. I could sell you in the morning."

"Please do not do so," I said. "I am a slave. I prefer to heel my Master."

"You," he said, "once a woman of Terra, now no more than a collared, branded, half-naked Gorean slave, wish to heel your Master?"

"With every bit of me, my Master," I said.

"You may speak," he said.

"I am a slave, Master," I said. "Take pity on me."

"You are lovely in your collar," he said.

"Thank you, Master," I said.

"Remove your clothing," he said.

"Yes, Master," I said.

ABOUT THE AUTHOR

John Norman is the creator of the Gorean Saga, the longest-running series of adventure novels in science fiction history. He is also the author of the science fiction series the Telnarian Histories, as well as *Ghost Dance, Time Slave, The Totems of Abydos, Imaginative Sex,* and *Norman Invasions*. Norman is married and has three children.

THE GOREAN SAGA

FROM OPEN ROAD MEDIA

OPEN ROAD
INTEGRATED MEDIA